PRAISE FOR RIC...
PREVIOUS YE... BEST
ANTHOLOGIES

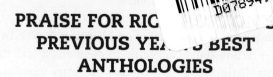

Fantasy: The Best of the Year, 2006 Edition

"The nineteen excellent short stories in this latest addition to the growing field of annual "best of" fantasy anthologies include works by established stars like Pat Cadigan and Peter S. Beagle. Distinguishing this anthology are many stories that first appeared in small press venues. . . . Horton has gathered a diverse mix of styles and themes that illustrate the depth and breadth of fantasy writing today."—*Publishers Weekly,* starred review

Science Fiction: The Best of the Year, 2006 Edition

"Horton's elegiac anthology of fifteen mostly hard sf stories illuminates a broad spectrum of grief over love thwarted through time, space, human frailty or alien intervention. This anthology reflects the concerns of the genre today—and the apparent inability of our society to do anything about them."—*Publishers Weekly*

Fantasy: The Best of the Year, 2007 Edition

"Horton's fantasy annual showcases the best short speculative fiction that steps beyond the established boundaries of science. The sixteen selections represent both magic-oriented fantasy and cross-genre slipstream fiction. Their inspired and resourceful authors range from veteran fantasists Geoff Ryman and Peter S. Beagle to such newer voices as Matthew Corradi and Ysabeau Wilce. Fantasy enthusiasts looking for stories that expand the genre's boundaries in unexpected ways will find them in this inventive, enticingly provocative collection."—*Booklist*

Science Fiction: The Best of the Year, 2007 Edition

"What with sf's current high literary standing, there is no shortage of gifted authors striving to produce outstanding short fiction, and editor Horton is more than happy to encourage them via this annual for which he sets no higher criterion than plain good writing. Dedicated genre fans may find some overlap of this with other genre annuals, but given the hours of mind-bending entertainment it provides, they'll hardly resent it."—*Booklist*

continued

THE YEAR'S BEST SCIENCE FICTION AND FANTASY

2011 EDITION

THE YEAR'S BEST SCIENCE FICTION AND FANTASY

2011 EDITION

EDITED BY
RICH HORTON

PRIME BOOKS

THE YEAR'S BEST SCIENCE FICTION AND FANTASY, 2011 EDITION

Prime Books
www.prime-books.com

ISBN: 978-1-60701-256-6

For two editors who got me started on the route
to putting together these books: Dave Truesdale and John O'Neill.

TABLE OF CONTENTS

TABLE OF CONTENTS

THE YEAR IN FANTASY AND SCIENCE FICTION, 2010

RICH HORTON

When we published the contents of this anthology, the first thing that attracted notice was the high proportion of stories from online venues. Sixteen of the twenty-eight stories in this book first appeared online. (Though actually one of those, K. J. Parker's "Amor Vincit Omnia" was published more or less simultaneously in the Australian print 'zine *Andromeda Spaceways Inflight Magazine*.) Other best of the year books also showed higher than previous totals of online stories. Is the web finally taking over?

Well, the proportion of short sf and fantasy first published online has been increasing steadily over time. So one would expect a concomitant increase in the proportion of online stories in Best of the Year books. In addition, the respectability of online sources has increased. Readers are more likely to expect good fiction there, and writers are happier to send their best stories there. (The pay has also increase, particularly at a site like *Subterranean*.) Mind you, one of the earliest online sites, Ellen Datlow's *Sci Fiction*, remains probably the best, but for some time it was seen as almost an outlier, buoyed by the presence of a revered editor and by high pay.

Other sites of a similar vintage battled image problems. One site that's been around seemingly forever in web years is *Strange Horizons*. It published some very strong fiction from the beginning, but had early on a reputation as to a great extent a slipstream site, and a site for new writers. This reputation was to a great extent deserved—but so what? Slipstream can be very good, and supporting new writers is a wonderful thing. *Strange Horizons* has parlayed a certain dogged persistence, and consistent high standards, into ever increasing reputation, so that by now they are as respectable a place to publish new sf and fantasy as anywhere. They are still hospitable to new writers, but some of the writers who were new when the site debuted have become, if not exactly grizzled veterans, at least established pros. So at *Strange Horizons* now we can expect fiction from a wider variety of contributors, and a vigorous mix of sf and fantasy.

Some sites built reputations first as print magazines. This is true of both *Fantasy Magazine* and *Subterranean Magazine*. Each transitioned online after several print issues. And each stand now among the very best venues of sf and fantasy (mainly fantasy of course at *Fantasy Magazine*). Another magazine that transitioned from print to online is *Apex* (formerly *Apex Digest*). The print magazine had a distinct focus on horror (albeit often sf horror), but the online version, though still prone to publish a fair amount of horror, seems more diverse in focus now. And in 2010 I thought it took a sharp leap upward in quality, partly perhaps due to the work of new editor Catherynne M. Valente (though I don't want to diminish previous editor (and still publisher) Jason Sizemore's contributions—the site was already on a definite upward path under his direction).

But nowadays an online site can build a strong reputation essentially from scratch, and fairly quickly, much like any print magazine. *Lightspeed*, the sf companion to *Fantasy Magazine*, began publication in mid-2010, and from the first were publishing outstanding stories. The editor—former *F&SF* assistant and busy anthologist John Joseph Adams—is a major factor, of course. Similarly, *Clarkesworld* and *Beneath Ceaseless Skies*, though they've been around longer than *Lightspeed*, have quickly become destination sites for those who love short sf and f.

Finally one must mention *Tor.com*, which, backed by a major publisher, also began with a built-in reputation, and has continued to back that up with strong fiction. *Tor.com*, like most of these sites, has other features besides the fiction that draw readers. In Tor's case, my favorite aspect is a vigorous blog with numerous contributors, on a variety of sf-related subjects. Most of the other sites have other interesting features, such as illustrations, interviews, and non-fiction of various kinds. Very notable in particular is the strong book review section at *Strange Horizons*.

Other worthwhile sites include *Abyss and Apex, Ideomancer, Reflection's Edge, Chiaroscuro, Flurb, Orson Scott Card's Intergalactic Medicine Show*, and *Heroic Fantasy Quarterly*.

Having sung the praises of online sites, it is incumbent on me to remind everyone that the print magazines, as well as original anthologies, are still an essential source of new stories. This year I felt that the magazines remained in a holding pattern. No major magazines folded or drastically changed format, though *Realms of Fantasy*, for the second year in a row, did temporarily fold, before being rescued by a new publisher. *F&SF* and *Asimov's* both had very good years as far as fiction quality goes. *Analog* was not as strong, but it remains unique, its own magazine, with a pretty clear sense of its market, its aims, which alas don't always square with mine. *Realms of Fantasy* is another magazine with a clear sense of mission—this is wholly Shawna McCarthy's domain, in the way that its style and sensibility have remained consistent over the years. In the UK, *Interzone* is featuring very good stuff, with a distinct personality of its own; one perhaps best summarized as being in alignment with a quasi-movement *Interzone* regular Jason Sanford has dubbed "Sci-Fi Strange."

There were quite a few fine original anthologies this year. What was missing were the major unthemed original anthology series we saw over the past few years. **The Solaris Book of New Science Fiction** and **Fast Forward** have died, and while a fourth number of **Eclipse** is planned, it won't appear until 2011.

Two of the most interesting original anthologies last year were big books that spanned genres, each mixing mainstream stories, and historical fiction, with a fair amount of sf and fantasy. These were **Stories**, edited by Neil Gaiman and Al Sarrantonio; and **Warriors**, edited by George R. R. Martin and Gardner Dozois. Martin and Dozois put out another strong book this year, this one more strictly fantastical in nature: **Songs of Love and Death**. Other top anthologies from 2010 included **Swords and Dark Magic**, edited by Lou Anders and Jonathan Strahan; **The Way of the Wizard**, edited by John Joseph Adams; and **The Beastly Bride**, edited by Ellen Datlow and Terri Windling. Strahan had another very strong book, the much delayed **Godlike Machines**, from the Science Fiction Book Club. The Frederik Pohl tribute anthology **Gateways**, edited by Elizabeth Anne Hull, was distinctly uneven but had nice stuff from the likes of Gene Wolfe and Cory Doctorow. And one of the most anticipated books of the year was Jetse de Vries's collection of "optimistic" sf, **Shine**, which was also uneven, but with some very good stories.

That's just a quick overview—there were probably a dozen more fairly solid anthologies last year, including several from Australia, and an interesting YA book, **Zombies vs. Unicorns**, edited by Justine Larbalestier and Holly Black.

As ever, there were a number of impressive novellas published as chapbooks. For a variety of reasons (primarily, length restrictions and contractual obligations), I haven't reprinted any of them here, but I urge the reader to seek out K. J. Parker's **Blue and Gold**, David Moles's **Seven Cities of Gold**, Ted Chiang's **The Lifecyle of Software Objects**, Elizabeth Bear's **Bone and Jewel Creatures**, and Lavie Tidhar's **Cloud Permutations**, just to list my five favorites in that format from 2010.

One odd sidelight to the year is the distribution of lengths of the stories I chose. In a typical year almost half the stories in my book are novelettes. For example, in 2009 I had one novella, thirteen novelettes, and sixteen short stories. But this year this book includes no fewer than five novellas (and I could easily have chose three or four more), and nineteen short stories. But only four novelettes. The novelette length has often been called the natural length for an sf story, and whatever you think of that argument from an artistic point of view; I think it does hold up that in most years there proportionately more outstanding novelettes than other lengths. But for whatever reason—just a statistical oddity, more than likely—that didn't seem to be the case this year.

Looked at as a whole, I think this was a fairly standard year for the field. The phrase "holding pattern" that I used for the magazine applies reasonably well to the entire field. I don't see an overwhelming movement at hand (though Sanford's "Sci-Fi Strange" idea is interesting), and despite the continuing increase in the influence of online sites and the ongoing stasis (it would appear) of the print magazines, what's happening to the short fiction market seems more a long term evolution than any sort of revolution. I remain, as every year so far, quite thrilled with the contents of this book—I am confident that it provides a varied and energetic set of exceptional stories, proof that despite the vagaries of the market, the creative powers of the collective sf/f world of writers remain amazing.

FLOWER, MERCY, NEEDLE, CHAIN

YOON HA LEE

The usual fallacy is that, in every universe, many futures splay outward from any given moment. But in some universes, determinism runs backwards: given a universe's state *s* at some time *t*, there are multiple previous states that may have resulted in *s*. In some universes, all possible pasts funnel toward a single fixed ending, Ω.

If you are of millenarian bent, you might call Ω Armageddon. If you are of grammatical bent, you might call it punctuation on a cosmological scale.

If you are a philosopher in such a universe, you might call Ω *inevitable*.

The woman has haunted Blackwheel Station for as long as anyone remembers, although she was not born there. She is human, and her straight black hair and brown-black eyes suggest an ancestral inheritance tangled up with tigers and shapeshifting foxes. Her native language is not spoken by anyone here or elsewhere.

They say her true name means things like *gray* and *ash* and *grave*. You may buy her a drink, bring her candied petals or chaotic metals, but it's all the same. She won't speak her name.

That doesn't stop people from seeking her out. Today, it's a man with mirror-colored eyes. He is the first human she has seen in a long time.

"Arighan's Flower," he says.

It isn't her name, but she looks up. Arighan's Flower is the gun she carries. The stranger has taken on a human face to talk to her, and he is almost certainly interested in the gun.

The gun takes different shapes, but at this end of time, origami multiplicity of form surprises more by its absence than its presence. Sometimes the gun is long and sleek, sometimes heavy and blunt. In all cases, it bears its maker's mark on the stock: a blossom with three petals falling away and a fourth about to follow. At the blossom's heart is a character that itself resembles a flower with knotted roots.

The character's meaning is the gun's secret. The woman will not tell it to you, and the gunsmith Arighan is generations gone.

"Everyone knows what I guard," the woman says to the mirror-eyed man.

"I know what it does," he says. "And I know that you come from people who worship their ancestors."

Her hand—on a glass of water two degrees from freezing—stops, slides to her side, where the holster is. "That's dangerous knowledge," she says. So he's figured it out. Her people's historians called Arighan's Flower the *ancestral gun*. They weren't referring to its age.

The man smiles politely, and doesn't take a seat uninvited. Small courtesies matter to him because he is not human. His mind may be housed in a superficial fortress of flesh, but the busy computations that define him are inscribed in a vast otherspace.

The man says, "I can hardly be the first constructed sentience to come to you."

She shakes her head. "It's not that." Do computers like him have souls? she wonders. She is certain he does, which is potentially inconvenient. "I'm not for hire."

"It's important," he says.

It always is. They want chancellors dead or generals, discarded lovers or rival reincarnates, bodhisattvas or bosses—all the old, tawdry stories. People, in all the broad and narrow senses of the term. The reputation of Arighan's Flower is quite specific, if mostly wrong.

"Is it," she says. Ordinarily she doesn't talk to her petitioners at all. Ordinarily she ignores them through one glass, two, three, four, like a child learning the hard way that you can't outcount infinity.

There was a time when more of them tried to force the gun away from her. The woman was a duelist and a killer before she tangled her life up with the Flower, though, and the Flower comes with its own defenses, including the woman's inability to die while she wields it. One of the things she likes about Blackwheel is that the administrators promised that they would dispose of any corpses she produced. Blackwheel is notorious for keeping promises.

The man waits a little longer, then says, "Will you hear me out?"

"You should be more afraid of me," she says, "if you really know what you claim to know."

By now, the other people in the bar, none of them human, are paying attention: a musician whose instrument is made of fossilized wood and silk strings, a magister with a seawrack mane, engineers with their sketches hanging in the air and a single doodled starship at the boundary. The sole exception is the tattooed traveler dozing in the corner, dreaming of distant moons.

In no hurry, the woman draws the Flower and points it at the man. She is aiming it not at his absent heart, but at his left eye. If she pulled the trigger, she would pierce him through the false pupil.

The musician continues plucking plangent notes from the instrument. The others, seeing the gun, gawk for only a moment before hastening out of the bar. As if that would save them.

"Yes," the man says, outwardly unshaken, "you could damage my lineage badly. I could name programmers all the way back to the first people who scratched a tally of birds or rocks."

The gun's muzzle moves precisely, horizontally: now the right eye. The woman says, "You've convinced me that you know. You haven't convinced me not to kill you." It's half a bluff: she wouldn't use the Flower, not for this. But she knows many ways to kill.

"There's another one," he says. "I don't want to speak of it here, but will you hear me out?"

She nods once, curtly.

Covered by her palm, engraved silver-bright in a language nobody else reads or writes, is the word *ancestor*.

Once upon a universe, an empress's favored duelist received a pistol from the empress's own hand. The pistol had a stock of silver-gilt and niello, an efflorescence of vines framing the maker's mark. The gun had survived four dynasties, with all their rebellions and coups. It had accompanied the imperial arsenal from homeworld to homeworld.

Of the ancestral pistol, the empire's archives said two things: *Do not use this weapon, for it is nothing but peril* and *This weapon does not function*.

In a reasonable universe, both statements would not be true.

The man follows the woman to her suite, which is on one of Blackwheel's tidier levels. The sitting room, comfortable but not luxurious by Blackwheeler standards, accommodates a couch sized to human proportions, a metal table shined to blurry reflectivity, a vase in the corner.

There are also two paintings, on silk rather than some less ancient substrate. One is of a mountain by night, serenely anonymous amid its stylized clouds. The other, in a completely different style, consists of a cavalcade of shadows. Only after several moments' study do the shadows assemble themselves into a face. Neither painting is signed.

"Sit," the woman says.

The man does. "Do you require a name?" he asks.

"Yours, or the target's?"

"I have a name for occasions like this," he says. "It is Zheu Kerang."

"You haven't asked me my name," she remarks.

"I'm not sure that's a meaningful question," Kerang says. "If I'm not mistaken, you don't exist."

Wearily, she says, "I exist in all the ways that matter. I have volume and mass and volition. I drink water that tastes the same every day, as water should. I kill when it moves me to do so. I've unwritten death into the history of the universe."

His mouth tilts up at *unwritten*. "Nevertheless," he says. "Your species never evolved. You speak a language that is not even dead. It never existed."

"Many languages are extinct."

"To become extinct, something has to exist first."

The woman folds herself into the couch next to him, not close but not far. "It's an old story," she says. "What is yours?"

"Four of Arighan's guns are still in existence," Kerang says.

The woman's eyes narrow. "I had thought it was three." Arighan's Flower is the last, the gunsmith's final work. The others she knows of are Arighan's Mercy, which always kills the person shot, and Arighan's Needle, which removes the target's memories of the wielder.

"One more has surfaced," Kerang says. "The character in the maker's mark resembles a sword in chains. They are already calling it Arighan's Chain."

"What does it do?" she says, because he will tell her anyway.

"This one kills the commander of whoever is shot," Kerang says, "if that's anyone at all. Admirals, ministers, monks. Schoolteachers. It's a peculiar sort of loyalty test."

Now she knows. "You want me to destroy the Chain."

Once upon a universe, a duelist named Shiron took up the gun that an empress with empiricist tendencies had given her. "I don't understand how a gun that doesn't work could possibly be perilous," the empress said. She nodded at a sweating man bound in monofilament so that he would dismember himself if he tried to flee. "This man will be executed anyway, his name struck from the roster of honored ancestors. See if the gun works on him."

Shiron fired the gun . . . and woke in a city she didn't recognize, whose inhabitants spoke a dialect she had never heard before, whose technology she mostly recognized from historical dramas. The calendar they used, at least, was familiar. It told her that she was 857 years too early. No amount of research changed the figure.

Later, Shiron deduced that the man she had executed traced his ancestry back 857 years, to a particular individual. Most likely that ancestor had performed some extraordinary deed to join the aristocracy, and had, by the reckoning of Shiron's people, founded his own line.

Unfortunately, Shiron didn't figure this out before she accidentally deleted the human species.

"Yes," Kerang says. "I have been charged with preventing further assassinations. Arighan's Chain is not a threat I can afford to ignore."

"Why didn't you come earlier, then?" Shiron says. "After all, the Chain might have lain dormant, but the others—"

"I've seen the Mercy and the Needle," he says, by which he means that he's copied data from those who have. "They're beautiful." He isn't referring to beauty in the way of shadows fitting together into a woman's profile, or beauty in the way of sun-colored liquor at the right temperature in a faceted glass. He means the beauty of logical strata, of the crescendo of axiom-axiom-corollary—*proof*, of *quod erat demonstrandum*.

"Any gun or shard of glass could do the same as the Mercy," Shiron says, understanding him. "And drugs and dreamscalpels will do the Needle's work, given time and expertise. But surely you could say the same of the Chain."

She stands again and takes the painting of the mountain down and rolls it tightly. "I was born on that mountain," she says. "Something like it is still there, on a birthworld very like the one I knew. But I don't think anyone paints in this style. Perhaps some art historian would recognize its distant cousin. I am no artist, but I painted it myself, because no one else remembers the things I remember. And now you would have it start again."

"How many bullets have you used?" Kerang asks.

It is not that the Flower requires special bullets—it adapts even to emptiness—it is that the number matters.

Shiron laughs, low, almost husky. She knows better than to trust Kerang, but she needs him to trust her. She pulls out the Flower and rests it in both palms so he can look at it.

Three petals fallen, a fourth about to follow. That's not the number, but he doesn't realize it. "You've guarded it so long," he says, inspecting the maker's mark without touching the gun.

"I will guard it until I am nothing but ice," Shiron says. "You may think that the Chain is a threat, but if I remove it, there's no guarantee that you will still exist—"

"It's not the Chain I want destroyed," Kerang says gently. "It's Arighan. Do you think I would have come to you for anything less?"

Shiron says into the awkward quiet, after a while, "So you tracked down descendants of Arighan's line." His silence is assent. "There must be many."

Arighan's Flower destroys the target's entire ancestral line, altering the past but leaving its wielder untouched. In the empire Shiron once served, the histories spoke of Arighan as an honored guest. Shiron discovered long ago that Arighan was no guest, but a prisoner forced to forge weapons for her captors. How Arighan was able to create weapons of such novel destructiveness, no one knows. The Flower was Arighan's clever revenge against a people whose state religion involved ancestor worship.

If descendants of Arighan's line exist here, then Arighan herself can be undone, and all her guns unmade. Shiron will no longer have to be an exile in this timeline, although it is true that she cannot return to the one that birthed her, either.

Shiron snaps the painting taut. The mountain disintegrates, but she lost it lifetimes ago. Silent lightning crackles through the air, unknots Zheu Kerang from his human-shaped shell, tessellates dead-end patterns across the equations that make him who he is. The painting had other uses, as do the other things in this room—she believes in versatility—but this is good enough.

Kerang's body slumps on the couch. Shiron leaves it there.

For the first time in a long time, she is leaving Blackwheel Station. What she does not carry she can buy on the way. And Blackwheel is loyal because they know, and they know not to offend her; Blackwheel will keep her suite clean and undisturbed, and deliver water, near-freezing in an elegant glass, night after night, waiting.

Kerang was a pawn by his own admission. If he knew what he knew, and lived long enough to convey it to her, then others must know what he knew, or be able to find it out.

Kerang did not understand her at all. Shiron unmazes herself from the station to seek passage to one of the hubworlds, where she can begin her search. If Shiron had wanted to seek revenge on Arighan, she could have taken it years ago.

But she will not be like Arighan. She will not destroy an entire timeline of people, no matter how alien they are to her.

Shiron had hoped that matters wouldn't come to this. She acknowledges her own naïveté. There is no help for it now. She will have to find and murder each child of Arighan's line. In this way she can protect Arighan herself, protect the accumulated sum of history, in case someone outwits her after all this time and manages to take the Flower from her.

In a universe where determinism runs backwards—where, no matter what you do, everything ends in the same inevitable Ω—choices still matter, especially if you are the last guardian of an incomparably lethal gun.

Although it has occurred to Shiron that she could have accepted Kerang's offer, and that she could have sacrificed this timeline in exchange for the one in which neither Arighan nor the guns ever existed, she declines to do so. For there will come a heat-death, and she is beginning to wonder: if a constructed sentience—a computer—can have a soul, what of the universe itself, the greatest computer of all?

In this universe, they reckon her old. Shiron is older than even that. In millions of timelines, she has lived to the pallid end of life. In each of those endings, Arighan's Flower is there, as integral as an edge is to a blade. While it is true that science never proves anything absolutely, that an inconceivably large but finite number of experiments always pales beside infinity, Shiron feels that millions of timelines suffice as proof.

Without Arighan's Flower, the universe cannot renew itself and start a new story. Perhaps that is all the reason the universe needs. And Shiron will be there when the heat-death arrives, as many times as necessary.

So Shiron sets off. It is not the first time she has killed, and it is unlikely to be the last. But she is not, after all this time, incapable of grieving.

Ω

AMOR VINCIT OMNIA

K. J. PARKER

Usually, the problem was getting the witnesses to talk.

. . . He just walked down the street looking at buildings and they caught fire. No, he didn't do anything, like wave his arms about or stuff like that, he just, I don't know, looked at them . . .

This time, the problem was getting them to shut up.

. . . Stared at this old guy and his head just sort of crumpled, you know, like a piece of paper when you screw it into a ball? Just stared at him, sort of annoyed, really, like the guy had trodden on his foot, and then his head just . . .

As he listened, the observer made notes; *Usque Ad Peric; Unam Sanc (twice); ?Mundus Verg ??variant.* He also nodded his head and made vague noises of sympathy and regret, and tried not to let his distaste show. But the smell bothered him; burnt flesh, which unfortunately smells just a bit like roasted meat (pork, actually), which was a nuisance because he'd missed lunch; burnt bone, which is just revolting. His moustache would smell of smoke for two days, no matter how carefully he washed it. He stopped to query a point; when he made the old woman vanish, was there a brief glow of light, or—? No? No, that's fine. And he jotted down; *Choris Anthrop, but no light; ?Strachylides?*

The witness was still talking, but he'd closed his eyes; *and then Thraso from the mill came up behind him and shot him in the back, and nothing happened, and then he turned around real slow and he pointed at Thraso, and Thraso just—*

He frowned, stopped the witness with a raised hand. "He didn't know—"

"What?"

"He didn't know he was there. This man—" Always hopeless at names. "The miller. He didn't know the miller was there."

"No, Thraso crept up on him real quiet. Shot him in the back at ten paces. Arrow should've gone right through him and out the other side. And then he turned round, like I just said, and—"

"You're sure about that. He didn't hear him, or look round."

"He was busy," the witness said. "He was making Cartusia's head come off, just by looking at it. And that's when Thraso—"

"You're *sure*?"

"Yes."

The witness carried on talking about stuff that clearly mattered to him, but which didn't really add anything. He tuned out the voice, and tried to write the word, but it was surprisingly difficult to make himself do it. Eventually, when he succeeded, it came out scrawled and barely legible, as though he'd written it with his left hand;

Lorica?

"Unam Sanctam," the Precentor said (and Gennasius was leaning back in his chair, hands folded on belly, his I've-got-better-things-to-do pose) "is, of course, commonly used by the untrained, since the verbal formula is indefinite and, indeed, often varies from adept to adept. Usque ad Periculum, by the same token, is frequently encountered in these cases, for much the same reason. They are, of course, basic intuitive expressions of frustration and rage, strong emotions which—"

"It says here," Poteidanius interrupted, "he also did Mundus Verg. That's not verbal-indefinite."

The Precentor glanced down at the notes on the table in front of him. "You'll note," he said, "that our observer was of the opinion that a variant was used, not Mundus Vergens itself. The variants, of which Licinianus lists twenty-six, include some forms which have been recorded as indefinite. The same would seem to apply to Choris Anthropou."

"Quite," said the very old man at the end, whose name he could never remember. "Strachylides' eight variants, three of which have been recorded as occurring spontaneously." *So there*, he thought, as Poteidanius shrugged ungraciously. "I remember a case back in 'Fifty-Six. Chap was a striker in a blacksmith's shop, didn't know a single word of Parol. But he could do five variants of Choris in the vernacular."

"Our observer," the Precentor said, "specifically asked if there was an aureola, and the witness was quite adamant."

"The third variant," Gennasius said. "Suggests an untrained of more than usual capacity, or else a man with a really deep-seated grudge. I still don't see why you had to drag us all out here. Surely your department can deal with this sort of thing without a full enclave."

He took a deep breath, but it didn't help. "If you'd care to look at paragraph four of the report," he said, trying to keep his voice level and reasonably pleasant, "you'll see that—"

"Oh, *that*." Gennasius was shaking his head in that singularly irritating way. "Another suspected instance of Lorica. If I had half an angel for every time some graduate observer's thought he's found an untrained who's cracked Lorica—"

"I have interviewed the observer myself," the Precentor said—trying to do gravitas, but it just came out pompous. "He is an intelligent young man with considerable field experience," he went on, "not the kind to imagine the impossible or to jump to far-fetched conclusions on the basis of inadequate evidence. Gentlemen, I would ask you to put aside your quite reasonable scepticism for one moment and simply look at the evidence with an open mind. If this really is Lorica—"

"It doesn't exist." Gennasius snapped out the words with a degree of passion the Precentor wouldn't have believed him capable of. "It's a legend. A fairy tale. There are some things that simply aren't possible. Lorica's one of them."

There was a short, rather painful silence. Raw emotion, like raw chicken, upset elderly gentlemen of regular habits. Then the Preceptor said gently, "Ninety-nine out of a hundred human beings would say exactly the same thing about *magic*." He allowed himself to dwell on the word, because Gennasius hated it so. "And of course, they would be right. There is no such thing as magic. Instead, there is a branch of natural philosophy of which we are adepts and the rest of the world is blissfully ignorant. Gentlemen, think about it, please. It may well not be Lorica. But if it is, if there's the slightest chance it could be, we have to do something about it. *Now.*"

"I'm sorry," the young man said. "I've never heard of it."

The Precentor smiled. "Of course you haven't." He half-filled two of his notoriously small glasses with wine and handed one to the young man, who took it as if the stem was red-hot. "For one thing, it doesn't exist."

The young man looked at him unhappily. "Ah," he said.

"At least," the Precentor went on, "we believe it doesn't exist. We hope like hell it doesn't exist. If it does—" He produced a synthetic shudder of horror that actually became a real one.

The young man put his glass down carefully on the table. "Is it some kind of weapon?"

The Precentor couldn't help smiling. "Quite the reverse," he said. "That's the whole point. Lorica's completely harmless, you might say. It's a defence."

"Ah."

"A total defence." The Preceptor paused and watched. He'd chosen young Framea for his intelligence and perceptiveness. This could be a test for him.

He passed. "A total defence," he said. "Against everything? All known forms?"

The Preceptor nodded slowly. "All known forms. And physical weapons too. And fire, water, death by suffocation and falling from a great height. Possibly some diseases too, we don't know."

"That would be—" Framea frowned, and the Preceptor imagined a great swelling cloud of implications filling the young man's mind. He didn't envy him that. "That could be bad," he said.

"Extremely. An individual we couldn't harm or kill; therefore outside our control. Even if he was a mediocre adept with limited power, knowledge of the basic offensive forms together with absolute invulnerability, it doesn't bear thinking about. Even if his intentions were benign to begin with, the mere possession of such power would inevitably turn him into a monster. Hence," he added gently, "our concern."

"But I still don't quite—" Framea looked at him, reminding him vaguely of a sheep. "If it doesn't exist—"

"Ah." The Preceptor held up a hand. "That's the question, isn't it? All we know is that it *could* exist. Blemmyes, a hundred and seventy years ago, proved that it could exist; his reasoning and his mathematics have been rigorously examined and found to be perfect. There is a potential for such a form. Of course, nobody has yet been able to produce it—"

"You mean people have tried?"

The Preceptor nodded slowly. "Unofficially, you might say, but yes. Well, you can imagine, the temptation would be irresistible. Some of the finest minds—But, thankfully, none of them succeeded. Several of them, indeed, wrote papers outlining their researches, basically arguing that if they couldn't do it, nobody could—flawed logic, you'll agree, but when you're dealing with men of such exceptional vanity—"

"I think I see," Framea interrupted. "Trained adepts have tried, using proper scientific method, and they've all failed. But an untrained—"

"Exactly." The Preceptor was relieved; he'd been right about the boy after all. "An untrained might well succeed where an adept would fail, because the untrained often possess a degree of intuitive power that tends to atrophy during the course of formal education. An untrained might be able to do it, simply because he doesn't know it's impossible."

Framea nodded eagerly. "And an untrained, by definition—"

"Quite. Unstable, probably mentally disturbed by the power inside him which he doesn't understand or know how to control; if not already malignant by nature, he would rapidly become so. And with Lorica—Really, it doesn't bear thinking about."

There was a long pause. Then Framea said, "And you want *me* to—"

Framea hadn't been cold for as long as he could remember. It was always warm in the Studium; warm, unpleasantly warm or downright hot, depending on who'd been nagging the Magister ad Necessariis most recently. Old men feel the cold, and the adepts of the Studium didn't have to worry about the cost of fuel.

He pulled his coat up round his ears and quickened his pace. He hadn't been out in the dark for a long time, either. It didn't frighten him ("an adept of the Studium fears nothing, because he has nothing to fear"; first term, first day, first lecture) but it made him feel uncomfortable. As did the task that lay ahead of him.

You will, of course, have to seduce a woman—

Well, fine. And the rest of the day's your own. He winced as he recalled his reaction.

("I see," he'd said, after a moment of complete silence. "I don't know how."

"Oh, it's quite straightforward. So I'm told."

"Is there, um, a book I could—?"

"Several.")

More than several, in fact; from Flaminian's *Art of Seduction*, three hundred years old, eight thousand lines of impeccable hexametric verse, to Bonosius Brunellus' *On the Seduction of Women*, three hundred pages with notes and appendices, entirely drawn from the works of earlier authors. The librarian had given him a not-you-as-well look when he'd asked for them, and they'd been no help at all. He'd asked Porphyrius, the only adept in the Studium who might possibly have had first-hand experience of such things, but he'd just laughed like a drain and walked away.

Lorica, he reminded himself.

The inn was, in fact, just another farmhouse, where the farmer's wife sold beer and cider in her kitchen, and you could pay a half-turner and sleep in the hayloft; not the sort of inn where you could rely on finding a prostitute at any hour of the day or night. In fact, he doubted very much whether they had prostitutes out here in the sticks. Probably, it was one of those areas of activity like brewing or laundry; you only got specialist professionals in the towns. Still, it couldn't hurt to ask.

"You what?" the woman demanded.

He repeated the question. It was unambiguous and politely phrased. The woman scowled at him and walked away.

He took his mug of beer, which he had no intention of drinking, and sat down in a corner the room. Everybody had turned to look at him when he came in, and again when he asked the question, but they'd lost interest. He stretched out his legs under the table, closed his eyes and tried to think.

("You will, of course, have to seduce a woman," the Preceptor had said. "To use as a source."

The second statement was infinitely more shocking than the first. "That's illegal," he said.

"Yes, well." The Preceptor had frowned at him. "I hereby authorise you to use all means necessary. I suppose you'll want that in writing."

"Yes, please. Also," he'd added, "I don't know how.")

He reached into his pocket and took out the book. It was only just light enough for reading, even with Bia Kai Kratos to enhance his eyesight.

He wondered if anybody had ever read a book in this room before and decided no, almost certainly not. He tried to concentrate on the analysis of the necessary forms, which were difficult, abstruse and in some cases downright bizarre; not all that different from the exercises he'd read about in Flaminian and Brunellus, come to that. The thought that he was going to have to perform both the forms and the other stuff *simultaneously* made him feel quite ill.

"Excuse me."

He looked up and saw a woman. At first he guessed she was about thirty-five, but she seemed to get younger as he looked at her. She was very pale, almost milk white, with mouse-coloured hair that seemed to drip off her head, like a leak in the roof. He wondered what she wanted.

"You were asking," she about. "About—"

Oh, he thought. "Yes, that's right."

She looked at him with a combination of hope and distaste. The latter he felt he deserved. "How much?" she said.

"I don't know," he replied. "What do you think?"

He didn't need to use Fortis Adiuvat to know what was going on in her mind. Think of a number and double it. "A thaler," she said.

Almost certainly way over the odds, but the Studium was paying. "Sure," he said quickly. "Now, or—?"

"Now," she said.

He reached in his coat pocket. The cellarer had issued him with money, along with spare clothes, stout walking boots and a waterproof hood. It had been so long since he'd had any dealings with the stuff that he didn't recognise the coins. But he seemed to recall that thalers were big silver things, and all he'd been given was small gold ones. "Here," he said, pressing a coin into her hand. It felt warm, soft, slightly clammy. "That's fine."

She stared at the coin and said nothing. "Now?" he said. She nodded.

Outside, it was raining hard. It wasn't far across the yard to the barn, but far enough for them both to get soaking wet. He couldn't face that, not on top of everything else, so he executed Scutum in coelis under his breath and hoped she wouldn't notice. As they climbed the ladder to the hayloft, something scuttled. He hoped she wasn't one of those people who had an irrational fear of mice, like he did.

"Use a general Laetitia," the Preceptor had said. It was the only specific piece of advice he'd given him. He tried it; the form to fill another person with unspeakable joy. He hadn't done it very often.

Either it worked, or he had a latent and unexpected talent for what Brunellus insisted on calling the subtleties of the bedchamber. His own impression of the activities involved was decidedly ambiguous. Predominant was the stress involved in doing two demanding and unfamiliar things at the same time. There was anxiety (though he calmed down a bit when he realised that the yelling and whimpering didn't mean she was in excruciating pain; bizarrely, the opposite). Guilt; partly because what he was doing was illegal—he had the Preceptor's written exemption, but it was still a crime; partly because he knew what would happen to the poor girl, who'd never done him any harm. Other than that, it was really just a blend of several different strains of acute embarrassment. The thought that people did that sort of thing for *fun* was simply bewildering.

In the morning he went to the village where it had happened. Sixteen dead, according to the report; four still comatose with shock and fear. He stopped at the forge and asked for directions.

The smith looked at him. "You're not from—"

"No," he said. "I'm from the city. I represent the Studium. It's about the incident."

It was the word they used when they had to talk to the public. He hated saying it; incident. Only stupid people used words like that.

The smith didn't say anything. He lifted his hand and pointed up the street. Framea followed the line, and saw a larger than average building at the end, white, with a sun-in-glory painted over the door. Which he could have found perfectly well for himself, had he bothered to look, and then the whole village wouldn't have known he was here.

Fortunately, the Brother was at home when he knocked on the door. A short man, with a round face, quite young but thin on top, tiny hands like a girl. According to the report, this little fat man had walked out of his house into the street after the perpetrator had killed sixteen people, and had tried to *arrest* him—And the perpetrator had turned and walked away.

"My name is Framea," he said. "I'm from the Studium."

The Brother stared at him for a moment, then stood aside to let him in through the door. He had to duck to keep from banging his head.

"I told the other man—"

"Yes, I've read the report," Framea cut him off. "But I need to confirm a few details. May I sit down?"

The Brother nodded weakly, as though Death had stopped by to borrow a cup of flour. "I told him everything I saw," he said. "I don't think there was anything—"

Framea got a smile from somewhere. "I'm sure that's right," he said. "But you know how it is. Important facts can get mangled in transmission. And the man who interviewed you was a general field officer, not a Fellow. He may have misunderstood, or failed to grasp the full significance of a vital detail. I'm sure you understand."

He went over it all again. Thrasea the miller had shot the perpetrator in the back with a crossbow, at close range, ten paces, but the arrow—No, he hadn't simply missed, you couldn't miss at that range. Well, you could, but not Thrasea, he'd won the spoon at shoot-the-popinjay the year before last, he was a good shot. And besides, the arrow had just *stopped*—

Technical details? For the report. Well, it was a hunting bow, you needed a windlass to draw it, you couldn't just span it with your hands. Well, it's possible, the man could have been wearing something under his coat, a mailshirt or a brigandine; but at that range the arrow would most likely have gone straight through, one of those things'll shoot clean through an oak door at point-blank range. Besides, if the man had been hot, even if he was wearing armour and it turned the arrow, he'd have moved; jerked like he'd been kicked by a horse, at that distance. And the arrowshaft would've splintered, or at the very least the tip would've snapped off or gotten bent. No; he'd picked up the arrow himself later that day, and it was good as new.

"And then he turned round and—"

"Yes, thank you," Framea said quickly. "That part of the account isn't in issue." He swallowed discreetly and went on; "Did you see any marks on the man? Scratches, bruises, anything like that?"

No, there wasn't a mark on him anywhere that the Brother could see, not that he'd expected to, since nobody had gotten closer to him than Thraso did. Cuts and scratches from flying debris, from when he made the houses fall down; no, nothing like that. There was stuff flying in the air, bits of tile and rafter, great slabs of brick and mortar, but none of them hit the man. Yes, he was right up close. No, he didn't make any warding-off gestures or anything like that. Too busy killing people. Didn't really seem interested in the effects of what he was doing, if Framea got his drift.

"And you're absolutely sure you'd never seen this man before."

"Quite sure. And the same goes for everybody else in the village. A complete stranger."

Framea nodded. "Don't suppose you get many of those."

"Carters," the Brother said, "pedlars occasionally, though they never come back. People here aren't very well off, you see. We don't tend to buy anything from outside."

"Can you think of anybody who'd have a grudge against the people here?" Framea asked. "Any feuds, or anything like that?"

The Brother looked blank, like he hadn't heard the word before.

"Inheritance disputes? Scandals? Anybody run off with someone else's wife lately?"

The Brother assured him that things like that simply didn't happen there. Framea thought of the girl, the previous night. She was probably a part-timer, like the smith and the wheelwright and the man who made coffins. Simply not enough business to justify going full time.

"There was one thing," the Brother said, as Framea stooped under the lintel on his way out. "But I'm sure it was just me imagining things."

"Well?"

"I don't know. " The Brother pulled a sad, indecisive face. "When I was looking at him, in the street, it's like he was sort of hard to see; you know, when you're looking at someone with the sun behind them? And at the time, I guess I must've thought that's what it was, only it didn't register, if you know what I mean."

"You noticed it without realising."

The Brother nodded. "But then later, thinking about it, I realised it couldn't have been that, because it was mid-morning, and I was looking *down* the street at him, I mean looking from my end, which is due east. So the sun was behind me, not him."

Framea blinked. Yes, he thought, it was just you imagining things. Or, just possibly, a really powerful Ignis in favellum; except why would anybody enchant himself to glow bright blue in broad daylight?

"Thank you," he said to the Brother. "You've been most helpful."

Your only viable approach will be to provoke him into attacking you.

Framea stopped at the crack in the wall where the fresh-waterspring trickled through. He'd seen women standing here, filling their jugs and bowls painfully slowly. It was the only clean water in the village. He knelt down and cupped his hands, then drank. It tasted of iron, and something nasty he couldn't quite place.

If it was such a poor village, how come Thrasea the miller could afford a good hunting bow? He shook his head. Urban thinking. He'd probably built it himself; carved the stock, traded flour with the smith for the steel bow. He could almost picture him in his mind—patiently, an hour each evening in the barn, by the light of a bulrush taper soaked in mutton-fat. People in the villages often used sharp flints for planing wood, because steel tools were luxuries. Or you might borrow a plane from the wheelwright, if he owed you a favour—

Motive. What motive would an untrained need? He tried to imagine what it must be like, to carry the gift inside you and not know what it was. You'd probably believe you were mad, because you knew they things you were able to do were impossible (but you'd seen them happen, but they were impossible, but you'd seen them) You wouldn't dare tell anyone else. But there'd be the times when you got angry (you'd have a shorter temper than most people, because of the stress you'd be under all the time) and you found you'd done something without realising. Something bad, inevitably. Your victim would tell people, in whispers; they wouldn't quite believe it, but they wouldn't quite disbelieve it either. You'd get a reputation. People would be nervous around you. Not much chance of a job, if you needed one, not much chance of help from your neighbours if something went wrong. It'd be a miracle if an untrained reached adulthood without being a complete mess.

He filled another handful and drank it. The taste was stronger, if anything. Iron and—

He stood up. Provoke a fight, the Precentor had said. Well, indeed. Easy peasy.

(But an untrained would *know*, wouldn't he? He'd feel the presence of another gift, he'd be drawn here. Would he dare come back to the village, where he'd be instantly recognised? It would all depend on exactly what he could do. Besides Lorica, of course. But untrained were always an unknown quantity. There were cases on record of untrained who could do seventh-degree translocations, but not a simple light or heat form. There was no way of knowing. Damn.)

He spent the rest of the day slouching round the village, trying to be conspicuous, something he'd spent his life avoiding. The idea was that news spreads like wildfire in small, remote rural communities, and he wanted everybody for miles around to know that there was a man from the Studium in the village, asking questions about the massacre. But the village chose that day to be empty, practically deserted; if anybody saw him , he didn't see them. It did cross his mind that it was deserted precisely because he was there. As darkness closed in, he began to feel rather desperate; he really didn't want to have to stay here any longer than was absolutely necessary. He went back to the spring-mouth, scrambled up onto a cart that someone and left there for some reason, and looked all around. Nobody in sight. Then he took a deep breath and shouted; "I AM FRAMEA OF THE STUDIUM! SURRENDER OR FIGHT ME TO THE DEATH!" Then he got down, feeling more ridiculous than he'd ever felt in his whole life.

He hadn't actually said anything about that night, but she was there waiting for him when he got back to the inn; standing alone, in the corner of the room. The five or six men sitting drinking acted as though she was invisible. Strictly speaking, it wasn't necessary; once was usually reckoned to be sufficient to form the connection. She looked up at him. Presumably, it was just about the money.

He nodded, and she left the room; as she did so, the men stopped talking, and there was dead silence for a while, as though they were at a religious service, or remembering the war dead on Victory Day. He'd thought about sitting down for a while and drinking a mug of the disgusting beer, but he decided against it. A man could catch his death of cold from a silence like that.

The subtleties of the hayloft, he thought, as he crossed the yard. The ground was still wet from yesterday's rain, and his muddy foot slipped on the bottom rung of the ladder. She was waiting for him, lying on her back, fully clothed. She looked as though she was waiting for the attentions of a surgeon, not a lover. Never again, he promised himself.

This time, he cast a number of specific Laetitias as well as a general one.

It was easier now that he knew what a woman's reproductive organs actually looked like (he'd seen drawings in a book, of course, but you couldn't get a real idea from a drawing. Besides, the illustrations in Coelius' *Anatomy* looked more like a sketch-map of a battlefield than anything to do with the human body). The results were quite embarrassingly effective, and he was worried the people in the inn might hear, and assume the poor woman was being murdered.

She fell asleep quite quickly afterwards. He lay on his back with his eyes closed, wishing more than anything that he was back in his warm chambers at the Studium, where he could wash properly and be alone. She snored. He realised he didn't know her name; though, to be fair, there was no compelling evidence to suggest she even had one.

Also, he wanted to wake her up and apologise. But of course she was better off not knowing.

If he'd been asleep, he was woken up by a soft white light filling the hayloft. He opened his eyes. It was as bright as day, lighter than lamplight, even the glare of a thousand candles in the Great Hall of the Studium at the Commemoration feast.

The light came from a man. He was standing at the entrance to the hayloft, where a beam ran across, separating the loft from the rest of the barn; he guessed it was used as the fulcrum for a rope, for hoisting up heavy weights. The man was leaning on his folded arms against the bar. It was impossible to make out his face, blindingly backlit. He was tall and slightly built.

"Hello," he said.

Framea sat up. "Hello."

"You wanted to see me."

Him. Framea felt terrified, for a moment or so. Then the fear stabilised; it didn't go away, but it settled down. It was something he could draw on. Maybe that's what courage is, he speculated later.

"You're Framea, right? The wizard."

Framea was pleased he'd said that. It triggered an automatic, well-practiced reponse. "We aren't wizards," he heard himself say. "There's no such thing. I'm a student of natural philosophy. A scientist."

"What's the difference?"

The man, he noticed, spoke with no accent; none at all. Also, his voice was strangely familiar. That's because it's inside my head, Framea realised. And the man isn't really there, this is a third-level translocation. But he wasn't sure about that. The light, for one thing.

"Are you here in this room?" he asked.

The man laughed. "You know," he said, "that's a bloody good question. I'm not sure, to be honest with you. Like, I can feel this wooden beam I'm resting on. But I definitely didn't leave the—where I'm staying. So I must still be there, mustn't I? Or can I be in two places at once?"

A *ninth*-level translocation. Under other circumstances, Framea would be on his knees, begging to be let in on the secret of how you did that. "Technically, no," he replied, his lecturer's voice, because it made him feel in control. Like hell he was; but the man didn't need to know that. "But there's a form we call Stans in duobus partibus which—theoretically—allows a person to be in two different places simultaneously. That's to say, his physical body. His mind—"

"Yes?" Eager.

"Opinions differ," Framea said. "Some maintain that the mind is present in both bodies. Others hold that it exists in another House entirely, and is therefore present in neither body."

"House," the man repeated. "You've lost me."

Framea shivered. "No doubt," he replied. "You would have to have studied for two years at the Studium to be in a position to understand the concept."

"That's what I wanted to see you about," the man said. "No, stay exactly where you are, or I'll kill her."

Her, Framea noted. "I'm sorry," he said. "A touch of cramp. Let me sit up so we can talk in a civilized manner."

"No." Maybe just a touch of apprehension in the voice, leading to a feather of hostility? "You can stay right there, or I'll burst her head. You know I can do it."

"I can, of course, protect her," Framea lied. "And I don't think we have anything to discuss. I have to inform you that you are under arrest."

The man laughed, just as if Framea had told the funniest joke ever. "Sure," he said. "I'll try and bear that in mind. Now, tell me about this Studium place of yours."

She was still fast asleep, breathing slow and deep. He could smell her spit where it had dried around his mouth. "I don't see that it's anything to do with you," he said.

"Come off it. You know I'm one of you lot. I want to come and be educated properly. That's what you're there for, isn't it?"

Framea winced. "Out of the question," he said. "For one thing, you're much too old. More to the point, you've committed a number of brutal murders. You should be aware that I'm authorised to use—"

"No, that's not right." A statement, not a question, or even an objection. "I've never done your lot any harm. Our lot," he amended. "I'm just like you. I'm not like them at all."

"They were human beings," Framea said. "You killed them. That is not acceptable."

"But we're not human, are we?" The man was explaining to him, as if to a small child. "We're better. I mean, wizards, we can do anything we like. That's the whole point, isn't it?"

Framea didn't answer. Far too much conversation already; he knew it was discouraged, since any interaction with a malignant could only serve to weaken one's position. The trouble was, he was on the defensive. Lorica . . .

"Well?"

"You will surrender now," Framea said, "or I shall have no option but to use force."

"Screw you, then," the man said, and he lashed out. It was Mundus vergens in a raw, inelegant variant, but backed up with enormous power. Framea barely held it with Scutum and a third-level translocation. Fortunately the man had fogotten about his threat to kill the girl, or else he'd never meant it. Framea replied tentatively with Hasta maiestatis, more as a test of the man's defences than anything else. The form stopped dead and washed back at him; he got out of the way of the backlash just in time with a fourth-level dissociation into the third House.

Lorica, he thought, and then; why *me*?

"Are you still there?" he heard the man ask. "Hello?"

Framea paused to consider the tactical options. If, as he suspected, the man was present only by way of a ninth-level translocation, the safest course would be to break the form and force him back into his other body, wherever the hell that was. He could manage that, he was fairly sure; but it would mean draining the source, because of the backlash, and how would he ever find him again? He wasn't here to protect himself, he was here to bring the malignant in, or kill him. In which case—

Oh well, he thought.

He concentrated all his mind on the sleeping girl. He imagined shoving his hand down her throat, grabbing her heart and ripping it out. On the count of three, he told himself; one, two, three.

He pulled, felt all of her strength flow into him, and immediately struck out with Fulmine. He put everything into it, all of her and all of him. It soaked into Lorica like water into sand, not even any backlash.

"Did you just do something?" the man asked curiously.

Framea felt empty. He had no strength left. By any normal standards he'd completely overdone the Fulmine—if he'd missed the target and overshot, they'd have to send to the City for cartographers to redraw all the maps—and the man was asking, did you just do something? It wasn't possible. It couldn't be happening. Lorica; which didn't exist.

The girl grunted in her sleep and turned over.

"This is pointless," the man said. "You can't hurt me, I can't hurt you, the hell with it. Don't come after me anymore, or I'll kill the village."

The light suddenly went out.

He spent the rest of the night crouched over the girl's body, watching her breathe.

She woke up just after dawn. As soon as she opened her eyes, he asked her, "Are you all right?"

She nodded. "Why? What's the matter?"

"Nothing." He hesitated. "Did you have nightmares?"

She frowned. "I think so. But I always forget my dreams. Why?"

He wanted to say, because I very nearly killed you, and I want to know if you remember any of it, because if you do, I'll have to erase your mind. He wanted to explain, at the very least. Dear God, he wanted to *apologise*. But he knew that would be to make him feel better. It would be self-indulgence, and they'd warned him about that on his second day as a student.

"Here," he said, and gave her two of the gold coins. She stared at them, and then at him. She was terrified.

"What happened?"

"Nothing," he said. "Well, you know. But that's all."

She went away, to wherever it was she went to. He pulled his clothes on, climbed down from the loft, crossed the yard and tried to wash in the rain-barrel. He felt disgusting (but that was probably just more self-indulgence; weren't there savages who washed by rolling in mud, then waiting till it caked dry and peeling it off, leaving their skins clean? Is that me, he wondered, and decided not to pursue that line of thought.) Then he crossed the yard and went into the kitchen, where the farmer's wife served him salted porridge and green beer with a face you could have sharpened knives on.

I could go home, he thought. I've failed, clearly this untrained is far too strong for me. If I stay here, the most likely outcome is that I'll be killed, the untrained will slaughter the innocent people here, and then they'll have to send someone else to sort out the mess. Somebody competent. Well, they might as well do that now. Out of my league. There'll be a certain amount of humiliation, and it won't do my career a lot of good, but at least I won't be dead. And they'll understand. After all, it really is Lorica. In fact, I'll probably get a mention in a book, as the man who proved Lorica existed.

And what about the girl, he asked himself, but of course he knew the answer to that. The reason why using another human being as a source was illegal was because of the risk of damaging them. In eighty-six cases out of a hundred, there was significant harm to the mind, the memory or both. In seventy-four cases studied by Sthenelaus and Arcadianus for their report to the Ninety-First Ecumenical, forty-one ex-sources killed themselves within five years of having been used. A further twelve died insane. Only eight were found to have emerged from the experience unscathed, and six of them were found to have latent abilities, which enabled them to repair the damage to some extent. There were further, worse effects when the source was female, as was usually the case, given that sexual intercourse was the simplest and most reliable means of forming the connection. Use of sources had been forbidden by the Sixty-Third Ecumenical, and the prohibition had subsequently been restated by the Seventy-Ninth and the Ninety-First, and by a series of orders in enclave; the discretion to ignore the prohibition, vested in an officer of Precentor rank or above, had only been granted by the Hundred and Seventh as an emergency measure during the Pacatian crisis. The intention had been to repeal the discretion as soon as the crisis was over, but presumably the repeal was still tied up in committee somewhere.

I'm not a hero, he told himself. None of us are, we're natural philosophers. Scientists. We shouldn't have to do this sort of thing, except there's nobody else to do it.

He went back to the hayloft, took his paper and portable inkwell out of his coat pocket, and wrote a report for the Precentor. As soon as the ink was dry, he burnt it, sending it into the fifth House. Thanks to intercameral distortion, the reply arrived a few minutes later.

Proceed as you think fit. You have full discretion. This matter must be resolved before you leave. Use any means necessary. Regret we cannot send further operatives at this time.

My mistake, he thought. I can't go home after all.

So he spent the day hanging around the village again, not doing anything much, pretending not to notice the overtly hostile stares of the villagers, the few of them who ventured into the street while he was there. He couldn't help being just a little angry at the injustice of it. Fairly soon, he assumed, he'd be giving his life for these people, and here they were scowling at him.

Giving, wasting; there'd be no point, since the untrained had Lorica and therefore couldn't be beaten.

The point struck him while he was sitting on the front step of some house, after a failed attempt to buy food. Such was the feeling against him that even a whole gold coin hadn't been enough to secure a loaf of bread. He'd been reduced to conjuring half-ripe apples off a tree in a walled orchard, when nobody was looking. As he bit into an apple and pulled a face, he remembered something the malignant had said.

You can't hurt me, I can't hurt you, the hell with it.

Factually inaccurate; but the malignant believed it—He let the apple fall from his hand, too preoccupied to maintain his grip on it. The untrained malignant believed that, if he could do Lorica, so could everyone else; he assumed it was perfectly normal, part of every adept's arsenal.

And why not? Perfectly reasonable assumption to make, in the circumstances. Something so fundamentally, incomparably useful—naturally, you'd think that it was basic stuff, the kind of thing you were taught at the same time as joined-up writing and the five-times table.

In which case—

It appeared to have worked the last time, so he did it again.

"I AM FRAMEA OF THE STUDIUM!" he roared, to an audience of three dogs, two small boys and an old woman who took absolutely no notice. "SURRENDER OR FIGHT ME! TONIGHT!" Then he scrambled down off the cart, turning his ankle over in the process, and hobbled back to the inn.

The farmer's wife was in the kitchen, cutting up pork for sausages. "What's that stuff all the people round here drink?" he asked.

She looked at him. "Beer," she said.

"Is it fit for human consumption?"

"Well, we drink it."

"That's not an answer. Never mind, the hell with it. Get me some. Lots."

You got used to it, after a while. At the Studium, wine was drunk four times a year (Commemoration, Ascension, Long Commons and the Election Dinner); two small glasses of exquisite ruby-red vintage wine from the best cellar in the City. Framea had never liked the stuff. He thought it tasted of vinegar and dust. The beer tasted of decay and the death of small rodents, but after a while it did things to his perception of the passage of time that no form had yet been able to accomplish. He slept through the afternoon and woke up in his chair in the kitchen just as it was starting to get dark. He had a headache, which he quickly disposed of with Salus cortis. He didn't feel hungry, even though he hadn't eaten all day.

He hauled himself to his feet, wincing as his turned-over ankle protested under his weight. An injury like that would be a death sentence if he'd been facing a conventional battle, with swords or fists. He limped across the yard, and the farm workers stared at him as he passed them. There were two young men in the barn, cutting hay in the loft with a big knife-blade, like a saw.

"Get out," he said. They left quickly.

He lay down on the hay, his hands linked behind his head. I do this for the people, he told himself. I do this so that there won't be another massacre like the last one. Then, because he didn't want what could well be his last meditation to be spoiled by such a flagrant lie, he amended it to; *we* do this for the people, for the reason stated. *I* do this because I was told to. I do this because if I refused a direct order from my superior, I'd be demoted from the Studium to a teaching post in the provinces. Hell of a reason for killing and dying.

I do this because of Lorica. Simple as that.

He considered the paradox of Lorica; the ultimate, intolerable weapon that hurt nobody, the absolute defence that could save the life of every adept who ever walked or strayed into harm's way. He couldn't help smiling at the absurdity of it. Half the cities in the Confederation forbade their citizens to own weapons; it never seemed to make any difference to the murder rate, but you could see a sort of logic to it. But no city anywhere banned the ownership of *armour*. Most of the scholars in the Studium spent at least some of their time developing weapon-grade forms, new ways of killing, wounding, forms directly or indirectly ancillary to such activities—all to be used only against the enemies of order and stability, of course, except that somehow the enemy always found out about them, which was why the Studium needed to develop even better weapons. Lorica, on the other hand, was pure anathema. The Studium didn't want to find Lorica and then try and keep it to itself; it was realistic enough to know that that wouldn't be possible. Most of all, they wanted it not to exist. If it did exist, they wanted it destroyed, without trace. Why? Because all government, all authority, no matter how civilised, enlightened, liberal, well-intentioned, ultimately depends on the use of force. If a man exists who is immune to force, even if he's the most blameless anchorite living on top of a column in the middle of the desert, he is beyond government, beyond authority, and cannot be controlled; and that would be intolerable. Imagine a rebel who stood in front of the entire army, invulnerable, untouchable, gently forgiving each spear-cast and arrow-shot while preaching his doctrine of fundamental change. It would mean the end of the world.

And *I*, he thought, am here because of Lorica because I'm expendable. Let's not lose sight of that along the way.

She came when it was dark outside. He'd hoped she wouldn't, but he couldn't help feeling a rush of joy when she climbed up the ladder and sat down beside him. It was too dark to see, so he had no way of knowing what, if any, signs of damage she was showing. He put his hand in his pocket, closed his fingers around all the remaining coins, and held it out to her.

"I don't want any more money," she said.

"I don't care what you want," he replied. "Take it, lie down and go to sleep."

She didn't move; didn't reach out her hand for the coins. He grabbed her left arm, prised the fingers apart and tipped the coins into it. "Please," he said. "It'll make me feel better."

(It didn't, though. It wasn't his money.)

She withdrew her hand, and he had no way of knowing if she pocketed the coins or dropped them into the hay. "You just want me to go to sleep," she said.

"Yes."

He felt her lie down, making a slight disturbance in the hay. He applied a light Suavi dormiente, and soon her breathing became slow and regular. He closed his eyes and went through the plan, for the hundredth time. The more he thought about it, the more problems, defects, disasters waiting to happen leapt out at him. It wasn't going to work, and any moment now the untrained would be here, and he'd have to fight—

He came in light, as before; it occurred to wonder how he did that, but of course he couldn't very well ask. He appeared where he'd been the first time, leaning against the cross-rafter, his face just as impossible to make out.

"I thought we'd been through all this," he said. "There's no point, is there?"

This time, though, his voice was different; accented (a City voice, but overlaid with the local flat vowels and ground-off consonants; so maybe he'd been one of the children evacuated in the War, who hadn't gone back again afterwards); more or less educated, so at least he'd been to school, even if it was just a few terms with a Brother. It wasn't much, but at least he knew something about him now. And he was *here*; not a ninth-level translocation, but an appearance in person, unified body and whole mind together in this place. *Thank you*, he thought.

"On the contrary," he replied. "We have to settle this."

"Why?"

That was a really good question, and he had no answer. "You might be able to hide," he said, "for a little while. But if you ever use your power again, we'll be able to trace you. We can kill you in your sleep if you'd rather. But I assumed you'd prefer to do the honourable thing."

The untrained laughed. "Can't say I'm bothered one way or the other," he said. "Sure, I'd like to join up, be a proper wizard, but you said I can't, so that's that. Don't see why I should want to play by your rules, in that case."

Framea could smell something. It took him back thirty years, to before he came to the City and joined the Studium; to when he'd lived with his mother in a small house, more of a shack, out back of the tannery. He could smell brains, which the tanners used to cure hides.

"You work in a tannery," he said.

"If you're reading my mind you're not very good at it," the man replied. "Six months since I left there. Five months and twenty-seven days since it burned down," he added. "Anyway, what's that got to do with anything?"

"Fight me," Framea said. "If you dare."

"If I think I'm hard enough, you mean?" The man laughed. "That's what they used to say at that place. Regretted it, later. But there's no point. We can't hurt each other. You know that."

Framea took a deep breath. "The defence you're referring to is called Lorica," he said.

"Fascinating."

"Take it down," Framea said. "I'll do the same. Then we can fight and really mean it. It's the way we do it."

He didn't dare breathe until the man replied, "Is that right?"

"Yes. Think about it. How do you suppose anything ever gets sorted out?"

Another pause. Then the man said, "How'll I know you've taken yours down?"

Framea muttered Ignis ex favellis, making his skin glow blue. "I've lit mine up, same as yours. When the lights go out, we'll both know the other one's taken down Lorica. Then we can put an end to this, once and for all." He waited a heartbeat, then added, "I'm taking mine down now. Don't disappoint me. I'm paying you a compliment."

He ended Ignis. Another heartbeat, and the white glow at the far end of the loft went out. With his mind's arm, he reached down into the girl's heart and took everything, at the same time as he ripped every last scrap out of himself, and launched it all in Ruans in defectum.

The form went through. The smallest fraction of time that he could perceive passed, and no counterstroke came. No backlash. With the last shreds of his strength, he moved into the second House.

As usual, it was light and cool there. Today it was a meadow, with a river in the distance, sheep in the pasture on the far bank. He looked round and saw the man, lying on his face, burned practically to charcoal. He ran across, lifted his head by his charred, crumbling hair and whispered in his ear, "Can you hear me?"

The reply was inside his own head. *Yes.*

"This is the second House," he said. "This is another place, not the place where you used to live. In that place, your body has been disintegrated. I used Ruans. There's nothing left for anyone to bury. You're dead."

I understand.

"I'm holding you here by Ensis spiritus. The second House is outside time, but it takes a huge amount of effort just to be here. In a moment I'll have to let you go, and then you'll just disappear, drain away. It won't hurt. Do you understand?"

Yes.

"Show me Lorica."

But you know—

"No. I don't know Lorica. Nobody does." He closed his eyes for a moment. "Nobody living. Show it to me. You're the only one who ever found it. Show it to me now."

The body was charred embers, it was ash, it was falling apart. Any moment now, the thing inside it would leak out into the air and be gone for good. Framea used Virtus et clementia, which was illegal, but who the hell would ever know?

He saw Lorica.

He wanted to laugh. It was absurdly simple, though it would take considerable strength of mind and talent; still, easier and more straightforward than some forms he'd learnt before his voice broke. It was nothing more than a wide dispersal through at least twenty different Houses, combined with a third-level dislocation. The weapon (or the form, or the collapsing wall or the falling tree) killed you in one House, or twelve, or nineteen; but there you were, safe and sound, also in the twentieth House, and a fraction of a second later, back you came, as though nothing had happened. All there was to it. Less skill and technique required than conjuring up a bunch of flowers.

The voice sighed in his head. A gentle breeze blew away the last of the ash. Framea felt the bitter cold that meant he'd stayed out too long and needed to get back. He slipped out of the second House just in time, and as soon as he got back he passed out.

Someone was shaking him. He opened his eyes and grunted,

"Are you all right?" The girl was leaning over him, looking worried. "You wouldn't wake up. I was afraid something had happened."

You could say that, he thought. Something did happen. "I'm fine," he said. "I had a bit too much to drink earlier, that's all. I'm going now," he added. "Thanks for everything."

He stood up. His ankle still hurt, and for some reason he couldn't be bothered to fix it with Salus or any of the other simple curative forms.

"Are you a wizard?" she asked.

He turned to face her. She looked all right, as far as he could tell, but in many cases there was a delay before the first symptoms manifested. "Me? God, no. Whatever gave you that idea?"

He walked away before she could say anything else.

"And was it," the Precentor said delicately, "the problem we discussed?"

Framea looked straight at him, as if taking aim. "No," he said. "I got that completely wrong. It was just an unusually powerful Scutum."

The Precentor's face didn't change. "That's just as well," he said. "I was concerned, when I received your letter."

"Yes. I'm sorry about that." Behind the Precentor's head he could just make out the golden wings of the Invincible Sun, the centrepiece of the elaborate fresco on the far wall. Had the Precentor deliberately arranged the chairs in his study so that, viewed from the visitor's seat, his head was framed by those glorious wings, imparting the subconscious impression of a halo? Wouldn't put it past him, Framea decided. "I guess I panicked, the first time I fought him. I'm new at this sort of thing, after all."

"You did exceedingly well," the Precentor said. "We're all very pleased with how you handled the matter. I myself am particularly gratified, since you were chosen on my personal recommendation."

Not long ago, that particular fragment of information would have filled him with terror and joy. "It was quite easy," he said, "once I'd figured it out. A simple translocation, change the angle, broke his guard." He licked his lips, which had gone dry, and added, "Needless to say, I regret having had to use lethal force. But he was very strong. I didn't want to take chances."

The Precentor smiled. "You did what had to be done. Now, will you join me in a glass of wine? I believe this qualifies as a special occasion."

Three weeks later, Framea was awarded the White Star, for exceptional diligence in the pursuit of duty, elevated to the Order of Distinguished Merit, and promoted to the vacant chaplaincy of the Clerestory, a valuable sinecure that would allow him plenty of time for his researches. He moved offices, from the third to the fifth floor, with a view over the moat, and was allocated new private chambers, in the Old Building, with his own sitting room and bath.

Nine months later, he wrote a private letter to the Brother of the village. He wrote back to say that the village whore (the Brother's choice of words) had recently given birth. The child was horribly deformed; blind, with stubs for arms and legs, and a monstrously elongated head. It had proved impossible to tell whether it was a boy or a girl. Fortuitously, given its sad condition, it had only lived a matter of hours. After its death, the woman hanged herself, presumably for shame.

Father Framea (as he is now) teaches one class a week at the Studium; fifth year, advanced class. He occasionally presents papers and monographs, which are universally well received. His most recent paper, in which he proves conclusively that the so-called Lorica form does not and cannot exist, is under consideration for the prestigious Headless Lance award.

THE GREEN BOOK

AMAL EL-MOHTAR

MS. Orre. 1013A Miscellany of materials copied from within Master Leuwin Orrerel's (*d.* Lady Year 673, Bright Be the Edges) library by Dominic Merrowin (*d.* Lady Year 673, Bright Be the Edges). Contains Acts I and II of Aster's *The Golden Boy's Last Ship*, Act III scene I of *The Rose Petal*, and the entirety of *The Blasted Oak*. Incomplete copy of item titled only THE GREEN BOOK, authorship multiple and uncertain. Notable for extensive personal note by Merrowin, intended as correspondence with unknown recipient, detailing evidence of personal connection between Orrerel and the Sisterhood of Knives. Many leaves regrettably lost, especially within text of THE GREEN BOOK: evidence of discussion of Lady Year religious and occult philosophies, traditions in the musical education of second daughters, and complex reception of Aster's poetry, all decayed beyond recovery. Markers placed at sites of likely omission.

My dear friend,

I am copying this out while I can. Leuwin is away, has left me in charge of the library. He has been doing that more and more, lately—errands for the Sisterhood, he says, but I know it's mostly his own mad research. Now I know why.

His mind is disturbed. Twelve years of teaching me, and he never once denied me the reading of any book, but this—this thing has hold of him, I am certain plays with him. I thought it was his journal, at first; he used to write in it so often, closet himself with it for hours, and it seemed to bring him joy. Now I feel there is something fell and chanty about it, and beg your opinion of the whole, that we may work together to Leuwin's salvation.

The book I am copying out is small—only four inches by five. It is a vivid green, quite exactly the color of sunlight through the oak leaves in the arbor, and just as mottled; its cover is pulp wrapped in paper, and its pages are thick with needle-thorn and something that smells of thyme.

There are six different hands in evidence. The first, the invocation, is archaic: large block letters with hardly any ornamentation. I place it during Journey Year 200-250, Long Did It Wind, and it is written almost in green paste: I observe a grainy texture to the letters, though I dare not touch them. Sometimes the green of them is obscured by rust-brown stains that I suppose to be blood, given the circumstances that produced the second hand.

The second hand is modern, as are the rest, though they vary significantly from each other.

The second hand shows evidence of fluency, practice, and ease in writing, though the context was no doubt grim. It is written in heavy charcoal, and is much faded, but still legible.

The third hand is a child's uncertain wobbling, where the letters are large and uneven; it is written in fine ink with a heavy implement. I find myself wondering if it was a knife.

The fourth is smooth, an agony of right-slanted whorls and loops, a gallows-cursive that nooses my throat with the thought of who must have written it.

The fifth hand is very similar to the second. It is dramatically improved, but there is no question that it was produced by the same individual, who claims to be named Cynthia. It is written in ink rather than charcoal—but the ink is strange. There is no trace of nib or quill in the letters. It is as if they welled up from within the page.

The sixth hand is Leuwin's.

I am trying to copy them as exactly as possible, and am bracketing my own additions.

Go in Gold,
Dominic Merrowin

[First Hand: invocation]
Hail!
To the Mistress of Crossroads, **[blood stain to far right]**
The Fetch in the Forest
The Witch of the Glen
The Hue and Cry of mortal men
Winsome and lissom and Fey!
Hail to the **[blood stain obscuring]** Mother of Changelings
of doubled paths and trebled means
of troubled dreams and salt and ash
Hail!

[Second Hand: charcoal smudging, two pages; dampened and stained]
Cold in here—death and shadows—funny there should be a book! the universe provides for last will and testament! **[illegible]**

[illegible] *I cannot write, mustn't* [illegible] *they're coming I hear them they'll hear scratching* [illegible] *knives to tickle my throat oh please*

They say they're kind. I think that's what we tell ourselves to be less afraid because how could anyone know? Do [blood stain] *the dead speak?*

Do the tongues blackening around their necks sing?

why do I write? save me, please, save me, stone and ivy and bone I want to live I want to breathe they have no right [illegible]

[Third Hand: block capitals. Implement uncertain—possibly a knife, ink-tipped.]

What a beautiful book this is. I wonder where she found it. I could write poems in it. This paper is so thick, so creamy, it puts me in mind of the bones in the ivy. Her bones were lovely! I cannot wait to see how they will sprout in it—I kept her zygomatic bone, but her lacrimal bits will make such pretty patterns in the leaves!

I could almost feel that any trace of ink against this paper would be a poem, would comfort my lack of skill.

I must show my sisters. I wish I had more of this paper to give them. We could write each other such secrets as only bones ground into pulpy paper could know. Or I would write of how beautiful are sister-green's eyes, how shy are sister-salt's lips, how golden sister-bell's laugh

[Fourth Hand: cursive, right-slanted; high quality ink, smooth and fine]

Strange, how it will not burn, how its pages won't tear. Strange that there is such pleasure in streaking ink along the cream of it; this paper makes me want to touch my lips. Pretty thing, you have been tricksy, tempting my little Sisters into spilling secrets.

There is strong magic here. Perhaps Master Leuwin in his tower would appreciate such a curiosity. Strange that I write in it, then—strange magic. Leuwin, you have my leave to laugh when you read this. Perhaps you will write to me anon of its history before that unfortunate girl and my wayward Sister scribbled in it.

That is, if I send it to you. Its charm is powerful—I may wish to study it further, see if we mightn't steep it in elderflower wine and discover what tincture results.

[Fifth Hand: ink is strange; no evidence of implement; style resembles Second Hand very closely]

Hello?

Where am I?

Please, someone speak to me

Oh

Oh no

[Sixth Hand: Master Leuwin Orrerel]

I will speak to you. Hello.

I think I see what happened, and I see that you see. I am sorry for you. But I think it would be best if you tried to sleep. I will shut the green over the black and you must think of sinking into sweetness, think of dreaming to fly. Think of echoes, and songs. Think of fragrant tea and the stars. No one can harm you now, little one. I will hide you between two great leather tomes—

[Fifth Hand—alternating with Leuwin's hereafter]

Do you know Lady Aster?

Yes, of course.

Could you put me next to her, please? I love her plays.

I always preferred her poetry.

Her plays ARE poetry!

Of course, you're right. Next to her, then. What is your name?

Cynthia.

I am Master Leuwin.

I know. it's very kind of you to talk to me.

You're—**[ink blot]** forgive the ink blot, please. Does that hurt?

No more than poor penmanship ever does.

Leuwin? Are you there?

Yes. What can I do for you?

Speak to me, a little. Do you live alone?

Yes—well, except for Dominic, my student and apprentice. It is my intention to leave him this library one day—it is a library, you see, in a tower on a small hill, seven miles from the city of Leech—do you know it?

No. I've heard of it, though. Vicious monarchy, I heard.

I do not concern myself overmuch with politics. I keep records, that is all.

How lucky for you, to not have to concern yourself with politics. Records of what?

Everything I can. Knowledge. Learning. Curiosities. History and philosophy. Scientific advances, musical compositions and theory—some things I seek out, most are given to me by people who would have a thing preserved.

How ironic.

. . . Yes. Yes, I suppose it is, in your case.

[[DECAY, SEVERAL LEAVES LOST]]

Were you very beautiful, as a woman?

What woman would answer no, in my position?

An honest one.

I doubt I could have appeared more beautiful to you as a woman than as a book.

. . . Too honest.

[[DECAY, SEVERAL LEAVES LOST]]

What else is in your library?

Easier to ask what isn't! I am in pursuit of a book inlaid with mirrors—the text is so potent that it was written in reverse, and can only be read in reflection to prevent unwelcome effects.

Fascinating. Who wrote it?

I have a theory it was commissioned by a disgruntled professor, with a pun on "reflection" designed to shame his students into closer analyses of texts.

Hah! I hope that's the case. What else?

Oh, there is a history of the Elephant War written by a captain on the losing side, a codex from the Chrysanthemum Year (Bold Did it Bloom) about the seven uses of bone that the Sisterhood would like me to find, and—

Cynthia I'm so sorry. Please, forgive me.

No matter. It isn't as if I've forgotten how I came to you in the first place, though you seem to quite frequently.

Why

Think VERY carefully about whether you want to ask this question, Leuwin.

Why did they kill you? . . . How did they?

Forbidden questions from their pet librarian? The world does turn. Do you really want to know?

Yes.

So do I. Perhaps you could ask them for me.

[[DECAY, SEVERAL LEAVES LOST]]

If I could find a way to get you out . . .

You and your ellipses. Was that supposed to be a question?

I might make it a quest.

I am dead, Leuwin. I have no body but this.

You have a voice. A mind.

I am a voice, a mind. I have nothing else.

Cynthia . . . What happens when we reach the end of this? When we run out of pages?

Endings do not differ overmuch from each other, I expect. Happy or sad, they are still endings.

Your ending had a rather surprising sequel.

True. Though I see it more as intermission—an interminable intermission, during which the actors have wandered home to get drunk.

[[DECAY, SEVERAL LEAVES LOST]]

Cynthia, I think I love you.

Cynthia?

Why don't you answer me?

Please, speak to me.

I'm tired, Leuwin.

I love you.

You love ink on a page. You don't lack for that here.

I love *you*.

Only because I speak to you. Only because no one but you reads these words. Only because I am the only book to be written to you, for you. Only because I allow you, in this small way, to be a book yourself.

I love you.

Stop.

Don't you love me?

Cynthia.

You can't lie, can you?

You can't lie, so you refuse to speak the truth.

I hate you.

Because you love me.

I hate you. Leave me alone.

I will write out Lady Aster's plays for you to read. I will write you her poetry. I will fill this with all that is beautiful in the world, for you, that you might live it.

Leuwin. No.

I will stop a few pages from the end, and you can read it over and over again, all the loveliest things . . .

Leuwin. No.

But I

STOP. I WANT TO LIVE. I WANT TO HOLD YOU AND FUCK YOU AND MAKE YOU TEA AND READ YOU PLAYS. I WANT YOU TO TOUCH MY CHEEK AND MY HAIR AND LOOK ME IN THE EYES WHEN YOU SAY YOU LOVE ME. I WANT TO LIVE!

And you, you want a woman in a book. You want to tremble over my binding and ruffle my pages and spill ink into me. No, I can't lie. Only the living can lie. I am dead. I am dead trees and dead horses boiled to glue. I hate you. Leave me alone.

[FINIS. Several blank pages remain]

You see he is mad.

I know he is looking for ways to extricate her from the book. I fear for him, in so deep with the Sisters—I fear for what he will ask them—

Sweet Stars, there's more. I see it appearing as I write this—unnatural, chanty thing! I shall not reply. I must not reply, lest I fall into her trap as he did! But I will write this for you—I am committed to completeness.

Following immediately after the last, then:

Dominic, why are you doing this?

You won't answer me? Fair enough.

I can feel when I am being read, Dominic. It's a beautiful feeling, in some ways—have you ever felt beautiful? Sometimes I think only people who are not beautiful can feel so, can feel the shape of the exception settling on them like a mantle, like a morning mist.

Being read is like feeling beautiful, knowing your hair to be just-so and your clothing to be well-put-together and your color to be high and bright, and to feel, in the moment of beauty, that you are being observed.

The world shifts. You pretend not to see that you are being admired, desired. You think about whether or not to play the game of glances, and you smile to yourself, and you know the person has seen your smile, and it was beautiful, too. Slowly, you become aware of how they see you, and without looking, quite, you know that they are playing the game too, that they imagine you seeing them as beautiful, and it is a splendid game, truly.

Leuwin reads me quite often, without saying anything further to me. I ache when he does, to answer, to speak, but ours is a silence I cannot be the one to break. So he reads, and I am read, and this is all our love now.

I feel this troubles you. I do not feel particularly beautiful when you read me, Dominic. But I know it is happening.

Will you truly not answer? Only write me down into your own little book? Oh, Dominic. And you think you will run away? Find him help? You're sweet enough to rot teeth.

You know, I always wanted someone to write me poetry.

If I weren't dead, the irony would kill me.

I wonder who the Mistress of the Crossroads was. Hello, I suppose, if you ever read this—if Dominic ever shares.

I am going to try and sleep. Sorry my handwriting isn't prettier. I never really was, myself.

I suppose Leuwin must have guessed, at some point. Just as he would have guessed you'd disobey him eventually. I am sorry he will find out about both, now. It isn't as if I can cross things out.

No doubt he will be terribly angry. No doubt the Sisters will find out you know something more of them than they would permit, as I did.

It's been a while since I've felt sorry for someone who wasn't Leuwin, but I do feel sorry for you.

Good night.

That is all. Nothing else appears. Please, you must help him. I don't know what to do. I cannot destroy the book—I cannot hide it from him, he seeks it every hour he is here—

I shall write more to you anon. He returns. I hear his feet upon the stair.

THE OTHER GRACES

ALICE SOLA KIM

See: I don't even need to wake you up anymore. Maybe you're exhausted, your eyeballs feeling tender and painful and peeled of their membranes, but when the alarm goes off at 6:00 AM, you jump out of bed and skitter across the chilly floor to the bathroom.

Every morning is thrilling; every morning you make an effort because this might be the day. It is April and you are a high school senior. Very soon you will be getting the letter that tells you that you've gotten into an Ivy League college. Any Ivy! Who gives a shit which one?

It wasn't easy to get in. You're all wrong for them. Your parents didn't put on identical polo shirts and take you on winding car tours through the Northeast to check out Princeton and Yale. No, you're part of the special category, species, family, genus, *thing* known as yellow trash. Yellow trash aren't supposed to go Ivy League—you've fooled them all, you cheater, you fake! Get ready for your new life.

It's all so thrilling. Too bad you thought you couldn't write about that in your college application essays. All of the things that make you what you had decided should be called yellow trash—the shouting matches in motel court-yards, the dirty hair, the histories of mental illness, the language barriers, the shoes, the silver fillings.

Grace, didn't you know? They eat that shit up. But you wanted a real do-over. You didn't want to be admitted only because they knew what you were. You like to think there's some honor in that.

Even though you may or may not have cheated on the SAT.

Breakfast is last night's dinner of chilly white rice and kimchi, which keeps your stomach full and your breath nasty, good things for a city girl on the go without a car. You like to think that this blast of prickly, fermented stink-breath might someday protect you from the next weirdo at the bus stop who sidles up to you to ask, "China or Japan?" So far, the most you've been able to do is flick up a middle finger in conjunction with a spat-out *"America,* asswipe!" And even that you've only been able to pull off once, but hey—good for you. If you were born unable to be pretty and quiet, then be loud and smelly. Own it.

When you leave the house for the day, your mother is gone and your brother is still at work. When you return, your brother will already be perched on the couch, watching TV. You pause at the door and rest your head on the jamb. The house is so quiet, all yours for now, and you will miss it.

Catch the bus, Grace! The bus!

It takes two city buses to get to your high school. You had started there right before your parents got divorced. You could walk seven blocks to go to a nearby, similarly shitty high school, but faced with the choice of shitty-familiar and shitty-new, you chose shitty-familiar.

Running across the street, you jam the hood of your sweatshirt over your damp head, creating tropical conditions under which your hair will steam and saran-wrap itself to your skull before giving up and drying itself. Why do people even use hair-dryers? They make you go deaf. You're just happy to have shampoo. It was not that long ago when your family could not afford shampoo and so used soap. People—as in, other ten-year-old girls—noticed. Perhaps being poor either turns one into an animal or a classy ascetic with eye-popping cheekbones; it made you into an animal, the fur on your head as oily and felted as a grizzly's.

The bus comes; you lunge inside, stepping tall; the doors slide shut like folding arms. On the sweating brown seat, you pull out a book to read—a charming little volume titled *Science Fiction Terror Tales*—but instead you wedge it under your thigh and close your eyes.

Last night you dreamed a familiar dream, so familiar that all you have to do is drift off in order to call it back. It's a Grace convention up in there, populated with girls and women who look exactly like you. GraceCon always meets in a different location—in hammocks that don't connect to anything you can see, a rainforest, the bottom of a swimming pool. Last night was the swimming pool. Graces were turning somersaults, sitting cross-legged on the bottom of the pool, knifing through the water. You just hung there, inhaling as if the heavy blue water was both fresh air and a nice cold drink.

Always, in the dreams, the Graces look at you and they go, "대황. 대황 대황 대황." You ask them, "대황?" Your accent is perfect. You sound like an ingénue on one of those K-dramas that your mother's addicted to. "대황," they answer. In the dreams, you understand every word.

On the bus, when you jerk awake, your face feels tired. It's the same way your face always felt after elementary school slumber parties—your eyebrows were unused to being hoisted so high, and your mouth-corners felt as though they had been pushed wide and pinned. Back then, your face didn't move much; when anyone in your family smiled, your pops got paranoid. He thought the joke was on him; now it is; it is.

Origin story. You first figured out that you were yellow trash when you were thirteen and attended a summer music day camp two hours away, in a nice neighborhood with a good school district. We both know that you're not that good at the violin. But already you were thinking about college applications, and searching for cheap and easy ways to make yourself appealing to admissions officials.

Anyway, you were getting off the bus in that nice neighborhood when the handle of the violin case slipped out of your hand. You stopped to wipe your sweaty hand on your T-shirt. Someone pushed up behind you and said, "Out of my way, chink."

Who does that? Surely the dickhead utterer of such words must have been green-skinned, a thousand feet tall, dragging a spiked club behind it as it picked and ate its own boogers. But, no, it was just some pretty white girl, a little older than you, high-ponytailed and tall. She didn't even look at you as she walked past. It was all so very racist that you felt as though you were watching a movie of yourself. A movie about racism! Oh, but for you it was playing in Extreme Feel-O-Vision, in that you felt everything, all the hurt and shock, and that despite your best efforts to blend in, to embody a Whiter Shade of Asian, this thing just happened to you, it had happened before, and it would happen again.

It was unfair how everyone could look at her and not see a—let's be blunt, Grace, a *racist asshole*—but just about anyone could look at you and see a chink.

You walked to the middle school where the music camp met, and spent a few minutes in quiet shock as everyone around you chattered and warmed up. Ann Li, who played the cello, asked you what was wrong.

"Someone called me a chink on the way over here," you said.

Ann opened her mouth, so you felt encouraged to spill. You said, "I didn't even do anything to her. I hate people."

"Wow," she said. She gave you a look of pity. "No one's ever called me a chink before."

At this, you crumpled like a soda can. *Never?* Bitch, please! You thought: if you believe *that* then I have a very lovely, like, pagoda to sell you. Admit it, you wondered how it could be that you got chinked about once a month but Ann never had in her entire life. Wasn't there enough racism to go around?

It was then you realized that there are many different kinds of Asian girls. one kind is yellow trash; that is what you are. No matter how you brush your hair and wear Neutrogena lip shimmer and speak perfect English with nary a trace of fobbiness and play a string instrument like, say, Ann Li, you are not like her and you will never be like her, because you are yellow trash and *people can tell*. Even if it takes them a while.

Because at first they only see an Asian girl carrying a violin case, and if they think about you at all, it's to wonder at what a dweeby little princess you must be. But then they realize that the violin is borrowed from the scanty school music equipment room, deep scratches next to the f-holes as if Wolverine himself had given classical music a brief try before roaring in frustration, that you can only ever understand about half of what your parents are saying (if that), that your father is a nutcase, that your mother—who, let it be known, is amazing at her job—periodically has clients who want to speak to her manager because does her manager know that *this woman totally cannot speak English?*, that your brother likes to spit on the floor inside the house, that you are trashy and weird and something is deeply wrong with you and it will never be right unless you do something drastic, like go away to an Ivy League college and return transmuted, if at all.

You like to think that the Ivy League is mystical, miraculous—that, in a biography, it erases everything that comes before it, or else imbues an ignoble childhood with a magical sense of purpose. And it goes without saying that it charms the life that comes after it.

Grace, you moron.

But I understand. Things were rough; you got single-minded.

Your high school is named after a Native American chief and is said to be one of the most ethnically diverse high schools in the state, which unfortunately gives ethnic diversity a terrible name because the high school is truly rubbish. They don't offer AP classes, which is a big part of what drove you to cheat on the SAT, because the SAT is then the only objective measure by which admissions officials will be able to determine if your waving and withered cold hand is the one they want to catch and yank out of the sea.

(You've thought this through. You chew your nails, a lot, and spit out keratin explosively like so many bitten-off ends of cigars. You like to think you fret in style.)

The school day is a long gray expanse. At lunch, you sit in the hallway with some friends. Tama is your best friend here. Tama's half-black half-white, her skin paler than yours. She's stupid-pretty. Not as in ridiculously pretty, but as in pretty in a way that initially makes people think she's not smart, with her jutting upper lip and her lashes so thick they pass for eyeliner. You and Tama have an unequal friendship of the type where she is your best friend and you are probably not hers.

You break Fritos in your mouth and listen to Tama talk about her mother's new painting. It is something sexually explicit involving satyrs and plums. Tama's parents are both artists.

You pull out *Science Fiction Terror Tales*, an act that might be rude if you were there, but you are not there. They, your friends, like you when you're there, but they don't miss you when you're not there. I don't read science fiction anymore, but I like to watch you do it. You get so lost, Grace. You're split in two: you're immersed in a story about a man who is confused about if he's really a man or a robot (truth: he's a bomb), but you're also dreamy for the better days to come.

Right now, you're a weirdo in a hooded sweatshirt, a skinny girl shapeless but for a gigantic ass. Think of a boa constrictor that's just eaten a goat. Stand the boa constrictor on its pointy end. The goat, sliding deeper into its body in one thick lump, is your ass. The rest of you, in this example, is the boa constrictor, which was chosen because obviously boa constrictors do not have tits.

But someday, far into the future, you will look fine. You will have money to spend on your clothes instead of going to the thrift store and pretending that the stuff there is cool but really everything's been picked over by tattooed twenty-somethings and all that's left are racks of sad tank tops with droopy armpits and flared stretch denim. Your hair will be washed with shampoo like the snot of unicorns and cruel hairstylists who are rude to everyone else but kind and complimentary to you will shear you into acceptability. Someday you'll learn on your own the things that no one bothered to teach you. You'll be a lovely young woman.

Yes you will.

Riding the bus home after school, you think about those letters that might be in the mailbox right now. Why not? You've got a perfect 4.0 (albeit the easiest 4.0 ever), crazy extracurriculars, a brilliant essay all about, like, realizing stuff at important moments, and an SAT score of 2400. A perfect score.

Around this time last year, you received a strange invitation to join a group on a social networking website. The group was called The Other Graces, and when you saw its members, you looked around the library in a panic and scooted your chair closer to the computer. Because the other members of The Other Graces looked just like you, but older, all different ages and hairstyles and clothing.

Well, you joined. The next day, you received a message from Grace Prime, as she called herself. Grace Prime got right to it:

> you have been chosen for a mentorship by the other graces
> the other graces are grace chos from alternate timelines of a high fidelity to yours
> we have decided to help you with your dream of acing the sat
> in order to do so i will have to open a subspace corridor into your brain
> please respond with your answer within two business days
> all best
> grace prime

You wrote back and asked her what a subspace corridor was and what it would do inside your brain. You told her that you needed more information before proceeding, duh. Grace Prime called you at home later that night. How she got your number you still don't know.

"It's a way of traveling between universes," said Grace Prime. "You won't feel anything. Well, you may experience a side effect of odd dreams, just here and there, but that's the nature of the beast. It's an invasion, dear. A kindly invasion. You don't need to be afraid."

The cordless handset rested on your face. You tapped your feet on the wall. "You'll all be inside my brain? For how long?"

Grace Prime's voice was old. Quavering-old, creaky screen door-old, gargling with Listerine for a thousand years-old. But strong and scary. "Once created, the subspace corridor remains open for a time before fading away. It has to close on its own. It'll take time, but eventually your mind will be all yours again."

"I don't want a bunch of strangers running through my brain." You laid back on your bed, stuck your big toe into a dent on the wall from that time you threw a desk drawer at it.

Grace Prime sighed. "Grace, privacy is overrated. Especially among those who've already thought your thoughts, or near enough. You think about that. We're no strangers. Think about what that means. Do you want a perfect score on the SAT or not? And those subject tests are killer. You've not exactly had a classical education. You need the help. But it's your decision to make."

You listened to the TV for a while. The way it sounded from the other room, the walls muffling its noise, made you think of someone being kidnapped. Oh, Grace: you composed an ecstatic letter in your head, like a *Penthouse* Forum letter except not to *Penthouse: Dear* Amazing Stories—*you'll never believe what happened to me* . . .

Then, slowly, you agreed to everything.

"Good," Grace Prime said. "You won't regret it. We get results. We change lives."

"Now what?"

"Now I tell you the truth," she said. "The subspace connection was already opened. It was the only way we could talk." She coughed, but not in an embarrassed way. "I'm sorry. I do hate to trick a Grace."

Your head jerked up, just a little. The phone stayed stuck to your cheek. "We're talking on the phone. You called me on the phone."

"Unfortunately not," she said. "Sorry."

The dial tone became louder, turned up and up, until it was all you could hear. And then you realized that it was all you had ever been hearing.

You never spoke to Grace Prime again. Grace Prime, ancient, weird, brilliant—you wonder how she's been. Moved on to another young Grace, you imagine.

She may have lied to you, but the subspace corridor worked. On the morning of the SAT, you got to the testing site and tied your hair back as solemnly as a kamizake pilot, sitting monolith-straight in a room full of slouchers.

The answers came to you unbidden, if not of you then from you. The room was silent but your mind was stuffed migraine-full. You wondered, as you do now, if the feeling of the panoply of Graces in your head, their voices as familiar as your own thoughts, is what it is like to be your father, who gets transmissions from a place he calls The Information Center. Sometimes you imagine how nice a place called The Information Center would be, so straightforward and honest, but then you remember that The Information Center only whispers lies to your father, lies that keep him awake all hours of the night, listening and scheming.

With the assistance of the other Graces over the subspace corridor, you aced test after test after test—Molecular Biology, English Literature, World History, Chemistry. That is how it happened. That is how you know you will get into any college you want. You know.

I am still with you, after all these months—*I can't pull myself away*—and I know this too.

The price you pay is that you'll never know how smart you really are.

When you finally get home, you yank open the mailbox door, prepared to gut it of its contents. There's nothing in there. Your face is tingly and your clothes are sticking to you, sweaty and wet as a pupal skin.

As expected, your brother Luke is sitting on the couch, watching the History Channel. Your mother and father are short, good-looking people, and it's unclear who, if anyone, inherited their looks. Both of you are patchy and unfinished. Luke is twenty-four. He finished college in a prudent and cheap way, by attending community college for two years and moving on afterward to the state university. Yet here he is. It just goes to show that escape must be a drastic endeavor. Otherwise you will loop ever closer back to the source, an orbit decaying into sodden trash.

"Where's the mail?" you say.

He rolls his eyes your way. "Kitchen table."

There's nothing there but catalogs and bills. "Nothing for me?"

"Nope."

"Are you sure?"

He sighs deeply. You know Luke is tired from his nocturnal job, making X-ray copies for hospitals. He also works at a discount department store. But you think this is no excuse for being such a butthead, a terrible brother, a faker, a conspiracy theorist.

"Uh," he finally says. "Dad came by earlier. I saw him through the window. He took something out of the mailbox."

"ARE YOU KIDDING ME? WHY DIDN'T YOU STOP HIM? DID YOU SEE WHAT IT WAS?"

"He would have made me let him into the house," your brother says simply. "It was a big envelope. Stop fucking yelling."

The last time your father got into the house, he went around cleaning everything up, which meant collecting a bunch of papers and magazines from your and your mother's rooms and ripping those up. Then he walked around the living room and took all the Christmas and birthday and congratulations cards that your mother had received over the years and put on the walls and he ripped those up too. You came home to three big grocery bags full of ripped-up paper clustered neatly by the front door, and your brother in his room with the door closed.

Your mother's not much of a yeller, but that night she really went off on your brother, which at first appeared ineffectual because Luke already has the mien of one who has just been yelled at, regardless. But after that, he never let your father into the house again.

Standing there in the living room, shoes still on (and your mother would kill you if she knew!), you consider your options. You're not going to call your mother. It will only stress her out, and then she will stress you out, and then you will feel sorry that you ever said anything. After their divorce, you discovered that your father had given your mother some kind of head injury, years and years ago. It's hard to picture now. He is like King Mr. Head Injury himself now, a man who got knocked straight out of a world in which he is a millionaire and people are conspiring against him in buzzing clusters, into this world, where he's a bum and no one believes a thing he says. He's not capable of hurting anyone now, but you must remember: once he was.

You worry so much that this head injury might bite your mother in the ass in thirty or so years. For now, her memory just sucks, kind of. She forgets when she's promised to take you shopping, because shopping makes her tired and always, always you demand far too much. Once upon a time she had three jobs (a main job at the shipping company, an occasional job at the nearby fried-fish fast food place, and the jewelry counter at JC Penney's on the weekends). Now she only needs one job, but the tiredness persists, deepened into something chronic.

It's also a language barrier thing—this occasionally drifty quality to her; after all, if your life began happening in the Korean language, you wouldn't be able to remember or express anything for shit.

You'll only call your mother when you tell her the good news about college. She'll be thrilled. She is the saddest and least trashy out of any of you. This is why life is hardest for her—you allow yourself to behave badly while she abstains.

"I need a ride downtown," you say to your brother.

"I'm busy," he says.

"It's the History Channel! They show everything five billion times!"

"Ancient astronauts," says Luke. "In the Chariots of the Gods. Chariots of the Gods." He grins stiffly and holds his head back in a way that makes him look seedy and double-chinned, unpleasantly taxidermied.

"Come on, Luke."

He's gotten into a state. He does this all the time and it is so awful. He'll repeat phrases from his conspiracy theory books over and over again, perform weird tics and squeaks (this is where the spitting on the floor thing comes in). You know he doesn't have Tourette's, you *know*, but he likes to act like he does. You will understand later that damage manifests itself in so many different ways. Later, you might have sympathy for Luke, with his fake Tourette's. Today, however, all you can think is that he is disgusting.

"Ancient astronauts."

"Shut the fuck up," you say, grabbing your backpack and moving out the door.

"Don't tell me to shut up," Luke says, suddenly angry.

You hate your brother! Yes you do, right now! You become even more furious when, turning back to Luke, you spy a glob of spit on the floor by the couch. He could stop himself from spitting in the house, but he just doesn't. The sight of it grosses you out but even more so it makes you feel existentially depressed and low and lonesome, all for your brother.

For there are times when you are near-friends, when you sit and watch The Simpsons reruns together and he forgets to spit on the floor and act crazy, or times when you ask him polite questions about his conspiracy theories and try to listen quietly, or times when he delivers unto you tiny kindnesses such as a new pair of ugly black socks from the department store where he works, but that's just not enough, it's not. The one time it's vital for you to get downtown very quickly and it takes about an hour to get there on the bus and the bus smells like poisonous butt-mushrooms when it rains (which it did last night), Luke completely shuts you down?

FUCK this STUPID family. You sail out the door; your brother gets up to lock it behind you; you kick the door; he opens it and yells at you again; you run away as the screen door squeaks shut and the door-door slams; and then, you assume, your brother lapses back into his History Channel stupor, because there's really nothing else to do.

You, as well as I, have had those times where you don't feel like trying anymore. You've thrown your SAT study books across the room. Big, flimsy blocks— they don't make much noise when they hit. You've laughed at your own words in the application essay: wah wah, please take me. I'm ethnic enough for you. But not ethnic in all the wrong ways. I'm poor enough for you. But not so poor I can't pay (let them find the truth out later).

You've made your blood go hot and speedy at the thought of what these colleges have done to you without their knowing it, making you bow and scrape, making you rewrite and redo your life, until you want to cursive your anger across the skies, or better yet, hack those .edus to scrawl in crude MS Paint on the home page banners I WOULDN'T GO TO YOUR FUCKING SCHOOL IF YOU PAID ME A MILLION DOLLARS TIMES A BILLION DOLLARS SO YOU CAN EAT MY ASS KTHXBYE. ALL BEST, GRACE CHO.

And yet, and yet. Every time, you picked up the books and brushed them off. You read each sentence in your essay aloud, searching for the perfect words, tamping down the parts of your brain that cringed at your asshattery, your mendaciousness.

Because:

Remember your brother. Remember your father, remember your mother.

Remember the Asian imposters at Stanford. Two recent news stories made you laugh, they scared you so much: an eighteen-year-old girl named Azia Kim (Azia? Seriously?) posed as a Stanford University freshman for almost a whole year. She lived in the dorms! She joined the ROTC! Just a week after, a woman named Elizabeth Okazaki was discovered to be posing as a visiting scholar in the physics department at—yes!—Stanford again, hanging out at Varian Physics Laboratory and accomplishing the heroic feat of being even weirder and creepier than a pack of physics grad students. Azia and Elizabeth were both kicked off campus.

To a certain extent, you had to admire them. They were too dumb or unlucky or crazy or poor to realize this one stupid dream of theirs, but that didn't stop them.

To a much greater extent, you had to separate yourself from any identification with them, because you were getting into college in a legit way (or, rather, your cheating would be so technologically advanced and devious that no one would ever find out), and they had ruined Stanford for you—you imagined campus police looking out for girls *just like you*, chasing you across the moist green lawns and under the Spanish tiles and demanding ID, except you were already late to class, and everyone was staring, and, and . . .

You didn't apply to Stanford.

Your father's shelter is on the outskirts of downtown, in an emptied neighborhood scattered with unsuccessful coffee shops, corner stores, dead brick businesses, and bus stops. The shelter is unobtrusive and looks like a tax office from the outside, except for a faded sign that reads FRANCIS-

HOLT HOUSE. The buzzer is broken, so you wait outside the door, peering in through the glass until a resident spots you and lets you in. You've never seen him before—a middle-aged black man wearing a maroon T-shirt with a stretched-out neck.

After opening the door, he smiles kindly and says, "Would you like some money?" He opens his hands and all these dollar bills fall on the ground. You help him pick them up, and then go down the hallway to the elevator. When you pass the main office, you wave at the girl inside and tell her you're there to see your father. Of course you don't tell her why you're here and what you might do, so she smiles and says that he's up in his room.

Everyone in this house has got something weird with their heads. Which should go without saying, but every time you come here it's as if you've stepped onto a stage, into a company of committed improv actors who incorporate you into skits with Oulipo-type parameters of which no one has informed you; you're just playing but they are wholly serious.

You take the elevator up to the fourth floor. The hallway is stuffy. It smells of madness, which is something like the smell of people who don't have the right soap and products to get fully clean in the shower, and who wear clothes that come in huge batches from churches. You knock on your father's door. He answers right away.

You say hello, leaning to give him a careful hug.

He smiles. You haven't seen him in a few months, so every time you visit you fear that he'll look like just another bum, just another crazy on the street. Always, he looks okay. His hair is neatly parted, and he is clad in clean-as-is-possible slacks and button-down shirts. The thing about yellow trash that you remember is that yellow trash can be visually deceptive.

"Grace," he says. "대황 [*you*] 대황 [*messy*] 대황 [*very tired-looking*]."

Every time you see him you are relieved that he looks so good but he gets upset at how awful you look.

"How are you doing?" you say.

"Ah," he says, like ten light bulbs have exploded above his head. "대황. 대황 [*Come in*]."

Your father has mellowed out extremely. There's a night you remember, a long time ago, when he left home. You and your mother and your brother went to retrieve him and had a huge shouting fight in a motel courtyard. People were smiling as they watched. The same people that liked watching your family fight probably liked watching that show *COPS*. Why else would they smile?

His place now looks like a motel room, everything petite and self-contained, an answer to the question, *How little do you need in order to feel like a respectable human being in today's America?* You stand by the round table next to his bed. Your father is on medication that makes his feet dance forward and back in a shuffling samba. You looked it up; it's called tardive dyskinesia, and it is the result of an evil White Elephant party in which one gives up psychosis in order to win a case of pseudo-Parkinson's. All the way home from the library you chanted "tardive dyskinesia, tardive dyskinesia" until it turned into "retarded synesthesia," which could have been yet another mental ailment lying in wait for your father.

"Come on, Dad, let's sit down." You put your hand on his elbow and help him down into the chair. He doesn't need the help, but it makes you feel better and maybe him too. He used to harsh you out every time you saw him, especially back when he still had money and his illness still seemed more like an overabundance of cruelty and suspicion than anything else.

These days, during the good visits, you two can walk arm-in-arm down the street to get tacos; this is something that never, ever would have happened before. So you have hope, now. Which is a terrible thing, Grace. I feel sorry for you.

"Dad," you say, "Luke saw you get some of the mail from our box."

He nods, and grins so widely you can see the spaces where teeth are missing.

"Was there anything for me?"

He opens his black satchel, which he keeps clean and polished, and pulls out a big flat envelope.

On that envelope are the colors of a school you've dreamed about. Inside that envelope must be a Yes, or at the very least a strong Maybe. Around that envelope are your father's fingers.

He says, "I am very proud of you," a sentence that you can understand in English or in Korean. You bask in it, you do, his pride and the fact that you finally understood something completely. Everything's so tenuous. Everything's about to be undone.

"Thanks, Dad," you say. You and your father smile at each other, and he reaches over to pat you on the shoulder. "Can I see it?" you say.

"No," he says loudly, "대황 대황 [keep safe] 대황 Information Center. 대황 대황."

He slides the envelope back into the satchel and rests his arm over it. "대황 [this is] 대황 [very good school]. 대황 대황 but you careful. 대황 대황 Information Center 대황 대황 대황 [your mother] 대황 대황 대황 대황 Catholic Church 대황 대황 대황 대황 대황 대황 lawyer 대황 대황 대황 대황 대황 [money] 대황 대황 대황 대황 대황 대황 Luke 대황 대황 대황 [millions] 대황 대황 [television news anchors] 대황 대황 대황 대황 sometimes you are not smart 대황u 대황 대황 대황olic [I need to make you study] 대황 대황 대황 대황 대황 I will call school 대황 대황. I'm coming with you. We go together."

You know that's not true and he can't, he just can't. It's all crazy talk.

How's this guy going to get on a plane and follow you anywhere? He couldn't even ride the bus if he didn't get a pass from the shelter.

But at the same time everything he is saying is so true that your heart and your head want to explode. You feel like crying, but your body is set up to not-cry, it's set up to shunt that impulse into thinking about crying, all the crying you will have to do later, in your your room at home. But by then it will be all gone. That's the problem with saving it up.

"Okay? Okay?" he is saying.

Heliumed with despair—because despair can make one oddly light, isn't that right? Everything lost, and what remains is so stupid and point-less it's lighter than popcorn—you rise up and stand over your father. He is small and thin in his paper-bag-cinched slacks and you feel huge. You're taller than both of your parents because you were bred on meat and white bread and hateful, indigestible milk. This can happen to guys who are afflicted with Bad Dads. They take it until they're fifteen, sixteen, until they discover that they're big enough to start hitting back. You're a girl, but over the years you've been getting angry and big too. So slowly that you had no idea it was happening.

He looks up at you. The reds of his eyes are showing, the skin underneath them lymphy and bagged. "Why you are so bad to me," he says.

"I'm not bad," you say.

"You know what happen 대황 대황," he says, "You don't help stop. You blame me."

"I don't know what to stop, Dad," you say. You're sinking again. You sink lower, catching your head in your arms, entirely exhausted.

There are things you've got to do now. You're too tired to do them. You've got to call the school and ask them for another packet, have them send it to your high school or your mom's workplace. They'll say, "Why?" maybe, and you will tell them a lie. Or maybe you'll say, "None of your fucking business!" and slam the phone down and then they'll un-admit you. Maybe it's all your father's fault that you are yellow trash and you will stay that way forever, but there must have been some way things could have been better. A way that is lost now. Plenty of people deal with plenty of things and they don't turn out trash.

He reaches into the briefcase and takes out the envelope again. This time he opens it and pulls out the letter to show you. He hands you the letter. It's nice. A seal's been punched into the paper, and someone is congratulating you. You barely read it.

"That's fine," you say, and slide it back to him.

The letter's not the thing. I told you, Grace. This story ends well, so never you worry; you don't need the fucking letter anyway. You're in, you're in, and no one can tell you that you're not. Don't cry please.

He says, "You study law, or medicine. If you study law you can do English too in undergrad 대황 대황e, ."

"Uh huh." A wailing rises up in your head.

Your father talks about getting an apartment—or, hey, even a house, because he'll have money to burn—near the campus, where he can visit you every day. And there comes a moment when you almost wish it could be true, all these delusions of his—houses and money and college degrees for anyone who wants sthose things so badly that they've dreamed themselves onto the streets and into homeless shelters.

"We can get cat or dog," he says. "대황 [which do you want?] 대황 대황 cat is cleaner."

"I hate cats," you say. This is the worst. A pet. Something he could very nearly have. But he will never, ever have a pet.

대황 [What?]" he says.

"I like cats."

"Ca-li-co," he says, "대황 [those are the prettiest]." How does he know that word?

Forget a wife, and kids, and a life to keep warm and solvent—I can't even imagine this man taking care of a pet. Suddenly I laugh. It surprises even me, but you get pissed off. You shake your head. *That's enough,* you think, *no more looking.* No more judging. Suddenly you lift a fist and punch the side of your head with a loud, inorganic-sounding thock. Inside your skull clangs and aches. It surprises even me. *Get out, get out,* you think. Go away.

Doing something crazy in front of someone crazy is interesting; you wonder, how will they explain this? Your father is staring at you with wide eyes, and you know he's not getting up to help you. He's figuring out how this all fits into the connected flow charts and diagrams and blueprints and toppling spires in his constructed world. Someone's gotten to his daughter. Someone's put poison into her drinking water and made her go crazy. His daughter is not his daughter.

"Dad," you say, "When you hear the Information Center, do you—"

But you interrupt by hitting yourself again. *Go away go away GO AWAY.* This time it takes. With a shock, I realize that it's my turn to feel, and what I feel is this: me and everything else receding into a rapidly shrinking circle, a tiny angry pupil.

The corridor's closing; I'm an ant up a vacuum cleaner.

Then I come to, and it's just me, all me—alone in my fancy house, chair tipped back onto the floor. There's a broken glass beside me. I want to see how it ends. But I think I know how it ends. I think it's you who doesn't, Grace. My back is killing me. I get up from the floor; I stumble to the kitchen and palm some pills down my throat and drink cold water from the dispenser.

I look at the clock on the wall.

Only minutes have passed for me, just a few of them, but for you, oh you, Grace, for you it's been years and years and years.

THE SULTAN OF THE CLOUDS

GEOFFREY A. LANDIS

When Leah Hamakawa and I arrived at Riemann orbital, there was a surprise waiting for Leah: a message. Not an electronic message on a link-pad, but an actual physical envelope, with *Doctor Leah Hamakawa* lettered on the outside in flowing handwriting.

Leah slid the note from the envelope. The message was etched on a stiff sheet of some hard crystal that gleamed a brilliant translucent crimson. She looked at it, flexed it, ran a fingernail over it, and then held it to the light, turning it slightly. The edges caught the light and scattered it across the room in droplets of fire. "Diamond," she said. "Chromium impurities give it the red color; probably nitrogen for the blue. Charming." She handed it to me. "Careful of the edges, Tinkerman; I don't doubt it might cut."

I ran a finger carefully over one edge, but found that Leah's warning was unnecessary; some sort of passivation treatment had been done to blunt the edge to keep it from cutting. The letters were limned in blue, so sharply chiseled on the sheet that they seemed to rise from the card. The title read, "Invitation from Carlos Fernando Delacroix Ortega de la Jolla y Nordwald-Gruenbaum." In smaller letters, it continued, "We find your researches on the ecology of Mars to be of some interest. We would like to invite you to visit our residences at Hypatia at your convenience and talk."

I didn't know the name Carlos Fernando, but the family Nordwald-Gruenbaum needed no introduction. The invitation had come from someone within the intimate family of the satrap of Venus.

Transportation, the letter continued, would be provided.

The satrap of Venus. One of the twenty old men, the lords and owners of the solar system. A man so rich that human standards of wealth no longer had any meaning. What could he want with Leah?

I tried to remember what I knew about the sultan of the clouds, satrap of the fabled floating cities. It seemed very far away from everything I knew. The society, I thought I remembered, was said to be decadent and perverse, but I knew little more. The inhabitants of Venus kept to themselves.

Riemann station was ugly and functional, the interior made of a dark anodized aluminum with a pebbled surface finish. There was a viewport in the lounge, and Leah had walked over to look out. She stood with her back to me, framed in darkness. Even in her rumpled ship's suit, she was beautiful, and I wondered if I would ever find the clue to understanding her.

As the orbital station rotated, the blue bubble of Earth slowly rose in front of her, a fragile and intricate sculpture of snow and cobalt, outlining her in a sapphire light. "There's nothing for me down there," she said.

I stood in silence, not sure if she even remembered I was there.

In a voice barely louder than the silence, she said, "I have no past."

The silence was uncomfortable. I knew I should say something, but I was not sure what. "I've never been to Venus," I said at last.

"I don't know anybody who has." Leah turned. "I suppose the letter doesn't specifically say that I should come alone." Her tone was matter of fact, neither discouraging nor inviting.

It was hardly enthusiastic, but it was better than no. I wondered if she actually liked me, or just tolerated my presence. I decided it might be best not to ask. No use pressing my luck.

The transportation provided turned out to be the *Suleiman*, a fusion yacht.

Suleiman was more than merely first-class, it was excessively extravagant. It was larger than many ore transports, huge enough that any ordinary yacht could have easily fit within the most capacious of its recreation spheres. Each of its private cabins—and it had seven—was larger than an ordinary habitat module. Big ships commonly were slow ships, but *Suleiman* was an exception, equipped with an impressive amount of delta-V, and the transfer orbit to Venus was scheduled for a transit time well under that of any commercial transport ship.

We were the only passengers.

Despite its size, the ship had a crew of just three: captain, and first and second pilot. The captain, with the shaven head and saffron robe of a Buddhist novice, greeted us on entry, and politely but firmly informed us that the crew was not answerable to orders of the passengers. We were to keep to the passenger section and we would be delivered to Venus. Crew accommodations were separate from the passenger accommodations and we should expect not to see or hear from the crew during the voyage.

"Fine," was the only comment Leah had.

When the ship had received us and boosted into a fast Venus transfer orbit, Leah found the smallest of the private cabins and locked herself in it.

Leah Hamakawa had been with the Pleiades Institute for twenty years. She had joined young, when she was still a teenager—long before I'd ever met her—and I knew little of her life before then, other than that she had been an orphan. The institute was the only family that she had.

It seemed to me sometimes that there were two Leahs. One Leah was shy and childlike, begging to be loved. The other Leah was cool and professional, who could hardly bear being touched, who hated—or perhaps disdained—people.

Sometimes I wondered if she had been terribly hurt as a child. She never talked about growing up, never mentioned her parents. I had asked her, once, and the only thing she said was that that was all behind her, long ago and far away.

I never knew my position with her. Sometimes I almost thought that she must love me, but couldn't bring herself to say anything. Other times she was so casually thoughtless that I believed she never thought of me as more than a technical assistant, indistinguishable from any other tech. Sometimes I wondered why she even bothered to allow me to hang around.

I damned myself silently for being too cowardly to ask.

While Leah had locked herself away, I explored the ship. Each cabin was spherical, with a single double-glassed octagonal viewport on the outer cabin wall. The cabins had every luxury imaginable, even hygiene facilities set in smaller adjoining spheres, with booths that sprayed actual water through nozzles onto the occupant's body.

Ten hours after boost, Leah had still not come out. I found another cabin and went to sleep.

In two days I was bored. I had taken apart everything that could be taken apart, examined how it worked, and put it back together. Everything was in perfect condition; there was nothing for me to fix.

But, although I had not brought much with me, I'd brought a portable office. I called up a librarian agent and asked for history.

In the beginning of the human expansion outward, transport into space had been ruinously expensive, and only governments and obscenely rich corporations could afford to do business in space. When the governments dropped out, a handful of rich men bought their assets. Most of them sold out again, or went bankrupt. A few didn't. Some stayed on due to sheer stubbornness, some with the fervor of an ideological belief in human expansion, and some out of a cold-hearted calculation that there would be uncountable wealth in space, if only it could be tapped. When the technology was finally ready, the twenty families owned it all.

Slowly, the frontier opened, and then the exodus began. First by the thousands: Baha'i, fleeing religious persecution; deposed dictators and their sycophants, looking to escape with looted treasuries; drug lords and their retinues, looking to take their profits beyond the reach of governments or rivals. Then, the exodus began by the millions, all colors of humanity scattering from the Earth to start a new life in space. Splinter groups from the Church of John the Avenger left the unforgiving mother church seeking their prophesied destiny; dissidents from the People's Republic of Malawi, seeking freedom; vegetarian communes from Alaska, seeking a new frontier; Mayans, seeking to reestablish a Maya homeland; libertarians, seeking their free-market paradise; communists, seeking a place outside of history to mold the new communist man. Some of them died quickly, some slowly, but always there were more, a never-ending flood of dissidents, malcontents, and rebels, people willing to sign away anything for the promise of a new start. A few of them survived. A few of them thrived. A few of them grew.

And every one of them had mortgaged their very balls to the twenty families for passage.

Not one habitat in a hundred managed to buy its way out of debt—but the heirs of the twenty became richer than nations, richer than empires.

The legendary war between the Nordwald industrial empire and the Gruenbaum family over solar-system resources had ended when Patricia Gruenbaum sold out her controlling interest in the family business. Udo Nordwald, tyrant and patriarch of the Nordwald industrial empire—now Nordwald-Gruenbaum—had no such plans to discard or even dilute his hard-battled wealth. He continued his consolidation of power with a merger-by-marriage of his only son, a boy not even out of his teens, with the shrewd and calculating heiress of la Jolla. His closest competitors gone, Udo retreated from the outer solar system, leaving the long expansion outward to others. He established corporate headquarters, a living quarters for workers, and his own personal dwelling in a place that was both central to the inner system, and also a spot that nobody had ever before thought possible to colonize. He made his reputation by colonizing what was casually called the solar system's Hell planet.

Venus.

The planet below grew from a point of light into a gibbous white pearl, too bright to look at. The arriving interplanetary yacht shed its hyperbolic excess in a low pass through Venus' atmosphere, rebounded leisurely into high elliptical orbit, and then circularized into a two-hour parking orbit.

Suleiman had an extravagant viewport, a single transparent pane four meters in diameter, and I floated in front of it, watching the transport barque glide up to meet us. I had thought *Suleiman* a large ship; the barque made it look like a miniature. A flattened cone with a rounded nose and absurdly tiny rocket engines at the base, it was shaped in the form of a typical planetary-descent lifting body, but one that must have been over a kilometer long, and at least as wide. It glided up to the *Suleiman* and docked with her like a pumpkin mating with a pea.

The size, I knew, was deceiving. The barque was no more than a thin skin over a hollow shell made of vacuum-foamed titanium surrounding a vast empty chamber. It was designed not to land, but to float in the atmosphere, and to float it required a huge volume and almost no weight. No ships ever landed on the surface of Venus; the epithet "hell" was well chosen. The transfer barque, then, was more like a space-going dirigible than a spaceship, a vehicle as much at home floating in the clouds as floating in orbit.

Even knowing that the vast bulk of the barque was little more substantial than vacuum, though, I found the effect intimidating.

It didn't seem to make any impression on Leah. She had come out from her silent solitude when we approached Venus, but she barely glanced out the viewport in passing. It was often hard for me to guess what would attract her attention. Sometimes I had seen her spend an hour staring at a rock, apparently fascinated by a chunk of ordinary asteroidal chondrite, turning it over and examining it carefully from every possible angle. Other things, like a spaceship nearly as big as a city, she ignored as if they had no more importance than dirt.

Bulky cargos were carried in compartments in the hollow interior of the barque, but since there were just two of us descending to Venus, we were invited to sit up in the pilot's compartment, a transparent blister almost invisible at the front.

The pilot was another yellow-robed Buddhist. Was this a common sect for Venus pilots, I wondered? But this pilot was as talkative as *Suleiman*'s pilot had been reclusive. As the barque undocked, a tether line stretched out between it and the station. The station lowered the barque toward the planet. While we were being lowered down the tether, the pilot pointed out every possible sight—tiny communications satellites crawling across the sky like turbocharged ants; the pinkish flashes of lightning on the night hemisphere of the planet far below; the golden spider's-web of a microwave power relay. At thirty kilometers, still talking, the pilot severed the tether, allowing the barque to drop free. The Earth and Moon, twin stars of blue and white, rose over the pearl of the horizon. Factory complexes were distantly visible in orbit, easy to spot by their flashing navigation beacons and the transport barques docked to them, so far away that even the immense barques were shrunken to insignificance.

We were starting to brush atmosphere now, and a feeling of weight returned and increased. Suddenly we were pulling half a gravity of over-g.

Without ever stopping talking, the pilot-monk deftly rolled the barque inverted, and Venus was now over our heads, a featureless white ceiling to the universe. "Nice view there, is it not?" the pilot said. "You get a great feel for the planet in this attitude. Not doing it for the view, though, nice as it is; I'm just getting that old hypersonic lift working for us, holding us down. These barques are a bit fragile; can't take them in too fast, have to play the atmosphere like a big bass fiddle. Wouldn't want us to bounce off the atmosphere, now, would you?" He didn't pause for answers to his questions, and I wondered if he would have continued his travelogue even if we had not been there.

The g-level increased to about a standard, then steadied.

The huge beast swept inverted through the atmosphere, trailing an ionized cloud behind it. The pilot slowed toward subsonic, and then rolled the barque over again, skipping upward slightly into the exosphere to cool the glowing skin, then letting it dip back downward. The air thickened around us as we descended into the thin, featureless haze. And then we broke through the bottom of the haze into the clear air below it, and abruptly we were soaring above the endless sea of clouds.

Clouds.

A hundred and fifty million square kilometers of clouds, a billion cubic kilometers of clouds. In the ocean of clouds the floating cities of Venus are not limited, like terrestrial cities, to two dimensions only, but can float up and down at the whim of the city masters, higher into the bright cold sunlight, downward to the edges of the hot murky depths.

Clouds. The barque sailed over cloud-cathedrals and over cloud-mountains, edges recomplicated with cauliflower fractals. We sailed past lairs filled with cloud-monsters a kilometer tall, with arched necks of cloud stretching forward, threatening and blustering with cloud-teeth, cloud-muscled bodies with clawed feet of flickering lightning.

The barque was floating now, drifting downward at subsonic speed, trailing its own cloud-contrail, which twisted behind us like a scrawl of illegible handwriting. Even the pilot, if not actually fallen silent, had at least slowed down his chatter, letting us soak in the glory of it. "Quite something, isn't it?" he said. "The kingdom of the clouds. Drives some people batty with the immensity of it, or so they say—cloud-happy, they call it here. Never get tired of it, myself. No view like the view from a barque to see the clouds." And to prove it, he banked the barque over into a slow turn, circling a cloud pillar that rose from deep down in the haze to tower thousands of meters above our heads. "Quite a sight."

"Quite a sight," I repeated.

The pilot-monk rolled the barque back, and then pointed, forward and slightly to the right. "There. See it?"

I didn't know what to see. "What?"

"There."

I saw it now, a tiny point glistening in the distance. "What is it?"

"Hypatia. The jewel of the clouds."

As we coasted closer, the city grew. It was an odd sight. The city was a dome, or rather, a dozen glistening domes melted haphazardly together, each one faceted with a million panels of glass. The domes were huge, the smallest nearly a kilometer across, and as the barque glided across the sky the facets caught the sunlight and sparkled with reflected light. Below the domes, a slender pencil of rough black stretched down toward the cloudbase like taffy, delicate as spun glass, terminating in an absurdly tiny bulb of rock that seemed far too small to counterbalance the domes.

"Beautiful, you think, yes? Like the wonderful jellyfishes of your blue planet's oceans. Can you believe that half a million people live there?"

The pilot brought us around the city in a grand sweep, showing off, not even bothering to talk. Inside the transparent domes, chains of lakes glittered in green ribbons between boulevards and delicate pavilions. At last he slowed to a stop, and then slowly leaked atmosphere into the vacuum vessel that provided the buoyancy. The barque settled down gradually, wallowing from side to side now that the stability given by its forward momentum was gone. Now it floated slightly lower than the counterweight. The counterweight no longer looked small, but loomed above us, a rock the size of Gibraltar. Tiny fliers affixed tow ropes to hardpoints on the surface of the barque, and slowly we were winched into a hard-dock.

"Welcome to Venus," said the monk.

The surface of Venus is a place of crushing pressure and hellish temperature. Rise above it, though, and the pressure eases, the temperature cools. Fifty kilometers above the surface, at the base of the clouds, the temperature is tropical, and the pressure the same as Earth normal. Twenty kilometers above that, the air is thin and polar cold.

Drifting between these two levels are the ten thousand floating cities of Venus.

A balloon filled with oxygen and nitrogen will float in the heavy air of Venus, and balloons were exactly what the fabled domed cities were. Geodetic structures with struts of sintered graphite and skin of transparent polycarbonate synthesized from the atmosphere of Venus itself, each kilometer-diameter dome easily lifted a hundred thousand tons of city.

Even the clouds cooperated. The thin haze of the upper cloud deck served to filter the sunlight so that the intensity of the Sun here was little more than the Earth's solar constant.

Hypatia was not the largest of the floating cities, but it was certainly the richest, a city of helical buildings and golden domes, with huge open areas and elaborate gardens. Inside the dome of Hypatia, the architects played every possible trick to make us forget that we were encapsulated in an enclosed volume.

But we didn't see this part, the gardens and waterfalls, not at first. Leaving the barque, we entered a disembarking lounge below the city. For all that it featured plush chaise lounges, floors covered with genetically engineered pink grass, and priceless sculptures of iron and jade, it was functional: a place to wait.

It was large enough to hold a thousand people, but there was only one person in the lounge, a boy who was barely old enough to have entered his teens, wearing a bathrobe and elaborately pleated yellow silk pants. He was slightly pudgy, with an agreeable, but undistinguished, round face.

After the expense of our transport, I was surprised at finding only one person sent to await our arrival.

The kid looked at Leah. "Doctor Hamakawa. I'm pleased to meet you." Then he turned to me. "Who the hell are you?" he said.

"Who are you?" I said. "Where's our reception?"

The boy was chewing on something. He seemed about to spit it out, and then thought better of it. He looked over at Leah. "This guy is with you, Dr. Hamakawa? What's he do?"

"This is David Tinkerman," Leah said. "Technician. And, when need be, pilot. Yes, he's with me."

"Tell him he might wish to learn some manners," the boy said.

"And who are you?" I shot back. "I don't think you answered the question."

The not-quite-teenager looked at me with disdain, as if he wasn't sure if he would even bother to talk to me. Then he said, in a slow voice as if talking to an idiot, "I am Carlos Fernando Delacroix Ortega de la Jolla y Nordwald-Gruenbaum. I own this station and everything on it."

He had an annoying high voice, on the edge of changing, but not yet there.

Leah, however, didn't seem to notice his voice. "Ah," she said. "You are the scion of Nordwald-Gruenbaum. The ruler of Hypatia."

The kid shook his head and frowned. "No," he said. "Not the scion, not exactly. I am Nordwald-Gruenbaum." The smile made him look like a child again; it make him look likable. When he bowed, he was utterly charming. "I," he said, "am the sultan of the clouds."

Carlos Fernando, as it turned out, had numerous servants indeed. Once we had been greeted, he made a gesture and an honor guard of twenty women in silken doublets came forward to escort us up.

Before we entered the elevator, the guards circled around. At a word from Carlos Fernando, a package was brought forward. Carlos took it, and, as the guards watched, handed it to Leah. "A gift," he said, "to welcome you to my city."

The box was simple and unadorned. Leah opened it. Inside the package was a large folio. She took it out. The book was bound in cracked, dark red leather, with no lettering. She flipped to the front. "Giordano Bruno," she read. "*On the Infinite Universe and Worlds*." She smiled, and riffled through the pages. "A facsimile of the first English edition?"

"I thought perhaps you might enjoy it."

"Charming." She placed it back in the box, and tucked it under her arm. "Thank you," she said.

The elevator rose so smoothly it was difficult to believe it traversed two kilometers in a little under three minutes. The doors opened to brilliant noon sunlight. We were in the bubble city.

The city was a fantasy of foam and air. Although it was enclosed in a dome, the bubble was so large that the walls nearly vanished into the air, and it seemed unencumbered. With the guards beside us, we walked through the city. Everywhere there were parks, some just a tiny patch of green surrounding a tree, some forests perched on the wide tops of elongated stalks, with elegantly sculpted waterfalls cascading down to be caught in wide fountain basins. White pathways led upward through the air, suspended by cables from impossibly narrow beams, and all around us were sounds of rustling water and birdsong.

At the end of the welcoming tour, I realized I had been imperceptibly but effectively separated from Leah. "Hey," I said. "What happened to Dr. Hamakawa?"

The honor guard of women still surrounded me, but Leah and the kid who was the heir of Nordwald-Gruenbaum had vanished.

"We're sorry," one of the women answered, one slightly taller, perhaps, than the others. "I believe that she has been taken to her suite to rest for a bit, since in a few hours she is to be greeted at the level of society."

"I should be with her."

The woman looked at me calmly. "We had no instructions to bring you. I don't believe you were invited."

"Excuse me," I said. "I'd better find them."

The woman stood back and gestured to the city. Walkways meandered in all directions, a three-dimensional maze. "By all means, if you like. We were instructed that you were to have free run of the city."

I nodded. Clearly, plans had been made with no room for me. "How will I get in touch?" I asked. "What if I want to talk to Leah—to Dr. Hamakawa?"

"They'll be able to find you. Don't worry." After a pause, she said, "Shall we show you to your place of domicile?"

The building to which I was shown was one of a cluster that seemed suspended in the air by crisscrossed cables. It was larger than many houses. I was used to living in the cubbyholes of habitat modules, and the spaciousness of the accommodations startled me.

"Good evening, Mr. Tinkerman." The person greeting me was a tall Chinese man perhaps fifty years of age. The woman next to him, I surmised, was his wife. She was quite a bit younger, in her early twenties. She was slightly overweight by the standards I was used to, but I had noticed that was common here. Behind her hid two children, their faces peeking out and then darting back again to safety. The man introduced himself as Truman Singh, and his wife as Epiphany. "The rest of the family will meet you in a few hours, Mr. Tinkerman," he said, smiling. "They are mostly working."

"We both work for His Excellency," Epiphany added. "Carlos Fernando has asked our braid to house you. Don't hesitate to ask for anything you need. The cost will go against the Nordwald-Gruenbaum credit, which is," she smiled, "quite unlimited here. As you might imagine."

"Do you do this often?" I asked. "House guests?"

Epiphany looked up at her husband. "Not too often," she said, "not for His Excellency, anyway. It's not uncommon in the cities, though; there's a lot of visiting back and forth as one city or another drifts nearby, and everyone will put up visitors from time to time."

"You don't have hotels?"

She shook her head. "We don't get many visitors from outplanet."

"You said 'His Excellency,' " I said. "That's Carlos Fernando? Tell me about him."

"Of course. What would you like to know?"

"Does he really—" I gestured at the city—"own all of this? The whole planet?"

"Yes, certainly, the city, yes. And also, no."

"How is that?"

"He will own the city, yes—this one, and five thousand others—but the planet? Maybe, maybe not. The Nordwald-Gruenbaum family does claim to own the planet, but in truth that claim means little. The claim may apply to the surface of the planet, but nobody owns the sky. The cities, though, yes. But, of course, he doesn't actually control them all personally."

"Well, of course not. I mean, hey, he's just a kid—he must have trustees or proxies or something, right?"

"Indeed. Until he reaches his majority."

"And then?"

Truman Singh shrugged. "It is the Nordwald-Gruenbaum tradition— written into the first Nordwald's will. When he reaches his majority, it is personal property."

There were, as I discovered, eleven thousand, seven hundred and eight cities floating in the atmosphere of Venus. "Probably a few more," Truman Singh told me. "Nobody keeps track, exactly. There are myths of cities that float low down, never rising above the lower cloud decks, forever hidden. You can't live that deep—it's too hot—but the stories say that the renegade cities have a technology that allows them to reject heat." He shrugged. "Who knows?" In any case, of the known cities, the estate to which Carlos Fernando was heir owned or held shares or partial ownership of more than half.

"The Nordwald-Gruenbaum entity has been a good owner," Truman said. "I should say, they know that their employees could leave, move to another city if they had to, but they don't."

"And there's no friction?"

"Oh, the independent cities, they all think that the Nordwald-Gruenbaums have too much power!" He laughed. "But there's not much they can do about it, eh?"

"They could fight."

Truman Singh reached out and tapped me lightly on the center of my forehead with his middle finger. "That would not be wise." He paused, and then said more slowly, "We are an interconnected ecology here, the independents and the sultanate. We rely on each other. The independents could declare war, yes, but in the end nobody would win."

"Yes," I said. "Yes, I see that. Of course, the floating cities are so fragile—a single break in the gas envelope—"

"We are perhaps not as fragile as you think," Truman Singh replied. "I should say, you are used to the built worlds, but they are vacuum habitats, where a single blow-out would be catastrophic. Here, you know, there is no pressure difference between the atmosphere outside and the lifesphere inside; if there is a break, the gas equilibrates through the gap only very slowly. Even if we had a thousand broken panels, it would take weeks for the city to sink to the irrecoverable depths. And, of course, we do have safeguards, many safeguards." He paused, and then said, "but if there were a war . . . we are safe against ordinary hazards, you can have no fear of that . . . but against metastable bombs . . . well, that would not be good. No, I should say that would not be good at all."

The next day I set out to find where Leah had been taken, but although everyone I met was unfailingly polite, I had little success in reaching her. At least, I was beginning to learn my way around.

The first thing I noticed about the city was the light. I was used to living in orbital habitats, where soft, indirect light was provided by panels of white-light diodes. In Hypatia City, brilliant Venus sunlight suffused throughout the interior. The next thing I noticed were the birds.

Hypatia was filled with birds. Birds were common in orbital habitats, since parrots and cockatiels adapt well to the freefall environment of space, but the volume of Hypatia was crowded with bright tropical birds, parrots and cockatoos and lorikeets, cardinals and chickadees and quetzals, more birds than I had names for, more birds than I had ever seen, a raucous orchestra of color and sound.

The floating city had twelve main chambers, separated from one another by thin, transparent membranes with a multiplicity of passages, each chamber well lit and cheerful, each with a slightly different style.

The quarters I had been assigned were in Sector Carbon, where individual living habitats were strung on cables like strings of iridescent pearls above a broad fenway of forest and grass. Within Sector Carbon, cable cars swung like pendulums on long strands, taking a traveler from platform to platform across the sector in giddy arcs. Carlos Fernando's chambers were in the highest, centermost bubble—upcity, as it was called—a bubble dappled with colored light and shadow, where the architecture was fluted minarets and oriental domes. But I wasn't, as it seemed, allowed into this elite sphere. I didn't even learn where Leah had been given quarters.

I found a balcony on a tower that looked out through the transparent canopy over the clouds. The cloudscape was just as magnificent as it had been the previous day; towering and slowly changing. The light was a rich golden color, and the Sun, masked by a skein of feathery clouds like a tracery of lace, was surrounded by a bronze halo. From the angle of the Sun it was early afternoon, but there would be no sunset that day; the great winds circling the planet would not blow the city into the night side of Venus for another day.

Of the eleven thousand other cities, I could detect no trace—looking outward, there was no indication that we were not alone in the vast cloudscape that stretched to infinity. But then, I thought, if the cities were scattered randomly, there would be little chance one would be nearby at any given time. Venus was a small planet, as planets go, but large enough to swallow ten thousand cities—or even a hundred times that—without any visible crowding of the skies.

I wished I knew what Leah thought of it.

I missed Leah. For all that she sometimes didn't seem to even notice I was there . . . our sojourn on Mars, brief as it had been . . . we had shared the same cubby. Perhaps that meant nothing to her. But it had been the very center of my life.

I thought of her body, lithe and golden-skinned. Where was she? What was she doing?

The park was a platform overgrown with cymbidian orchids, braced in the air by the great cables that transected the dome from the stanchion trusswork. This seemed a common architecture here, where even the ground beneath was suspended from the buoyancy of the air dome. I bounced my weight back and forth, testing the resonant frequency, and felt the platform move infinitesimally under me. Children here must be taught from an early age not to do that; a deliberate effort could build up destructive oscillation. I stopped bouncing, and let the motion damp.

When I returned near the middle of the day, neither Truman nor Epiphany were there, and Truman's other wife, a woman named Triolet, met me. She was perhaps in her sixties, with dark skin and deep gray eyes. She had been introduced to me the previous day, but in the confusion of meeting numerous people in what seemed to be a large extended family, I had not had a chance to really talk to her yet. There were always a number of people around the Singh household, and I was confused as to how, or even if, they were related to my hosts. Now, talking to her, I realized that she, in fact, was the one who had control of the Singh household finances.

The Singh family were farmers, I discovered. Or farm managers. The flora in Hypatia was decorative or served to keep the air in the dome refreshed, but the real agriculture was in separate domes, floating at an altitude that was optimized for plant growth and had no inhabitants. Automated equipment did the work of sowing and irrigation and harvest. Truman and Epiphany Singh were operational engineers, making those decisions that required a human input, watching that the robots kept on track and were doing the right things at the right times.

And there was a message waiting for me, inviting me in the evening to attend a dinner with His Excellency, Carlos Fernando Delacroix Ortega de la Jolla y Nordwald-Gruenbaum.

Triolet helped me with my wardrobe, along with Epiphany, who had returned by the time I was ready to prepare. They both told me emphatically that my serviceable but well-worn jumpsuit was not appropriate attire. The gown Triolet selected was far gaudier than anything I would have chosen for myself, an electric shade of indigo accented with a wide midnight black sash. "Trust us, it will be suitable," Epiphany told me. Despite its bulk, it was as light as a breath of air.

"All clothes here are light," Epiphany told me. "Spider's silk."

"Ah, I see," I said. "Synthetic spider silk. Strong and light; very practical."

"Synthetic?" Epiphany asked, and giggled. "No, not synthetic. It's real."

"The silk is actually woven by spiders?"

"No, the whole garment is." At my puzzled look, she said, "Teams of spiders. They work together."

"Spiders."

"Well, they're natural weavers, you know. And easy to transport."

I arrived at the banquet hall at the appointed time and found that the plasma-arc blue gown that Epiphany had selected for me was the most conservative dress there. There were perhaps thirty people present, but Leah was clearly the center. She seemed happy with the attention, more animated than I'd recalled seeing her before.

"They're treating you well?" I asked, when I'd finally made it through the crowd to her.

"Oh, indeed."

I discovered I had nothing to say. I waited for her to ask about me, but she didn't. "Where have they given you to stay?"

"A habitat next section over," she said. "Sector Carbon. It's amazing—I've never seen so many birds."

"That's the sector I'm in," I said, "but they didn't tell me where you were."

"Really? That's odd." She tapped up a map of the residential sector on a screen built into the diamond tabletop, and a three-dimensional image appeared to float inside the table. She rotated it and highlighted her habitat, and I realized that she was indeed adjacent, in a large habitat that was almost directly next to the complex I was staying in. "It's a pretty amazing place. But mostly I've been here in the upcity. Have you talked to Carli much yet? He's a very clever kid. Interested in everything—botany, physics, even engineering."

"Really?" I said. "I don't think they'll let me into the upcity."

"You're kidding; I'm sure they'll let you in. Hey—" she called over one of the guards. "Say, is there any reason Tinkerman can't come up to the centrum?"

"No, madam, if you want it, of course not."

"Great. See, no problem."

And then the waiters directed me to my place at the far end of the table.

The table was a thick slab of diamond, the faceted edges collecting and refracting rainbows of color. The top was as smooth and slippery as a sheet of ice. Concealed inside were small computer screens so that any of the diners who wished could call up graphics or data as needed during a conversation. The table was both art and engineering, practical and beautiful at the same time.

Carlos Fernando sat at the end of the table. He seemed awkward and out of place in a chair slightly too large for him. Leah sat at his right, and an older woman—perhaps his mother?—on his left. He was bouncing around in his chair, alternating between playing with the computer system in his table and sneaking glances over at Leah when he thought she wasn't paying attention to him. If she looked in his direction, he would go still for a moment, and then his eyes would quickly dart away and he went back to staring at the graphics screen in front of him and fidgeting.

The server brought a silver tray to Carlos Fernando. On it was something the size of a fist, hidden under a canopy of red silk. Carlos Fernando looked up, accepted it with a nod, and removed the cloth. There was a moment of silence as people looked over, curious. I strained to see it.

It was a sparkling egg.

The egg was cunningly wrought of diamond fibers of many colors, braided into intricate lacework resembling entwined Celtic knots. The twelve-year-old satrap of Venus picked it up and ran one finger over it, delicately, barely brushing the surface, feeling the corrugations and relief of the surface.

He held it for a moment, as if not quite sure what he should do with it, and then his hand darted over and put the egg on the plate in front of Leah. She looked up, puzzled.

"This is for you," he said.

The faintest hint of surprise passed through the other diners, almost subvocal, too soft to be heard.

A moment later the servers set an egg in front of each of us. Our eggs, although decorated with an intricate filigree of finely painted lines of gold and pale verdigris, were ordinary eggs—goose eggs, perhaps.

Carlos Fernando was fidgeting in his chair, half grinning, half biting his lip, looking down, looking around, looking everywhere except at the egg or at Leah.

"What am I to do with this?" Leah asked.

"Why," he said, "perhaps you should open it up and eat it."

Leah picked up the diamond-laced egg and examined it, turned it over and rubbed one finger across the surface. Then, having found what she was looking for, she held it in two fingers and twisted. The diamond eggshell opened, and inside it was a second egg, an ordinary one.

The kid smiled again and looked down at the egg in front of him. He picked up his spoon and cracked the shell, then spooned out the interior.

At this signal, the others cracked their own eggs and began to eat. After a moment, Leah laid the decorative shell to one side and did the same. I watched her for a moment, and then cracked my own egg.

It was, of course, excellent.

Later, when I was back with the Singh family, I was still puzzled. There had been some secret significance there that everybody else had seen, but I had missed. Mr. Singh was sitting with his older wife, Triolet, talking about accounts.

"I must ask a question," I said.

Truman Singh turned to me. "Ask," he said, "and I shall answer."

"Is there any particular significance," I said, "to an egg?"

"An egg?" Singh seemed puzzled. "Much significance, I would say. In the old days, the days of the asteroid miners, an egg was a symbol of luxury.

Ducks were brought into the bigger habitats, and their eggs were, for some miners, the only food they would ever eat that was not a form of algae or soybean."

"A symbol of luxury," I said, musing. "I see. But I still don't understand it." I thought for a moment, and then asked, "Is there any significance to a gift of an egg?"

"Well, no," he said, slowly, "not exactly. An egg? Nothing, in and of itself."

His wife Triolet asked, "You are sure it's just an egg? Nothing else?"

"A very elaborate egg."

"Hmmm," she said, with a speculative look in her eye. "Not, maybe, an egg, a book, and a rock?"

That startled me a little. "A book and a rock?" The Bruno book—the very first thing Carlos Fernando had done on meeting Leah was to give her a book. But a rock? I hadn't see anything like that. "Why that?"

"Ah," she said. "I suppose you wouldn't know. I don't believe that our customs here in the sky cities are well known out there in the outer reaches."

Her mention of the outer reaches—Saturn and the Beyond—confused me for a moment, until I realized that, viewed from Venus, perhaps even Earth and the built worlds of the orbital clouds would be considered "outer."

"Here," she continued, "as in most of the ten thousand cities, an egg, a book, and a rock is a special gift. The egg is symbolic of life, you see; a book symbolic of knowledge; and a rock is the basis of all wealth, the minerals from the asteroid belt that built our society and bought our freedom."

"Yes? And all three together?"

"They are the traditional gesture of the beginning of courtship," she said.

"I still don't understand."

"If a young man gives a woman an egg, a book, and a rock," Truman said, "I should say this is his official sign that he is interested in courting her. If she accepts them, then she accepts his courtship."

"What? That's it, just like that, they're married?"

"No, no, no," he said. "It only means that she accepts the courtship—that she takes him seriously and, when it comes, she will listen to his proposal. Often a woman may have rocks and eggs from many young men. She doesn't have to accept, only take him seriously."

"Oh," I said.

But it still made no sense. How old was Carlos Fernando, twenty Venus years? What was that, twelve Earth years or so? He was far too young to be proposing.

"No one can terraform Venus," Carlos Fernando said.

Carlos Fernando had been uninterested in having me join in Leah's discussion, but Leah, oblivious to her host's displeasure (or perhaps simply not caring), had insisted that if he wanted to talk about terraforming, I should be there.

It was one room of Carlos Fernando's extensive palaces, a rounded room, an enormous cavernous space that had numerous alcoves. I'd found them sitting in one of the alcoves, an indentation that was cozy but still open. The ubiquitous female guards were still there, but they were at the distant ends of the room, within command if Carlos Fernando chose to shout, but far enough to give them the illusion of privacy.

The furniture they were sitting on was odd. The chairs seemed sculpted of sapphire smoke, yet were solid to the touch. I picked one up and discovered that it weighed almost nothing at all. "Diamond aerogel," Carlos Fernando said. "Do you like it?"

"It's amazing," I said. I had never before seen so much made out of diamond. And yet it made sense here, I thought; with carbon dioxide an inexhaustible resource surrounding the floating cities, it was logical that the floating cities would make as much as they could out of carbon. But still, I didn't know you could make an aerogel of diamond. "How do you make it?"

"A new process we've developed," Carlos Fernando said. "You don't mind if I don't go into the details. It's actually an adaptation of an old idea, something that was invented back on Earth decades ago, called a molecular still."

When Carlos Fernando mentioned the molecular still, I thought I saw a sharp flicker of attention from Leah. This was a subject she knew something about, I thought. But instead of following up, she went back to his earlier comment on terraforming.

"You keep asking questions about the ecology of Mars," she said. "Why so many detailed questions about Martian ecopoiesis? You say you're not interested in terraforming, but are you really? You aren't thinking of the old idea of using photosynthetic algae in the atmosphere to reduce the carbon dioxide, are you? Surely you know that that can't work."

"Of course." Carlos Fernando waved the question away. "Theoretical," he said. "Nobody could terraform Venus, I know, I know."

His pronouncement would have been more dignified if his voice had finished changing, but as it was, it wavered between squeaking an octave up and then going back down again, ruining the effect. "We simply have too much atmosphere," he said. "Down at the surface, the pressure is over ninety bars—even if the carbon dioxide of the atmosphere could be converted to oxygen, the surface atmosphere would still be seventy times higher than the Earth's atmospheric pressure."

"I realize that," Leah said. "We're not actually ignorant, you know. So high a pressure of oxygen would be deadly—you'd burst into flames."

"And the leftover carbon," he said, smiling. "Hundreds of tons per square meter."

"So what are you thinking?" she asked.

But in response, he only smiled. "Okay, I can't terraform Venus," he said. "So tell me more about Mars."

I could see that there was something that he was keeping back. Carlos Fernando had some idea that he wasn't telling.

But Leah did not press him, and instead took the invitation to tell him about her studies of the ecology on Mars, as it had been transformed long ago by the vanished engineers of the long-gone Freehold Toynbee colony. The Toynbee's engineers had designed life to thicken the atmosphere of Mars, to increase the greenhouse effect, to melt the frozen oceans of Mars.

"But it's not working," Leah concluded. "The anaerobic life is being out-competed by the photosynthetic oxygen-producers. It's pulling too much carbon dioxide out of the atmosphere."

"But what about the Gaia effect? Doesn't it compensate?"

"No," Leah said. "I found no trace of a Lovelock self-aware planet. Either that's a myth, or else the ecology on Mars is just too young to stabilize."

"Of course on Venus, we would have no problem with photosynthesis removing carbon dioxide."

"I thought you weren't interested in terraforming Venus," I said.

Carlos Fernando waved my objection away. "A hypothetical case, of course," he said. "A thought exercise." He turned to Leah. "Tomorrow," he said, "would you like to go kayaking?"

"Sure," she said.

Kayaking, on Venus, did not involve water.

Carlos Fernando instructed Leah, and Epiphany helped me.

The "kayak" was a ten-meter long gas envelope, a transparent cylinder of plastic curved into an ogive at both ends, with a tiny bubble at the bottom where the kayaker sat. One end of the kayak held a huge, gossamer-bladed propeller that turned lazily as the kayaker pedaled, while the kayaker rowed with flimsy wings, transparent and iridescent like the wings of a dragonfly.

The wings, I discovered, had complicated linkages; each one could be pulled, twisted, and lifted, allowing each wing to separately beat, rotate, and camber.

"Keep up a steady motion with the propeller," Epiphany told me. "You'll lose all your maneuverability if you let yourself float to a stop. You can scull with the wings to put on a burst of speed if you need to. Once you're comfortable, use the wings to rise up or swoop down, and to maneuver. You'll have fun."

We were in a launching bay, a balcony protruding from the side of the city. Four of the human-powered dirigibles that they called kayaks were docked against the blister, the bulge of the cockpits neatly inserted into docking rings so that the pilots could enter the dirigible without exposure to the outside atmosphere. Looking out across the cloudscape, I could see dozens of kayaks dancing around the city like transparent squid with stubby wings, playing tag with each other and racing across the sky. So small and transparent compared to the magnificent clouds, they had been invisible until I'd known how to look.

"What about altitude?" I asked.

"You're about neutrally buoyant," she said. "As long as you have airspeed, you can use the wings to make fine adjustments up or down."

"What happens if I get too low?"

"You can't get too low. The envelope has a reservoir of methanol; as you get lower, the temperature rises and your reservoir releases vapor, so the envelope inflates. If you gain too much altitude, vapor condenses out. So you'll find you're regulated to stay pretty close to the altitude you're set for, which right now is," she checked a meter, "fifty-two kilometers above local ground level. We're blowing west at a hundred meters per second, so local ground level will change as the terrain below varies; check your meters for altimetry."

Looking downward, nothing was visible at all, only clouds, and below the clouds, an infinity of haze. It felt odd to think of the surface, over fifty kilometers straight down, and even odder to think that the city we were inside was speeding across that invisible landscape at hundreds of kilometers an hour. There was only the laziest feeling of motion, as the city drifted slowly through the ever-changing canyons of clouds.

"Watch out for wind shear," she said. "It can take you out of sight of the city pretty quickly, if you let it. Ride the conveyor back if you get tired."

"The conveyor?"

"Horizontal-axis vortices. They roll from west to east and east to west. Choose the right altitude, and they'll take you wherever you want to go."

Now that she'd told me, I could see the kayakers surfing the wind shear, rising upward and skimming across the sky on invisible wheels of air.

"Have fun," she said. She helped me into the gondola, tightened my straps, looked at the gas pressure meter, checked the purge valve on the emergency oxygen supply, and verified that the radio, backup radio, and emergency locator beacons worked.

Across the kayak launch bay, Leah and Carlos Fernando had already pushed off. Carlos was sculling his wings alternatingly with a practiced swishing motion, building up a pendulum-like oscillation from side to side.

Even as I watched, his little craft rolled over until for a moment it hesitated, inverted, and then rolled completely around.

"Showing off," Epiphany said, disdainfully. "You're not supposed to do that. Not that anybody would dare correct him."

She turned back to me. "Ready?" she asked.

"Ready as I'm going to be," I said. I'd been given a complete safety briefing that explained the backup systems and the backups to the backups, but still, floating in the sky above a fifty-two kilometer drop into the landscape of hell seemed an odd diversion.

"Go!" she said. She checked the seal on the cockpit and then with one hand she released the docking clamp.

Freed from its mooring, the kayak sprang upward into the sky. As I'd been instructed, I banked the kayak away from the city. The roll made me feel suddenly giddy. The kayak skittered, sliding around until it was moving sideways to the air, the nose dipping down so that I was hanging against my straps. Coordinate the turn, I thought, but every slight motion I made with the wings seemed amplified drunkenly, and the kayak wove around erratically.

The radio blinked at me, and Epiphany's voice said, "You're doing great. Give it some airspeed."

I wasn't doing great; I was staring straight down at lemon-tinted haze and spinning slowly around like a falling leaf. Airspeed? I realize that I had entirely forgotten to pedal. I pedaled now, and the nose lifted. The sideways spin damped out, and as I straightened out, the wings bit into the air. "Great," Epiphany's voice told me. "Keep it steady."

The gas envelope seemed too fragile to hold me, but I was flying now, suspended below a golden sky. It was far too complicated, but I realized that as long as I kept the nose level, I could keep it under control. I was still oscillating slightly—it was difficult to avoid over-controlling—but on the average, I was keeping the nose pointed where I aimed it.

Where were Leah and Carlos Fernando?

I looked around. Each of the kayaks had different markings—mine was marked with gray stripes like a tabby cat—and I tried to spot theirs.

A gaggle of kayaks was flying together, rounding the pylon of the city. As they moved around the pylon they all turned at once, flashing in the sunlight like a startled school of fish.

Suddenly I spotted them, not far above me, close to the looming wall of the city; the royal purple envelope of Carlos Fernando's kayak and the blue and yellow stripes of Leah's. Leah was circling in a steady climb, and Carlos Fernando was darting around her, now coming in fast and bumping envelopes, now darting away and pulling up, hovering for a moment with his nose pointed at the sky, then skewing around and sliding back downward.

Their motions looked like the courtship dance of birds.

The purple kayak banked around and swooped out and away from the city; and an instant later, Leah's blue and yellow kayak banked and followed. They both soared upward, catching a current of air invisible to me. I could see a few of the other fliers surfing on the same updraft. I yawed my nose around to follow them, but made no progress; I was too inexperienced with the kayak to be able to guess the air currents, and the wind differential was blowing me around the city in exactly the opposite of the direction I wanted to go. I pulled out and away from the city, seeking a different wind, and for an instant I caught a glimpse of something in the clouds below me, dark and fast moving.

Then I caught the updraft. I could feel it, the wings caught the air and it felt like an invisible giant's hand picking me up and carrying me—

Then there was a sudden noise, a stuttering and ripping, followed by a sound like a snare drum. My left wing and propeller ripped away, the fragments spraying into the sky. My little craft banked hard to the left. My radio came to life, but I couldn't hear anything as the cabin disintegrated around me. I was falling.

Falling.

For a moment I felt like I was back in zero-g. I clutched uselessly to the remains of the control surfaces, connected by loose cords to fluttering pieces of debris. Pieces of my canopy floated away and were caught by the wind and spun upward and out of sight. The atmosphere rushed in and my eyes started to burn. I made the mistake of taking a breath, and the effect was like getting kicked in the head. Flickering purple dots, the colors of a bruise, closed in from all directions. My vision narrowed to a single bright tunnel. The air was liquid fire in my lungs. I reached around, desperately, trying to remember the emergency instructions before I blacked out, and my hands found the back-up air-mask between my legs. I was still strapped into my seat, although the seat was no longer attached to a vehicle, and I slapped the breathing mask against my face and sucked hard to start the airflow from the emergency oxygen. I was lucky; the oxygen cylinder was still attached to the bottom of the seat, as the seat, with me in it, tumbled through the sky. Through blurred eyes, I could see the city spinning above me. I tried to think of what the emergency procedure could be and what I should do next, but I could only think of what had gone wrong. What had I done? For the life of me I couldn't think of anything that I could have done that would have ripped the craft apart.

The city dwindled to the size of an acorn, and then I fell into the cloud layer and everything disappeared into a pearly white haze. My skin began to itch all over. I squeezed my eyes shut against the acid fog. The temperature was rising. How long would it take to fall fifty kilometers to the surface?

Something enormous and metallic swooped down from above me, and I blacked out.

Minutes or hours or days later I awoke in a dimly lit cubicle. I was lying on the ground and two men wearing masks were spraying me with jets of a foaming white liquid that looked like milk but tasted bitter. My flight suit was in shreds around me.

I sat up and began to cough uncontrollably. My arms and my face itched like blazes, but when I started to scratch, one of the men reached out and slapped my hands away.

"Don't scratch."

I turned to look at him, and the one behind me grabbed me by the hair and smeared a handful of goo into my face, rubbing it hard into my eyes.

Then he picked up a patch of cloth and tossed it to me. "Rub this where it itches. It should help."

I was still blinking, my face dripping, my vision fuzzy. The patch of cloth was wet with some gelatinous slime. I grabbed it from him, and dabbed it on my arms and then rubbed it in. It did help, some.

"Thanks," I said. "What the hell—"

The two men in facemasks looked at each other. "Acid burn," the taller man said. "You're not too bad. A minute or two of exposure won't leave scars."

"What?"

"Acid. You were exposed to the clouds."

"Right."

Now that I wasn't quite so distracted, I looked around. I was in the cargo hold of some sort of aircraft. There were two small round portholes on either side. Although nothing was visible through them but a blank white, I could feel that the vehicle was in motion. I looked at the two men. They were both rough characters. Unlike the brightly colored spider's-silk gowns of the citizens of Hypatia, they were dressed in clothes that were functional but not fancy, jumpsuits of a dark gray color with no visible insignia. Both of them were fit and well muscled. I couldn't see their faces, since they were wearing breathing masks and lightweight helmets, but under their masks I could see that they both wore short beards, another fashion that had been missing among the citizens of Hypatia. Their eyes were covered with amber-tinted goggles, made in a crazy style that cupped each eye with a piece that was rounded like half an eggshell, apparently stuck to their faces by some invisible glue. It gave them a strange, bug-eyed look. They stared at me, but behind their facemasks and goggle-eyes I was completely unable to read their expressions.

"Thanks," I said. "So, who are you? Some sort of emergency rescue force?"

"I think you know who we are," the taller one said. "The question is who the hell are you?"

I stood up and reached out a hand, thinking to introduce myself, but both of the men took a step back. Without seeming to move his hand, the taller one now had a gun, a tiny omniblaster of some kind. Suddenly a lot of things were clear.

"You're pirates," I said.

"We're the Venus underground," he said. "We don't like the word pirates very much. Now, if you don't mind, I have a question, and I really would like an answer. Who the hell are you?"

So I told him.

The first man started to take off his helmet, but the taller pirate stopped him. "We'll keep the masks on for now. Until we decide he's safe." The taller pirate said he was named Esteban Jaramillo, the shorter one Esteban Francisco. That was too many Estebans, I thought, and decided to tag the one Jaramillo and the other Francisco.

I discovered from them that not everybody in the floating cities thought of Venus as a paradise. Some of the independent cities considered the clan of Nordwald-Gruenbaum to be well on its way to becoming a dictatorship. "They own half of Venus outright, but that's not good enough for them, no, oh no," Jaramillo told me. "They're stinking rich, but not stinking rich enough, and the very idea that there are free cities floating in the sky, cities that don't swear fealty to them and pay their goddamned taxes, that pisses them off. They'll do anything that they can to crush us. Us? We're just fighting back."

I would have been more inclined to see his point if I didn't have the uncomfortable feeling that I'd just been abducted. It had been a tremendous stroke of luck for me that their ship had been there to catch me when my kayak broke apart and fell. I didn't much believe in luck. And they didn't bother to answer when I asked about being returned to Hypatia. It was pretty clear that the direction we were headed was not back toward the city.

I had given them my word that I wouldn't fight or try to escape—where would I escape to?—and they'd accepted it. Once they realized that I wasn't whom they had expected to capture, they'd pressed me for news of the outside.

There were three of them in the small craft: the two Estebans and the pilot, who was never introduced. He did not bother to turn around to greet me and all I ever saw of him was the back of his helmet. The craft itself they called a manta; an odd thing that was partly an airplane, partly dirigible, and partly a submarine. Once I'd given my word that I wouldn't escape, I was allowed to look out, but there was nothing to see but a luminous golden haze.

"We keep the manta flying under the cloud decks," Jaramillo said. "Keeps us invisible."

"Invisible to whom?" I asked, but neither one of them bothered to answer. It was a dumb question anyway; I could very well guess who they wanted to keep out of sight of. "What about radar?" I said.

Esteban looked at Esteban, and then at me. "We have means to deal with radar," he said. "Just leave it at that and stop it with the questions you should know enough not to ask."

They seemed to be going somewhere, and eventually the manta exited the cloudbank into the clear air above. I pressed toward the porthole, trying to see out. The cloudscapes of Venus were still fascinating to me. We were skimming the surface of the cloud deck—ready to duck under if there were any sign of watchers, I surmised. From the cloudscape it was impossible to tell how far we'd come, whether it was just a few leagues or halfway around the planet. None of the floating cities were visible, but in the distance I spotted the fat torpedo shape of a dirigible. The pilot saw it as well, for we banked toward it and sailed slowly up, slowing down as we approached, until it disappeared over our heads, and the hull resonated with a sudden impact, then a ratcheting clang.

"Soft dock," Jaramillo commented, and then a moment later another clang, and the nose of the craft was suddenly jerked up. "Hard dock," he said. The two Estebans seemed to relax a little, and a whine and a rumble filled the little cabin. We were being winched up into the dirigible.

After ten minutes or so, we came to rest in a vast interior space. The manta had been taken inside the envelope of the gas chamber, I realized. Half a dozen people met us.

"Sorry," Jaramillo said, "but I'm afraid we're going to have to blind you. Nothing personal."

"Blind?" I said, but actually that was good news. If they did not intend to release me, they wouldn't care what I saw.

Jaramillo held my head steady while Francisco placed a set of the goggle-eyed glasses over my eyes. They were surprisingly comfortable. Whatever held them in place, they were so light that I could scarcely feel that they were there. The amber tint was barely noticeable. After checking that they fit, Francisco tapped the side of the goggles with his fingertip, once, twice, three times, four times. Each time he touched the goggles, the world grew darker, and with a fifth tap, all I could see was inky black. Why would sunglasses have a setting for complete darkness, I thought? And then I answered my own question: the last setting must be for e-beam welding. Pretty convenient, I thought. I wondered if I dared to ask them if I could keep the set of goggles when they were done.

"I am sure you won't be so foolish as to adjust the transparency," one of the Estebans said.

I was guided out the manta's hatch and across the hangar, and then to a seat.

"This the prisoner?" a voice asked.

"Yeah," Jaramillo said. "But the wrong one. No way to tell, but we guessed wrong, got the wrong flyer."

"Shit. So who is he?"

"Technician," Jaramillo said. "From the up and out."

"Really? So does he know anything about the Nordwald-Gruenbaum plan?"

I spread my hands out flat, trying to look harmless. "Look, I only met the kid twice, or I guess three times, if you—"

That caused some consternation; I could hear a sudden buzz of voices, in a language I didn't recognize. I wasn't sure how many of them there were, but it seemed like at least half a dozen. I desperately wished I could see them, but that would very likely be a fatal move. After a moment, Jaramillo said, his voice now flat and expressionless, "You know the heir of Nordwald-Gruenbaum? You met Carlos Fernando in person?"

"I met him. I don't know him. Not really."

"Who did you say you were again?"

I went through my story, this time starting at the very beginning, explaining how we had been studying the ecology of Mars, how we had been summoned to Venus to meet the mysterious Carlos Fernando. From time to time I was interrupted to answer questions—what was my relationship with Leah Hamakawa? (I wished I knew). Were we married? Engaged? (No. No.) What was Carlos Fernando's relationship with Dr. Hamakawa? (I wished I knew). Had Carlos Fernando ever mentioned his feelings about the independent cities? (No.) His plans? (No.) Why was Carlos Fernando interested in terraforming? (I don't know.) What was Carlos Fernando planning? (I don't know.) Why did Carlos Fernando bring Hamakawa to Venus? (I wished I knew.) What was he planning? What was he planning? (I don't know. I don't know.)

The more I talked, the more sketchy it seemed, even to me.

There was silence when I had finished talking. Then the first voice said, "Take him back to the manta."

I was led back inside and put into a tiny space, and a door clanged shut behind me. After a while, when nobody answered my call, I reached up to the goggles. They popped free with no more than a light touch, and, looking at them, I was still unable to see how they attached. I was in a storage hold of some sort. The door was locked.

I contemplated my situation, but I couldn't see that I knew any more now than I had before, except that I now knew that not all of the Venus cities were content with the status quo, and some of them were willing to go to some lengths to change it. They had deliberately shot me down, apparently thinking that I was Leah—or possibly even hoping for Carlos Fernando? It was hard to think that he would have been out of the protection of his bodyguards. Most likely, I decided, the bodyguards had been there, never letting him out of sight, ready to swoop in if needed, but while Carlos Fernando and Leah had soared up and around the city, I had left the sphere covered by the guards, and that was the opportunity the pirates in the manta had taken. They had seen the air kayak flying alone and shot it out of the sky, betting my life on their skill, that they could swoop in and snatch the falling pilot out of mid-air.

They could have killed me, I realized.

And all because they thought I knew something—or rather, that Leah Hamakawa knew something—about Carlos Fernando's mysterious plan.

What plan? He was a twelve-year-old kid, not even a teenager, barely more than an overgrown child! What kind of plan could a kid have?

I examined the chamber I was in, this time looking more seriously at how it was constructed. All the joints were welded, with no obvious gaps, but the metal was light, probably an aluminum-lithium alloy. Possibly malleable, if I had the time, if I could find a place to pry at, if I could find something to pry with.

If I did manage to escape, would I be able to pilot the manta out of its hangar in the dirigible? Maybe. I had no experience with lighter than air vehicles, though, and it would be a bad time to learn, especially if they decided that they wanted to shoot at me. And then I would be—where? A thousand miles from anywhere. Fifty million miles from anywhere I knew.

I was still mulling this over when Esteban and Esteban returned.

"Strap in," Esteban Jaramillo told me. "Looks like we're taking you home."

The trip back was more complicated than the trip out. It involved two or more transfers from vehicle to vehicle, during some of which I was again "requested" to wear the opaque goggles.

We were alone in the embarking station of some sort of public transportation. For a moment, the two Estebans had allowed me to leave the goggles transparent. Wherever we were, it was unadorned, drab compared to the florid excess of Hypatia, where even the bus stations—did they have bus stations?—would have been covered with flourishes and artwork.

Jaramillo turned to me and, for the first time, pulled off his goggles so he could look me directly in the eye. His eyes were dark, almost black, and very serious,

"Look," he said, "I know you don't have any reason to like us. We've got our reasons, you have to believe that. We're desperate. We know that his father had some secret projects going. We don't know what they were, but we know he didn't have any use for the free cities. We think the young Gruenbaum has something planned. If you can get through to Carlos Fernando, we want to talk to him."

"If you get him," Esteban Francisco said, "Push him out a window. We'll catch him. Easy." He was grinning with a broad smile, showing all his teeth, as if to say he wasn't serious, but I wasn't at all sure he was joking.

"We don't want to kill him. We just want to talk," Esteban Jaramillo said. "Call us. Please. Call us."

And with that, he reached up and put his goggles back on. Then Francisco reached over and tapped my goggles into opacity, and everything was dark. With one on either side of me, we boarded the transport—bus? Zeppelin? Rocket?

Finally I was led into a chamber and was told to wait for two full minutes before removing the goggles, and after that I was free to do as I liked.

It was only after the footsteps had disappeared that it occurred to me to wonder how I was supposed to contact them, if I did have a reason to. It was too late to ask, though; I was alone, or seemed to be alone.

Was I being watched to see if I would follow orders, I wondered? Two full minutes. I counted, trying not to rush the count. When I got to a hundred and twenty, I took a deep breath and finger-tapped the goggles to transparency.

When my eyes focused, I saw I was in a large disembarking lounge with genetically engineered pink grass and sculptures of iron and jade. I recognized it. It was the very same lounge at which we had arrived at Venus three days ago—was it only three? Or had another day gone by?

I was back in Hypatia city.

Once again I was surrounded and questioned. As with the rest of Carlos Fernando's domain, the questioning room was lushly decorated with silk-covered chairs and elegant teak carvings, but it was clearly a holding chamber.

The questioning was by four women, Carlos Fernando's guards, and I had the feeling that they would not hesitate to tear me apart if they thought I was being less than candid with them. I told them what had happened, and at every step they asked questions, making suggestions as to what I could have done differently. Why had I taken my kayak so far away from any of the other fliers and out away from the city? Why had I allowed myself to be captured without fighting? Why didn't I demand to be returned and refuse to answer any questions? Why could I describe none of the rebels I'd met, except for two men who had—as far as they could tell from my descriptions—no distinctive features?

At the end of their questioning, when I asked to see Carlos Fernando, they told me that this would not be possible.

"You think I allowed myself to be shot down deliberately?" I said, addressing myself to the chief among the guards, a lean woman in scarlet silk.

"We don't know what to think, Mr. Tinkerman," she said. "We don't like to take chances."

"What now, then?"

"We can arrange transport to the built worlds," she said. "Or even to the Earth."

"I don't plan to leave without Dr. Hamakawa," I said.

She shrugged. "At the moment, that's still your option, yes," she said. "At the moment."

"How can I get in contact with Dr. Hamakawa?"

She shrugged. "If Dr. Hamakawa wishes, I'm sure she will be able to contact you."

"And if I want to speak to her?"

She shrugged. "You're free to go now. If we need to talk to you, we can find you."

I had been wearing one of the gray jumpsuits of the pirates when I'd been returned to Hypatia; the guard women had taken that away. Now they gave me a suit of spider-silk in a lavender brighter than the garb an expensive courtesan would wear in the built worlds surrounding Earth, more of an evening gown than a suit. It was nevertheless subdued compared to the day-to-day attire of Hypatia citizens, and I attracted no attention. I discovered that the goggle-eyed sunglasses had been neatly placed in a pocket at the knees of the garment. Apparently people on Venus keep their sunglasses at their knees. Convenient when you're sitting, I supposed. They hadn't been recognized as a parting gift from the pirates, or, more likely, had been considered so trivial as to not be worth confiscating. I was unreasonably pleased; I liked those glasses.

I found the Singh habitat with no difficulty, and when I arrived, Epiphany and Truman Singh were there to welcome me and to give me the news.

My kidnapping was already old news. More recent news was being discussed everywhere.

Carlos Fernando Delacroix Ortega de la Jolla y Nordwald-Gruenbaum had given a visitor from the outer solar system, Dr. Leah Hamakawa—a person who (they had heard) had actually been born on Earth—a rock.

And she had not handed it back to him.

My head was swimming.

"You're saying that Carlos Fernando is proposing marriage? To Leah? That doesn't make any sense. He's a kid, for Jove's sake. He's not old enough."

Truman and Epiphany Singh looked at one another and smiled. "How old were you when we got married?" Truman asked her. "Twenty?"

"I was almost twenty-one before you accepted my book and my rock," she said.

"So, in Earth years, what's that?" he said. "Thirteen?"

"A little over twelve," she said. "About time I was married up, I'd say."

"Wait," I said. "You said you were twelve years old when you got married?"

"Earth years," she said. "Yes, that's about right."

"You married at twelve? And you had—" I suddenly didn't want to ask, and said, "Do all women on Venus marry so young?"

"There are a lot of independent cities," Truman said. "Some of them must have different customs, I suppose. But it's the custom more or less everywhere I know."

"But that's—" I started to say, but couldn't think of how to finish. Sick? Perverted? But then, there were once a lot of cultures on Earth that had child marriages.

"We know the outer reaches have different customs," Epiphany said. "Other regions do things differently. The way we do it works for us."

"A man typically marries up at age twenty-one or so," Truman explained. "Say, twelve, thirteen years old, in Earth years. Maybe eleven. His wife will be about fifty or sixty—she'll be his instructor, then, as he grows up. What's that in Earth years—thirty? I know that in old Earth custom, both sides of a marriage are supposed to be the same age, but that's completely silly, is it not? Who's going to be the teacher, I should say?

"And then, when he grows up, by the time he reaches sixty or so he'll marry down, find a girl who's about twenty or twenty-one, and he'll serve as a teacher to her, I should say. And, in time, she'll marry down when she's sixty, and so on."

It seemed like a form of ritualized child abuse to me, but I thought it would be better not to say that aloud. Or, I thought, maybe I was reading too much into what he was saying. It was something like the medieval apprentice system. When he said teaching, maybe I was jumping to conclusions to think that he was talking about sex. Maybe they held off on the sex until the child grew up some. I thought I might be happier not knowing.

"A marriage is braided like a rope," Epiphany said. "Each element holds the next."

I looked from Truman to Epiphany and back. "You, too?" I asked Truman. "You were married when you were twelve?"

"In Earth years, I was thirteen when I married up Triolet," he said. "Old. Best thing that ever happened to me. God, I needed somebody like her to straighten me out back then. And I needed somebody to teach me about sex, I should say, although I didn't know it back then."

"And Triolet—"

"Oh, yes, and her husband before her, and before that. Our marriage goes back a hundred and ninety years, to when Raj Singh founded our family; we're a long braid, I should say."

I could picture it now. Every male in the braid would have two wives, one twenty years older, one twenty years younger. And every female would have an older and a younger husband. The whole assembly would indeed be something you could think of as a braid, alternating down generations. The interpersonal dynamics must be terribly complicated. And then I suddenly remembered why we were having this discussion. "My god," I said. "You're serious about this. So you're saying that Carlos Fernando isn't just playing a game. He actually plans to marry Leah."

"Of course," Epiphany said. "It's a surprise, but then, I'm not at all surprised. It's obviously what His Excellency was planning right from the beginning. He's a devious one, he is."

"He wants to have sex with her."

She looked surprised. "Well, yes, of course. Wouldn't you? If you were twenty—I mean, twelve years old? Sure you're interested in sex. Weren't you? It's about time His Excellency had a teacher." She paused a moment. "I wonder if she's any good? Earth people—she probably never had a good teacher of her own."

That was a subject I didn't want to pick up on. Our little fling on Mars seemed a long way away, and my whole body ached just thinking of it.

"Sex, it's all that young kids think of," Truman cut in. "Sure. But for all that, I should say that sex is the least important part of a braid. A braid is a business, Mr. Tinkerman, you should know that. His Excellency Carlos Fernando is required to marry up into a good braid. The tradition, and the explicit terms of the inheritance, are both very clear. There are only about five braids on Venus that meet the standards of the trust, and he's too closely related to half of them to be able to marry in. Everybody has been assuming he would marry the wife of the Telios Delacroix braid; she's old enough to marry down now, and she's not related to him closely enough to matter. His proposition to Dr. Hamakawa—yes, that has everybody talking."

I was willing to grasp at any chance. "You mean his marriage needs to be approved? He can't just marry anybody he likes?"

Truman Singh shook his head. "Of course he can't! I just told you. This is business as well as propagating the genes for the next thousand years. Most certainly he can't marry just anybody."

"But I think he just outmaneuvered them all," Epiphany added. "They thought they had him boxed in, didn't they? But they never thought that he'd go find an outworlder."

"They?" I said. "Who's they?"

"They never thought to guard against that," Epiphany continued.

"But he can't marry her, right?" I said. "For sure, she's not of the right family. She's not of any family. She's an orphan, she told me that. The institute is her only family."

Truman shook his head. "I think Epiphany's right," he said. "He just may have outfoxed them, I should say. If she's not of a family, doesn't have the dozens or hundreds of braided connections that everybody here must have, that means they can't find anything against her."

"Her scientific credentials—I bet they won't be able to find a flaw there." Epiphany said. "And an orphan? That's brilliant. Just brilliant. No family ties at all. I bet he knew that. He worked hard to find just the right candidate, you can bet." She shook her head, smiling. "And we all thought he'd be another layabout, like his father."

"This is awful," I said. "I've got to do something."

"You? You're far too old for Dr. Hamakawa." Epiphany looked at me appraisingly. "A good looking man, though—if I were ten, fifteen years younger, I'd give you another look. I have cousins with girls the right age. You're not married, you say?"

Outside the Singh quarters in Sector Carbon, the Sun was breaking the horizon as the city blew into the daylit hemisphere.

I hadn't been sure whether Epiphany's offer to find me a young girl had been genuine, but it was not what I needed, and I'd refused as politely as I could manage.

I had gone outside to think, or as close to "outside" as the floating city allowed, where all the breathable gas was inside the myriad bubbles. But what could I do? If it was a technical problem, I would be able to solve it, but this was a human problem, and that had always been my weakness.

From where I stood, I could walk to the edge of the world, the transparent gas envelope that held the breathable air in and kept the carbon dioxide of the Venus atmosphere out. The Sun was surrounded by a gauzy haze of thin high cloud, and encircled by a luminous golden halo, with mock suns flying in formation to the left and the right. The morning sunlight slanted across the cloud tops. My eyes hurt from the direct sun. I remembered the sun goggles in my knee pocket and pulled them out. I pressed them onto my eyes and tapped on the right side until the world was comfortably dim.

Floating in the air, in capital letters barely darker than the background, were the words LINK: READY.

I turned my head, and the words shifted with my field of view, changing from dark letters to light depending on the background.

A communications link was open? Certainly not a satellite relay; the glasses couldn't have enough power to punch through to orbit. Did it mean the manta was hovering in the clouds below?

"Hello, hello," I said, talking to the air. "Testing. Testing?"

Nothing.

Perhaps it wasn't audio. I tapped the right lens: dimmer, dimmer, dark; then back to full transparency. Maybe the other side? I tried tapping the left eye of the goggle, and a cursor appeared in my field of view.

With a little experimentation, I found that tapping allowed input in the form of Gandy-encoded text. It seemed to be a low bit-rate text only; the link power must be minuscule. But Gandy was a standard encoding, and I tapped out "CQ CQ."

Seek you, seek you.

The LINK: READY message changed to a light green, and in a moment the words changed to HERE.

WHO, I tapped.

MANTA 7, was the reply. NEWS?

CF PROPOSED LH, I tapped. !

KNOWN, came the reply. MORE?

NO.

OK. SIGNING OUT.

The LINK: READY message returned.

A com link, if I needed one. But I couldn't see how it helped me any.

I returned to examining the gas envelope. Where I stood was an enormous transparent pane, a square perhaps ten meters on an edge. I was standing near the bottom of the pane, where it abutted to the adjacent sheet with a joint of very thin carbon. I pressed on it and felt it flex slightly. It couldn't be more than a millimeter thick; it would make sense to make the envelope no heavier than necessary. I tapped it with the heel of my hand and could feel it vibrate; a resonant frequency of a few Hertz, I estimated. The engineering weak point would be the joint between panels: if the pane flexed enough, it would pop out from its mounting at the join.

Satisfied that I had solved at least one technical conundrum, I began to contemplate what Epiphany had said. Carlos Fernando was to have married the wife of the Telios Delacroix braid. Whoever she was, she might be relieved at discovering Carlos Fernando making other plans; she could well think the arranged marriage as much a trap as he apparently did. But still. Who was she, and what did she think of Carlos Fernando's new plan?

The guards had made it clear that I was not to communicate with Carlos Fernando or Leah, but I had no instructions forbidding access to Braid Telios Delacroix.

The household seemed to be a carefully orchestrated chaos of children and adults of all ages, but now that I understood the Venus societal system a little, it made more sense. The wife of Telios Delacroix—once the wife-apparent of His Excellency Carlos Fernando—turned out to be a woman only a few years older than I was, with closely cropped gray hair. I realized I'd seen her before. At the banquet, she had been the woman sitting next to Carlos Fernando. She introduced herself as Miranda Telios Delacroix and introduced me to her up-husband, a stocky man perhaps sixty years old.

"We could use a young husband in this family," he told me. "Getting old, we are, and you can't count on children—they just go off and get married themselves."

There were two girls there, who Miranda Delacroix introduced as their two children. They were quiet, attempting to disappear into the background, smiling brightly but with their heads bowed, looking up at me through lowered eyelashes when they were brought out to be introduced. After the adults' attention had turned away from them, I noticed both surreptitiously studying me. A day ago I wouldn't even have noticed.

"Now, either come and sit nicely and talk, or else go do your chores," Miranda told them. "I'm sure the outworlder is quite bored with your buzzing in and out."

They both giggled and shook their heads and then disappeared into another room, although from time to time one or the other head would silently pop out to look at me, disappearing instantly if I turned to look.

We sat down at a low table that seemed to be made of oak. Miranda's husband brought in some coffee and then left us alone. The coffee was made in the Thai style, in a clear cup, in layers with thick sweet milk.

"So you are Dr. Hamakawa's friend," she said. "I've heard a lot about you. Do you mind my asking, what exactly is your relationship with Dr. Hamakawa?"

"I would like to see her," I said.

She frowned. "So?"

"And I can't."

She raised an eyebrow.

"He has these woman, these bodyguards—"

Miranda Delacroix laughed. "Ah, I see! Oh, my little Carli is just too precious for words. I can't believe he's jealous. I do think that this time he's really infatuated." She tapped on the tabletop with her fingers for a moment, and I realized that the oak tabletop was another one of the embedded computer systems. "Goodness, Carli is not yet the owner of everything, and I don't see why you shouldn't see whoever you like. I've sent a message to Dr. Hamakawa that you would like to see her."

"Thank you."

She waved her hand.

It occurred to me that Carlos Fernando was about the same age as her daughters, perhaps even a classmate of theirs. She must have known him since he was a baby. It did seem a little unfair to him—if they were married, she would have all the advantage, and for a moment I understood his dilemma. Then something she had said struck me.

" 'He's not yet owner of everything,' " I repeated. "I don't understand your customs, Mrs. Delacroix. Please enlighten me. What do you mean, yet?"

"Well, you know that he doesn't come into his majority until he's married," she said.

The picture was beginning to make sense. Carlos Fernando desperately wanted to control things, I thought. And he needed to be married to do it. "And once he's married?"

"Then he comes into his inheritance, of course," she said. "But since he'll be married, the braid will be in control of the fortune. You wouldn't want a twenty-one-year-old kid in charge of the entire Nordwald-Gruenbaum holdings. That would be ruinous. The first Nordwald knew that. That's why he married his son into the la Jolla braid. That's the way it's always been done."

"I see," I said. If Miranda Delacroix married Carlos Fernando, she—not he—would control the Nordwald-Gruenbaum fortune. She had the years of experience, she knew the politics, how the system worked. He would be the child in the relationship. He would always be the child in the relationship.

Miranda Delacroix had every reason to want to make sure Leah Hamakawa didn't marry Carlos Fernando. She was my natural ally.

And also, she—and her husband—had every reason to want to kill Leah Hamakawa.

Suddenly the guards that followed Carlos Fernando seemed somewhat less of an affectation. Just how good were the bodyguards? And then I had another thought. Had she or her husband hired the pirates to shoot down my kayak? The pirates clearly had been after Leah, not me. They had known that Leah was flying a kayak; somebody must have been feeding them information. If it hadn't been her, then who?

I looked at her with new suspicions. She was looking back at me with a steady gaze. "Of course, if your Dr. Leah Hamakawa intends to accept the proposal, the two of them will be starting a new braid. She would nominally be the senior, of course, but I wonder—"

"But would she be allowed to?" I interrupted. "If she decided to marry Carlos Fernando, wouldn't somebody stop her?"

She laughed. "No, I'm afraid that little Carli made his plan well. He's the child of a Gruenbaum, all right. There are no legal grounds for the families to object; she may be an outworlder, but he's made an end run around all the possible objections."

"And you?"

"Do you think I have choices? If he decides to ask me for advice, I'll tell him it's not a good idea. But I'm halfway tempted to just see what he does."

And give up her chance to be the richest woman in the known universe? I had my doubts.

"Do you think you can talk her out of it?" she said. "Do you think you have something to offer her? As I understand it, you don't own anything. You're hired help, a gypsy of the solar system. Is there a single thing that Carli is offering her that you can match?"

"Companionship," I said. It sounded feeble, even to me.

"Companionship?" she echoed, sarcastically. "Is that all? I would have thought most outworlder men would promise love. You are honest, at least, I'll give you that."

"Yes, love," I said, miserable. "I'd offer her love."

"Love," she said. "Well, how about that. Yes, that's what outworlders marry for; I've read about it. You don't seem to know, do you? This isn't about love. It's not even about sex, although there will be plenty of that, I can assure you, more than enough to turn my little Carlos inside out and make him think he's learning something about love.

"This is about business, Mr. Tinkerman. You don't seem to have noticed that. Not love, not sex, not family. It's business."

Miranda Telios Delacroix's message had gotten through to Leah, and she called me up to her quarters. The woman guards did not seem happy about this, but they had apparently been instructed to obey her direct orders, and two red-clad guardswomen led me to her rooms.

"What happened to you? What happened to your face?" she said, when she saw me.

I reached up and touched my face. It didn't hurt, but the acid burns had left behind red splotches and patches of peeling skin. I filled her in on the wreck of the kayak and the rescue, or kidnapping, by pirates. And then I told her about Carlos. "Take another look at that book he gave you. I don't know where he got it, and I don't want to guess what it cost, but I'll say it's a sure bet it's no facsimile."

"Yes, of course." she said. "He did tell me, eventually."

"Don't you know it's a proposition?"

"Yes; the egg, the book, and the rock," she said. "Very traditional here. I know you like to think I have my head in the air all the time, but I do pay some attention to what's going on around me. Carli is a sweet kid."

"He's serious, Leah. You can't ignore him."

She waved me off. "I can make my own decisions, but thanks for the warnings."

"It's worse than that," I told her. "Have you met Miranda Telios Delacroix?"

"Of course," she said.

"I think she's trying to kill you." I told her about my suspicion that the pirates had been hired to shoot me down, thinking I was her.

"I believe you may be reading too much into things, Tinkerman," she said. "Carli told me about the pirates. They're a small group, disaffected; they bother shipping and such, from time to time, but he says that they're nothing to worry about. When he gets his inheritance, he says he will take care of them."

"Take care of them? How?"

She shrugged. "He didn't say."

But that was exactly what the pirates—rebels—had told me: that Carlos had a plan, and they didn't know what it was. "So he has some plans he isn't telling," I said.

"He's been asking me about terraforming," Leah said. "But it doesn't make sense to do that on Venus. I don't understand what he's thinking. He could split the carbon dioxide atmosphere into oxygen and carbon; I know he has the technology to do that."

"He does?"

"Yes, I think you were there when he mentioned it. The molecular still. It's solar-powered micromachines. But what would be the point?"

"So he's serious?"

"Seriously thinking about it, anyway. But it doesn't make any sense. Nearly pure oxygen at the surface, at sixty or seventy bars? That atmosphere would be even more deadly than the carbon dioxide. And it wouldn't even solve the greenhouse effect; with that thick an atmosphere, even oxygen is a greenhouse gas."

"You explained that to him?"

"He already knew it. And the floating cities wouldn't float any more. They rely on the gas inside—breathing air—being lighter than the Venusian air. Turn the Venus carbon dioxide to pure O2, the cities fall out of the sky."

"But?"

"But he didn't seem to care."

"So terraforming would make Venus uninhabitable and he knows it. So what's he planning?"

She shrugged. "I don't know."

"I do," I said. "And I think we'd better see your friend Carlos Fernando."

Carlos Fernando was in his playroom.

The room was immense. His family's quarters were built on the edge of the upcity, right against the bubble-wall, and one whole side of his playroom looked out across the cloudscape. The room was littered with stuff: sets of interlocking toy blocks with electronic modules inside that could be put together into elaborate buildings; models of spacecraft and various lighter-than-air aircraft, no doubt vehicles used on Venus; a contraption of transparent vessels connected by tubes that seemed to be a half-completed science project; a unicycle that sat in a corner, silently balancing on its gyros. Between the toys were pieces of light, transparent furniture. I picked up a chair, and it was no heavier than a feather, barely there at all. I knew what it was now, diamond fibers that had been engineered into a foamed, fractal structure. Diamond was their chief working material; it was something that they could make directly out of the carbon dioxide atmosphere, with no imported raw materials. They were experts in diamond, and it frightened me.

When the guards brought us to the playroom, Carlos Fernando was at the end of the room farthest from the enormous window, his back to the window and to us. He'd known we were coming, of course, but when the guards announced our arrival he didn't turn around, but called behind him, "It's okay—I'll be with them in a second."

The two guards left us.

He was gyrating and waving his hands in front of a large screen. On the screen, colorful spaceships flew in three-dimensional projection through the complicated maze of a city that had apparently been designed by Escher, with towers connected by bridges and buttresses. The viewpoint swooped around, chasing some of the spaceships, hiding from others. From time to time bursts of red dots shot forward, blowing the ships out of the sky with colorful explosions as Carlos Fernando shouted "Gotcha!" and "In your eye, dog!"

He was dancing with his whole body; apparently the game had some kind of full-body input. As far as I could tell, he seemed to have forgotten entirely that we were there.

I looked around.

Sitting on a padded platform no more than two meters from where we had entered, a lion looked back at me with golden eyes. He was bigger than I was. Next to him, with her head resting on her paws, lay a lioness, and she was watching me as well, her eyes half open. Her tail twitched once, twice. The lion's mane was so huge that it must have been shampooed and blow-dried.

He opened his mouth and yawned, then rolled onto his side, still watching me.

"They're harmless," Leah said. "Bad-Boy and Knickers. Pets."

Knickers—the female, I assumed—stretched over and grabbed the male lion by the neck. Then she put one paw on the back of his head and began to groom his fur with her tongue.

I was beginning to get a feel for just how different Carlos Fernando's life was from anything I knew.

On the walls closer to where Carlos Fernando was playing his game were several other screens. The one to my left looked like it had a homework problem partially worked out. Calculus, I noted. He was doing a chain-rule differentiation and had left it half-completed where he'd gotten stuck or bored. Next to it was a visualization of the structure of the atmosphere of Venus. Homework? I looked at it more carefully. If it was homework, he was much more interested in atmospheric science than in math; the map was covered with notes and had half a dozen open windows with details. I stepped forward to read it more closely.

The screen went black.

I turned around, and Carlos Fernando was there, a petulant expression on his face. "That's my stuff," he said. His voice squeaked on the word "stuff." "I don't want you looking at my stuff unless I ask you to, okay?"

He turned to Leah, and his expression changed to something I couldn't quite read. He wanted to kick me out of his room, I thought, but didn't want to make Leah angry; he wanted to keep her approval. "What's he doing here?" he asked her.

She looked at me and raised her eyebrows.

I wish I knew myself, I thought, but I was in it far enough that I had better say something.

I walked over to the enormous window and looked out across the clouds. I could see another city, blue with distance, a toy balloon against the golden horizon.

"The environment of Venus is unique," I said. "And to think, your ancestor Udo Nordwald put all this together."

"Thanks," he said. "I mean, I guess I mean thanks. I'm glad you like our city."

"All of the cities," I said. "It's a staggering accomplishment. The genius it must have taken to envision it all, to put together the first floating city; to think of this planet as a haven, a place where millions can live. Or billions—the skies are nowhere near full. Someday even trillions, maybe."

"Yeah," he said. "Really something, I guess."

"Spectacular." I turned around and looked him directly in the eye. "So why do you want to destroy it?"

"What?" Leah said.

Carlos Fernando had his mouth open, and started to say something, but then closed his mouth again. He looked down, and then off to his left, and then to the right. He said, "I . . . I . . . " but then trailed off.

"I know your plan," I said. "Your micromachines—they'll convert the carbon dioxide to oxygen. And when the atmosphere changes, the cities will be grounded. They won't be lighter than air, won't be able to float anymore. You know that, don't you? You want to do it deliberately."

"He can't," Leah said, "it won't work. The carbon would—" and then she broke off. "Diamond," she said. "He's going to turn the excess carbon into diamond."

I reached over and picked up a piece of furniture, one of the foamed-diamond tables. It weighed almost nothing.

"Nanomachinery," I said. "The molecular still you mentioned. You know, somebody once said that the problem with Venus isn't that the surface is too hot. It's just fine up here where the air's as thin as Earth's air. The problem is the surface is just too darn far below sea level.

"But for every ton of atmosphere your molecular machines convert to oxygen, you get a quarter ton of pure carbon. And the atmosphere is a thousand tons per square meter."

I turned to Carlos Fernando, who still hadn't managed to say anything. His silence was as damning as any confession. "Your machines turn that carbon into diamond fibers and build upward from the surface. You're going to build a new surface, aren't you? A completely artificial surface. A platform up to the sweet spot, fifty kilometers above the old rock surface. And the air there will be breathable."

At last Carlos found his voice. "Yeah," he said. "Dad came up with the machines, but the idea of using them to build a shell around the whole planet—that idea was mine. It's all mine. It's pretty smart, isn't it? Don't you think it's smart?"

"You can't own the sky," I said, "but you can own the land, can't you? You will have built the land. And all the cities are going to crash. There won't be any dissident cities, because there won't be any cities. You'll own it all. Everybody will have to come to you."

"Yeah," Carlos said. He was smiling now, a big goofy grin. "Sweet, isn't it?" He must have seen my expression, because he said, "Hey, come on. It's not like they were contributing. Those dissident cities are full of nothing but malcontents and pirates."

Leah's eyes were wide. He turned to her and said, "Hey, why shouldn't I? Give me one reason. They shouldn't even be here. It was all my ancestor's idea, the floating city, and they shoved in. They stole his idea, so now I'm going to shut them down. It'll be better my way."

He turned back to me. "Okay, look. You figured out my plan. That's fine, that's great, no problem, okay? You're smarter than I thought you were, I admit it. Now, just, I need you to promise not to tell anybody, okay?"

I shook my head.

"Oh, go away," he said. He turned back to Leah. "Dr. Hamakawa," he said. He got down on one knee, and, staring at the ground, said, "I want you to marry me. Please?"

Leah shook her head, but he was staring at the ground and couldn't see her. "I'm sorry, Carlos," she said. "I'm sorry."

He was just a kid, in a room surrounded by his toys, trying to talk the adults into seeing things the way he wanted them to. He finally looked up, his eyes filling with tears. "Please," he said. "I want you to. I'll give you anything. I'll give you whatever you want. You can have everything I own, all of it, the whole planet, everything."

"I'm sorry," Leah repeated. "I'm sorry."

He reached out and picked up something off the floor—a model of a space-ship—and looked at it, pretending to be suddenly interested in it. Then he put it carefully down on a table, picked up another one, and stood up, not looking at us. He sniffled and wiped his eyes with the back of his hand—apparently forgetting he had the ship model in it—trying to do it casually, as if we wouldn't have noticed that he had been crying.

"Okay," he said. "You can't leave, you know. This guy guessed too much. The plan only works if it's secret, so that the malcontents don't know it's coming, don't prepare for it. You have to stay here. I'll keep you here, I'll—I don't know. Something."

"No," I said. "It's dangerous for Leah here. Miranda already tried to hire pirates to shoot her down once, when she was out in the sky kayak. We have to leave."

Carlos looked up at me, and with sudden sarcasm said, "Miranda? You're joking. That was me who tipped off the pirates. Me. I thought they'd take you away and keep you. I wish they had."

And then he turned back to Leah. "Please? You'll be the richest person on Venus. You'll be the richest person in the solar system. I'll give it all to you. You'll be able to do anything you want."

"I'm sorry," Leah repeated. "It's a great offer. But no."

At the other end of the room, Carlos' bodyguards were quietly entering. He apparently had some way to summon them silently. The room was filling with them, and their guns were drawn, but not yet pointed.

I backed toward the window, and Leah came with me.

The city had rotated a little, and sunlight was now slanting in through the window. I put my sun goggles on.

"Do you trust me?" I said quietly.

"Of course," Leah said. "I always have."

"Come here."

LINK: READY blinked in the corner of my field of view.

I reached up, casually, and tapped on the side of the left lens. CQ MANTA, I tapped. CQ.

I put my other hand behind me and, hoping I could disguise what I was doing as long as I could, I pushed on the pane, feeling it flex out.

HERE, was the reply.

Push. Push. It was a matter of rhythm. When I found the resonant frequency of the pane, it felt right, it built up, like oscillating a rocking chair, like sex.

I reached out my left hand to hold Leah's hand, and pumped harder on the glass with my right. I was putting my weight into it now, and the panel was bowing visibly with my motion. The window was starting to make a noise, an infrasonic thrum too deep to hear, but you could feel it. On each swing, the pane of the window bowed further outward.

"What are you doing?" Carlos shouted. "Are you crazy?"

The bottom bowed out, and the edge of the pane separated from its frame.

There was a smell of acid and sulfur. The bodyguards ran toward us, but—as I'd hoped—they were hesitant to use their guns, worried that the damaged panel might blow completely out.

The window screeched and jerked, but held, fixed in place by the other joints. The way it was stuck in place left a narrow vertical slit between the window and its frame. I pulled Leah close to me and shoved myself backward, against the glass, sliding along against the bowed pane, pushing it outward to widen the opening as much as I could.

As I fell, I kissed her lightly on the edge of the neck.

She could have broken my grip, could have torn herself free.

But she didn't.

"Hold your breath and squeeze your eyes shut," I whispered, as we fell through the opening and into the void, and then with my last breath of air, I said, "I love you."

She said nothing in return. She was always practical, and knew enough not to try to talk when her next breath would be acid. "I love you too," I imagined her saying.

With my free hand, I tapped, MANTA.

NEED PICK-UP. FAST.

And we fell.

"It wasn't about sex at all," I said. "That's what I failed to understand." We were in the manta, covered with slime, but basically unhurt. The pirates had accomplished their miracle, snatched us out of mid-air. We had information they needed, and in exchange they would give us a ride off the planet, back where we belonged, back to the cool and the dark and the emptiness between planets. "It was all about finance. Keeping control of assets."

"Sure it's about sex," Leah said. "Don't fool yourself. We're humans. It's always about sex. Always. You think that's not a temptation? Molding a kid into just exactly what you want? Of course it's sex. Sex and control. Money? That's just the excuse they tell themselves."

"But you weren't tempted," I said.

She looked at me long and hard. "Of course I was." She sighed, and her expression was once again distant, unreadable. "More than you'll ever know."

THE MAGICIAN AND THE MAID AND OTHER STORIES

CHRISTIE YANT

———◆———

She called herself Audra, though that wasn't her real name; he called himself Miles, but she suspected it wasn't his, either.

She was young (how young she would not say), beautiful (or so her Emil had told her), and she had a keen interest in stories. Miles was old, tattooed, perverted, and often mean, but he knew stories that no one else knew, and she was certain that he was the only one who could help her get back home.

She found him among the artists, makers, and deviants. They called him Uncle, and spoke of him sometimes with loathing, sometimes respect, but almost always with a tinge of awe—a magician in a world of technicians, they did not know what to make of him.

But Audra saw him for what he truly was.

There once was a youth of low birth who aspired to the place of King's Magician. The villagers scoffed, "Emil, you will do naught but mind the sheep," but in his heart he knew that he could possess great magic.

The hedge witches and midwives laughed at the shepherd boy who played at sorcery, but indulged his earnestness. He learned charms for love and marriage (women's magic, but he would not be shamed by it) and for wealth and luck, but none of this satisfied him, for it brought him no nearer to the throne. For that he needed real power, and he did not know where to find it.

He had a childhood playmate named Aurora, and as they approached adulthood Aurora grew in both beauty and cleverness. Their childhood affection turned to true love, and on her birthday they were betrothed.

The day came when the youth knew he had learned all that he could in the nearby villages and towns. The lovers wept and declared their devotion with an exchange of humble silver rings. With a final kiss Emil left his true love behind, and set out to find the source of true power.

It was not hard to meet him, once she understood his tastes. A tuck of her skirt, a tug at her chemise; a bright ribbon, new stockings, and dark kohl to line her eyes. She followed him to a club he frequented, where musicians played discordant arrangements and the patrons were as elaborately costumed as the performers. She walked past his booth where he smoked cigarettes and drank scotch surrounded by colorful young women and effeminate young men.

"You there, Bo Peep, come here."

She met his dark eyes, turned her back on him, and walked away. The sycophants who surrounded him bitched and whined their contempt for her. He barked at them to shut up as she made her way to the door.

Once she had rejected him it was easy. She waited for his fourth frustrated overture before she joined him at his table.

"So," she said as she lifted his glass to her lips uninvited, "tell me a story."

"What kind of story?"

"A fairy tale."

"What—something with elves and princes and happily-ever-after?"

"No," she said and reached across the corner of the table to turn his face toward her. He seemed startled but complied, and leaned in until their faces were just inches apart. "A real fairy tale. With wolves and witches, jealous parents, woodsmen charged with murdering the innocent. Tell me a story, Miles—" she could feel his breath against her cheek falter as she leaned ever closer and spoke softly into his ear "—tell me a story that is true."

Audra was foot-sore and weary when they reached the house at dawn. She stumbled on the stone walk, and caught Miles's arm to steady her.

"Are you sure you don't need anything from home?" he asked as he worked his key in the lock.

At his mention of *home,* she remembered again to hate him.

"Quite sure," she said. He faced her, this time with a different kind of appraisal. There was no leer, no suspicion. He touched her face, and his habitual scowl relaxed into something like a smile.

"You remind me of someone I knew once, long ago." The smile vanished and he opened the front door, stepping aside to let her pass.

His house was small and filled with a peculiar collection of things that told her she had the right man. Many of them where achingly familiar to Audra: a wooden spindle in the entryway, wound with golden thread; a dainty glass shoe on the mantle, almost small enough to fit a child; in the corner, a stone statue of an ugly, twisted creature, one arm thrown protectively over its eyes.

"What a remarkable collection," she said and forced a smile. "It must have taken a long time to assemble."

"Longer than I care to think of." He picked a golden pear off the shelf and examined it. "None of it is what I wanted." He returned it to the shelf with a careless toss. "I'll show you the bedroom."

The room was bare, in contrast with the rest of the house. No ornament hung on the white plaster walls, no picture rested on the dresser. The bed was small, though big enough for two, and covered in a faded quilt. It was flanked by a table on one side, and a bent wood chair on the other.

Audra sat stiffly at the foot of the bed.

The mattress creaked as Miles sat down beside her. She turned toward him with resolve, and braced herself for the inevitable. She would do whatever it took to get back home.

She had done worse, and with less cause.

He leaned in close and stroked her hair; she could smell him, sweet and smoky, familiar and foreign at the same time. She lifted a hand to caress his smooth head where he lingered above her breast. He caught her wrist and straightened, pressed her palm to his cheek—eyes closed, forehead creased in pain—then abruptly dropped her hand and rose from the bed.

"If you need more blankets, they're in the wardrobe. Sleep well," he said, and left Audra to wonder what had gone wrong, and to consider her next move.

Aurora was as ambitious as Emil, but of a different nature. She believed that the minds of most men were selfish and swayed only by fear or greed. In her heart there nestled a seed of doubt that Emil could get his wish through pure knowledge and practice. She resolved in her love for him to secure his place through craft and wile.

Aurora knew the ways of tales. She planted the seed of rumor in soil in which it grew best: the bowry; the laundry; anywhere the women gathered, she talked of his power.

But word of the powerful sorcerer had to reach the King himself, and to get close enough she would need to use a different craft.

The hands of guards and pikemen were rougher than Emil's; the mouths of servants less tender. She ignited the fire of ambition in their hearts with flattery, and fanned it with promises that Emil, the most powerful sorcerer in the kingdom, would repay those who supported him once he was installed in the palace.

And if she had regrets as she hurried from chamber to cottage in the cold night air, she dismissed them as just a step on the road toward realizing her lover's dream.

Audra woke at mid-day to find a note on the chair in the corner of the room.

In deep black ink and an unpracticed hand was written:

"Stay if you like, or go as you please. I am accountable to only one, and that one is not you. If that arrangement suits you, make yourself at home.—M."

It suited her just fine.

She searched the house. She wasn't sure what she was looking for, but she was certain that any object of power great enough to rip her from her own world would be obvious somehow. It would be odd, otherworldly, she thought—but that described everything here. Like a raven's hoard, every nook contained some shiny, stolen object.

On a shelf in the library she found a clear glass apothecary jar labeled "East Wind." *Thief,* she thought. Audra hoped that the East Wind didn't suffer for the lack of the contents of the jar. She would keep an eye on the weather vane and return it at the first opportunity.

Something on the shelf caught her eye, small and shining, and her contempt turned to rage.

Murderer.

She pocketed Emil's ring.

Miles seemed to dislike mirrors. There were none in the bedroom; none even in the washroom. The only mirror in the house was an ornate, gilded thing that hung in the library. She paused in front of it, startled at her disheveled appearance. She smoothed her hair with her fingers and leaned in to examine her blood-shot eyes—and found someone else's eyes looking back at her.

The gaunt, androgynous face that gazed dolefully from deep within the mirror was darker and older than her own.

"Hello," she said to the Magic Mirror. "I'm Audra."

The Mirror shook its head disapprovingly.

"You're right," she admitted. "But we don't give strangers our true names, do we?"

She considered her new companion. The long lines of its insubstantial face told Audra that it had worn that mournful look for a long time.

"Did he steal you, as well? Perhaps we can help each other find a way home. The answer is here somewhere."

The face in the Mirror brightened, and it nodded.

Audra had an idea. "Would you like me to read to you?"

Emil travelled a bitter road in search of the knowledge that would make his fortune. By day he starved, by night he froze. But one day Luck was with him, and he caught two large, healthy hares before sunset. As he huddled beside his small fire, the hares roasting over the flames, a short and grizzled man came out of the forest, carrying a sack of goods.

"Good evening, Grandfather," Emil said to the little man. "Sit, share my fire and supper." The man gratefully accepted. "What do you sell?" Emil asked.

"Pots and pans, needles, and spices," the old man said.

"Know you any magic?" Emil asked, disappointed. He was beginning to think the knowledge he sought didn't exist, and he was losing hope.

"What does a shepherd need with magic?"

"How did you know I'm a shepherd?" Emil asked in surprise.

"I know many things," the man said, and then groaned, and doubled over in pain.

"What ails you?" Emil cried, rushing to the old man's side.

"Nothing that you can help, lad. I've a disease of the gut that none can cure, and my time may be short."

Emil questioned the man about his ailment, and pulled from his pack dozens of pouches of herbs and powders. He heated water for a medicinal brew while the old man groaned and clutched his stomach.

The man pulled horrible faces as he drank down the bitter tea, but before long his pain eased, and he was able to sit upright again. Emil mixed another batch of the preparation and assured him that he would be cured if he drank the tea for seven days.

"I was wrong about you," the man said. "You're no shepherd." He pulled a scroll from deep within his pack. "For your kindness I'll give you what you've traveled the world seeking."

The little man explained that the scroll contained three powerful spells, written in a language that no man had spoken in a thousand years. The first was a spell to summon a benevolent spirit, who would then guide him in his learning.

The second summoned objects from one world into another, for every child knew that there were many worlds, and that it was possible to pierce the veil between them.

The third would transport a person between worlds.

If he could decipher the three spells, he would surely become the most powerful sorcerer in the kingdom.

Emil offered the old man what coins he had, but he refused. He simply handed over the scroll, bade Emil farewell, and walked back into the forest.

Audra filled her time reading to the Mirror. The shelves were filled with hundreds of books: old and new, leather-bound and gilt-edged, or flimsy and sized to be carried in a pocket.

She devoured them, looking for clues. How she got here. How she might get back.

On a bottom shelf in the library, in the sixth book of a twelve-volume set, she found her story.

The illustrations throughout the blue, cloth-bound book were full of round, cheerful children and curling vines. She recognized some of her friends and enemies from her old life: there was Miska, who fooled the Man-With-The-Iron-Head and whom she had met once on his travels; on another page she found the fairy who brought the waterfall to the mountain, whom Audra resolved to visit as soon as she got home.

She turned the page, and her breath caught in her throat.

"The Magician and the Maid," the title read. Beneath the illustration were those familiar words, "Once upon a time."

A white rabbit bounded between birch trees toward Audra's cottage. Between the tree tops a castle gleamed pink in the sunset light, the place where her story was supposed to end. Audra traced the outline of the rabbit with her finger, and then traced the two lonely shadows that followed close behind.

Two shadows: one, her own, and the other, Emil's.

Audra was reading to the Mirror, a story it seemed to particularly like. It did tricks for her as she read, creating wispy images in the glass that matched the prose.

She had just reached the best part, where the trolls turn to stone in the light of the rising sun, when she heard footsteps outside the library door. The Mirror looked anxiously toward the sound, and then slipped out of sight beyond the carved frame.

The door burst open.

"Who are you talking to?" Miles demanded. "Who's here?" He smelled of scotch and sweat, and his overcoat had a new stain.

"No one. I like to read aloud. I am alone here all day," she said.

"Don't pretend I owe you anything." He slouched into the chair and pulled a cigarette from his coat. "You might make yourself useful," he said. "Read to me."

The room was small, and she stood no more than an arm's length away, feeling like a school girl being made to recite. She opened to a story she did not know, a tale called "The Snow Queen," and began to read. Miles closed his eyes and listened.

"Little Kay was quite blue with cold, indeed almost black, but he did not feel it; for the Snow Queen had kissed away the icy shiverings, and his heart was already a lump of ice," she read.

She glanced down at him when she paused for breath to find him looking at her in a way that she knew all too well.

Finally, an advantage.

She let her voice falter when he ran a finger up the side of her leg, lifting her skirt a few inches above her knee.

She did not stop reading—it was working, something in him had changed as she read. Sex was a weak foothold, but it was the only one she had, and perhaps it would be a step toward getting into his mind.

"He dragged some sharp, flat pieces of ice to and fro, and placed them together in all kinds of positions, as if he wished to make something out of them. He composed many complete figures, forming different words, but there was one word he never could manage to form, although he wished it very much. It was the word 'Eternity.' "

He fingered the cord tied at her waist, and tugged it gently at first, then more insistently. He leaned forward in the chair, and unfastened the last hook on her corset.

"Just at this moment it happened that little Gerda came through the great door of the castle. Cutting winds were raging around her, but she offered up a prayer and the winds sank down as if they were going to sleep; and she went on till she came to the large empty hall, and caught sight of Kay; she knew him directly; she flew to him and threw her arms round his neck, and held him fast, while she exclaimed, "Kay, dear little Kay, I have found you at last.' "

His fingers stopped their manipulations. His hands were still on her, the fastenings held between his fingertips.

She dared not breathe.

Whatever control she had for those few minutes was gone. She tried to reclaim it, to keep going as if nothing had happened. She even dropped a hand from the book and reached out to touch him. His hand snapped up and caught hers; he stood, pulling hard on her arm.

"Enough." He left the room without looking back. She heard the front door slam.

Audra straightened her clothes in frustration and wondered again what had gone wrong.

It took only a moment's thought for Audra to decide to follow him. She peered out into the street: there he was, a block away already, casting a long shadow in the lamp light on the wet pavement.

Her feet were cold and her shoes wet through by the time he finally stopped at a warehouse deep in a maze of brick complexes. He manipulated a complex series of locks on the dented and rusting steel door, and disappeared inside.

So this was where he went at night? Not to clubs and parlors as she had thought, but here, on the edge of the inhabited city, to a warehouse only notable for having all its window glass.

The windows were too high for her to see into, but a dumpster beneath one of them offered her a chance. The metal bin was slick with mist, and she slipped off it twice, but on her third try she hoisted herself on top and nervously peered through the filthy glass of the window.

In the dim light she could just make out the shape of Miles, rubbing his hands fiercely together as if to warm them, then unrolling something—paper, or parchment—spreading it out carefully in front of him on the concrete floor. He stood, and began to speak.

The room grew brighter, and a face appeared in front of him, suspended in the air—a familiar face made of dim green light; Audra could see little of it through the dirty glass. She could hear Miles's voice, urgent and almost desperate, but the words he shouted at the thing made no sense to her.

She shifted her weight to ease the pain of her knee pressing against the metal of the dumpster, and slipped. She fell, and cried out in pain as she landed hard on the pavement. She didn't know if Miles had heard, but she did not wait to find out. She picked herself up—now wet, filthy, and aching—and ran.

When she reached the house she went straight to the library. Audra shifted the books on the shelf so that the remaining volumes were flush against each other, and she hid her book in the small trunk where she kept her few clothes.

The Mirror's face emerged from its hiding place behind the frame, looking worried and wan.

"It's my story, after all," she told it. "I won't let him do any more damage. What if he takes the cottage? The woods? Where would I have to go home to? No, he can't have any more of our story."

The language of the scroll was not as impossible as the little man had said—while it was not his own, it was similar enough that someone as clever as Emil could puzzle it out. He applied himself to little else, and before long Emil could struggle through half of the first spell. But when he thought of arriving home after so long, still unable to execute even the simplest of the three, the frustration in him grew.

Surely, he thought, he should begin with the hardest, for having mastered that the simpler ones will come with ease.

So thinking, he set out to learn the last of the three spells before he arrived home.

When Miles finally returned the following evening at dusk, he looked exhausted and filthy, as if he had slept on the floor of the warehouse. She met him in the kitchen, and didn't ask questions.

He brooded on a chair in the corner while she chopped vegetables on the island butcher block, never taking his eyes off her, then stood abruptly and left the room.

The hiss and sputter of the vegetables as they hit the pan echoed the angry, inarticulate hiss in her mind. She had been here for days, and she was no closer to getting home.

The knife felt heavy and solid in her hand as she cubed a slab of marbled meat. She imagined Miles under the knife, imagined his fear and pain. She would get it out of him—how to get home—and he would tell her what he had done to her Emil before the miserable bastard died.

Sounds from the next room were punctuated with curses. The crack of heavy books being unshelved made her flinch.

"Where is it?" he first seemed to ask himself; then louder, "*Where?*" he demanded of the room at large; then a roar erupted from the doorway: "*What have you done with it, you vicious witch?*"

A cold wash of fear cleared away her thoughts of revenge.

"What are you talking about?"

"My book," he said. "Where is it? What have you done with it?"

He came at her hunched like an advancing wolf. They circled the butcher block. She gripped the knife and dared not blink, for fear that he would take a split second advantage and lunge for her.

"You have many books."

"*And I only care about one!*" His hand shot out and caught her wrist, bringing her arm down against the scarred wood with a painful shock. The knife fell from her hand.

He dragged her into the library. "There," he said, pointing to the shelf where her book had been. "Six of twelve. It was there and now it's not." He relaxed his grip without letting go. "If you borrowed it, it's fine. I just want it back." He released her and forced a smile. "Now, where is it?"

"You're right," she said, "I borrowed it. I didn't realize it was so important to you."

"It's very special."

"Yes," she said, her voice low and hard, "it is."

And with that, she knew she had given herself away.

Miles shoved her away from him. She fell into the bookcase as he left the small library and shut door behind him. A key turned in the lock.

It was too late.

She rested with her forehead against the door and caught her breath. She tried to pry open the small window, but it was sealed shut with layers of paint. She considered breaking the glass, and then thought better of it; she could escape from this house, it was true, but not from this world. For that, she still needed Miles.

She watched the sun set through the dirty window, and tried to decide what to do when he let her out. She heard him pacing through the house, talking to himself with ever greater stridency, but the words made no sense to her. It gave her a headache.

The sound of the key in the door woke her. She grabbed at the first thing that might serve as a weapon, a sturdy hardcover. She held in front of her like a shield.

Miles stood in the doorway, a long, wicked knife in his hand.

"Who are you?" he finally asked, his eyes narrowed with suspicion. "And how did you know?"

"Someone whose life you destroyed. Liar. Thief. Murderer." She produced Emil's ring.

He seemed frozen where he stood, his eyes darting back and forth between the ring in her hand and her face. "I am none of those things," he said.

"You took all of this," she gestured around the room. "You took him, and you took me. And what did you do with the things that were of no use to you?"

She had been edging toward him while he talked. She threw the book at his arm and it struck him just as she had hoped. The knife fell to the floor and she dove for it, snatching it up before Miles could stop her.

She had him now, she thought, and pressed the blade against his throat. He tried to push her off but she had a tenacious grip on him and he ceased his struggle when the knife pierced his thin skin. She felt his body tense in her hands, barely breathing and perfectly still.

"You still haven't told me who you are."

"Where is he?" she demanded.

"Where is who?" His voice was smooth and controlled.

"The man you stole, like you stole me. Like you stole all of it. Where is he?"

"You're obviously very upset. Put that down, let me go, and we'll talk about it. I don't know about any stolen man, but maybe I can help you find him."

He voice was calm, slightly imploring, asking for understanding and offering help. She hesitated, wondering what threat she was really willing to carry out against an enemy who was also her only hope.

She waited a moment too long. Miles grabbed a heavy jar off the shelf and hurled it at the wall.

The East Wind ripped through the room, finally free.

Fatigued and half-starved, Emil made his way slowly toward his home, and tried to unlock the spell. Soon he had three words, and then five, and soon a dozen. He would say them aloud, emphasizing this part or that, elongating a sound or shortening it, until the day he gave voice to the last character on the page, and something happened: a spark, a glimmer of magic.

He had ciphered out the spell.

Finally, on the coldest night he could remember, with not a soul in sight, he raised his voice against the howling wind, and shouted out the thirteen words of power.

As weeks turned into months the stories of Emil the Sorcerer grew, until finally even the King had heard, and wanted his power within his own control.

But Emil could not be found.

The angry vortex threw everything off the shelves. Audra ducked and covered her head as she was pummeled by books and debris. Miles crouched behind the trunk, which offered little protection from the gale.

There was a crash above Audra's head; her arms flew up to protect her eyes; broken glass struck her arms and legs, some falling away, some piercing her skin.

The window broke with a final crash and the captive wind escaped the room. The storm was over. Books thumped and glass tinkled to the ground.

Audra opened her eyes to the wreckage. Miles was already sifting through the pages and torn covers.

"No," he said, "no! It has to be here, my story has to be here . . . " He bled from a hundred small cuts but he paid them no mind. Audra plucked shards of dark glass out of her flesh. The shards gave off no reflection at all.

A cloud drifted from where the Mirror had hung over the wreckage-strewn shelves, searching. On the floor beside Audra's trunk, the lid torn off in the storm, it seemed to find what it was looking for. It slipped between the pages of a blue cloth-bound volume and disappeared.

"Here!" Audra said, clutching the volume to her chest. He scrambled toward her until they kneeled together in the middle of the floor, face to face.

Smoke curled out of the pages, only a wisp at first. Then more, green and glowing like a sunbeam in a mossy pond, crept out and wrapped itself around both them.

"The Guide you sought was always here," a voice whispered. "Your captive, Emil, and your friend, Aurora." Audra—Aurora—looked at the man she had hated and saw what was there all along: her Emil, thirty years since he had disappeared, with bald head and graying beard. Miles, who kept her because she looked like his lost love, but who wouldn't touch her, in faith to his beloved.

Emil looked back at her, tears in the eyes that had seemed so dead and without hope until now.

"Now, Emil, speak the words," the voice said, "and we will go home."

So should you happen across a blue cloth-bound book, the sixth in a set of twelve, do not look for "The Magician and the Maid," because it is not there.

Read the other stories, though, and in the story of the fairy who brought the waterfall to the mountain, you may find that she has a friend called Audra, though you will know the truth: it is not her real name.

If you read further you may find Emil as well, for though he never did become the King's magician, every story needs a little magic.

LETTER FROM THE EMPEROR

STEVE RASNIC TEM

A mishap occurred four sleeps from landfall. Jacob had been logging observations when he heard the alarm, so by the time he got down to the cargo bay it was all over. The bay door was breached. He stared at the switch through the window—it had been opened from inside the bay. Whatever had been inside the bay had been swept out into space.

"Anders?" he called through com. He waited. There was no answer. Ship command buzzed in his ear. *There are indications that Anders Nils . . .* Jacob shut the communication off. He didn't want to hear what command had to say. He went looking for Anders.

The forward crew cabin was empty. As were the toilets, the shower, records, navigation, engineering, recreation, general stores. Jacob had been in the recording room when the alarm went off. He systematically tried every compartment, passage, pipe, even the output trays of the garbage grinders. There was no place left to look. "Anders, please report your whereabouts," he called through com. Again no answer.

He waited. He turned the link to ship command back on. "Please report the whereabouts of Anders Nils," he said aloud.

Anders Nils is not on board, a woman's voice spoke softly into his ear. *Procedure is to query ship command first when there is an unscheduled breach of the cargo bay. Why did you fail to query ship command? Why did you shut off initial communications from ship command?*

Jacob didn't answer. He didn't know why he hadn't followed procedure. Maybe he already knew Anders was gone, but didn't want to hear command's confirmation. Was that it? It made very little sense—despite their long service together on messaging and data collection ships he and Anders weren't even friends, as far as he understood. Suddenly he wasn't sure. Was that possible?

How had they not become friends, enemies, something? Somehow he had avoided entanglement. He'd spent his long hours listening, the job they'd been trained to do, snatching the words out of space and trying to understand, and whenever possible delivering these stray messages to their intended destinations.

Please respond to official queries. Command's voice had lost some of its warmth, its naturalness. *You have a duty to respond to these questions.* Command was beginning to show its mechanical roots.

He was a professional, a sensor for the emperor, or for who- or whatever passed for the emperor these days, capturing the nuances machinery was still incapable of. "You record every stray fart," was the usual, vulgar summation of their duties. Such attention to detail discouraged both amity and enmity, as far as he was concerned.

He would be finishing the assignment alone. Perhaps even the entire tour of duty. The realization left him cold, furious. How was he supposed to manage it? Besides recording local observations and handling messaging, the ship delivered statements of regulation, and proclamations to the outlying settlements. But a quick replacement was impossible, out here on the farthest reaches of the empire, where the dividing line between empire and not-empire wasn't all that clear.

Did Anders Nils speak to you before going to the cargo bay?

Jacob gathered Anders's spare clothing into a bag. He catalogued his former crewmate's personal effects, his toiletries, his player, various small art objects.

Please respond. Did Anders Nils speak to you of his intentions?

Jacob ignored command's transmissions. He separated out all written notes and recordings, checking the storage on Anders's personal devices for data files and images. Anders's diary files were extensive and detailed, and he only had time to go through a sampling. The entries surprised him, but he had no time or inclination to be surprised.

Did Anders Nils show observable signs of depression?

He'd never liked talking to ship command. The fact that it appeared to possess more charisma and compassion than he did . . . grated.

He caught his first yawn while carefully placing Anders's personal documents into a sealed container. Over the next brief interval the yawns multiplied rapidly. There was no way to fight ship command's enforced sleep—he barely made it back to his bunk before oblivion wiped him away.

After sleep, command brought him up to dialogue regarding the incident. The temperature in the recording room had dropped noticeably into the discomfort zone.

"Please change your uniform to the appropriate formality." The voice out of the speaker was soft again, lush. He considered how brittle his own voice was in comparison. He brushed two fingers over his cuff until the correct dark blue color swam beneath them. "Correct." Pause. "The Emperor expresses his condolences for the loss of crewman reporter Anders Nils." The voice sounded achingly sincere. It made Jacob ashamed of his own underdeveloped powers of empathy. Another, awkwardly long pause. "How long did you serve with Anders Nils?"

"It would have been four years in a few sleeps."

"More precise, please."

"You have this information." He didn't bother to mask his annoyance,

"Answer please. We understand this may be a difficult time." Command rarely said "we." Suddenly Jacob felt quite unsure whom he was talking to.

Jacob ran his fingers over the table, accessing his personal diary. "Three years. Eleven months. Three weeks. Seventy-three hours. And four minutes, at least until the time of the hatch alarm."

Another long pause. Jacob knew this wasn't processing inefficiency. Com could formulate appropriate questions instantly. It was giving him time to think and remember, and it was measuring and analyzing that process. But as far as he knew, he had nothing to remember. So he waited.

"Did you know Anders had been depressed?"

"Was he?"

"Do you know why Anders would commit suicide?"

"Is that what he did? What is your percentage of certitude on that?"

"Forty-three percent."

"Then you don't know to a certainty."

Quite a long pause, then, "We do not know to a certainty."

"Then you don't know what you're talking about."

A red light glowed unsteadily on the panel. Jacob thought about Anders, concluded they'd never really been friends.

"You have heard the personal diaries of Anders Nils."

It wasn't a question. Wasn't command supposed to be asking questions? He answered anyway, thinking that at least he was doing *his* part. "I listened to some of it. There wasn't time for a full examination."

"What was your impression of the personal diaries of Anders Nils?"

"I . . . well, that's hard to say. He recorded a great deal. I suppose that surprised me. And they were well-composed, I think. Somewhat poetic, I suppose."

"Did any of the events described in the diaries of Anders Nils actually occur?"

"No, none that I heard. They were pretty outlandish."

"Please define 'outlandish,' as you understand it."

"Oh, unusual. Crazy. Impossible. We never went to the locations he describes. You know that very well. We did not visit those places, or have those adventures."

"You did not have the kind of relationship with Anders Nils he describes?"

"Well, no. No, I did not. I didn't know him all that well, actually."

"You were not friends?"

"Well, not close, not like that. We were acquaintances. We worked together. We had a working relationship."

"Why were you not friends?"

Jacob never would have expected command to ask such a thing. "I really don't know how to answer that," he finally replied.

"Why did you not know Anders was thinking of committing suicide?"

Jacob would not answer. He sat there silently, staring into the red eye lens mounted in the panel, until the countdown for landing preparations began.

The planet's surface was that light-trapping coating they'd used for official installations and supporting structures back before his grandfather was born. The fact that here and there it glistened and flowed with bits of color only emphasized how basically drab it all was. But it was durable and resistant to the attempts of most planetary ecologies to reclaim it.

"Welcome to Joy," the officer said, with what appeared to be a genuinely warm smile.

Jacob blinked. This wasn't the official designation. "From the looks of things, someone had a sense of humor."

"It would appear so," she said, still smiling. "Nine six oh gee four dash thirty-two."

"Then I'm in the correct place."

The com link in his ear murmured, *You may inform her that her uniform color has shifted out of sequence,* but he ignored that. True, her outfit appeared slightly on the purplish side, but it was probably the best she could do. It was no doubt decades old and difficult to calibrate.

"I'm pleased. We don't get many visitors."

Protocols were loose here, he observed. Not that he really cared. "I'm only scheduled for two sleeps," he said, not really wanting to discourage her friendly manner, although he was sure it came across that way.

"Well, we'll see what we can show you during that time. I know that the reporter ships like to record as much as possible during their limited visits."

Com buzzed his ear. *There are currently 432 undelivered regulatory messages due for 960G4-32. Too many for practical application. Please select at your discretion.* He had no intention of passing along any of these messages. In any case, how could they be enforced?

He nodded, thinking she probably hadn't even been born yet when the last such ship arrived. She'd probably briefed herself from some aging manual. The truth was the system didn't care that much about the outlying bases—just some basic facts on population and armaments for the statistical grids. He'd heard that the assumption had always been that such far-flung installations would fade in and out of participation in the empire over time. Otherwise their construction would have been made more pleasing.

"Anya, you should have called me." The man's voice was somewhat frail, but commanding as he trotted into the room. He raised a palm. Jacob returned the gesture tentatively, no longer accustomed to the act.

"I believe I did, Colonel," she said softly, stepping back from her post as the man stepped onto the platform.

"Terrible bother, this scan business," he said, face slightly red. "But required. Looking for tentacles, I suppose."

It was an old joke. Jacob waited for the inefficient sensors to grind to a halt. "Have you ever turned up any?"

"Certainly not with this device. There were Strangers about in the old days, and I might have run into a few during the sweeps. But hard to say. Back then they had these tag lines attached to every communication, 'If they're not a Friend, they might be a Stranger.' Remember those? Of course not—you're far too young. In any case, we were told they were all about. Problem is they were, are, so hard to identify. Has the process gotten any easier? Surely, with all the advances."

Jacob wondered what advances the old man could have been talking about. People could be so gullible out on the reaches. "Not that I know of. I've never seen a Stranger myself. Friends all, I suppose."

The aging officer stared at him. "You shouldn't make light of such things. I'm surprised that you haven't seen one of the enemy, as much as you travel. Do you have word, official of course, on the progress of the war?"

Jacob had the uneasy feeling that the man might keep him quarantined and under scan if he didn't provide a satisfactory answer. He wished he had Anders's ability at complete fabrication. His ear buzzed. *The war ebbs and flows, but remains constant. The empire continues to maintain.* Ashamed of himself, Jacob repeated command's answer word for word.

"Very well then." The officer motioned and Jacob was propelled forward up the ramp. The man's hand thrust forward, gripping his arm. "Welcome to our humble landing. Anya—Officer Bolduan—is preparing the statistical feed. Any specific observations you'd like to make?"

"Not really, as I was explaining to the other officer I'm only here two sleeps."

"Very well. You do realize your sleep regulation isn't enforced here. If you'd like to continue your accustomed sleep cycle you can return to your vessel at the appropriate intervals—"

"I'd like to give it a try."

"Certainly. Some have a difficult time transitioning." The officer looked down suddenly, as if intent on something on the instrument panel. "Do you have messages to deliver?" he asked without looking up.

Buzz. *432 undelivered regulatory messages.* Jacob shook his head in annoyance. "There are a few, probably obsolete, regulatory messages."

The officer laughed to himself. "Well, we hardly need more of those." He wetted his lips. "Anything for specific persons?"

Buzz. *Specific name is required for an adequate search. Misdirects now at over 62% due to addressing and time-delimiting malfunctions.*

"I'm not sure. I will certainly—"

"My father is retiring tomorrow," Anya spoke up, entering from the hall. "He's been waiting for his letter from the emperor."

They skittered across the dull-sealed surface of the world in a shallow vehicle looking somewhat like a huge sandal. An old geo-magnetic skimmer, as far as he could tell, although it had a home-made, jerry-built feel. Regulation replacement parts were unheard of out here (or in most of the empire, if the full truth were known). Now and then they'd pass over a deteriorated portion of the coating and the skimmer would fishtail with a twittering sound.

"It's really more stable than it seems." She was obviously amused by his discomfort. "I'm sorry about my father back there."

"He didn't do anything wrong. You embarrassed him."

She sighed. "Yes, I'm afraid I did. It's just that he's been waiting for that stupid letter for so long, and I knew he'd never ask about it directly."

"Well, yes, I surmised that. The way he began immediately apologizing for your uniform, and his, obviously to change the subject. 'My uniform is currently twenty-two points out of color phase. Officer Anya Bolduan's is currently thirty-six points out of color phase.'"

"The sad thing is he tracks those figures every day, and at the end of the month he graphs the progress. He worries about that sort of thing. It's like he expects my uniform will turn transparent in another year."

Jacob thought he might actually blush. The notion filled him with self-loathing. He couldn't look at her. "They're old uniforms. It can't be helped. I don't suppose it even matters."

"It matters very much to my father. And he only has another day for it to matter. So, is there a letter, Crewman Reporter Jacob Westman? Do you know anything, or is it all in that thing in your ear?"

She might not have seen his kind before, but she read manuals. "Patience, please. My ear is attempting to tell me what it knows."

Letters from the emperor were given at one time to higher officers, including provisional officers in charge of outposts and settlements, upon the occasion of their retirement. The practice has been largely discontinued, declining rapidly as chains of command have become increasingly ambivalent. Rarely did such letters receive the emperor's personal attention. Last recorded incident of such a letter . . . records here are incomplete.

"He knew the emperor at one time," she said. "They were friends. He served with him when they were both young. I think that's why he has his hopes so high."

Monitoring this statement due to its high probability of fabrication. Positing truthfulness, such a relationship might possibly make a difference. Is it a friendship? Please note the lower case "f." Probabilities difficult to determine, high inaccuracy due to questions as to whether a singular figure known as the "emperor" in fact now exists. Parameters classified.

"Does your ear need more time?"

"Apparently. I'm sorry."

"So how does it feel, having that voice in your head all the time? I can't manage even the low volume of communications we deal with on Joy. Don't tell my father, but sometimes I unplug."

"Truthfully it becomes annoying at times. But it is," he stopped, watched her eyes, "company."

She nodded. "It does get lonely here, you know. Even after all this time, the older staff will be talking to you, and it feels like a genuine conversation, then suddenly they're treating you like you were a Stranger."

"From my observations in these outlying posts, that isn't unusual behavior."

"So are they still out there?"

. . . speculations here are ill-advised . . .

"Honestly, I really have no idea. Possibly."

"Is the emperor even still alive? We never hear anything out here."

. . . lack of complete information is no excuse for misleading statements by crewmembers acting in their official capacity . . .

"I'm afraid I can't help you there, either. Some things work, I know that. We receive communications, including new regulations and orders. Although infrequently, supply ships arrive at destinations." Com buzzed his ear aggressively, but he ignored it. "Other military ships are encountered. The empire runs, although its borders apparently continue to change. And from my observation, most of the settlements appear to be running themselves. Maybe there's still an emperor, maybe there's a committee. People talk about the Strangers, but no one I know has ever seen one. Some people say there are no Strangers, and no emperor either."

"Well, there *was* an emperor. My father knew him. He says in the old days before he took command the emperor was expected to serve just like everyone else."

"He must have some interesting stories from that time."

The world's surface coating stopped abruptly, and the skimmer almost as quickly. The unsettled portion of Joy rolled out in front of them, its multicolored layers of stone swirling into cones, peaks, and shallow valleys. The late-afternoon light emphasized its strangeness, and its random highlighting of geologic features gave the landscape an appearance of constant movement.

"Very pretty," he said, feeling inadequate to the task of responding to such an exotic vision.

"Yes, but I'm afraid that ends the tour. Bad enough I go out there by myself without orders, but if you were to be injured—you can imagine, I'm sure. But it has such beauty and strangeness—I'm not sure I could handle so much Joy without it." She laughed. "That was a silly thing to say, I guess."

He wanted to tell her how much he enjoyed hearing her laughter, but of course did not. "You stay because of your father?"

"He retires tomorrow and I'm supposed to take over. Maybe then we can stretch things a bit, and I can find excuses to go out there more. Besides, he needs me for now. There are so many things he's unsure of."

"I can't promise any particular results, but I'll keep searching for some sort of message, at least some official recognition of his retirement."

"He *knew* the emperor, I'm sure of it. My father isn't the sort of person to fabricate things."

. . . fabrication is always a potential hazard when inadequate information is present . . .

"I believe you."

"But he doesn't have any *stories.* His memory stops after meeting the emperor, going out on those first tentative incursions. At some point his entire platoon came back with the emperor, and the powers that be must have suspected a Stranger was among them, because they were all examined, if that's even an adequate word for it. He's lost most of his memories of that period, and although his official record provides dates and locations, details are sparse."

. . . possibilities of message retrieval using insufficient search parameters are questionable . . .

"I hope a message comes through. I'll return to the ship, spend the rest of the day in queries."

"Even if you can't find anything, please come to the ceremony tomorrow? Having someone from outside in attendance, in official capacity or not—"

"Of course. Of course. I'll be there," he said, even though the idea of standing within a gathering of people he did not know made him cringe.

That evening he sat alone in the recording room in the hours before enforced sleep, as he would sit alone before many sleeps until the powers above (and there were thousands of layers, he thought, of powers above) chose someone to replace Anders. As he had sat alone time after time when Anders had still been alive and only a few meters away, simply another stranger listening for voices in the dark, recording what those voices had to say. Tonight there were a thousand such voices, most chronicling the minutiae of rulings and orders, specifications and principles, some calling out for contact from worlds not visited in generations, some pleading for assistance, remuneration, or the simple return of a greeting, and a few hesitant inquiries concerning Strangers, and fewer still wondering aloud if Strangers had at last taken over all that could be seen, heard, or imagined. The emperor himself, however, was conspicuously silent, as he had been silent, and invisible, all of Jacob's life. The possibility the sought-after letter might miraculously arrive seemed almost infinitely remote.

"Continue to parse and deliver all incoming and previously uncategorized communications," Jacob said aloud. "But please intersperse with entries from the diaries of Anders Nils."

Command remained silent, as it had all evening, but swiftly complied.

The hall where the ceremony was held was small, but so was the attendance. Official banners had been hung, each one a few points off in color as far as Jacob could determine, lending a not-entirely unpleasant but unmistakable disharmony to the proceedings.

The walls cycled images of the retiring colonel at various points in his career, but there were numerous, obvious gaps. A few of the images portrayed groups of officers and enlisted. Jacob wondered if any of the blurred, shadowed faces was that of their emperor.

People stood up one at a time and offered chronicles of their experiences serving with the colonel. Some talked about his skills as an administrator, a supervisor. One or two said he was a visionary, but provided no evidence for this claim. A man appearing older than the colonel told a semi-humorous story of their time serving together in the campaigns, but stopped abruptly and sat down. Jacob then realized the man must have also been part of the group suffering the examination which had scattered the colonel's memories.

Anya stood and told everyone what a good father he had been. She talked about his patience, and how much she respected him. When she sat down Jacob saw her warily eyeing the thin sheet of film Jacob held in his shaking hand.

"Is there anyone else?" a small man in a faded clerk's uniform asked.

Jacob stood and unsteadily made his way to the front of the room. When he turned around he looked for someone to focus on. He discovered he couldn't begin to look at the colonel, but watching Anya's face as he read was pleasant and barely possible. He held the sheet tightly to minimize the shaking.

"The vast spaces between us are filled with messages. In these scattered times few seem to find their intended destinations, or satisfy us with the things we've always wanted to hear. But sometimes you can stitch together a voice here, a voice there, until some clarity of feeling emerges. I cannot vouch for the complete accuracy of what I am about to read—it is difficult to verify the messages that come to us out of the vast unknown. But I intuit its general true feeling.

"To Colonel William Bolduan, officer in custody of Joy, from Joseph, once acquaintance and always friend, emperor of all he loves, hates, or imagines, on the occasion of the colonel's retirement from a lifetime of most meritorious service.

"Now, you may not remember because of measures taken both terrible and necessary, but when I hungered so long for sustenance, and courage, you made us a meal out of the wings of some glorious bird whose name was unfamiliar to all, whose face bore a map of the hard world we'd traveled, and while we ate, our eyes became like white jewels, and we paid each other out of laughter and song. For us there were no soldiers or emperors, no desperate orders or misguided honor to separate us, and we swore to each other the peace that comes with age. I would stand by you as your children were married, and we would tolerate no serious disagreement, and think nothing of the worlds that separated us, but praise the fineness of difference.

"When we woke I could see your embarrassment, the shame you felt for being so familiar, and you would not hear when I explained what all emperors know, that sometimes the heart must be lubricated if any truth is to be told.

"Still, we were no strangers to adventure. We were not strangers in our hearts. Without regret I followed you into the fires at Weilung, where the breath of the dying fliers erased our uniforms and then our hair. In agony you carried me to the fountains of that fading world, where those beautiful ghosts regretted our injuries, and we lay swaddled in their manes as the battles raged without us, until finally I could open my eyes without screaming, and you had that ship waiting, and past the eighty-two falls of those unfortunate worlds you transported me, until the rest of the fleet arrived, and there began our first separation.

"And you should know my people thought it improper. They called themselves my people but in truth I was irretrievably theirs. Some beings must remain separate, they told me, and a friendship of equals is a lie we tell children. So I had to content myself with reports of your exploits, your rescue mission between the two green seas, the time you brought the children (those oh-so-gullible children!) out of the mines at Debel 'Schian, and your long voyage out of the Cheylen clouds.

"If you could only remember our next meeting at the Hejen Temples! How broken I was over those jokes you told! I painted my cheeks like a little girl, and danced until you were too hoarse to sing. Later, when you were afraid your honor could not bear such frivolous and insane behavior, I somehow convinced you that sometimes insanity is the only reasonable response to atrocity, and the death of everything, and long voyages home, alone in the dark.

"But all this ends. And even I with such a grand, fully augmented memory, cannot remember the last time we laughed together, any more than you, my friend. It all has to end. And strangeness comes, and there is no science deep enough to explicate the secrets of the heart. An empire separates us, but still I think of you.

"Signed Joseph, your emperor."

Jacob returned immediately to his ship. His dialogue with command continued in the recording room, even as the vessel departed that atmosphere, trailing unanswered messages from the occupants of Joy.

"This is a continuation of queries related to the death of Anders Nils, crewman reporter third. Are you prepared to answer these queries?"

"Ask me anything. You may also repeat questions from our first session. Obviously, I have nothing better to do."

"Before proceeding to those queries we would like to ask you some possibly related questions concerning your stay on *960G4-32*."

"Yes, I imagine you do."

"The letter you read from the Emperor Joseph—that was a complete fabrication, was it not?"

"Yes, a complete fabrication."

"The letter was fabricated from fabrications previously entered by Anders Nils in his diaries, concerning imaginary adventures you and he experienced while visiting a variety of worlds."

"Yes, that was the principal source—Ander's imaginary adventures and the imaginary friendship he invented for us. But I filled it in with a few details from the colonel's service record, some stray descriptive passages from this soup of transmissions I have travelled in these past nine years. The style came out of Li Po's *Exile's Letter*. Have you read it?"

"The poem is in the database."

"I admit I've hardly done it justice."

"So you admit the emperor's letter was a lie?"

Jacob waited, thinking, then said, "It is not a lie. It is an accurate depiction of the way Anders Nils felt about me, felt about the loneliness of the voyage. It is an accurate depiction of his yearnings. I also believe it is an accurate depiction of Colonel Bolduan's yearnings, and perhaps those of our maybe-living, maybe-not emperor as well. It is certainly an accurate depiction of my own feelings."

"But the events you've narrated, events which were supposedly experienced by Colonel Bolduan, are fictional."

"Those events, those memories are gone forever. They were taken from the colonel. If the colonel had lost a leg in combat, the service would have provided him with a prosthetic. The events I have narrated in the emperor's letter are a prosthetic for what he has lost."

"Do you know why Anders would commit suicide?"

"I cannot be sure. I will never be sure. But I believe the stories he had made up, or fabricated, to use your word, had ceased to work for him. He must have been terribly, terribly lonely."

"He should have spoken to you. He could have asked us for assistance."

"Some people are unable to ask, or tell. People do what they can do."

"Why did you not know Anders was thinking of committing suicide?"

"Because I failed at the one thing I have been so thoroughly trained to do. I failed to listen."

And there ended the interview. Jacob returned to his long nights listening, alone, waiting for Anders's replacement, wondering if there would even be a replacement. Now and then he would listen to Anders's diaries. Now and then he would make up diary entries of his own.

Command wrapped up its report and transmitted it into the empty space between its reported location and a vague approximation of the location called home, not knowing, or caring, if contact was made.

HOLDFAST

MATTHEW JOHNSON

Irrel was halfway through milking Black-Eye when the sky went dark with dragons. He looked up to see what had happened and saw dozens of winged shapes obscuring the sun in the east. They were flying low to the ground; that might mean rain, but if they were riding-dragons it meant battle was coming. He shrugged and turned back to his work, resuming his interrupted song:

> Five riders in a ring
> Round Bessie's udder
> Bessie bring milk
> Milk bring butter

Milk fell into the bucket with each pull, thick and yellow with cream drawn by the charm. Irrel's daughter Niiv sat on a stool across the yard churning the milk: With every fourth stroke she clapped the churn-staff down hard to catch the hands of any witches or devils that might try to spoil the butter. She stopped partway through a stroke and pointed over Irrel's head.

He turned just in time to see the load of worm-cast falling a short distance away to the west. Irrel gave one more pull of Black-Eye's udder and patted her on the side. "Good girl," he said as he stood. Then he called out: "Sifrid, get the wagon and shovels."

Sifrid, the season-man, was over by the house. He waved and then headed for the carriage-house.

Niiv stood up and threw a glance in Sifrid's direction. "Let me get the cows back inside, and I'll come with you."

Irrel shook his head. "Black-Eye's too full to wait. Besides, someone has to keep watch over Tyrrel."

His daughter frowned. "Where is he?"

"Chicken coop, should be."

Niiv crossed her arms. "Well, am I to be a milkmaid or a nursemaid?"

Irrel fought to keep himself from smiling at her pout and her wrinkled nose. It was far from the only thing she had got from her mother, but it was the one that most recalled Eliis. "Fetch him first. Black-Eye will keep for a few moments, and then perhaps you can persuade him to try milking her." He took the tally sticks from his apron pocket and handed them to her; she took them, gave Black-Eye a pat and walked off toward the chicken coop, sighing loudly.

Once she was gone he made his way to the stable, unbarred the small door and stepped inside, pausing until his eyes adjusted to the dimmer light. Along the wall hung a dozen rope harnesses, each one tight and unfrayed. He cast his eye over the harnesses, his fingers twitching with the memory of having tied them, until finally he reached out and chose a Ram's Knot.

Grunting a little with the effort, he lifted the harness off of the wooden hook and went to the stalls. Sviput and Svegjut whickered as he passed, impatient to be let out into the yard; he called Sviput, the gelding, with a whistle and then led him to where the leather collars hung. Once the horse was dressed Irrel brought him outside, shading his own eyes against the change in light.

Sifrid had loaded the dray with shovels and drawn it up by the gate. His shirt was soaked with sweat. His childhood in the city had not left him well prepared for farm work, and he stooped with exhaustion as he drew the cart into position to be harnessed.

"Where are we going?" he asked as he dumb-tied the tug to the horse's collar.

Irrel pointed down the road to the west, then gave the gelding a pat and tossed the halter over its neck. He leaned down to loosen the holdfast on the gate, then lifted it carefully and hung it on the fencepost before leading the horse and dray forward with a tug of the harness-rope. He kept a tight hand on it. The Ram's Knot would give Sviput strength to pull the load when the cart was full, but for now it only made him headstrong. Sifrid closed the gate and followed along a few steps behind.

The road was rough, holed by hoof-prints and stranger spoors. After they had been walking for a while they saw a man ahead leading a donkey-drawn cart. Irrel gave the lead a tug, letting Sviput go more quickly, and they soon drew up close enough to see that it was Allren, who worked the farm on the other side of Slow Creek.

"Morning find you," Allren said, touching the brim of his hat and tugging it.

Irrel touched his hat in response. "And you," he said. He gave the lead a pull to slow the horse and found himself breathing harder than he was used to. His years had mostly spared his strength, but he had lost much of his wind.

"You saw it too, I suppose?"

Irrel nodded.

"And there's been men this way, looks like." Allren pointed to a break in the fencing at the side of the road. Beyond it the wheat had been trampled and torn from the ground, the heads broken and kernels scattered. "Or almost men. Only the Margrave's beasts would eat plain rye, and before harvest-time too."

"People will eat the same as pigs if they're hungry enough."

"That's true as you say it," Allren said, nodding. "That's not your fence there, is it?"

Irrel shook his head. "My hide ends back at the crooked tree."

"Didn't think so. Never saw your fence in such a state."

The wind, which had been blowing from the south all morning, had shifted to the west: It brought the smell of worm-cast, acrid and sulphurous. It grew stronger as they kept walking, passing beyond the fenced land and into marshy country. Finally they began to see the first drops of worm-cast, pats of manure about a hand around that were fibrous like a horse's droppings but dark, oily and resinous. Irrel had Sifrid gather them as they passed. Each drop clung to the season-man's gloves, needing a hard shake to fall into the cart.

The largest concentration lay ahead, in a pile about a cow-hide around that had fallen on a stretch of peatland at the edge of the marsh. Two more men with carts were standing at the side of the road, having come from the opposite direction: One Irrel knew as Karten, a brinker whose tiny strip of land stood just outside the marsh; the other one he did not know at all. Both touched their hats at he and Allren's arrival.

"Fair morning," Karten said. He was thinner than he was the last time Irrel had seen him, sometime in the winter.

"To you," Irrel said.

Allren looked back the way they had come, then further down the road. "Do either of you claim a stake by law in this find?" he asked. After a moment the two men shook their heads. "Then I propose we divide equal stakes. Do you all agree?"

Karten and the other man both looked to Irrel; after a moment he nodded, took his shovel from the cart and began to walk towards where the worm-cast had fallen. The others followed him as they walked first across the spongy peatland and then through the thick shit, which reached nearly to the tops of their boots by the time they were at the center of it. Once there they clasped hands and then turned away from one another, walking towards the edge of the worm-cast and drawing their shovels behind them to quarter it. Sifrid brought his shovel and they began to work, separating sticky spadefuls from the pat and ferrying it back to their carts.

As they were both bringing loads to the cart, Sifrid cleared his throat. "There's something I need to talk to you about," he said.

Irrel grunted, levering the shovel high to drop the worm-cast into the cart. "And now's the time, is it?"

"Well, it's, I guess it's as good a time as any, but I couldn't wait any longer. With the harvest coming, I mean."

"Hm." Irrel planted the shovel on the ground and leaned his weight on it, catching his breath. "And so?"

"Well—well I, I suppose you know that I have—I've known Niiv, I've known your daughter a long time, and . . . well. Perhaps you know already."

"I hadn't thought a goldsmith's son was working as a season-man because he needed the coin," Irrel said.

Sifrid was silent for a moment. "Yes, of course," he said. "And, well, the thing is, I'd like to marry her. I'd like to marry your daughter, to marry Niiv."

"Well," Irrel said, "I suppose I should talk to Niiv about this."

"She feels the same as I do, sir."

"I'm sure she does, but I'll talk to her just the same."

Sifrid laughed nervously. "Of course. I only meant—"

Irrel held up a hand. There was a sound he couldn't quite identify, something out of place. After a moment he realized it was a voice, quietly chanting:

> Ten little men all in a ring
> Ten little men bow to the king

He closed his eyes and turned his head slightly from side to side, still listening.

> Ten little men dance all day
> Ten little men hide a—

Irrel reached out and seized the boy by his shirt-collar. Of course it was Tyrrel, his son, his hands still splayed out in the dancing part of the charm. "What are you doing here?" Irrel said. "Your sister's sure to be beside herself."

"She didn't even go look for me!" Tyrrel said. He was a handsome boy, a bit small for ten but already bearing the lean, serious face of a man: A thatch of chestnut hair, his mother's legacy, fell over his eyes. "I watched her before I followed you. She just went into the house."

"And you showed her right," Irrel said, frowning.

"But I needed to come with you," Tyrrel said. "I have to start learning about things like this. I'll be a man soon enough, you know."

Irrel nodded slowly. "So you will," he said. "Well then, get in the cart and see if you can find any worm-coal in that mess."

Tyrrel wrinkled his nose in distaste. "What's worm-coal?"

Irrel held his thumb and forefinger about an inch apart. "Shiny black balls, say this big. Burns purer than sea-coal or charcoal—might be we'll sell what we find to Sifrid's father."

"Is it just smiths that use it in their craftings, or is it wizards too? We could give it to Uncle Allel."

"Could be we would, if you find any. Now hop to."

Tyrrel's eyes widened, and Irrel turned to see what he was looking at: More dragons were flying in from the east. Tyrrel began counting as they flew overhead: "One for sorrow, two for joy. Three for a wedding." A moment later another appeared on the horizon and he laughed, a child again. "And four for a baby boy!"

Irrel looked over at Sifrid, who was blushing. He took a deep breath and went back to his work.

By the time they had gone back to the farm and finished shoveling the worm-cast onto the dung-hill, Niiv had dinner ready. Irrel kept his eyes on his plate as they ate the meal: dark bread, beet pickle and cheese.

"Fetch me some rope and meet me on the afternoon porch," he said to Tyrrel as he stood. He looked over at Sifrid: The young man was a careful distance from Niiv, keeping the firepit between them. "There might be some trouble tonight. I need you to walk the fences today, make sure they're all holding. Be sure you go sunwise, not widdershins."

Sifrid nodded.

"And me?" Niiv asked.

"Hex signs need freshening," Irrel said. "You know where the paint is."

He stepped out of the summer kitchen, then turned and went through the door that led into the storage room. He drew a rope-cutting knife from its drawer, then took four thunderstones from their box and went back through the long hall and out onto the afternoon porch. Tyrrel was waiting for him there, sitting on a stool with a pile of rope at his feet.

Irrel settled into the empty stool across from him and put down the knife. "That was quite a charm you did this morning," he said. "Kept it up all the way to the marsh, and with five men there too."

"It's just a children's charm," Tyrrel said; he shrugged, but there was pride evident in his voice. He had always excelled at the craftings children did for mischief: making a leaf fly through the air or a thrown stick return to your hand. His hands were quick like his mother's had been, and he was able to hold his concentration much longer than any other boy his age.

"Well, it's time you learned some proper crafts," Irrel said. He gestured at the coil of rope. "We'll start with knots. Do you know any of those?"

Tyrrel nodded. "Niiv taught me the one to stop a nosebleed with a red thread."

"All right, let's see you do that one—but with a rope."

Frowning, Tyrrel picked up the knife and cut off an arm's-length of rope. He drew it into a loop, then crossed the standing part and brought it back up through the loop, drawing it tight. He regarded the knot for a moment and then held it up to his father.

"That's the knot your sister taught you?" Irrel asked.

Tyrrel nodded. "I think so. She only showed me once."

"And does it work?"

"Sometimes."

"Maybe to stop a nosebleed, but it won't hold for much else. Untie that and let me show you a real knot." Tyrrel held the rope out to his father, but Irrel shook his head. "No—I'll tell you what to do, and you tie the knot. Hold up the rope and let one end drop. The part you're holding is the *standing part*. Between that and the end is the *bight*. Do you have that?"

"Yes, father," Tyrrel said, rolling his eyes a little.

Irrel took a breath and went on. "Drop the end under the standing part and bring it back over. Now draw it back through the loop you've made."

"That's the same knot I did," Tyrrel said.

"It's not—and that's the difference between a knot that holds and one that betrays you. Now make a loop big enough to go over a cow or a horse's head. Mark the point where the loop closes, then tie the knot I just showed you right there. Now make the loop again, so that it crosses just below the first knot—crosses under. Bring the end around and over the standing part, now pass it under and up through the loop."

Tyrrel's hands moved hesitantly, finally pulling hard at the end: It slipped the length of the rope and his knot vanished. "Why can't you just *show* me?" he asked.

Irrel shook his head. "You have to feel it in your hands."

"Is that what makes a wizard?" Tyrrel asked, looking at his hands. "Did Uncle Allel have clever hands as a boy?"

"Try that knot again," Irrel said. He repeated his instructions, slowly, and this time Tyrrel's knot resolved into a figure eight. "Do you see? That knot brings the loop closed, but the first one keeps it from closing too tight on the animal's neck."

Tyrrel frowned. "That didn't feel like making a charm."

"It wasn't—not yet. The craft comes from doing it *right*: from tying it so well that your hands move the rope themselves, and you just step out of the way."

"What will it do if I do it right?"

Irrel reached out to touch the loop of rope his son had tied. "That's the Lamb's Knot. It'll keep an animal gentled so long as it's around him."

"Oh," Tyrrel said. "What about the other knots? What do they do?"

"There's no end to them," Irrel said. "There's clever knots that will slip under a thief's fingers or bite like a snake, and wise knots that know the hand that touches them before they loosen or hold. But you be careful, and not just with knots. When you work a craft, it works you too." He looked Tyrrel in the eyes. "Do you understand?"

"Yes," Tyrrel said after a moment.

Irrel held his son's gaze for a moment and then stood. "Here," he said, placing his hands flat against Tyrrel's elbows. "Push against my hands as hard as you can, as though you were trying to spread your wings like a bird."

Tyrrel nodded and began to push. Irrel had to work harder than he had expected to keep the boy's arms at his side, but after a few dozen heartbeats Tyrrel gave up. "Now what?" he asked.

Irrel released the boy's arms and they rose up of their own accord, as though he had been charmed. He looked from one arm to another in amazement.

"D'you see now?" Irrel asked. "Whatever you craft, you're always pushing against something—and it pushes you too."

"I understand," Tyrrel said, in the deadly serious tone he used when he was trying to be grown-up. He frowned. "If I learn knots well enough, do you think I could do magic? Wizard magic?"

"A wizard's just a crafter who doesn't make anything useful. Your mam could craft a candle that brought warmth to anyone in the home, a shoe that made a horse never stumble and jam that let you remember the day the berries were picked: That's magic enough."

Tyrrel said nothing. After a few moments he turned away, untied his knot and began to tie it again, his brow furrowed.

Irrel watched him for a while and then stood. "When it feels like a craft, you'll know," he said. "When that happens, tie a half-dozen or so more. There's like to be some noise tonight, and I want the cattle to stay in their places."

When he went to the barn he could see the work Niiv had done, repainting the hex signs. She had been doing them for years, since she had been about Tyrrel's age, and while he could still discern the shapes of his originals underneath they were clearly her work: much more ornate, with his simple sunwheel shapes fractured and filigreed, and more colorful as well. He admired them for a moment and then took his spade to the northeast corner of the barn. He dug a hole a hand deep and then took from his pouch one of four thunderstones—flat stones shaped like ax-heads, which had been left buried in the ground where lightning bolts had struck—and sang:

Roll, thunder, roll
Down from mountains tall
Where lightning touched once
Let never lightning fall.

With haying time so soon past, the barn might as well be a box of tinder—and he had seen enough to expect fire in the sky tonight. He went sunwise from corner to corner, burying a stone and singing the charm at each one. When he rounded the northwest corner he saw Niiv up on the ladder, freshening the paint on that side's hex signs. When she saw him she stopped her work and came down the ladder.

"Did Sifrid talk to you this morning?" she asked.

Irrel frowned. "Did you not ask him that?"

She laughed. "I think you scared him, father. I haven't seen even his shadow since dinner-time."

"Well. Yes, he did talk to me."

"And?"

He took a slow breath. "And you already know what he said, so what questions could you have of me?"

"Are you *happy* for me?" she asked, wrinkling her nose with exasperation. "Do you approve? Will you bless our wedding?"

"This is not some fancy then? You haven't just cooked him up a love-apple, or twisted your belt to get him hot?" Like her brother, she had always been skilled at the children's charms: Like her mother, hers had served to get the village boys running around after her like puppies.

She crossed her arms. "Father. No. This is real—we both want this. And we . . . "

He let her silence hang in the air. "Your mam could have taught you a crafting for that," he said quietly. "I haven't given you everything she would have, I know. But the wise woman owes me for winter corn—she could . . . "

"It's what I want," Niiv said.

Irrel nodded. "It's love, then? Truly?"

"I don't know," she said. "His father is the best goldsmith in Rebenstod. We could craft a charm that would make me the most beautiful woman there is."

He smiled. "You are the most beautiful woman there is."

She smiled too, sighing. "I know, Father. But *really*."

"And do either of you know any handfasts?"

Niiv shrugged. "Sifrid doesn't. I've tied a few, with boys from the village, but . . . well, they weren't ever meant to last." She looked away, towards the farm-house, then back to him. "I thought . . . I was hoping you could teach us the handfast you and mother tied."

Irrel said nothing, holding his hands in front of him. He curled his fingers and then straightened them again, slowly. "No," he said at last. "That's past me now—and besides I needed your mam to tie that."

"Of course," Niiv said.

He let his hands drop, put them on his hips. "You know, when your mam and I were young we spent our winter nights learning handfasts. There was none of that sledding around to farm and village you have today."

"I know, Father."

"There are plenty of fine handfasts I could teach you, ones that will last you a lifetime." He brushed his hands against the front of his pants. "I've got to finish burying these thunderstones and then get on my other work. I'll see you at supper."

When he passed by the porch he saw that Tyrrel was not there. There were about a dozen knotted harnesses lying abandoned on the ground—the first few tangled messes, the rest perfectly tied Lamb's Knots. He sighed and set out to find out how Sifrid was doing with the fence.

He followed the fence's circuit until he heard voices ahead, one a young man's and one a child's—answering the question of where Tyrrel had gone. Irrel looked at his hands and began to move them, stiffly at first, to do the charm his son had done that morning. He had not crafted it since he himself had been a boy, but he found his fingers remembered the motions—held up flat, then turned inwards, then coiled into a ring, bowing, dancing, tucked away into fists—as he quietly chanted the charm:

Ten little men standing straight
Ten little men open the gate
Ten little men all in a ring
Ten little men bow to the king
Ten little men dance all day
Ten little men hide away

Irrel could feel the craft working through him as he did the charm, and unlike his son he did not need to repeat it to keep it going. Sifrid was leaning against the fence, his face covered with dust and his shirt damp with sweat; Tyrrel sat on the fence-post, curled like a gargoyle as he interrogated the young man.

"Will you and Niiv live in Rebenstod?" Tyrrel was asking.

"I expect we will, if we get married," Sifrid said.

"Is it a big place? Are there wizards there? Did you ever see my uncle there?"

Sifrid turned to look at the boy. "He passes through from time to time. And it's not as big a place as some, but it's bigger than others. Bigger than your village."

"Does it have a schoolhouse?"

"Several."

Tyrrel nodded sagely. "In the schoolhouses there, do they just teach you children's crafts or do they teach you to be a wizard?"

"I don't know," Sifrid said. He held his fingers splayed out in front of him. "I was never in a schoolhouse: I was apprenticed as soon as I could hold a graver. Every time my hands grew, my father wept." He was silent for a moment. "But you don't need a school to teach you crafting, or your uncle for that matter. I'm sure your father could teach you anything you might want to know."

"Father?" Tyrrel asked. "All he ever does is farm-craftings. He won't even do knots, because of his fingers."

"Maybe now, but he did a great one once—he and your mother, that is. Didn't you ever notice how you're never short of water here? How spring comes a little sooner than in the other farms, and summer stays a little later—fruits ripen without rotting and keep without spoiling? That's from the handfast they tied at their wedding. It bound them to each other in a way no other handfast had ever done—bound them to this farm and it to them, bound even time itself. My father said it was the finest working he ever saw—as great as anything the Margrave or the Thaumaturge ever did."

"Is that why you want to marry my sister?" Tyrrel asked. "To learn our magic?"

Sifrid was silent for a moment. "No," he said. "I want to marry her because I love her."

Tyrrel jumped down from the fence-post. "I think that would be a good reason to marry somebody," he said.

A growing noise had been coming from up the road, and now it resolved itself into the tread of dozens or hundreds of men, marching together in ragged rhythm: soldiers, as many leaning on their spears as carrying them, and each with a holed coin sewn over his heart to protect him. Not the Margrave's things, Irrel could see. These had to be the Prince's men.

"Come back to the house," he called to Tyrrel and Sifrid.

"I want to watch."

"Tyrrel. To the house, now."

The boy threw him an angry look and then began walking slowly toward the house. Irrel kept his eyes on the Prince's soldiers; they were not nearly so wild as the Margrave's beasts, but desperate men could do desperate things.

"Karten told me they're letting people shelter inside the walls at Rebenstod," Sifrid said quietly. "We could be there by nightfall if we rode."

"I'll tie the holdfast," Irrel said. "We'll be safe."

"Yes, I know," Sifrid said. "I just thought—"

"We'll be safe."

Without another word they went back to the farmhouse. Irrel and Niiv brought the animals from the pasture back into the barn, dropping the tally sticks into the pail to keep from counting the cattle too closely. Then it was time for supper: Irrel sat on a bench facing his daughter, eating his bread and soup in silence, while Tyrrel sat beside Sifrid, peppering the young man with questions.

They sat around the small fire for a while after supper while Niiv did the dishes; then it was time for Tyrrel to go to bed. Irrel opened the bedcloset and crouched to tuck his son into the quilts, reciting the night-charm:

> Touch your collar
> Touch your toes
> Never catch a fever
> Touch your knee
> Touch your chin
> Never let the burglar in

Tyrrel giggled when his father tapped his chin, then smiled sleepily. "Do you think Uncle Allel will ever come to see us here?" he asked.

"I don't know," Irrel said. "He's a busy man."

"Could we go to visit him? It's not right, you know, that I've never seen my uncle, and I'm almost a man."

Irrel shook his head. "I can't be traveling, you know that. I've the farm to care for, and in the winter the roads are no good." He took a breath. "But you might, perhaps—now that you're almost a man. Or perhaps he'll come to Rebenstod to see your sister, when she marries, and you can see him then."

"Yes," Tyrrel said, his eyes half-shut. "Yes, I think so."

Irrel crouched there for a few moments more, listening to his son's breathing settle into the slow rhythm of sleep; then he rose, with some difficulty, and went back out into the long hall. It was nearly dark, lit only by the embers of the small fire in the main room, and he did not know where Sifrid and Niiv had gone. Sighing, he went out the main door and up the path to the gate.

He took the previous night's holdfast from where he had hung it on the fencepost and began to untie it; his clawed hands struggled with the knot, plucking at it and fraying the rope. Holding the end of the rope toward himself he made an overhand loop and then, his arm shaking, passed the end through it and up behind the standing part. He had made the base of the holdfast, a Sheep's Tail knot, and the shaking in his arms was gone.

By the time he passed the end down through the loop again his fingers were softening like butter, and he began to more fully elaborate the knot. A few more twists and loops and he had made a holdfast that would hold against the Margrave and the Thaumaturge both, but he did not stop. The rope danced in his hands, twisting around and around itself and slipping over and under the loops he had made, and he knew that if he only kept on going he would tie a knot that would be greater even than the handfast he and Eliis had made: a knot that would hold everything just as it was, bind them all and hold fast against time and chance. He held the end of the rope in his hand and took a breath.

The night passed, as all nights eventually do, but it never grew very dark, with spells, lightning and dragon-fire lighting the sky. Unable to sleep, Irrel went to the summer kitchen, kicked at the coals in the firepit until he exposed a glowing ember and lit a candle from it. Then he went to the storage room and hauled up the trap-door to the cellar before going carefully down the stairs. In the dim light of the candle it took him a while to find what he was looking for: a few jars of blackberry jam, hidden away in memory of the day he and Niiv had gone foraging in the bush and Eliis had preserved the few berries they had brought home. He went back upstairs and sat on the bench by the cold ashes of the fire, licking the dark jam from his fingers.

When true dawn finally arrived he went outside and surveyed the farm. The barn was entirely intact, even the hex signs unmarked, and the stable door still held. He walked down the path to the gate and kneeled down to untie the holdfast, feeling the craft dissipate as he loosened the knot.

"Morning find you!" Allren was coming down the road toward him, the front of his hat pulled down low to block out the morning sun.

"And you."

Allren stood on the other side of the gate, his hands on his hips. "Did you hear? The Prince's men prevailed, if you can believe it. Why, they say the Thaumaturge himself took part in the battle." He tilted his hat upwards as a grin crossed his face. "The Margrave is overthrown!"

Irrel undid the last loop and hung the now-slack rope on the fencepost. He stood up and nodded slowly, brushing the dirt from his knees.

"Well, there's that."

STANDARD LONELINESS PACKAGE

CHARLES YU

—◆—

Root canal is one fifty, give or take, depending on who's doing it to you. A migraine is two hundred.

Not that I get the money. The company gets it. What I get is twelve dollars an hour, plus reimbursement for painkillers. Not that they work.

I feel pain for money. Other people's pain. Physical, emotional, you name it.

Pain is an illusion, I know, and so is time, I know, I know. I know. The shift manager never stops reminding us. Doesn't help, actually. Doesn't help when you are on your third broken leg of the day.

I get to work late and already there are nine tickets in my inbox. I close my eyes, take a deep breath, open the first ticket of the day:

I am at a funeral.

I am feeling grief.

Someone else's grief.

I am feeling a mixture of things.

Grief, mostly, but I also detect that there is some guilt in there. There usually is.

I hear crying.

I am seeing crying faces. Pretty faces. Crying, pretty, white faces.

Nice clothes.

Our services aren't cheap. As the shift manager is always reminding us.

Need I remind you? That is his favorite phrase these days. He is always walking up and down the aisle tilting his head into our cubicles and saying it. *Need I remind you*, he says, *of where we are on the spectrum?* In terms of low-end/high-end? We are solidly towards the highish-end. So the faces are usually pretty, the clothes are usually nice. The people are usually nice, too.

Although, I imagine that it's easy to be nice when you are rich and pretty. Even when you're at a funeral.

There's a place in Hyderabad that is doing what we're doing, a little more towards the budget end of things. Precision Living Solutions, it's called. And of course there are hundreds of emotional engineering firms in Bangalore. Springing up everywhere you look. I read in the paper that a new call center opens, on average, like every three days.

Okay. Body is going into the ground now. The crying is getting more serious.

Here it comes.

I am feeling that feeling. The one that these people get a lot, near the end of a funeral service. These sad and pretty people. It's a big feeling. Different operators have different ways to describe it. For me, it feels something like a huge boot. Huge, like it fills up the whole sky, the whole galaxy, all of space. Some kind of infinite foot. And it's stepping on me. The infinite foot is stepping on my chest.

The funeral ends, and the foot is still on me, and it is hard to breathe. People are getting into black town cars. I also appear to have a town car. I get in. The foot, the foot. So heavy. Here we go, yes, this is familiar, the foot, yes, the foot. It doesn't hurt, exactly. It's not what I would call comfortable, but it's not pain, either. More like pressure.

Deepak, who used to be in the next cubicle, once told me that this feeling, which I call the infinite foot—to him it felt more like a knee—is actually the American experience of the Christian God.

"Are you sure it is the Christian God?" I asked him. "I always thought God was Jewish."

"You're an idiot," he said. "It's the same guy. Duh. The Judeo-Christian God."

"Are you sure?" I said.

He just shook his head at me. We'd had this conversation before. I figured he was probably right, but I didn't want to admit it. Deepak was the smartest guy in our cube-cluster, as he would kindly remind me several times a day.

I endure a few more minutes of the foot, and then, right before the hour is up, right when the grief and guilt are almost too much and I wonder if I am going to have to hit the safety button, there it is, it's usually there at the end of a funeral, no matter how awful, no matter how hard I am crying, no matter how much guilt my client has saved up for me to feel. You wouldn't expect it—I didn't—but anyone who has done this job for long enough knows what I'm talking about. It seems unbelievable, but it's there, it's almost always there, even if it's just a glimmer of it, and even though you know it's coming, even when you are waiting for it, in fact, when it comes, it is always still a little bit of a shock.

Relief.

Death of a cousin is five hundred. Death of a sibling is twelve-fifty. Parents are two thousand a piece, but depending on the situation people will pay all kinds of money, for all kinds of reasons, for bad reasons, or for no reason at all.

The company started in corporate services. Ethical qualm transference. Plausible deniability. That kind of stuff. Good cash flow, which the founder—now retired to philanthropy and heli-skiing—plowed right back into R&D, and turned Transfer Corp. into a specialist: a one-feeling shop. Cornered the early market in guilt.

Then the technology improved. Some genius in Delhi figured out a transfer protocol to standardize and packetize all different kinds of experiences. Qualia in general. *Don't feel like having a bad day?* That's a line from one of our commercials. *Let someone else have it for you.* It shows a rich executive-looking-type sitting and rubbing his temples, making the TV face to communicate the stress of his situation. There are wavy lines on either side of his temples to indicate that the Executive is! really! stressed! Then he places a call to his broker, and in the next scene, the Executive is lying on a beach, drinking golden beer from a bottle and looking at the bluest ocean I have ever seen.

I saw this on American television at the lunch counter across the street that has a satellite feed. I was eating at the counter and next to me was a girl, maybe four or five, scooping rice and peas into her mouth a little at a time. She watched the commercial in silence, and after it was over, turned to her mother and softly asked her what the blue liquid was. I was thinking about how sad it was that she had never seen water that color in real life until I realized that I was thirty-nine years old and hey, you know what, neither had I.

That someone else they are talking about in the commercial is me—me and the other six hundred terminal operators in building D, cubicle block 4. Don't feel like having a bad day? Let me have it for you.

It's okay for me, a good job. I didn't do that well in school, after all. It was tougher for Deep. He did three semesters at technical college. He was always saying he deserved better. Better than this, anyway. I would nod and agree with him, but I never told him what I wanted to tell him, which was hey, Deepak, when you say that you deserve better, even if I agree with you, you are kind of also implying that I don't deserve better, which, maybe I don't, maybe this is about where I belong in the grand scheme of things, in terms of high-end/low-end for me as a person, but I wish you wouldn't say it, because whenever you do, it makes me feel a sharp bit of sadness and then, for the rest of the day, a kind of low-grade crumminess.

Deep and I used to go to lunch, and he always tried to explain to me how it works:

"Okay, so, the clients," he would say, "they call into their account reps and book the time."

He liked to start sentences with, *okay, so*. It was a habit he had picked up from the engineers. He thought it made him sound smarter, thought it made him sound like them, those code geeks, standing by the coffee machine, talking faster than he could think, every word a term of art, every sentence packed with logic, or small insights or a joke. He liked to stand near them, pretending to stir sugar into his coffee, listening in on them as if they were speaking a different language. A language of knowing something, a language of being an expert at something. A language of being something more than an hourly unit.

Okay, so, he said, they book the time, and then at the appointed hour, a switch in their implant chip kicks on and starts transferring their consciousness over. Perceptions, sensory data, all of it. Okay, so, then it goes first to an intermediate server for processing and then gets bundled with other jobs, and then a huge block of the stuff gets zapped over here, where it gets downloaded onto our servers and then dumped into our queue management system, which parcels out the individual jobs to all of us in the cubicle farm.

Okay, so, it's all based on some kind of efficiency algorithm—our historical performance, our current emotional load. Sensors in our head assembly unit measure our stress levels, sweat composition, to see what we can handle. Okay?

(He would say, *okay*, when he was done. Like a professor. He wanted so badly to be an expert at something.)

I always appreciated Deepak trying to help me understand. But it's just a job, I would say. I never really understood why Deep thought so much of those programmers, either. In the end, we're all brains for hire. All I know is they seem to have gotten it down to a science. How much a human being can take in a given twelve-hour shift. Grief, embarrassment, humiliation, all different, of course, so they calibrate our schedules, mix it up, the timing and the order, and the end result is you leave work every day right about at your exact breaking point.

A lot of people smoke to take the edge off. I quit twelve years ago, so sometimes when I get home, I'm still shaking for a little bit. I sit on my couch and drink a beer and let it subside. Then I heat up some bread and lentils and read a newspaper or, if it's too hot to stay inside, walk down to the street and eat my dinner there.

When I get to work the next morning, there's a woman sitting in the cubicle across from mine. She's young, at least a couple of years younger than me, looks right out of school. She has the new employee set-up kit laid out in front of her and is reading the trainee handbook. I think about saying hi, but who am I kidding, I am still me, so instead I just say nothing.

My first ticket of the day is a death bed. Death beds are not so common. They are hard to schedule—we require at least twenty-four hours advance booking, and usually clients don't know far enough in advance when the ailing beloved one is going to go—so we don't see these too often. But this isn't regular death bed. It's pull-the-plug.

They are pulling the plug on grandpa this morning.

I open the ticket.

I am holding grandpa's hand.

I cry.

He squeezes my hand, one last burst of strength. It hurts. Then his hand goes limp and his arm falls away.

I cry, and also, I really cry. Meaning, not just as my client, but I start crying, too. Sometimes it happens. I don't know why, exactly. Maybe because he was somebody's grandpa. And he looked like a nice one, a nice man. Maybe something about the way his arm fell against the guard rail on the hospital bed. Maybe because I could sort of tell, when grandpa was looking at his grandson for the last time, looking into his eyes, looking around in there trying to find him, he didn't find him, he found me instead, and he knew what had happened, and he didn't even look mad. Just hurt.

I am at a funeral.

I am in a dentist's chair.

I am in a queen-sized motel bed, feeling guilty.

I am quitting my job. This is a popular one. Clients like to avoid the awkwardness of quitting their jobs, so they set an appointment and walk into their bosses' offices and tell them where they can stick this effing job, and right before their boss starts to reply, the switch kicks in and I get yelled at.

My teeth throb.

My kidneys seethe.

My lungs burn.

My heart aches.

On a bridge.

My heart aches on a bridge.

My heart aches on a cruise ship.

My heart aches on an airplane, taking off at night.

Some people think it's not so great that we can do this. Personally, I don't really see the problem. Press one to clear your conscience. Press two for fear of death. Consciousness is like anything else. I'm sure when someone figures out how to sell time itself, they'll have infomercials for that, too.

I am at a funeral.

I am losing someone to cancer.

I am coping with something vague.

I am at a funeral.

I am at a funeral.

I am at a funeral.

Fourteen tickets today in twelve hours. Four half-hours and ten full.

On my way out, I can hear someone wailing and gnashing his teeth in his cubicle. He is near the edge. Deepak was always like that, too. I always told him, hey man, you have to let go a little. Just a little. Don't let it get to you so much.

I peek my head to see if I can steal a glance at the new woman, but she is in the middle of a ticket. She appears to be suffering. She catches me looking at her. I look at my feet and keep shuffling past.

It used to be that the job wasn't all pain and suffering. Rich American man outsources the nasty bits of his life. He is required to book by the hour or the day or some other time unit, but in an hour or two or twenty-four hours of unpleasantness, there are always going to be some parts of it that are not so bad. Maybe just boring. Maybe even not so bad. Maybe even more okay than not. Like if a guy books his colonoscopy and he hires us for two hours, but for the first eight minutes, he's just sitting there in the waiting room, reading a magazine, enjoying the air conditioning, admiring someone's legs. Or something. Anyway, it used to be that we would get the whole thing, so part of my job here could be boring or neutral or even sometimes kind of interesting.

But then the technology improved again and the packeting software was refined to filter out those intervals and collect them. Those bits, the extras, the slices of life that were left over were lopped off by the program, and smushed all together, into a kind of reconstituted life slab. Like American baloney lunchmeat. A life-loaf. They take the slabs and process them and sell them as prepackaged lives.

I've had my eye on one for a while, at a secondhand shop that's on my way home from work. Not ideal, but it's something to work for.

So now, what's left over, what we get to feel at work, it's all pretty much just pure undiluted badness. The only thing left that can be a surprise is when, even in the middle of badness, there is something not so awful mixed in there. Like the relief in the middle of a funeral, or sometimes when you get someone who is really religious, not just religious, but a true believer, then mixed in with the sadness and loss at a funeral, you get faith, and you get to try different flavors, depending on the believer. You get the big foot on your chest, or you get the back of your head on fire. (A cold fire, it tickles.) You get to know what it is like to know that your dead lover, your dead mother, father, brother, sister, that they are all standing in front of you, tall as the universe, and they have huge, infinite feet, and their heads are all ablaze with this brilliant, frozen fire. You get the feeling of being inside of a room and at the same time, the room being inside of you, and the room is the world, and so are you.

The next day is more of the same. Eleven tickets, including a two-hour adultery confession. To my husband of twenty-six years.

After lunch, I pass her in the hall. The new woman. Her name badge says Kirthi. She doesn't look at me this time.

Walking home I swing a block out of the way to check in on the secondhand shop.

Someone bought my life.

It was there in the window yesterday, and now it's gone.

It wasn't my life, technically. Not yet. It was the life I wanted, the life I've been saving for. Not a DreamLife®, not top of the line, but a starter model, a good one. Standard Possibility. Normal Volatility. A dark-haired, soulful wife. 0.35 kids, no actuals—certainties are too expensive—but some potential kids, a solid thirty-five percent chance of having one or more. Normal life expectancy, average health, median aggregate amount of happiness. I test-drove it once, and it felt good, it felt right. It fit just fine.

I don't know. I'm trying not to feel sorry for myself. I just thought there might be more to it all than this.

Still, I've got it better than some people. I mean, I'm renting my life out one day at a time, but I haven't sold it yet.

My father sold his life on a cold, clear afternoon in November. He was thirty. It was the day before my fourth birthday.

We went to the brokerage. It felt like a bank, but friendlier. My father had been carrying me on his back, but he put me down when we got inside. There was dark wood everywhere, and also bright flowers and classical music. We were shown to a desk, and a woman in an immaculate pantsuit asked if we would like anything to drink. My father didn't say anything, just looked off at the far wall. I remember my mother asked for a cup of tea for my father.

I don't want to sell my life. I'm not ready to do that yet.

So I sell it bit by bit. Scrape by.

Sell it by the hour.

Pain, grief, terror, worse.

Or just mild discomfort.

Social anxiety.

Boredom.

I ask around about Kirthi. People are talking. The guys are talking. Especially the married guys. They do the most talking.

I pass her in the hall again, and again she doesn't look at me. No surprise there. Women never look at me. I am not handsome or tall. But I am nice.

I think it is actually that which causes the not-looking at me. The niceness, I mean, not the lack of handsomeness or tallness. They can see the niceness and it is the kind of niceness that, in a man, you instinctively ignore. What good is a nice man? No good to women. No good to other men.

She doesn't look at me, but I feel, or maybe I wish or I imagine, that something in the way she does not look at me is not quite the same. She is not-looking at me in a way that feels like she is consciously not-looking at me. And from the way she is not-looking at me, I can tell she knows I am trying to not-look at her. We are both not-looking at each other. For some reason, for the first time in a long while, I have hope.

I don't know why, but I do.

I am at a funeral.

I'm flipped to green.

You can be flipped to green, or flipped to red.

You can be there, or can just feel the feeling.

This is the one improvement they have made that actually benefits us workers. There's a toggle switch on the headset. Flip it to green and you get a rendering of the client's visual field. You see what he sees. Flip it to red and you still feel all of the feelings, but you see what you see.

You can do whatever you want, so long as you don't leave your cubicle. You can just stare at the cube-divider wall, or play computer solitaire, or even chat with neighbors, although that is strongly discouraged.

I was hesitant at first, but more and more these days I am usually flipped to red. Except for funerals. Funerals, I like to be there, just out of some kind of respect thing.

This morning's first ticket is your standard affair. Sixtyish rich guy, heart attack in the home office, millions in the bank, five kids from three marriages, all hate him.

The client is one of those kids, trust fund baby, paid extra for amnesia after the event. No feeling, no pre-feeling, no hangover, no residue, no chance of actually having any part of it, long enough to ensure that he will be halfway in the bag before any of the day's events start nibbling at the corners of his awareness.

I see the fresh, open plot. A little rain falls on the funeral procession as they get out of the cars, but there's a break in the clouds so that it's raining and the sun is shining at the same time.

As usual, everyone is well-dressed. A lot of the rich look mildly betrayed in the face of death, as if they are a little bit surprised that good style and enough money weren't quite enough to protect them from the unpleasantness of it all. I'm standing next to what I am guessing is widow number two, late thirties, probably, with beautiful sand-colored hair. We make eye contact and she is staring at me and I am trying not to stare at her and then we both realize the same thing at the same time. Raj, I say, under my breath. She smiles. Rajiv is on night shift now, but back in the day, we had beers once in a while.

The pastor talks about a full life lived, and the limits of earthly rewards, and everyone nods affirmatively, and then there is music as the body goes into the ground, I've heard it at a lot of funerals. Mozart, I think, but I am not sure.

Death of an aunt is seven hundred. Death of an uncle is six.

Bad day in the markets is a thousand. Kid's recital is a one twenty-five an hour. Church is one-fifty.

The only category that we will not quote a price on is death of a child. Death of a child is separately negotiated. Hardly anyone can afford it. And not all operators can handle it. We have to be specially trained to be eligible for those tickets. People go on sick leave, disability. Most people just physically cannot do it. There hasn't been one booked the whole time I've been here, so most of us aren't even sure what is true and what isn't. The rumor is that if you do one, you are allowed to take the rest of the month off.

Deep was always tempted. It's not worth it, I would tell him. Okay, so, maybe not for you, Deep said. Okay, so, mind your own business, he would say.

The first time I talk to Kirthi is by the water fountain. I tell her we are neighbors, cubicle-wise. She says she knows. I feel a bit stupid.

The second time we talk, we are also by the water fountain, and I try to make a joke, one of those we have to stop meeting like this things. I probably saw it on TV and it just came out. Stupid. She doesn't laugh, but she doesn't frown, either.

The third time we talk, I kiss her. By the microwave in the snack room. I don't know what got into me. I am not an aggressive person. I am not physically strong. I weigh one hundred and fifty-five pounds. She doesn't laugh. She actually makes a face like disgust. But she doesn't push me away, either. Not right away. She accepts the kiss, doesn't kiss back, but after a couple of seconds, breaks it off and leans back and turns her head and says, under her breath, you shouldn't have done that. And she doesn't say it in a nice way. Or like a threat. Just real even, like she is stating a fact.

Still, I am happy. I've got three more tickets in the bucket before lunch, and then probably eight or nine before I go home, but the whole rest of the day, I am having an out of body experience. Even when I am in someone else's body, I am still out of my body. I am double out of my body.

I weep.

I wail.

I gnash my teeth.

Underneath it all, I am smiling. I am giggling.

I am at a funeral. My client's heart aches, and inside of it is my heart, not aching, the opposite of aching—doing that, whatever it is.

Kirthi and I start dating. That's what I call it. She calls it letting me walk her to the bus stop. She lets me buy her lunch. She tells me I should stop. She still never smiles at me.

I'm a heartbreak specialist, she says.

When I see her in the hallway, I walk up behind her and slip my arm around her waist.

She has not let me in yet. She won't let me in.

Why won't you let me in, I ask her?

You don't want in, she says. You want around. You want near. You don't want in.

There are two hundred forty seven ways to have your heartbroken, she says, *and I have felt them all.*

I am in a hospice.

I have been here before. A regular client.

I am holding a pen.

I have just written something on a notepad in front of me.

My husband is gone.

He died years ago.

Today is the tenth anniversary of his death.

I have Alzheimer's, I think.

A memory of my husband surfaces, like a white-hot August afternoon, resurfacing in the cool water of November.

I tear off the sheet on the notepad.

I read it to myself.

It is a suicide note.

I raise a glass to my mouth, swallow a pill. Catch a glance of my note to the world.

The failsafe kicks on, just in time. The system overrides. I close the ticket.

It's her father.

That's what Sunil tells me, one day over a beer.

Kirthi hasn't been to work for the past two days.

Sunil is in Tech Support. He has seen all of the glitches. He knows what can go wrong in the mechanics of feeling transfers. He has seen some ugliness. He is fond of saying that there is no upper bound on weirdness.

Her father is still mortgaged, Sunil explains. Locked in. A p-zombie, he says. Sold his life.

"This is going to end badly, man," he says. "You have to trust me on this. Kirthi is damaged. And she knows it."

Sunil means well, but what he doesn't know is that I am fine with damaged. I want damage. I've looked down the road I'm on and I see what's coming. A lot of nothing. No great loves lost. And yet, I feel like I lost something. Better to have loved and lost than never to have loved at all? How about this: I lost without the love. I've lost things I've never even had. A whole life. Just like my father, I get to have my cake and eat it, too. Except that it's a great big crap cake.

Still, as the weeks go on, I am starting to think Sunil is right.

"Kirthi won't let me in," I tell him. "She tells me to get away from her, to run."

"She is doing you a favor, man. Take her advice."

I ask her about her father.

She doesn't talk to me for a week.

And then, on Friday night, after we walk for an hour in silence, before going into her apartment, she turns to me and says, how awful it is to look at him in that state.

We draw closer for a moment.

Why won't you just love me, I ask her.

She says it's not possible to make someone feel something.

Even yourself, she says.

Even if you want to feel it.

I tell her about the life I had my eye on.

It's gone, she says.

I'll find another one just like it, I tell her. Standard happiness package. Decent possibility. The chance of a kid. It wouldn't be enough for us, not quite, but we could share it, take turns living the life. One works while the other one lives, maybe I work the weekdays and she gives me a break on weekends.

She looks at me. For a few long seconds, she seems to be thinking about it, living the whole life out in her head.

She doesn't say anything. She touches the side of my head.

It's a start.

When Deep was happy, before it got bad and then worse and then even worse, he was always talking about how he knew a guy who knew a guy who knew a guy. Stuff like that. He talked like that, he really did. He loved telling stories. About a week before he cracked up, he told me a story while we were in the coffee room about a guy at Managed Life Solutions, a physical suffering shop across town, who somehow made arrangements with a prominent banker who wanted to kill his wife. The banker was going to do it, he'd made up his mind, but he didn't want the guilt. Plus, he thought it might help with his alibi if he didn't have any memory.

Bullshit, I said. That would never work.

No, really, he says. He tells me all about it, how they met, how they arranged it all while talking in public, at work in fact, but they talked in code, etc.

Could never happen, I say. There are twenty reasons why that wouldn't work.

Why not, he said.

It's just too much, I said.

Too much what? There is no upper bound on cruelty, he said.

The next Monday, I came to work, and they were pulling Deep out the door, two paramedics, each one with an arm under Deep's arms, and two security guards trailing behind. I wanted to say something, anything, to make them stop. I knew I would never see him again. But I froze. As they dragged him past me, I tried to make eye contact, but I looked in there, and no one was left. He had gone somewhere else. He was saying, okay, so. Okay, so.

And then the next day, there it was, in the newspaper. The whole story about the banker. Exactly how Deepak told it to me. There were rumors that he was the one the banker hired; he was living with murderous guilt. Other people gossiped that he had done death of a child.

I don't think it was either. I don't think it was any one thing that did it. Deep just knew. He knew what was out there. There is no upper bound on sadness. There is no lower bound on decency. Deep saw it, he understood it, what was out there, and he let it seep in, and once it was in, it got all the way in, and it will never come out.

I open tickets. I do the work. I save up money.

Weeks go by. Kirthi opens up. (Just a little.)

She still refuses to look me in the eyes when we are kissing.

That's weird, she says. No one does that.

How am I supposed to know that? I have not kissed many people, but I don't want her to know it. I have seen in American movies that people close their eyes, but I have also seen that sometimes one person or the other will sneak open an eye and take a peek at the other one. I think it makes sense. Otherwise, how would you know what the other person is feeling? That seems to me to be the only way to be sure, the only way to understand, through the look on their face, what they are feeling, to be able to feel what they feel for you. So we kiss, she with her eyes closed, me looking at her, trying to imagine what she is feeling. I hope she is feeling something.

I am at a funeral.

I am having a bypass.

I am in drug rehabilitation.

I am in withdrawal.

She takes me to see her father.

He has the look. I remember this look. This is how my father looked.

He is living someone else's life. He is a projection screen, a vessel, a unit of capacity for pain, like an external hard drive, a peripheral device for someone's convenience, a place to store frustration and guilt and unhappiness.

We stand there in silence.

We go back to work.

I am at a funeral.

I am at a root canal.

The thing it is uncomfortable to talk about is: we could do it. We could get him out.

Finally, she can't take it.

He has only four years left on his mortgage, Kirthi tells me.

The thing is, the way the market works, sellers like us never get full value on our time. It's like a pawnshop. You hock your pocketwatch to put dinner on the table, you might get fifty bucks. Go to get it after payday and you'll have to pay four times that to get it back.

Same principle here. I love Kirthi, I do. But I don't know if I could give sixteen years of my life to get her father out. I could do it if I knew she loved me, but I don't know it yet. I want to be a better man than this, I want to be more selfless. My life isn't so great as it is, but I just don't know if I could do it.

I am in surgery.

I am bleeding to death.

It doesn't hurt at all.

Things progress. We move in together. We avoid planning for the future. We hint at it. We talk around it.

I am being shot at.

I am being slapped in the face.

I go home.

I rest.

I come back and do it again.

When I turned thirteen, my mother told me the story. She sat me down in the kitchen and explained.

"The day your father sold his life," she said, "I wore my best dress, and he wore a suit. He combed his hair. He looked handsome and calm. You wore your only pair of long pants. We walked to the bank. You rode on his back."

"I remember that," I said.

"A man with excellent hair came out from some office in the back and sat down behind the desk."

I remember that, too, I told her.

You get—we got—forty thousand a year, she said.

My dad sold his life for a fixed annuity, indexed to inflation at three percent annually, and a seventy percent pension if he made it full term: forty years, age seventy, and he could stop, he could come back to us, to his life.

There were posters everywhere, my mother said, describing that day, the reunion day. The day when you've made it, you've done it, you're done.

There was a video screen showing a short film describing the benefits of mortgage, the glorious day of reunion. We would all drink lemonade in the hot summer air.

Just forty years, it said.

In the meantime, your family will be taken care of. You will have peace of mind.

"Time is money," the video said. "And money is time. Create value out of the most valuable asset you own."

"Don't miss out on a chance of a lifetime."

When we went home, I remember, my father went to lie down. He slept for twelve hours, twice as long as normal, and in the morning, while I was still asleep, he went and sold his life.

Things stop progressing with Kirthi.

Things go backward.

And then, one day, whatever it is we had, it's gone. It won't come back. We both know it.

Whatever it is she let me have, she has taken it away. Whatever it is when two people agree to briefly occupy the same space, agree to allow their lives to overlap in some small area, some temporary region of the world, a region they create through love or convenience, or for us, something even more meager, whatever that was, it has collapsed, it has closed. She has closed herself to me.

A week after Kirthi moves out, her father passes away.

My shift manager will not let me off to go to the funeral.

Kirthi doesn't even ask if I would like to go anyway.

I should go.

I will be fired if I go.

But I don't have her anymore. If I leave, I won't have a job, either. I'll never get her back if I don't have a job.

I'm never getting her back anyway.

I don't even know if I want her back.

But maybe this is why I don't have her, could never, would never have had her. Maybe the problem isn't that I don't have a life. Maybe the problem is that I don't *want* a life.

I go to work.

I open tickets.

I close tickets.

When I get home my apartment seems empty. It's always empty, but today, more empty. The emptiness is now empty.

I call her. I don't know what to say. I breathe into the phone.

I call her again. I leave a message. I know a guy in the billing department, I say. We could get some extra capacity, no one would know, find an open line. I could feel it for you. Your grief. I could bury your father for you.

I would say that I am tired of this substitute life, except that this is the only life I will ever have. It is a substitute for itself. A substitute for nothing. A substitute for something that never existed in the first place.

Three days later, when I get to work, there is a note on my desk, giving the time of the funeral service. Just the time and, underneath it, she scrawled, okay.

Okay.

I arrange for the hour. At the time, I open the ticket.

I am expecting a funeral.

I am not at a funeral.

I can't tell exactly where I am, but I am far away. In a place I don't recognize. She has moved to a place where I will never find her. Probably where no one will ever find her. A new city. A new life.

She paid for this time herself. She wanted to let me in. For once. Just once. She must have used up everything she had saved. The money was supposed to be for her father but now, no need.

She is walking along a road. The sun is hot, the air is dusty, but the day is alive; she feels alive, I feel alive for her.

She is looking at a picture we took—the only picture we took together, in a photo booth in the drugstore. Our faces are smashed together and in the picture she is not smiling, as usual, and I am smiling, a genuine smile, or so I have always thought about myself, but now, looking at myself through her eyes, I see that she sees that my own smile starts to decompose, like when you say a word over and over again, so many times, over and over, and you begin to feel silly, but you keep saying it, and then after a short while, something happens and the word stops being a word and it resolves into its constituent sounds, and then all of a sudden what used to be a word is not a word at all, it is now the strangest thing you have ever heard.

I am inside of her head.

I am a nice person, she is thinking. I deserve more, she wants to believe. She wants to believe it, but I can feel that she doesn't. If only she could see herself through my eyes. If only she could see herself through my eyes looking through her eyes. I deserve to be loved, she thinks, but she doesn't believe it. If only I could believe it for her. I want to believe in her, believe inside of her. Believe hard enough inside of her that it somehow seeps through.

She turns up the road and the hill gets steeper. The air gets hotter. I feel her sadness with every step, and then, right near the top of the hill, just the faintest hint of it: a smile. She is remembering us. The few happy moments we had.

I am standing on a hill. I am not at a funeral. I am thinking of someone I once loved. I don't know if I am her thinking of me, or if I am me thinking of her, or if maybe, right at this moment, there is no difference.

THE LADY WHO PLUCKED RED FLOWERS BENEATH THE QUEEN'S WINDOW

RACHEL SWIRSKY

My story should have ended on the day I died. Instead, it began there.

Sun pounded on my back as I rode through the Mountains where the Sun Rests. My horse's hooves beat in syncopation with those of the donkey that trotted in our shadow. The queen's midget Kyan turned his head toward me, sweat dripping down the red-and-blue protections painted across his malformed brow.

"Shouldn't . . . we . . . stop?" he panted.

Sunlight shone red across the craggy limestone cliffs. A bold eastern wind carried the scent of mountain blossoms. I pointed to a place where two large stones leaned across a narrow outcropping.

"There," I said, prodding my horse to go faster before Kyan could answer. He grunted and cursed at his donkey for falling behind.

I hated Kyan, and he hated me. But Queen Rayneh had ordered us to ride reconnaissance together, and we obeyed, out of love for her and for the Land of Flowered Hills.

We dismounted at the place I had indicated. There, between the mountain peaks, we could watch the enemy's forces in the valley below without being observed. The raiders spread out across the meadow below like ants on a rich meal. Their women's camp lay behind the main troops, a small dark blur. Even the smoke rising from their women's fires seemed timid. I scowled.

"Go out between the rocks," I directed Kyan. "Move as close to the edge as you can."

Kyan made a mocking gesture of deference. "As you wish, Great Lady," he sneered, swinging his twisted legs off the donkey. Shamans' bundles of stones and seeds, tied with twine, rattled at his ankles.

I refused to let his pretensions ignite my temper. "Watch the valley," I instructed. "I will take the vision of their camp from your mind and send it to the Queen's scrying pool. Be sure to keep still."

The midget edged toward the rocks, his eyes shifting back and forth as if he expected to encounter raiders up here in the mountains, in the Queen's dominion. I found myself amused and disgusted by how little provocation it took to reveal the midget's true, craven nature. At home in the Queen's castle, he strutted about, pompous and patronizing. He was like many birth-twisted men, arrogant in the limited magic to which his deformities gave him access. Rumors suggested that he imagined himself worthy enough to be in love with the Queen. I wondered what he thought of the men below. Did he daydream about them conquering the Land? Did he think they'd make him powerful, that they'd put weapons in his twisted hands and let him strut among their ranks?

"Is your view clear?" I asked.

"It is."

I closed my eyes and saw, as he saw, the panorama of the valley below. I held his sight in my mind, and turned toward the eastern wind which carries the perfect expression of magic—flight—on its invisible eddies. I envisioned the battlefield unfurling before me like a scroll rolling out across a marble floor. With low, dissonant notes, I showed the image how to transform itself for my purposes. I taught it how to be length and width without depth, and how to be strokes of color and light reflected in water. When it knew these things, I sang the image into the water of the Queen's scrying pool.

Suddenly—too soon—the vision vanished from my inner eye. Something whistled through the air. I turned. Pain struck my chest like thunder.

I cried out. Kyan's bundles of seeds and stones rattled above me. My vision blurred red. Why was the midget near me? He should have been on the outcropping.

"You traitor!" I shouted. "How did the raiders find us?"

I writhed blindly on the ground, struggling to grab Kyan's legs. The midget caught my wrists. Weak with pain, I could not break free.

"Hold still," he said. "You're driving the arrow deeper."

"Let me go, you craven dwarf."

"I'm no traitor. This is woman's magic. Feel the arrow shaft."

Kyan guided my hand upward to touch the arrow buried in my chest. Through the pain, I felt the softness of one of the Queen's roc feathers. It was particularly rare and valuable, the length of my arm.

I let myself fall slack against the rock. "Woman's magic," I echoed, softly. "The Queen is betrayed. The Land is betrayed."

"Someone is betrayed, sure enough," said Kyan, his tone gloating.

"You must return to court and warn the Queen."

Kyan leaned closer to me. His breath blew on my neck, heavy with smoke and spices.

"No, Naeva. You can still help the Queen. She's given me the keystone to a spell—a piece of pure leucite, powerful enough to tug a spirit from its rest. If I blow its power into you, your spirit won't sink into sleep. It will only rest, waiting for her summons."

Blood welled in my mouth. "I won't let you bind me . . . "

His voice came even closer, his lips on my ear. "The Queen needs you, Naeva. Don't you love her?"

Love: the word caught me like a thread on a bramble. Oh, yes. I loved the queen. My will weakened, and I tumbled out of my body. Cold crystal drew me in like a great mouth, inhaling.

I was furious. I wanted to wrap my hands around the first neck I saw and squeeze. But my hands were tiny, half the size of the hands I remembered. My short, fragile fingers shook. Heavy musk seared my nostrils. I felt the heat of scented candles at my feet, heard the snap of flame devouring wick. I rushed forward and was abruptly halted. Red and black knots of string marked boundaries beyond which I could not pass.

"O, Great Lady Naeva," a voice intoned. "We seek your wisdom on behalf of Queen Rayneh and the Land of Flowered hills."

Murmurs rippled through the room. Through my blurred vision, I caught an impression of vaulted ceilings and frescoed walls. I heard people, but I could only make out woman-sized blurs—they could have been beggars, aristocrats, warriors, even males or broods.

I tried to roar. My voice fractured into a strangled sound like trapped wind. An old woman's sound.

"Great Lady Naeva, will you acknowledge me?"

I turned toward the high, mannered voice. A face came into focus, eyes flashing blue beneath a cowl. Dark stripes stretched from lower lip to chin: the tattoos of a death whisperer.

Terror cut into my rage for a single, clear instant. "I'm dead?"

"Let me handle this." Another voice, familiar this time. Calm, authoritative, quiet: the voice of someone who had never needed to shout in order to be heard. I swung my head back and forth trying to glimpse Queen Rayneh.

"Hear me, Lady Who Plucked Red Flowers beneath My Window. It is I, your Queen."

The formality of that voice! She spoke to me with titles instead of names? I blazed with fury.

Her voice dropped a register, tender and cajoling. "Listen to me, Naeva. I asked the death whisperers to chant your spirit up from the dead. You're inhabiting the body of an elder member of their order. Look down. See for yourself."

I looked down and saw embroidered rabbits leaping across the hem of a turquoise robe. Long, bony feet jutted out from beneath the silk. They were swaddled in the coarse wrappings that doctors prescribed for the elderly when it hurt them to stand.

They were not my feet. I had not lived long enough to have feet like that.

"I was shot by an enchanted arrow . . . " I recalled. "The midget said you might need me again . . . "

"And he was right, wasn't he? You've only been dead three years. Already, we need you."

The smugness of that voice. Rayneh's impervious assurance that no matter what happened, be it death or disgrace, her people's hearts would always sing with fealty.

"He enslaved me," I said bitterly. "He preyed upon my love for you."

"Ah, Lady Who Plucked Red Flowers beneath My Window, I always knew you loved me."

Oh yes, I had loved her. When she wanted heirs, it was I who placed my hand on her belly and used my magic to draw out her seedlings; I who nurtured the seedlings' spirits with the fertilizer of her chosen man; I who planted the seedlings in the womb of a fecund brood. Three times, the broods I catalyzed brought forth Rayneh's daughters. I'd not yet chosen to beget my own daughters, but there had always been an understanding between us that Rayneh would be the one to stand with my magic-worker as the seedling was drawn from me, mingled with man, and set into brood.

I was amazed to find that I loved her no longer. I remembered the emotion, but passion had died with my body.

"I want to see you," I said.

Alarmed, the death whisperer turned toward Rayneh's voice. Her nose jutted beak-like past the edge of her cowl. "It's possible for her to see you if you stand where I am," she said. "But if the spell goes wrong, I won't be able to—"

"It's all right, Lakitri. Let her see me."

Rustling, footsteps. Rayneh came into view. My blurred vision showed me frustratingly little except for the moon of her face. Her eyes sparkled black against her smooth, sienna skin. Amber and obsidian gems shone from her forehead, magically embedded in the triangular formation that symbolized the Land of Flowered Hills. I wanted to see her graceful belly, the muscular calves I'd loved to stroke—but below her chin, the world faded to grey.

"What do you want?" I asked. "Are the raiders nipping at your heels again?"

"We pushed the raiders back in the battle that you died to make happen. It was a rout. Thanks to you."

A smile lit on Rayneh's face. It was a smile I remembered. *You have served your Land and your Queen*, it seemed to say. *You may be proud.* I'd slept on Rayneh's leaf-patterned silk and eaten at her morning table too often to be deceived by such shallow manipulations.

Rayneh continued, "A usurper—a woman raised on our own grain and honey—has built an army of automatons to attack us. She's given each one a hummingbird's heart for speed, and a crane's feather for beauty, and a crow's brain for wit. They've marched from the Lake Where Women Wept all the way across the fields to the Valley of Tonha's Memory. They move faster than our most agile warriors. They seduce our farmers out of the fields. We must destroy them."

"A usurper?" I said.

"One who betrays us with our own spells."

The Queen directed me a lingering, narrow-lidded look, challenging me with her unspoken implications.

"The kind of woman who would shoot the Queen's sorceress with a roc feather?" I pressed.

Her glance darted sideways. "Perhaps."

Even with the tantalizing aroma of revenge wafting before me, I considered refusing Rayneh's plea. Why should I forgive her for chaining me to her service? She and her benighted death whisperers might have been able to chant my spirit into wakefulness, but let them try to stir my voice against my will.

But no—even without love drawing me into dark corners, I couldn't renounce Rayneh. I would help her as I always had from the time when we were girls riding together through my grandmother's fields. When she fell from her mount, it was always I who halted my mare, soothed her wounds, and eased her back into the saddle. Even as a child, I knew that she would never do the same for me.

"Give me something to kill," I said.

"What?"

"I want to kill. Give me something. Or should I kill your death whisperers?"

Rayneh turned toward the women. "Bring a sow!" she commanded.

Murmurs echoed through the high-ceilinged chamber, followed by rushing footsteps. Anxious hands entered my range of vision, dragging a fat, black-spotted shape. I looked toward the place where my ears told me the crowd of death whisperers stood, huddled and gossiping. I wasn't sure how vicious I could appear as a dowager with bound feet, but I snarled at them anyway. I was rewarded with the susurration of hems sliding backward over tile.

I approached the sow. My feet collided with the invisible boundaries of the summoning circle. "Move it closer," I ordered.

Hands pushed the sow forward. The creature grunted with surprise and fear. I knelt down and felt its bristly fur and smelled dry mud, but I couldn't see its torpid bulk.

I wrapped my bony hands around the creature's neck and twisted. My spirit's strength overcame the body's weakness. The animal's head snapped free in my hands. Blood engulfed the leaping rabbits on my hem.

I thrust the sow's head at Rayneh. It tumbled out of the summoning circle and thudded across the marble. Rayneh doubled over, retching.

The crowd trembled and exclaimed. Over the din, I dictated the means to defeat the constructs. "Blend mustard seed and honey to slow their deceitful tongues. Add brine to ruin their beauty. Mix in crushed poppies to slow their fast-beating hearts. Release the concoction onto a strong wind and let it blow their destruction. Only a grain need touch them. Less than a grain—only a grain need touch a mosquito that lights on a flower they pass on the march. They will fall."

"Regard that! Remember it!" Rayneh shouted to the whisperers. Silk rustled. Rayneh regarded me levelly. "That's all we have to do?"

"Get Lakitri," I replied. "I wish to ask her a question."

A nervous voice spoke outside my field of vision. "I'm here, Great Lady."

"What will happen to this body after my spirit leaves?"

"Jada will die, Great Lady. Your spirit has chased hers away."

I felt the crookedness of Jada's hunched back and the pinch of the strips binding her feet. Such a back, such feet, I would never have. At least someone would die for disturbing my death.

Next I woke, rage simmered where before it had boiled. I stifled a snarl, and relaxed my clenched fists. My vision was clearer: I discerned the outlines of a tent filled with dark shapes that resembled pillows and furs. I discovered my boundaries close by, marked by wooden stakes painted with bands of cinnamon and white.

"Respected Aunt Naeva?"

My vision wavered. A shape: muscular biceps, hard thighs, robes of heir's green. It took me a moment to identify Queen Rayneh's eldest daughter, who I had inspired in her brood. At the time of my death, she'd been a flat-chested flitling, still learning how to ride.

"Tryce?" I asked. A bad thought: "Why are you here? Has the usurper taken the palace? Is the Queen dead?"

Tryce laughed. "You misunderstand, Respected Aunt. I am the usurper."

"You?" I scoffed. "What does a girl want with a woman's throne?"

"I want what is mine." Tryce drew herself up. She had her mother's mouth, stern and imperious. "If you don't believe me, look at the body you're wearing."

I looked down. My hands were the right size, but they were painted in Rayneh's blue and decked with rings of gold and silver. Strips of tanned human flesh adorned my breasts. I raised my fingertips to my collarbone and felt the raised edges of the brand I knew would be there. Scars formed the triangles that represented the Land of Flowered Hills.

"One of your mother's private guard," I murmured. "Which?"

"Okilanu."

I grinned. "I never liked the bitch."

"You know I'm telling the truth. A private guard is too valuable for anyone but a usurper to sacrifice. I'm holding this conference with honor, Respected Aunt. I'm meeting you alone, with only one automaton to guard me. My informants tell me that my mother surrounded herself with sorceresses so that she could coerce you. I hold you in more esteem."

"What do you want?"

"Help winning the throne that should be mine."

"Why should I betray my lover and my Land for a child with pretensions?"

"Because you have no reason to be loyal to my mother. Because I want what's best for this Land, and I know how to achieve it. Because those were my automatons you dismantled, and they were good, beautiful souls despite being creatures of spit and mud. Gudrin is the last of them."

Tryce held out her hand. The hand that accepted drew into my vision: slender with shapely fingers crafted of mud and tangled with sticks and pieces of nest. It was beautiful enough to send feathers of astonishment through my chest.

"Great Lady, you must listen to The Creator of Me and Mine," intoned the creature.

Its voice was a songbird trill. I grimaced in disgust. "You made male automatons?"

"Just one," said Tryce. "It's why he survived your spell."

"Yes," I said, pondering. "It never occurred to me that one would make male creatures."

"Will you listen, Respected Aunt?" asked Tryce.

"You must listen, Great Lady," echoed the automaton. His voice was as melodious as poetry to a depressed heart. The power of crane's feathers and crow's brains is great.

"Very well," I said.

Tryce raised her palms to show she was telling truth. I saw the shadow of her mother's face lurking in her wide-set eyes and broad, round forehead.

"Last autumn, when the wind blew red with fallen leaves, my mother expelled me from the castle. She threw my possessions into the river and had my servants beaten and turned out. She told me that I would have to learn to live like the birds migrating from place to place because she had decreed that no one was to give me a home. She said I was no longer her heir, and she would dress Darnisha or Peni in heir's green. Oh, Respected Aunt! How could either of them take a throne?"

I ignored Tryce's emotional outpouring. It was true that Tryce had always been more responsible than her sisters, but she had been born with an heir's heaviness upon her. I had lived long enough to see fluttering sparrows like Darnisha and Peni become eagles, over time.

"You omit something important," I said. "Why did your mother throw you out, Imprudent Child?"

"Because of this."

The automaton's hand held Tryce steady as she mounted a pile of pillows that raised her torso to my eye level. Her belly loomed large, ripe as a frog's inflated throat.

"You've gotten fat, Tryce."

"No," she said.

I realized: she had not.

"You're pregnant? Hosting a child like some brood? What's wrong with you, girl? I never knew you were a pervert. Worse than a pervert! Even the lowest worm-eater knows to chew mushrooms when she pushes with men."

"I am no pervert! I am a lover of woman. I am natural as breeze! But I say we must not halve our population by splitting our females into women and broods. The raiders nip at our heels. Yes, it's true, they are barbaric and weak—now. But they grow stronger. Their population increases so quickly that already they can match our numbers. When there are three times as many of them as us, or five times, or eight times, they'll flood us like a wave crashing on a naked beach. It's time for women to make children in ourselves as broods do. We need more daughters."

I scoffed. "The raiders keep their women like cows for the same reason we keep cows like cows, to encourage the production of calves. What do you think will happen if our men see great women swelling with young and feeding them from their bodies? They will see us as weak, and they will rebel, and the broods will support them for trinkets and candy."

"Broods will not threaten us," said Tryce. "They do as they are trained. We train them to obey."

Tryce stepped down from the pillows and dismissed the automaton into the shadows. I felt a murmur of sadness as the creature left my sight.

"It is not your place to make policy, Imprudent Child," I said. "You should have kept your belly flat.

"There is no time! Do the raiders wait? Will they chew rinds by the fire while I wait for my mother to die?"

"This is better? To split our land into factions and war against ourselves?"

"I have vowed to save the Land of Flowered Hills," said Tryce, "with my mother or despite her."

Tryce came yet closer to me so that I could see the triple scars where the gems that had once sealed her heirship had been carved out of her cheeks. They left angry, red triangles. Tryce's breath was hot; her eyes like oil, shining.

"Even without my automatons, I have enough resources to overwhelm the palace," Tryce continued, "except for one thing."

I waited.

"I need you to tell me how to unlock the protections you laid on the palace grounds and my mother's chambers."

"We return to the beginning. Why should I help you?"

Tryce closed her eyes and inhaled deeply. There was shyness in her posture now. She would not direct her gaze at mine.

She said, "I was young when you died, still young enough to think that our strength was unassailable. The battles after your death shattered my illusions. We barely won, and we lost many lives. I realized that we needed more power, and I thought that I could give us that power by becoming a sorceress to replace you." She paused. "During my studies, I researched your acts of magic, great and small. Inevitably, I came to the spell you cast before you died, when you sent the raiders' positions into the summoning pool."

It was then that I knew what she would say next. I wish I could say that my heartfelt as immobile as a mountain, that I had always known to suspect the love of a Queen. But my heart drummed, and my mouth went dry, and I felt as if I were falling.

"Some of mother's advisers convinced her that you were plotting against her. They had little evidence to support their accusations, but once the idea rooted into mother's mind, she became obsessed. She violated the sanctity of woman's magic by teaching Kyan how to summon a roc feather enchanted to pierce your heart. She ordered him to wait until you had sent her the vision of the battleground, and then to kill you and punish your treachery by binding your soul so that you would always wander and wake."

I wanted to deny it, but what point would there be? Now that Tryce forced me to examine my death with a watcher's eye, I saw the coincidences that proved her truth. How else could I have been shot by an arrow not just shaped by woman's magic, but made from one of the Queen's roc feathers? Why else would a worm like Kyan have happened to have in his possession a piece of leucite more powerful than any I'd seen?

I clenched Okilanu's fists. "I never plotted against Rayneh."

"Of course not. She realized it herself, in time, and executed the women who had whispered against you. But she had your magic, and your restless spirit bound to her, and she believed that was all she needed."

For long moments, my grief battled my anger. When it was done, my resolve was hardened like a spear tempered by fire.

I lifted my palms in the gesture of truth telling. "To remove the protections on the palace grounds, you must lay yourself flat against the soil with your cheek against the dirt, so that it knows you. To it, you must say, 'The Lady Who Plucked Red Flowers beneath the Queen's Window loves the Queen from instant to eternity, from desire to regret.' And then you must kiss the soil as if it is the hem of your lover's robe. Wait until you feel the earth move beneath you and then the protections will be gone."

Tryce inclined her head. "I will do this."

I continued, "When you are done, you must flay off a strip of your skin and grind it into a fine powder. Bury it in an envelope of wind-silk beneath the Queen's window. Bury it quickly. If a single grain escapes, the protections on her chamber will hold."

"I will do this, too," said Tryce. She began to speak more, but I raised one of my ringed, blue fingers to silence her.

"There's another set of protections you don't know about. One cast on your mother. It can only be broken by the fresh life-blood of something you love. Throw the blood onto the Queen while saying, 'The Lady Who Plucked Red Flowers beneath Your Window has betrayed you.' "

"Life-blood? You mean, I need to kill—"

"Perhaps the automaton."

Tryce's expression clouded with distress. "Gudrin is the last one! Maybe the baby. I could conceive again—"

"If you can suggest the baby, you don't love it enough. It must be Gudrin."

Tryce closed her mouth. "Then it will be Gudrin," she agreed, but her eyes would not meet mine.

I folded my arms across Okilanu's flat bosom. "I've given you what you wanted. Now grant me a favor, Imprudent Child Who Would Be Queen. When you kill Rayneh, I want to be there."

Tryce lifted her head like the Queen she wanted to be. "I will summon you when it's time, Respected Aunt." She turned toward Gudrin in the shadows. "Disassemble the binding shapes," she ordered.

For the first time, I beheld Gudrin in his entirety. The creature was tree-tall and stick-slender, and yet he moved with astonishing grace. "Thank you on behalf of the Creator of Me and My Kind," he trilled in his beautiful voice, and I considered how unfortunate it was that the next time I saw him, he would be dead.

I smelled the iron-and-wet tang of blood. My view of the world skewed low, as if I'd been cut off at the knees. Women's bodies slumped across lush carpets. Red ran deep into the silk, bloodying woven leaves and flowers. I'd been in this chamber far too often to mistake it, even dead. It was Rayneh's.

It came to me then: my perspective was not like that of a woman forced to kneel. It was like a child's. Or a dwarf's.

I reached down and felt hairy knees and fringed ankle bracelets. "Ah, Kyan . . . "

"I thought you might like that." Tryce's voice. These were probably her legs before me, wrapped in loose green silk trousers that were tied above the calf with chains of copper beads. "A touch of irony for your pleasure. He bound your soul to restlessness. Now you'll chase his away."

I reached into his back-slung sheath and drew out the most functional of his ceremonial blades. It would feel good to flay his treacherous flesh.

"I wouldn't do that," said Tryce. "You'll be the one who feels the pain."

I sheathed the blade. "You took the castle?"

"Effortlessly." She paused. "I lie. Not effortlessly." She unknotted her right trouser leg and rolled up the silk. Blood stained the bandages on a carefully wrapped wound. "Your protections were strong."

"Yes. They were."

She re-tied her trouser leg and continued. "The Lady with Lichen Hair tried to block our way into the chamber." She kicked one of the corpses by my feet. "We killed her."

"Did you."

"Don't you care? She was your friend."

"Did she care when I died?"

Tryce shifted her weight, a kind of lower-body shrug. "I brought you another present." She dropped a severed head onto the floor. It rolled toward me, tongue lolling in its bloody face. It took me a moment to identify the high cheekbones and narrow eyes.

"The death whisperer? Why did you kill Lakitri?"

"You liked the blood of Jada and Okilanu, didn't you?"

"The only blood I care about now is your mother's. Where is she?"

"Bring my mother!" ordered Tryce.

One of Tryce's servants—her hands marked with the green dye of loyalty to the heir—dragged Rayneh into the chamber. The Queen's torn, bloody robe concealed the worst of her wounds, but couldn't hide the black and purple bruises blossoming on her arms and legs. Her eyes found mine, and despite her condition, a trace of her regal smile glossed her lips.

Her voice sounded thin. "That's you? Lady Who Plucked Red Flowers beneath My Window?"

"It's me."

She raised one bloody, shaking hand to the locket around her throat and pried it open. Dried petals scattered onto the carpets, the remnants of the red flowers I'd once gathered for her protection. While the spell lasted, they'd remained whole and fresh. Now they were dry and crumbling like what had passed for love between us.

"If you ever find rest, the world-lizard will crack your soul in its jaws for murdering your Queen," she said.

"I didn't kill you."

"You instigated my death."

"I was only repaying your favor."

The hint of her smile again. She smelled of wood smoke, rich and dark. I wanted to see her more clearly, but my poor vision blurred the red of her wounds into the sienna of her skin until the whole of her looked like raw, churned earth.

"I suppose our souls will freeze together." She paused. "That might be pleasant."

Somewhere in front of us, lost in the shadows, I heard Tryce and her women ransacking the Queen's chamber. Footsteps, sharp voices, cracking wood.

"I used to enjoy cold mornings," Rayneh said. "When we were girls. I liked lying in bed with you and opening the curtains to watch the snow fall."

"And sending servants out into the cold to fetch and carry."

"And then! When my brood let slip it was warmer to lie together naked under the sheets? Do you remember that?" She laughed aloud, and then paused. When she spoke again, her voice was quieter. "It's strange to remember lying together in the cold, and then to look up, and see you in that body. Oh, my beautiful Naeva, twisted into a worm. I deserve what you've done to me. How could I have sent a worm to kill my life's best love?"

She turned her face away, as if she could speak no more. Such a show of intimate, unroyal emotion. I could remember times when she'd been able to manipulate me by trusting me with a wince of pain or a supposedly accidental tear. As I grew more cynical, I realized that her royal pretense wasn't vanishing when she gave me a melancholy, regretful glance. Such things were calculated vulnerabilities, intended to bind me closer to her by suggesting intimacy and trust. She used them with many ladies at court, the ones who loved her.

This was far from the first time she'd tried to bind me to her by displaying weakness, but it was the first time she'd ever done so when I had no love to enthrall me.

Rayneh continued, her voice a whisper. "I regret it, Naeva. When Kyan came back, and I saw your body, cold and lifeless—I understood immediately that I'd been mistaken. I wept for days. I'm weeping still, inside my heart. But listen—" her voice hardened "—we can't let this be about you and me. Our Land is at stake. Do you know what Tryce is going to do? She'll destroy us all. You have to help me stop her—"

"Tryce!" I shouted. "I'm ready to see her bleed."

Footsteps thudded across silk carpets. Tryce drew a bone-handled knife and knelt over her mother like a farmer preparing to slaughter a pig. "Gudrin!" she called. "Throw open the doors. Let everyone see us."

Narrow, muddy legs strode past us. The twigs woven through the automaton's skin had lain fallow when I saw him in the winter. Now they blazed in a glory of emerald leaves and scarlet blossoms.

"You dunce!" I shouted at Tryce. "What have you done? You left him alive."

Tryce's gaze held fast on her mother's throat. "I sacrificed the baby."

Voices and footsteps gathered in the room as Tryce's soldiers escorted Rayneh's courtiers inside.

"You sacrificed the baby," I repeated. "What do you think ruling is? Do you think Queens always get what they want? You can't dictate to magic, Imprudent Child."

"Be silent." Tryce's voice thinned with anger. "I'm grateful for your help, Great Lady, but you must not speak this way to your Queen."

I shook my head. Let the foolish child do what she might. I braced myself for the inevitable backlash of the spell.

Tryce raised her knife in the air. "Let everyone gathered here behold that this is Queen Rayneh, the Queen Who Would Dictate to a Daughter. I am her heir, Tryce of the Bold Stride. Hear me. I do this for the Land of Flowered Hills, for our honor and our strength. Yet I also do it with regret. Mother, I hope you will be free in your death. May your spirit wing across sweet breezes with the great bird of the sun."

The knife slashed downward. Crimson poured across Rayneh's body, across the rugs, across Tryce's feet. For a moment, I thought I'd been wrong about Tryce's baby—perhaps she had loved it enough for the counter-spell to work—but as the blood poured over the dried petals Rayneh had scattered on the floor, a bright light flared through the room. Tryce flailed backward as if struck.

Rayneh's wound vanished. She stared up at me with startled, joyful eyes. "You didn't betray me!"

"Oh, I did," I said. "Your daughter is just inept."

I could see only one solution to the problem Tryce had created—the life's blood of something I loved was here, still saturating the carpets and pooling on the stone.

Magic is a little bit alive. Sometimes it prefers poetic truths to literal ones. I dipped my fingers into the Queen's spilled blood and pronounced, "The Lady Who Plucked Red Flowers beneath Your Window has betrayed you."

I cast the blood across the Queen. The dried petals disintegrated. The Queen cried out as my magical protections disappeared.

Tryce was at her mother's side again in an instant. Rayneh looked at me in the moment before Tryce's knife descended. I thought she might show me, just this once, a fraction of uncalculated vulnerability. But this time there was no vulnerability at all, no pain or betrayal or even weariness, only perfect regal equanimity.

Tryce struck for her mother's heart. She let her mother's body fall to the carpet.

"Behold my victory!" Tryce proclaimed. She turned toward her subjects. Her stance was strong: her feet planted firmly, ready for attack or defense. If her lower half was any indication, she'd be an excellent Queen.

I felt a rush of forgiveness and pleasure and regret and satisfaction all mixed together. I moved toward the boundaries of my imprisonment, my face near Rayneh's where she lay, inhaling her last ragged breaths.

"Be brave," I told her. "Soon we'll both be free."

Rayneh's lips moved slowly, her tongue thick around the words. "What makes you think . . . ?"

"You're going to die," I said, "and when I leave this body, Kyan will die, too. Without caster or intent, there won't be anything to sustain the spell."

Rayneh made a sound that I supposed was laughter. "Oh no, my dear Naeva . . . much more complicated than that . . . "

Panic constricted my throat. "Tryce! You have to find the piece of leucite—"

" . . . even stronger than the rock. Nothing but death can lull your spirit to sleep . . . and you're already dead . . . "

She laughed again.

"Tryce!" I shouted. "Tryce!"

The girl turned. For a moment, my vision became as clear as it had been when I lived. I saw the Imprudent Child Queen standing with her automaton's arms around her waist, the both of them flushed with joy and triumph. Tryce turned to kiss the knot of wood that served as the automaton's mouth and my vision clouded again.

Rayneh died a moment afterward.

A moment after that, Tryce released me.

If my story could not end when I died, it should have ended there, in Rayneh's chamber, when I took my revenge.

It did not end there.

Tryce consulted me often during the early years of her reign. I familiarized myself with the blur of the paintings in her chamber, squinting to pick out placid scenes of songbirds settling on snowy branches, bathing in mountain springs, soaring through sun-struck skies.

"Don't you have counselors for this?" I snapped one day.

Tryce halted her pacing in front of me, blocking my view of a wren painted by The Artist without Pity.

"Do you understand what it's like for me? The court still calls me the Imprudent Child Who Would Be Queen. Because of you!"

Gudrin went to comfort her. She kept the creature close, pampered and petted, like a cat on a leash. She rested her head on his shoulder as he stroked her arms. It all looked too easy, too familiar. I wondered how often Tryce spun herself into these emotional whirlpools.

"It can be difficult for women to accept orders from their juniors," I said.

"I've borne two healthy girls," Tryce said petulantly. "When I talk to the other women about bearing, they still say they can't, that 'women's bodies aren't suited for childbirth.' Well, if women can't have children, then what does that make me?"

I forebore responding.

"They keep me busy with petty disputes over grazing rights and grain allotment. How can I plan for a war when they distract me with pedantry? The raiders are still at our heels, and the daft old biddies won't accept what we must do to beat them back!"

The automaton thrummed with sympathy. Tryce shook him away and resumed pacing.

"At least I have you, Respected Aunt."

"For now. You must be running out of hosts." I raised my hand and inspected young, unfamiliar fingers. Dirt crusted the ragged nails. "Who is this? Anyone I know?"

"The death whisperers refuse to let me use their bodies. What time is this when dying old women won't blow out a few days early for the good of the Land?"

"Who is this?" I repeated.

"I had to summon you into the body of a common thief. You see how bad things are."

"What did you expect? That the wind would send a hundred songbirds to trill praises at your coronation? That sugared oranges would rain from the sky and flowers bloom on winter stalks?"

Tryce glared at me angrily. "Do not speak to me like that. I may be an Imprudent Child, but I am the Queen." She took a moment to regain her composure. "Enough chatter. Give me the spell I asked for."

Tryce called me in at official occasions, to bear witness from the body of a disfavored servant or a used-up brood. I attended each of the four ceremonies where Tryce, clad in regal blue, presented her infant daughters to the sun: four small, green-swathed bundles, each borne from the Queen's own body. It made me sick, but I held my silence.

She also summoned me to the court ceremony where she presented Gudrin with an official title she'd concocted to give him standing in the royal circle. Honored Zephyr or some such nonsense. They held the occasion in autumn when red and yellow leaves adorned Gudrin's shoulders like a cape. Tryce pretended to ignore the women's discontented mutterings, but they were growing louder.

The last time I saw Tryce, she summoned me in a panic. She stood in an unfamiliar room with bare stone walls and sharp wind creaking through slitted windows. Someone else's blood stained Tryce's robes. "My sisters betrayed me!" she said. "They told the women of the grasslands I was trying to make them into broods, and then led them in a revolt against the castle. A thousand women, marching! I had to slay them all. I suspected Darnisha all along. But Peni seemed content to waft. Last fall, she bore a child of her own body. It was a worm, true, but she might have gotten a daughter next. She said she wanted to try!"

"Is that their blood?"

She held out her reddened hands and stared at them ruefully as if they weren't really part of her. "Gudrin was helping them. I had to smash him into sticks. They must have cast a spell on him. I can't imagine . . . "

Her voice faltered. I gave her a moment to tame her undignified excess.

"You seem to have mastered the situation," I said. "A Queen must deal with such things from time to time. The important thing will be to show no weakness in front of your courtiers."

"You don't understand! It's much worse than that. While we women fought, the raiders attacked the Fields That Bask under Open Skies. They've taken half the Land. We're making a stand in the Castle Where Hope Flutters, but we can't keep them out forever. A few weeks, at most. I told them this would happen! We need more daughters to defend us! But they wouldn't listen to me!"

Rayneh would have known how to present her anger with queenly courage, but Tryce was rash and thoughtless. She wore her emotions like perfume. "Be calm," I admonished. "You must focus."

"The raiders sent a message describing what they'll do to me and my daughters when they take the castle. I captured the messenger and burned out his tongue and gave him to the broods, and when they were done with him, I took what was left of his body and catapulted it into the raiders' camp. I could do the same to every one of them, and it still wouldn't be enough to compensate for having to listen to their vile, cowardly threats."

I interrupted her tirade. "The Castle Where Hope Flutters is on high ground, but if you've already lost the eastern fields, it will be difficult to defend. Take your women to the Spires of Treachery where the herders feed their cattle. You won't be able to mount traditional defenses, but they won't be able to attack easily. You'll be reduced to meeting each other in small parties where woman's magic should give you the advantage."

"My commander suggested that," said Tryce. "There are too many of them. We might as well try to dam a river with silk."

"It's better than remaining here."

"Even if we fight to a stalemate in the Spires of Treachery, the raiders will have our fields to grow food in, and our broods to make children on. If they can't conquer us this year, they'll obliterate us in ten. I need something else."

"There is nothing else."

"Think of something!"

I thought.

I cast my mind back through my years of training. I remembered the locked room in my matriline's household where servants were never allowed to enter, which my cousins and I scrubbed every dawn and dusk to teach us to be constant and rigorous.

I remembered the cedar desk where my aunt Finis taught me to paint birds, first by using the most realistic detail that oils could achieve, and then by reducing my paintings to fewer and fewer brushstrokes until I could evoke the essence of bird without any brush at all.

I remembered the many-drawered red cabinets where we stored Leafspine and Winterbrew, powdered Errow and essence of Howl. I remembered my bossy cousin Alne skidding through the halls in a panic after she broke into a locked drawer and mixed together two herbs that we weren't supposed to touch. Her fearful grimace transformed into a beak that permanently silenced her sharp tongue.

I remembered the year I spent traveling to learn the magic of foreign lands. I was appalled by the rituals I encountered in places where women urinated on their thresholds to ward off spirits, and plucked their scalps bald when their eldest daughters reached majority. I walked with senders and weavers and whisperers and learned magic secrets that my people had misunderstood for centuries. I remembered the terror of the three nights I spent in the ancient ruins of The Desert which Should Not Have Been, begging the souls that haunted that place to surrender the secrets of their accursed city. One by one my companions died, and I spent the desert days digging graves for those the spirits found unworthy. On the third dawn, they blessed me with communion, and sent me away a wiser woman.

I remembered returning to the Land of Flowered Hills and making my own contribution to the lore contained in our matriline's locked rooms. I remembered all of this, and still I could think of nothing to tell Tryce.

Until a robin of memory hopped from an unexpected place—a piece of magic I learned traveling with herders, not spell-casters. It was an old magic, one that farmers cast when they needed to cull an inbred strain.

"You must concoct a plague," I began.

Tryce's eyes locked on me. I saw hope in her face, and I realized that she'd expected me to fail her, too.

"Find a sick baby and stop whatever treatment it is receiving. Feed it mosquito bellies and offal and dirty water to make it sicker. Give it sores and let them fill with pus. When its forehead has grown too hot for a woman to touch without flinching, kill the baby and dedicate its breath to the sun. The next morning, when the sun rises, a plague will spread with the sunlight."

"That will kill the raiders?"

"Many of them. If you create a truly virulent strain, it may kill most of them. And it will cut down their children like a scythe across wheat."

Tryce clapped her blood-stained hands. "Good."

"I should warn you. It will kill your babies as well."

"What?"

"A plague cooked in an infant will kill anyone's children. It is the way of things."

"Unacceptable! I come to you for help, and you send me to murder my daughters?"

"You killed one before, didn't you? To save your automaton?"

"You're as crazy as the crones at court! We need more babies, not fewer."

"You'll have to hope you can persuade your women to bear children so that you can rebuild your population faster than the raiders can rebuild theirs."

Tryce looked as though she wanted to level a thousand curses at me, but she stilled her tongue. Her eyes were dark and narrow. In a quiet, angry voice, she said, "Then it will be done."

They were the same words she'd used when she promised to kill Gudrin. That time I'd been able to save her despite her foolishness. This time, I might not be able to.

Next I was summoned, I could not see at all. I was ushered into the world by lowing, distant shouts, and the stench of animals packed too closely together.

A worried voice cut through the din. "Did it work? Are you there? Laverna, is that still you?"

Disoriented, I reached out to find a hint about my surroundings. My hands impacted a summoning barrier.

"Laverna, that's not you anymore, is it?"

The smell of manure stung my throat. I coughed. "My name is Naeva."

"Holy day, it worked. Please, Sleepless One, we need your help. There are men outside. I don't know how long we can hold them off."

"What happened? Is Queen Tryce dead?"

"Queen Tryce?"

"She didn't cast the plague, did she? Selfish brat. Where are the raiders now? Are you in the Spires of Treachery?"

"Sleepless One, slow down. I don't follow you."

"Where are you? How much land have the raiders taken?"

"There are no raiders here, just King Addric's army. His soldiers used to be happy as long as we paid our taxes and bowed our heads at processions. Now they want us to follow their ways, worship their god, let our men give us orders. Some of us rebelled by marching in front of the governor's theater, and now he's sent sorcerers after us. They burned our city with magical fire. We're making a last stand at the inn outside town. We set aside the stable for the summoning."

"Woman, you're mad. Men can't practice that kind of magic."

"These men can."

A nearby donkey brayed, and a fresh stench plopped into the air. Outside, I heard the noise of burning, and the shouts of men and children.

"It seems we've reached an impasse. You've never heard of the Land of Flowered Hills?"

"Never."

I had spent enough time pacing the ruins in the Desert which Should Not Have Been to understand the ways in which civilizations cracked and decayed. Women and time marched forward, relentless and uncaring as sand.

"I see."

"I'm sorry. I'm not doing this very well. It's my first summoning. My aunt Hetta used to do it but they slit her throat like you'd slaughter a pig and left her body to burn. Bardus says they're roasting the corpses and eating them, but I don't think anyone could do that. Could they? Hetta showed me how to do this a dozen times, but I never got to practice. She would have done this better."

"That would explain why I can't see."

"No, that's the child, Laverna. She's blind. She does all the talking. Her twin Nammi can see, but she's dumb."

"Her twin?"

"Nammi's right here. Reach into the circle and touch your sister's hand, Nammi. That's a good girl."

A small hand clasped mine. It felt clammy with sweat. I squeezed back.

"It doesn't seem fair to take her sister away," I said.

"Why would anyone take Laverna away?"

"She'll die when I leave this body."

"No, she won't. Nammi's soul will call her back. Didn't your people use twins?"

"No. Our hosts died."

"Yours were a harsh people."

Another silence. She spoke the truth, though I'd never thought of it in such terms. We were a lawful people. We were an unflinching people.

"You want my help to defeat the shamans?" I asked.

"Aunt Hetta said that sometimes the Sleepless Ones can blink and douse all the magic within seven leagues. Or wave their hands and sweep a rank of men into a hurricane."

"Well, I can't."

She fell silent. I considered her situation.

"Do you have your people's livestock with you?" I asked.

"Everything that wouldn't fit into the stable is packed inside the inn. It's even less pleasant in there if you can imagine."

"Can you catch one of their soldiers?"

"We took some prisoners when we fled. We had to kill one but the others are tied up in the courtyard."

"Good. Kill them and mix their blood into the grain from your larder, and bake it into loaves of bread. Feed some of the bread to each of your animals. They will fill with a warrior's anger and hunt down your enemies."

The woman hesitated. I could hear her feet shifting on the hay-covered floor.

"If we do that, we won't have any grain or animals. How will we survive?"

"You would have had to desert your larder when the Worm-Pretending-to-Be-Queen sent reinforcements anyway. When you can safely flee, ask the blind child to lead you to the Place where the Sun Is Joyous. Whichever direction she chooses will be your safest choice."

"Thank you," said the woman. Her voice was taut and tired. It seemed clear that she'd hoped for an easier way, but she was wise enough to take what she received. "We'll have a wild path to tame."

"Yes."

The woman stepped forward. Her footsteps released the scent of dried hay. "You didn't know about your Land, did you?"

"I did not."

"I'm sorry for your loss. It must be—"

The dumb child whimpered. Outside, the shouts increased.

"I need to go," said the woman.

"Good luck," I said, and meant it.

I felt the child Laverna rush past me as I sank back into my restless sleep. Her spirit flashed as brightly as a coin left in the sun.

I never saw that woman or any of her people again. I like to think they did not die.

I did not like the way the world changed after the Land of Flowered Hills disappeared. For a long time, I was summoned only by men. Most were a sallow, unhealthy color with sharp narrow features and unnaturally light hair. Goateed sorcerers too proud of their paltry talents strove to dazzle me with pyrotechnics. They commanded me to reveal magical secrets that their peoples had forgotten. Sometimes I stayed silent. Sometimes I led them astray. Once, a hunched barbarian with a braided beard ordered me to give him the secret of flight. I told him to turn toward the prevailing wind and beg the Lover of the Sky for a favor. When the roc swooped down to eat him, I felt a wild kind of joy. At least the birds remembered how to punish worms who would steal women's magic.

I suffered for my minor victory. Without the barbarian to dismiss me, I was stuck on a tiny patch of grass, hemmed in by the rabbit heads he'd placed to mark the summoning circle. I shivered through the windy night until I finally thought to kick away one of the heads. It tumbled across the grass and my spirit sank into the ground.

Men treated me differently than women had. I had been accustomed to being summoned by Queens and commanders awaiting my advice on incipient battles. Men eschewed my consult; they sought to steal my powers. One summoned me into a box, hoping to trap me as if I were a minor demon that could be forced to grant his wishes. I chanted a rhyme to burn his fingers. When he pulled his hand away, the lid snapped shut and I was free.

Our magic had centered on birds and wind. These new sorcerers made pets of creatures of blood and snapping jaws, wolves and bears and jaguars. We had depicted the sun's grace along with its splendor, showing the red feathers of flaming light that arc into wings to sweep her across the sky. Their sun was a crude, jagged thing—a golden disk surrounded by spikes that twisted like the gaudy knives I'd seen in foreign cities where I traveled when I was young.

The men called me The Bitch Queen. They claimed I had hated my womb so much that I tried to curse all men to infertility, but the curse rebounded and struck me dead. Apparently, I had hanged myself. Or I'd tried to disembowel every male creature within a day's walk of my borders. Or I'd spelled my entire kingdom into a waking death in order to prevent myself from ever becoming pregnant. Apparently, I did all the same things out of revenge because I became pregnant. I eschewed men and impregnated women with sorcery. I married a thousand husbands and murdered them all. I murdered my husband, the King, and staked his head outside my castle, and then forced all the tearful women of my kingdom to do the same to their menfolk. I went crazy when my husband and son died and ordered all the men in my kingdom to be executed, declaring that no one would have the pleasure I'd been denied. I had been born a boy, but a rival of my father's castrated me, and so I hated all real men. I ordered that any woman caught breastfeeding should have her breasts cut off. I ordered my lover's genitals cut off and sewn on me. I ordered my vagina sewn shut so I could never give birth. I ordered everyone in my kingdom to call me a man.

They assumed my magic must originate with my genitals: they displayed surprise that I didn't strip naked to mix ingredients in my vagina or cast spells using menstrual blood. They also displayed surprise that I became angry when they asked me about such things.

The worst of them believed he could steal my magic by raping me. He summoned me into a worthless, skinny girl, the kind that we in the Land of Flowered Hills would have deemed too weak to be a woman and too frail to be a brood. In order to carry out his plans, he had to make the summoning circle large enough to accommodate the bed. When he forced himself on top of me, I twisted off his head.

The best of them summoned me soon after that. He was a young man with nervous, trembling fingers who innovated a way to summon my spirit into himself. Books and scrolls tumbled over the surfaces of his tiny, dim room, many of them stained with wax from unheeded candles. Talking to him was strange, the two of us communicating with the same mouth, looking out of the same eyes.

Before long, we realized that we didn't need words. Our knowledge seeped from one spirit to the other like dye poured into water. He watched me as a girl, riding with Rayneh, and felt the sun burning my back as I dug graves in the Desert which Should Not Have Been, and flinched as he witnessed the worm who attempted to rape me. I watched him and his five brothers, all orphaned and living on the street, as they struggled to find scraps. I saw how he had learned to read under the tutelage of a traveling scribe who carried his books with him from town to town. I felt his uncomfortable mixture of love, respect, and fear for the patron who had set him up as a scribe and petty magician in return for sex and servitude. *I didn't know it felt that way*, I said to him. *Neither did I*, he replied. We stared at each other cross-eyed through his big green eyes.

Pasha needed to find a way to stop the nearby volcano before it destroyed the tiny kingdom where he dwelled. Already, tremors rattled the buildings, foreshadowing the coming destruction.

Perhaps I should not have given Pasha the spell, but it was not deep woman's magic. Besides, things seemed different when I inhabited his mind, closer to him than I had been to anyone.

We went about enacting the spell together. As we collected ash from the fireplaces of one family from each of the kingdom's twelve towns, I asked him, *Why haven't you sent me back? Wouldn't it be easier to do this on your own?*

I'll die when your spirit goes, he answered, and I saw the knowledge of it which he had managed to keep from me.

I didn't want him to die. *Then I'll stay,* I said. *I won't interfere with your life. I'll retreat as much as I can.*

I can't keep up the spell much longer, he said. I felt his sadness and his resolve. Beneath, I glimpsed even deeper sadness at the plans he would no longer be able to fulfill. He'd wanted to teach his youngest brother to read and write so that the two of them could move out of this hamlet and set up shop in a city as scribes, perhaps even earn enough money to house and feed all their brothers.

I remembered Laverna and Nammi and tried to convince Pasha that we could convert the twins' magic to work for him and his brother. He said that we only had enough time to stop the volcano. *The kingdom is more important than I am,* he said.

We dug a hole near the volcano's base and poured in the ashes that we'd collected. We stirred them with a phoenix feather until they caught fire, in order to give the volcano the symbolic satisfaction of burning the kingdom's hearths. A dense cloud of smoke rushed up from the looming mountain and then the earth was still.

That's it, said Pasha, exhaustion and relief equally apparent in his mind. *We did it.*

We sat together until nightfall when Pasha's strength began to fail.

I have to let go now, he said.

No, I begged him, *Wait. Let us return to the city. We can find your brother. We'll find a way to save you.*

But the magic in his brain was unwinding. I was reminded of the ancient tapestries hanging in the Castle Where Hope Flutters, left too long to moths and weather. Pasha lost control of his feet, his fingers. His thoughts began to drift. They came slowly and far apart. His breath halted in his lungs. Before his life could end completely, my spirit sank away, leaving him to die alone.

After that, I did not have the courage to answer summons. When men called me, I kicked away the objects they'd used to bind me in place and disappeared again. Eventually, the summons stopped.

I had never before been aware of the time that I spent under the earth, but as the years between summons stretched, I began to feel vague sensations: swatches of grey and white along with muted, indefinable pain.

When a summons finally came, I almost felt relief. When I realized the summoner was a woman, I did feel surprise.

"I didn't expect that to work," said the woman. She was peach-skinned and round, a double chin gentling her jaw. She wore large spectacles with faceted green lenses like insect eyes. Spines like porcupine quills grew in a thin line from the bridge of her nose to the top of her skull before fanning into a mane. The aroma of smoke—whether the woman's personal scent or some spell remnant—hung acrid in the air.

I found myself simultaneously drawn to the vibrancy of the living world and disinclined to participate in it. I remained still, delighting in the smells and sights and sounds.

"No use pretending you're not there," said the woman. "The straw man doesn't usually blink on its own. Or breathe."

I looked down and saw a rudimentary body made of straw, joints knotted together with what appeared to be twine. I lifted my straw hand and stretched out each finger, amazed as the joints crinkled but did not break. "What is this?" My voice sounded dry and crackling, though I did not know whether that was a function of straw or disuse.

"I'm not surprised this is new to you. The straw men are a pretty new development. It saves a lot of stress and unpleasantness for the twins and the spirit rebounders and everyone else who gets the thankless job of putting up with Insomniacs taking over their bodies. Olin Nimble—that's the man who innovated the straw men—he and I completed our scholastic training the same year. Twenty years later? He's transfigured the whole field. And here's me, puttering around the library. But I suppose someone has to teach the students how to distinguish Pinder's Breath from Summer Twoflower."

The woman reached into my summoning circle and tugged my earlobe. Straw crackled.

"It's a gesture of greeting," she said. "Go on, tug mine."

I reached out hesitantly, expecting my gesture to be thwarted by the invisible summoning barrier. Instead, my fingers slid through unresisting air and grasped the woman's earlobe.

She grinned with an air of satisfaction that reminded me of the way my aunts had looked when showing me new spells. "I am Scholar Misa Meticulous." She lifted the crystal globe she carried and squinted at it. Magical etchings appeared, spelling words in an unfamiliar alphabet. "And you are the Great Lady Naeva who Picked Posies near the Queen's Chamber, of the Kingdom Where Women Rule?"

I frowned, or tried to, unsure whether it showed on my straw face. "The Land of Flowered Hills."

"Oh." She corrected the etching with a long, sharp implement. "Our earliest records have it the other way. This sort of thing is commoner than you'd think. Facts get mixed with rumor. Rumor becomes legend. Soon no one can remember what was history and what they made up to frighten the children. For instance, I'll bet your people didn't really have an underclass of women you kept in herds for bearing children."

"We called them broods."

"You called them—" Misa's eyes went round and horrified. As quickly as her shock had registered, it disappeared again. She snorted with forthright amusement. "We'll have to get one of the historians to talk to you. This is what they *live* for."

"Do they."

It was becoming increasingly clear that this woman viewed me as a relic. Indignation simmered; I was not an urn, half-buried in the desert. Yet, in a way, I was.

"I'm just a teacher who specializes in sniffing," Misa continued. "I find Insomniacs we haven't spoken to before. It can take years, tracking through records, piecing together bits of old spells. I've been following you for three years. You slept dark."

"Not dark enough."

She reached into the summoning circle to give me a sympathetic pat on the shoulder. "Eternity's a lonely place," she said. "Even the academy's lonely, and we only study eternity. Come on. Why don't we take a walk? I'll show you the library."

My straw eyes rustled as they blinked in surprise. "A walk?"

Misa laughed. "Try it out."

She laughed again as I took one precarious step forward and then another. The straw body's joints creaked with each stiff movement. I felt awkward and graceless, but I couldn't deny the pleasure of movement.

"Come on," Misa repeated, beckoning.

She led me down a corridor of gleaming white marble. Arcane symbols figured the walls. Spell-remnants scented the air with cinnamon and burnt herbs, mingling with the cool currents that swept down from the vaulted ceiling. Beneath our feet, the floor was worn from many footsteps and yet Misa and I walked alone. I wondered how it could be that a place built to accommodate hundreds was empty except for a low-ranking scholar and a dead woman summoned into an effigy.

My questions were soon answered when a group of students approached noisily from an intersecting passageway. They halted when they saw us, falling abruptly silent. Misa frowned. "Get on!" she said, waving them away. They looked relieved as they fled back the way they'd come.

The students' shaved heads and shapeless robes made it difficult to discern their forms, but it was clear I had seen something I hadn't been meant to.

"You train men here," I ascertained.

"Men, women, neuters," said Misa. "Anyone who comes. And qualifies, of course."

I felt the hiss of disappointment: another profane, degraded culture. I should have known better than to hope. "I see," I said, unable to conceal my resentment.

Misa did not seem to notice. "Many cultures have created separate systems of magic for the male and female. Your culture was extreme, but not unusual. Men work healing magic, and women sing weather magic, or vice versa. All very rigid, all very unscientific. Did they ever try to teach a man to wail for a midnight rain? Oh, maybe they did, but if he succeeded, then it was just that one man, and wasn't his spirit more womanly than masculine? They get noted as an exception to the rule, not a problem with the rule itself. Think Locas Follow with the crickets, or Petrin of Atscheko, or for an example on the female side, Queen Urté. And of course if the man you set up to sing love songs to hurricanes can't even stir up a breeze, well, there's your proof. Men can't sing the weather. Even if another man could. Rigor, that's the important thing. Until you have proof, anything can be wrong. We know now there's no difference between the magical capabilities of the sexes, but we'd have known it earlier if people had asked the right questions. Did you know there's a place in the northern wastes where they believe only people with both male and female genitals can work spells?"

"They're fools."

Misa shrugged.

"Everyone's a fool, sooner or later. I make a game of it with my students. What do we believe that will be proven wrong in the future? I envy your ability to live forever so you can see."

"You should not," I said, surprised by my own bitterness. "People of the future are as likely to destroy your truths as to uncover your falsehoods."

She turned toward me, her face drawn with empathy. "You may be right."

We entered a vast, mahogany-paneled room, large enough to quarter a roc. Curving shelf towers formed an elaborate labyrinth. Misa led me through the narrow aisles with swift precision.

The shelves displayed prisms of various shapes and sizes. Crystal pyramids sat beside metal cylinders and spheres cut from obsidian. There were stranger things, too, shapes for which I possessed no words, woven out of steel threads or hardened lava.

Overhead, a transparent dome revealed a night sky strewn with stars. I recognized no patterns among the sparkling pinpricks; it was as if all the stars I'd known had been gathered in a giant's palm and then scattered carelessly into new designs.

Misa chattered as she walked. "This is the academy library. There are over three hundred thousand spells in this wing alone and we've almost filled the second. My students are taking bets on when they'll start construction on the third. They're also taking bets on whose statue will be by the door. Olin Nimble's the favorite, wouldn't you know."

We passed a number of carrel desks upon which lay maps of strange rivers and red-tinted deserts. Tubes containing more maps resided in cubby holes between the desks, their ends labeled in an unfamiliar alphabet.

"We make the first year students memorize world maps," said Misa. "A scholar has to understand how much there is to know."

I stopped by a carrel near the end of the row. The map's surface was ridged to show changes in elevation. I tried to imagine what the land it depicted would look like from above, on a roc's back. Could the Mountains where the Sun Rests be hidden among those jagged points?

Misa stopped behind me. "We're almost to the place I wanted to show you," she said. When we began walking again, she stayed quiet.

Presently, we approached a place where marble steps led down to a sunken area. We descended, and seemed to enter another room entirely, the arcs of the library shelves on the main level looming upward like a ring of ancient trees.

All around us, invisible from above, there stood statues of men and women. They held out spell spheres in their carved, upturned palms.

"This is the Circle of Insomniacs," said Misa. "Every Insomniac is depicted here. All the ones we've found, that is."

Amid hunched old women and bearded men with wild eyes, I caught sight of stranger things. Long, armored spikes jutted from a woman's spine. A man seemed to be wearing a helmet shaped like a sheep's head until I noticed that his ears twisted behind his head and became the ram's horns. A child opened his mouth to display a ring of needle-sharp teeth like a leech's.

"They aren't human," I said.

"They are," said Misa. "Or they were." She pointed me to the space between a toothless man and a soldier whose face fell in shadow behind a carved helmet. "Your statue will be there. The sculptor will want to speak with you. Or if you don't want to talk to him, you can talk to his assistant, and she'll make notes."

I looked aghast at the crowd of stone faces. "This—this is why you woke me? This sentimental memorial?"

Misa's eyes glittered with excitement. "The statue's only part of it. We want to know more about you and the Kingdom Where Women Rule. Sorry, the Land of Flowered Hills. We want to learn from you and teach you. We want you to stay!"

I could not help but laugh, harsh and mirthless. Would this woman ask a piece of ancient stone wall whether or not it wanted to be displayed in a museum? Not even the worms who tried to steal my spells had presumed so much.

"I'm sorry," said Misa. "I shouldn't have blurted it out like that. I'm good at sniffing. I'm terrible with people. Usually I find the Great Ones and then other people do the summoning and bring them to the library. The council asked me to do it myself this time because I lived in a women's colony before I came to the academy. I'm what they call woman-centered. They thought we'd have something in common."

"Loving women is fundamental. It's natural as breeze. It's not some kind of shared diversion."

"Still. It's more than you'd have in common with Olin Nimble."

She paused, biting her lip. She was still transparently excited even though the conversation had begun to go badly.

"Will you stay a while at least?" she asked. "You've slept dark for millennia. What's a little time in the light?"

I scoffed and began to demand that she banish me back to the dark—but the scholar's excitement cast ripples in a pond that I'd believed had become permanently still.

What I'd learned from the unrecognizable maps and scattered constellations was that the wage of eternity was forgetfulness. I was lonely, achingly lonely. Besides, I had begun to like Misa's fumbling chatter. She had reawakened me to light and touch—and even, it seemed, to wonder.

If I was to stay, I told Misa, then she must understand that I'd had enough of worms and their attempts at magic. I did not want them crowding my time in the light.

The corners of Misa's mouth drew downward in disapproval, but she answered, "The academy puts us at the crossroads of myriad beliefs. Sometimes we must set aside our own." She reached out to touch me. "You're giving us a great gift by staying. We'll always respect that."

Misa and I worked closely during my first days at the academy. We argued over everything. Our roles switched rapidly and contentiously from master to apprentice and back again. She would begin by asking me questions, and then as I told her about what I'd learned in my matriline's locked rooms, she would interrupt to tell me I was wrong, her people had experimented with such things, and they never performed consistently. Within moments, we'd be shouting about what magic meant, and what it signified, and what it wanted—because one thing we agreed on was that magic was a little bit alive.

Misa suspended her teaching while she worked with me, so we had the days to ourselves in the vast salon where she taught. Her people's magic was more than superficially dissimilar from mine. They constructed their spells into physical geometries by mapping out elaborate equations that determined whether they would be cylinders or dodecahedrons, formed of garnet or lapis lazuli or cages of copper strands. Even their academy's construction reflected magical intentions, although Misa told me its effects were vague and diffuse.

"Magic is like architecture," she said. "You have to build the right container for magic to grow in. The right house for its heart."

"You fail to consider the poetry of magic," I contended. "It likes to be teased with images, cajoled with irony. It wants to match wits."

"Your spells are random!" Misa answered. "Even you don't understand how they work. You've admitted it yourself. The effects are variable, unpredictable. It lacks rigor!"

"And accomplishes grandeur," I said. "How many of your scholars can match me?"

I soon learned that Misa was not, as she claimed, an unimportant scholar. By agreement, we allowed her female pupils to enter the salon from time to time for consultations. The young women, who looked startlingly young in their loose white garments, approached Misa with an awe that verged on fear. Once, a very young girl who looked barely out of puberty, ended their session by giving a low bow and kissing Misa's hand. She turned vivid red and fled the salon.

Misa shook her head as the echoes of the girl's footsteps faded. "She just wishes she was taking from Olin Nimble."

"Why do you persist in this deception?" I asked. "You have as many spells in the library as he does. It is you, not he, who was asked to join the academy as a scholar."

She slid me a dubious look. "You've been talking to people?"

"I have been listening."

"I've been here a long time," said Misa. "They need people like me to do the little things so greater minds like Olin Nimble's can be kept clear."

But her words were clearly untrue. All of the academy's scholars, from the most renowned to the most inexperienced, sent to Misa for consultations. She greeted their pages with good humor and false humility, and then went to meet her fellow scholars elsewhere, leaving her salon to me so that I could study or contemplate as I wished.

In the Land of Flowered Hills, there had once been a famous scholar named The Woman Who Would Ask the Breeze for Whys and Wherefores. Misa was such a woman, relentlessly impractical, always half-occupied by her studies. We ate together, talked together, slept together in her chamber, and yet I never saw her focus fully on anything except when she was engrossed in transforming her abstract magical theories into complex, beautiful tangibles.

Sometimes, I paused to consider how different Misa was from my first love. Misa's scattered, self-effaced pursuit of knowledge was nothing like Rayneh's dignified exercise of power. Rayneh was like a statue, formed in a beautiful but permanent stasis, never learning or changing. Misa tumbled everywhere like a curious wind, seeking to understand and alter and collaborate, but never to master.

In our first days together, Misa and I shared an abundance of excruciating, contentious, awe-inspiring novelty. We were separated by cultures and centuries, and yet we were attracted to each other even more strongly because of the strangeness we brought into each other's lives.

The academy was controlled by a rotating council of scholars that was chosen annually by lots. They made their decisions by consensus and exercised control over issues great and small, including the selection of new mages who were invited to join the academy as scholars and thus enter the pool of people who might someday control it.

"I'm grateful every year when they don't draw my name," Misa said.

We were sitting in her salon during the late afternoon, relaxing on reclining couches and sipping a hot, sweet drink from celadon cups. One of Misa's students sat with us, a startle-eyed girl who kept her bald head powdered and smooth, whom Misa had confided she found promising. The drink smelled of oranges and cinnamon; I savored it, ever amazed by the abilities of my strange, straw body.

I looked to Misa. "Why?"

Misa shuddered. "Being on the council would be . . . terrible."

"Why?" I asked again, but she only repeated herself in a louder voice, growing increasingly frustrated with my questions.

Later, when Misa left to discuss a spell with one of the academy's male scholars, her student told me, "Misa doesn't want to be elevated over others. It's a very great taboo for her people."

"It is self-indulgent to avoid power," I said. "Someone must wield it. Better the strong than the weak."

Misa's student fidgeted uncomfortably. "Her people don't see it that way."

I sipped from my cup. "Then they are fools."

Misa's student said nothing in response, but she excused herself from the salon as soon as she finished her drink.

The council requested my presence when I had been at the academy for a year. They wished to formalize the terms of my stay. Sleepless Ones who remained were expected to hold their own classes and contribute to the institution's body of knowledge.

"I will teach," I told Misa, "but only women."

"Why!" demanded Misa. "What is your irrational attachment to this prejudice?"

"I will not desecrate women's magic by teaching it to men."

"How is it desecration?"

"Women's magic is meant for women. Putting it into men's hands is degrading."

"But why!"

Our argument intensified. I began to rage. Men are not worthy of woman's magic. They're small-skulled, and cringing, and animalistic. It would be wrong! *Why, why, why?* Misa demanded, quoting from philosophical dialogues, and describing experiments that supposedly proved there was no difference between men's and women's magic. We circled and struck at one another's arguments as if we were animals competing over territory. We tangled our horns and drew blood from insignificant wounds, but neither of us seemed able to strike a final blow.

"Enough!" I shouted. "You've always told me that the academy respects the sacred beliefs of other cultures. These are mine."

"They're absurd!"

"If you will not agree then I will not teach. Banish me back to the dark! It does not matter to me."

Of course, it did matter to me. I had grown too attached to chaos and clamor. And to Misa. But I refused to admit it.

In the end, Misa agreed to argue my intentions before the council. She looked at turns furious and miserable. "They won't agree," she said. "How can they? But I'll do what I can."

The next day, Misa rubbed dense, floral unguents into her scalp and decorated her fingers with arcane rings. Her quills trembled and fanned upward, displaying her anxiety.

The circular council room glowed with faint, magical light. Cold air mixed with the musky scents favored by high-ranking scholars, along with hints of smoke and herbs. Archways loomed at each of the cardinal directions. Misa led us through the eastern archway, which she explained was for negotiation, and into the center of the mosaic floor.

The council's scholars sat on raised couches arrayed around the circumference of the room. Each sat below a torch that guttered, red and gold, rendering the councilors' bodies vivid against the dim. I caught sight of a man in layered red and yellow robes, his head surmounted by a brass circlet that twinkled with lights that flared and then flitted out of existence, like winking stars. To his side sat a tall woman with mossy hair and bark-like skin, and beside her, a man with two heads and torsos mounted upon a single pair of legs. A woman raised her hand in greeting to Misa, and water cascaded from her arms like a waterfall, churning into a mist that evaporated before it touched the floor.

Misa had told me that older scholars were often changed by her people's magic, that it shaped their bodies in the way they shaped their spells. I had not understood her before.

A long, narrow man seemed to be the focal point of the other councilors' attention. Fine, sensory hairs covered his skin. They quivered in our direction like a small animal's sniffing. "What do you suggest?" he asked. "Shall we establish a woman-only library? Shall we inspect our students' genitalia to ensure there are no men-women or women-men or twin-sexed among them?"

"Never mind that," countered a voice behind us. I turned to see a pudgy woman garbed in heavy metal sheets. "It's irrelevant to object on the basis of pragmatism. This request is exclusionary."

"Worse," added the waterfall woman. "It's immoral."

The councilors around her nodded their heads in affirmation. Two identical-looking men in leather hoods fluttered their hands to show support.

Misa looked to each assenting scholar in turn. "You are correct. It is exclusionist and immoral. But I ask you to think about deeper issues. If we reject Naeva's conditions, then everything she knows will be lost. Isn't it better that some know than that everyone forgets?"

"Is it worth preserving knowledge if the price is bigotry?" asked the narrow man with the sensory hairs, but the other scholars' eyes fixed on Misa.

They continued to argue for some time, but the conclusion had been foregone as soon as Misa spoke. There is nothing scholars love more than knowledge.

"Is it strange for you?" I asked Misa. "To spend so much time with someone trapped in the body of a doll?"

We were alone in the tiny, cluttered room where she slept. It was a roughly hewn underground cavity, its only entrance and exit by ladder. Misa admitted that the academy offered better accommodations, but claimed she preferred rooms like this one.

Misa exclaimed with mock surprise. "You're trapped in the body of a doll? I'd never noticed!"

She grinned in my direction. I rewarded her with laughter.

"I've gotten used to the straw men," she said more seriously. "When we talk, I'm thinking about spells and magic and the things you've seen. Not straw."

Nevertheless, straw remained inescapably cumbersome. Misa suggested games and spells and implements, but I refused objects that would estrange our intimacy. We lay together at night and traded words, her hands busy at giving her pleasure while I watched and whispered. Afterward, we lay close, but I could not give her the warmth of a body I did not possess.

One night, I woke long after our love-making to discover that she was no longer beside me. I found her in the salon, her equations spiraling across a row of crystal globes. A doll hung from the wall beside her, awkwardly suspended by its nape. Its skin was warm and soft and tinted the same sienna that mine had been so many eons ago. I raised its face and saw features matching the sketches that the sculptor's assistant had made during our sessions.

Misa looked up from her calculations. She smiled with mild embarrassment.

"I should have known a simple adaptation wouldn't work," she said. "Otherwise, Olin Nimble would have discarded straw years ago. But I thought, if I worked it out . . . "

I moved behind her, and beheld the array of crystal globes, all showing spidery white equations. Below them lay a half-formed spell of polished wood and peridot chips.

Misa's quill mane quivered. "It's late," she said, taking my hand. "We should return to bed."

Misa often left her projects half-done and scattered. I like to think the doll would have been different. I like to think she would have finished it.

Instead, she was drawn into the whirl of events happening outside the academy. She began leaving me behind in her chambers while she spent all hours in her salon, almost sleepwalking through the brief periods when she returned to me, and then rising restless in the dark and returning to her work.

By choice, I remained unclear about the shape of the external cataclysm. I did not want to be drawn further into the academy's politics.

My lectures provided little distraction. The students were as preoccupied as Misa. "This is not a time for theory!" one woman complained when I tried to draw my students into a discussion of magic's predilections. She did not return the following morning. Eventually, no one else returned either.

Loneliness drove me where curiosity could not and I began following Misa to her salon. Since I refused to help with her spells, she acknowledged my presence with little more than a glance before returning to her labors. Absent her attention, I studied and paced.

Once, after leaving the salon for several hours, Misa returned with a bustle of scholars—both men and women—all brightly clad and shouting. They halted abruptly when they saw me.

"I forgot you were here," Misa said without much contrition.

I tensed, angry and alienated, but unwilling to show my rage before the worms. "I will return to your chamber," I said through tightened lips.

Before I even left the room, they began shouting again. Their voices weren't like scholars debating. They lashed at each other with their words. They were angry. They were afraid.

That night, I went to Misa and finally asked for explanations. It's a plague, she said. A plague that made its victims bleed from the skin and eyes and then swelled their tongues until they suffocated.

They couldn't cure it. They treated one symptom, only to find the others worsening. The patients died, and then the mages who treated them died, too.

I declared that the disease must be magic. Misa glared at me with unexpected anger and answered that, no! It was not magic! If it was magic, they would have cured it. This was something foul and deadly and *natural*.

She'd grown gaunt by then, the gentle cushions of fat at her chin and stomach disappearing as her ribs grew prominent. After she slept, her head-rest was covered with quills that had fallen out during the night, their pointed tips lackluster and dulled.

I no longer had dialogues or magic or sex to occupy my time. I had only remote, distracted Misa. My world began to shape itself around her—my love for her, my concern for her, my dread that she wouldn't find a cure, and my fear of what I'd do if she didn't. She was weak, and she was leading me into weakness. My mind sketched patterns I didn't want to imagine. I heard the spirits in The Desert Which Should Not Have Been whispering about the deaths of civilizations, and about choices between honor and love.

Misa stopped sleeping. Instead, she sat on the bed in the dark, staring into the shadows and worrying her hands.

"There is no cure," she muttered.

I lay behind her, watching her silhouette.

"Of course there's a cure."

"Oh, *of course*," snapped Misa. "We're just too ignorant to find it!"

Such irrational anger. I never learned how to respond to a lover so easily swayed by her emotions.

"I did not say that you were ignorant."

"As long as you didn't say it."

Misa pulled to her feet and began pacing, footsteps thumping against the piled rugs.

I realized that in all my worrying, I'd never paused to consider where the plague had been, whether it had ravaged the communities where Misa had lived and loved. My people would have thought it a weakness to let such things affect them.

"Perhaps you are ignorant," I said. "Maybe you can't cure this plague by building little boxes. Have you thought of that?"

I expected Misa to look angry, but instead she turned back with an expression of awe. "Maybe that's it," she said slowly. "Maybe we need your kind of magic. Maybe we need poetry."

For the first time since the plague began, the lines of tension began to smooth from Misa's face. I loved her. I wanted to see her calm and curious, restored to the woman who marveled at new things and spent her nights beside me.

So I did what I knew I should not. I sat with her for the next hours and listened as she described the affliction. It had begun in a swamp far to the east, she said, in a humid tangle of roots and branches where a thousand sharp and biting things lurked beneath the water. It traveled west with summer's heat, sickening children and old people first, and then striking the young and healthy. The children and elderly sometimes recovered. The young and healthy never survived.

I thought back to diseases I'd known in my youth. A very different illness came to mind, a disease cast by a would-be usurper during my girlhood. It came to the Land of Flowered Hills with the winter wind and froze its victims into statues that would not shatter with blows or melt with heat. For years after Rayneh's mother killed the usurper and halted the disease, the Land of Flowered Hills was haunted by the glacial, ghostly remains of those once-loved. The Queen's sorceresses sought them out one by one and melted them with memories of passion. It was said that the survivors wept and cursed as their loved ones melted away, for they had grown to love the ever-present, icy memorials.

That illness was unlike what afflicted Misa's people in all ways but one—that disease, too, had spared the feeble and taken the strong.

I told Misa, "This is a plague that steals its victims' strength and uses it to kill them."

Misa's breaths came slowly and heavily. "Yes, that's it," she said. "That's what's happening."

"The victims must steal their strength back from the disease. They must cast their own cures."

"They must cast your kind of spells. Poetry spells."

"Yes," I said. "Poetry spells."

Misa's eyes closed as if she wanted to weep with relief. She looked so tired and frail. I wanted to lay her down on the bed and stroke her cheeks until she fell asleep.

Misa's shoulders shook but she didn't cry. Instead, she straightened her spectacles and plucked at her robes.

"With a bit of heat and . . . how would obsidian translate into poetry? . . . " she mused aloud. She started toward the ladder and then paused to look back. "Will you come help me, Naeva?"

She must have known what I would say.

"I'll come," I said quietly, "but this is woman's magic. It is not for men."

What followed was inevitable: the shudder that passed through Misa as her optimism turned ashen. "No. Naeva. You wouldn't let people die."

But I would. And she should have known that. If she knew me at all.

She brought it before the council. She said that was how things were to be decided. By discussion. By consensus.

We entered through the western arch, the arch of conflict. The scholars arrayed on their raised couches looked as haggard as Misa. Some seats were empty, others filled by men and women I'd not seen before.

"Why is this a problem?" asked one of the new scholars, an old woman whose face and breasts were stippled with tiny, fanged mouths. "Teach the spell to women. Have them cast it on the men."

"The victims must cast it themselves," Misa said.

The old woman scoffed. "Since when does a spell care who casts it?"

"It's old magic," Misa said. "Poetry magic."

"Then what is it like?" asked a voice from behind us.

We turned to see the narrow man with the fine, sensory hairs, who had demanded at my prior interrogation whether knowledge gained through bigotry was worth preserving. He lowered his gaze onto my face and his hairs extended toward me, rippling and seeking.

"Some of us have not had the opportunity to learn for ourselves," he added.

I hoped that Misa would intercede with an explanation, but she held her gaze away from mine. Her mouth was tight and narrow.

The man spoke again. "Unless you feel that it would violate your ethics to even *describe* the issue in my presence."

"No. It would not." I paused to prepare my words. "As I understand it, your people's magic imprisons spells in clever constructions. You alter the shape and texture of the spell as you alter the shape and texture of its casing."

Dissenting murmurs rose from the councilors.

"I realize that's an elementary description," I said. "However, it will suffice for contrast. My people attempted to court spells with poetry, using image and symbol and allusion as our tools. Your people give magic a place to dwell. Mine woo it to tryst awhile."

"What does that," interjected the many-mouthed old woman, "have to do with victims casting their own spells?"

Before I could answer, the narrow man spoke. "It must be poetry—the symmetry, if you will. Body and disease are battling for the body's strength. The body itself must win the battle."

"Is that so?" the old woman demanded of me.

I inclined my head in assent.

A woman dressed in robes of scarlet hair looked to Misa. "You're confident this will work?"

Misa's voice was strained and quiet. "I am."

The woman turned to regard me, scarlet tresses parting over her chest to reveal frog-like skin that glistened with damp. "You will not be moved? You won't relinquish the spell?"

I said, "No."

"Even if we promise to give it only to the women, and let the men die?"

I looked toward Misa. I knew what her people believed. The council might bend in matters of knowledge, but it would not bend in matters of life.

"I do not believe you would keep such promises."

The frog-skinned woman laughed. The inside of her mouth glittered like a cavern filled with crystals. "You're right, of course. We wouldn't." She looked to her fellow councilors. "I see no other option. I propose an Obligation."

"No," said Misa.

"I agree with Jian," said a fat scholar in red and yellow. "An Obligation."

"You can't violate her like that," said Misa. "The academy is founded on respect."

The frog-skinned woman raised her brows at Misa. "What is respect worth if we let thousands die?"

Misa took my hands. "Naeva, don't let this happen. Please, Naeva." She moved yet closer to me, her breath hot, her eyes desperate. "You know what men can be. You know they don't have to be ignorant worms or greedy brutes. You know they can be clever and noble! Remember Pasha. You gave him the spell he needed. Why won't you help us?"

Pasha—kin of my thoughts, closer than my own skin. It had seemed different then, inside his mind. But I was on my own feet now, looking out from my own eyes, and I knew what I knew.

When she'd been confronted by the inevitable destruction of our people, Tryce had made herself into a brood. She had chosen to degrade herself and her daughters in the name of survival. What would the Land of Flowered Hills have become if she'd succeeded? What would have happened to we hard and haughty people who commanded the sacred powers of wind and sun?

I would not desecrate our knowledge by putting it in the hands of animals. This was not just one man who would die from what he learned. This would be unlocking the door to my matriline's secret rooms and tearing open the many-drawered cupboards. It would be laying everything sacrosanct bare to corruption.

I broke away from Misa's touch. "I will tell you nothing!"

The council acted immediately and unanimously, accord reached without deliberation. The narrow man wrought a spell-shape using only his hands, which Misa had told me could be done, but rarely and only by great mages. When his fingers held the right configuration, he blew into their cage.

An Obligation.

It was like falling through blackness. I struggled for purchase, desperate to climb back into myself.

My mouth opened. It was not I who spoke.

"Bring them water from the swamp and damp their brows until they feel the humidity of the place where the disease was born. The spirit of the disease will seek its origins, as any born creature will. Let the victims seek with their souls' sight until they find the spirit of the disease standing before them. It will appear differently to each, vaporous and foul, or sly and sharp, but they will know it. Let the victims open the mouths of their souls and devour the disease until its spirit is inside their spirit as its body is inside their body. This time, they will be the conquerors. When they wake, they will be stronger than they had been before."

My words resonated through the chamber. Misa shuddered and began to retch. The frog-skinned woman detached a lock of her scarlet hair and gave it, along with a sphere etched with my declamation, to their fleetest page. My volition rushed back into me as if through a crashing dam. I swelled with my returning power.

Magic is a little bit alive. It loves irony and it loves passion. With all the fierceness of my dead Land, I began to tear apart my straw body with its own straw hands. The effigy's viscera fell, crushed and crackling, to the mosaic floor.

The narrow man, alone among the councilors, read my intentions. He sprang to his feet, forming a rapid protection spell between his fingers. It glimmered into being before I could complete my own magic, but I was ablaze with passion and poetry, and I knew that I would prevail.

The fire of my anger leapt from my eyes and tongue and caught upon the straw in which I'd been imprisoned. Fire. Magic. Fury. The academy became an inferno.

They summoned me into a carved rock that could see and hear and speak but could not move. They carried it through the Southern arch, the arch of retribution.

The narrow man addressed me. His fine, sensory hairs had burned away in the fire, leaving his form bald and pathetic.

"You are dangerous," he said. "The council has agreed you cannot remain."

The council room was in ruins. The reek of smoke hung like a dense fog over the rubble. Misa sat on one of the few remaining couches, her eyes averted, her body etched with thick ugly scars. She held her right hand in her lap, its fingers melted into a single claw.

I wanted to cradle Misa's ruined hand, to kiss and soothe it. It was an unworthy desire. I had no intention of indulging regret.

"You destroyed the academy, you bitch," snarled a woman to my left. I remembered that she had once gestured waterfalls, but now her arms were burned to stumps. "Libraries, students, spells . . . " her voice cracked.

"The council understands the grave injustice of an Obligation," the narrow man continued, as if she had not interjected. "We don't take the enslavement of a soul lightly, especially when it violates a promised trust. Though we believe we acted rightfully, we also acknowledge we have done you an injustice. For that we owe you our contrition.

"Nevertheless," he continued, "it is the council's agreement that you cannot be permitted to remain in the light. It is our duty to send you back into the dark and to bind you there so that you may never answer summons again."

I laughed. It was a grating sound. "You'll be granting my dearest wish."

He inclined his head. "It is always best when aims align."

He reached out to the women next to him and took their hands. The remaining council members joined them, bending their bodies until they, themselves, formed the shape of a spell. Misa turned to join them, the tough, shiny substance of her scar tissue catching the light. I knew from Misa's lessons that the texture of her skin would alter and shape the spell. I could recognize their brilliance in that, to understand magic so well that they could form it out of their own bodies.

As the last of the scholars moved into place, for a moment I understood the strange, distorted, perfect shape they made. I realized with a slash that I had finally begun to comprehend their magic. And then I sank into final, lasting dark.

I remembered.

I remembered Misa. I remembered Pasha. I remembered the time when men had summoned me into unknown lands.

Always and inevitably, my thoughts returned to the Land of Flowered Hills, the place I had been away from longest, but known best.

Misa and Rayneh. I betrayed one. One betrayed me. Two loves ending in tragedy. Perhaps all loves do.

I remembered the locked room in my matriline's household, all those tiny lacquered drawers filled with marvels. My aunt's hand fluttered above them like a pale butterfly as I wondered which drawer she would open. What wonder would she reveal from a world so vast I could never hope to understand it?

"To paint a bird, you must show the brush what it means to fly," my aunt told me, holding my fingers around the brush handle as I strove to echo the perfection of a feather. The brush trembled. Dip into the well, slant, and press. Bristles splay. Ink bleeds across the scroll and—there! One single graceful stroke aspiring toward flight.

What can a woman do when love and time and truth are all at odds with one another, clashing and screeching, wailing and weeping, begging you to enter worlds unlike any you've ever known and save this people, this people, this people from king's soldiers and guttering volcanoes and plagues? What can a woman do when beliefs that seemed as solid as stone have become dry leaves blowing in autumn wind? What can a woman cling to when she must betray her lovers' lives or her own?

A woman is not a bird. A woman needs ground.

All my aunts gathering in a circle around the winter fire to share news and gossip, their voices clat-clat-clatting at each other in comforting, indistinguishable sounds. The wind finds its way in through the cracks and we welcome our friend. It blows through me, carrying scents of pine and snow. I run across the creaking floor to my aunts' knees which are as tall as I am, my arms slipping around one dark soft leg and then another as I work my way around the circle like a wind, finding the promise of comfort in each new embrace.

Light returned and shaded me with grey.

I stood on a pedestal under a dark dome, the room around me eaten by shadow. My hands touched my robe which felt like silk. They encountered each other and felt flesh. I raised them before my face and saw my own hands, brown and short and nimble, the fingernails jagged where I'd caught them on the rocks while surveying with Kyan in the Mountains where the Sun Rests.

Around me, I saw more pedestals arranged in a circle, and atop them strange forms that I could barely distinguish from shade. As my eyes adjusted, I made out a soldier with his face shadowed beneath a horned helmet, and a woman armored with spines. Next to me stood a child who smelled of stale water and dead fish. His eyes slid in my direction and I saw they were strangely old and weary. He opened his mouth to yawn, and inside, I saw a ring of needle-sharp teeth.

Recognition rushed through me. These were the Insomniacs I'd seen in Misa's library, all of them living and embodied, except there were more of us, countless more, all perched and waiting.

Magic is a little bit alive. That was my first thought as the creature unfolded before us, its body a strange darkness like the unrelieved black between stars. It was adorned with windows and doors that gleamed with silver like starlight. They opened and closed like slow blinking, offering us portals into another darkness that hinted at something beyond.

The creature was nothing like the entities that I'd believed waited at the core of eternity. It was no frozen world lizard, waiting to crack traitors in his icy jaws, nor a burning sun welcoming joyous souls as feathers in her wings. And yet, somehow I knew then that this creature was the deepest essence of the universe—the strange, persistent thing that throbbed like a heart between stars.

Its voice was strange, choral, like many voices talking at once. At the same time, it did not sound like a voice at all. It said, "You are the ones who have reached the end of time. You are witnesses to the end of this universe."

As it spoke, it expanded outward. The fanged child staggered back as the darkness approached. He looked toward me with fear in his eyes, and then darkness swelled around me, too, and I was surrounded by shadow and pouring starlight.

The creature said, "From the death of this universe will come the birth of another. This has happened so many times before that it cannot be numbered, unfathomable universes blinking one into the next, outside of time. The only continuity lies in the essences that persist from one to the next."

Its voice faded. I stretched out my hands into the gentle dark. "You want us to be reborn?" I asked.

I wasn't sure if it could even hear me in its vastness. But it spoke.

"The new universe will be unlike anything in this one. It will be a strangeness. There will be no 'born,' no 'you.' One cannot speak of a new universe. It is anathema to language. One cannot even ponder it."

Above me, a window opened, and it was not a window, but part of this strange being. Soothing, silver brilliance poured from it like water. It rushed over me, tingling like fresh spring mornings and newly drawn breath.

I could feel the creature's expectancy around me. More windows opened and closed as other Sleepless Ones made their choices.

I thought of everything then—everything I had thought of during the millennia when I was bound, and everything I should have thought of then but did not have the courage to think. I saw my life from a dozen fractured perspectives. Rayneh condemning me for helping her daughter steal her throne, and dismissing my every subsequent act as a traitor's cowardice. Tryce sneering at my lack of will as she watched me spurn a hundred opportunities for seizing power during centuries of summons. Misa, her brows drawn down in inestimable disappointment, pleading with me to abandon everything I was and become like her instead.

They were all right. They were all wrong. My heart shattered into a million sins.

I thought of Pasha who I should never have saved. I thought of how he tried to shield me from the pain of his death, spending his last strength to soothe me before he died alone.

For millennia, I had sought oblivion and been denied. Now, as I approached the opportunity to dissipate at last . . . now I began to understand the desire for something unspeakably, unfathomably new.

I reached toward the window. The creature gathered me in its massive blackness and lifted me up, up, up. I became a woman painted in brush-strokes of starlight, fewer and fewer, until I was only a glimmer of silver that had once been a woman, now poised to take flight. I glittered like the stars over The Desert which Should Not Have Been, eternal witnesses to things long forgotten. The darkness beyond the window pulled me. I leapt toward it, and stretched, and changed.

ARVIES

ADAM-TROY CASTRO

―――◆―――

STATEMENT OF INTENT

This is the story of a mother, and a daughter, and the right to life, and the
dignity of all living things, and of some souls granted great destinies at the
moment of their conception, and of others damned to remain society's useful
idiots.

CONTENTS

Expect cute plush animals and amniotic fluid and a more or less happy
ending for everybody, though the definition of happiness may depend on the
truncated emotional capacity of those unable to feel anything else. Some of
the characters are rich and famous, others are underage, and one is legally
dead, though you may like her the most of all.

APPEARANCE

We first encounter Molly June on her fifteenth deathday, when the
monitors in charge of deciding such things declare her safe for passengers.
Congratulating her on completing the only important stage of her development, they truck her in a padded skimmer to the arvie showroom where she
is claimed, right away, by one of the Living.

The fast sale surprises nobody, not the servos that trained her into her
current state of health and attractiveness, not the AI routines managing the
showroom, and least of all Molly June, who has spent her infancy and early
childhood having the ability to feel surprise, or anything beyond a vague
contentment, scrubbed from her emotional palate. Crying, she'd learned
while still capable of such things, brought punishment, while unconditional
acceptance of anything the engineers saw fit to provide brought light and
flower scent and warmth. By this point in her existence she'll greet anything
short of an exploding bomb with no reaction deeper than vague concern. Her
sale is a minor development by comparison: a happy development, reinforcing
her feelings of dull satisfaction. Don't feel sorry for her. Her entire life, or

more accurately death, is happy ending. All she has to do is spend the rest of it carrying a passenger.

VEHICLE SPECIFICATIONS

You think you need to know what Molly June looks like. You really don't, as it plays no role in her life. But as the information will assist you in feeling empathy for her, we will oblige anyway.

Molly June is a round-faced, button-nosed gamin, with pink lips and cheeks marked with permanent rose: her blonde hair framing her perfect face in parentheses of bouncy, luxurious curls. Her blue eyes, enlarged by years of genetic manipulation and corrective surgeries, are three times as large as the ones imperfect nature would have set in her face. Lemur-like, they dominate her features like a pair of pacific jewels, all moist and sad and adorable. They reveal none of her essential personality, which is not a great loss, as she's never been permitted to develop one.

Her body is another matter. It has been trained to perfection, with the kind of punishing daily regimen that can only be endured when the mind itself remains unaware of pain or exhaustion. She has worked with torn ligaments, with shattered joints, with disfiguring wounds. She has severed her spine and crushed her skull and has had both replaced, with the same ease her engineers have used, fourteen times, to replace her skin with a fresh version unmarked by scars or blemishes. What remains of her now is a wan amalgam of her own best-developed parts, most of them entirely natural, except for her womb, which is of course a plush, wired palace, far safer for its future occupant than the envelope of mere flesh would have provided. It can survive injuries capable of reducing Molly June to a smear.

In short, she is precisely what she should be, now that she's fifteen years past birth, and therefore, by all standards known to modern civilized society, Dead.

HEROINE

Jennifer Axioma-Singh has never been born and is therefore a significant distance away from being Dead.

She is, in every way, entirely typical. She has written operas, climbed mountains, enjoyed daredevil plunges from the upper atmosphere into vessels the size of teacups, finagled controlling stock in seventeen major multinationals, earned the hopeless devotion of any number of lovers, written her name in the sands of time, fought campaigns in a hundred conceptual wars, survived twenty regime changes and on three occasions had herself turned off so she could spend a year or two mulling the purpose of existence while her bloodstream spiced her insights with all the most fashionable hallucinogens.

She has accomplished all of this from within various baths of amniotic fluid.

Jennifer has yet to even open her eyes, which have never been allowed to fully develop past the first trimester and which still, truth be told, resemble black marbles behind lids of translucent onionskin. This doesn't actually deprive her of vision, of course. At the time she claims Molly June as her arvie, she's been indulging her visual cortex for seventy long years, zipping back and forth across the solar system collecting all the tourist chits one earns for seeing all the wonders of modern-day humanity: from the scrimshaw carving her immediate ancestors made of Mars to the radiant face of Unborn Jesus shining from the artfully re-configured multicolored atmosphere of Saturn. She has gloried in the catalogue of beautiful sights provided by God and all the industrious living people before her.

Throughout all this she has been blessed with vision far greater than any we will ever know ourselves, since her umbilical interface allows her sights capable of frying merely organic eyes, and she's far too sophisticated a person to be satisfied with the banal limitations of the merely visual spectrum. Decades of life have provided Jennifer Axioma-Singh with more depth than that. And something else: a perverse need, stranger than anything she's ever done, and impossible to indulge without first installing herself in a healthy young arvie.

ANCESTRY

Jennifer Axioma-Singh has owned arvies before, each one customized from the moment of its death. She's owned males, females, neuters, and several sexes only developed in the past decade. She's had arvies designed for athletic prowess, arvies designed for erotic sensation, and arvies designed for survival in harsh environments. She's even had one arvie with hypersensitive pain receptors: that, during a cold and confused period of masochism.

The last one before this, who she still misses, and sometimes feels a little guilty about, was a lovely girl named Peggy Sue, with a metabolism six times baseline normal and a digestive tract capable of surviving about a hundred separate species of nonstop abuse. Peggy Sue could down mountains of exotic delicacies without ever feeling full or engaging her gag reflex, and enjoyed taste receptors directly plugged into her pleasure centers. The slightest sip of coconut juice could flood her system with tidal waves of endorphin-crazed ecstasy. The things chocolate could do to her were downright obscene.

Unfortunately, she was still vulnerable to the negative effects of unhealthy eating, and went through four liver transplants and six emergency transfusions in the first ten years of Jennifer's occupancy.

The cumulative medical effect of so many years of determined gluttony mattered little to Jennifer Axioma-Singh, since her own caloric intake was regulated by devices that prevented the worst of Peggy Sue's excessive consumption from causing any damage on her side of the uterine wall. Jennifer's umbilical cord passed only those compounds necessary for keeping her alive and healthy. All Jennifer felt, through her interface with Peggy Sue's own sensory spectrum, was the joy of eating; all she experienced was the sheer, overwhelming treasury of flavor.

And if Peggy Sue became obese and diabetic and jaundiced in the meantime—as she did, enduring her last few years as Jennifer's arvie as an immobile mountain of reeking flab, with barely enough strength to position her mouth for another bite—then that was inconsequential as well, because she had progressed beyond prenatal development and had therefore passed beyond that stage of life where human beings can truly be said to have a soul.

PHILOSOPHY

Life, true life, lasts only from the moment of conception to the moment of birth. Jennifer Axioma-Singh subscribes to this principle, and clings to it in the manner of any concerned citizen aware that the very foundations of her society depend on everybody continuing to believe it without question. But she is capable of forming attachments, no matter how irrational, and she therefore felt a frisson of guilt once she decided she'd had enough and the machines performed the Caesarian Section that delivered her from Peggy Sue's pliant womb. After all, Peggy Sue's reward for so many years of service, euthanasia, seemed so inadequate, given everything she'd provided.

But what else could have provided fair compensation, given the shape Peggy Sue was in by then? Surely not a last meal! Jennifer Axioma-Singh, who had not been able to think of any alternatives, brooded over the matter until she came to the same conclusion always reached by those enjoying lives of privilege, which is that such inequities are all for the best and that there wasn't all that much she could do about them, anyway. Her liberal compassion had been satisfied by the heartfelt promise to herself that if she ever bought an arvie again she would take care to act more responsibly.

And this is what she holds in mind, as the interim pod carries her into the gleaming white expanse of the very showroom where fifteen-year-old Molly June awaits a passenger.

INSTALLATION

Molly June's contentment is like the surface of a vast, pacific ocean, unstirred by tide or wind. The events of her life plunge into that mirrored surface without effect, raising nary a ripple or storm. It remains unmarked even now, as the anesthetician and obstetrician mechs emerge from their recesses to guide her always-unresisting form from the waiting room couch where she'd been left earlier this morning, to the operating theatre where she'll begin the useful stage of her existence. Speakers in the walls calm her further with an arrangement of melodious strings designed to override any unwanted emotional static.

It's all quite humane: for even as Molly June lies down and puts her head back and receives permission to close her eyes, she remains wholly at peace. Her heartbeat does jog, a little, just enough to be noted by the instruments, when the servos peel back the skin of her abdomen, but even that instinctive burst of fear fades with the absence of any identifiable pain. Her reaction to the invasive procedure fades to a mere theoretical interest, akin to what Jennifer herself would feel regarding gossip about people she doesn't know living in places where she's never been.

Molly June drifts, thinks of blue waters and bright sunlight, misses Jennifer's installation inside her, and only reacts to the massive change in her body after the incisions are closed and Jennifer has recovered enough to kick. Then her lips curl in a warm but vacant smile. She is happy. Arvies might be dead, in legal terms, but they still love their passengers.

AMBITION

Jennifer doesn't announce her intentions until two days later, after growing comfortable with her new living arrangements. At that time Molly June is stretched out on a lounge on a balcony overlooking a city once known as Paris but which has undergone perhaps a dozen other names of fleeting popularity since then; at this point it's called something that could be translated as Eternal Night, because its urban planners have noted that it looks best when its towers were against a backdrop of darkness and therefore arranged to free it from the sunlight that previously diluted its beauty for half of every day.

The balcony, a popular spot among visitors, is not connected to any actual building. It just sits, like an unanchored shelf, at a high altitude calculated to showcase the lights of the city at their most decadently glorious. The city itself is no longer inhabited, of course; it contains some mechanisms important for the maintenance of local weather patterns but otherwise exists only to confront the night sky with constellations of reflective light. Jennifer, experiencing its beauty through Molly June's eyes, and the bracing high-altitude wind through Molly June's skin, feels a connection with the place that goes beyond aesthetics. She finds it fateful, resonant, and romantic, the perfect location to begin the greatest adventure of a life that has already provided her with so many.

She cranes Molly June's neck to survey the hundreds of other arvies sharing this balcony with her: all young, all beautiful, all pretending happiness while their jaded passengers struggle to plan new experiences not yet grown dull from surfeit. She sees arvies drinking, arvies wrestling, arvies declaiming vapid poetry, arvies coupling in threes and fours; arvies colored in various shades, fitted to various shapes and sizes; pregnant females, and impregnated males, all sufficiently transparent, to a trained eye like Jennifer's, for the essential characters of their respective passengers to shine on through. They all glow from the light of a moon that is not *the* moon, as the original was removed some time ago, but a superb piece of stagecraft designed to accentuate the city below to its greatest possible effect.

Have any of these people ever contemplated a stunt as over-the-top creative as the one Jennifer has in mind? Jennifer thinks not. More, she is certain not. She feels pride, and her arvie Molly June laughs, with a joy that threatens to bring the unwanted curse of sunlight back to the city of lights. And for the first time she announces her intentions out loud, without even raising her voice, aware that any words emerging from Molly June's mouth are superfluous, so long as the truly necessary signal travels the network that conveys Jennifer's needs to the proper facilitating agencies. None of the other arvies on the balcony even hear Molly June speak. But those plugged in hear Jennifer speak the words destined to set off a whirlwind of controversy.

I want to give birth.

CLARIFICATION

It is impossible to understate the perversity of this request.

Nobody gives Birth.

Birth is a messy and unpleasant and distasteful process that ejects living creatures from their warm and sheltered environment into a harsh and unforgiving one that nobody wants to experience except from within the protection of wombs either organic or artificial.

Birth is the passage from Life, and all its infinite wonders, to another place inhabited only by those who have been forsaken. It's the terrible ending that modern civilization has forestalled indefinitely, allowing human beings to live within the womb without ever giving up the rich opportunities for experience and growth. It's sad, of course, that for Life to even be possible a large percentage of potential Citizens have to be permitted to pass through that terrible veil, into an existence where they're no good to anybody except as spare parts and manual laborers and arvies, but there are peasants in even the most enlightened societies, doing the hard work so the important people don't have to. The best any of us can do about that is appreciate their contribution while keeping them as complacent as possible.

The worst thing that could ever be said about Molly June's existence is that when the Nurseries measured her genetic potential, found it wanting, and decided she should approach Birth unimpeded, she was also humanely deprived of the neurological enhancements that allow first-trimester fetuses all the rewards and responsibilities of Citizenship. She never developed enough to fear the passage that awaited her, and never knew how sadly limited her existence would be. She spent her all-too-brief Life in utero ignorant of all the blessings that would forever be denied her, and has been kept safe and content and happy and drugged and stupid since birth. After all, as a wise person once said, it takes a perfect vassal to make a perfect vessel. Nobody can say that there's anything wrong about that. But the dispossession of people like her, that makes the lives of people like Jennifer Axioma-Singh possible, remains a distasteful thing decent people just don't talk about.

Jennifer's hunger to experience birth from the point of view of a mother, grunting and sweating to expel another unfortunate like Molly June out of the only world that matters, into the world of cold slavery, thus strikes the vast majority as offensive, scandalous, unfeeling, selfish, and cruel. But since nobody has ever imagined a Citizen demented enough to want such a thing, nobody has ever thought to make it against the law. So the powers that be indulge Jennifer's perversity, while swiftly passing laws to ensure that nobody will ever be permitted such license ever again; and all the machinery of modern medicine is turned to the problem of just how to give her what she wants. And, before long, wearing Molly June as proxy, she gets knocked up.

IMPLANTATION

There is no need for any messy copulation. Sex, as conducted through arvies, still makes the world go round, prompting the usual number of bittersweet affairs, tempestuous breakups, turbulent love triangles, and silly love songs.

In her younger days, before the practice palled out of sheer repetition, Jennifer had worn out several arvies fucking like a bunny. But there has never been any danger of unwanted conception, at any time, not with the only possible source of motile sperm being the nurseries that manufacture it as needed without recourse to nasty antiquated testes. These days, zygotes and embryos are the province of the assembly line. Growing one inside an arvie, let alone one already occupied by a human being, presents all manner of bureaucratic difficulties involving the construction of new protocols and the rearranging of accepted paradigms and any amount of official eye-rolling, but once all that is said and done, the procedures turn out to be quite simple, and the surgeons have little difficulty providing Molly June with a second womb capable of growing Jennifer Axioma-Singh's daughter while Jennifer Axioma-Singh herself floats unchanging a few protected membranes away.

Unlike the womb that houses Jennifer, this one will not be wired in any way. Its occupant will not be able to influence Molly June's actions or enjoy the full spectrum of Molly June's senses. She will not understand, except in the most primitive, undeveloped way, what or where she is or how well she's being cared for. Literally next to Jennifer Axioma-Singh, she will be by all reasonable comparisons a mindless idiot. But she will live, and grow, for as long as it takes for this entire perverse whim of Jennifer's to fully play itself out.

GESTATION (1)

In the months that follow, Jennifer Axioma-Singh enjoys a novel form of celebrity. This is hardly anything new for her, of course, as she has been a celebrity several times before and if she lives her expected lifespan, expects to be one several times again. But in an otherwise unshockable world, she has never experienced, or even witnessed, that special, nearly extinct species of celebrity that comes from eliciting shock, and which was once best-known by the antiquated term, *notoriety.*

This, she glories in. This, she milks for every last angstrom. This, she surfs like an expert, submitting to countless interviews, constructing countless bon mots, pulling every string capable of scandalizing the public.

She says, "I don't see the reason for all the fuss."

She says, "People used to share wombs all the time."

She says, "It used to happen naturally, with multiple births: two or three or four or even seven of us, crowded together like grapes, sometimes absorbing each other's body parts like cute young cannibals."

She says, "I don't know whether to call what I'm doing pregnancy or performance art."

She says, "Don't you think Molly June looks special? Don't you think she glows?"

She says, "When the baby's born, I may call her Halo."

She says, "No, I don't see any problem with condemning her to Birth. If it's good enough for Molly June, it's good enough for my child."

And she says, "No, I don't care what anybody thinks. It's my arvie, after all."

And she fans the flames of outrage higher and higher, until public sympathies turn to the poor slumbering creature inside the sac of amniotic fluid, whose life and future have already been so cruelly decided. Is she truly limited enough to be condemned to Birth? Should she be stabilized and given her own chance at life, before she's expelled, sticky and foul, into the cold, harsh world inhabited only by arvies and machines? Or is Jennifer correct in maintaining the issue subject to a mother's whim?

Jennifer says, "All I know is that this is the most profound, most spiritually fulfilling, experience of my entire life." And so she faces the crowds, real or virtual, using Molly June's smile and Molly June's innocence, daring the analysts to count all the layers of irony.

GESTATION (II)

Molly June experiences the same few months in a fog of dazed, but happy confusion, aware that she's become the center of attention, but unable to comprehend exactly why. She knows that her lower back hurts and that her breasts have swelled and that her belly, flat and soft before, has inflated to several times its previous size; she knows that she sometimes feels something moving inside her, that she sometimes feels sick to her stomach, and that her eyes water more easily than they ever have before, but none of this disturbs the vast, becalmed surface of her being. It is all good, all the more reason for placid contentment.

Her only truly bad moments come in her dreams, when she sometimes finds herself standing on a gray, colorless field, facing another version of herself half her own size. The miniature Molly June stares at her from a distance that Molly June herself cannot cross, her eyes unblinking, her expression merciless. Tears glisten on both her cheeks. She points at Molly June and she enunciates a single word, incomprehensible in any language Molly June knows, and irrelevant to any life she's ever been allowed to live: "Mother."

The unfamiliar word makes Molly June feel warm and cold, all at once. In her dream she wets herself, trembling from the sudden warmth running down her thighs. She trembles, bowed by an incomprehensible need to apologize. When she wakes, she finds real tears still wet on her cheeks, and real pee soaking the mattress between her legs. It frightens her.

But those moments fade. Within seconds the calming agents are already flooding her bloodstream, overriding any internal storms, removing all possible sources of disquiet, making her once again the obedient arvie she's supposed to be. She smiles and coos as the servos tend to her bloated form, scrubbing her flesh and applying their emollients. Life is so good, she thinks. And if it's not, well, it's not like there's anything she can do about it, so why worry?

BIRTH (I)

Molly June goes into labor on a day corresponding to what we call Thursday, the insistent weight she has known for so long giving way to a series of contractions violent enough to reach her even through her cocoon of deliberately engineered apathy. She cries and moans and shrieks infuriated, inarticulate things that might have been curses had she ever been exposed to any, and she begs the shiny machines around her to take away the pain with the same efficiency that they've taken away everything else. She even begs her passenger—that is, the passenger she knows about, the one she's sensed seeing through her eyes and hearing through her ears and carrying out conversations with her mouth—she begs her passenger *for mercy*. She hasn't ever asked that mysterious godlike presence for anything, because it's never occurred to her that she might be entitled to anything, but she needs relief now, and she demands it, shrieks for it, can't understand why she isn't getting it.

The answer, which would be beyond her understanding even if provided, is that the wet, sordid physicality of the experience is the very point.

BIRTH (II)

Jennifer Axioma-Singh is fully plugged in to every cramp, every twitch, every pooled droplet of sweat. She experiences the beauty and the terror and the exhaustion and the certainty that this will never end. She finds it resonant and evocative and educational on levels lost to a mindless sack of meat like Molly June. And she comes to any number of profound revelations about the nature of life and death and the biological origins of the species and the odd, inexplicable attachment brood mares have always felt for the squalling sacks of flesh and bone their bodies have gone to so much trouble to expel.

CONCLUSIONS

It's like any other work, she thinks. Nobody ever spent months and months building a house only to burn it down the second they pounded in the last nail. You put that much effort into something and it belongs to you, forever, even if the end result is nothing but a tiny creature that eats and shits and makes demands on your time.

This still fails to explain why anybody would invite this kind of pain again, let alone the three or four or seven additional occasions common before the unborn reached their ascendancy. Oh, it's interesting enough to start with, but she gets the general idea long before the thirteenth hour rolls around and the market share for her real-time feed dwindles to the single digits. Long before that, the pain has given way to boredom. At the fifteenth hour she gives up entirely, turns off her inputs, and begins to catch up on her personal correspondence, missing the actual moment when Molly June's daughter, Jennifer's womb-mate and sister, is expelled head-first into a shiny silver tray, pink and bloody and screaming at the top of her lungs, sharing oxygen for the very first time, but, by every legal definition, Dead.

AFTERMATH (JENNIFER)

As per her expressed wishes, Jennifer Axioma-Singh is removed from Molly June and installed in a new arvie that very day. This one's a tall, lithe, gloriously beautiful creature with fiery eyes and thick, lush lips: her name's

Bernadette Ann, she's been bred for endurance in extreme environments, and she'll soon be taking Jennifer Axioma-Singh on an extended solo hike across the restored continent of Antarctica.

Jennifer is so impatient to begin this journey that she never lays eyes on the child whose birth she has just experienced. There's no need. After all, she's never laid eyes on anything, not personally. And the pictures are available online, should she ever feel the need to see them. Not that she ever sees any reason for that to happen. The baby, itself, was never the issue here. Jennifer didn't want to be a mother. She just wanted to give birth. All that mattered to her, in the long run, was obtaining a few months of unique vicarious experience, precious in a lifetime likely to continue for as long as the servos still manufacture wombs and breed arvies. All that matters now is moving on. Because time marches onward, and there are never enough adventures to fill it.

AFTERMATH (MOLLY JUNE)

She's been used, and sullied, and rendered an unlikely candidate to attract additional passengers. She is therefore earmarked for compassionate disposal.

AFTERMATH (THE BABY)

The baby is, no pun intended, another issue. Her biological mother Jennifer Axioma-Singh has no interest in her, and her birth-mother Molly June is on her way to the furnace. A number of minor health problems, barely worth mentioning, render her unsuitable for a useful future as somebody's arvie. Born, and by that precise definition Dead, she could very well follow Molly June down the chute.

But she has a happier future ahead of her. It seems that her unusual gestation and birth have rendered her something of a collector's item, and there are any number of museums aching for a chance to add her to their permanent collections. Offers are weighed, and terms negotiated, until the ultimate agreement is signed, and she finds herself shipped to a freshly constructed habitat in a wildlife preserve in what used to be Ohio.

AFTERMATH (THE CHILD)

She spends her early life in an automated nursery with toys, teachers, and careful attention to her every physical need. At age five she's moved to a cage consisting of a two-story house on four acres of nice green grass, beneath what looks like a blue sky dotted with fluffy white clouds. There's even a playground. She will never be allowed out, of course, because there's no place for her to go, but she does have human contact of a sort: a different arvie almost every day, inhabited for the occasion by a long line of Living who now think it might be fun to experience child-rearing for a while.

Each one has a different face, each one calls her by a different name, and their treatment of her ranges all the way from compassionate to violently abusive.

Now eight, the little girl has long since given up on asking the good ones to stay, because she knows they won't. Nor does she continue to dream about what she'll do when she grows up, since it's also occurred to her that she'll never know anything but this life in this fishbowl. Her one consolation is wondering about her real mother: where she is now, what she looks like, whether she ever thinks about the child she left behind, and whether it would have been possible to hold on to her love, had it ever been offered, or even possible.

The questions remain the same, from day to day. But the answers are hers to imagine, and they change from minute to minute: as protean as her moods, or her dreams, or the reasons why she might have been condemned to this cruelest of all possible punishments.

MERRYTHOUGHTS

BILL KTE'PI

Jaima Coleman isn't eating dessert tonight because they're cutting Duncan's wings off. Mama and Papa have him pressed against the wall, pinning his wings against the mud room's bluebell wallpaper, Grandpa feeling for the spot like the knuckle of a drumstick, the place where you can put the saw and cut between bones instead of through one. No cobbler is worth having to see that, not even Grandma's best Redhaven Peach with the clove sprinkled on top. Duncan's thirteen and he's the only boy, the last boy. His wings are the last to go, and he's awfuldamn loud.

They cut Jaima's wings off when she was a baby. She doesn't remember, but she says she does if they ask, says she remembers what the choir sounded like before she was cut off from it, and what the sky looked like when she could still see the eleven secret colors. They cut Jaima's off when she was a baby, because "girls can't take the pain," at least that's what they say, that's the tradition. Boys wait until they're thirteen, but "girls can't take it." It won't matter now. Duncan's the last, and unless him and Jaima were to marry, there won't be any more. It takes two to tango, Mama says, and peoplefolk are pretty, but there ain't no more having babies with them than there is with the moon or the spoon. May as well bang two rocks together and hope you make a puppy, is how Grandma puts it. Jaima drew pictures of it in kindergarten, magic stone puppies like gargoyles falling out of struck stones.

After Jaima finished her peanut soup and Awendaw spoonbread, she'd excused herself and gone outside to the fallow hill west of the tobacco fields, and now she's sitting on the stone wall where the old well used to be, watching the ravens in the peach tree play cats cradle with a piece of twine they fished from somewheres or other. Peach cobbler's Duncan's favorite, warm so the ice cream would melt against it. He got to have a Cheerwine from the garage fridge and a shot of Grandpa's brandy mixed with honey, too. He strutted about it all day, but Jaima wouldn't trade places with him now. It's not the first time she's glad she's not a boy. Boys get it worst, and they aren't supposed to play make-believe.

The trees that grow along the stone wall look mean when it gets dark, and she doesn't like to play out here when that happens. But right now it's still hot and bright, sunset still a summer ways off. There's time enough she could play cowboys if she wanted. She can't have any friends over until the end of the week, when Duncan will be better. *Entertain yourself, Jaima,* Mama said. It isn't long before Papa comes out, walking back to town where he lives with That Woman, with his shoulders hunched and his hands stuffed in the pockets of pants that need mending. That makes Jaima want to go inside even less.

She plays Princess of the Meadow and If I Had a Pony What Would I Name It, and the sun wanes but it'll be a while yet before Mama'll ring the dinner bell that means you gotta come back to the house no matter what. Jaima's trying to decide whether she wants to be the good guy or the bad guy in cowboys when a man lands in the field. She probably can't tell it's a man at first, not for real, but even without her wings she usually knows things before she sees them for sure. The sky scars yellow, the trees whistle their leaves off right before he slams into the dirt, and the ground buckles like that part of the carpet where the pipe leaked. Layers of grass, soil, and rock intermingle around him, and smoke or steam or something thick as fog rises, smelling like barbecues and laundromats.

When she sees the costume, she recognizes him—the Typhoon, the most famous of all superheroes, and the best and strongest. His costume is green and black and dashing, but now it's torn and scorched, and his handsome face is bruised. The superheroes have been fighting. It's on the news all the time. Something went wrong, and the superheroes are fighting each other. Her favorite is the Black Hole, because she saw him once, like everyone did, the time the sun came to life and he saved the world from it. She saw him clear as the creek, even though he was a million miles away and eight minutes before.

"Little girl," the Typhoon says as he brushes dirt from himself, "why are you crying?"

Is she? She didn't realize it. When he sits up, his elbow dislodges from a ledge of rock. She's never heard before the sound of rock breaking without any impact like a sledgehammer—rock breaking just because something very strong breaks it. It isn't a sound she'll forget. She wipes her cheeks with the back of her hands because her palms are grimy from playing outside, and sure enough, her face is wet. "I dunno," she says.

"Where are your wings?" He winces as he gets up, his arm funny against his side. "Shite."

"They cut them off," she says, vaguely waving at the house. "How did you know?"

He points to her chest. "X-ray vision," he says. "You have a wishbone. It's the bone on the sternum that connects the wing muscles, keeps you strong so you can fly. We used to call them 'merrythoughts', but that was hundreds of years ago."

She does? She has a wishbone? "What happened to you?" she asks. "Are you okay? Why can you fly without wings?" She didn't mean to ask this last one, but she's always wondered, because she can't fly, and at least she used to have wings. Duncan used to fly sometimes, wasn't supposed to but she caught him sometimes, saw him in the sky. Up up in that hard blue sky. Be no more of that now.

"Tell you the truth," he says, "I'm not even sure myself anymore." He smiles, and it's a sad smile, with another wince. But he sure is handsome, in a noble swashbuckling way, like Will Turner.

Jaima cups her hands together and looks down at them the way she would if she were holding water in them, the way Grandma does when she wishes she could pray. Then she gets up and straightens out her dress, which is too dirty to be presentable by half, and patched where brambles loved her a little too well. Jaima's never prayed cause it ain't allowed, not for her and hers, and it ain't allowed to tell anybody that either, so she can't ever ask anyone to pray for her. *It just is as it is, Jaima*, is what everyone tells her. Even Duncan, though she knows he don't get it any better than she does. "I guess you oughta come inside, Mister Typhoon," she says. "Get you cleaned up, huh? No house closer'n our'n and my brother Duncan he'll sure be glad to meet you, I bet."

There is faint surprise in his eyes and she realizes with that same knowing-before-seeing that he is still always startled when someone recognizes him, still after all this time. Like he ain't never heard of the teevee, this one. "That'd be a kindness," he says. "Long as it's all right by your parents."

She nods, takes his hand and leads him. He shudders in pain when she touches his hand, and moves to the other side of her, lets her take the other hand as they walk. "Papa's gone, but I'll ask my Mama."

"I'm sorry to hear that," he says, misunderstanding, and it ain't for her to set him right.

The Typhoon finishes the leftovers and sits by Duncan's bed for an hour talking to him, having been told the boy's sick and recovering. No one is much in awe of him, which seems to put him at ease. Duncan's too hurt for awe, and the grown-ups, well, it takes more than superheroes to widen their eyes.

Not Jaima's, though. She's full of questions, and he doesn't mind answering as long as she doesn't interrupt. Yes, he knows the Black Hole, and they're friends. He's a nice man. No, he doesn't think the superheroes should be fighting either. Yes, Majestia is very pretty in person, just like on teevee. No, he doesn't have any pets, but he used to have a crocodile.

"For real?" she asks, and he laughs.

"Yeah," he says. "For real. When I was still a boy, before I left the island I grew up on. It was a long growin' up, with all manner o' thing." There's a lilt to his voice like when Duncan watches *Doctor Who*.

"Why'd you leave it?" Mama asks. "Why'd you come here, why'd you become the Typhoon?" There is a challenge in her voice.

"I don't know," he says, and he sounds tired—no, he sounds like Papa, sounds like Papa when he's tired of something just as it starts. "No, I do. Everyone knows. I've talked about it before."

"The Hook," Duncan says, and the Typhoon nods.

"The Hook escaped the destruction of the Never. I knew no one else would know how to deal with him." He sounds sad, he sounds like Papa and Grandpa do when they talk about losing their wings, which they stopped doing about a year ago, knowing Duncan would be next. "No one else would take him seriously until it was too late."

"But if you hadn't come," Jaima says, "there'd be no Shadow, and maybe the Hook would be the only bad guy." She takes a bite of her butter-and-sugar sandwich, happy that she's getting a snack so late at night and nobody's told her to go to bed yet.

"That's not true," Duncan protests. "There's the Clockwork Pirate and the whole Mischief Brigade, you know that. There's Mistress Sputnik and Injun Joe and the Beatnik."

"But maybe that's because of the Shadow. Maybe if it was only the Hook, somebody else would've beaten him, and once he was beaten, all these other supervillains wouldn't have entered the picture at all cause they'd see there weren't no chance in it."

The Typhoon holds up a hand when Mama swats her. "It's nothing I haven't heard before," he says. "There's really no knowing one way or the other what would have happened, Jemma."

"Jaima," Mama corrects him curtly.

He looks hurt. "Jaima. Of course. I'm sorry, Moira."

That's the wrong name too, Mama's name is Mary, but she doesn't correct him, just rolls her eyes. Jaima frowns at her last bite of sandwich, the soft Bunny bread practically showing her fingertips, and kicks at the table.

"That's enough, Jaima," Mama says.

"I didn't do nothing!"

"I think it's somebody's bed time."

"I wanna stay up until Mister Typhoon goes home!"

Mama eyes the Typhoon, whose arm is bandaged up now in a sling. "It's late. You can stay in the spare room if you want."

"If there's no objection, that'd be a kindness."

Grandma's in the door with pillows and blankets. "It sure would," she says. "But you won't get a better breakfast in town. That damn Susan Piker at the Evangeline can't cook eggs worth a damn."

"Well," the Typhoon says. "I'd hate to subject myself to a terrible breakfast."

When Jaima wakes up in the morning, the Typhoon is still asleep on the cot in the sewing room, the covers bunched up and the pillows folded in half under his head. He's not a sound sleeper, and she peers at him from the cracked-open doorway in her feetie pajamas. She used to have a stuffed rabbit named Black Hole and got him a stuffed kitty named Typhoon so they could play together, but they're both away in the box in the closet now that she's older.

"Grandma," she says when she sits down at the breakfast table. Grandma's making soft grits and waffle syrup for Duncan, food for when you're sick. "Mister Typhoon says I got a wishbone. He says he can see it with his X-rays vision."

"That boy says a mite too much," Grandma says absently. "You want eggs or pancakes, youngun?"

"Cain't I have both? We got company."

"We got company, so there ain't enough eggs for both. Now which it gonna be?"

"I reckon syrup on eggs is better than hot sauce on pancakes," Jaima muses.

"I reckon you're a crazy little pigeon, but long as you eat your eggs, that's not today's bother."

"Course I'll eat 'em," she says. "I need my energy. Mister Typhoon's gonna show me how to fly today, without wings."

Grandma stops what she's doing, turns around and looks at her. When the spoon clatters against the bowl of grits, she sets it down atable. "He put that fool notion on your head?"

"Naw," she says, "but I know he can do it. Even if he did fall down, I seen him fly on teevee."

"See all kindsa things on teevee," Grandma says, and brings Duncan his breakfast. When she comes back, she makes pancakes for everyone, forgetting Jaima said eggs, but she doesn't complain. There's a wrong current in the house, and even Jaima knows that, knows it ain't just about Duncan. She rubs her chest while they eat, feeling for the wishbone.

"You think I could make a wish on my wishbone, Mister Typhoon?" she asks.

The Typhoon coughs on a bite of pancake and then laughs, and so does Grandpa, and even Grandma smiles. Mama scowls, not at Jaima but the rest of them. "It's no laughing matter," she says. "Nothing funny about it, not a thing."

No one says anything. The Typhoon starts to, but doesn't even get a whole sound out.

"So could I?" Jaima asks, because whether it's funny or not doesn't answer her question any.

"No, honey," Grandpa says.

Mama puts her hand on Grandpa's, instead of outright telling him he's wrong. "But everyone does," she says, not looking straight at any of them, hiding her eyes. "Everyone makes a wish when she breaks, Jaima."

Everyone finishes their pancakes in the silence of forks scraping against plates, eyes on the table and knees too close together. "They used to call them Mary thoughts," Jaima says, but nobody answers.

"Don't expect me to think it's coincidence, do you?" Grandpa asks the Typhoon. Jaima can hear them on the front step of the barn, which is where Grandpa keeps his pouch and his flask. "You showin' up here of all places, to lick your wounds."

"I got hit," the Typhoon says. They're talkin' hushed. "I got hit hard and I fell."

"Yeah," Grandpa says, and Jaima sits against the side of the barn where sometimes she plays shouting games because the sound doesn't carry as well to the house from here, so she won't bother anybody. "You're a damn fool, but not too much to know who loves you."

"Moira?" the Typhoon asks.

"All right, 'Moira', and Kate too, damn it. And Kate's mama, and her before that. All the women of the family. You ain't here for Jaima, is what I come to tell you."

"Johnny!" the Typhoon says. "You know that's not why I'm here."

"And I'm remindin' you. Even when she's older. This family's quit of you, Peter. We'll mend you when you're sick, we'll feed you an' you're hungry, but no more. You understand? You keep to your cot."

"You don't have to worry about me and Kate," the Typhoon says.

"Damn right I don't!" The air around the corner smells like the tobacco that grows all over the east fields, a smell Jaima's lived with all her life. It smells better curin' than it does burnin',' but she reckons that's true of most the world. "Kate may love you, but it don't make her love me any less. You got to understand that about Mary too, kid. Christ, you never did grow up, did you? Not really. You get hurt, you still come lookin' for somebody to mother you. It don't matter to you whether she's Moira or Mary or the next one. You play dress-up and go off on adventures."

"I'm given to understand that Moira's husband passed on?"

Grandpa laughs. "Passed on down the street for a woman he isn't tired of yet! I love Mary, but she's a hard soul, you understand. Tom's a chickenshit, but he ain't all the way out of the picture yet, she just keeps driving him off in the hopes he'll fight her on it. You don't mess where you oughtn't, you understand?"

The Typhoon shakes his head, Jaima can see his shadow moving, and the shadow of smoke rising around them. "There was another like you, you know. Like all you all, someone who used to have wings, someone who saw things a little differently."

"Yeah?" This is a new tone in Grandpa's voice.

"Gabriel. You seen him on the newsreels?"

"Used to did, when Mary was a girl."

"That was him. Passed on now. Years ago, I guess."

"He didn't have any kids, did he? Brothers, sisters?"

"No. No, it was just him."

Grandpa sighs. "That's a damn shame."

"Johnny, come on. Are you ever going to let me know what's going on?"

"Ain't nothing going on anymore. That's the thing of it. We fought a war a long time ago. Not me, not my father, but a father long before him. The war ended centuries ago, and there wasn't nothing much left for them that survived it, so they came here, settled down. Old soldiers retirin' to raise families."

"Georgia?"

Grandpa snorts. "Earth, Peter. Christ's sake. This family ain't even been in Macon County two hundred years, you know that. It don't none of it matter now. The war's long ended, one way or the other, and what did we get for it? We're the last of us, now. Jaima and Duncan, there won't be no more. I had a sister died of pox, and you know about Kate's brother."

"You don't know you have to be the last."

Jaima peers around the corner, and the Typhoon's sitting with his elbows on his knees, leaning over smoking a hand-rolled cigarette with Grandpa, who keeps taking sips from the flask, licking his lips.

"There ain't nobody left. You won't be surprised to know we don't breed with humans. Just don't work."

"Well," the Typhoon says. "Maybe I'm not a hundred percent human, though. When you think about it."

Grandpa doesn't say anything to that, until he's finished his cigarette and there's just a tiny nub left that he crushes between his old fingertips. "Don't put your nose on anything you shouldn't be sniffin' around. I can still lick you, Peter. Now or then, it don't matter. Put that on your mind and don't dawdle about getting back to your fancy work up in the sky. If you think that just cause we help you means we need you, you're humaner than you think."

Jaima plays Princess Jaima of the Winged Folk, running down the fallow hill with her arms spread, running as fast as she can so she can feel the air in her hair and her sweat, and it's almost like flying. It almost is. She runs along the stones of the old wall, jumping as high and as far as she can with each stride so she can feel that hanging moment in the air when she isn't falling yet and isn't jumping anymore. She keeps touching her chest, where her wishbone is. She skins both her knees and one of her elbows, and gets a bump on her head, but there's no one around so she doesn't cry. She might later if Grandma notices she tore her shirt at the collar.

"There's no need to take a stand," someone says, voice rising from a quiet she hadn't heard. She's been climbing up in the trees, among those three trees near the base of the hills that are so old that she can climb from the branch of one to the branch of the next, as long as Mama and Papa aren't looking and distracting her by yelling that she'll break her fool neck.

"There's no need to take a stand, I'm the one who started it," the Typhoon says. He has Mama in his arms, in the sumac grove where Grandma goes sometimes to get sumac for lemonade. Mama has her back to him, so that the Typhoon's arms are around her waist, and she has her own arms folded against her chest like she's pretending she isn't letting him. "Jaima's right about that much. Without me, there'd be no Shadow. Without the Shadow, no war. I came to help, but maybe I set it all off. Maybe I should have trusted them to handle the Hook on their own."

"Maybe you should have killed him," Mama says. "Maybe you just should have killed him before it was ever a problem, or after you came here and saw all he done."

"You know the Typhoon doesn't kill," he murmurs, and she snorts. "We could make a fresh start," he says. "We're different now, older."

"I am," she says.

"I am too. Look at me, look how I'm dressed! Look how plain."

"In my husband's clothes." They almost fit him, but not well.

"We could have a family. We could start a family."

She shakes her head, but leans back against his chest. "Jaima was the last. I—can't have more children. It was a hard birth. Harder than most."

"You don't seem to hold it against her."

Mama peers up at him. He's so tall he towers over her, and Mama's not a slight woman. "Love her more for it. But we'd never be able to start a family, Peter. The one I've got's more than enough."

"Well," the Typhoon says. "Jaima—when she's older—there's no saying I can't, I mean I could conceive—"

She turns around, wriggling in his arms, to fully face him. "You're sayin' we could be together and have a family of you putting children on my daughter. When she's old enough."

His face screws up and he sighs. "It sounds so crazy when you put it like that, but how can you stand to be the last? How can anyone, Moira?"

"I guess you could tell me that."

They neither of them say anything more, and he leans to kiss her when there's the grind of gravel from the road, the spin of wheels and an old horn leaned on. They both freeze, and Jaima turns to look up the hill. She can see what they can't from the ground, the old blue pickup rounding the bend.

"Tom," Mama says, amused and surprised. "He finally fixed that fucking truck like I been naggin' him to do." She pushes her way out of the Typhoon's arms.

"Moira—" he says. "No, wait—Mary. It's Mary. Mary—"

"No," she says. "That's enough. A little flattering attention is fun and all at my age, but I've had all I need, 'Mister Typhoon.' Just touch my cheek, and get on your way. That busted wing of yours looks like it's healed up all right. You always did heal fast."

"Not so fast as some." He leans to kiss her and she presses her cheek against his mouth and stalks up the hill without looking back at him.

Jaima and the Typhoon both watch her go, and Jaima jumps down to the ground. The Typhoon doesn't seem surprised to see her. They walk a little ways up the hill towards the old well, in time to see Mama and Papa embracing. Their arms are tight around each other and their mouths together, nothing like the way the Typhoon held Mama.

She looks up at the superhero. "Are you gonna teach me to fly like you do, without wings?" she asks.

He looks back at her, and finally puts his hand out. "I'll tell you a secret. Every time I fly, I think I've forgotten how. I don't think I can teach it anymore, but I can show you what it's like. Would you like that?"

She takes his hand and nods. "But you gotta bring me back, Mister Typhoon."

The Typhoon cradles her against his chest, a hand on the back of her head like you'd hold a baby, and the ground falls away. It's fast but it feels floaty, the wind rushes less than it does running down the hill. Like swimming without the wet. The sky surrounds them and the dots of Mama and Papa and the house and the barn become smaller until you'd hardly remember where they were.

"Wow," Jaima says, and the Typhoon laughs.

"You're not scared," he says.

She shakes her head. "Grandpa could still lick you."

He laughs hard at that, and she feels sad for him because he doesn't believe it. "What would you like to see?" A V-formation of birds passes underfoot, and clouds take on wispier shapes here. It's strange seeing a cloud from the side.

"Show me where the winged people came," she says. "When we first came to Earth like Grandpa said."

"I—I don't know where that is," he says. "Somewhere in Europe, I guess. Maybe the Middle East. Jerusalem would make sense, or Babylon. That's Iraq now."

"Well," she says. "Show me where the superheroes are fighting."

He shakes his head violently. "No. No, it's dangerous there. Rules aren't the same there."

They soar in silence, in a high blue where you can see both the sun and stars.

"I guess you can just bring me home, then, Mister Typhoon," Jaima says.

He lands softly, his feet touching the ground like she imagines you would if you were parachuting, and places her down gently. "I think I need to go now," he says, looking up the hill, at Mama and Papa laughing in the back of the pickup.

Jaima looks up at him and stands on tip-toes and he leans down to her. She presses her palm against his chest. "You need to be more careful with this," she says very seriously to him. "You don't get a wish if it breaks. You're not like us."

He grins at that and kisses the crown of her head. "Be careful yourself," he says. "Be careful growing up."

"It's not as scary as you think," she says, but he might not hear her as he disappears into the sky.

She walks back up the hill, thinking if Mama and Papa are happy enough, maybe they can all get in the pickup and go into town and get ice cream, in the nice little glass dishes that curve like petals. Rum raisin. Or chocolate orange. By the time she gets to the top of the hill, she's changed her mind about which flavor four times, and has just taken it for granted that ice cream will be in her near future. She touches her chest and tells herself to save the wish until she really needs it, because you only get one.

THE RED BRIDE

SAMANTHA HENDERSON

You are to imagine, Twigling, the Red Bride to be a human, such as yourself, although she is in truth a creature of the Var.

I'm guessing you've heard the kitchen staff speak of the Red Bride, because you've a quick ear and the wit to pick up a few words of Varian, and you're not so arrogant as most of your race, to think the back-chatter of servants and slaves as no account. You're small for your species, and quiet, and I'm wise to that trick of yours of tucking up under the table and staying so still everyone forgets you're there. Still, they should be cannier than to imagine a human Twigling like you wouldn't overhear.

You must be patient. The Red Bride isn't a story I've pondered back and forth in my head and made like a Terran bedtime tale, all chopped up nicely for your eager birdlike gape. I must think it through in the telling and you must open up your mind and believe that a dog-which-is-not-a-dog may be hatched from an egg with all the knowledge it needs to hunt. The story of the Red Bride is a slave's tale in slave speech, which I do not generally hold in my head around humans lest my face betray me, so I must shift words around from one meaning to another like stones on a reckoning-board, each stone taking meaning from a square where another stone was a moment before.

Also, I think the story of the Red Bride is Varian entirely, nothing human at all, and doesn't come from the shared tales the scholars say that all the Seeded Races share in common.

If your mother overheard me mention the Seeded Races, and that the scholars begin to say that human and the Var are alike, she would have me whipped. You know that yourself, Twigling. But past this night, I do not think that your mother's whip will be used for anything after tonight save lashing a bundle of fiber-thorn.

The Red Bride is a Var and so squat, stunted, and ape-like to you, but you are to see her as we do and therefore beautiful, straight and strong, with piercing eyes and poised like a warrior. However you think of those princesses of yours, that you watch in your holo-stories and then beg me to weave into your bedtime tales—however you think of the most beautiful of them, or the most adventurous, the one you want to be—that is what she looks like.

You must understand, Twigling, that your princesses are all very ugly to me.

The Red Bride is born again and again, as our holy people are, over the span of many years. In the story in your head you might say that she is one of a long line of women that are born each from another. I notice that in the stories humans tell their young a woman who lives forever is a monstrous thing—a demon that kills the newborn, or that runs about on chicken-feet, and not to be honored as we would honor her.

The story doesn't start with the Bride, but with the Vallhan, a leader that is born, unknowing, when the Var have greatest need of him. He is not born a dreamer, or a gatherer, or an arbiter, as are our males, but all these things together. In your story, you must think of a village boy who has found an ancient sword. The Vallhan's mind is like a prism, gathering and scattering light, and information, and knowledge, and pain.

It's quiet—yes, it's very quiet. You don't hear the clatter from the kitchen, the servants getting ready for tomorrow's anniversary feast and celebrations. They're not preparing the Great Room, or polishing the silver. I wonder if your parent's guests, come to the ambassador's house for this holiday, snug in their bedrooms with a Var outside each door to supply their every need—I wonder if they notice anything strange about it.

There comes a time when the Vallhan has seen enough, and bears all he can bear, but he cannot act without his bride, the Red Bride, beside him.

So far this tale is easy to tell but now it gets difficult, for I don't have time to shift from what the words mean in slave talk to Semla-Varian (we have as many languages as bloodlines, you know, although as far as the humans are concerned we all speak the same debased patois), to bedtime-speak. My mind's rusty—I've been living among the Terrans too long. You are to imagine that the Red Bride must be sought, hunted down by a dog, a hound. This hound hatches from an egg laid by a monstrous bird, like the ones whose bones are stone in the Vandian Mountains, that the scholars say are like those dug out of Terran soil. The egg is made from the belly-stones of the Var that go to the mountain-lakes to die; the bird eats them, and crushes them inside it, and makes it all as one: egg and shell and hound.

You remember the lake, and the belly-stones, don't you, Twigling? I know you followed us that day we took old Impiti to the mountain on his dying-day. I didn't say anything, because I know you were fond of Impiti and brought him water when he was thirsty and he feared to move from his place in the children's wing. And also I know that you lied to your mother and said you had sent him on an errand when he was really sleeping. I didn't say anything, because I thought that it might be a good thing for a human child to see how a Var died.

When I saw that you understood that the moonstones your people find on the shores of lakes and small seas, which are sacred to us, are the belly-stones of the Var that die there, I almost killed you. I saw you look from the white bare ribs of the dead to the opalescent spill of pebbles beneath, and I know you are clever. If humans learned that in time the grey coating of our belly-stones wore away and they became such pretty baubles, we would be bred and slaughtered for them as your species breeds cattle.

But I am curious, and I wanted to see what you would do. At that time, I knew the hound had been hatched and was hunting the cities, the mines and the salt-flats for the Bride. And you said nothing. That's why I'm here tonight, telling you stories, instead of gathering with the others or guarding your door, ready to strike.

No, Twigling, you can't move. I put stillweed in your tea tonight. You can hear, and see and breathe, but your limbs will not obey you. Let me finish the story.

The hound hunts the alleys where my people scrape for a living in the soaring cities their ancestors built. It sniffs the banks of rivers where mothers throw their children, either because they have died or because they don't want them to live in slavery. It finds the places where the Var have been whipped, and kicked, and killed.

I'm sure it found that post beside the back door, where your mother has her servants whipped. I have bled there myself, more times than I care to remember. I will admit to you that I won't miss your mother, or your father, who occupied himself with his ambassador's duties and did nothing.

So the hound hunts until he finds the Red Bride, with her veils and scarlet slippers and ruby bracelets, waiting for him. You understand that because this is not a story of your time, or race, or planet, that the hound is not a hound as the Bride is not a Bride as the rubies are not rubies, but the Bride is certainly red, because both Var and human blood are red.

Ah—you hear them now? It won't be long.

The hound leads the Bride to the Vallhan, and the hearts of the Var quicken and their seeming inaction—simply a slow, hidden birth, a process of decision that would make impatient humans jibe—ends.

No—hush. They won't come in; they know I am here. I gave you stillweed because I need you to be quiet, and not incite the others to kill you when you try to run away.

Yes, they're in your sister's room next door. I gave her stillweed as well, and I thought a long time about whether I could save her too. But I can only carry one and I'll need to protect you a while, while the Red Bride runs rampant and the Var carry her onward with their anger. And in truth I can't forget the time your sister misplaced her necklace and blamed it on Sencha, and the poor little thing was whipped at your mother's post.

You didn't know Sencha was mine, did you? It's not the habit of humans to pay attention to such things. When you live with us, you will have to learn to pay attention.

The others disagreed with me. They want none of your kind to live. But I have been living among humans a long time, and I know many of your stories, and I think it is worth the risk. I think perhaps I have a part in the tale of the Red Bride as well, because in the old stories there is a little bird that sings on the Red Bride's shoulder, and flies to the Vallhan when they meet, and causes him to stay behind at the worst of the raging and keep his hands clean. I think I may be that bird.

I gave this kindness to your sister—I gave her enough stillweed that she fell asleep, and opened her veins myself. I've no wish for her to be frightened, as Sencha was frightened.

Sencha died after her whipping, did you know that? Small wonder. We don't speak of it. You might have asked, I think.

Don't try to speak. It's important that they think you're dead. I'll tell them I'm taking you to the lake to bury you—they know I'm half-mad, anyway. It's a good thing I'm stronger than I look, and that you're little for your kind, Twigling.

Come now, the house is burning. We'll stay in the long woods until the Red Bride has ended her reign and the Var remember, as the humans have not, that we are the Seeded Races, and one under the skin, as the scholars say.

Then, perhaps, we can try this again.

GHOSTS DOING THE ORANGE DANCE

(The Parke Family Scrapbook Number IV)

PAUL PARK

1. Phosphorescence

Before her marriage, my mother's mother's name and address took the form of a palindrome. I've seen it on the upper left-hand corner of old envelopes:

Virginia Spotswood McKenney
Spotswood
McKenney
Virginia

Spotswood was her father's farm in a town named after him, outside of Petersburg. He was a congressman and a judge who had sent his daughters north to Bryn Mawr for their education, and had no reason to think at the time of his death that they wouldn't live their lives within powerful formal constraints. He died of pneumonia in 1912. He'd been shooting snipe in the marshes near his home.

I have a footlocker under my desk that contains the remains of my grandmother's trousseau, enormous Irish-linen tablecloths and matching napkins—never used. The silver and china, a service for twenty-five, was sold when my mother was a child. My grandmother married a Marine Corps captain from a prominent family, a graduate of the University of Virginia and Columbia Law School. But their money went to his defense during his court-martial.

For many years she lived a life that was disordered and uncertain. But by the time I knew her, when she was an old woman, that had changed. This was thanks to forces outside her control—her sister Annie had married a lawyer who defended the German government in an international case, the Black

Tom explosion of 1916. An American gunboat had blown up in the Hudson River amid suspicions of sabotage.

The lawyer's name was Howard Harrington. Afterward, on the strength of his expectations, he gave up his practice and retired to Ireland, where he bought an estate called Dunlow Castle. Somewhere around here I have a gold whistle with his initials on it, and also a photograph of him and my great-aunt, surrounded by a phalanx of staff.

But he was never paid. America entered the First World War, and in two years the Kaiser's government collapsed. Aunt Annie and Uncle Howard returned to New York, bankrupt and ill. My grandmother took them in, and paid for the sanatorium in Saranac Lake where he died of tuberculosis, leaving her his debts. In the family this was considered unnecessarily virtuous, because he had offered no help when she was most in need. Conspicuously and publicly he had rejected her husband's request for a job in his law firm, claiming that he had "committed the only crime a gentleman couldn't forgive."

She had to wait forty years for her reward. In the 1970s a West German accountant discovered a discrepancy, an unresolved payment which, with interest, was enough to set her up in comfort for the rest of her life.

At that time she was director of the Valentine Museum in Richmond. Some of her father's household silver was on display there in glass cases, along with various antebellum artifacts, and General Jeb Stuart's tiny feathered hat and tiny boots. She was active in her local chapter of the United Daughters of the Confederacy. She used to come to Rhode Island during the summers and make pickled peaches in our kitchen. I was frightened of her formal manners, her take-no-prisoners attitude toward children, and her southern accent, which seemed as foreign to me as Turkish or Uzbeki. She had white hair down her back, but I could only see how long it was when I was spying on her through the crack in her bedroom door, during her morning toilette. She'd brush it out, then braid it, then secure the braids around her head in tight spirals, held in place with long tortoiseshell hairpins.

She wore a corset.

One night there was a thunderstorm, and for some reason there was no one home but she and I. She appeared at the top of the stairs, her hair undone. She was breathing hard, blowing her cheeks out as she came down, and then she stood in the open door, looking out at the pelting rain. "Come," she said—I always obeyed her. She led me out onto the front lawn. We didn't wear any coats, and in a moment we were soaked. Lightning struck nearby. She took hold of my arm and led me down the path toward the sea; we stood on the bluff as the storm raged. The waves were up the beach. Rain wiped clean the surface of the water. For some reason there was a lot of phosphorescence.

She had hold of my arm, which was not characteristic. Before, she'd never had a reason to touch me. Her other hand was clenched in a fist. The lenses of her glasses were streaked with rain. The wind blew her white hair around her head. She pulled me around in a circle, grinning the whole time. Her teeth were very crooked, very bad.

2. THE GLASS HOUSE

It occurs to me that every memoirist and every historian should begin by reminding their readers that the mere act of writing something down, of organizing something in a line of words, involves a clear betrayal of the truth. Without alternatives we resort to telling stories, coherent narratives involving chains of circumstance, causes and effects, climactic moments, introductions and denouements. We can't help it.

This is even before we start to make things up. And it's in spite of what we already know from our own experience: that our minds are like jumbled crates or suitcases or cluttered rooms, and that memory cannot be separated from ordinary thinking, which is constructed in layers rather than sequences. In the same way history cannot be separated from the present. Both memory and history consist not of stories but of single images, words, phrases, or motifs repeated to absurdity. Who could tolerate reading about such things? Who could even understand it?

So our betrayal of experience has a practical justification. But it also has a psychological one. How could we convince ourselves of progress, of momentum, if the past remained as formless or as pointless as the present? In our search for meaning, especially, we are like a man who looks for his vehicle access and ignition cards under a streetlamp regardless of where he lost them. What choice does he have? In the darkness, it's there or nowhere.

But stories once they're started are self-generating. Each image, once clarified, suggests the next. Form invents content, and so problems of falsehood cannot be limited entirely to form. A friend of mine once told me a story about visiting his father, sitting with him in the VA hospital the morning he died, trying to make conversation, although they had never been close. "Dad," he said, "there's one thing I've never forgotten. We were at the lake house the summer I was twelve, and you came downstairs with some army stuff, your old revolver that you'd rediscovered at the bottom of a drawer. You told Bobby and me to take it out into the woods and shoot it off, just for fun. But I said I didn't want to, I wanted to watch *Gilligan's Island* on TV, and you were okay with that. Bobby went out by himself. And I think that was a turning point for me, where I knew you would accept me whatever I did, even if it was, you know, intellectual things—books and literature. Bobby's in jail, now, of course. But I just wanted you to know how grateful I was for that, because you didn't force me to conform to some. . . . "

Then my friend had to stop because the old man was staring at him and trying to talk, even though the tubes were down his throat. What kind of deranged psychotic asshole, he seemed to want to express, would give his teenage sons a loaded gun of any kind, let alone a goddamned .38? The lake house, as it happened, was not in Siberia or fucking Wyoming, but suburban Maryland; there were neighbors on both sides. The woods were only a hundred yards deep. You could waste some jerkoff as he sat on his own toilet in his own home. What the fuck? And don't even talk to me about Bobby. He's twice the man you are.

Previously, my friend had told variations of this childhood memory to his wife and his young sons, during moments of personal or family affirmation. He had thought of it as the defining moment of his youth, but now in the stark semiprivate hospital room it sounded ridiculous even to him. And of course, any hope of thoughtful tranquility or reconciliation was impeded, as the old man passed away immediately afterward.

Everyone has had experiences like this. And yet what can we do, except pretend what we say is accurate? What can we do, except continue with our stories? Here is mine. It starts with a visit to my grandfather, my father's father, sometime in the early 1960s.

His name was Edwin Avery Park, and he lived in Old Mystic in eastern Connecticut, not far from Preston, where his family had wasted much of the seventeenth, the entire eighteenth, and half of the nineteenth centuries on unprofitable farms. He had been trained as an architect, but had retired early to devote himself to painting—imitations, first, of John Marin's landscapes, and then later of Georgio di Chirico's surrealist canvases; he knew his work derived from theirs. Once he said, "I envy you. I know I'll never have what you have. Now here I am at the end of my life, a fifth-rate painter." His eyes got misty, wistful. "I could have been a third-rate painter."

He showed no interest in my sisters. But I had been born in a caul, the afterbirth wrapped around my head, which made me exceptional in his eyes. According to my father, this was a notion he had gotten from his own mother, my father's grandmother, president of the New Haven Theosophist Society in the 1880s and '90s and a font of the kind of wisdom that was later to be called "new age," in her case mixed with an amount of old Connecticut folklore.

When we visited, my grandfather was always waking me up early and taking me for rambles in old graveyards. Once he parked the car by the side of the road, and he—

No, wait. Something happened first. At dawn I had crept up to his studio in the top of the house and looked through a stack of paintings: "Ghosts Doing the Orange Dance." "The Waxed Intruder." "Shrouds and Dirges, Disassembled."

This was when I was seven or eight years old. I found myself examining a pencil sketch of a woman riding a horned animal. I have it before me now, spread out on the surface of my desk. She wears a long robe, but in my recollection she is naked, and that was the reason I was embarrassed to hear the heavy sound of my grandfather's cane on the stairs, why I pretended to be looking at something else when he appeared.

His mother, Lucy Cowell, had been no larger than a child, and he also was very small—five feet at most, and bald. Long, thin nose. Pale blue eyes. White moustache. He knew immediately what I'd been looking at. He barely had to stoop to peer into my face. Later, he parked the car beside the road, and we walked out through a long field toward an overgrown structure in the distance. The sky was low, and it was threatening to rain. We took a long time to reach the greenhouse through the wet, high grass.

Now, in my memory it is a magical place. Maybe it didn't seem so at the time. I thought the panes were dirty and smudged, many of them cracked and broken. Vines and creepers had grown in through the lights. But now I see immediately why I was there. Standing inside the ruined skeleton, I look up to see the sun break through the clouds, catch at motes of drifting dust. And I was surrounded on all sides by ghostly images, faded portraits. The greenhouse had been built of large, old-fashioned photographic exposures on square sheets of glass.

A couple of years later, in Puerto Rico, I saw some of the actual images made from these plates. I didn't know it then. Now, seated at my office desk, I can see the greenhouse in the long, low, morning light, and I can see with my imagination's eye the bearded officers and judges, the city fathers with their families, the children with their black nannies. And then other, stranger images: My grandfather had to swipe away the grass to show me, lower down, the murky blurred exposure of the horned woman on the shaggy beast, taken by firelight, at midnight—surely she was naked there! "These were made by my great-uncle, Benjamin Cowell," he said. "He had a photography studio in Virginia. After the war he came home and worked for his brother. This farm provided all the vegetables for Cowell's Restaurant."

Denounced as a Confederate sympathizer, Benjamin Cowell had had a difficult time back in Connecticut, and had ended up by taking his own life. But in Petersburg in the 1850s, his studio had been famous—Rockwell & Cowell. Robert E. Lee sat for him during the siege of the city in 1864. That's a matter of record, and yet the greenhouse itself—how could my grandfather have walked that far across an unmowed field? The entire time I knew him he was very lame, the result of a car accident. For that matter, how could he have driven me anywhere when he didn't, to my knowledge, drive? And Cowell's Restaurant, the family business, was in New Haven, seventy miles away. My great-great-grandfather personally shot the venison and caught the fish. Was it likely he would have imported his vegetables over such a distance?

Middle-aged, I tried to find the greenhouse again, and failed. My father had no recollection. "He'd never have told him," sniffed Winifred, my grandfather's third wife. "He liked you. You were born in a caul. He liked that. It was quite an accomplishment, he always said."

Toward the end of her life I used to visit her in Hanover, New Hampshire, where they'd moved in the 1970s when she was diagnosed with multiple sclerosis. It was her home town. Abused by her father, a German professor at Dartmouth, she had escaped to marry my grandfather, himself more than thirty years older, whom she had met in a psychiatric art clinic in Boston, a program run by his second wife. It surprised everyone when Winifred wanted to move home, most of all my grandfather, who didn't long survive the change. He had spent the 1930s in Bennington, Vermont, teaching in the college there, and had learned to loathe those mountains. In addition, I believe now, he had another, more complicated fear, which he associated with that general area.

Because of her illness, Winifred was unable to care for him, and he ended his life in a nursing home. He was convinced, the last time I saw him, that I was visiting him during half-time of the 1908 Yale-Harvard game. "This is the worst hotel I've ever stayed in," he confided in a whisper, when I bent down to kiss his cheek. But then he turned and grabbed my arm. "You've seen her, haven't you?"

I didn't even ask him what he meant, he was so far gone. Later, when I used to visit Winifred in New Hampshire, she got in the habit of giving me things to take away—his paintings first of all. She'd never cared for them. Then old tools and odds and ends, and finally a leather suitcase, keyless and locked, which I broke open when I got home. There in an envelope was the drawing of the horned woman riding the horned beast.

There also were several packages tied up in brown paper and twine, each with my name in his quavering handwriting. I brought them to my office at Williams College and opened them. The one on top contained the first three volumes of something called *The Parke Scrapbook*, compiled by a woman named Ruby Parke Anderson: exhaustive genealogical notes, which were also full of errors, as Winifred subsequently pointed out. Folded into Volume Two was his own commentary, an autobiographical sketch, together with his annotated family tree. This was familiar to me, as he had made me memorize the list of names when I was still a child, starting with his immigrant ancestor in Massachusetts Bay—Robert, Thomas, Robert, Hezekiah, Paul, Elijah, Benjamin Franklin, Edwin Avery, Franklin Allen, Edwin Avery, David Allen, Paul Claiborne, Adrian Xhaferaj. . . .

But I saw immediately that some of the names were marked with asterisks, my grandfather's cousin Theo, Benjamin Cowell, and the Reverend Paul Parke, an eighteenth-century Congregationalist minister. At the bottom of the page, next to another asterisk, my grandfather had printed CAUL.

3. The Battle of the Crater

Not everyone is interested in these things. Already in those years I had achieved a reputation in my family as someone with an unusual tolerance for detritus and memorabilia. Years before I had received a crate of stuff from Puerto Rico via my mother's mother in Virginia. These were books and papers from my mother's father, also addressed to me, though I hadn't seen him since I was nine years old, in 1964. They had included his disbarment records in a leather portfolio, a steel dispatch case without a key, and a bundle of love letters to and from my grandmother, wrapped in rubber bands. I'd scarcely looked at them. I'd filed them for later when I'd have more time.

That would be now. I sat back at my desk, looked out the open window in the September heat. There wasn't any air conditioning anymore, although someone was mowing the lawn over by the Congo church. And I will pretend that this was my Proustian moment, by which I mean the moment that introduces a long, false, coherent memory—close enough. I really hadn't thought about Benjamin Cowell during the intervening years, or the greenhouse or the horned lady. My memories of Puerto Rico seemed of a different type, inverted, solid, untransparent. In this way they were like the block of pasteboard images my mother's father showed me at his farm in Maricao, and then packed up for me later to be delivered after his death, photographs made, I now realized, by Rockwell & Cowell in Petersburg, where he was from.

I closed my eyes for a moment. Surely in the greenhouse I'd seen this one, and this one—images that joined my mother's and my father's families. Years before on my office wall I'd hung "Ghosts Doing the Orange Dance" in a simple wooden frame, and beside it the military medallion in gilt and ormolu: General Lee surrounded by his staff. Under them, amid some boxes of books, I now uncovered the old crate, still with its stickers from some Puerto Rican shipping line. I levered off the top. Now I possessed two miscellaneous repositories of words, objects, and pictures, one from each grandfather. And because of this sudden connection between them, I saw immediately a way to organize these things into a pattern that might conceivably make sense. Several ways, in fact—geographically, chronologically, thematically. I imagined I could find some meaning. Alternately from the leather satchel and the wooden crate, I started to lay out packages and manuscripts along the surface of my desk and the adjoining table. I picked up a copy of an ancient Spanish tile, inscribed with a stick figure riding a stag—it was my maternal grandfather in Puerto Rico who had shown me this. He had taken me behind the farmhouse to a cave in the forest, where someone had once seen an apparition of the devil. And he himself had found there, when he first bought the property, a Spanish gold doubloon. "You've seen her, haven't you?" he said.

"Who?"

A lawyer, he had left his wife and children to resettle in the Caribbean, first in the Virgin Islands and then in San Juan. He'd won cases and concessions for the Garment and Handicrafts Union, until he was disbarred in the 1950s. Subsequently he'd planted citrus trees in a mountain ravine outside of Maricao. His name was Robert W. Claiborne.

In my office, I put my hand on the locked dispatch case, and then moved down the line. In 1904, his father, my great-grandfather, had published a memoir called *Seventy-Five Years in Old Virginia.* Now I picked up what looked like the original manuscript, red-lined by the editor at Neale Publishing, and with extensive marginal notes.

Years before I'd read the book, or parts of it. Dr. John Herbert Claiborne had been director of the military hospital in Petersburg during the siege, and subsequently the last surgeon-general of the Army of Northern Virginia, during the retreat to Appomattox. A little of his prose, I remembered, went a long way:

> We would not rob the gallant Captain or his brave North Carolinians of one feather from their plume. Where there were North Carolinians, there were brave men always, and none who ever saw them in a fight, or noted the return of their casualties after a fight, will gainsay that; but there were other brave men, of the infantry and of the artillery,—men whom we have mentioned,—who rallied promptly, and who shared with our Captain and his game crew that generous rain of metal so abundantly poured out upon their devoted heads.

Or:

> We were descendents of the cavalier elements that settled in that State and wrested it from the savage by their prowess, introducing a leaven in the body politic, which not only bred a high order of civilization at home, but spread throughout the Southern and Western States, as the Virginian, moved by love of adventure or desire of preferment, migrated into the new and adjoining territories. And from this sneered-at stock was bred the six millions of Southrons who for four long years maintained unequal war with thirty millions of Northern hybrids, backed by a hireling soldiery brought from the whole world to put down constitutional liberty—an unequal war, in which the same Southron stock struck undaunted for honor and the right, until its cohorts of starved and ragged heroes perished in their own annihilation. . . .

Or even:

> But how many of our little band, twenty years afterward, rode with Fitz Lee, and with Stuart, and with Rosser—rode upon the serried squares of alien marauders on their homes and their country,—I know not. As the war waged I would meet one of them sometimes, with the same firm seat in the saddle, the same spirit of dash and deviltry—but how many were left to tell to their children the story of battle and of bivouac is not recorded. I only know that I can not

recall a single living one to-day. As far as I can learn, every one has responded to the last Long Roll, and every one has answered *adsum*—here—to the black sergeant—Death.

In other words, what you might call an unreconstructed Southerner, gnawing at old bones from the Civil War. I glanced up at a copy of the finished book on the shelf above my desk. And I could guess immediately that the typescript underneath my hand was longer. Leafing through it, I could see whole chapters were crossed out.

For example, in the section that describes the siege of Petersburg, there is an odd addendum to an account of the Battle of the Crater, which took place on the night and early morning of July 30, 1864:

But now at certain nights during the year, between Christmas Night and New Year's Day, or else sometimes during the Ember Days, I find myself again on the Jerusalem Plank Road, or else retreading in the footsteps of Mahone's doughty veterans, as they came up along the continuous ravine to the east of the Cameron house, and on to near the present location of the water works. From there I find myself in full view of the captured salient, and the fortifications that had been exploded by the mine, where Pegram's Battery had stood. On these moon-lit nights, I see the tortured chasm in the earth, the crater as it was,—two hundred feet long, sixty feet wide, and thirty feet deep. To my old eyes it is an abyss as profound as Hell itself, and beyond I see the dark, massed flags of the enemy, as they were on that fatal morning,—eleven flags in fewer than one hundred yards,—showing the disorder of his advance. Yet he comes in great strength. As before, because of the power of the exploded mine, and because of the awful destruction of the Eighteenth and Twenty-Second South Carolina Regiments, the way lies open to Cemetery Hill, and then onward to the gates of the doomed city, rising but two hundred yards beyond its crest. As before and as always, the Federals advance into the gap, ten thousand, twelve thousand strong. But on the shattered lip of the Crater, where Mahone brought up his spirited brigade, there is no one but myself, a gaunt and ancient man, holding in his hand neither musket nor bayonet, but instead a tender stalk of maize. Weary, I draw back, because I have fought this battle before, in other circumstances. As I do so, as before, I see that I am not alone, and in the pearly dawn that there are others who have come down from the hill, old veterans like myself, and boys also, and even ladies in their long gowns, as if come immediately from one of our 'starvation balls,' in the winter of '64, and each carrying her frail sprig of barley, or wheat, or straw. On these nights, over and again, we must defend the hearths and houses of the town, the kine in their fields, the horses in their stalls. Over and again, we must obey the silent trumpet's call. Nor in this battle without end can we expect or hope for the relief of Col. Wright's proud Georgians, or Saunders's gallant heroes from Alabama, who, though out-numbered ten to one, stopped the Federals' charge and poured down such a storm of fire upon their heads, that they were obliged to pile up barricades of slaughtered men, trapped as they were in that terrible pit, which was such as might be fitly portrayed by the pencil of Dante after he had trod 'nine-circled Hell,' where the very air seemed darkened by the flying of human limbs. Then the tempest came down on Ledlie's men like the rain of Norman arrows at Hastings, until the white handkerchief was displayed from the end of a ramrod or bayonet—there is no hope for that again, for even such a momentary victory. This is not Burnsides's Corps, but in its place an army of the dead, commanded by a fearsome figure many times his superior in skill and fortitude, a figure which I see upon the ridge, her shaggy mount trembling beneath her weight. . . .

This entire section is crossed out by an editor's pen, and then further qualified by a note in the margin—"Are we intended to accept this as a literal account of your actual experience?" And later, "Your tone here cannot be successfully reconciled."

Needless to say, I disagreed with the editors' assessments. In my opinion they might have published these excised sections and forgotten all the rest. I was especially interested in the following paragraph, marked with a double question mark in the margin:

Combined with unconsciousness, it is a condition that is characterized by an extreme muscular rigidity, particularly in the sinews of the upper body. But the sensation is difficult to describe. [. . .] Now the grass grows green. In the mornings, the good citizens of the town bring out their hampers. But through the hours after midnight I must find a different landscape as, neck stiff, hands frozen into claws, I make my way from my warm bed, in secret. Nor have I once seen any living soul along the way, unless one might count that single, odd, bird-like, Yankee 'carpet-bagger' from his 'atelier,' trudging through the gloom, all his cases and contraptions over his shoulders, including his diabolical long flares of phosphorus. . . .

4. A UFO in Preston

Benjamin Cowell had made his exposures on sheets of glass covered with a silver emulsion. There were none of his photographs in Edwin Avery Park's leather valise. Instead I found daguerreotypes and tintypes from the 1850s and earlier. And as I dug farther into the recesses of the musty bag, I found other images—a framed silhouette of Hannah Avery, and then, as I pushed back into the eighteenth century, pen and pencil sketches of other faces, coarser and coarser and worse-and-worse drawn, increasingly cartoonish and indistinct, the lines lighter and lighter, the paper darker and darker.

The sketch of the Reverend Paul Parke is particularly crude, less a portrait than a child's scribble: spidery silver lines on a spotted yellow card: bald pate, round eyes, comically seraphic smile, suggesting the death's head on an ancient grave. It was in an envelope with another artifact, a little handwritten booklet about three by six inches, sewn together and covered in rough brown paper. The booklet contained the text of a sermon preached at the Preston Separate Church on July 15, 1797, on the occasion of the fiftieth anniversary of the Rev. Parke's public ministry. Because of its valedictory nature—he was at the time almost eighty years old—the sermon includes an unusual admixture of personal reflection and reminiscence. Immensely long, it is not interesting in its totality, and I could not but admire the stamina of the Preston Separatists, dozing, as I imagined, in their hot, uncomfortable pews.

For the Reverend Parke, the most powerful and astonishing changes of his lifetime had been spiritual in nature, the various schisms and revivals we refer to as the Great Awakening. Independence, and the rebellion of the American Colonies, seemed almost an afterthought to him, a distant social echo of a more profound and significant rebellion against established doctrine, which had resulted in the manifest defeat of the Anti-Christ, and the final destruction of Babylon.

Moving through the sermon, at first I thought I imagined an appealing sense of modesty and doubt:

> . . . it wood not Do to trust in my knowledge: or doings or anything of men of means that sentered in Selfishness: and tried to avoid Self Seeking: but in this I was baffled for while I was Giting out of Self in one Shap I should find I was Giting into another and whilst I endeavored not to trust in one thing I found I was trusting in Something else: and they Sem all to be but refuges of lies as when I fled from a lion I met a fox or went to lean on the wall a Serpent wood bite me and my own hart dyed and my every way I Could take and when I could find no way to escape and as I thought no Divine assistance or favour: I found Dreadful or it was my hart murmuring in emity against God himself that others found mercy and were Safe and happy: whilst I that had Sought as much was Denied of help and was perishing. I knew this timper was blasphmonthy wicked and Deserved Damnation: and it appeared to be of Such a malignant nature that the pains of hell wood

not allow or make me any bettor thoug I Greatly feared it wood be my portion: but this Soon Subsided and other Subjects drew my sight.

As is so often the case, these subjects were, and now became, the problems of other people. Nor did the Reverend Parke's self-doubt translate automatically into compassion:

> . . . if any one was known to err in principle or practisee or Did Not walk everly there was Strickt Disapline attended according to rule, bee the sin private and publick, as the Case required: and the offender recovered or admenished that theire Condition be all ways plaine, their Soberiety and Zeal for virtue and piety was Such theire Common language and manners was plaine and innocent Carefully avoiding Jesting rude or profain Communications with all Gamblings and Gamings: excessive festevity frolicking Drinking Dressing and even all fashenable Divertions that appeared Dangerous to Virtue: and observed the Stricktest rules of prudence and economy in Common life and to have no felloship with the unfruitful works of Darkness but reprove them.

Even though my office window was open, the heat was still oppressive. I sat back, listening to the buzz of the big mowers sweeping close across the lawn. This last paragraph seemed full of redirected misery, and it occurred to me to understand why, having given me my ancestor's name, my parents had never actually used it, preferring to call me by a nickname from a 1950s comic strip. I slouched in my chair, letting my eyes drift down the page until I found some other point of entry. But after a few lines I was encouraged, and imagined also a sudden, mild stir of interest, moving through the ancient congregation like a breeze:

> . . . in Embr Weeke, this was pasd the middle of the night when I went out thoug my wife would not Sweare otherwise but that I had not shifted from my bed. But in Darkness I betoke myself amongst the hils of maise and having broken of a staff of it I cam out from the verge and into the plouged field wher I saw others in the sam stile. Amongst them were that sam Jonas Devenport and his woman that we had still Givn mercyfull Punishment and whipd as I have menshoned on that publick ocation befor the entire congregation. But on this night when I had come out with the rest: not them but others to that we had similarly Discomforted. So I saw an army of Sinners that incluyded Jho Whitside Alice Hster and myself come from the maise with ears and tasills in our hands. I was one amongst them So Convinced in my own Depravity and the Deceitfullness of

my own Hart of Sin the body of Death and ungodlyness that always lyes in wait to Deceive. On that bar ground of my unopned mind these ours wood apear as like a Morning without ligt of Gospill truth and all was fals Clouds and scret Darkness. Theire I saw printed on the earth the hoof of mine enimy: a deep print up on the ground. In the dark I could still perceive her horns and her fowl wind. Nor thougt I we could hold her of with our weak armes. But together lnking hands we strugld upward up the hill by Preston Grang nto the appel trees led by that enimy common to al who movd befor us like a hornd beast togther with her armee of walking corses of dead men. Nor could I think she was not leding us to slaghter by the ruind hutts of the Pecuods theire: exsept When I saw a Greate Ligt at the top of the hill coming throug the trees as lik a cold fire and a vessel or a shipe com down from heavn theire and burning our fases as we knelt and prayd. Those hutts bursd afire and a Great Ligt and a vessill on stakes or joyntd legs was come for our delivrance: with Angels coming down the laddr with theire Greate Heads and Eys. Nor could I Scersely refrain my Mouth from laughter and my tongue from Singing: for the Lord God omnipotent reigneth: or singing like Israel at the Red Sea: the hors and his rider he has thrown into the Sea: or say with Debarah he rode in the heavens for our help, the heavens Droped the Clouds Droped Down Water: the Stars in theire Courses fought against Ceera: who was deliverd into the Hand and slain by a woman: with a Sinful weapon. If any man doubt it theire is stil now upon that hill the remnts of that battel. Or I have writ a copy of that Shipe that otherwse did flie away and leving ondly this scrape of scin ript from man's enimny in that hour of Tryumph. . . .

In my office, in the late afternoon, I sat back. The diagram was there, separately drawn on a small, stiff card, the lines so light I could hardly make them out. But I saw a small sphere atop three jointed legs.

Then I unwrapped the piece of skin, which was tied up in a shred of leather. It was hard as coal and blackish-green, perhaps two inches by three, the scales like goose-bumps.

I looked up at my grandfather's painting above my desk, "Ghosts Doing the Orange Dance." I had examined it many times. The ghosts are like pentagrams, five-pointed stars, misty and transparent. They are bowing to each other in a circle, clutching the oranges in their hands. In the misty landscape, under the light of what must be the full moon behind the clouds, there are cabinets and chests of drawers where other ghosts lie folded up.

But now I noticed an odd detail for the first time. The furniture is littered across a half-plowed field. And in the background, against a row of faux-gothic windows, there are men and women hiding, peering out from a row of corn placed incongruously along the front. Their faces glint silver in the moonlight. Their eyes are hollow, their cheeks pinched and thin.

I got up to examine the painting more closely. I unhooked it from the wall and held it up close to my nose. Then I laid it among the piles of paper on my desk.

These similarities, these correspondences between my mother's family and my father's—I give the impression they are obvious and clear. But that is the privilege of the memoirist or the historian, searching for patterns, choosing what to emphasize: a matter of a few lines here and there, sprinkled over thousands of pages. Turning away, I wandered around my office for a little while, noticing with despair the boxes of old books and artifacts, the shelves of specimens, disordered and chaotic. A rolled-up map had fallen across the door. How had everything gotten to be like this? Soon, I thought, I'd need a shovel just to dig myself out.

But through the open window I could smell cut grass. I turned toward the screen again, searching for a way to calm myself and to arrange in my mind these disparate narratives. Because of my training as a literary scholar, I found it easy to identify some similarities, especially the repeating motif of the corn stalk, and the conception of a small number of unworthy people, obliged to protect their world or their community from an awful power. And even in the scene of triumph described by the Reverend Parke—achieved, apparently, through some type of extraterrestrial intervention—was I wrong to catch an odor of futility? This was no final victory, after all. These struggles were nightly, or else at certain intervals of the year. The enemy was too strong, the stakes too high. Our weapons are fragile and bizarre, our allies uncertain and unlike ourselves—no one we would have chosen for so desperate a trial.

I sat back down again, touched my computer, googled Ember Days, idly checked my email, not wanting to go home. The buzz of the lawnmower was gone. The campus was underutilized, of course. The building was almost empty.

I cleared a place on my desk, crossed my arms over it, laid down my cheek. Not very comfortable. But in a few minutes I was asleep. I have always been a lucid dreamer, and as I have gotten older the vividness of my dreams has increased and not diminished, the sense of being in some vague kind of control. This is in spite of the fact that I sleep poorly now, never for more than a few hours at a time, and if a car goes by outside my bedroom, or if someone were to turn onto her side or change her breathing, I am instantly awake. As a result, the experience of sleeping and not sleeping has lost the edge between them. But then at moments my surroundings are sufficiently distorted and bizarre for me to say for certain, "I am dreaming," and so wake myself up.

With my cheek and mouth pressed out of shape against the wooden surface, I succumbed to this type of double experience. I had a dream in which I was sufficiently alert to ponder its meaning while it was still going on. Not that I have any clear preconceptions about the language of dreams, but in a general way I can see, or pretend I can see, how certain imagery can reflect or evoke the anxieties of waking life—the stresses on a relationship or a marriage, say, or the reasons I was sitting here in my office on a sweltering afternoon, instead of going home. I dreamed I was at one of those little private cave-systems that are a roadside feature of the Shenandoah Valley Interstate—I had visited a few with Nicola and Adrian when he was four or five and we were still living in Baltimore. But I was alone this time. I felt the wind rush by me as I stood at the entrance to the main cavern, a function of the difference in temperature outside and inside. It gives the illusion that the cave is "breathing," an illusion fostered in this case by the soft colors and textures of the stone above my head, the flesh-like protuberances, and the row of sharp white stalactites. Perhaps inevitably I now realized I was in the mouth of a sleeping giant, and that the giant was in fact myself, collapsed over my office desk. And as I ran out over the hard, smooth surface, I realized further that I had taken the shape of a small rodent; now I jumped down to the floor and made a circuit of the room, trying to find a hole to hide in, or (even better!) a means of egress through the towering stacks of books.

5. A Detour

When I woke, I immediately packed my laptop, locked my office. It was late. I went down to my car in the lot below Stetson Hall, seeing no one along the way. I passed what once had been known as the North Academic Building— subsequently they'd made the basement classroom into a storeroom. The glass they had replaced with bricks, so that you couldn't look in. But even so I always walked this way, in order to remember my first trip to Williams College years before, and the class where I had met my wife. In this dark, cannibalized building, Professor Rosenheim had taught his 100-level course on meta-fiction. Andromeda Yoo (as I will call her for these purposes) had been a first-year student then.

These days we also live in a town called Petersburg, though the coincidence had never struck me until now. It is across the border in New York State, and there are two ways to drive home. One of them, slightly longer, loops north into Vermont.

Usually I take the shorter way, because I have to stop and show my identification and vaccination cards at only one state inspection booth and not two. There's hardly ever a line, and usually you just breeze through. Of course I accept the necessity. The world has changed. Even so, there's something that rubs against the grain.

But that afternoon I headed north. On my way along Route 346, it occurred to me suddenly that I recognized the façade in the painting of the star-shaped ghosts. It belongs to a gingerbread construction, a mansion in North

Bennington called the Park-McCullough House, at one time open to the public, and not far from the campus where Edwin Park taught architecture and watercolor painting in the 1930s, until he was dismissed (my father once claimed) for some kind of sexual indiscretion.

But apparently, much later, subsequent to his marriage to Winifred, he had revisited the place. I knew this because of a strange document in a battered envelope, part of the contents of his leather valise, a scribbled note on the stationery of the Hanover nursing home where he had ended his life, and then a few typed pages, obviously prepared earlier, about the time, I imagined, that he had painted "Ghosts Doing the Orange Dance." And then some more pages in a woman's writing—when I first glanced at them, I had discounted the whole thing as some sort of meandering and abortive attempt at fiction. Now, as I drove home, I found I wasn't so sure.

The note was attached to the pages with a paperclip, and the thin, spidery lines were almost illegible. Yet even though the letters were distorted, I could still see vestiges of my grandfather's fine hand: "Ghosts; ghosts in the moon."

And here is the typed text of the manuscript: "Now that I'm an old man, dreams come so hard I wake up choking. Now at midnight, with my wife asleep, I sit down hoping to expunge a crime—a tiny crime I must insist—that I committed in the Park-McCullough mansion on one autumn night when I was there alone.

"In 1955 I moved to Boston and married Winifred Nief, who had been a patient of my deceased wife. Within a few years I retired from my architectural practice and removed to Old Mystic to devote myself to painting. About this time I became a member of the Park Genealogical Society, an organization of modest ambitions, though useful for determining a precise degree of consanguinity with people whose names all sound like variations of Queen Gertrude the Bald. Its standards of admission, as a consequence and fortunately, are quite lax.

"Starting in the early 1960s, the society had its annual meeting each Halloween weekend in the Park-McCullough House, a boxy Second-Empire structure in Bennington, which was no longer by that time in private hands. At first I had no wish to go. Quite the contrary. Winifred was bored speechless by the prospect, and I couldn't blame her. But something perverse about the idea nagged at me, and finally I thought I might like to revisit that town, without saying why. Enough time had passed, I thought.

"Winifred said she might like to drive down to Williamstown and visit David and Clara. She could drop me off for the afternoon and pick me up later. I had no desire to see the children go out trick-or-treating. In those days I didn't concern myself with my son's family, except for Paul, though in many ways he was the least interesting of the four. He'd been born in a caul, which my daughter-in-law had not seen fit to preserve. The youngest daughter was retarded, of course.

"Winifred dropped me off under the porte-cochere on a beautiful autumn day. Among a dozen or so genealogists, it was impossible for me to pretend any relation to the former owners, who by that time had died out. But we traipsed around the house, listening with modest interest to the shenanigans of the Parks and the McCulloughs—Trenor Park had made his money in the Gold Rush. Even so, he seemed a foolish sort. Success, even more than accomplishment, is the consolation of a mediocre mind.

"The house itself interested me more, designed by Henry Dudley (of the euphonious New York firm of Diaper & Dudley) in the mid 1860s, and displaying some interesting features of the Romantic Revival. It was a shameless copy of many rather ugly buildings, but I have often thought that true originality in architecture, or in anything, can only be achieved through a self-conscious process of imitation. I was especially taken with the elegant way the staff's rooms and corridors and staircases were folded invisibly into the structure, as if two separate houses were located on the same floor plan, intersecting only through a series of hidden doors. In fact there were many more secret passageways and whatnot than were usual. I was shown the secret tunnel under the front. There was a large dumbwaiter on the first floor.

"The docent told me stories of the family, and stories also about screams in the night, strange sounds and footsteps, lights turned on, a mysterious impression on the mattress of the great four-poster in the master bedroom. These are standard stories in old houses, but it seemed to me that an unusual quantity had accumulated here, a ghost in almost every room, and this over a mere hundred years of occupation. For example, there was a servant who had disappeared after his shift, never to be heard of again. A fellow named John Kepler, like the philosopher. He had left a wife and child in the village.

"I had thought I would go to the morning session and then use the afternoon to stroll about the town. As things turned out, I found my leg was bothering me too much. I could not bear to walk the streets or even less to climb the hill to the campus, for fear I might be recognized. I berated myself for coming within a hundred miles of the place, and so I took refuge in the mansion past the time everyone else had departed, and the staff was preparing for a special children's program, putting up paper spiderwebs and bats. The docents were so used to me they left me to my own devices. Waiting for Winifred to pick me up, I found myself sitting in an alcove off Eliza McCullough's bedroom, where she had written her correspondence at a small, Italianate, marble-topped table.

"I sat back in the wicker chair. I've always had an instinct for rotten wood, and for any kind of anomaly. I happened to glance at the parquet floor beneath my feet and saw at once a place where the complicated inlay had been cut apart and reassembled not quite perfectly. In old houses sometimes there are secret compartments put in for the original owners, and that secret is often lost and forgotten in the second generation or the third. And in this house I thought I could detect a mania for secrecy. I put my foot on the anomaly and pressed, and was rewarded by a small click. I could tell a box was hidden under the surface of the floor.

"I confess I was nervous and excited as I listened at the door for the footsteps of the staff. Then I returned and knelt down on the floor. I could see immediately the secret was an obvious one, a puzzle like those child's toys, plastic sliding squares with letters on them in a little frame, and because one square is missing, the rest can be rearranged. Words can be spelled. The little squares of parquetry moved under my fingers until one revealed a deeper hole underneath. I reached in and found the clasp, and the box popped open.

"The hole contained a document. I had already been shown a sample of Eliza Park-McCullough's handwriting, the distinctively loopy, forceful, slanting letters, which I recognized immediately. I enclose the pages, pilfered from the house. But because they are difficult to read, I also transcribe them here:

God I think I will go mad if I don't put this down and put this down. Esther tells me to say nothing, to tell nothing and say nothing, but she does not live here. Nor will she come back she says as long as she lives. And the rest are all gone and will not come back for an old woman, nor can I tell them. It would be prison if they knew or an asylum. So here I am alone in the nights when the servants go back behind the wall, and I take the elevator to the second floor. And I cannot always keep the lights burning and the victrola playing and the radio on, and then I am alone. It has been twenty years since Mr. McCullough died and left me here, a crippled bird who cannot fly to him! So in the night I drink my sherry and roll my chair back and forth along the hall. I spy from the front windows, and I can almost see them gather on the lawn, not just one or two. But they nod shyly to each other as they join in the dance. The lamps that they carry glow like fireflies. But they are also lit from above as if from an enormous fire behind the clouds, an engine coming down. Some nights I think it must land here on the roof, and if I could I would climb to the top of the house, and it would take me up. Or else I lie on my bed and listen for the sounds I know must come, the clink of the billiard balls on the green baize, and the smell of cigar smoke even though it has been two years since I had them take the balls and cues away. I asked them to burn them. I am sure they thought me insane, but I'm not insane. Nor was I even unhappy till the monster came into this house, and if I'm punished now it is for giving him his post and not dismissing him. But how could I do that? John McCullough, do you forgive me? It was for his high forehead and curling brown moustaches and strong arms like your arms. Do you know when I first saw him, when he first stood there in the hall with his cap in his hands, I thought I saw your ghost. No one is alive now who remembers you when you were young, but

I remember. That boy was my John brought back, and when he lifted me in his arms and carried me upstairs before the elevator went in, when he put me down in my wheel-chair at the top of the stairs, I scarcely could let go his neck. Do they think because I'm paralyzed that I feel nothing? Even now, past my eightieth year I can remember how it felt when you would carry me up those stairs and to my room, me like a little bird in your arms, though I could walk then and fly, too. Do not think I was unfaithful when I put my face into his shirt when he was carrying me upstairs. And when he put me down and asked me in his country voice if there was anything more, why then the spell was broken.

I do not say these things to excuse myself. There is no excuse. Though even now I marvel I was able to do it, able to find a way that night when they were all asleep and I was reading in my room. Or perhaps I had gone asleep. 'Is that you?' I cried when I heard the click of the billiard balls and smelled the cigar. I thought it was you, the way you put the house to bed before you came up. I pulled myself into my chair and wheeled myself down the hall. 'Is that you?' And when I saw him coming up the stairs, you ask me why I didn't ring the bell. I tell you it was all a dream until he spoke in his loud voice. I had no money about the place. Perhaps he thought I'd be asleep. He smiled when he saw me. He was drunk. I am ashamed to say I do not think he would have hurt me. But I could not forgive him because he knew my secret. I could tell it in his smiling face as he came down the hall. He knew why I could not cry out or ring the bell. Oh my John, he was nothing like you then as he turned my chair about and rolled me down away from the servants' door. 'Is that right, old bird?' he said. He would not let go of my chair. Once he put his hand over my mouth. And he went through my jewel case and he turned out my closets and my drawers. He could not guess the secret of this box where I keep the stone. Then he was angry and he took hold of my arms. He put his face against my face so that our noses touched, and he smiled and I could smell his cologne and something else, the man's smell underneath. I could not forgive him. 'There in the closet,' I said, meaning the water closet, though he didn't understand me. I let him wheel me over the threshold, and then I reached out on the surface of the cabinet where Mr. McCullough's man had shaved him every morning. There was no electric light, and so I reached out my hand in the darkness. The man's head was near my head and I struck at him with the razor. Oh, I could not get it out of my head that I had committed a great crime! It was you, John, who put that thought into my head, and I did not deserve it! I pulled myself into my room again. I found a clean nightgown and took off my other one and lay down on my bed. When I made my telephone call it was to Esther who drove up from the town. I think I was a little insane, then. She scrubbed the floor with her own hands. She told me we must tell no one, and that no one would believe us. She said there was a space where the dumb-waiter comes into the third floor, a fancy of the builder's she'd discovered when she and Bess were children. It is a three-sided compartment set into the top of the shaft. Esther does not live in the real world, though that is hard to say of your own child. She said the stone would keep the man away. But otherwise he would come back. She laughed and said it would be an eye for him. We'd put it into his head and it would be his eye. We'd claim he'd stolen it and run away. We'd claim a rat had died inside the wall.

"I sat reading these notes as it grew dark. Then I folded up the pages and slipped them into my jacket. I sat at Mrs. McCullough's desk and stared out the window. Darkness was falling. I poked at the floor with the end of my cane. Winifred was late. The box in the parquetry was closed.

"The docent's name was Jane Mears, and she was a beautiful, shy woman, with soft hair, if you care about that sort of thing. She stood in the doorway with a question on her lips. I asked her whether there was any story of a famous jewel that appertained to the house. And she told me about a massive stone, a ruby or sapphire or topaz or tourmaline the size of an orange that Trenor Park had won in a poker game in San Francisco. According to the story, it was delivered to his hotel room in a blood-spattered box, the former owner having shot himself after he packed it up.

"'It disappeared around 1932,' she said.

"I didn't say anything. I was not like other members of my family, or like my cousin Theodora who had died. I had never heard the voices. There had been no membrane over my eyes when I was born, no secret screen of images between me and the world. But even so I was interested in the anomaly, the corpse at the top of the shaft, a jewel in his mouth, as I imagined. A ghost's footprint in the dust, or else the men and women who had come out of the corn to follow my great-great-great-grandfather up Bartlett Hill in Preston, where there was a machine, or a mechanical robot, or an automaton with the cold light behind it and the stag running away.

"When Winifred drove up, I was waiting in the drive. She had stories to tell me about my son's family. I asked her to take the long way round, to circle by the campus, and we drove through North Bennington and watched the children dressed as witches and Frankensteins. There was a little ghost running after his mother, carrying a pumpkin.

"I motioned with my finger, and Winifred drove me toward the Silk Road and the covered bridge, then past it toward the corner where my car had spun out of control. She chattered about her day, and I responded in monosyllables. She made the turn past the tree where I had lost control. She didn't know, and at first I didn't think I would say anything about it. But then I changed my mind. 'Stop,' I said, and I made her pull over onto the side of the road. I gave her some foolish story, and left her in the car while I limped back in the darkness to deliver my gift."

6. ANDROMEDA YOO

As I sped home at dusk, I wondered if I should retrace my grandfather's steps and drive up to the Park-McCullough House along Silk Road—it wasn't so far out of the way. Perhaps I could find the tree he was talking about. But I passed the turnoff and continued, pondering as I did so the differences and connections between this narrative and the previous ones. That Halloween night, I thought, there had been no ghosts in the cornrows, and no cornrows at all, lining the front of the mansion or surrounding the elaborate porte-cochere. But then why had my grandfather chosen that image or motif for his portrait of the house? Though it was obvious he had read the Reverend Parke's sermon, he had no way of knowing how it corresponded or overlapped with various documents from my mother's family—manuscripts he'd never seen, composed by people he'd never met.

But after I had crossed into New York State, I left behind my obsessive thoughts of those dry texts. Instead I imagined my wife waiting for me. And so when I arrived home at my little house beside the river, there she was. She had brought Chinese food from Pittsfield, where she worked as a lawyer for Sabic Plastics.

What was it my grandfather had said? " . . . A beautiful, shy woman with long black hair, if you care about that sort of thing. She stood in the doorway with a question on her lips . . . "—when I first read the description I had thought of my wife. Driving home, remembering that first reading, I thought of her again, and wondered how I would answer her question, and whether she would be angry or impatient, as the docent at the Park-McCullough house, I imagined, had had every right to be. But Andromeda was just curious; she often got home late after supper, and in the long September light, everything tended to seem earlier than it was. We made Bombays-and-tonic and went to sit on the deck looking down toward the swamp willows, and ate seaweed salad and chicken with orange sauce out of the white containers with wire handles—very civilized. Andromeda raised her chopsticks, a further interrogation.

And so I told her about the mystery, the ghosts in the corn. As I did so, I remembered the first time I saw her in Professor Rosenheim's class, fresh-faced, eager to engage. Rosenheim had given them an early novel of mine, *A Princess of Roumania*, and it was obvious to me that Andromeda had liked it very much. The class itself was about meta-fiction, which is a way of doubling a story back upon itself, in a fashion similar to my grandfather's description of the double nature of the Park-McCullough mansion with its manifest anomalies. It was possible to see these kinds of patterns in my own work, although I always warned students against complexity for its own sake, and to consider the virtues of the simple story, simply told.

Rosenheim had invited me up from Baltimore to discuss *A Princess of Roumania*, a novel that had become infected almost against my will with references to the past, with descriptions of locations from my own life, and people I had once known or would come to know—all writing, after all, is a mixture of experience and imagination, fantasy and fact. I had accepted his offer because the trip enabled me to revisit the town where I'd grown up, and where part of the novel was set. Already by that time, Baltimore had ceased to feel like home.

And so I spent the weekend visiting as if for the first time the locations where I had set *A Princess of Roumania*. It was strange to see how I had misread my own memory, how little the text recalled the actual places. Lakes had become ponds. Rivers had become streams. Subdued, I met Rosenheim the night before the class, and we sat in a bar called "The Red Herring," and it was there that he first told me about his student, Andromeda. "You'll see what I mean tomorrow. None of this will be difficult for her. She'll figure out not just what you said, but what you meant to say. If only the rest had half her brains," he said, peering at me through glasses as thick as hockey pucks.

But then he roused himself, brandishing in his right hand the text of something else I had been working on, a "memoir," or fragment of science-fiction, which I would finish many years later, and which, ill-advisedly maybe, I had emailed to his class a couple of days before. "How dare you?" he said. "How dare you send this without my permission? Did you think I wouldn't find out about it?

"Did you think I'd be jazzed about this?" he complained, indicating the phrase "whispered drunkenly" in the text. "Did you think I'd want them to think I'm an alcoholic? Though in a way it's the least of my problems: Right now they are reading this," he whispered drunkenly, conspiratorially, "and they have no idea why. Right here, right here, this is confusing them," he said, pressing his pudgy thumb onto the manuscript a couple lines later, a fractured and contradictory passage. "Andromeda Yoo is reading this," he said, his voice hoarse with strain. "You . . . you'll see what I mean tomorrow."

Now, years later, as we sat with our drinks in Petersburg, she was supremely sensible. "I agree with you. There must be something else besides the sermon, some other manuscript." She smiled. "You know, this is like what I do all day. I took a Bible history course in college, and I think the thing that made me want to be a lawyer was the discussion of the Q Gospel—you know, how you can deduce the existence of a missing source. It's all meta-fiction, all the time.

That's what I learned in college. So that's what we have here. Where's the actual text?"

. For the purposes of this memoir, I have narrated it verbatim, as if I carried the document with me, or else had committed it to heart. But that's not so. "It's in my office," I told her. Some birds were squawking down by the stream.

"What do you think your father means by a 'sexual indiscretion'? It couldn't have been just sleeping with students. That's what Bennington College was all about, wasn't it? Its founding philosophy. In the 1930s? Didn't you get fired for *not* doing that?"

"I don't think my father knows anything about it. He's just guessing."

This was true, or at least it was true that I thought so. "But it must have been something pretty humiliating," continued Andromeda. "I mean, thirty years later he couldn't even walk around the town."

"I guess."

"Although maybe the only reason he joined the genealogical society was to go back there, to have an excuse. The way he talks about it, it's not like he had any real interest."

"You're wrong about that," I said. "He made me memorize a list of all the Parks, although we tended to stop before Gertrude the Bald."

"Hmm—so maybe it's about the jewel. But the problem is, there must be at least one other source for this business about the cornfields, something that doesn't involve anything about the Claibornes. Because there are two sources from that side, aren't there? Doctor Claiborne and his son? Was there anything about it in the court-martial?"

"Maybe, but I don't know anything about that yet. I was saving it for later. I haven't told anyone."

She frowned. "Who would you tell?"

"Well, I mean the people who might be reading about this. I've told them about Doctor Claiborne and the Battle of the Crater. But the court-martial, I guess I'm already foreshadowing it a little. Part of it, anyway."

Andromeda looked around. There was no one in the neighbor's yard. Not a living soul, unless you counted the cat jumping in and out of the bee's balm.

"That sounds crazy," she said indulgently. "Particularly since now you've mentioned it to me."

"Never mind about that," I interrupted. "We don't want to pay attention to everything at once. One thing after another. Speaking of which, isn't there something else you want to tell me? I mean about this. Now might be a convenient time."

I didn't like to bully her or order her around, especially since it felt so good to talk to her, to let our conversation develop naturally, as if unplanned. All day I had been listening to people's voices inside my head, ghosts long departed, and in some sense I had been telling them what to say.

The sun had gone down, and we watched the bats veer and blunder through the purple sky. The yard was deep and needed mowing. Suddenly it was quite cold.

Petersburg, New York, is a small village in the hollows of the Taconic hills. Quite recently, people like Andromeda and me had started buying up semi-derelict Victorians and redoing them. The town hadn't figured out yet what it thought about that. As a result, we kept to ourselves; we were busy anyway. Andromeda had a gift for interior spaces, and a special talent for making things seem comfortable and organized at the same time. She liked Chinese antiques.

She turned to me and smiled. "Okay, so let's get it over with," she said, raising her glass. "You know that Bible Studies class I told you about? Well, the second semester was all about heresy. And when you talk about this stuff, I'm so totally reminded of these trials in this one part of northern Italy. It was kind of the same thing—these peasants were being prosecuted for witchcraft. But they were the opposite of witches, that's what they claimed. They talked about a tradition, father to son, mother to daughter, going back generations. On some specific nights their souls would leave their bodies and go out to do battle with the real witches and warlocks, who were out to steal the harvest and, you know, poison the wells, make the women miscarry, spread diseases, the usual. I remember thinking, Jesus, we need more people like this. And they never gave in, they never confessed, even though this was part of the whole witchcraft mania of the sixteenth century. I'm sure they were tortured, but even so, they were just so totally convinced that the entire Inquisition was part of the same diabolic plot to keep them from their work—they'd seen it all before."

Andromeda Yoo was so beautiful at that moment, her golden skin, her black hair down her back. I felt she understood me. "Another interesting thing," she said, "was that these people were never the model citizens. There was always something dodgy or damaged about them. You could tell it in the way they talked about each other, not so much about themselves. And of course the judges were always pointing out that they were sluts and whores and drunks and sodomites and village idiots. But they had a place in the community. Everyone was on their side. They had to bring people in from neighboring counties just to have a quorum at the executions."

"That's a relief," I murmured.

She got up from her chair and came to stand behind me, bent down to embrace me—I didn't deserve her! "I'm glad I got that off my chest," she said, a puzzled expression on her face. "Now, where were we?"

And we proceeded to talk about other things. "What do you think he left next to the tree?" she asked. "I'll bet it was the jewel. The tourmaline the size of a pumpkin or whatever. I'll bet that was what was in the secret box under the floor."

"That's crazy. It never would have fit."

"What do you mean? That's what it was for. Do you really think Esther would have left it in the dead man's mouth? Or in his eye—Kepler's eye, wasn't that it? No, she wanted to see where it was hidden. That was probably how she'd found the compartment at the top of the shaft—looking for the jewel. Maybe she had hired the guy in the first place, or she was his lover—no, scratch that. She was probably a lesbian. That's what her mother probably meant about not living in the real world."

"Really. But then why wouldn't she have stolen it that night? Why leave it in the box?"

"I'm not sure. But that's what your grandfather meant about a tiny crime. He just had it for a few minutes. He'd taken it on impulse, and he had time to think during the drive. How could you dispose of such a thing?"

Andromeda had been adopted from a Korean orphanage and then orphaned again when her American parents died in a fire. And they themselves were also orphans, had met in an orphanage, possessed no family or traditions or history on either side—I don't think I had ever known their names. Maybe they had never even had any names. This was one of the things I found comforting about Andromeda, together with her calmness and common sense. She was so different from me.

Our bedroom, underneath the eaves, was always warmer than the rest of the house. Later, I had already dozed off when I heard her say, "I think it probably has to do with his cousin, Theodora. Didn't she kill herself?"

"Yes, when she was a teenager. It was a terrible thing. He was an only child, and she was his only cousin, too. My father always said it was some kind of romantic disappointment. Maybe a pregnancy."

"You mean a 'sexual indiscretion.'"

"I suppose so. But not the same one. The dates don't work out."

"Well, what do you know about her? Is there anything in your boxes?"

"I think there's a photograph. A locket."

"Where?"

I had hung up my pants before we lay down, and put my wallet on the dresser with some loose change, a pocket knife, and a number of other small objects. The locket wasn't among them. It's not as if I carried it around. "I don't know," I said.

But then I felt something in my closed fist. "Wait," I said, opening my hand, revealing it on my palm. It was round and gold, as big as an old-fashioned watch, and had an ornate "T" engraved on the lid. Inside there were two photographs, a smiling young woman on one side, and an older man in a bowler hat on the other, my grandfather's uncle Charlie, perhaps.

"Turn on the light," Andromeda said. "I can't see anything."

There was a reading light beside the bed. I switched it on. Andromeda lay naked on her back, one hand scratching her pubic hair. She turned onto her side, raised herself on one elbow, and her breasts reformed. "Look at the depth of the case," she said. "Maybe there's some kind of secret message inside, under the photograph. There's enough room for a letter folded six or seven times. Look—that's a place where it might lever up," she said, sliding her fingernail under the circle of gold that held the image. Because of her legal work for Sabic Plastics, she had all kinds of special expertise.

Theodora Park had a pleasant, happy face with a big round nose like a doorknob. I thought to myself she might have made a good clown in the circus, though no doubt that was partly because of her distended lips, the white circles on her cheeks, and the fright wig she was wearing underneath the potted geranium that served her for a hat.

"Look," said Andromeda, her beautiful young (Why not? What the hell? She had been a non-traditional student at Williams, older than her classmates, but even so—) body curved around the locket, which we held between us. And under her fingernail, whether it was just a trick of the light, but the woman in the photograph seemed to shift and move and change expression—a sudden, exaggerated grimace, while at the same time the man in the bowler hat and big moustache frowned in disapproval. And that was certainly enough, because Andromeda's black eyes filled with tears. "No," she said, "oh, no, no, no, no, no, no, no. . . . "

7. SECOND LIFE

In fact no one was there when I got home. I feel I can pretend, as long as it is obvious: I had lived by myself for many, many years, and the house was a wreck. Andromeda Yoo is a confabulation, though I suppose she carries a small resemblance to the underdressed avatar of a woman I once met in a sex club in Second Life, or else the lawyer who handled my wife's divorce long ago—not just that poor girl in Rosenheim's class.

No, the other stuff—the peasants from the Friuli—I had discovered for myself, through a chance reference in one of my sister Katy's books. I've always had an interest in European history. Nor do I think there is any surviving information about Theo Park, any diary or letter or written text that might explain her suicide, or if she suffered from these vivid dreams. There isn't a living person who knows anything about her. And I suppose it can be a kind of comfort to imagine that our passions or our difficulties might at some time be released into the air, as if they never had existed. But it is also possible to imagine that the world consists of untold stories, each a little package of urgent feelings that might possibly explain our lives to us. And even if that's an illusion or too much to hope for, it is still possible to think that nothing ever goes away, that the passions of the dead are still intact forever, sealed up irrevocably in the past. No one could think, for example, that if you lost an object that was precious to you, then it would suddenly stop existing. It would be solipsistic arrogance to think like that. No, the object would always be bumping around somewhere, forgotten in someone else's drawer, a compound tragedy.

I got myself a gin and tonic—that much is true—and sat at the kitchen table under the fluorescent light, studying a pack of well-thumbed photographs of my son when he was small. My wife had taken so many, I used to say you could make of a flip-book of his childhood in real time—enough for both of us, as it turned out. More than enough. I could look at them forever, and yet I always felt soiled, somehow, afterward, as if I had indulged myself in something dirty. In the same way, perhaps, you can look at photographs of naked women on the Internet for hours at a time, each one interesting for some tiny, urgent fraction of a second.

I went upstairs to lie down. In the morning, I telephoned the offices of *The Bennington Banner*, where someone was uploading the biweekly edition. I didn't have a precise date, and I didn't even know exactly what I was looking for. But a good part of the archives was now online, and after a couple of hours I found the story. On the first of November, 1939, a Bennington College student had died in a car accident. The road was slippery after a rainstorm. She hadn't been driving. The details were much as I'd suspected.

"What do you think about what's happening in Virginia," said the woman on the phone.

"Virginia?"

The Bennington Banner is about small amounts of local news, if it's about anything. But this woman paid attention to the blogs. "There's some kind of disturbance," she told me. "Riots in the streets."

Subsequent to this conversation, I took a drive. I drove out to the Park-McCullough House. The place was boarded up, the grounds were overgrown. After ten minutes I continued on toward the former Bennington College campus and took a left down the Silk Road through the covered bridge. Along the back way to the monument I looked for likely trees, but it was impossible to tell. When I reached Route 7, I continued straight toward Williamstown. I thought if there was a message for me—a blog from the past, say—it might be hidden in my grandfather's painting, which was, I now imagined, less a piece of De Chirico surrealism than an expression of regret.

It had rained during the night, and toward three o'clock the day was overcast and humid. In my office, I sat in the wreckage with my feet on the desk. I looked up at the painting, and I could tell there was something wrong with it. I just had a feeling, and so I turned on my computer, IM'd my ex-wife in Richmond, and asked her to meet me in Second Life.

Which meant Romania, where she was working, supposedly, as some kind of virtual engineer. In Second Life, her office is in a hot air balloon suspended above the Piata Revolutiei in Bucharest; you'd have to teleport. It was a lovely place, decked out with a wood-burning stove, but she didn't want to meet me there. Too private. Instead we flew east to the Black Sea coast, past Constanta to the space park, the castle on the beach, where there was always a crowd. We alighted on the boardwalk and went into a café. We both got lattés at the machine, and sat down to talk.

God knows what Romania is like now. God knows what's going on there. But in Second Life it's charming and picturesque, with whitewashed buildings painted with flowers and livestock, and red tile roofs. In Second Life my ex-wife's name is Nicolae Quandry. She wears a military uniform and a handlebar mustache—a peculiar transformation from the time I knew her. It's hard not to take it personally, even after all these years—according to the *Kanun*, or tribal code, women under certain circumstances can take a vow of celibacy and live as men, with all the rights and privileges. Albanian by heritage, Nicola—Nicolae, here—had a great-aunt who made that choice, after the death of her father and brothers. Of course her great-aunt had not had a grown autistic son.

It was always strange to see her in her hip boots, epaulettes, and braid. She had carried this to extremes, because once I had told her that her new name and avatar reminded me of Nicolae Ceausescu, the Romanian dictator whom I'd researched extensively for my novel—not that she looked like him. He was a drab little bureaucrat, while she carried a pistol on her hip. With Saturn hanging low over the Black Sea, its rings clearly visible, she stood out among all the space aliens that were walking around. "My psychiatrist says I'm not supposed to talk to you," I typed.

"Hey, Matt," she typed—my name in Second Life is Matthew Wirefly. "I figured you would want to bring Adrian a birthday present."

It was hard to tell from her face, but I imagined she sounded happy to hear from me, a function of my strategy in both marriage and divorce, to always give her everything she wanted. Besides, everything had happened so long ago. Now I was an old man, though you wouldn't necessarily have known it from my avatar. "Yes, that's right," I typed. "I bought him a sea turtle at the aquarium. I'll bring it to his party. Where's it going to be?"

"Oh, I don't know. Terra Nova. You know how he likes steampunk."

Actually, I didn't know. I'd thought he was still in his sea-mammal stage, which had lasted ten years or so. The previous year he'd had his party on the beach in Mamaia Sat, and I'd ridden up on the back of a beluga whale.

Now we typed about this and that. A man with six arms wandered by, gave us an odd look, it seemed to me. The name above his head was in Korean characters.

After a few minutes I got down to business. She had never known my grandfather, but I tried to fill her in. After a certain amount of time, she interrupted. "I don't even believe you have a psychiatrist," she typed. "What do you pay him?"

"Her," I corrected. "Nowadays they work for food."

"Hunh. Maybe you could ask her to adjust your meds. Remember when you thought the graffiti on the subway was a message for you? 'Close Guantanamo'—that's good advice! 'Call Mark'—you're probably the only person who ever called. And you didn't even get through."

Good times, I thought. "Hey, I misdialed. Or he moved. Hey, *le monde n'est qu'un texte.*"

"Fine—whatever. That's so true. For twenty years I've thanked God it's not my responsibility anymore, to act as your damn filter."

She knew what I meant, and I knew what she meant. It's possible for me to get carried away. But I hadn't ever told her during the eight years of our relationship, and I didn't tell her now, that I had always, I think, exaggerated certain symptoms for dramatic effect.

Once, when New York City was still New York City, I'd belonged to a squash club on Fifth Avenue. Someone I played with got it into his head that I was Canadian, introduced me to someone else—I let it go. It seemed impolite to insist. Within weeks I was tangled up in explanations, recriminations, and invented histories. When I found myself having to learn French, to memorize maps of Montreal, I had to quit the club.

This was like that. When Nicola and I first got together, I pretended to have had a psychiatric episode years before, thinking that was a good way to appeal to her—a short-term tactic that had long-term effects. It was a story she was amusingly eager to believe, a story confirmed rather than contradicted by my parents' befuddled refusal to discuss the issue, a typical (she imagined) Episcopalian reticence that was in itself symptomatic. And it was a story I had to continue embellishing, particularly after Adrian was first diagnosed.

But like all successful lies, it was predominantly true. These things run in families, after all. And sometimes I have a hard time prioritizing: "What's happening in Richmond?" I asked her. "What's happening down there?"

Nicolae took a sip from her latte, wiped her mustache. Above us, from the deck of the space park, you could see the solar system trying to persevere, while behind it the universe was coming to an end. Stars exploded and went cold. "Matt," she typed. "You don't want to know. It would just worry you. I don't even know. Something downtown. Abigail has gone out and I—fuck, what could you do, anyway?" She touched the pistol at her hip.

After we logged off, I sat for a while in peace. Then I got up on my desk so I could look at the picture, "Ghosts Doing the Orange Dance."

Kneeling, my nose up close, I saw a few things that were new. No, that's not right. I noticed a few things I hadn't seen before. This is partly because I'd just been to the house, circled the drive. But now I saw some differences.

My grandfather had never been able to paint human beings. Trained as an architect, he had excelled in façades, ruins, urban landscapes. But people's faces and hands were mysterious to him, and so instead he made indistinct stylized figures, mostly in the distance. Shapes of light and darkness. Star-shaped ghosts with oranges in their hands. The haunted house in the moonlight, or else a burning light behind the clouds, descending to the roof. Men and women in the corn, beyond the porte-cochere. A single light at the top of the house, and a shadow against the glass. Kepler's eye. I wondered if this was where the dumbwaiter reached the third floor.

Down below, along the garden wall, a woman lay back against a tree trunk. Her face was just a circle of white, and she had long white hair. She was holding an orange, too, holding it out as if in supplication. Her legs were white. Her skirt had ridden up.

I thought I had not seen that tree against that wall that morning, when I had stopped my Toyota on the drive. My grandfather was good at trees. This was a swamp willow, rendered in miniature, so that the branches drooped over the woman's head. I thought there was no tree like that on the grounds of the Park-McCullough house. So instead I went to look for it.

8. In Quantico

Naturally, after forty years I didn't find anything valuable. But there was a willow tree along the Silk Road, set back on the other side of a ditch. He must have been going very fast.

I dug down through the old roots. And I did find something, a key ring with two stainless steel keys, in good condition. One of them, I assumed, was a secret or back-door key to the abandoned McCullough mansion. The other was much smaller, more generic, the kind of key that could open many cheap little locks. After a detour to my office, I took it home. I unpacked my satchel, took out my laptop. I arranged various stacks of paper on the kitchen table. And then I used the little key to unlock the steel dispatch case that had come to me from Puerto Rico. I knew what I'd find, the various documents and exhibits from the court-martial of Captain Robert Watson Claiborne, USMC.

After dinner (Indian takeout and a beer), I began my search. The trial had taken place at the Marine barracks at Quantico, Virginia, during the second and third weeks in January, 1919. There were about eight hundred pages of testimony, accusations and counter-accusations regarding my grandfather's behavior aboard the USS *Cincinnati* during the previous November, the last month of the European war. Captain Claiborne was only recently attached to the ship, in command of a detachment of Marines. But during the course of twenty-seven days there were complaints against him from four Marine Corps privates and a Navy ensign, when the vessel was anchored off Key West.

Colonel Dion Williams, commander of the barracks at Quantico, presided over the court, and the judge advocate was Captain Leo Horan. On the fourth day of the trial, my grandfather took the stand in his own defense. Here's what I found on page 604 of the transcript, during Captain Horan's cross-examination:

463. Q. In his testimony you heard him say in substance that he came into your room on the occasion when he came there to see a kodak, and that you and he lay on your bunk or bed and that he slept, or pretended to fall asleep, and that at that time you put your hands on his private parts; that he roused himself, and that you desisted, and this was repeated some two or three times, and that at the last time when he feigned sleep, you reached up and pulled his hand down in the direction of your private parts. Is that true or not?

A. That is not true.

464. Q. Did anything like that happen?

A. Nothing whatsoever.

465. Q. Did you fondle his person?

A. I did not fondle his person.

466. Q. Or touch him in any way except as you might have—

A. I only touched him in the manner as one might touch another, as one would come in contact with another lying down next to each other on a bed, the approximate width of which was about as that table (indicating).

467. Q. I see. Referring to another matter, will you tell the court, Captain Claiborne, what kind of a school this was you say you started at Sharon, Connecticut?

A. A school for boys.

468. Q. Average age?

A. Average age was twelve or thirteen.

469. Q. The length of time you ran it?

A. One year, just before the war.

470. Q. I see. Did you sleep soundly on board the *Cincinnati*, as a general rule?

A. I did.

471. Q. Now Captain Claiborne, in your original response to the complaint against you, in the matter of Ensign Mowbray's testimony as to your behavior on the night of the sixth of November, I have here your response saying that you could not have knowingly or consciously done such a thing. I believe your words to Commander Moses, as he testified, were that you had done nothing of the sort in any conscious moment. What did you mean by that?

A. I meant that this could not be true, that I had a clean record behind me, and that I surely did nothing of the sort in any conscious moment. He immediately interrupted me and went on to say, "Oh, I know what you are going to say about doing it in your sleep," or something of that sort. I said, "Nor in any unconscious moment, for surely no one who has had a record behind him such as I can show you would do such things as these in unconscious moments, or asleep." This is what he must have meant when he referred to a qualified denial.

472. Q. I see. The alleged conduct of you toward Ensign Mowbray—do you now deny that that might have been in an unconscious manner?

A. I do.

473. Q. I see. About this radium-dialed watch: as I recall your testimony, you had a little pocket watch?

A. I had quite a large pocket watch, a normal watch, too large to be fixed into any leather case which would hold it onto the wrist.

474. Q. Mr. Mowbray's statement about seeing a wrist-watch, radium dialed, on your wrist the night of the first sleeping on the divan is a fabrication?

A. Yes.

475. Q. You deny wearing a wrist-watch on that night?

A. I deny wearing a wrist-watch on that night.

476. Q. I see. Now, taking up the matter of this first hike, before you turned in with Walker, will you tell the court how far you went on this hike, approximately?

A. About three or four miles.

477. Q. Along the beach from Key West?

A. We went through Key West and out into the country.

478. Q. On these hikes they went swimming along the beach?

A. On that hike they went in swimming at my orders.

479. Q. Yes. What happened afterward?

A. They came out and dried themselves and put on their clothes and took physical exercise.

480. Q. How were they clad when they took this physical exercise?

A. Some of them had on underwear and some of them did not. The majority of them had on underwear.

481. Q. How were you dressed at the time that the men were undressed going through this physical drill on the beach?

A. I don't recall.

482. Q. I want a little bit more than that. Do you deny that you were undressed at the time?

A. I either had on part of my underwear, or my entire underwear, or had on none.

483. Q. Or had on what?

A. None.

484. Q. In front of the guard, were you?

A. I don't recall.

485. Q. But you do admit that you may have been entirely naked.

A. I may have been.

486. Q. You admit that? They went through these Swedish exercises, whatever they were? Physical drill?

A. Physical drill, yes.

487. Q. I see. Now, Captain Claiborne, you admit to sleeping soundly on board ship, as a general rule?

A. As a general rule.

488. Q. No problem with somnambulism, or anything of that sort?

Counsel for the accused (Mr. Littleton): If the court please, I began by saying I would desist from making any objections in this case. Nevertheless, I could not then anticipate that counsel would profit from my forbearance by making these insinuations about the conduct of the accused, in these matters that are irrelevant to the complaints against him. I did not anticipate that counsel would undertake to go all over the world asking this sort of question about conduct which, if Captain Claiborne had not acted as he did, would have constituted a dereliction. I am going to withdraw my statement that I will not object, and I am going to insist upon the rules in reference to this witness. He needs protection in some way from the promiscuous examination regarding every Tom, Dick, and Harry in the universe. I insist that the counsel shall confine his examination to things which are somewhere within the range of these charges. We cannot be called upon to meet every ramification that comes up here. We cannot be called on to suffer the imputation which a mere question itself carries.

The judge advocate: Are you objecting to that question, the last question about somnambulism?

Counsel for the accused (Mr. Littleton): Yes, the last question is the only one I could object to. The others were all answered. I am objecting to it on the basis that it is irrelevant.

By a member: Mr. President, I also would like to arise to ask the point of these questions, so that we may know, at the time they are asked, whether they are relevant or not.

Counsel assisting the judge advocate: Does the court wish enlightenment on that?

The president: Yes.

Counsel assisting the judge advocate: If the court please, we would be very ready and willing to tell you what our purpose is, but it would disclose the purpose of the cross examination, and I don't think we are required to state before the court and before the witness what our purpose may be in bringing out this subject of somnambulism. But it is perfectly proper cross examination, inasmuch as the witness has testified to sleeping soundly at the time of these alleged incidents.

The accused: I am perfectly willing to answer the question.

Counsel assisting the judge advocate: The witness and the judge advocate are at one on that now, if the judge advocate will ask that question.

The president: As I understood, the question of the member was, "Is it relevant or not."

The member: Yes, that is right.

Counsel assisting the judge advocate: Yes, sir, I state from my study of the case that it is relevant. Does that answer the member's question?

The court was cleared.

The court was opened. All parties to the trial entered, and the president announced that the court overruled the objection.

489. Q. Very well, Captain Claiborne. Have you ever suffered from somnambulism?

Counsel for the accused (Mr. Littleton): I object—

The judge advocate: Let me rephrase the question. Did you experience an episode of somnambulism while on board the U.S.S. *Cincinnati*, between the first and twenty-seventh of November of last year?

A. I can't remember exactly what day. But I had a sensation of being awake and dreaming at the same time. This is not unusual with me, and from time to time I have had this experience ever since I was a boy. This is only the most extreme example, and I imagine that I was affected by a sort of nervous excitement, due to the end of the hostilities in Europe, and of course my own catastrophic reversal of fortune. This was in the very early morning when I saw myself at the top of a great cliff, while below me I could see the streets of a town laid out with lines of lamp-posts, glowing in a sort of a fog. I thought to myself that I was overlooking a town or city of the dead. There were houses full of dead men, and hospitals full of soldiers of every nationality, and also influenza patients who were laid outside in an open field or empty lot. I thought there were thousands of them. At the same time there was a long, straight boulevard cutting through the town from north to south. I saw a regiment or a battalion march along it toward a dark beach along the sea, which had a yellow mist and a yellow froth on the water. Other men climbed toward me up a narrow ravine. I thought to myself that I must fight them to protect the high plain, and I had a stick in my hand to do it. As they clambered up I struck at them one by one. The first fellow over the ledge was Captain Harrington, whom I replaced on board the *Cincinnati*, because he had died of the influenza in October—the bloom was on his face. It was a fight, but I struck and struck until the stick burst in my hand. Then I woke up and found myself outside on the balcony, long past midnight—

490 Q. By balcony I presume you mean the ship's rail—

A. No, no, I mean the balcony of my hotel where I was staying with my wife. I mean I had left the bed and climbed out onto the balcony, dressed only in my shirt. It was four A.M., judging from my wristwatch. This was in New York City before Christmas, less than a month ago, several weeks after I had been detached from the ship.

Counsel assisting the judge advocate: Captain Claiborne, please restrict your answers to the time covered in the complaint, prior to the twenty-seventh of November.

Counsel for the accused (Mr. Littleton): Again I must object to this entire line of questioning, on the grounds that it is irrelevant.

The judge advocate: I withdraw the question—

The president: The objection is overruled. The court would like the witness to continue.

The member: This was during the third week in Advent, was it not? During what is commonly called the "Ember Days"?

The president: The stick that was in your hand, the court would like to know what type of stick it was.

The member: Captain Claiborne, will you tell the court whether you were born still wrapped inside an afterbirth membrane, which is a trait or condition that can run in certain families—

The judge advocate: Mr. President, I must agree with my esteemed colleague, the counsel for the accused—

The president: The objection is overruled. The witness will answer the question. Now, Captain Claiborne, the court would like to know if you experienced any stiffness or muscular discomfort prior to this event, especially in your neck or jaw.

A. Well, now that you mention it, I did have a discomfort of that kind.

The president: The court would like you to expand on your answer to an earlier question, when you described your encounter with Captain Harrington. You said the bloom was on his face, or words of that effect. Did you see any marks or symptoms of the influenza epidemic on him at that time?

Counsel for the accused (Mr. Littleton): I object—

The judge advocate: Mr. President—

The president: The objection is overruled. The witness will answer the question.

A. Now that you mention it, there is a great deal more I could say about the events of that night, between the time I recognized Captain Harrington and the time I came to myself on the balcony above Lexington Avenue. If the court wishes, I could proceed. Captain Harrington was the first but by no means the last who were climbing up along the precipice, and all of them bore traces of the epidemic. Pale skin, dull eyes, hair lank and wet. Hectic blossoms on their cheeks, and in this way they were different than the soldiers marching below them in the streets of the necropolis, most of whom, I see now, were returning from France. I remember Captain Harrington because I was able to dislodge his fingers and thrust him backward with a broken head. But soon I was forced to retreat, because these ones who had climbed the cliffs and spread out along the plain were too numerous for us to resist. I had no more than a company of raw recruits under my command. Against us marched several hundred of the enemy, perhaps as many as a battalion of all qualities and conditions, while behind them I could see a large number of women in their hospital gowns. Severely outnumbered, we gave way before them. But I brought us to the high ground, where we attempted to defend a single house on a high hill, a mansion in the French style. The weather had been calm, but then I heard a roll of distant thunder. A stroke of lightning split the sky, followed by a pelting rain, and a wind strong enough to flatten the wide, flat stalks as the fire burned. By then it was black night, and whether from some stroke of lightning or some other cause, but the roof of the house had caught on fire. By its light I could see the battle in the corn, while at the same time we were reinforced quite unexpectedly in a way that is difficult for me to describe. But a ship had come down from the clouds, a great metal airship or dirigible, while a metal stair unrolled out of its belly . . .

9. Ember Days

My grandfather was immediately acquitted of all charges. The president of the court, and at least one of its members, came down to shake his hand. Nevertheless, he did not linger in the Marine Corps, but put in for his release as quickly as he could. In some ways he was not suited to a soldier's life. You can't please everyone: There were some—among them his brother-in-law, Howard Harrington—who thought his acquittal had not fully restored his reputation.

Subsequently he ran a music school in Rye, New York, hosted a classical music radio program in New York City, and even wrote a book, before he left the United States to practice law in the Caribbean. Prior to his disbarment he was full of schemes—expensive kumquat jellies, Nubian goats delivered to the mainland by submarine during the Second World War—all of which my grandmother dutifully underwrote. His farm in Maricao was called the Hacienda Santa Rita, and it was there that we visited him when I was nine years old, my father, my two older sisters, and myself. My mother hadn't seen him since she was a teenager, and did not accompany us. She could never forgive the way he'd treated her and her brother when they were children. This was something I didn't appreciate at the time, particularly since he went out of his way to charm us. He organized a parade in our honor, roasted a suckling pig. And he showed an interest in talking to me—the first adult ever to do so—perhaps from some mistaken idea of primogeniture. In those days he was a slender, elegant, white-haired old man.

Later I was worried that my own life would follow his trajectory of false starts and betrayals and dependency. Early on he had staked out the position that ordinary standards of civilized behavior had no hold on people like him. On the contrary, the world owed him a debt because of his genius, which had been thwarted and traduced at every turn—a conspiracy of jealous little minds. It was this aspect of her father's personality that my mother hated most of all, and regularly exposed to ridicule. A moderately gifted musician, he had the pretensions of genius, she used to say, without the talent. Moreover, she said, even if he'd been Franz Liszt himself, he could not have justified the damage that he caused. When I asked why her mother had stayed with him, she retorted that you don't turn a sick dog out to die. But I suspected there was more to her parents' marriage than that, and more to his sense of privilege. Laying the record of his court-martial aside, I imagined that any summary of his life that did not include the valiant battle he had waged—one of many, I guessed—against the victims of the Spanish Influenza epidemic of 1918, would seem truncated and absurd. Maybe the goats and the kumquats were the visible, sparse symptoms of a secret and urgent campaign, the part of the ice above the water.

When my mother talked about her father, I always thought she was advising me, because it was obvious from photographs that I took after him. She had no patience for anything old, either from her or my father's family, and she was constantly throwing things away. My father's father never forgave her for disposing of the caul I was born in, and she never forgave him for pressing on me, when I was seven, a bizarre compensation for this supposed loss. He had wrapped it up for me, or Winifred had: a sequined and threadbare velvet pouch, which contained, in a rubberized inner compartment, his cousin Theo's caul, her prized possession, which she had carried with her at all times. She had embroidered her name in thick gold thread; furious, my mother snatched up the pouch and hid it away. I only rediscovered it years later, when she asked me to move some boxes in the attic.

When I was a child I kept the thought of this velvet pouch as a picture in my mind, and referred to it mentally whenever I heard a story about something large contained in something small, as often happens in fairy tales. I had seen it briefly, when my grandfather had first pressed it into my hands. It was about six inches long, red velvet worn away along the seams. Some of the stitches on the "T" and the "h" had come undone.

But I wondered when I was young, was I special in any way? Perhaps it was my specialness that could explain my failures, then and always. At a certain moment, we cannot but hope, the ordinary markers of success will show themselves to be fraudulent, irrelevant, diversionary. All those cheating hucksters, those athletes and lovers, those trusted businessmen and competent professionals, those good fathers, good husbands, and good providers will hang their heads in shame while the rest of us stand forward, unapologetic at long last.

Thinking these inspirational thoughts, in the third week of September—the third sequence of ember days of the liturgical year, as I had learned from various wikipedias—I drove up to the Park-McCullough house again. As usual that summer and fall, I had not been able to fall asleep in my own bed. Past two o'clock in the morning, Theodora Park's velvet purse in my pocket, I sidled up to each of the mansion's doors in turn, and tried the second key I had found among the roots of the willow. Some windows on the upper floor were broken. Ghosts, I thought, were wandering through the building and the grounds, but I couldn't get the key to work. Defeated, I stepped back from the porte-cochere; it was a warm night. Bugs blundered in the beam of my flashlight. The trees had grown up over the years, and it was too much to expect that a ship or dirigible would find the space to land here safely. The same could be said of Bartlett Hill in Preston, which I had visited many years before. Logged and cleared during Colonial times, now it was covered with second- or third-growth forest. From the crest overlooking the Avery-Parke Cemetery, you could barely see the lights and spires of Foxwoods Casino, rising like the Emerald City only a few miles away. I found myself wondering if the casino was still there, and if the "ruind hutts of the Pecuods" had "burst afire" as a result of the ship coming down, or as some kind of signal to indicate a landing site. Whichever, it was certainly interesting that in Robert Claiborne's account of the battle on the French-style mansion's lawn, "the roof of the house had caught on fire."

Interesting, but not conclusive. As a scholar, I was trained to discount these seductive similarities. I had not yet dared to unbutton the velvet pouch or slip my hand inside, but with my hand firmly in my pocket I stepped back through the broken, padlocked, wrought-iron fence and stumbled back to the main road, where I had left my car. And because, like three-quarters of the faculty at Williams College, I was on unpaid leave for the fall semester, I thought I would drive down to Richmond and see Adrian, who was now thirty years old—a milestone. That was at least my intention. I had a reliable automobile, one of the final hydrogen-cell, solar-panel hybrids before Toyota discontinued exports. I would take Route 2 to 87, making a wide semicircle around the entire New York City area, before rejoining 95 in central New Jersey. I would drive all night. There'd be no traffic to speak of, except the lines of heavy trucks at all the checkpoints.

So let's just say I went that way. Let's just say it was possible to go. And let's just say that nothing happened on that long, dark drive, until morning had come.

Beyond the Delaware Bridge I saw the army convoys headed south along I-95. North of Baltimore it became clear I couldn't continue much farther, because there was no access to Washington. There were barricades on the interstate, and flashing lights. Shortly before noon I got off the 695 bypass to drive through Baltimore itself—sort of a nostalgia tour, because Nicola and I had lived on North Calvert Street and 31st, near the Johns Hopkins campus, when Adrian was born. I drove past the line of row houses without stopping. Most of them were boarded up, which could not fail to depress me and throw me back into the past. I took a left and turned into the east gate of the Homewood campus. I wanted to see if my old ID would still get me into the Eisenhower Library, so I parked and gave it a try. It was a bright, cool day, and I was cheered to see a few students lying around the lawn.

I needn't have worried—there was no one at the circulation desk. Once inside the library, I took the stairs below street level to one of the basements, a peculiar place that I remembered from the days when I had taught at the university. The electricity wasn't functioning, but some vague illumination came from the airshafts, and I had my flashlight. With some difficulty I made my way toward the north end of that level, where a number of books by various members of my family were shelved in different sections that nevertheless came together in odd proximity around an always-deserted reading area. Within a few steps from those dilapidated couches you could find a rare copy of Robert W. Claiborne's book *How Man Learned Music*. A few shelves farther on there were six or seven volumes by his son, my uncle, on popular science or philology. In the opposite direction, if you didn't mind stooping, you would discover three books on autism by Clara Claiborne Park, while scarcely a hundred feet away there were a whole clutch of my father's physics textbooks and histories of science. Still on the same level it was possible to unearth Edwin Avery Park's tome (Harcourt, Brace, 1927) on modernist architecture, *New Backgrounds for a New Age*, as well as other books by other members of the family. And filling out the last corner of a rough square, at comfortable eye-level, in attractive and colorful bindings, stood a row of my own novels, including *A Princess of Roumania*. It was one of the few that had come out while I was living in Baltimore, and I was touched to see they had continued to acquire the later volumes, either out of loyalty or bureaucratic inertia—certainly not from need—up to the point where everything turned digital.

It is such a pleasure to pick up a book and hold it. I will never get used to reading something off a screen. I gathered together an assortment of texts and went back to the reading area, rectangular vinyl couches around a square table. Other people had been there recently; there were greasy paper bags, and a bedroll, and a gallon jug of water. The tiled floor was marred with ashes and charred sticks, and the skylight was dark with soot. But I had proprietary instincts, and would not be deterred. I put down my leather satchel and laid the books down in a pile, squared the edges, and with my flashlight in my hand I played a game I hadn't played in years, since the last time I was in that library.

The game was called "trajectories," my personal version of the *I Ching*. I would choose at random various sentences and paragraphs, hoping to combine them into a kind of narrative, or else whittle them into an arrow of language that might point into the future. For luck I took Cousin Theo's velvet pouch out of my pocket, ran my thumb along the worn places. I did not dare unbutton it, thinking, as usual, that whatever had once been inside of it had probably dried up and disappeared. The pouch, I imagined, was as empty as Pandora's box or even emptier. How big was a caul, anyway? How long did it take for it to crumble into dust?

I set to work. Here was my first point of reference, from my uncle Bob (Robert W. Jr.) Claiborne's book on human evolution, *God or Beast* (Norton, 1974), page 77:

> . . . To begin with, then, in that the women to whom I have been closest during my lifetime have all of them been bright, intellectually curious, and independent-minded. My mother was involved in the women's rights movement before World War I, and until her retirement worked at administrative jobs; at this writing she is, at eighty-six, still actively interested in people, ideas, and public affairs. My sister is a college teacher and author. . . .
>
> Given this sort of background, it will probably not surprise the reader much to learn that for most of my life I have preferred the company of women—interesting ones—to that of men. Not just some of my best friends but nearly all of them have been women. Evolution and genetics aside, then, I obviously find women distinctly different from men—and so far as I am concerned, *vive la différence!*

And on page 84:

> Thus it seems to me very probable that human males possess a built-in tolerance for infants and young children, as well as a built-in interest in them and capacity to become emotionally involved with them—a conclusion that seems wholly consistent with what we know about human societies. I would also suspect that, like both baboon and chimp males, the human male has a less powerful tendency to become involved with the young than does the female. I can't prove this, and indeed am not certain that it can ever be either proved or disproved. Nonetheless, it seems to me at least arguable that the emotional rewards of fatherhood are somewhat less than those of motherhood. Be that as it may, however, the rewards exist and I, for one, would hate to have forgone them.

In these passages I could see in my uncle a wistful combination of pedantry and 1960s masculinity. As I read, I remembered him telling me about a trip to visit his father in the Virgin Islands when he was a teenager. He had found him living with an alumnus of the music school, a boy also named Robert, whom he had already passed off to the neighbors as his son, Robert Jr. Loud and gleeful, sitting on his leather sofa in the West Tenth Street apartment, my uncle had described the farcical misunderstandings and logistical contortions that had accompanied his stay.

But what about this, a few more pages on? Here in the flashlight's small tight circle, when I brought it close:

> The point bears repetition, because it is important, and because no one else is willing to make it (I've checked.) . . .

I thought this was a promising place to start, and so I laid the book down, picked up another at random. It was *The Grand Contraption*, a book about comparative cosmologies that my father—the husband, as it happens, of the "college teacher and author" mentioned above—published in 2005. Here's what he had to say to me, on page 142:

> . . . Once more the merchant looked around him. Far away on the road someone walked toward the hill, but there was still time. A little smoke still came out of the eastern pot. There was no sound but he went on, softly reciting *Our Father*. He crossed himself, stepped into the center of the triangle, filled his lungs, and bellowed into the quiet air, "Make the chair ready!"
>
> But it is time for us to leave the demons alone. Even if supernatural beings are an important part of many people's vision of the world, they belong to a different order of nature and should be allowed some privacy.

I didn't think so. Looking up momentarily, glancing down the long dark layers of books, reflecting briefly on the diminished condition of the world, it didn't occur to me that privacy was in short supply. It didn't occur to me that it had any value whatsoever, since a different order of nature was what I was desperate to reveal.

But I was used to these feelings of ambivalence. Leafing forward through the book, I remembered how studiously my father had competed with his own children. After my sister started publishing her own histories of science, he switched from physics to a version of the same field, claiming it was the easier discipline, and therefore suitable to his waning powers. Princeton University Press had been her publisher before it was his. And after I had started selling science fiction stories in the 1980s, he wrote a few himself. He sent them off to the same magazines, claiming that he wanted to start out easy, just like me. Though unprintable, all his stories shared an interesting trait—they started out almost aggressively conventional, before taking an unexpected science-fiction turn. At the time I'd wondered if he was trying to mimic aspects of my style. If so, could it be true that he had found no emotional rewards in fatherhood?

Disappointed by this line of thought, I glanced down at the book again, where my thumb had caught. The beam of the flashlight, a red rim around a yellow core, captured these words: "The point bears repetition."

That was enough. I closed *The Grand Contraption* with a bang that reverberated through the library. Apprehensive, I shined the light back toward the stairway, listening for an answering noise.

After a moment, to reassure myself, I opened a novel written by my father's mother, Edwin Avery Park's first wife. It was called *Walls Against the Wind*, and had been published by Houghton Mifflin. On the strength of the advance, my grandmother had taken my father on a bicycle tour through Western Ireland in 1935. This, from the last pages:

> 'I'm going to Moscow,' Miranda told him. 'They have another beauty and a different God—' The tones of her voice were cool as spring rain. 'It's what I have to do. It's all arranged.'
>
> 'Yes . . . I wish you'd understand.'
>
> 'I'm going almost immediately. I'm going to work there and be part of it.' Her voice came hard and clipped like someone speaking into a long-distance telephone. 'Will you come to Russia with me?' she challenged her brother. 'Will you do that?'
>
> Adrian flung back his head, unexpectedly meeting her challenge. His eyes were blue coals in the white fire of his face.
>
> 'All right,' he said. 'I'll go with you.'
>
> She wanted them to go to Russia. It was the only thing she wanted to do. There was a fine clean world for them there, with hard work and cold winters. It was the kind of world she could dig into and feel at home in. She did not want to live in softness with Adrian. Only in the clean cold could the ripe fruit of his youth keep firm and fresh. She gave him her hand across the table. Perhaps it would work out—some way. Russia. In Russia, she thought, anything can happen. . . .

Anything could happen. Of course not much information had come out of Russia for a long time, not even the kind of disinformation that might have convinced a cultivated Greenwich Village *bohemienne* like my grandmother that Russia might be a bracing place to relocate in the 1930s. Now, of course, in Moscow there wasn't even Second Life.

But maybe my thinking was too literal. Parts of what had been Quebec, I knew from various websites, were experimenting with a new form of socialism. Maybe, I thought, my impersonation of a Canadian in New York City long before had constituted some kind of preparation, or at least some caul-induced clairvoyance. Maybe my grandmother's text was telling me to move up there, to escape my responsibilities or else bring them with me to attempt something new. Or if that was impossible, maybe I was to reorganize my own life along socialistic or even communistic lines, clear away what was unneeded, especially this bourgeois obsession with dead objects and the dead past. The world would have a future, after all, and I could choose to share it or else not.

And of course all this frivolous thinking was meant to hide a disturbing coincidence. Adrian was my son's name. Furthermore, my wife had miscarried a few years before he was born, a girl we were intending to name Miranda. But I don't think, in my previous trajectories, I had ever glanced at this particular book. The library contained several other romances by Frances Park.

Was I to think that if Miranda had lived, she would have been able to reach her brother as I and his mother had not, break him out of his isolation? Briefly, idly, I wondered if, Abigail now dead in some unfortunate civil disturbance, I could swoop down on Richmond like Ulysses S. Grant. . . .

After a few moments, I tightened my flashlight's beam. What did I possess so far? A deluded vision of a fine clean world, with hard work and cold winters. Demons, rapid transformations, and the diluted pleasures of fatherhood. Almost against my will, a pattern was beginning to materialize.

But now I turned to something else, a Zone book from 2006 called *Secrets of Women*, page 60:

> . . . In addition to these concerns about evidence, authenticity, and female corporeality, a second factor helps explain why anatomies were performed principally or exclusively on holy women: the perceived similarities between the production of internal relics and the female physiology of conception. Women, after all, generated other bodies inside their own. God's presence in the heart might be imagined as becoming pregnant with Christ.

It was true that I had many concerns about evidence, authenticity, and female corporeality, although it had not occurred to me until that moment to wonder why anatomies had been performed (either principally or exclusively) on holy women. These words had been written by my sister, Katy Park, who had been a history professor at Harvard University.

She had left Boston in 2019, when the city was attacked, but up until her death she was still working in Second Life. Her lectures were so popular, she used to give them in the open air, surrounded by hundreds of students and non-students. For a course in utopias, she had created painstaking reproductions of Plato's Republic, Erewhon, Islandia, and Kim Stanley Robinson's Orange County. Or once I'd seen her give a private seminar in Andreas Veselius's surgical amphitheater, while he performed an autopsy down below.

She had not had children. But her words could not but remind me of my ex-wife's pregnancy, and how miraculous that had seemed. Anxious, I took the laptop from my satchel and tried to contact Nicola in Richmond, but everything was down. Or almost everything—there was information available on almost any year but this one.

So maybe it wasn't even true, that I could choose to share in the world's future. It wasn't a matter of simple nostalgia: For a long time, for many people and certainly for me, the past had taken the future's place, as any hope or sense of forward progress had dried up and disappeared. But now, as I aged, more and more the past had taken over the present also, because the past was all we had. Everywhere, it was the past or nothing. In Second Life, frustrated, I pulled up some of the daily reconstructions of the siege of 1864-65—why not? I could see the day when my New Orleans great-great-grandmother, Clara Justine Lockett, crossed the line with food and blankets for her brother, who was serving with the Washington Artillery. Crossing back, she'd been taken for a spy, and had died of consumption while awaiting trial.

Or during the previous July, I could see at a glance that during the Battle of the Crater, inexplicably, unforgivably, General Burnsides had waited more than an hour after the explosion to advance, allowing the Confederates to re-form their ranks. If he had attacked immediately, before dawn, he might have ended the war that day.

Exasperated by his failure, I logged off. I picked up a book my mother had written about my younger sister, published in 1967 when she was nine years old. As if to reassure myself, I searched out a few lines from the introduction where my mother introduced the rest of the family under a selection of aliases. Katy was called Sara. Rachel was called Becky. I was called Matthew:

> If I were to describe them this would be the place to do it. Their separate characteristics. The weaknesses and strengths of each one of them, are part of Elly's story. But it is a part that must remain incomplete, even at the risk of unreality. Our children have put up with a lot of things because of Elly; they will not have to put up with their mother's summation of their personalities printed in a book . . .

This seemed fair and just to me, though it meant we scarcely appeared or existed in our own history. I wouldn't make the same mistake; finding nothing more of interest, I laid the book aside. Instead I picked up its sequel, *Exiting Nirvana* (Little, Brown, 2001, in case you want to check).

In that book, Elly has disappeared, and Jessy has resumed her real name. Autism is already so common, there is no longer any fear of embarrassment. But when I was young, Jessy was an anomaly. The figure I grew up with was one child out of 15,000—hard to believe now, when in some areas, if you believe the blogs, the rates approach twenty percent. Spectrum kids, they call them. In the 1960s the causes were thought to be an intolerable and unloving family. Larger environmental or genetic tendencies were ignored. But toward the end of her life, my mother resembled my sister more and more, until finally in their speech patterns, their behavior, their obsessions, even their looks, they were virtually identical.

Now I examined the pictures. My autistic sister, like her grandfather, had not excelled in portraiture. Her frail grasp of other people's feelings did not allow her to render faces or gestures or expressions. But unlike him, for a while she had enjoyed a thriving career, because her various disabilities were explicit in her work, rather than (as is true for the rest of us, as is true, for example, right now) its muddled subtext. For a short time before her death she was famous for her meticulous acrylic paintings of private houses, or bridges, or public buildings—the prismatic colors, the night skies full of constellations and atmospheric anomalies. When I lived in Baltimore, I had commissioned one for a colleague. Here it was, printed in color in the middle of the book: "The House on Abell Avenue."

I looked at the reproduction of Jessy's painting—one of her best—and tried to imagine the end of my trajectory, the house of a woman I used to know. I tried to imagine a sense of forward progress, but in this I was hindered by another aspect of the game, the way it threw you back into the past, the way it allowed you to see genetic and even stylistic traits in families. Shared interests, shared compulsions, a pattern curling backward, a reverse projection, depressing for that reason. This was the shadow portion of the game, which wouldn't function without it, obviously. But even the first time I had stumbled on these shelves, I had been careful not to look at my own books, or bring them to the table, or even think about them in this context. There had been more future then, not as much past.

I was not yet done. There were some other texts to be examined, the only one not published by a member of my family, or published at all. But I had collected in a manila envelope some essays on the subject of *A Princess of Roumania*, forwarded to me by Professor Rosenheim after my appearance in his class. To these I had added the letters I'd received from the girl I called Andromeda, not because that was her name, but because it was the character in the novel she had most admired. While she was alive, I had wanted to hide them from my wife, not that she'd have cared. And after her death I had disposed of them among the "R" shelves of the Eisenhower Library, thinking the subject closed.

I opened the envelope, and took out Rosenheim's scribbled note: "I was disappointed with their responses to *A Princess of Roumania*. I was insulted by proxy, me to you. These students have no sympathy for failure, for lives destroyed just because the world is that way. They are so used to reading cause and effect, cause and effect, cause and effect, as if that were some kind of magic template for understanding. With what I've gone through this past year. . . . "

I assumed he was referring to the painful breakup of his own marriage, which he'd mentioned in the bar. Here is an excerpt from the essay he was talking about:

The novel ends before the sexual status of Andromeda can be resolved. It ends before the confrontation between Miranda and the baroness, Nicola Ceausescu, her surrogate mother, though one assumes that will be covered in the sequels. And it ends before the lovers consummate their relationship, which we already know won't last. Park's ideas about love are too cynical, too "sad" to be convincing here, though the novel seems to want to turn that way, a frail shoot turning toward the sun. Similarly, the goal of the quest narrative, the great jewel, Kepler's Eye (dug from the brain of the famous alchemist) is too ambiguous a symbol, representing enlightenment and blindness at the same time. . . .

"How dare he put 'sad' in quotation marks?" commented Rosenheim.

And on the same page he had scribbled a little bit more about his prize student, who apparently hadn't made such mistakes, and who had requested my address on North Calvert Street in Baltimore ("You made quite an impression. I hope she ends up sending you something. I've gotten to know her a little bit outside of class, because she's been baby-sitting for the twins . . . ").

Dear Mr. Park: What I liked most about the book was the experience of living inside of it as I was reading it, because it was set where I live, and I could walk around to those places, there was never anyone there but me. Although I noticed some mistakes, especially with the street names, and I wondered . . .

Dear Mr. Park: What I liked best about the book was all those portraits of loving fathers and understanding husbands, so many different kinds. I hadn't known there were so many kinds . . .

Dear Mr. Park: I know we're supposed to like the heroine, but I can't. I find the others much more convincing, because they are so incomplete, holes missing, and the rest of them pasted together like collages. I mean Nicola Ceausescu, but especially Andromeda . . .

I couldn't read any more. How was it possible to care about these things, after all these years? Tears were in my eyes, whatever that means. Now I tried to remember the face of a woman I'd met only once, with whom I'd swapped a half a dozen letters and perhaps as many emails, before she and Rosenheim had died together in a car crash, when he was driving her home. There was no suggestion of a scandal. A drunk had crossed the line. I'd read about it in the newspaper.

Because I had been up all night, I stretched out on the vinyl sofa and fell asleep. I had switched off the flashlight, and when I woke up I was entirely in darkness, and I was no longer alone.

No—wait. There was a time when I was lying awake. I remember thinking it was obvious that I had made an error, because the sun had obviously gone down. The light was gone from the stairwells and the air shafts. I remember worrying about my car, and whether it was safe where I had parked it. And I remember thinking about Adrian and Nicola, about the way my fantasies had pursued in their footsteps and then changed them when I found them into distortions of themselves—all, I thought, out of a sense of misplaced guilt.

As I lay there in the dark, my mind was lit with images of her and of Adrian when he was young. Bright figures running through the grass, almost transparent with the sunlight behind them. Subsequent to his diagnosis, the images darkened. Nowadays, of course, no one would have given Adrian's autism a second's thought: It was just the progress of the world. No one cared about personal or family trauma anymore. No one cared about genetic causes. But there was something in the water or the air. You couldn't help it.

Now there was light from the stairwell, and the noise of conversation. For a moment I had wondered if I'd be safe in the library overnight. But it was too tempting a refuge; I packed away my laptop, gathered together my satchel and my flashlight. I stuffed my velvet pouch into my pocket, and moved into the stacks to replace my books on their shelves. I knew the locations almost without looking. I felt my way.

I thought the owner or owners of the bedroll had returned, and I would relinquish the reading area and move crabwise though the stacks until I found the exit, and he or she or they would never see me. I would make a break for it. Their voices were loud, and at first I paid no attention to the words or the tone, but only to the volume. The light from their torches lapped at my feet. I stepped away as if from an advancing wave, turned away, and saw something glinting in the corner. I risked a quick pulse from my flashlight, my finger on the button. And I was horrified to see a face looking up at me, the spectacled face of a man lying on his side on the floor, motionless, his cheek against the tiles.

I turned off the flashlight.

Was it a corpse I had seen? It must have been a corpse. In my mind, I could not but examine my small glimpse of it: a man in his sixties, I thought—in any case, younger than I. Bald, bearded, his cap beside him on the floor. A narrow nose. Heavy, square, black glasses. The frame had lifted from one ear. In the darkness I watched him. I did not move, and in my stillness and my fear I found myself listening to the conversation of the strangers, who had by this time reached the vinyl couches and were sitting there. Perhaps I had caught a glimpse of them as they passed by the entrance to the stacks where I was hiding, or perhaps I was inventing details from the sound of their voices, but I pictured a boy and a girl in their late teens or early twenties, with pale skin, pale, red-rimmed eyes, straw hair. I pictured chapped lips, bad skin, ripped raincoats, fingerless wool gloves, though it was warm in the library where I stood. I felt the sweat along my arms.

Girl: "Did you use a condom?"

Boy: "Yes."

Girl: "Did you use it, please?"

Boy: "I did use it."

Girl: "What kind did you use?"

Boy: "I don't know."

Girl: "Was it the ribbed kind?"

Boy: (inaudible)

Girl: "Or with the receptacle?"

Boy: "No."

Girl (anxiously): "Maybe with both? Ribbed and receptacle?"

Boy: (inaudible)

Girl: "No. I didn't feel it. Was it too small? Why are you smiling at me?"

Girl (after a pause, and in a nervous sing-song): "Because I don't want to get pregnant."

Girl (after a pause): "I don't want to get up so early."

Girl (after a pause): "And not have sleep."

Girl (after a pause): "Because of the feeding in the middle of the night. What are you doing?"

Boy (loudly and without inflection): "You slide it down like this. First this way and then this. Can you do that?"

Girl (angrily): "Why do you ask me?"

Boy: "For protection. This goes here. Yes, you see it. You point it like this, with both hands."

Girl: "I don't want to use it. Because it's too dangerous."

Boy: "For protection from any people. Because you are my girlfriend. Here's where you press the switch, and it comes out."

Girl: "I don't want to use it."

Girl (after a pause): "What will you shoot?"

Girl (after a pause): "Will you shoot animals? Or a wall? Or maybe a target?"

Boy: "Because you are my girlfriend. Look in the bag. Those are many condoms of all different kinds. Will you choose one?"

Girl (after a pause): "Oh, I don't know which one to choose."

Girl (after a pause): "This one. Has it expired, please?"

Boy: (inaudible)

Girl: "Is it past the expiration date?"

As I listened, I was thinking of the dead man on the floor. His body was blocking the end of the stacks, and I didn't want to step over him. But I also didn't want to interrupt the young lovers, homeless people somewhere on the spectrum, as I guessed, and armed. At the same time, I felt an irrational desire to replace in their proper spaces the books I held in my hands, because I didn't think, if I was unable now to take the time, that they would ever be reshelved.

I couldn't bear to tumble them together, the Parks and the Claibornes, on some inappropriate shelf. And this was not just a matter of obsessiveness or vanity. Many of these people disliked each other, had imagined their work as indirect reproaches to some other member of the family. Even my parents, married sixty-five years. That was how "trajectories" functioned, as I imagined it: forcing the books together would create a kinetic field. Repulsed, the chunks of text would fly apart and make a pattern. Without even considering the dead man on the floor, the library was full of ghosts. At the same time, I had to get out of there.

Of course it was also possible that the spectrum kids would end up burning the place down, and I was surprised that the girl, who seemed like a cautious sort, had not noticed the possibility. Light came from a small fire, laid (as I could occasionally see as I moved among the shelves, trusting my memory, feeling for the gaps I had left—in each case I had pulled out an adjoining book a few inches, as if preparing for this eventuality) in a concave metal pan, like an oversized hubcap. Evidently it had been stored under the square table in the reading area, though in the uncertain light I had not seen it there.

I still had one book in my hand when I heard the girl say, "What is that noise?"

I waited. "What is that noise?" she said again.

Then I had to move. I burst from my hiding place, and she screamed. As I rounded the corner, heading toward the stairwell, I glanced her way, and was surprised to see (considering the precision of the way I had imagined her) that she was older and smaller and darker than I'd thought—a light-skinned black woman, perhaps. The man I scarcely dared glance at, because I imagined him pointing his gun; I turned my head and was gone, up the stairs and into the big atrium, which formerly had housed the reference library. Up the stairs to the main entrance, and I was conscious, as I hurried, that there were one or two others in that big dark space.

Outside, in the parking lot, I found no cars at all.

It was a chilly autumn night, with a three-quarter moon. I stood with my leather satchel over my shoulder, looking down toward St. Charles Avenue. The Homewood campus sits on a hill overlooking my old neighborhood, which was mostly dark. But some fires were burning somewhere, it looked like.

I had my mother's book in my hand. Because of it, and because a few hours before I had been looking at "The House on Abell Avenue," I wondered if my friend still lived in that house, and if I could take refuge there. Her name was Bonni Goldberg, and she had taught creative writing at the School for Continuing Studies long ago. What with one thing and another, we had fallen out of touch.

All these northeastern cities had lost population over the years since the pandemics. Baltimore had been particularly hard hit. North of me, in gated areas like Roland Park, there was still electricity. East, near where I was going, the shops and fast-food restaurants were open along Greenmount Avenue. I could see the blue glow from the carbide lanterns. But Charles Village was mostly dark as I set off down the hill and along 33rd Street, and took the right onto Abell Avenue.

Jessy had painted the house from photographs, long before. According to her habit she had drawn a precise sketch, every broken shingle and cracked slate in place—a two-story arts & crafts with an open wraparound porch and deep, protruding eaves. A cardinal was at the bird feeder, a bouquet of white mums at the kitchen window. Striped socks were on the clothesline—I remembered them. In actuality they had been red and brown, but in the painting the socks were the pastels that Jessy favored. It was the same with the house itself, dark green with a gray roof. But in the painting each shingle and slate was a different shade of lavender, pink, light green, light blue, etc. The photograph had been taken during the day, and in the painting the house shone with reflected light. But above it the sky was black, except for the precisely rendered winter constellations—Orion, Taurus, the Pleiades. And then the anomaly: a silver funnel cloud, an Alpine lighting effect known as a Brocken Spectre, and over to the side, the golden lines from one of Jessy's migraine headaches.

I was hoping Bonni still lived there, but the house was burned. The roof had collapsed from the south end. I stood in the garden next to the magnolia tree. In Jessy's painting, it had been in flower. I stood there trying to remember some of the cocktail parties, dinner parties, or luncheons I'd attended in that house. Bonni had put her house portrait up over the fireplace, and I remembered admiring it there. She'd joked about the funnel cloud, which suggested to her the arrival of some kind of flying saucer, and she'd hinted that an interest in such things must run in families.

Remembering this, I found myself wondering if the painting, or some remnant of it, was still hanging inside the wreckage of the house. Simultaneously, and this was also a shadow trajectory, I was already thinking it was a stupid mistake to have come here, even though I'd seen very few people on my walk from the campus, and Abell Avenue was deserted. But I was only a block or so from Greenmount, which I imagined still formed a sort of a frontier. And so inevitably I was accosted, robbed, pushed to the ground, none of which I'll describe. If it's happened to you recently, it was like that. They didn't hit me hard.

I listened to them argue over my laptop and my velvet purse, and it took me a while to figure out they were talking in a foreign language—Cambodian, perhaps. They unbuttoned the purse, and I could hear their expressions of disappointment and disgust, though I couldn't guess what they were actually touching as they thrust their fingers inside. Embarrassed, humiliated, I lay on my back on the torn-up earth—it is natural in these situations to blame yourself. A cold but reliable comfort—if not victims, whom else does it make sense to blame? You have to start somewhere. Besides, these people in an instant had done something I had never dared.

It won't amaze you to hear that as I lay there, a dazed old man on the cold ground, I was conscious of a certain stiffness in my joints, especially in my shoulders and the bones of my neck. As my attackers moved off across a vacant lot, I raised myself onto my elbows. I was in considerable pain, and I didn't know what I was supposed to do without money or credit cards. I thought I should try to find a policeman or a community health clinic.

How was it possible that what happened next took my by surprise? It is, once again, because how you tell a story, or how you hear it, is different from how you experience it, different in every way. Cold hands grabbed hold of me and raised me to my feet. Cold voices whispered words of comfort—"Here, here."

Walking from Homewood I'd seen almost no one, as I've said. St. Paul, North Calvert, Guilford—I'd passed blocks of empty houses and apartments. But now I could sense that doors were opening, people were gathering on the side streets. I could hear laughter and muted conversation. Two men turned the corner, arm in arm. Light came from their flashlight beams. In the meantime, the woman who had raised me up was dusting off my coat with her bare palms, and now she stooped to retrieve my own flashlight, which had rolled away among the crusts of mud. She pressed it into my hands, closed my fingers over it, and then looked up at me. In the moonlight I was startled to see a face I recognized, the black woman in the library whom I had overheard discussing prophylactics. She smiled at me, a shy, natural expression very rare inside the spectrum—her front teeth were chipped.

Overhead, the moon moved quickly through the sky, because the clouds were moving. A bright wind rattled the leaves of the magnolia tree. People came to stand around us, and together we moved off toward Merrymans Lane, and the parking lot where there had been a farmers' market in the old days. "Good to see you," a man said. "It's General Claiborne's grandson," murmured someone, as if explaining something to someone else. "He looks just like him."

The clouds raced over us, and the moon rode high. As we gathered in the parking lot, a weapon was passed along to me, a sharp stick about three feet long. There was a pile of weapons on the shattered asphalt: sticks and stones, dried cornstalks, old tomatoes, fallen fruit. My comrades chose among them. More of them arrived at every minute, including a contingent of black kids from farther south along Greenmount. There was some brittle high-fiving, and some nervous hilarity.

"Here," said the spectrum girl. She had some food for me, hot burritos in a greasy paper bag. "You need your strength."

"Thanks."

Our commander was an old man like me, a gap-toothed old black man in an Argyle vest and charcoal suit, standing away from the others with a pair of binoculars. I walked over. Even though my neck was painfully stiff, I could turn from my waist and shoulders and look north and east. I could see how the land had changed. Instead of the middle of the city, I stood at its outer edge. North, the forest sloped away from me. East, past Loch Raven Boulevard, the land opened up around patches of scrub oak and ash, and the grass was knee-high as far as I could see. There was no sign of any structure or illumination in either direction, unless you count the lightning on the eastern horizon, down toward Dundalk and the river's mouth. The wind blew from over there, carrying the smell of ozone and the bay. Black birds hung above us. Thirty-third Street was a wide, rutted track, and as I watched I could see movement down its length, a deeper blackness there.

The commander handed me the binoculars. "She's brought them up from the Eastern Shore on flatboats," he said.

I held the binoculars in my hand. I couldn't bear to look. For all I knew, among the pallid dead I would perceive people that I recognized—Shawn Rosenheim, perhaps, a bayonet in his big fist. And one young woman, of whose face I'd be less sure.

"She'll try and take the citadel tonight," murmured the commander by my side. Behind us, the road ran over a bridge before ending at the gates of Homewood. St. Charles Avenue was hidden at the bottom of a ravine. The campus rose above us, edged with cliffs, a black rampart from the art museum to the squash courts. And at the summit of the hill, light gleamed from between the columns of the citadel.

I had to turn in a complete circle to see it all. But I was also imagining what lay behind the hill, the people those ramparts housed and protected, not just here but all over the world. Two hundred miles south, in Richmond, a boy and his mother crouched together in the scary dark.

"I fought with your grandfather when I was just a boy," said the commander. "That was on Katahdin Ridge in 1963. That was the first time I saw her." He motioned back down the road toward Loch Raven. I put the binoculars to my eyes, and I could see the black flags.

"Her?"

"Her."

I knew whom he meant. "What took you so long, anyway?" he asked. I might have tried to answer, if there was time, because I didn't hear even the smallest kind of reproach in his voice, but just simple curiosity. I myself was curious. What had I been doing all these years, when there was work to be done? Others, evidently, started as children—there were kids among us now.

I was distracted from my excuses by the sight of them building up a bonfire of old two-by-fours and plywood shards, while the rest of us stood around warming our hands. I heard laughter and conversation. People passed around bottles of liquor. They smoked cigarettes or joints. A woman uncovered a basket of corn muffins. A man had a bag of oranges, which he passed around. I could detect no sense of urgency, even though the eastern wind made the fire roar, while lightning licked the edges of the plain. The crack of thunder was like distant guns.

"Here they come," said the commander.

BLOODSPORT

GENE WOLFE

Sit down and I'll tell you.

I was but a youth when I was offered for the Game. I would have refused had that been possible; it was not—those offered were made to play. As I was already large and strong, I became a knight. Our training was arduous; two of my fellows died as a result, and one was crippled for life. I had known and liked him, drank with him, and fought him once. Seeing him leave the school in a little cart drawn by his brothers, I did not envy him.

After two years, I was knighted. I had feared that I would rank no higher than bowman; so it was a glad day for me. Later that same day I was given three stallions, the finest horses ever seen—swift golden chargers with manes and tails dark as the darkest shadows. Many an hour I spent tending and training them; and I stalled them apart, never letting them graze in the same meadow or even an adjoining meadow, lest they war. If I were refused that many meadows on a given day, one remained in his stall while the other two grazed; but I was never refused after my first Game.

But I shall say here and say plainly that it was never my intention to slay my opponent. Never, or at least very seldom. It was my task to defeat my opponent—if I could. And his to defeat me. Well do I recall my first fight. It was with another knight, and those engagements are rarest of all. I had been ordered to a position in which a moon knight might attack me. It seemed safe enough, since our own dear queen would be sure to attack him if he triumphed. Yet attack he did.

Under the rules, the attacker runs or rides to the defender's position, a great advantage. I had been taught that; but never so well as I learned it then, when I did not know I was to be attacked until I heard the thunder of his charger's hooves. That white charger cleared the lists with a leap that might have made mock of two, and he was upon me. The ax was his weapon, mine the mace. We fought furiously until some blow of mine struck the helm from his head and left him—still in the saddle—half-stunned. To yield, one must drop one's weapon; so long as the weapon remains in hand, the fight continues. His eyes were empty, his flaccid hand scarce able to grasp his ax.

Yet he did not drop it. I might have slain him then and there; I struck his gauntlet instead. A spike breached the steel, nailing his hand—for a moment only—to the haft of his ax. I jerked my mace away and watched him fall slowly from his game saddle. His head struck the wretched stony soil of the black square first, and I feared a broken neck. Yet he lived, and was mewing and moving when they bore him away. The spectators were not pleased with me, but I was pleased with myself; it is winning that matters, not slaying.

My next was with a pawn. She was huge, as they all are; bred like chargers, some say. Others declare that it is only a thing the mages do to baby girls. As you are doubtless aware, pawn's arms are the simplest of all: a long sword and a shield nearly as tall as the pawn herself, and wider. Other than those, sandals and a loincloth, for pawns wear no armor. I thought to ride her down, or else to slay her readily with my sword. One always employs the sword against pawns.

It was not to be. She sprang to my left, my stroke came too late, and she stripped me from the saddle.

A moment more and I lay upon the fair green grass of a sun square, with her sword's point tickling my throat. "I yield!" I cried, and she grinned her triumph.

I was taken from the game, and Dhorie, my trainer, found me sitting alone, my head in my hands. He slapped my back and told me he was proud of me.

"I charged a pawn," I mumbled.

"Who bested you."

I nodded.

"Could happen to anybody. Lurn is the best of the moon pawns, and you had been charged by a knight scarcely a hundred breaths before." (This last was an exaggeration.) "You had given mighty blows and received them. Two moves and you were sent again. Do you know how often a knight is charged by another, but defeats him? The stands are still abuzz with your name."

I did not believe him but was comforted nonetheless. Soon I learned that he had been correct, for my bruises had not yet faded when I was put forward in a new game. That game I shall not describe. Nor the others.

The Hunas swept down upon us, and the games were ended. There was talk of employing us in battle; and I believe—yes, I believe still—that we might have turned them back. Before it could be done, they rushed upon the city by night. We fought and fled as best we could, I on Flare, my finest charger. For four days and three nights he and I hid in the hills, where I bandaged our wounds and applied poultices of borage and the purple-flowered high-heal that none but a seventh son may find.

The city had been put to the torch, but we returned to it. My father had been a mage of power, I knew, and I felt that his house might somehow have survived. In that I was mistaken; yet it had not been destroyed wholly. The south wing stood whole, and thus I was able to return to the very chamber I had called my own as a boy. My bed was there and waiting, and I felt an attraction to it by no means strange in a weary, wounded man. I saw to Flare as well as I could—water, a roof, and a little stale bread I found in the larder—and slept where I had slept for nights that had seemed endless so long ago. In the hills I had not dreamt; the imps and fiends that sought me out there had been those of waking. Returned to my own bed in the bedchamber that had been my own, I dreamt indeed.

In dream, my father sat before me, his head cloven to the jaw. He could not speak, but wrote upon the ground for me to read: I blessed and I cursed you, Valorius, and my blessing and my curse are the same. You will inherit.

I woke with his words ringing in through my thoughts, and I have never forgotten them. Whether they be so or no, who is to say? Perhaps I have inherited already, and know not of it. Perhaps they are as false as most dreams—false as most words, I ought to have said. For it is only those words that hold power over the thing they represent that are not false, and they are few and seldom found.

A league beyond the Gate of Exile, I saw Lurn sleeping in the shade of a spreading chestnut.

Dismounting, I went to her; I cannot say why. Seeing that she slept soundly and was not liable to waken soon, I unsaddled Flare and let him graze, which he was eager to do. After that I sat near her, my back propped by the bole of the tree, and thought upon many things.

"What puzzles you so?"

Hearing her voice for the first time, I knew it was hers, deeper than my own yet a woman's. I smiled, I hope not impudently, and said, "Gaining your friendship. I fear that you will wish to engage, and that would be but folly as the world stands today."

"Folly indeed, for it stands not but circles the moon as both swim among stars." She laughed like a river over stones. "As for engaging, Valorius, why, I bested you. I choose to stand upon my victory, for you might die were we to engage again."

"You would not see me dead."

"No," she said; and when I did not speak, she said, "Would you see me so? You might have killed me while I slept."

"You would have sprung up and wrested the sword from my hand."

"Yes! Let us say that." The river flowed again. "Let us say it, that I may be joyful."

"You would not see me dead," I repeated, "and you troubled to learn my name, Lurn."

"And you mine." She sat up.

"I have seen sun and moon in the same sky," I told her. "They did not engage."

"They do but rarely." She smiled as she spoke, and there was something in her smile of the maid no man has bussed. "When they do she bests him, as is only to be expected. Bests him, and brings darkness over the earth."

"Is that true?"

"It is. She bests him, but having bested him she bids him rise. Someday—do you credit prophesy?"

I do not, but said I did.

"Someday he will best her and, besting her, take her life. So is it written. When the evil day comes, you men will walk in blind dark from twilight to dawn and much harm come of it."

"And what of women?"

"Women will have no warning, so that they bleed in the market. Will you come and sit by me, Valorius?"

"Gladly," I said. I rose and did so.

"Have the Hunas killed everyone save you and me?"

"They have slain many," I said, "but they can scarcely have slain everyone."

"When they have looted the towns and burned them, not many will remain. Those of our people who can still hold the hilt might be rallied to resist."

"Are they really our people?" I inquired.

"I was born among them. So were you, I think. I took shelter in this deep shade because my skin can't bear your noonday sun. When your sun is low, I'll walk again. Then we'll see what a lone woman can accomplish."

I shrugged. "Much, perhaps, with a knight to assist her. We must get you a wide hat, however, and a gown with long sleeves."

When the sun declined, we journeyed on together, and very pleasant journeying it was, for her head was level with my own when I rode Flare. We chattered and joked, and in time—not that day, I think, but the next—I beheld something in Lurn's eyes that I had never seen in the eyes of any woman.

That day we discovered a crone who knew the weaving of hats; she made such hat as Lurn required, a hat woven of straw, with a crown like a sugar loaf and brim wide as a shield. She sent us to a little man with a crooked back, who for a silver piece made Lurn not one long gown but three, all of coarse white cloth. Of our rallying of the people, I shall say little or nothing. We armed them with whatever could be made or found, and ere long enlisted a forester. Bradan knew the longbow, and taught some youths how to make and use war-arrows, bows, bowcases, bracers, quivers, and all such things—a great blessing.

That day we discovered a crone who knew the weaving of hats; she made such hat as Lurn required, a hat woven of straw, with a crown like a sugar loaf and brim wide as a shield. She sent us to a little man with a crooked back, who for a silver piece made Lurn not one long gown but three, all of coarse white cloth. Of our rallying of the people, I shall say little or nothing. We armed them with whatever could be made or found, and ere long enlisted a forester. Bradan knew the longbow, and taught some youths how to make and use war-arrows, bows, bowcases, bracers, quivers, and all such things—a great blessing.

A mountain town called Scarp was besieged, and we marched to its relief. It lay in the valley of the Bright, and while one may go up that valley, or down it, a mounted man may not leave it for many a long league. Lurn and I flipped a crown; I lost and took two hundred or so of the rabble we tried to make foot soldiers, seventeen archers, and twenty-five horsemen upstream, skirting the town by night. Ere the sun was high, we found a place where the mountains pressed in on either side and the land on both sides of the road was rough and thickly wooded. I set out sentries, stationed my horsemen a thousand paces higher to prevent desertion, ordered the rest to get some sleep, and led by example.

Flare stamped to wake me. When I sat up, I could hear, though but faintly, the sounds he had heard more clearly—our trumpets, the drums of the Hunas, and the shouts, clashing blades, and screams of war. Then I could picture Lurn as I had seen her so often, leading the half-armed men she alone made bold. She had held her attack until the sun declined. Now her wide hat and white gown had been laid aside, and she would be fighting in sandals and a loincloth as she had as a pawn, a woman who towered above every man as those men towered above children, and the target of every Hunas horse-bow.

I knew the Hunas had broken when their drums fell silent. Lurn's trumpets shrilled orders, call after call:

"Form up!" "Give way for the horse!" "Canter!" And again, "Canter!"

The Hunas had turned and fled. Our archers had the best of targets then, the riders' backs. We wanted to capture uninjured horses almost as much as we wanted to slay Hunas. And that moment—the moment when they turned and fled—would be the best of all moments to do it. If our horsemen galloped after them, they would flee the faster, which we did not want. Besides, our horsemen would soon break up, the best mounted outdistancing the rest. Then the Hunas might rally and charge, and our best mounted would go down. We did not want that, either.

"Here they come!"

It was a sentry upon a rocky outcrop. He waved and yelled, and soon another was waving and yelling, too. I formed up my men, halberds in front and pikes behind the halberds. Archers on the flanks, half-protected by trees and stones.

"I'll be in front. Stand firm behind me when I stand. Advance behind me when I advance. I'll not retreat. Come forward to take the place of those who fall. If the Hunas get past us, we've lost. If they don't, we've won. Do we mean to win?"

They shouted their determination; and not long after, when the first Hunas rode into sight, someone struck up the battle hymn. They were farmers and farriers, tinkers, tailors, and trades-men, not soldiers and certainly not Game pieces. Would they run? They will not run, I told myself, if I do not run.

Not all the Hunas carry lances, but a good many do. Their lances are shorter than ours, thus easier to control. Lighter, too, and thus quick to aim. Now they positioned five lancers in front—enough to fill the road side-to-side. There were more behind, and I was glad to see them there, sensing that if the first were stopped (and I meant to stop them) they might be ridden down by those pressing forward.

My shield slipped the too-high lance-head, sending it over my left shoulder, and my point took his knee. Perhaps he yowled; if so, it could not be heard above the thudding drums and thundering hooves.

No more could the singing of our bows, but I saw the lancer next to him fall with an arrow in his throat. I had warned our pikemen to spare the horses. A horse screamed nonetheless, screamed and reared with the pike still in his vitals.

Then all was silence.

Though I did not dare look behind me, I glanced to right and left and counted the five—five lancers and one charger. Four lay still. One lancer writhed until a halberd-blade split his skull. The charger struggled to regain its feet; it would never succeed, but it would not cease to try until it died.

I waited for the next five lancers, but they did not charge. They must have known, as I did, that Lurn was behind them, strengthened by whatever troops had joined her from the town. And knowing that, known that they were caught between jaws. But they did not charge. We received a shower of arrows from their horse-bows; a few men cried out, and it may be that some died. Still, they did not charge.

Our battle hymn had ceased. I waved my sword above my head and began the hymn again myself.

When I advanced, I heard the rest behind me, advancing as I did.

The road was no wider here, but its shoulders were clearer.

More Hunas could front us now. They were more likely to attack, and we more likely to scatter. I wanted the first, and felt sure the last was little risk enough. They dismounted and came for us on foot; I knew the gods fought beside us then.

They had light horse-axes and serpent swords. Both were more dangerous than they appeared. They had helmets, too, and seeing them I hoped my own men would have sense enough to strip them from the dead Hunas—and wear them. There were pikes to either side of me; those Hunas who came straight at me died, unable to parry my thrusts. Again and again I stepped forward over the bodies of our foes. In a hundred Games, no knight would ever slay half so many. It ought to have sickened me. It did not because I thought only of Lurn; each Hunas who fell to me was one who would never shed her blood.

I have never liked slaying men, and slaying women—I have done that, too—is worse. No doubt slaying children would be worse still. I have never done it and am glad, though I have met children who should be slain. Slaying animals is, for me, the worst of all. A stag fell to my bow yesterday; and I was glad, for I (I had almost said "we") needed the meat. That stag has haunted me ever since. What a fine, bold beast he was! It was not until now, when I have already told so much, that I kenned why I feel as I do.

Animals have no evil in them. Men have much, women (I think) half as much or less. Children have still less. Yet all humanity is touched by evil. Possibly there are men who have never been cruel. I have tried to be such a man, but is there a man above grass who would say I have succeeded? Certainly I will not say it.

Yonder stands my stag. I see him each time I look up, standing motionless where the shadows are thickest. He watches me with innocent eyes. There are always ghosts in a forest. My father taught me that a year, perhaps, before he gave me over to the games. Ghosts in forests, and few demons. In a desert, he said, that situation is reversed. Deserts call to demons and not to ghosts. (Yet not to demons only.) Among hills and mountains, their numbers are about equal—but who shall count them?

Yonder stands my stag. I see him each time I look up, standing motionless where the shadows are thickest. He watches me with innocent eyes. There are always ghosts in a forest. My father taught me that a year, perhaps, before he gave me over to the games. Ghosts in forests, and few demons. In a desert, he said, that situation is reversed. Deserts call to demons and not to ghosts. (Yet not to demons only.) Among hills and mountains, their numbers are about equal—but who shall count them?

Let me gather more wood.

When we were no longer wanted, Lurn and I passed through this forest, which covers the hills at the feet of the mountains. She pressed forward eagerly and I hurried because she did. It was no easy thing for me to keep pace with her long strides, though most of my armor had been cast away.

It was these mountains, she assured me, that had given rise to the Game. The little mounds upon which we stand at the beginning of each playing of the Game are but the toys men have fashioned in imitation of these works of the gods. "It will mean nothing to you," she told me, "but it will mean the world and more to me." As I have said, I do not credit prophesy. Gods can prophesy, perhaps. No woman can, and no man.

If I recalled more of our journey, I would tell it now. I remember only hunger and cold, for it grew colder and colder as the land rose. There was less game, too. The mountain sheep are very wise, dwelling where the land lies open to their gaze. To hunt them, one must climb behind them, disturbing not one stone. They leap at the sound of the bow, though by then it is too late—leap and fall, always breaking the arrow and too often falling into bottomless clefts where they are devoured by demons.

Oh, yes! They eat as men do, and more. They cannot starve, though they grow lean; yet they eat nevertheless. The flesh of infants is what they like best. Witches offer it to them to gain their favor. We do not do that.

In time, I gave up all hope of finding one of the forty palaces of which she spoke. I only knew that if we went far enough, the mountains would cease their climb to the clouds and diminish again. Lurn would want to turn back; I would insist that we press forward, and we would see who would prevail.

It rained and we took shelter. A day exhausted the little food we had. Famished, we waited for a second day. On the third we went forth to hunt, knowing that we must hunt or starve. I knowing, too, that I dared not use my bow lest the string be wetted. Toward afternoon we flushed a flight of deer. Lurn could run more swiftly than they, they turn more sharply than she. She turned them and turned them until at last I was able to dash among them like a wolf, stabbing and slashing. I have no doubt that some escaped us, and that some of those who thus escaped soon perished of their wounds. We got three, even so, and chewed raw meat that night, and roasted meat the night following when we were able at last to kindle a fire, and so hungry as to abide the smoke of the twigs and fallen branches we collected.

We slept long that night. Day had come when we awoke, the clouds had lifted, and far away—yet not so distant as to be beyond our sight—we beheld a white palace on the side of the mountain looming before us. "There will be a garden!" Lurn's left hand closed on my shoulder with such strength that I nearly cried out.

"I see none," I told her.

"That green . . ."

"A mountain meadow. We've seen many."

"There must be a garden!" She spun me around. "A coronation garden for me. There must be!"

There was none, but we went there even so, a half-starved journey of two days through a forest filled with birdsong. There had been a wall about the palace, a low stone wall that might readily have been stormed. In many places it had fallen, and the gate of twisted bars had fallen into rust.

The rich chambers of centuries past had been looted, and here and there defiled. Their carpets were gone, and their hangings likewise. In many chambers we saw where fires of broken furniture had once blazed. Their ashes had been cold for heaped years no man could count, and their half-burned ends of wood, their strong square nails, and their skillfully wrought bronze screws had been scattered long ago, perhaps by the feet of the great-grandsons of those who had kindled them.

"This is a palace of ghosts," I told Lurn.

"I see none."

"I have seen many, and heard them, too. If we stay the night here . . . " I let the matter drop.

"Then we will go." She shrugged. "This was an error, and an error of my doing. We must first find food, and afterward another."

"No. We must go into the vaults." My own words surprised me.

She looked incredulous, but the ghost in the dark passage ahead nodded and smiled; it seemed almost a living man, though its eyes were the eyes of death.

"What's gotten into you?"

"I must go, and you with me," I told her. "I must go and bring you. You are afraid. I—"

"You lie!"

"Fear better suits a woman than a man. Even so, I am the more frightened. Yet I will go, and you will come with me." I set off, following the ghost, and very soon I heard Lurn's heavy tread behind me.

The corridor we traversed was dark as pitch. I slung my shield over my back, traced the damp stone walls with my left hand, and groped the dark before me with my sword point, testing the flagstones with every step. None of which mattered in the least. The ghost led me, and there was no treachery.

We descended a stair, narrow and steep, and I saw light below. Here was a cresset, filled with blazing wood and dripping embers. The ghost, which ought to have dimmed in the firelight, seemed almost a living man, a man young and nearly as tall as I, in livery of grey and crimson.

"Who is that?" Lurn's voice came from behind me, but not far behind.

I did not speak, but followed our guide.

He led us to a second stair, a winding stair that seemed at first to plunge into darkness. We had descended this for many steps when I took notice of a faint, pale light below.

"Where are we going?" Lurn asked.

I was harkening to a nightingale. It was our guide who answered her: "Where you wished to go, O pawn."

"Why are you talking to me like that, Valorius?"

I shrugged, and followed our guide into a garden lit by stars and the waning moon. He led us over smooth lawns and past tinkling fountains. The statues we saw were of pieces, of kings and queens, of slingers and spearmen, of knights such as I and pawns like Lurn. Winged figures stood among them, figures whiter than they and equally motionless; though these did not move or appear to breathe, it seemed to me they were not statues. They might have moved, I thought, this though they did not live.

"There can be no such place underground!" Lurn exclaimed.

I turned to face her. "We are not there. Surely you can see that. We entered into the stone of the mountain, and emerged here."

"It was broad day!"

"And is now night. Be silent."

That last I said because our guide stood behind her, his finger to his lips. He pointed, but I saw only a thick growth of cypress. I went to it, nonetheless; and when I stood before it I heard a muted creaking and squeaking, as though some portal long closed were opening. I pushed aside the boughs to look.

There my eyes saw nothing. My father (who seemed to sit before me, his head cloven by the ax) had entered my mind and let me see him there.

I knelt.

He took his mantle from his shoulders and fastened it about mine. For a moment only I knew the freezing cold of the gold brooch that had held it. I reached for it. My fingers found nothing, yet I knew then (as I know now) where that mantle rests.

"What's in there?" Lurn asked.

"A tomb," I told her. "You did not come here to see a tomb, but to become a queen. See you the moon?"

"My lady? Yes, of course I see her."

"She rises to behold your coronation, and is already near the zenith. There is a circle of white stones, just there." I pointed. "Do you see it?"

It appeared as I spoke.

"No—yes. Yes, I see it now."

"Stand there—and wait. When the moon-shadows are short and every copse and course in bathed in moonlight, you will become a queen."

She went gladly. I stood before her; the distance was half as far, perhaps, as a boy might fling a stone.

I recall that she said this: "Won't you sit, Valorius? You must be tired."

"Are you not?"

"I? When I am to become a queen? No, never!"

That was all. That, and this: "Why do you rub your head?"

"It is where the ax went in. I rub it because the place is healed and my father at rest."

The moon rose higher yet, and one of the white figures came to kneel before me. She held a pillow of white silk; upon it lay a great visored helm white as any pearl, and upon that a silver crown.

I accepted it and rose. Six more were arming Lurn, armor of proof that no sword could cleave: breastplate and gorget, tasset and tace. As earth circles moon, I circled her; and when her arming was complete save for the helm, poised that as high as I might. "From the goddess whom you serve, receive the crown that is your due." Standing, her head was higher than my upstretched arms; but she knelt before me to receive helm and crown, and I set them upon her head. They felt no heavier than their own pale plumes.

Rising, she pulled down the visor to try it; and I saw that there was a white face graven upon the visor now—and that white face was her own.

"I am a queen!" It might have been ten-score trumpets speaking.

I nodded.

"We will restore the kingdom, Valorius!"

I nodded as before. It had been my own thought.

"I shall restore the kingdom, and the Game will be played again. The Game, Valorius, and I a queen!"

I knew then that she whom I had kissed so often must die. Men have said my sword springs to my hand.

That is not so, yet few draw more swiftly. She parried my first thrust with her gauntlet and sought to seize the blade; it escaped her—thus I lived.

Of our fight in that moonlit garden I will say little. She could parry my blows, and did. I could not parry hers; she was too strong for it. I dodged and ducked and was knocked sprawling again and again. I hoped for help, and received none. If longing could foal a horse from air, I would have had two score.

No horse appeared.

What came at last was Our Lord the Sun, and that was better. I turned her until she faced it and put my point through her eye-slot. The steel that went in was not so long as my hand and less wide than two fingers together, yet it was enough. It sufficed.

Now I wander the land. Asked to prophesy, I say we shall overthrow the tyrants and make a new nation for ourselves and our children. Should our folk require a sword, I am the sword that springs to their hands. Asked to heal, I cure their sick—when I can. If they bring food, I eat it. If they do not, I fast or find my own. And that is all, save that from time to time I entertain a lost traveler, such as yourself.

East lies the past, west the future. Go north to find the gods, south to find the blessed. Above stands the All High, and below lies Pandemonium. Choose your road and keep to it, for if you stray from it, you may encounter such as I. Fare you well! We shall not meet again.

NO TIME LIKE THE PRESENT

CAROL EMSHWILLER

A lot of new rich people have moved into the best houses in town—those big ones up on the hill that overlook the lake. What with the depression, some of those houses have been on the market for a long time. They'd gotten pretty run down, but the new people all seem to have plenty of money and fixed them up right away. Added docks and decks and tall fences. It was our fathers, mine included, who did all the work for them. I asked my dad what their houses were like and he said, "Just like ours only richer."

As far as we know, none of those people have jobs. It's as if all the families are independently wealthy.

Those people look like us only not exactly. They're taller and skinnier and they're all blonds. They don't talk like us either. English does seem to be their native language, but it's an odd English. Their kids keep saying, "Shoe dad," and, "Bite the boot." They shout to each other to, "Evolve!"

At first their clothes were funny, too—the men had weird jackets with tight waists and their pants were too short. The girls and women actually wore longish wide skirts. They don't have those anymore. They must have seen right away how funny they looked compared to us, and gone to Penny's and got some normal clothes like ours.

They kept their odd shoes, though, like they couldn't bear not to have them. (They look really soft, they're kind of square and the big toe is separate.) And they had to wait for their hair to grow out some before they could get haircuts like ours. This year our boys have longer hair than the girls, so their boys were all wrong.

Every single one of those new people, first thing, put two flamingos out on their front lawns, but then, a few days later, they wised up and took them away. It wasn't long before every single one of them had either a dog or a cat.

When Sunday came, they all went to the Unitarian church and the women wore the most ridiculous hats, but took them off as soon as they saw none of us wore any. They wore their best clothes, too, but only a few of us do.

Even though they come to church, Mom says I shouldn't make friends with their kids until we know more about them and I especially shouldn't visit any of their houses. She says the whole town doesn't trust them even though everybody has made money on them one way or another.

Their kids have a funny way of walking. Not *that* funny, actually, but as if they don't want anybody to talk to them, and as if they're better than we are—maybe just because they're taller. But we don't look *that* different. It seems as if they're pretending we're not here. Or maybe that *they're* not here. In school they eat lunch together at the very farthest table and bring their own food, like our cafeteria food isn't good enough. They obviously—all of them—don't want to be here.

I've got one of the new people in my class. I feel sorry for her. Marietta . . . Smith? (I'll bet. All those new people are Smiths and Joneses and Browns and Blacks.) She's tall and skinny like they all are. She's by herself in my class; usually there's two or three of them in each class. She's really scared. I tried to help her the first days—I thought she needed a girl friend really badly—but she didn't even smile back when I smiled straight at her.

The boys are all wondering if those new boys would be on the basketball team, but so far they don't even answer when they're asked. Jerry asked Huxley Jones, and Huxley said, under his breath, "Evolve, why don't you?"

Trouble is, my name is Smith, too, but it's *really* Smith. I've always wanted to change it to something more complicated. I'd rather be Karpinsky or Jesperson or Minnifee like some of the kids in my class.

I kind of understand those new kids. I have to eat a special diet, and I'm too tall, too. I tower over most of the town boys. And I'm an only child and I'm not at all popular. I don't care what Mom says, I don't see what harm there can be in helping Marietta and I'm curious. I like her odd accent. I try saying things as she does and I say, "Shoe Dad," to my dad even though I don't know what those kids mean by it. Maybe it's really *Shoo* Dad.

One of these days I'm going to sneak into her house and see what I can find out.

But I don't have a lot of time for finding out things because I have to practice the violin so much. Funny though, when I took my violin to school because I had my lesson that afternoon, Marietta looked at the case as if she couldn't imagine what was in it. I said, "violin," even though she hadn't asked. And then she looked as if she wanted to ask, "What's a violin?"

Those kids are all so dumb about ordinary things. Every single one of them has been kept back a grade. I don't know how they can walk around looking so snooty. It's as if they think being dumb is better.

Marietta is awful in school, too. The teacher asked her who was the vice president and she didn't know. So the teacher asked who was president and she didn't know that either.

That gave me the courage to ask her if she wanted help. But then she said her mother doesn't want her to be friends with any of us and I said my mother says the exact same thing. Finally she laughs, we both do, and she says, "Shoe Dad, if we can keep it secret."

(Those kids never say "Okay.")

She says, "But I shouldn't be too smart either. We don't want anybody to notice us."

So far I don't think she has anything to worry about in that direction. I don't say that, though. What I say is, "You're getting noticed for the opposite reason. You need my help."

I'm really curious about her house, but she wouldn't dare invite me and I wouldn't dare go there. And she can't come to my house because Mom would be horrified. Too bad they look a little bit different otherwise Mom would never know. So we mostly meet in the woods by the railroad tracks where the bums used to hide out back when there were bums. Mom doesn't like me to go there either. She thinks maybe there might still be bums around. Marietta and I always scope out the place first, not for bums, but because boys sometimes go there to smoke.

I discovered Marietta was so bad at math because she was used to writing out the problems in an entirely different way. Once I got that straightened out she got a lot better. But she said Huxley told her there was no need for her ever to know who was president here now. I said, "Why not?" She started to say it wasn't important but she stopped in the middle. Then she said, it was just that there were some things she wasn't going to bother knowing.

She tells me she really likes Judson Jesperson, but she says she's not supposed to go outside her own group. And me, I like Huxley Jones, but Marietta says he can't go outside their group either. She's supposed to like Huxley and I'm supposed to like Judd. I asked her if this was some sort of religious thing? I didn't dare say racial but Judson has very dark hair and eyes though his skin is just like hers. She said, no, it was something entirely different and she wasn't supposed to talk about it. She said it would be *very* dangerous for any of her group to marry outsiders. She said, "Who knows who would be president in a couple a hundred years if Judd and I got married?"

So anyway, we're unhappy together and I can tell her all about Judson's family but she can't tell me anything about Huxley.

A dozen more families of the tall people move into town. They can't take the best houses because they're already gone, but when they get through with the second best houses, they turn out be almost as good except for not being on top of a hill and next to the lake.

The first group of kids is getting a little friendlier. Huxley even let himself get talked into being on the basketball team but he didn't know how to play and had to be taught from scratch. Judd says they're sorry now. All he has going for him is being tall.

I don't care, I like him. I like his stooped over posture. As if he doesn't want to be that tall. I like his kind of scholarly face. I like his pixie grin. At first he was always frowning at all of us, but pretty soon he wasn't and especially not at me.

The first thing I said to him was, "I like your name," and he actually did smile.

By now everybody is saying Shoe Dad.

Then we have the first snow and a snow day. It's so beautiful. I want to see Marietta right away, but no school so I start out towards her house. I'm not going to disobey Mom. Besides, that's our only good hill for sledding. Everybody will be up there.

And there everybody is, with sleds and garbage can lids and folded up cardboard boxes. Some kids even have skis. The new kids are even more excited about the snow than we are. They act as though they've never made snowmen and never thrown snow balls. They're like little kids. Well, actually we all are.

Those new kids have skis and fancy boots. But not a single one knows how to ski.

Marietta's there. I knew she would be. She says first off, "Look . . . these great boots . . . "

She has the fancy kind you can't walk around in. They're white with dozens of black buckles. I admit they're beautiful. I say, "Shoe Dad."

" . . . and they only cost five hundred dollars."

She's always saying things like that. Everything is cheap to her. I wish something was cheap to me. I'd like to say, "Evolve!" but I don't want to make her feel bad. I say, "Bite the . . . oh yeah, bite the *ski* boot."

We don't hear about it till lunch time, but that night in the middle of the storm, odd things disappeared. Half the fish at the fish hatchery, and that very same night, a big pile of lumber from the lumber mill disappeared. The night watchman swears he made his rounds every hour. Sometime between his two o'clock and three o'clock a whole section of lumber was gone and not a sound. The fish people are there early and late. They went to feed the fish at eight and found half the tanks empty. Some of us say the new people are getting blamed just because they're richer than we are and just because they're new, though nobody can figure out how they could have done it. Even so, I'm suspicious, too. Dad says the town is going to have a meeting about them.

Then we hear that exactly the same night, north of us, in Washington State they also lost a lot of lumber. And another place in Nevada lost half their grass-fed beef.

Funny though, Huxley said all this was *our* fault. Even that they're here in the first place is *our* fault. He said we should have stopped cutting down trees. He won't say anything more about it. That shows how odd these new kids are. But I guess that's fair, we blame them for everything and they blame us.

Except for Marietta, those kids still don't like it here at all, but Marietta says she's getting to like it, partly because of being friends with me—where she was before she never had such a good friend as I am—and she also likes it because she always did like camping out and making do with what's at hand. That makes me wonder all the more where she came from.

The new people often have meetings in one of the larger houses up on the hill. They can't hide that because all the best cars in town are parked outside. After the fish and lumber disappear, the next time those cars gather, a whole batch of the town's people storm the house. It isn't fair, but the cops are on our side; they're just like all the town's people, they don't trust those new people either. And it isn't as if the new people had any higher up connections in the town that would help them. So the cops arrest *them* instead of *us*, even though we're the ones that broke into their meeting. Did a lot of damage, too, and not only to the furniture. Six of the new people are in the hospital.

That leaves a lot of those kids with nobody looking after them. The school principal asks the town parents if they'll take in some of the children temporarily until their parents can get themselves straightened out with the police. I get my folks to take in Marietta. Mom doesn't mind it under these circumstances. In fact she acts nice. She even bakes cookies. Marietta can't believe Mom made these right here at home. She's so fascinated she forgets to feel worried for a while.

As usual I have to practice the violin. Marietta tries it out. All she makes is squeaks. She can't believe how hard it is. She's only played computer instruments. "Aided," she says, so you don't have to know anything. But you can have any sound you want and you sound good right at the beginning.

I have twin beds in my room so we get to be right in together.

At first Marietta seems to like it as much as I do. We talk until Mom comes in and tells us we have to stop because of school tomorrow. But a little bit after I turn out the light, I'm pretty sure Marietta is crying. I ask if there's anything I can do.

She says, "I wish I could go home."

I say, "It won't be long before your parents come back."

"I mean I want to go back where we used to live. My real home."

"Where is it?"

"We're not supposed to say."

"Was it so much better there?"

"Sort of . . . some ways . . . except it's nice being so rich for a change. Of course there's lots you don't have. . . . Oh well."

"*I'm* glad you're here."

"Well, I'm glad for having you."

"Can I go up and see your house now that there's nobody there?"

"It's just like yours only richer. That's because everything is so cheap here otherwise we couldn't afford stuff. It's *supposed* to be just like yours. Our parents made it special to be like that."

"Can we go anyway? I like rich stuff and I hardly ever get to see rich things except on TV. Besides, don't you need to go get more clothes?"

So we do that—skip school and go up. She's right. There's nothing odd about it . . . except there is. There's a fancy barbeque thing in the backyard, but obviously never used. There's a picnic table beside it but no chairs. The two flamingos are in a corner, lying on their sides. Inside it's awfully—I don't know how to describe it—cold and stiff, and kind of empty. It's as if nobody lives there. There's a *National Geographic* on one side of the coffee table and a *Consumers Report* on the other, and that's *all*. No clutter. Mom would like it.

Upstairs, her room has all the right stuff. There's a brand new teddy bear on the pillow and a small bookcase with brand new books, all very girlie. They don't look read either. There's not a single Tarzan or John Carter. I ask, and she never even heard of Tarzan. I tell her I'll lend her some. Even though we're too old for those, she'll like them.

She has one whole drawer with nothing but fancy sweaters and blouses. We gather some up to bring back and she says I can have half of them.

On the way out, I open the hall closet and there's a tangle of wires and silvery things along them like Christmas tree lights. At first Marietta tries to keep the door shut as if she doesn't want me to see them, but then she says she trusts me as much as anybody she ever knew so she says, "Take a good look."

I say, "I don't know what it is, anyway."

She says, "Time machine," and starts laughing hysterically. And then we both laugh so hard we fall on the floor and I don't know what's the truth and what isn't, except maybe I do.

I'm glad we went there. I don't need to feel jealous after all. Even though Mom would probably like living like that, I wouldn't.

The police hang on to those new people to see if any of them are guilty of anything at all and also as a sort of punishment, I suppose for being rich and taking up all the best places. That means Marietta and I have even more time together.

The lumber mill now has three night watchmen. They're sitting right next to the biggest piles of lumber. The fish hatchery has people practically in with the fish.

But then—again in the middle of the night—all the new people disappear. The grown-ups, that is. So then we know who did the fish and lumber. But now there's nobody to blame but their children. Some townspeople are so angry they want to put them in jail, too. Most of the townspeople don't go that far, though. My parents and lots of others say they won't let that happen. Besides, now that they know Marietta they like her.

But it's not safe for the new kids to walk the streets anymore—two kids got beat up by a gang of boys and they weren't even the new kids, they were just blond and tall and skinny. Mom dyes Marietta's hair black so she'll be safer. Some of the other new kids do that too.

Marietta looks good with dark hair. That doesn't cheer her up, though. All those kids feel terrible. Naturally. But it's odd, they keep saying they're not surprised, they just wondered when it would happen.

We talk a lot in bed at night and Mom doesn't tell us to shut up until it gets really late.

"How can your parents leave you like this?"

"We're not allowed to say, but it's for our own good."

"Parents always say that."

I try to cheer up Marietta. We go to lots of movies. She does like the Tarzan and John Carter books and there are lots of those to go through yet. Mom gives her valerian and chamomile tea almost every night. At first Marietta didn't want hugs from my mom, but now she does.

I go around wearing her expensive sweaters and I wear her white jacket when she wears her shiny black one. That turns out to be a big mistake because I get taken for one of them. I'm as tall and skinny as they are. And here I am, wearing fancy clothes like they always do. And here we are, Marietta and me, one of us with dyed black hair and me, a darker blond than they are but that doesn't matter to this bunch. They're not high school boys. I don't know who they are but they're grown men—waiting for us after the movie.

They don't think Marietta is one of the new people—they think *I* am. She's wearing my faded blue jeans and my sweatshirt and I'm in her cashmere sweater and that white jacket.

They push her aside—so hard they knock her down—and come after me. They yank at Marietta's jacket so hard the zipper breaks, and then pull the sweater up over my face so I don't see what happens next. All I know is they suddenly stop and Marietta is pulling the sweater down so I can see. She yells, "Run," and we do. When I look back I see all three of them collapsed on the ground.

"Don't stop." Marietta grabs my arm and pulls me along with her.

"What did you do?"

"I'm not allowed to say."

We run all the way home and collapse in our front hall. That white jacket is lost and ruined out there somewhere and the sweater is all pulled out of shape.

Marietta right away says, "Don't tell."

"How did you do that?"

"I thought you had those here. Tazers. Don't you? This is just a different form."

"Where is your tazer?"

"I'm not supposed to say. See, where I come from it's not safe anymore since the revolt of . . . . My drones—I mean my parents—they wanted me to be able to defend myself. Besides, they thought everybody here had guns."

"Where is it? You can tell me."

"Here." She points to her earlobe. (There's not even a mark that I can see.) "I have some control over the direction." She twists her earlobe. "I can even point it back."

I touch it, but I don't feel anything.

"They left us here, my drones. They said they would if anything happened. And things did happen. I guess it *is* better here. I mean the air and water and space to move around in. . . . And the food . . . it isn't what we're used to, and it's awfully primitive, everything is, but it's better some ways and we're rich. I have a million dollars in the bank in my name."

She's about to tell me more but Mom comes in right then and finds us sitting on the floor, and me, all bedraggled and the sweater ruined. She gets really upset when she hears about it. (We don't tell her the tazer part.) She insists that she's going to dye my hair that very night no matter how long it takes, and I have to stop wearing Marietta's nice clothes.

For once I agree with her. I let her do all that, even though I know the kids at school will tease me.

I wonder if those men are going to tell what happened to them? Maybe not, though, because they were breaking the law.

I'm going to stick close to Marietta from now on. I feel safe with her.

Most of those new kids are physically awkward—like Huxley trying to be on the basketball team—but Marietta isn't so bad. She says it's because her parents didn't believe in the education boxes most kids had. She says those were like being inside a TV set. But she kept calling hers "Mommy" by mistake and that upset her mother so much she actually had her playing outside even though the air wasn't that good anymore and even when it was too hot.

She's been telling me everything, even about the air-conditioned sweater her mom got her.

She says, "Even so, it was getting worse and worse. Food riots sometimes. I know this is best for us. But we have to be so careful and not change anything. Nobody knows what would happen if we upset things. Shoe Dad, I might not even exist. I'd go *poof*! Just like that."

And then Huxley gets in trouble and that changes everything. He didn't dye his hair like the others did. It might not have worked anyway. Three men attack him; maybe the same three that came after us. (You'd think they'd learn.) Marietta and I have to guess what happened: that he not only used his tazer, but tied up the men when they were down. Dragged them into the woods. Then he walked all the way home with bruises all over. Nobody found out about the men out in the woods till two days later. It rained all the next day and one of the men suffocated with his head in the mud. Marietta and I know Huxley didn't use his tazer until he was practically all beat up. He was trying so hard not to cause any changes in the people living here but then he caused more of a problem.

The townspeople are blaming him. Of course they are. Besides, who knows what story those men told? So the police come to arrest him, but he takes off. They even shoot at him, but he gets away. We don't know if he got shot or not.

All the new kids are even scareder than they already were. About going "poof." They keep saying, "It's gotta be even worse than that butterfly back in the Jurassic era." I don't know what they mean by that.

They stand there staring at nothing, as if thinking: Any minute and I never existed. They stop in mid sentence as if: Is it right now that I disappear?

On the other hand, they could disappear by going back home. We'd never know which it was. Marietta hangs on to me whenever she can. It's as if she thinks as long as she has a good grip on my arm, she won't disappear. It's a bother but I let her.

I know where Huxley isn't. He's not at that place where the bums used to go and where the boys go to smoke. That's too easy. But I do know where he could be. I don't even tell Marietta. I get up real early before anybody is up. I make a couple of peanut butter sandwiches and take some nuts and apples and go. Good that Huxley and I never got together or the cops would be watching me.

So I head out into the woods. It's a good place to get lost since there are so many crisscrossing paths and there's a lot of undergrowth for hiding. I think Huxley is somewhere in there but I'll have a hard time finding him. I whistle. I sing. I make a lot of noise and wander all over. I think I'm going to get lost myself.

But what if he's disappeared already? What if he's never been at all?

Then I hear a bird chirping above me, I look up and there he is and he's not been shot. I climb up and give him the sandwiches. He's changed a lot from when he first came. I don't think he'd have been able to climb a tree. He looks kind of wild and haunted and dirty. That makes me like him all the more. I'm always embarrassed, being so close to a boy I like so much, and now even more so. I don't ask anything I really want to. I'm too nervous.

He gobbles up both sandwiches and apples and nuts all in about five minutes. When everything is gone he thinks maybe one of the sandwiches might have been for me and apologizes. But I say none of it was for me and I'll bring more tomorrow.

He admires my new black hair, but I think he's just trying to be nice.

I move up closer to the branch he's on. Turns out I don't have to ask anything. He tells me he always did like me but didn't dare show it. Now he does dare. He thinks everything is all messed up anyway so he might as well like me and he wants me to know it.

Then we hear the swishing of underbrush and voices of people coming closer.

We shut up. He moves higher and I move lower.

In a few minutes the woods are packed with people walking all over the place looking for him. Some of them are cops in uniform. Lots are just townspeople. Mostly men but a few women.

I jump down and move away from his tree. I shout, "Let's look over by the little cave next to the stream." So I and a group of others including one cop, head over there.

The cop says, "Aren't you supposed to be in school?"

"Yeah, but isn't this important?"

"You're lucky I'm not a truant officer."

"What will you do when you find him?"

He pulls his cuffs out of his back pocket and rattles them. Says, "He's dangerous."

I know this whole woods better than a lot of them do. I lead them around to all sorts of good hiding places. I talk loud and make a lot of noise. I don't ever look up.

It's a tiring day for everybody. I had no idea I was going to get caught up in the search and get home so late. My folks and Marietta have been worried about me. I didn't tell Mom where I'd been, but I tell Marietta. She feels bad that I didn't ask her to come along, but I convinced her it was safer for Huxley if it's just me.

Next day I don't think I should keep on skipping school so I just skip my last class. This time I make four peanut butter sandwiches. It's late so I bring a flashlight.

I head for that same tree first, but he's not there. As before, I sing. I whistle. I keep looking up and chirping. I go to all the good spots. It gets dark and I'm worried about using the flashlight. There's only a little moon so I stumble around tripping on things.

Pretty soon I know I'd better go home. I leave the sandwiches up in the tree where I first found Huxley. I leave the flashlight for him, too, and try to find my way out without it.

But I can't. I thought if I just came to one of the streams and followed it, I'd be okay, but it's muddy and slippery near the stream and I keep falling down. I decide it's best to just wait till dawn. I huddle down against a tree. I wish I'd kept one of those sandwiches for myself.

In the morning I go back to the tree where I left the sandwiches. Something got into them and ate most of them and scattered what was left all over.

When I get back my folks are so worried and the police are all over looking for me. Thing is, Marietta disappeared, too, and first they thought we were off somewhere together. Then they thought that I got disappeared with all the others.

It turns out they're *all* gone. I'll never know if Marietta got to go home or if she never existed in the first place or maybe they decided it was a bad and dangerous idea to leave their kids here. Or maybe things got better so it was okay to go home. Or maybe they found better stuff from other times. Like way, way back before there were other people to get in their way.

She left a lot of her clothes in my room. Funny though, my old Tarzan and John Carter books—the ones she was in the middle of reading—are gone. That makes me feel that she didn't disappear completely like she was afraid would happen. She's still someplace, I'm sure of it, reading my books.

I wonder if I could write her a letter. I'll bet there is a way, like sealed up in stainless steel. I wish we'd talked about that before she left. I wish I knew how long my letter would have to last to get to her. Maybe I'll have to carve it in stone.

BRAIDING THE GHOSTS

C.S.E. COONEY

That first year, when Nin was eight, she wanted her mother so desperately. But Noir was dead, she was dead, and *would always be dead*, thanks to Reshka.

Reshka liked to say, "I'm not above keeping ghosts in the house for handmaids and men-of-all-work. There must be ghosts for sweeping, for scrubbing, ghosts for plunging the toilets or repairing the roof, ghosts to fix the swamp cooler and to wash and dry the dishes. But," said Reshka, "but *I will be damned*—I will be damned and in hell and dancing for the Devil—before I summon any daughter of mine from the grave."

So Reshka had Noir cremated three days after her death. Afterward, she prepared the funeral feast in Noir and Nin's small apartment kitchen.

"This is a family affair," she told Nin, who sat numb at the table, feet dangling above the floor. "*This* is a meal no ghost may touch."

Instead of salt or herbs, Reshka scattered ashes over the meat. The buttered bread and the broccoli she dusted with Noir's remains. Ash in Reshka's wineglass, and in Nin's chocolate milk.

The taste never left Nin's mouth. Everything she ate or drank after that was death and dust—but it was also Noir. So Nin ate and drank and did not complain.

When they drove away from the apartment where Noir had quietly died, Nin did not cry. She sat with the black cat Behemoth purring on her lap, and she looked out the window, her thoughts a great buzzing silence.

Behemoth was warm and indolent, matted at the back, soft at the belly. A large cat at full stretch, he possessed the ability to curl up into improbably kittenish proportions. Now, though he seemed asleep, his tail danced. Like most cats, Behemoth was a very good liar.

Nin stroked her mother's cat, playing catch with his clever tail. She had nothing else of Noir's. Reshka had sold it all, or given it to Goodwill.

The sunlight glinted off a crack in the windshield, lancing her dry, dry eyes. Ahead, the road sign read, *Lake Argentine, 2 miles.*

Nin was pretty sure they had hundreds of miles to drive. Reshka said at the outset that they wouldn't arrive at Stix Haunt 'til midnight. But at the Lake Argentine exit, they swerved off the freeway and jounced down the narrow lake road. Reshka offered no explanations. Nin did not ask. Something in her grandmother's tight, pink, unpleasant smile put a padlock to Nin's curiosity.

Noir used to tease her daughter about her constant questioning, saying, "Nin, my love, you live in the Age of Information—just Google it!" This, even if all Nin asked was, "What's for dinner?"

But Reshka was not Noir. Noir who had died with wrinkles on her brow and bruises under her eyes. Reshka's face was perfectly made up, in peaches and corals and cream. Her complexion had neither the flush nor pliancy of flesh, but seemed to ring like pure hard porcelain. Her hair, plaited into two dozen tiny braids, was golden in color, but of a bright and brittle gold, like autumn oak leaves that rattle juicelessly from jaded stems. Nin could not understand how a woman with no wrinkles or gray hairs could be the mother of Noir.

Noir's last words?

"Nin—my love. Have I. Told you. About your . . . grandmother?"

If tissue paper had a heartbeat, that was Noir's heartbeat. When cobwebs breathed, they exhaled more vigorously than she. Nin touched the hem of Noir's nightgown. Contact with any part of Noir's skin made her cry out.

"Her name is Reshka." For comic effect, to make her mother's eyes smile, Nin rolled her own, the way Noir did whenever mentioning Reshka's name. *"She lives in a place called Haunt and you two do not get on."*

"No—we never . . . did." Noir's voice was shy of a whisper. Still it laughed. *"Nin. Come. Close. Hand . . . shears?"*

Nin brought the shears. Noir could not close her fingers over the handle.

"I'll do it," Nin said. *"What do you want cut?"*

Noir told her, and Nin performed the small, bloodless surgery.

"Keep," Noir said. *"Hide it. Don't . . . Reshka."*

"I won't tell her."

Nin did not ask why Reshka must come; of course she must. Under her mother's bright, fading gaze, she put the curl of gray hair away, in an envelope, in a plastic bag, in a metal box. Which rode in the truck with Nin now, in her ratty old Superman backpack.

Reshka's truck humped along the lumpy lake road. The sun shone on gentle hills and flashed on the rumps of small wild things running. Reshka drove her truck right up to the gravelly shore, her tires rolling over the bravest waves. Then she turned off the ignition.

Without looking at Nin, Reshka said, "Give me the cat."

Bemused, a little sleepy, Nin did so. Reshka opened the driver's side door. "Stay here."

Nin stayed. She watched her grandmother walk, straight-legged in her high heels and stockings, into Lake Argentine. Reshka walked into the lake as if she did not see it, stopping only when the hem of her tea-length linen skirt began to drag the waters. Nin stayed, watching, as Reshka squatted suddenly, and with one violent thrust slammed the black cat Behemoth into the lake water and held him under.

The world whited out. Nin clawed her seat belt. She heard herself breathing in ragged gasps. Her thoughts raced ahead of her body, already diving down beneath the lake.

"No!" she shouted. But she was sealed in the truck, and Reshka did not hear. "No!" she shouted anyway, scrabbling for the lock on her door. Finding it, she flicked it up and spilled out onto the shore. The stony ground cut her bare feet. Nin ignored the stones, her feet, the blood, everything but running, dashing into the water.

"No!" she screamed, dividing air and water in a breaststroke. "No, you *can't!*"

Reshka was not a large woman and Nin was tall for her age. She leapt onto her grandmother's back, pummeling and kicking and scratching and shrieking.

"Stop it! Stop! Please! Give him back! Give him back!"

But her grandmother remained solid in her squat, both arms straight down and rigid, showing no strain though surely the black cat Behemoth struggled. No sign of the writhing thing in her hands or on her back fretted Reshka's artful and implacable face.

When the deed was done—Nin still screaming—Reshka stood up, abrupt and smooth, the way she had gone down. This overset Nin, who fell backwards into the lake. Green water closed over her, cool and silent.

Nin thought, Just let me stay.

One-armed, Reshka hauled her out. One-armed, Reshka forced Nin upright, her polished yellow claws sunk into her shoulder.

"Hey, you!" Reshka said, shaking her. "You!"

She slapped Nin on one cheek, then the other.

"None of that from you!" she said, slapping her mouth. Until the blow fell, Nin had not realized she was still screaming. Had been, even underwater. Even choking.

"Listen!" ordered Reshka, sounding more exasperated than angry. "Listen to me, you." Her voice, like her fingernails, was older than her face and hair. It was old and dry and it shook.

"Cats can't abide ghosts," she said. "Nor do ghosts bide well with cats. I'd keep a crazy household if I kept a live cat at Stix Haunt. Here." And Reshka thrust something soggy and awful and dead into Nin's arms. "Put it in the truck bed. If it bothers you so much, I'll give it a raising up when we get home. It'll be just the same, only you won't have to feed it."

Nin clutched the sodden black drowned dead thing close to her chest.

"He won't be just the same!" Her raw voice carried weirdly across the water. "He'll be dead! He's dead! And you killed him! I won't let you touch him! I'll burn him first! I'll burn him myself!"

"Suit yourself, Little Miss Nin It's My Whim," said Reshka coolly.

Nin turned her head and spat.

Later, she came to wonder if burning was what her grandmother had intended all along. She was to discover that Reshka considered it beneath her dignity to bind and braid the ghosts of dumb animals.

Life before Reshka had been quiet. Life after Noir was silent.

Noir used to say, "Let's have an hour of quiet time, Nin, my love. Read if you want, or draw. Mama's just going to lie down and shut her eyes."

But at Stix Haunt, all hours were quiet. The house was a sprawling shamble of gray stone and stucco, with peeling columns, peaked roof and dark cupola, its rotten porches and balconies webbed all about with decrepit scrollwork. It could not have been more different from that cozy, shabby apartment in the city. Woodland and wetland bordered the property on all sides. Only one dark road under dark trees led to a small town that did not like to remember it had a Haunt at all.

Nin never saw Reshka sleep, never caught her still or off her guard. Reshka prowled the house and grounds day and night. Making her rounds. Check the saltshakers for sugar and the shampoo bottles for honey. Was there superglue in the conditioner? Was there sawdust in the Quaker Oats? Sometimes the ice cube trays were full of flies. Sometimes the meat crawled with maggots.

Because sometimes the ghosts got things wrong.

"Death doesn't cure stupidity," Reshka was fond of saying. She did not talk to Nin much, and tended to repeat herself when she did. "Death makes a dumbie dumber. So keep your eyes open!"

Nin did not think the ghosts were stupid. She thought maybe they were angry. Or, scarier still, that they had a sly, prankish sense of humor. Or both.

Many nights Nin went to bed short-sheeted or with crickets in her pillowcase. She was careful not to gasp or laugh or do anything to draw attention. She did not want the ghosts to notice her at all.

Reshka depended on them for everything. They drew her bath and chose her clothes, groomed her, perfumed her, prepared her meals. They did what they were told, silent and unseen, slight freezing breezes in Reshka's great grey house.

The first year was the hardest. Nin was always cold, and her skin—

especially her face—was chapped. Asleep or awake, she wept. And she was not awake often.

The second year, she started reading again. The few books she owned palled quickly, so Nin stole Reshka's, who had hundreds but never touched them. Reshka did not own a TV. She had a dinosaur of a computer that she kept unplugged most of the time. It had a dial-up connection that she used when ordering food or clothes online. Delivery vans dropped the boxes at the gate and never ventured an inch beyond it.

The mistress of Stix Haunt had little contact with the outside world. Nin had none.

When Nin was not reading, she wrote letters to Noir. She drew pictures of live cats and dead grandmothers. She never spoke. Most days she slept. Not in her bed, which, due to the ghosts, was not to be trusted, but out under the willow tree. This was where Nin had buried the little curl of Noir's hair, safe in its white envelope, the envelope sealed in a plastic bag, and the plastic bag placed in a metal box. A small grave. Nin's special place.

The willow tree marked the boundary between Reshka's ghost-kept gardens and the wild Heron Marsh that ruffled and rippled and sprawled beyond. It was not quiet beneath that green umbrella. There were flies and mosquitoes and curious bees. Bird chatter and squirrel quarrels drifted down like leaves, and the marsh grass hissed under a constant low wind.

This was where Nin slept, dreaming through those first sad years. She dreamed of Noir.

"Nin, my love," said her mother, the day after Nin's birthday.

"Yes, Noir, my love?" Nin replied.

Noir sighed. Immediately, Nin crawled straight onto her mother's lap, even though she was thirteen now and tall for her age.

"Nin," said Noir, "Reshka's going to begin teaching you soon."

Nin grimaced. "Teach me what? She can barely stand to hear me breathe." She paused. "But she doesn't have much practice with people who can breathe, does she?"

"No!" Noir laughed. "She's useless with the living. Always was."

When Noir laughed, she threw back her head, giving her full throat to the sky. They sat on a large boulder in the middle of Lake Argentine, the waters flat as ink and cobalt blue, the sky glowing like a dome of jade above them. There was never any sun that Nin could see—only her mother, who sometimes seemed to glow.

"Listen." Noir stroked the nape of Nin's neck. "Reshka will teach you the four winds. Piccolo, flute, oboe, bass recorder. She will teach you songs of luring, of binding and braiding. She will teach you how to break a gravestone and make a grave-ring. She will teach you about silver, about lilies and bitter red myrrh, for you are the last of her line, now that I am gone."

"You're not gone," replied Nin in a soft voice, hugging her mother. "You're right here."

She bent her head and took a deep whiff of Noir's hair. Noir wore it short and dark and curly, never long enough to braid. Her mother smelled sweet and slightly messy, like baby oil.

"My darling," murmured Noir, tightening her arms around Nin. "How's school?"

Nin's laughter was rusty, like a lawnmower left out in the rain.

"I don't go," she said. "Reshka says school is for morons, and the bus won't stop at the Haunt, and she won't drive me. Everyone's afraid of her. Reshka says sorcerers like her are revered as gods among men."

Noir snorted.

"Sorcerers!" she said scornfully. "Reshka talks of sorcerers as if there were others like her. There aren't, Nin. There *aren't!* Before I had you, I traveled—well—I traveled everywhere, wherever I could, searching for others. Reshka was always whispering warnings about them: to beware, to guard my tongue, to learn everything and grow strong. A day will come, she said, when my powers would be pitted against another like me, only far more puissant and merciless. There were nights I couldn't sleep for terror."

"I'm sorry, Mama."

But Noir merely patted her head. "There are no sorcerers in the real world, Nin. There are used car salesmen. And lawyers. Boys in black overcoats who pretend to be wizards. Pregnant teenagers working at McDonalds who call themselves High Priestesses of Discord. Peyote-swallowers and acid-tasters—even true shamans. But there is no one like Reshka Stix of Stix Haunt, or like her mother before her. There was no one like me, born of a sorcerer and a ghost on Dark Eve. And no one like you, my Nin, although I chose for you a living father, that you might be more alive than dead when you came into this world."

By now both Noir and Nin were sitting upright, arms locked wrist to forearm. Two pairs of gray eyes gazed at each other.

"Noir?" Nin's voice was very small.

Noir's grip on her daughter relaxed.

"Reshka has no equal," she said. "She has no living friends and her enemies are not alive. The house she lives in was built by the dead. That's why people are afraid. Reshka is unnatural."

"Are you unnatural?" Nin asked. She wanted to ask, "Am I?" but knew better, even dreaming.

Her mother pinched Nin's chin and smiled, and her smile was like a lilac blooming in the snow. All she said was, "Reshka will start teaching you soon."

Nin cocked her head to one side. "And should I learn?"

"Oh, yes," breathed Noir. "Learn everything. Grow bold and strong. And stay awake!"

Nin woke.

Learning the instruments took the better part of the next two years. There were only four songs, one for each wind, but Nin had to learn them pitch perfect, note perfect. She had to be able to play them dancing, or lying down, or walking barefoot on the ridge of the roof. Four songs for the four winds: lure with the piccolo, bind with the flute, braid with the oboe, and with the bass recorder break the stone.

But songs were not all she learned. When Nin turned fourteen, Reshka taught her how to make grave-rings out of silver clay, a substance made of fine silver powder, water, and organic binder. Nin learned to etch the entire alphabet on the inner band of a ring, in tiny, precise letters so small they could only be read by magnifying glass. She learned how to fire the rings in a kiln until they were hard, how to tumble them and finish them until they shone like mirrors, smooth as satin.

"Why silver?" Nin asked her grandmother. "Why not gold?"

"Silver's a repellent," Reshka said. "Like salt. Some say running water—but they lie."

They worked in the Ring Room, as Nin called the small chamber off Reshka's bedroom. Illuminated by dazzling electric lights, it was the brightest, harshest room in the house. Reshka had installed salt trenches along threshold and windowsills. Silver wire ran all around the room at the baseboards so that no ghosts could enter. An enormous worktable and two long wooden benches took up most of the space. Supply shelves crowded the walls.

In that room, Nin fashioned hundreds of silver rings, and Reshka destroyed them all. The work of hours, weeks, months gone in an instant, slapped to the floor, and the worker slapped too, for good measure. Nothing satisfied her grandmother.

"No!" she would croak. "Another! Again! They must be beautiful. They must be perfect."

"Why?" asked Nin.

"Because, Nin the Dim—" dry, dry, Reshka was dry as an old well with bones at the bottom "—they are each to become a tombstone."

As Nin's fifteenth birthday neared, the new difficulty became choosing her first ghost.

Pieta Cemetery lay between the town and its woodland like a farm that grew only corpses. Nin sat beside her grandmother in the parked truck, staring out over the desolate miscellany. Mausoleums and monuments, tablets and tombs, vaults, angels, cherubs, reapers, veiled Madonnas, all spread out before them in orderly serenity. Like a country girl come to the big city for the first time, Nin felt flushed and giddy. She was used to the dead outnumbering the living—but not on this scale!

Smiling to herself, she muttered, "Pick a gravestone, any gravestone."

"Not *any* gravestone!" Reshka shouted. "Stupid girl!"

Nin smoothed out her smile.

"You must choose your ghost with care," Reshka explained in her raspy, exasperated way. "It must not be an infant. Infants are fractious, unformed. Nothing appeases them. They teethe on the furniture. They break things. They're always underfoot. Nor do you want an old ghost—imagine!" And here Reshka laughed, a skeletal sound. "Imagine! Raising *me* as your ghost! You couldn't boss her around. *She'd* boss *you!* She'd own you! Never let a ghost own you, Little Miss Nin the Grim. *You* own *it.* You got that? *You* own your ghost! Or she'll eat you up, all but your teeth."

Nin nodded. The cab of the truck, she decided, smelled like mildew. She was surprised the engine had coughed to life in the first place. Probably Reshka kept a ghost as a mechanic.

"No," concluded Reshka, "you do not want the very old, or the very young. You do not want a teenager—don't I know? How tiresome they are, moping around and popping pimples. Choose a ghost in the full strength of its youth, a beautiful ghost in its prime, who will do as you bid or be whipped for it. Go."

Nin slipped out of the truck and entered the deserted cemetery. The grass underfoot was warm and wet. Nin, who never went shod at Stix Haunt, had gotten out of the habit of shoes. The grass tickled her ankles and the sun pounded on her scalp. She began perusing the stones.

1896-1909. A boy. An adolescent. Timothy Hearn. No.

1890-1915. A soldier. Robert John Henehan. Nin did not want a soldier.

1856-1934. Mary Pritchett had outlived all of her children and her husband. Too sad. Too sad and too old.

At Reshka's step behind her, Nin asked carefully, "How do you whip a ghost?"

"Ah!" cried Reshka. "Ha! Why, you have his name! With the song of breaking, you destroy his gravestone. He can't remember who he is. Nobody alive knows or cares. This site," she gestured around with her manicured claws, "is a historical landmark. No one uses it anymore. But you—you've got his name, his birth and death, etched in silver on a ring. You wear it against your flesh, and he must return to you. You're his gravestone. You're his home. Your power over him is complete. With the songs of binding and braiding, you've trapped his soul; you've twisted his spirit into your hair, until he's so tangled in the strands, he'll never come loose. Say he misbehaves. All you have to do is this."

She pinched one of her skinny blonde braids between her fingers. From the very tip of it, she plucked a single hair.

Then she dug around awhile in her large suede purse, at last drawing out a lighter.

Flick of the wheel—flame. It made nothing of that little hair in an acrid instant.

Howling filled the steamy August afternoon. A great coldness rushed over Nin, followed by sobbing. One of her grandmother's ghosts was near, she knew. Must have followed them from Stix Haunt.

Even with her hands clapped over her ears, Nin could hear the ghost crying.

Reshka held out one hand to the air, like a queen to her vassal. The silver rings she wore, two for each finger and three on her thumbs, glinted smugly. The sobbing quieted, replaced by a whispering unwet suction, like fervent kisses.

If she squinted at the air around Reshka's hand, Nin could almost make out the ghost. It was more difficult in daylight. But, yes, there was a haze—a disturbance, colorless, like a mirage, not of heat but of deep and biting cold.

Reshka waved the ghost away.

"Do you see?" she asked.

Nin nodded.

"They must be disciplined." Reshka's pursed pink mouth smiled. "When you have a ghost of your own," her outthrust fingernail caught Nin squarely on the nose, "I expect your bed to be made every morning. I don't understand why you've salted my ghosts from your room, but your slovenliness is intolerable. Of course, what else is to be expected of Noir's daughter? She was a slob too, and ungrateful. But come your first raising, you'll have no excuse for your messes. Either in your room or on your person. Do you hear me?"

"Yes, Reshka."

But Nin was no longer paying attention. She had found what she was looking for.

The gravestone read:

Mason Ezekiel Gont

1901-1924

Son, Brother, Friend

Mason Ezekiel Gont.

The words rang like bells. The sweetest, most clangorous, most dangerous clamor. Mason. Ezekiel. Gont. Mason Ezekiel Gont.

Son. Brother. *Friend*.

The night of the raising, Nin dressed with care.

She had grown up wearing Reshka's castoffs, or ancient garments rifled from attic and cupola. But for this special occasion, which marked her fifteenth birthday and her very first ghost, Nin ordered a new wardrobe from online catalogues like Gypsy Moon and the Tudor Shoppe. She used Reshka's credit card.

Most of what Nin bought came in some shade of red.

Her poppy-petal skirt fell to her ankles, embroidered and deeply flounced. Her shirt was dyed a vibrant arterial red, with scarlet ribbons running through the collar and cuffs. Around her waist she tied a golden scarf with firebird patterns and a beaded fringe. She wore bells on her ankles. Her hair, black and rough and loose, covered her bare arms. Her skin, scrubbed with salted water, shone pink as hope.

She did not want her ghost to mistake her for a mere shade. She wanted to be seen.

Reshka had commissioned Nin a carrying case for the four winds. It was ebony, lined in blue velvet, with separate compartments for the instruments. Flute, piccolo, oboe, bass recorder, each fit cunningly in its own place.

"It's better than you deserve," Reshka said.

Nin did not argue. Neither did she say thank you.

They accomplished the drive to Pieta Cemetery in their customary silence, arriving at an hour so late it was technically morning. There was no telling sky from tomb, everything was so black and still. Pulling up outside the gates, Reshka let the truck idle. Old Stix and young Stix stared straight ahead, neither looking at the other.

"Tonight," said Reshka, "we'll see if the sorcery runs true in you. I'll never know why Noir insisted on diluting your bloodline with a living sire. You favor your bag boy father in everything but the eyes."

Nin sprang out of the truck. Before slamming the door, she leaned in and stared Reshka dead in the eye.

"I look like Noir, except I'm taller and my hair is black. I look like Noir Stix, you old bitch. Don't wait up."

And she turned and stalked away.

But no sooner did Nin step through the gates than she felt the ire slipping from her shoulders. To be alone at last, and a year older, and dressed to tryst! All around the graveyard sang, in cricket song, frog-throb, and the call of night birds from hundred-year-old trees. Moss fell from low branches like silver veils.

The dead are close, Nin thought, but not awake. The dead are underfoot.

She knew the way to his grave by heart. Since discovering him, Nin had visited often, sneaking off early from Stix Haunt to tramp those five miles down the dark road on foot, just to bring him wildflowers. Wooing him, she hoped.

Mason Ezekiel Gont. 1901-1924. She wished there had been room to etch,

"Son, Brother, Friend," on the inner band of the grave-ring, but she carried the words hard in her heart, that they would not be destroyed when his headstone fell.

And there it was, his quiet resting place.

Nin laid a shallow bowl of alabaster before his headstone, lighting the coals inside it. Then, sifting resin of red myrrh over the smolder, she knelt and placed a circle of white lilies in her hair. Bitter smoke snaked skyward, leaving a pale echo of vanilla in the air. She opened the ebony carrying case.

First, the luring song.

Pipe it on the piccolo, high and sweet and blithe. Pipe it playful on your tiptoes, and dance you 'round his grave. Three times three, you dance—and trill and tease and coax:

Come out to me!

Come dance and leap!

Rise up, rise out!

Come play!

Nin played the lure perfectly. But it was very, very hard.

Reshka never told her that it would hurt. Or of the horrors.

Her lips burned. Her tongue burst into blisters, which burst into vile juices that ran down her throat. The sky ripped open and a bleak wind dove down from the stars, beating black wings and shrieking. Reshka never said how a greater darkness would fall over the night like a hand smothering heaven, how every note she played would cost her a heartbeat, how the earth shuddered away from her naked, dancing feet as though it could not bear her touch.

And then Mason Ezekiel Gont appeared in the smoke of the burning myrrh.

"Ghosts can't take flesh," Reshka had said. "But they can take form. In water, in windows, in smoke and mirror, in steam and flame. If you are lucky and if they're strong, they can shape a shadow you can almost touch."

He was there. The lure was over. Nin stopped playing and stood still and looked her fill.

The ghost rose uncertainly from the burning coals, upright and blinking, but not quite awake. His hands, which were vague, which were vapor, moved to touch his face, before falling to his sides again, in fists. A look of terrible confusion made his whole body waver, shred apart, form again. He could not feel himself.

Remembering just in time, Nin snatched the crown of lilies from her hair and tossed it over his head. The flowers fell through him, landing in a perfect circle around the alabaster bowl. She had practiced that toss a hundred thousand times.

The ghost glanced down at the lilies, then back up at Nin. She was not supposed to speak until he was hers for sure, but she smiled, hoping to reassure him.

Don't worry, she wanted to say. *They're to keep you safe. Keep you from straying.*

She put the piccolo away and picked up the flute.

The binding song was a lightning series of notes, arpeggios and scales both wild and shrill (Nin had never really mastered the flute; Reshka kept telling her she played like a flock of slaughtered turkeys), and even the ghost winced to hear them.

The flute screamed, and then it seemed the ghost screamed, and frost settled over Pieta Cemetery. It came from nowhere and everywhere. The graves began to glisten. The trees were draped in diamonds. Nin's lips froze to the lip of the flute. Her fingers slowed on the notes, turned blue, stiffened and stuck. It was like she played an instrument made of angry ice.

It was not music anymore. Nothing like music. Only one long, sustained, horrible noise, like a stake hammered into frozen ground, making a claim.

You are mine

You will stay with me

For all eternity

And then the binding was over. The flute fell from Nin's nerveless hands.

The ghost stared at her. His eyes were the color of burning myrrh. The trees were white and still beneath a sheen of frost, and he was still too, trapped within the chain of lilies.

Nin began to braid a single lock of her hair. It was no simple braid, but a sturdy rope of many strands, with a series of intricate knots at the end. She had spent a year practicing this braid, first with embroidery thread, then with spiderwebs, then on a doll with human hair that had been from the head of her great-grandmother's grandmother.

"The hair of a madwoman," Reshka had said. "So you know what lunacy feels like."

Nin had practiced the braid in her own hair too, but it had not been like this. There was a song of braiding. She hummed it now, and would later seal the braid with the same tune on the oboe, after the last knot was tied.

The song filled her mouth with wasps. She kept humming, though the wasps stung her tongue and crawled over her teeth. She hummed and braided, even though her hair was suddenly tough as steel, sharp as needles, poisonous as nettles. Already burnt and frozen, now her hands stung, now they trembled and bled, until her hair was wet with her own blood.

And still she braided and hummed, and the ghost watched.

Bind and wind and knot and weave

A labyrinth of grief and need

Way and wall and maze and path
A labyrinth of want and wrath
Mason Ezekiel Gont—
I braid thee, my ghost I braid thee in my hair

She tied the end of the braid with silver thread, coughing out a mouthful of crawling white wasps as she did so, and took up the oboe, and sealed the braid with a song. When it was over, Nin wept.

The ghost looked on her tears with curiosity, maybe even pity, but his fists did not relax.

The bass recorder was a lean length of polished ivory, ending in a gentle bell. It shook in her hands.

Break, she played
Break, stone, and be forgotten
Nothing but bones beneath, and those are dust
Break stone, break name, break birth and death
Break old, forgotten words and go to dust
I will keep him, I will hold him
My flesh shall be his gravestone
I alone shall name him
Break, break, stone—and be forgotten . . .

Nin did not know how long she played. She played until "Son, Brother, Friend," collapsed to pebbly rubble. Until the day her ghost was born and the day he died turned to gravel, and his name, his beautiful name, decayed to dirt and fell to dirt, indistinguishable from the rest of the earth.

When the song was done, she packed up the lilies and the alabaster bowl so that nothing would mark the place. She slung the strap of her carrying case over her shoulder.

From her pocket, she drew the silver grave-ring and slipped it over her finger.

"Mason Ezekiel Gont," said Nin Stix. "Follow me home."

Even the silence changed after that. Everything was music.

When the last of her wounds healed, the frostbite and heat blisters and wasp stings leaving numb spots and small scars, Nin started reading to her ghost. All her old favorites, Pushkin to Pratchett, Yourcenar to Yolen, J.M. Barrie to Gene Wolfe: dog-eared and thumbed-through as these books were, she took them out and began them again, this time out loud. She read the ghost her old letters to Noir, showed him her sketchbooks, and led him to her secret place beneath the willow tree. She even vacuumed the salt from her threshold and windowsill that the ghost might come and go as he pleased.

Because he shared it with her, Nin straightened her room every day. She made her bed with what Noir had called "Marine Corps precision"—hoping that Reshka would never suspect it was Nin's work and none of the ghost's. She began to wear perfume and dressed in her new clothes every day. For the first time in seven years, Nin was happy.

And she was beginning to see the ghost more clearly.

One night, several weeks after the raising, Nin sat at the edge of her bed and lit a candle. Like magic, the ghost's shadow sprang to the wall, man-sized, as though he were standing right in front of her, with her flame shining bright upon him. Nin smiled. The shadow stepped off the wall and sat down at the foot of the bed.

"Mason," she whispered.

He turned towards her, rayless, faceless, dense. She could not see through him.

"I'm sorry you can't sleep," she said. "You must miss dreaming."

The ghost gave a small shrug, out of courtesy or despair. It might have meant a thousand things.

"Rest, please, you must rest—if you can," said Nin. "On the bed, if you want. I'll sleep on the floor. If you want."

In answer, the ghost drew back her covers, his shadow hands deliberate and careful, and then gestured Nin beneath the sheets. The moment her bare feet brushed the footboard, he pulled the blankets up to her chin, smoothed them, and lay down beside her, on top of the white eyelet lace. Nin turned onto her side, facing away from him, barely breathing. The ghost gathered her against him, one arm tucked snug against her stomach. For a long time, wrapped in his shadow, Nin stared at the candle and did not sleep.

She awoke with dark blue bruises on the places he had pressed against all night. Her stomach, the back of her neck, all along her spine. Frost hung in her black hair where he had breathed on her, a mist of crystals everywhere but on a single braid.

Soon after this, she took him to meet her mother.

Beneath the willow tree, Nin dreamed her willow dreams.

It was September, and the Heron Marsh was restless. Greens bled to gold, gold grew dense and dry. Insects chafed. Long-legged birds took wing. The ghost followed Nin into dreaming.

"Oh, my," said Noir the first time she saw him.

They were curled on the boulder, out in the middle of Lake Argentine. A warm green breeze moved down from the languid sky.

Mother and daughter regarded the ghost as he treaded the too-blue water, splashing about, sometimes diving under to swim with the black fish-cat who lived beneath, a sleekly furred beast with the head of a panther and the body of an eel.

Once or twice, it twined with the ghost's feet as he swam, trying to pull him under.

Mason dodged the fish-cat and swam up to rest against Nin's legs where they dangled in the water. His dark, wet head nudged her knobbly knees. Nin stroked his hair.

"I can see him so clearly here," Nin said. "He's like a silhouette that grew dimensions. And he's not cold at all!"

Her mother ran her fingers through her own short curls, her smile rueful, and glanced from Nin's face to the ghost.

"Well," said Noir. "Nice to meet you finally. What's your name?"

The ghost glanced at Nin, radiating inquiry.

"Mason Ezekiel Gont," Nin replied with a proud smile. She could never say his name without smiling. She said it whenever she could. "Mason Gont. The Gont of Haunt. Mason. His name is Mason."

"Mason," Noir repeated, never taking her eyes from the ghost's face. "Mason."

"Mason," said the ghost. Then, "I won't remember it."

Nin clapped a hand to her mouth in shock. Her ghost had never spoken before. Her mother did not look surprised, only compassionate. And a little angry.

"I know you won't remember, Mason. But while you're here, we'll do what we can."

The ghost spread his hands, palms up, treading water. Noir leaned down to touch his shoulder.

"Is my daughter kind to you?"

"Is she kind?" He lifted his head from Nin's knees to stare at her. His eyes were darker than the rest of him, a deep and glossy black beaming like volcano glass from the chiseled planes and contours of his face. Every eyelash showed in spiky, sharp relief.

Nin and her ghost watched each other, forgetting to breathe. Both remembered the shower they had shared that morning. How he had spilled into shape, hot spray and viscid steam, touching her with hands that were rivulets, that were waterfalls, soaping her body and washing the suds from her hair. Nin had not asked him into the bathroom with her. But he had entered anyway, uninvited, and she did not order him away.

After the shower, when she was clean and sweet smelling, when his icy and invisible arms wrapped the towel around her flushed body, she had wiped the steam from the mirror with the heel of her hand and saw them both inside it. The ghost stood behind her, vivid as any man.

Mason's nose was too large for his face. His eyebrows grew straight and ferocious, very dark. Most of his skin was luminous with spectral pallor, wet and bare, steaming from the shower, but his cheekbones were hectic, as though fever-eaten. His hair was shaggy, almost as curly as Noir's, almost as black as Nin's—a warm black, with hints of brown and glints of red. His lips were thin and seemed naturally pensive.

Nin wondered if she could ever make him laugh.

Even as she thought this, he began to smile, matching the thoroughness of her inspection with the intensity of his own.

And then he bent his head. And placed his mouth on her neck.

Soft as lilies, sore as stinging nettles. The shock went through her like a bitter wind. And when he lifted his head again, they stared at each other in the glass, stunned, and she knew that he had felt what she had felt, on his side of the mirror.

"Yes," Mason Ezekiel Gont told her mother, in the water of Nin's willow dream. "Nin has been very kind."

"My name is Noir," said Noir, with a terrible pity in her eyes. "You are welcome beneath my tree any time."

In the second week of October, Reshka summoned Nin to the Ring Room. The ghost accompanied Nin up to the door but no further; the salt trenches on the threshold stopped him.

When she stepped through the doorway, Nin could no longer see him, or even sense his presence. The braid in her hair hung listless, but the silver grave-ring burned against her finger. By this alone she knew the ghost was disturbed. He could not find her. He could not follow her. He could not even know the room existed.

"What do you want?" Nin asked, not patiently.

Reshka hunched like a harpy on one of the benches. Mockery whetted her round blue eyes.

"All Souls' soon," she said.

Nin never paid attention to the holidays. Mostly, she slept through them.

"So?"

"So?" Reshka sneered. Her voice was like taking ice cubes to a cheese grater, always at odds with her varnished face. "So? You've not lived through a Souls' Day yet, girl. Or the Eve of it, either."

Nin sighed.

"Every Dark Eve," Reshka went on, "I've drugged your food and drink to make you sleep. I've circled your bed with salt and locked your door with a silver key. I've kept you safe from the ghosts of Stix Haunt—and *so*, you ask? So! You have no idea, do you, girl, what happens when the dead walk? *When the dead take flesh and come walking!*"

That parched old voice, never less than awful, now cracked under the strain of something more. Nin had never seen Reshka's fear. She did not know how to respond to it.

"They come walking?" she asked. "In the flesh? But you said . . . "

Reshka ignored her. "I won't drug you this year. You're grown—got a ghost of your own now, don't you, girl? I've seen. You're careless, treat him like a pet, let him walk all over you. Let him take liberties. You'll deserve what happens when he walks. He'll destroy everything you own, searching for that little ring you wear. Might be he'll gobble you in your bed. But I don't know." Reshka's pink lips curled. "Might be you want that, to die as ghoul food? Noir's daughter is fool enough for such, I guess."

Nin clenched her hands. "Leave Noir out of this, Reshka! If you have something to teach me, teach me!"

Her grandmother's immaculate claws shot out, quick and callous as they had been seven years ago at Lake Argentine, when they drowned the black cat Behemoth. Now they closed around Nin's wrist and sunk deep, drawing blood.

Nin's grave-ring flared—agony! agony!—and her knees gave out. She fell hard at Reshka's feet, her arm twisted in her grandmother's grip, seized fast.

"The dead will come walking." Reshka's voice shook, but her talons never faltered. "They come looking for their names. You stay in your salt circle, with a silver veil cast over your braid, and you keep still. You don't move. You barely breathe. They'll take the house apart searching. That's of no matter—I make them put it to rights again the next day. They'll do it, or I'll hurt them as only the dead can be hurt, I'll burn little bits of them to dust.

"But that's for morning. At night, on Dark Eve, so long as they walk, you stay still, you never leave the circle. And you never, *ever* remove your silver veil. Or else they'll *see*. The salt might stop them—maybe, maybe not—but best not test it. Do this and don't stray, Noir's daughter, or I'll hang you from that willow tree you love. Then I'll raise you up again by the four winds, and you'll be scrubbing my back and brushing my teeth for all eternity. You got that, Nin the Necrophilian? Am I clear enough, Miss Nin?"

"Clear!" Nin gasped, hating herself. She might as well have cried mercy. Reshka flung her wrist away with a disgusted hiss.

"Then get out," said her grandmother. "And prepare while you still can."

It rained all day on the Dark Eve.

No trick-or-treaters came skipping down the road from town, plastic pumpkin heads in hand. No teens dressed in black T-shirts and glow-in-the-dark bones came to teepee the lawns and throw stones at the windows of Stix Haunt.

Nin stayed at her window all day, pretending to watch the rain. But it was Mason she watched, following his restlessness as he paced wall to wall in the reflection of her room.

"It's all right," she told him. "You'll walk tonight."

He paused long enough to give her a single, unfathomable look.

"I wish I could go to the willow tree," Nin said. "But on a day like this I'd drown."

The ghost drifted towards her in the window. Nin felt him at her back. But before he touched her, before his arctic breath sent chills down her neck, he turned away. He walked through one of her walls, and he did not return.

Nin tried not to cry. She'd wanted him out anyway. Now she could begin her preparations. The first part was easy. All she needed was scissors.

The hour before midnight, Nin lit a line of red pillar candles. Hot cinnamon wax scented the air. She had covered her windows with shawls and scarves, so that no one outside—alive or dead—could look in.

By candlelight, Nin laid her circle of salt, three thick lines of it. Sea salt, then road salt, then perfumed bath salts that smelled like lavender. When the circle met itself, when even Nin forgot where it began and ended, she stepped out of her clothes and shoes, folded them neatly and put them away, and flung a dark gray veil, heavy with silver embroidery and longer than she was tall, over her head. Then she moved over the lines of salt into the heart of the circle, and sat on the floor to wait.

Reshka's grandfather clock struck midnight. Dark Eve was over, and All Souls' began. So did the noises.

Downstairs, down the hall, starting in the kitchen, a great clashing started up. Glass broke. Drawers pulled out and upended. Knives hurled at the walls. A huge, frightening crash—perhaps the refrigerator tipping over. Bookcases toppled. Books ripped apart. Curtain rods torn down. Someone singing an awful song. Someone flushing and flushing the toilet. (Nin wondered what they were flushing.) Cabinet doors ripped off. Doors slamming. Outside, shrubs uprooted, banged against the house, tossed through the windows. Someone pounding holes in the porch with something blunt. A furious gibbering. People who had forgotten how to speak. Whistlings and whispers and wet slobbering sobs sliding through the cracks in the plaster.

The ghosts walked in flesh. The search was on.

Below, Nin knew, Reshka was in hiding, sealed in the Ring Room behind salt and silver. The ghosts could not harrow her from that secret place, to reclaim what she wore on her fingers, in her hair. Thwarted, they grew restless. Further and further out they ranged, into the woods and the marshes, maybe as far as the town, knocking on doors, rapping on windows, searching for their names. The calamity of their passing faded to a distant wailing.

Nin's door opened and Mason Ezekiel Gont stepped inside.

He did not see Nin, invisible behind her barrier of salt, with the gray veil over her. He walked to her bed and stared at it for some time, then stroked the white eyelet lace. He could feel what he touched. He did not, precisely, smile.

Mason moved through the candlelight, a ghost in the flesh, casting no shadow. He ran his fingers over everything, the fringes of her scarves, the beads hanging from her ceiling fan, the cotton underwear in her drawer. Always with that expression that was not entirely sweet or bitter, but concentrated. Perhaps hungry.

Three times he passed the mirror before he dared look at himself. When he did, he stepped right up to the glass, pressed his nose to it. Forehead to reflected forehead, he studied himself. His left palm flattened to his breastbone, where no heart beat. Mason and Mason-in-the-mirror stayed that way for a long time.

While he stared, Nin stood up in her circle. Almost carelessly, almost by accident, she stretched one bare big toe towards him. The toe smudged a few grains of salt out of place. It took only that, and Mason Ezekiel Gont turned to look at her.

Two strides, and he reached through the circle, pulling the veil from her face.

He said, "Your hair."

"Yes," said Nin. "Now I know why Noir kept it so short."

He shook his head, wordlessly reaching out again. But Nin sidestepped his grasp and backed away, until the back of her knees met the edge of her bed and she sank down. She rubbed the stubble on her head, more acutely aware of its unpredictable tufts than of her nakedness.

Frowning down at her feet, Nin could not see him coming, but she heard his tread. And then he was there, standing knee to knee with her.

"Will you sit?" she invited him.

"Do you command it?"

"No."

"I will not sit."

Nin glanced up. For the first time since he had entered her room, she recognized the expression on his face as anger. He was so angry, heat simmered off his skin. He looked not into her eyes, but at her skull, her scalp, the absence of her hair—the absence of the braid where his soul was bound. Once she saw his gaze flicker to her ring finger, which was bare.

"It—it—was never right to call you," she stammered. "Or, having called you, to keep you. But I was so . . ." She shrugged. She could not say the words she had practiced a hundred times.

"Where is it?" asked Mason in his soft way. "You still have it somewhere. You have not released me. It's here. Very near. My soul, braided and bound in you. Do you think I can't feel it? Is this a trick? What did you do with your hair?"

"I was going to give it to you . . ."

"Do it now," he said. "Do it, please, before the others come back and pull me into their madness. I am that close to going over . . . I am so close, Nin."

Nin, he said, and his rage broke a little.

Nin began to weep. The ghost placed his hands on her naked shoulders. His hands, heavy with borrowed life, were smooth and lineless, without fingerprints or scars or calluses. They bore her against the mattress, and she did not fight, knowing that he was no more relentless than she had been.

"Nin," he said, "I need my name. I need it. I need it back. Where did you put it? Where is your hair?"

Her nose was clogged from crying. "You are my only friend."

"And I'm here, Nin," he whispered. His breath was white waste and winter night. "I'm right here. And I am your friend. But I have neither eaten nor drunk for one hundred years. I have not felt flesh beneath my fingers in one hundred years. Nin, I am hungry—and I have no name to recall me to myself, or the honor I once believed in!"

His hands were warm, and his breath was cold, and her own breath was coming too fast.

"Please," said Nin.

"Stop me," begged the ghost. "Nin, stop me."

"I can't."

"Please." His voice grew ragged. His hands moved down her body, fingers hard on her thighs. His mouth suckled at her skin, not so much kissing as tasting raised flesh, heartbeat, the pulse of the artery running through her belly. She grasped his curls and his head slid lower. Even his hair was alive, twining around her fingers like damp, sleepy ferns.

Nin reached one hand beneath her pillow to draw out a silver-embroidered sack ungainly with salt. The knot that bound it was simple, but Mason's mouth complicated everything. When her trembling fingers finally undid the knot, salt spilled everywhere, along with a single black braid, which she had bound on both ends in silver, and looped through a little silver ring. The inner band of the ring was engraved with a name and two dates.

Mason raised his head and saw the braid.

"It's for you," Nin said. "It's yours."

His hand shot out so fast she did not see it move. The braid and the silver ring disappeared into his clenched fist.

"I am Nin Stix," Nin said. "What's your name?"

"I am Mason Ezekiel Gont," said the ghost, and then he laughed. The sound seemed to surprise him. Then, surprising Nin, he dipped his head and brushed her belly with a kiss.

"And I am pleased," he said, "I am most pleased to meet you, Nin Stix." He kissed her belly again, the spot between her breasts, the side of her throat.

Then, in a whisper she almost missed: "Stop me, Nin."

"No," she said. "You're free. You're my friend. You're the only one I want."

His tongue licked a few grains of salt from the spill across her belly. His exhale moved, frozen, across her skin. Nin felt a thin ice crust her stomach.

"Mason," she began.

"Nin Stix."

"Mason Ezekiel Gont."

"Nin Stix, sorceress." His tongue worked on her, his lips, his teeth. The hunger of a hundred years. "Nin, gentle mistress. Nin of the Four Winds . . ."

"Mason . . ."

"Nin, do not stop me now . . ."

"Mason—finish it!"

And he did.

All Souls' day passed in a dream, and then night came.

Nin and Mason lay together, foreheads touching, and Nin wept to realize that Mason's kiss had driven the taste of ash from her mouth. She burrowed against him, driving her flesh to his, knowing she would not be able to touch him again after midnight.

"Nin." His breath was warm now, warm on her scalp, and it smelled of lily and of myrrh. "Nin, my Nin, what will you do now?"

She knew what he was asking. He was asking, "What are you going to do without me?" He was asking, "How will you live, when I leave you alone— more alone than anyone has ever been alone?"

Nin shook her head. "It doesn't matter."

"It does," he insisted. "I know it does. What will you do?"

The answer came to her then, like a bruise behind the eyes, or a freezer-burn of the marrow bone, and she put both her hands over her face and stayed that way for some time.

"Nin?"

"This can't continue."

"What can't?" the ghost asked carefully.

Nin rolled onto her back, her neck cradled in the crook of his arm. "Any of it."

Reshka Stix waited out the day in her Ring Room.

She had lived through one hundred eight All Souls', midnight to midnight; she knew what to do. For twenty-three hours, she had been supine upon her worktable, covered in a net of silver that glittered under the bright electric lights. She barely breathed, keeping a light trance that let her listen for the ghosts. Even when they left the Haunt, she could hear them. Reshka Stix could always hear them, screaming through the marshes, baying in the woods, frightening the water moccasins and the foxes and the owls to stony deaths. Searching for their names.

She could name them all.

No one in the house now but Noir's mouse, mooning for her ghost boy. That girl would end up gobbled. Or she'd end up too weepy and weak for the sorcery, and abandon the Haunt as Noir had done, salting her footsteps so the ghosts could not bring her back . . .

Shimmering under silver and memory, Reshka did not hear her grand-daughter creep up to the Ring Room door. Reshka never heard the living so well as the dead. So when Nin poured water into the salt trenches at the Ring Room's threshold, Reshka did not know it.

Only when the ghosts came back did she know. She knew, and they knew, and they poured back into the Haunt so fast they blew the front door off its hinges and left it for splinters on the floor. A horde of ghosts descended upon her, twenty-two shrieking things, crowding the bright-lit chamber where silver rings were made. Reshka Stix could name them all.

The oldest saw her first. Perhaps her foot twitched beneath the net of silver. Or her breathing gave her away. In a flash, in a blink, moving as only a ghost could move—he was upon her, ripping off the silver veil with one hand, while the other lunged for her braided hair.

Each ghost who could reach one seized a braid, and those who could not started chewing, chomping, gnawing the rings off her fingers with their teeth, gnawing off her fingers one by one.

Reshka Stix did not scream. Even when they tore the braids out of her scalp, taking chunks of skin and clots of blood, she kept her tight pink lips compressed. And when they sucked the flesh from her severed fingers to get to the grave-rings, even then, proud Reshka made no sound. Of course, by that time, she was dead.

So there was no one alive at Stix Haunt that night to stop the ghosts from setting it ablaze.

"Nin, my love?"

"Yes, Noir, my love?"

"Is it over?"

"Yes. It's over and he is gone."

"It's morning, Nin. It's very late, in fact. I think you should wake."

"Did I really . . . Is Reshka . . . ?"

"*Wake* . . ."

The morning smelled like a funeral feast. Ashy air filled Nin's mouth, and she coughed, then turned onto her side and retched.

She had no recollection of leaving Stix Haunt after Reshka's ghosts came ravening back through. Mason must have done something, put her to sleep somehow and carried her to the willow tree—but she remembered nothing of that. Nin rubbed her head. She missed her hair, but not as much as she missed the braid and what it had bound. On hands and knees, she crawled from her damp shelter. It was in this genuflection that she had her first sight of the Haunt—what it had become.

Smoke filtered the sweet colors from the air. Reshka's house was a charred shell, clung about with trembling curtains of heat. A few piles of rubble smoldered yet. Nin made a sound between a cough and a cry.

"Oh, Noir! Oh, Mason—what have I done?"

The distance from willow to ruin might have been the distance between stars. She could not bear to go any closer. Palms pressed to eyes, she dropped until her forehead rested on the ground. Something cold kissed her forehead.

Nin did not have to see the ring to recognize it. His ring, his name, his birth and death—his broken and stolen tombstone—the ring she had returned to him, encircled her finger once again. Mason had put it there, he must have done, had bequeathed it to her, making her his resting place.

"Nin, my Nin," the ghost had asked, "what will you do now?"

Nin pushed to her knees and wiped her face.

THE THING ABOUT CASSANDRA

NEIL GAIMAN

—◆—

So there's Scallie and me wearing Starsky-and-Hutch wigs, complete with sideburns, at five o'clock in the morning by the side of a canal in Amsterdam. There had been ten of us that night, including Rob, the groom, last seen handcuffed to a bed in the Red Light District with shaving foam covering his nether regions and his brother-in-law giggling and patting the hooker holding the straight razor on the arse, which was the point I looked at Scallie and he looked at me, and he said, "Maximum deniability?" and I nodded, because there are some questions you don't want to be able to answer when a bride starts asking pointed questions about the stag weekend, so we slipped off for a drink, leaving eight men in Starsky-and-Hutch wigs (one of whom was mostly naked, attached to a bed by fluffy pink handcuffs, and seemed to be starting to think that this adventure wasn't such a good idea after all) behind us, in a room that smelled of disinfectant and cheap incense, and we went and sat by a canal and drank cans of Danish lager and talked about the old days.

Scallie—whose real name is Jeremy Porter, and these days people call him Jeremy, but he had been Scallie when we were eleven—and the groom to be, Rob Cunningham, had been at school with me. We had drifted out of touch, more or less, had found each other the lazy way you do these days, through Friends Reunited and Facebook and such, and now Scallie and I were together for the first time since we were nineteen. The Starsky-and-Hutch wigs, which had been Scallie's idea, made us look like we were playing brothers in some made-for-TV movie—Scallie the short, stocky brother with the thick moustache, me, the tall one. Given that I've made a significant part of my income since leaving school modeling, I'd add the tall good-looking one, but nobody looks good in a Starsky-and-Hutch wig, complete with sideburns.

Also, the wig itched.

We sat by the canal, and when the lager had all gone we kept talking and we watched the sun come up.

Last time I saw Scallie he was nineteen and filled with big plans. He had just joined the RAF as a cadet. He was going to fly planes, and do double duty using the flights to smuggle drugs, and so get incredibly rich while helping his country. It was the kind of mad idea he used to have all the way through school. Usually the whole thing would fall apart. Sometimes he'd get the rest of us into trouble on the way.

Now, twelve years later, his six months in the RAF ended early because of an unspecified problem with his right knee, he was a senior executive in a firm that manufactured double-glazed windows, he told me, with, since the divorce, a smaller house than he felt that he deserved and only a golden retriever for company.

He was sleeping with a woman in the double-glazing firm, but had no expectations of her leaving her boyfriend for him, seemed to find it easier that way. "Of course, I wake up crying sometimes, since the divorce. Well, you do," he said at one point. I could not imagine him crying, and anyway he said it with a huge Scallie grin.

I told him about me: still modelling, helping out in a friend's antique shop to keep busy, more and more painting. I was lucky; people bought my paintings. Every year I would have a small gallery show at the Little Gallery in Chelsea, and while initially the only people to buy anything had been people I knew—photographers, old girlfriends, and the like—these days I have actual collectors. We talked about the days that only Scallie seemed to remember, when he and Rob and I had been a team of three, inviolable, unbreakable. We talked about teenage heartbreak, about Caroline Minton (who was now Caroline Keen, and married to a vicar), about the first time we brazened our way into an 18 film, although neither of us could remember what the film actually was.

Then Scallie said, "I heard from Cassandra the other day."

"Cassandra?"

"Your old girlfriend. Cassandra. Remember?"

" . . . No."

"The one from Reigate. You had her name written on all your books." I must have looked particularly dense or drunk or sleepy, because he said, "You met her on a skiing holiday. Oh, for heaven's sake. *Your first shag.* Cassandra."

"Oh," I said, remembering, remembering everything. "Cassandra."

And I did remember.

"Yeah," said Scallie. "She dropped me a line on Facebook. She's running a community theatre in East London. You should talk to her."

"Really?"

"I think, well, I mean, reading between the lines of her message, she may still have a thing for you. She asked after you."

I wondered how drunk he was, how drunk I was, staring at the canal in the early light. I said something, I forget what, then I asked whether Scallie remembered where our hotel was, because I had forgotten, and he said he had forgotten too, and that Rob had all the hotel details and really we should go and find him and rescue him from the clutches of the nice hooker with the handcuffs and the shaving kit, which, we realised, would be easier if we knew how to get back to where we'd left him, and looking for some clue to where we had left Rob, I found a card with the hotel's address on it in my back pocket, so we headed back there and the last thing I did before we walked away from the canal and that whole strange evening was to pull the itchy Starsky-and-Hutch wig off my head and throw it into the canal.

It floated.

Scallie said, "There was a deposit on that, you know. If you didn't want to wear it, I'd've carried it." Then he said, "You should drop Cassandra a line."

I shook my head. I wondered who he had been talking to online, who he had confused for her, knowing it definitely wasn't Cassandra.

The thing about Cassandra is this: I'd made her up.

I was fifteen, almost sixteen. I was awkward. I had just experienced my teenage growth spurt and was suddenly taller than most of my friends, self-conscious about my height. My mother owned and ran a small riding stables, and I helped out there, but the girls—competent, horsey, sensible types—intimidated me. At home I wrote bad poetry and painted water colours, mostly of ponies in fields; at school—there were only boys at my school—I played cricket competently, acted a little, hung around with my friends playing records (the CD was around, but they were expensive and rare, and we had all inherited record players and hi-fis from parents or older siblings). When we didn't talk about music, or sports, we talked about girls.

Scallie was older than me. So was Rob. They liked having me as part of their gang, but they liked teasing me, too. They acted like I was a kid, and I wasn't. They had both done it with girls. Actually, that's not entirely true. They had both done it with the same girl, Caroline Minton, famously free with her favours and always up for it once, as long as the person she was with had a moped.

I did not have a moped. I was not old enough to get one, my mother could not afford one (my father had died when I was small, of an accidental overdose of anaesthetic, when he was in hospital to have a minor operation on an infected toe. To this day, I avoid hospitals). I had seen Caroline Minton at parties, but she terrified me and even had I owned a moped, I would not have wanted my first sexual experience to be with her.

Scallie and Rob also had girlfriends. Scallie's girlfriend was taller than he was, had huge breasts, and was interested in football, which meant that Scallie had to feign an interest in football, Crystal Palace, while Rob's girlfriend thought that Rob and she should have things in common, which meant that Rob stopped listening to the mid-80s electropop the rest of us liked and started listening to hippy bands from before we were born, which was bad, and that Rob got to raid her dad's amazing collection of old TV series on video, which was good.

I had no girlfriend.

Even my mother began to comment on it.

There must have been a place where it came from, the name, the idea: I don't remember though. I just remember writing "Cassandra" on my exercise books. Then, carefully, not saying anything.

"Who's Cassandra?" asked Scallie.

"Nobody," I said.

"She must be somebody. You wrote her name on your maths exercise book."

"She's just a girl I met on the skiing holiday." My mother and I had gone skiing, with my aunt and cousins, the month before, in Austria.

"Are we going to meet her?"

"She's from Reigate. I expect so. Eventually."

"Well, I hope so. And you *like* her?"

I paused, for what I hoped was the right amount of time, and said, "She's a really good kisser." Then Scallie laughed and Rob wanted to know if this was French kissing, with tongues and everything, and I said, "What do *you* think," and by the end of the day, they both believed in her.

My mum was pleased to hear I'd met someone. Her questions—what Cassandra's parents did, for example—I simply shrugged away.

I went on three "dates" with Cassandra. On each of our dates, I took the train up to London, and took myself to the cinema. It was exciting, in its own way.

I returned from the first trip with more stories of kissing, and of breast-feeling.

Our second date (in reality, spent watching *Weird Science* on my own in Leicester Square) was, as told to my mum, holding hands together at what she still called "the pictures," but as told to Rob and Scallie (and over that week, to several other school friends who had heard rumours from sworn-to-secrecy Rob and Scallie, and now needed to find out if it was true), the day I lost my virginity, in Cassandra's aunt's flat in London: The aunt was away, Cassandra had a key. I had (for proof) a packet of three condoms missing the one I had thrown away and a strip of four black-and-white photographs I had found on my first trip to London, abandoned in the basket of a photo booth on Victoria Station. The photo strip showed a girl about my age with long straight hair (I could not be certain of the colour. Dark blond? Red? Light brown?) and a friendly, freckly, not unpretty, face. I pocketed it. In art class I did a pencil sketch of the third of the pictures, the one I liked the best, her head half-turned as if calling out to an unseen friend beyond the tiny curtain. She looked sweet, and charming.

I put the drawing up on my bedroom wall, where I could see it from my bed.

After our third date (it was *Who Framed Roger Rabbit*) I came back to school with bad news: Cassandra's family was going to Canada (a place that sounded more convincing to my ears than America), something to do with her father's job, and I would not see her for a long time. We hadn't really broken up, but we were being practical: Those were the days when transatlantic phone calls were too expensive for teenagers. It was over.

I was sad. Everyone noticed how sad I was. They said they would have loved to have met her, and maybe when she comes back at Christmas? I was confident that by Christmas, she would be forgotten.

She was. By Christmas I was going out with Nikki Blevins and the only evidence that Cassandra had ever been a part of my life was her name, written on a couple of my exercise books, and the pencil drawing of her on my bedroom wall, with "Cassandra, February 19, 1985" written underneath it.

When my mother sold the riding stables in 1989, the drawing was lost in the move. I was at art college at the time, considered my old pencil-drawings as embarrassing as the fact that I had once invented a girlfriend, and did not care.

I do not believe I had thought of Cassandra for twenty years.

My mother sold the riding stables, the attached house, and the meadows to a property developer, who built a housing estate where it had once been, and as part of the deal, gave her a small, detached house at the end of Seton Close. I visit her at least once a fortnight, arriving on Friday night, leaving Sunday morning, a routine as regular as the grandmother clock in the hall.

Mother is concerned that I am happy in life. She has started to mention that various of her friends have eligible daughters. This trip we had an extremely embarrassing conversation that began with her asking if I would like to meet the church organist, a very nice young man of about my age.

"Mother. I'm not gay."

"There's nothing wrong with it, dear. All sorts of people do it. They even get married. Well, not proper marriage, but it's the same thing."

"I'm still not gay."

"I just thought, still not married, and the painting, and the modelling."

"I've had girlfriends, Mummy. You've even met some of them."

"Nothing that ever stuck, dear. I just thought there might be something you wanted to tell me."

"I'm not gay, Mother. I would tell you if I was." And then I said, "I snogged Tim Carter at a party when I was at art college, but we were drunk and it never went beyond that."

She pursed her lips. "That's quite enough of that, young man." And then, changing the subject, as if to get rid of an unpleasant taste in her mouth, she said, "You'll never guess who I bumped into in Tesco's last week."

"No, I won't. Who?"

"Your old girlfriend. Your first girlfriend, I should say."

"Nikki Blevins? Hang on, she's married, isn't she? Nikki Woodbridge?"

"The one before her, dear. Cassandra. I was behind her in the line. I would have been ahead of her, but I forgot that I needed cream for the berries today, so I went back to get it, and she was in front of me, and I knew her face was familiar. At first I thought she was Joanie Simmond's youngest, the one with the speech disorder—what we used to call a stammer but apparently you can't say that anymore—but then I thought, *I* know where I know that face. It was over your bed for five years. Of course I said, 'It's not Cassandra, is it?' and she said, 'It is,' and I said, 'You'll laugh when I say this, but I'm Stuart Innes's mum.' She says, 'Stuart Innes?' and her face lit up. Well, she hung around while I was putting my groceries in my shopping bag, and she said she'd already been in touch with your friend Jeremy Porter on Bookface, and they'd been talking about you—"

"You mean Facebook? She was talking to Scallie on Facebook?"

"Yes, dear."

I drank my tea and wondered who my mother had actually been talking to. I said, "You're quite sure this was the Cassandra from over my bed?"

"Oh yes, dear. She told me about how you took her to Leicester Square, and how sad she was when they had to move to Canada. They went to Vancouver. I asked her if she ever met my cousin Leslie—he went to Vancouver after the war—but she said she didn't believe so, and it turns out it's actually a big sort of place. I told her about the pencil drawing you did, and she seemed very up-to-date on your activities. She was thrilled when I told her that you were having a gallery opening this week."

"You *told* her that?"

"Yes, dear. I thought she'd like to know." Then my mother said, almost wistfully, "She's very pretty, dear. I think she's doing something in community theatre." Then the conversation went over to the retirement of Dr. Dunnings, who had been our GP since before I was born, and how he was the only non-Indian doctor left in his practice and how my mother felt about this.

I lay in bed that night in my small bedroom at my mother's house and turned over the conversation in my head. I am no longer on Facebook and thought about rejoining to see who Scullie's friends were, and if this pseudo-Cassandra was one of them, but there were too many people I was happy not to see again, and I let it be, certain that when there was an explanation, it would prove to be a simple one, and I slept.

I have been showing in the Little Gallery in Chelsea for over a decade now. In the old days, I had a quarter of a wall and nothing priced at more than three hundred pounds. Now I get my own show, every October for a month, and it would be fair to say that I have to sell only a dozen paintings to know that my needs, rent, and life are covered for another year. The unsold paintings remain on the gallery walls until they are gone and they are always gone by Christmas.

The couple who own the gallery, Paul and Barry, still call me "the beautiful boy" as they did twelve years ago, when I first exhibited with them, when it might actually have been true. Back then, they wore flowery, open-necked shirts and gold chains; now, in middle age, they wear expensive suits and talk too much for my liking about the stock exchange. Still, I enjoy their company. I see them three times a year; in September, when they come to my studio to see what I've been working on and select the paintings for the show; at the gallery, hanging and opening in October; and in February, when we settle up.

Barry runs the gallery. Paul co-owns it, comes out for the parties, but also works in the wardrobe department of the Royal Opera House. The preview party for this year's show was on a Friday night. I had spent a nervous couple of days hanging the paintings. Now my part was done, and there was nothing to do but wait, and hope people liked my art, and not to make a fool of myself. I did as I had done for the previous twelve years, on Barry's instructions, "Nurse the champagne. Fill up on water. There's nothing worse for the collector than encountering a drunk artist, unless he's a famous drunk, and you are not, dear. Be amiable but enigmatic, and when people ask for the story behind the painting, say 'My lips are sealed.' But for God's sake, imply there *is* one. It's the story they're buying."

I rarely invite people to the preview any longer: Some artists do, regarding it as a social event. I do not. While I take my art seriously, as art, and am proud of my work (the latest exhibition was called "People in Landscapes," which pretty much says it all about my work anyway), I understand that the party exists solely as a commercial event, a come-on for eventual buyers and those who might say the right thing to other eventual buyers. I tell you all this so that you will not be surprised that Barry and Paul manage the guest list to the preview, not I.

The preview begins at 6:30 P.M. I had spent the afternoon hanging paintings, making sure everything looked as good as it could. The only thing that was different about this particular event was how excited Paul looked, like a small boy struggling with the urge to tell you what he had bought you for a birthday present. That, and Barry, who said, while we were hanging, "I think tonight's show will put you on the map."

I said, "I think there's a typo on the Lake District one." An oversized painting of Windemere at sunset, with two children staring lostly at the viewer from the banks. "It should say three thousand pounds. It says three hundred thousand."

"Does it?" said Barry, blandly. "My, my."

It was perplexing, but the first guests had arrived, a little early, and the mystery could wait. A young man invited me to eat a mushroom puff from a silver tray. Then I took my glass of nurse-this-slowly champagne and I prepared to mingle.

All the prices were high, and I doubted that the Little Gallery would be able to sell them at those prices, and I worried about the year ahead.

Barry and Paul took responsibility for moving me around the room, saying, "This is the artist, the beautiful boy who makes all these beautiful things, Stuart Innes," and I would shake hands and smile. By the end of the evening I will have met everyone, and Paul and Barry are very good about saying, "Stuart, you remember David, he writes about art for the *Telegraph* . . . " and I for my part am good about saying, "Of course, how are you? So glad you could come."

The room was at its most crowded when a striking red-haired woman to whom I had not yet been introduced began shouting, "Representational bullshit!"

I was in conversation with *The Daily Telegraph* art critic and we turned. He said, "Friend of yours?" I said, "I don't think so."

She was still shouting, although the sounds of the party had now quieted. She shouted, "Nobody's interested in this shit! Nobody!" Then she reached her hand into her coat pocket and pulled out a bottle of ink, shouted, "Try selling this now!" and threw ink at *Windemere Sunset*. It was blue-black ink.

Paul was by her side then, pulling the ink bottle away from her, saying, "That was a three-hundred-thousand-pound painting, young lady." Barry took her arm, said, "I think the police will want a word with you," and walked her back into his office. She shouted at us as she went, "I'm not afraid! I'm proud! Artists like him, just feeding off you gullible art buyers. You're all sheep! Representation crap!"

And then she was gone, and the party people were buzzing, and inspecting the ink-fouled painting and looking at me, and the *Telegraph* man was asking if I would like to comment and how I felt about seeing a three-hundred-thousand-pound painting destroyed, and I mumbled about how I was proud to be a painter, and said something about the transient nature of art, and he said that he supposed that tonight's event was an artistic happening in its own right, and we agreed that, artistic happening or not, the woman was not quite right in the head.

Barry reappeared, moving from group to group, explaining that Paul was dealing with the young lady, and that her eventual disposition would be up to me. The guests were still buzzing excitedly as he was ushering people out of the door, apologising as he did so, agreeing that we lived in exciting times, explaining that he would be open at the regular time tomorrow.

"That went well," he said, when we were alone in the gallery.

"*Well?* That was a disaster!"

"Mm. 'Stuart Innes, the one who had the three-hundred-thousand-pound painting destroyed.' I think you need to be forgiving, don't you? She was a fellow artist, even one with different goals. Sometimes you need a little something to kick you up to the next level."

We went into the back room.

I said, "Whose idea was this?"

"Ours," said Paul. He was drinking white wine in the back room with the red-haired woman. "Well, Barry's mostly. But it needed a good little actress to pull it off, and I found her." She grinned modestly: managed to look both abashed and pleased with herself.

"If this doesn't get you the attention you deserve, beautiful boy," said Barry, smiling at me, "nothing will. *Now* you're important enough to be attacked."

"The Windemere painting's ruined," I pointed out.

Barry glanced at Paul, and they giggled. "It's already sold, ink splatters and all, for seventy-five thousand pounds," he said. "It's like I always say, people think they are buying the art, but really, they're buying the story."

Paul filled our glasses: "And we owe it all to you," he said to the woman. "Stuart, Barry, I'd like to propose a toast. *To Cassandra.*"

"Cassandra," we repeated, and we drank. This time I did not nurse my drink. I needed it.

Then, as the name was still sinking in, Paul said, "Cassandra, this ridiculously attractive and talented young man is, as I am sure you know, Stuart Innes."

"I know," she said. "Actually, we're very old friends."

"Do tell," said Barry.

"Well," said Cassandra, "twenty years ago, Stuart wrote my name on his maths exercise notebook."

She looked like the girl in my drawing, yes. Or like the girl in the photographs, all grown up. Sharp-faced. Intelligent. Assured.

I had never seen her before in my life.

"Hello, Cassandra," I said. I couldn't think of anything else to say.

We were in the wine bar beneath my flat. They serve food there, too. It's more than just a wine bar.

I found myself talking to her as if she was someone I had known since childhood. And, I reminded myself, she wasn't. I had only met her that evening. She still had ink stains on her hands.

We had glanced at the menu, ordered the same thing—the vegetarian meze—and when it had arrived, both started with the dolmades, then moved on to the hummus.

"I made you up," I told her.

It was not the first thing I had said: First we had talked about her community theatre, how she had become friends with Paul, his offer to her—a thousand pounds for this evening's show—and how she had needed the money, but mostly said yes because it sounded like a fun adventure. Anyway, she said, she couldn't say no when she heard my name mentioned. She thought it was fate.

That was when I said it. I was scared she would think I was mad, but I said it. "I made you up."

"No," she said. "You didn't. I mean, obviously you didn't. I'm really here." Then she said, "Would you like to touch me?"

I looked at her. At her face, and her posture, at her eyes. She was everything I had ever dreamed of in a woman. Everything I had been missing in other women. "Yes," I said. "Very much."

"Let's eat our dinner first," she said. Then she said, "How long has it been since you were with a woman?"

"I'm not gay," I protested. "I have girlfriends."

"I know," she said. "When was the last one?"

I tried to remember. Was it Brigitte? Or the stylist the ad agency had sent me to Iceland with? I was not certain. "Two years," I said. "Perhaps three. I just haven't met the right person yet."

"You did once," she said. She opened her handbag then, a big floppy purple thing, pulled out a cardboard folder, opened it, removed a piece of paper, tape browned at the corners. "See?"

I remembered it. How could I not? It had hung above my bed for years. She was looking around, as if talking to someone beyond the curtain. "Cassandra," it said, "February 19, 1985." And it was signed, "Stuart Innes." There is something at the same time both embarrassing and heartwarming about seeing your handwriting from when you were fifteen.

"I came back from Canada in eighty-nine," she said. "My parents' marriage fell apart, and Mum wanted to come home. I wondered about you, what you were doing, so I went to your old address. The house was empty. Windows were broken. It was obvious nobody lived there anymore. They'd knocked down the riding stables already—that made me so sad. I'd loved horses as a girl, obviously, but I walked through the house until I found your bedroom. It was obviously your bedroom, although all the furniture was gone. It still smelled like you. And this was still pinned to the wall. I didn't think anyone would miss it."

She smiled.

"Who *are* you?"

"Cassandra Carlisle. Aged thirty-four. Former actress. Failed playwright. Now running a community theatre in Norwood. Drama therapy. Hall for rent. Four plays a year, plus workshops, and a local panto. Who are *you*, Stuart?"

"You know who I am." Then, "You know I've never met you before, don't you?"

She nodded. She said, "Poor Stuart. You live just above here, don't you?"

"Yes. It's a bit loud sometimes. But it's handy for the tube. And the rent isn't painful."

"Let's pay, and go upstairs."

I reached out to touch the back of her hand. "Not yet," she said, moving her hand away before I could touch her. "We should talk first."

So we went upstairs.

"I like your flat," she said. "It looks exactly like the kind of place I imagine you being."

"It's probably time to start thinking about getting something a bit bigger," I told her. "But it does me fine. There's good light out the back for my studio—you can't get the effect now, at night. But it's great for painting."

It's strange, bringing someone home. It makes you see the place you live as if you've not been there before. There are two oil paintings of me in the lounge, from my short-lived career as an artists' model (I did not have the patience to stand and wait), blown-up advertising photos of me in the little kitchen and the loo, book covers with me on—romance covers, mostly, over the stairs.

I showed her the studio, and then the bedroom. She examined the Edwardian barber's chair I had rescued from an ancient barbers' that closed down in Shoreditch. She sat down on the chair, pulled off her shoes.

"Who was the first grown-up you liked?" she asked.

"Odd question. My mother, I suspect. Don't know. Why?"

"I was three, perhaps four. He was a postman called Mr. Postie. He'd come in his little post van and bring me lovely things. Not every day. Just sometimes. Brown paper packages with my name on, and inside would be toys or sweets or something. He had a funny, friendly face with a knobby nose."

"And he was real? He sounds like somebody a kid would make up."

"He drove a post van inside the house. It wasn't very big."

She began to unbutton her blouse. It was cream-coloured, still flecked with splatters of ink. "What's the first thing you actually remember? Not something you were told you did. That you really remember?"

"Going to the seaside when I was three, with my mum and my dad."

"Do you remember it? Or do you remember being *told* about it?"

"I don't see what the point of this is . . . ?"

She stood up, wiggled, stepped out of her skirt. She wore a white bra, dark green panties, frayed. Very human: not something you would wear to impress a new lover. I wondered what her breasts would look like, when the bra came off. I wanted to stroke them, to touch them to my lips.

She walked from the chair to the bed, where I was sitting.

"Lie down, now. On that side of the bed. I'll be next to you. Don't touch me."

I lay down, my hands at my sides. She said, "You're so beautiful. I'm not honestly sure whether you're my type. You would have been when I was fifteen, though. Nice and sweet and unthreatening. Artistic. Ponies. A riding stable. And I bet you never make a move on a girl unless you're sure she's ready, do you?"

"No," I said. "I don't suppose that I do."

She lay down beside me.

"You can touch me now," said Cassandra.

I had started thinking about Stuart again late last year. Stress, I think. Work was going well, up to a point, but I'd broken up with Pavel, who may or may not have been an actual bad hat although he certainly had his finger in many dodgy East European pies, and I was thinking about Internet dating. I had spent a stupid week joining the kind of Web sites that link you to old friends, and from there it was no distance to Jeremy "Scallie" Porter, and to Stuart Innes.

I don't think I could do it anymore. I lack the single-mindedness. The attention to detail. Something else you lose when you get older.

Mr. Postie used to come in his van when my parents had no time for me. He would smile his big gnomey smile, wink an eye at me, hand me a brown-paper parcel with "Cassandra" written on in big block letters, and inside would be a chocolate, or a doll, or a book. His final present was a pink plastic microphone, and I would walk around the house singing or pretending to be on TV. It was the best present I had ever been given.

My parents did not ask about the gifts. I did not wonder who was actually sending them. They came with Mr. Postie, who drove his little van down the hall and up to my bedroom door, and who always knocked three times. I was a demonstrative girl, and the next time I saw him, after the plastic microphone, I ran to him and threw my arms around his legs.

It's hard to describe what happened then. He fell like snow, or like ash. For a moment I had been holding someone, then there was just powdery white stuff, and nothing.

I used to wish that Mr. Postie would come back after that, but he never did. He was over. After a while, he became embarrassing to remember: I had fallen for *that*.

So strange, this room.

I wonder why I could ever have thought that somebody who made me happy when I was fifteen would make me happy now. But Stuart was perfect: the riding stables (with ponies), and the painting (which showed me he was sensitive), and the inexperience with girls (so I could be his first) and how very, very tall, dark, and handsome he would be. I liked the name, too: it was vaguely Scottish and (to my mind) like the hero of a novel.

I wrote Stuart's name on my exercise books.

I did not tell my friends the most important thing about Stuart: that I had made him up.

And now I'm getting up off the bed and looking down at the outline of a man, a silhouette in flour or ash or dust on the black satin bedspread, and I am getting into my clothes.

The photographs on the wall are fading too. I didn't expect that. I wonder what will be left of his world in a few hours, wonder if I should have left well enough alone, a masturbatory fantasy, something reassuring and comforting. He would have gone through his life without ever really touching anyone, just a picture and a painting and a half memory for a handful of people who barely ever thought of him anymore.

I leave the flat. There are still people at the wine bar downstairs. They are sitting at the table, in the corner, where Stuart and I had been sitting. The candle has burned way down, but I imagine that it could almost be us. A man and a woman, in conversation. And soon enough, they will get up from their table and walk away, and the candle will be snuffed and the lights turned off, and that will be that for another night.

I hail a taxi. Climb in. For a moment—for, I hope, the last time—I find myself missing Stuart Innes.

Then I sit back in the seat of the taxi, and I let him go. I hope I can afford the taxi fare, and find myself wondering whether there will be a cheque in my bag in the morning, or just another blank sheet of paper. Then, more satisfied than not, I close my eyes, and I wait to be home.

THE INTERIOR OF MISTER BUMBLETHORN'S COAT

WILLOW FAGAN

Mister Bumblethorn slept through the morning, as he usually did, rising from his dry-as-dust bathtub just after noon. He stood in the weak light of the shaded window, his massive blue coat rumpled but still imposing. He did not even remember getting into the bathtub the night before, much less falling asleep in it. He yawned and shook out his arms. An antelope or a gazelle, tiny as a beetle, tumbled out of his coat sleeve and splatted on the floor below. Mister Bumblethorn studiously ignored this.

Bleary-eyed, he walked across his tiny apartment to rummage through the cupboards, finding no food except some stale crackers. Worse, his water flask was empty as a thimble; he held the thing upside down for a full minute and not a drop appeared, not a whiff of moisture.

Mister Bumblethorn sighed heavily. Into the blank space of his empty stomach, memories began to flow like saliva. *Once, adoring folk had thrust gifts of cheese and honeycakes at him wherever he walked: through the streets of grand Abadore, through the humble thoroughfares of nameless hamlets.* Fingers shaking, Mister Bumblethorn rolled himself a fat spliff of redleaf. *No matter how little the peasants had, they shared their suppers with him and refused any offer of payment.* Damn it, light already. *After all, he was*—Ah, there it was, that sweet smoke filling his mouth, translating the stream of memories into a language as meaningless to him as the clicking prayers of the insectile priests in their hive temple on Wingcleft Avenue, his old life grown as insubstantial as their flowery incense, drifting away in the wind.

Pleasantly hazy, in search of a more expansive view, Mister Bumblethorn pulled down on the windowshade, a membrane as thin as his own eyelid. At his touch, the shade twitched—and Mister Bumblethorn's skin answered with its own shudders at the unpleasant reminder that the building he lived in was alive. Was tower-kren. The windowshade crept up and disappeared into its pouch above and Mister Bumblethorn confronted the naked window—was it an eye? Was it looking back at him? Mister Bumblethorn looked away, held his breath, tried to determine once more if the walls were breathing, were expanding and contracting rhythmically, ever so slightly. This was a game he never won, even when he was sober.

The light coming through the window was blueish, and Mister Bumblethorn felt as if he were underwater, as if any moment a fish might swim by, as if he could feel the currents tugging at his long coat, tugging so insistently that he felt dizzy and unsteady on his feet (No, Mister Bumblethorn, you are simply a little too high), so unsteady that he grabbed the window frame to hold himself in place. He raised his head in surrender and gazed out the window at the reality of the city he lived in.

Fleet City. Even near noon, the sky was lit up hardly at all, as if the pale blue sun were pouring light and light and light into a vessel so vast that there was no hope of ever filling it. Tower-kren rose up into the desolate bowl of the sky, tower-kren after tower-kren, clustered near his own building and standing far away, at the edges of Fleet City, and filling up the middle distance as well. The tower-kren shone red and scarlet, somehow snatching up enough of the meager light that they gleamed bright, their scales glittering like the segmented metal armor of—no, Mister Bumblethorn would not think of that. He looked down, to the streetworm far below, flat and black with the little yellow ridges running along its spine, blurring, from this distance, into a single line. Up and down the streetworm, the motor-kren clattered and the lamp-kren glowed and the many varied denizens of Fleet City walked or glided or skittered or swam-through-the-air.

So many strange creatures lived in this city with him. Mister Bumblethorn did not even know which were native and which were emigres like himself. He knew as little about Fleet City as possible; it was like a living book of symbols written in a language of flesh and movement, a language he could not read. The meaninglessness was a comfort to him.

Eventually, the haze receded enough that Mister Bumblethorn became aware of the hunger gnawing at his stomach, the thirst scrabbling at the back of his throat like clawed feet. He would have to go out.

He picked up his key, which was large and knobby and white. He took one last hit from his spliff, for courage. He brushed off imaginary lint from his long, dark coat.

The keyhole was dark and warm, like a deep mouth. Mister Bumblethorn rooted the key around in it, eyes carefully averted. The walls of the keyhole responded to the touch of the key, shuddering and grasping until the whole door vibrated and let out a soft, whistling sigh and swung open. The space where the door met the wall, exposed now, was red and wet. Mister Bumblethorn stepped through quickly. The door closed with a squishing sound.

Mister Bumblethorn held the key out from himself carefully, away from his coat. Something dripped from the tip.

Down on the streetworm, the air smelled of sulfur and citrus, cedar and unnamed spices. A fine spray of pink sand blew into his face. Someone called out, "Maps! Hot off the presses! Fresh maps of the latest migration!" But Mister Bumblethorn had no money: no goldbloom tea or even water. He had his blood, but the mapseller would not take that. He would have to find a florist. He scanned the moving crowd for familiar shapes. There was the two headed horse man in his fancy clothes, checking some kind of spherical instrument on a chain without pausing in his long strides. There were three of the blobby orange things with wings like rusty yellow knives, hovering above a cart selling fruit. Mister Bumblethorn looked away; something about the shape of the flying things brought bubbles of nausea to his stomach. On the other side of the streetworm, near the dark entryway of another tower-kren, which hung open like a giant's gullet, strolled an orange-skinned woman. She must have been obscenely wealthy, for she wore a dress made of enchanted water. As she walked, the water fountained and swirled in intricate patterns over her sunset skin. Behind her trailed three tame ghosts on tethers, bobbing up and down in the wind like balloons. The ghosts were dolled up, with ribbons in their cloudy hair and rouge on their flimsy cheeks but Mister Bumblethorn knew that if some destitute (such as himself) so much as tried to squeeze a droplet of water from the fountaining dress, the ghosts would be on him like wild dogs.

Distracted, Mister Bumblethorn bumped into a stopped motor-kren. A tiny furred creature with huge eyes, standing atop the motor-kren's smooth red shell, scolded Mister Bumblethorn with a series of clipped chirps, making an incomprehensible sign with its delicate, naked fingers. Mister Bumblethorn shook his head and backed away. He had seen such creatures before, riding on other motor-kren, but he refused to consider what this might mean or imply. In the noise and blur of the streetworm, the jostling, ever-moving, alien crowd, Mister Bumblethorn's high had faded to a dull headache, a slight membrane between his skin and his thoughts. Slight but enough, with the chaos of the street itself. He had learned, in his time in Fleet City, that the one thing the city could be relied on to provide was an endless stream of distractions, of bewildering sensations.

By the time Mister Bumblethorn found a florist, his throat ached with thirst, his feet throbbed with each step and he was worryingly sober. He looked at the florist's shop and it was disconcertingly familiar, a place he was returning to, a place he remembered. Or, at least, a place indistinguishable, to his eyes, from the other florist shops. There was the pavilion carved from the rocky, jeweled shell of a slumbering mound-turtle, holding a wealth of flowers of all colors and shapes and sizes which were framed by four pillars of red stone and wrapped around, on three sides, by heavy curtains rich with pattern and gloss. As Mister Bumblethorn walked up the ramshackle stone staircase beside the mound-turtle, the florist craned its long neck to peer at him.

The florist had a white head like a bird's, with a prehensile beak. Its long neck ended in a nest of feathers, mottled grey and black and white. These feathers sat on broad, furry shoulders, on a body like a sasquatch's. The florist had two legs, thick as tree trunks and no other visible limbs. In the center of its furry chest there was a broad, black opening like a mouth without any teeth. Protruding from this maw were six wings, plastered flat against the chest like the petals of pinwheel, alternating between white and black.

The florist clicked and squeaked at Mister Bumblethorn. It did not recognize him.

"I'm sorry, I do not speak that language," he said.

At the sound of his voice, a cluster of dark red roses turned towards him. Mister Bumblethorn started at the sight of eyes in the center of the crimson layers of petals.

The florist tried again, this time in a voice like mournful singing arising from beneath water.

Mister Bumblethorn shook his head.

"Good day," the florist said. "Tell me why you have sought me out, and we shall see if I can meet your desires."

"I need to make an exchange. Blood for water."

"Such a commonplace request," the florist tutted. "Are you certain you have no more extravagant dreams? A mottled spywing, perhaps, to trace the steps of your unmet love through these shifting streets? A heartsblack bulb to hold your grief and nightmares till Fleet City reaches—"

"Please," Mister Bumblethorn said, clenching his teeth. "I have no money and I am very thirsty."

"He who drinks his wealth in haste will thirst in leisure."

Mister Bumblethorn hated this platitude, but he did not want to risk offending the florist. As far as he understood the arcane laws of Fleet City, only florists were allowed to exchange blood for water. Water. The shape the word made in his mouth, in his throat, was a paroxysm of longing. He held out his arm and pulled up the sleeve of his great blue coat. "Just take it," he said.

"First, your name," the florist said.

Mister Bumblethorn stated his name.

The florist clucked and slid its head inside of the hole in its chest. The six wings fluttered gently, as if half-heartedly trying to escape. After a moment, the florist's head re-emerged. "Our guild records indicate that you have already exchanged your blood for water twice this month. I will not take more blood from you so soon. I can't have your death on my beak. I couldn't afford the care and feeding of your ghost."

Mister Bumblethorn felt as if he might faint. His tongue was like paper in his mouth. "Could you, possibly, lend or give me water? I need—"

"Have you not heard the words of the Wandering Sage? 'To give charity is to toss poison into the mouths of children.' But I am a reasonable birdbeast. Surely you must have something else to sell?"

Reluctantly, Mister Bumblethorn opened his coat.

There was a world inside.

The interior of Mister Bumblethorn's coat teemed with life and movement, as if it were an intricately detailed model of a continent, brought to life and hung suspended and sideways, its own gravity still somehow intact: the rivers meandered or rushed, according to their temperament, through the miniature landscape, specks of birds flew vertically from tree to tree or wheeled above the mountain peaks, smoke drifted horizontally from pencil small chimneys on cabins and manors, people as tiny as toys worked the fields and walked the streets of towns and cities, oblivious to their strange circumstances.

On the edges of this landscape were great black maggots chewing away at trees and valleys and towns, slowly consuming the very fabric of the world. Two or three of them had grown so bloated they could no longer move; shadowy threads of webbing encased these blobs, indicating an unimaginable chrysalis might be underway. Seeing these maggots, Mister Bumblethorn could not help but remember their name: the Shadowscraw. And with this single incursion, the dam burst and out swept a flood of memories—

—*rancid licorice scent of the Shadowscraw's gummy, purple black blood—*

—*eyes open, nothing but darkness, head throbbing where the dragonewt's tail had struck—*

—*rubbery shudders of monstrous flesh wrenching his sword back and forth—*

—*the Blessed Sword, aglow, white light piercing the blacks of his eyes—*

—*his mother's tears, "Goodbye!"—*

—*the salt of the merman's kiss—*

Eventually, narrative emerged. He had been a hero. His name had been Lavender. Lavender the Swift and Sure. He had rescued a prominent mayor's dimwitted daughter from a dragonewt, and had been summoned to Queens Hall and feted as a hero. The Snow Regent Herself had whispered thanks and praise into his ear. The next day, while he slept late, still pleasantly drunk in his slumber, word had come: the son of a governor of some farflung province had been killed by one of the Shadowscraw's fearful servants. That night, the Queen's Council had unveiled a convenient prophecy which declared Lavender chosen defender of the realm and rightful bearer of the Blessed Sword, a relic which had been gathering dust in a crypt for nearly four hundred years. Armed with this fearsome weapon, he had outwitted and killed hundreds upon hundreds of the minions of the Shadowscraw. He had proven victorious, at least through the first leg of his quest; he made his way to the cavern at the heart of the world, where the voice of the light which surrounded him there had said,

"Now that you have beheld the Crown of Awe, the world is yours to command. You can kill one of the Gods in this cavern and take their place for your own. Or you can don the Armor of the Sun and claim the chance to finally purge the world of the Shadowscraw's deadly infection. Know this: if you do not so, the Shadowscraw will eat away at the world until only a rind remains. But if you fight them, only your deathblood will cleanse all their blight from this world."

Lavender stood, filthy and exhausted, the swells of light nearly overpowering his ability to think, to receive and form words. Nonetheless, the last words echoed in his mind. *This world.* "This world?" he said. "There are others?"

"Oh, yes. Many worlds, like drops of drew caught in a spider's web, like bubbles in a glass of brew wine, like links of silver in a long necklace."

"If this world is mine to command, can I order it to leave me alone? Can I escape to another?" Motes of color, like tiny crystalline fish, rushed and twinkled through the light, echoed by rippling tinkles, like the ringing of a bell shattered across time. Was the Crown of Awe laughing?

"You are thoughtful for a warrior, Lavender Swift and Sure. You can indeed journey to another world. But you can never leave this one behind; it is bound to you, and you to it, by birth and prophecy and blood."

Blood. He was so tired of blood, of killing, of the weight and heft of the Blessed Sword in his right hand, of the terrible burden of so many hopes invested in him, in the strength of his arms, the endurance of his heart, the swiftness and surety of his killing blows. The worst had been the little girl, her eyes blackened from the kiss of the Shadowscraw. If he did not kill her, she would screech with her tumor-tongue and call down the gnats on her town, dooming half of it to death or worse. There was no choice. But when he sliced through her tiny frame, something died or broke in him too. And the faces of her parents, afterward—he could never scrub his memory clean of them, no matter how hard he tried.

"I do not want to fight anymore," he said. "I want to go away, go somewhere else where no one will expect me to be a hero." A killer.

"Very well," the light replied, and flashed white before ebbing away. When Lavender's eyes cleared, he found that he was no longer in the cavern at the heart of the world, but in the grassy field just outside the vast honeycomb of tunnels. He stood under the night sky and laughed. "I'm free!"

And then the stars spoke to him, in the voice of the Crown of Awe, "Perhaps. But though you can leave—" with each word, a star winked out of existence "—this world must shrink to accompany you." And then all the stars streaked down and disappeared, and then the sky itself began to shrink and fall, sweeping up mountains and islands and rivers in its night blue folds, shrinking and falling, gathering and concealing all the history of the world, all the times and travels of Lavender the Swift and Sure, the memories curling up into the places of their occurrence like roots retreating, the places themselves shrinking, the whole world falling, wrapped around by sky, until it hung from his shoulders as a long, dark, heavy coat.

He stood in the streetworms of a strange new place, a city full of shining reptilian towers. Before him, amid the clatter of the varied crowd, perched a bird with a single eye and a long lizard's tail.

"Excuse me," he said to the bird. "I seem to have forgotten my name. Well, everything. Would you be so kind as to tell me who I am?"

"Bumblethorn," the bird squawked. "Bumble-thorn!" In a flurry of green and blue feathers, the bird took off.

Mister Bumblethorn took his first tentative steps in Fleet City.

Mister Bumblethorn could hardly stand to have the florist see the interior of his coat. His clothes, revealed to daylight for the first time in years, were a ragged leather breastplate and coarse wool leggings.

He looked up at the florist, at its strange, blue, bird eyes, which gave away nothing. "Please!" Mister Bumblethorn cried. "Just take something. Take this forest!" Mister Bumblethorn gestured towards the interior of his coat without looking at it. "Take these hills!" He swallowed, and his throat was so dry it felt as if one side of it was scraping against the other, rough and caved in. "Take a whole city! I don't care, just take something and give me some blasted water."

The florist cocked its head this way and that, and rippled the edges of its stationary wings. "But Mister Bumblethorn, it looks as if you already have some water." The florist pointed with its beak, at the rivers running through the world inside Mister Bumblethorn's coat.

Mister Bumblethorn felt dizzy and faint. A sudden fear stabbed through him, like a fuzzy knife. What if he collapsed, here, in front of the inscrutable florist?

"Here," the florist said, passing him a tall cup.

Mister Bumblethorn closed his eyes and moved the cup towards the river. As his hand neared the surface of his coat, it began to tingle and felt heavier and heavier. As if the weight of an entire world were pulling down on it. As if he were falling through the sky, plummeting downwards. Vertigo spiraled behind his eyes. Then, the lips of the cup touched the rushing water of the river and his fingers slid through the wetness, and he pulled up. His arm swung back fast, propelled by momentum, and he opened his eyes with a jolt.

The shimmering scales of the tower-kren were like slippery rainbows to his eyes, which would not stop sliding down the living buildings, along the yellow lines of the streetworms, back up another tower-kren, jumping from taloned tip to taloned tip and down again. Mister Bumblethorn tore his gaze away. The still pool of water in his cup was calm, a respite. It was easy to ignore the few flecks of fish swimming through the precious liquid, it was a relief. He tipped back the cup, careful even in his state of extremity to limit his intake of water. He poured the rest into his waterpurse.

When he had finished he closed his coat with a shudder, then buttoned each button. "Are you sure," he said, not looking at the florist, "that there's nothing in my coat that you want to buy?"

"I deal exclusively in liquids and flowers," the florist said.

Mister Bumblethorn wanted to shout out, "Take it! Take the whole damn thing from me! For free," but he did not.

Now that he had water in his purse, merchants flocked to him, as if they could smell it. He needed to find some redleaf, and fast. His hands shook like branches in a furious storm, and the only safe path through his thoughts was like a sliver of a ledge around the bottomless pit which had been revealed when he opened his coat. He would not trip, would not tumble, would not allow his eyes to wander from the security of this inner wall. He recited recipes and relived the experiences of his favorite Fleet City foods—the tender, subdued sweetness of solemncakes, which only ghosts could properly make; the heady, thick brew offered for free by the insectile priests of Wingcleft Avenue; the simple savory stuffed birds sold by the catkin.

Ah, here was someone selling redleaf joints—a creature with its face on top of its head and long green tentacles dangling from the edges of its scalp like willow branches, animate and ending in tiny hands.

After he inhaled the earthy red smoke, breathing it in like the scent of a lover he had not seen in far too long, he imagined himself floating above that bottomless pit, serene. He floated through the streetworms and, despite the jostling crowds, the many-shaped appendages and bodies which brushed against him, nothing could touch him. Nothing could reach him, in his mind. The rich scents and sounds and images of the city flowed over him like water, slippery and clean. Until one caught—a green-skinned, horned being stabbing a creature of its same kind, either with a sword or a sharp metallic arm. The second being writhed in apparent pleasure as bright yellow liquid oozed from the newly opened hole in its flesh, its movement growing increasingly frenzied as the first being bent down to lick up the goo with a tongue convoluted as a flower. Seeing this, Mister Bumblethorn could not help but think of the times when he himself had stabbed his sword into the flesh of misshapen beasts and, with this thought, he plunged downwards into the abyss, like a balloon sucked in by a tornado—

—*the blood of the Lice Queen pumping out of her torn open leg, her lips still smiling obscenely, the crown of white symbiotes on her otherwise bald head dancing like drunken, dying children—*

—*the girl, oh god the girl, how she squeaked when he sliced through her, how her chest slid from off her torso—*

—*scrambling, scrambling to get away, someplace safe, anywhere—torso— safe torso—*

—*the arms of Leonine the Archer wrapped tight around him, the scent of cinnamon and sweat, the soft touch of his long golden hair a blessed relief, like a curtain—*

—*the veiled faces of the Palimpcine as they chanted and scrubbed the tiles that were all that remained of their temple, as if it mattered now to restore the cleanliness of white stones, to wash away the muck—*

—*blood, always blood—*

—*blood circling down the drain in the bathtub, in the ivory bathtub of the Lord of Abadore, his first true cleanse after months and months of fighting, so that the color of his own skin came as a surprise to him, a revelation—*

"Bumblethorn. Bumble-thorn!" He had not seen the bird since his first day in Fleet City. He did not know, now, if the bird was speaking to him or if "Bumblethorn" were simply its call. Before he could struggle through his dizziness to ask, another voice spoke to him.

"Bald monkey,
brown skin,
desires to trade
seven drops
for sweet
sweet roast rhomba?"

The speaker peered at him with a chimpanzee's face over a wispy body of smoke and leaves, the suggestion of a robe.

"Y-yes," Mister Bumblethorn sputtered. "I do desire to trade."

The roast rhomba filled his mouth with its sinewy texture and taste of smoke and pears, rooting him to the present, the pleasant pressure of food passing down his throat. He walked as he ate, buying more food each time he ran out so that he made his way back to his apartment on a wave of chewing and swallowing.

Mister Bumblethorn could not sleep that night. No matter how much redleaf he smoked, when he lay down and closed his eyes, the shapes of his past, of the world before, bobbed up and threatened to play out their scenes, which were old and new at once but most of all *threatening*. He tossed and he turned, imagining that he could feel the mountains and towers and trees poking into his back, the gruesome popping of peasants and lords crushed beneath him, chickens and donkeys and dragonewts, and, worst of all, the gnawing of the Shadowscraw on the bare skin of his wrists. Mister Bumblethorn shuddered and opened his eyes. He could not bear the interior of his own mind. He got up out of bed, shook his beetle-lamp awake, and set about finding a distraction. He had only one book to his name, a curious story told in pictures and words, the pages divided into boxes. In the story, there was a man with a mask and antlers who kept dying and rising again, whose flesh, if consumed, could cure almost any illness, who could use mirrors as gateways between worlds. This man was being pursued by a cabal of mechanical creations who threw razor-edged gears and who could combine and reconfigure their forms, trading body parts like articles of clothing. They chased him across worlds many and strange, despite the masked man's continued pleas to simply be left alone. Finally, the masked man found his way to the great clock which stood at the center of all worlds like the hub of a wheel, and confronted the creator of his mechanical foes. The man or god was so old that his beard flowed throughout the clock, catching in the gears, causing time itself to glitch and stutter like a nervous child, and so lonely that he cried and cried at the sight of the masked man. The masked man gently trimmed the old man's beard and watered the old man's many houseplants, and they sat and drank tea together. In gratitude, the old man dismantled his mechanical creations and the masked man was finally allowed to die in peace.

Mister Bumblethorn read the book three times in a row and was halfway through his fourth read when the periwinkle light of dawn fell on the pages. He looked up. Normally, he slept through the mornings. He did not want to watch Fleet City's migration but he stood up, as if hypnotized, and walked to the window. The room lurched to one side and Mister Bumblethorn had to grab hold of the windowframe to keep his balance. The shade flew open, an alarmed eye. Mister Bumblethorn looked out.

All across the skyline, tower-kren were rocking back and forth, uprooting themselves from the dirt, exposing boney appendages curved like fangs or claws. Soon, Mister Bumblethorn knew, the tower-kren would race across the land like obscenely tall crabs, leaving behind a pink, blowing desert and running towards places as yet unspoiled, towards the silhouette of a forest and the hint of a river that Mister Bumblethorn could just make out at the horizon. Soon, but not yet. The lamp-kren too were pulling themselves out of the pink sand, scuttling towards the waiting motor-kren and fitting their sockets together smoothly. A few inhabitants not safely holed up in their rooms within the tower-kren raced to get home in time. The mound-turtles yawned and stretched their jeweled legs and began to trudge forward. Finally, the streetworms puffed up and pulled away, rolling and squiggling across the suddenly naked sand like great black caterpillars. It was then that Mister Bumblethorn realized how much the streetworms resembled the Shadowscraw, those malignant maggots—no, he would not go back there. He scrunched his eyes closed. He curled up in his bathtub, his coat wrapped around him like blanket. He felt like a parasite: tiny, trapped within a great lumbering beast that moved with terrifying speed and carried him along. He may have chosen to come here, to Fleet City, but now that he was here, the City itself would choose where he went, and when, and how fast they would go.

THE THINGS

PETER WATTS

—❦—

I am being Blair. I escape out the back as the world comes in through the front.

I am being Copper. I am rising from the dead.

I am being Childs. I am guarding the main entrance.

The names don't matter. They are placeholders, nothing more; all biomass is interchangeable. What matters is that these are all that is left of me. The world has burned everything else.

I see myself through the window, loping through the storm, wearing Blair. MacReady has told me to burn Blair if he comes back alone, but MacReady still thinks I am one of him. I am not: I am being Blair, and I am at the door. I am being Childs, and I let myself in. I take brief communion, tendrils writhing forth from my faces, intertwining: I am BlairChilds, exchanging news of the world.

The world has found me out. It has discovered my burrow beneath the tool shed, the half-finished lifeboat cannibalized from the viscera of dead helicopters. The world is busy destroying my means of escape. Then it will come back for me.

There is only one option left. I disintegrate. Being Blair, I go to share the plan with Copper and to feed on the rotting biomass once called Clarke; so many changes in so short a time have dangerously depleted my reserves. Being Childs, I have already consumed what was left of Fuchs and am replenished for the next phase. I sling the flamethrower onto my back and head outside, into the long Antarctic night.

I will go into the storm, and never come back.

I was so much more, before the crash. I was an explorer, an ambassador, a missionary. I spread across the cosmos, met countless worlds, took communion: the fit reshaped the unfit and the whole universe bootstrapped upwards in joyful, infinitesimal increments. I was a soldier, at war with entropy itself. I was the very hand by which Creation perfects itself.

So much wisdom I had. So much experience. Now I cannot remember all the things I knew. I can only remember that I once knew them.

I remember the crash, though. It killed most of this offshoot outright, but a little crawled from the wreckage: a few trillion cells, a soul too weak to keep them in check. Mutinous biomass sloughed off despite my most desperate attempts to hold myself together: panic-stricken little clots of meat, instinctively growing whatever limbs they could remember and fleeing across the burning ice. By the time I'd regained control of what was left the fires had died and the cold was closing back in. I barely managed to grow enough antifreeze to keep my cells from bursting before the ice took me.

I remember my reawakening, too: dull stirrings of sensation in real time, the first embers of cognition, the slow blooming warmth of awareness as body and soul embraced after their long sleep. I remember the biped offshoots surrounding me, the strange chittering sounds they made, the odd uniformity of their body plans. How ill-adapted they looked! How inefficient their morphology! Even disabled, I could see so many things to fix. So I reached out. I took communion. I tasted the flesh of the world—

—and the world attacked me. It attacked me.

I left that place in ruins. It was on the other side of the mountains—the Norwegian camp, it is called here—and I could never have crossed that distance in a biped skin. Fortunately there was another shape to choose from, smaller than the biped but better adapted to the local climate. I hid within it while the rest of me fought off the attack. I fled into the night on four legs, and let the rising flames cover my escape.

I did not stop running until I arrived here. I walked among these new offshoots wearing the skin of a quadruped; and because they had not seen me take any other shape, they did not attack.

And when I assimilated them in turn—when my biomass changed and flowed into shapes unfamiliar to local eyes—I took that communion in solitude, having learned that the world does not like what it doesn't know.

I am alone in the storm. I am a bottom-dweller on the floor of some murky alien sea. The snow blows past in horizontal streaks; caught against gullies or outcroppings, it spins into blinding little whirlwinds. But I am not nearly far enough, not yet. Looking back I still see the camp crouched brightly in the gloom, a squat angular jumble of light and shadow, a bubble of warmth in the howling abyss.

It plunges into darkness as I watch. I've blown the generator. Now there's no light but for the beacons along the guide ropes: strings of dim blue stars whipping back and forth in the wind, emergency constellations to guide lost biomass back home.

I am not going home. I am not lost enough. I forge on into darkness until even the stars disappear. The faint shouts of angry frightened men carry behind me on the wind.

Somewhere behind me my disconnected biomass regroups into vaster, more powerful shapes for the final confrontation. I could have joined myself, all in one: chosen unity over fragmentation, resorbed and taken comfort in the greater whole. I could have added my strength to the coming battle. But I have chosen a different path. I am saving Child's reserves for the future. The present holds nothing but annihilation.

Best not to think on the past.

I've spent so very long in the ice already. I didn't know how long until the world put the clues together, deciphered the notes and the tapes from the Norwegian camp, pinpointed the crash site. I was being Palmer, then; unsuspected, I went along for the ride.

I even allowed myself the smallest ration of hope.

But it wasn't a ship any more. It wasn't even a derelict. It was a fossil, embedded in the floor of a great pit blown from the glacier. Twenty of these skins could have stood one atop another, and barely reached the lip of that crater. The timescale settled down on me like the weight of a world: how long for all that ice to accumulate? How many eons had the universe iterated on without me?

And in all that time, a million years perhaps, there'd been no rescue. I never found myself. I wonder what that means. I wonder if I even exist any more, anywhere but here.

Back at camp I will erase the trail. I will give them their final battle, their monster to vanquish. Let them win. Let them stop looking.

Here in the storm, I will return to the ice. I've barely even been away, after all; alive for only a few days out of all these endless ages. But I've learned enough in that time. I learned from the wreck that there will be no repairs. I learned from the ice that there will be no rescue. And I learned from the world that there will be no reconciliation. The only hope of escape, now, is into the future; to outlast all this hostile, twisted biomass, to let time and the cosmos change the rules. Perhaps the next time I awaken, this will be a different world.

It will be aeons before I see another sunrise.

This is what the world taught me: that adaptation is provocation. Adaptation is incitement to violence.

It feels almost obscene—an offense against Creation itself—to stay stuck in this skin. It's so ill-suited to its environment that it needs to be wrapped in multiple layers of fabric just to stay warm. There are a myriad ways I could optimize it: shorter limbs, better insulation, a lower surface:volume ratio. All these shapes I still have within me, and I dare not use any of them even to keep out the cold. I dare not adapt; in this place, I can only hide.

What kind of a world rejects communion?

It's the simplest, most irreducible insight that biomass can have. The more you can change, the more you can adapt. Adaptation is fitness, adaptation is survival. It's deeper than intelligence, deeper than tissue; it is cellular, it is axiomatic. And more, it is pleasurable. To take communion is to experience the sheer sensual delight of bettering the cosmos.

And yet, even trapped in these maladapted skins, this world doesn't want to change.

At first I thought it might simply be starving, that these icy wastes didn't provide enough energy for routine shapeshifting. Or perhaps this was some kind of laboratory: an anomalous corner of the world, pinched off and frozen into these freakish shapes as part of some arcane experiment on monomorphism in extreme environments. After the autopsy I wondered if the world had simply forgotten how to change: unable to touch the tissues the soul could not sculpt them, and time and stress and sheer chronic starvation had erased the memory that it ever could.

But there were too many mysteries, too many contradictions. Why these particular shapes, so badly suited to their environment? If the soul was cut off from the flesh, what held the flesh together?

And how could these skins be so empty when I moved in?

I'm used to finding intelligence everywhere, winding through every part of every offshoot. But there was nothing to grab onto in the mindless biomass of this world: just conduits, carrying orders and input. I took communion, when it wasn't offered; the skins I chose struggled and succumbed; my fibrils infiltrated the wet electricity of organic systems everywhere. I saw through eyes that weren't yet quite mine, commandeered motor nerves to move limbs still built of alien protein. I wore these skins as I've worn countless others, took the controls and left the assimilation of individual cells to follow at its own pace.

But I could only wear the body. I could find no memories to absorb, no experiences, no comprehension. Survival depended on blending in, and it was not enough to merely look like this world. I had to act like it—and for the first time in living memory I did not know how.

Even more frighteningly, I didn't have to. The skins I assimilated continued to move, all by themselves. They conversed and went about their appointed rounds. I could not understand it. I threaded further into limbs and viscera with each passing moment, alert for signs of the original owner. I could find no networks but mine.

Of course, it could have been much worse. I could have lost it all, been reduced to a few cells with nothing but instinct and their own plasticity to guide them. I would have grown back eventually—reattained sentience, taken communion and regenerated an intellect vast as a world—but I would have been an orphan, amnesiac, with no sense of who I was. At least I've been spared that: I emerged from the crash with my identity intact, the templates of a thousand worlds still resonant in my flesh. I've retained not just the brute desire to survive, but the conviction that survival is meaningful. I can still feel joy, should there be sufficient cause.

And yet, how much more there used to be.

The wisdom of so many other worlds, lost. All that remains are fuzzy abstracts, half-memories of theorems and philosophies far too vast to fit into such an impoverished network. I could assimilate all the biomass of this place, rebuild body and soul to a million times the capacity of what crashed here—but as long as I am trapped at the bottom of this well, denied communion with my greater self, I will never recover that knowledge.

I'm such a pitiful fragment of what I was. Each lost cell takes a little of my intellect with it, and I have grown so very small. Where once I thought, now I merely react. How much of this could have been avoided, if I had only salvaged a little more biomass from the wreckage? How many options am I not seeing because my soul simply isn't big enough to contain them?

The world spoke to itself, in the same way I do when my communications are simple enough to convey without somatic fusion. Even as dog I could pick up the basic signature morphemes—this offshoot was Windows, that one was Bennings, the two who'd left in their flying machine for parts unknown were Copper and MacReady—and I marveled that these bits and pieces stayed isolated one from another, held the same shapes for so long, that the labeling of individual aliquots of biomass actually served a useful purpose.

Later I hid within the bipeds themselves, and whatever else lurked in those haunted skins began to talk to me. It said that bipeds were called guys, or men, or assholes. It said that MacReady was sometimes called Mac. It said that this collection of structures was a camp.

It said that it was afraid, but maybe that was just me.

Empathy's inevitable, of course. One can't mimic the sparks and chemicals that motivate the flesh without also feeling them to some extent. But this was different. These intuitions flickered within me yet somehow hovered beyond reach. My skins wandered the halls and the cryptic symbols on every surface—Laundry Sched, Welcome to the Clubhouse, This Side Up—almost made a kind of sense. That circular artefact hanging on the wall was a clock; it measured the passage of time. The world's eyes flitted here and there, and I skimmed piecemeal nomenclature from its—from his—mind.

But I was only riding a searchlight. I saw what it illuminated but I couldn't point it in any direction of my own choosing. I could eavesdrop, but I could only eavesdrop; never interrogate.

If only one of those searchlights had paused to dwell on its own evolution, on the trajectory that had brought it to this place. How differently things might have ended, had I only known. But instead it rested on a whole new word:

Autopsy.

MacReady and Copper had found part of me at the Norwegian camp: a rearguard offshoot, burned in the wake of my escape. They'd brought it back—charred, twisted, frozen in mid-transformation—and did not seem to know what it was.

I was being Palmer then, and Norris, and dog. I gathered around with the other biomass and watched as Copper cut me open and pulled out my insides. I watched as he dislodged something from behind my eyes: an organ of some kind.

It was malformed and incomplete, but its essentials were clear enough. It looked like a great wrinkled tumor, like cellular competition gone wild—as though the very processes that defined life had somehow turned against it instead. It was obscenely vascularised; it must have consumed oxygen and nutrients far out of proportion to its mass. I could not see how anything like that could even exist, how it could have reached that size without being outcompeted by more efficient morphologies.

Nor could I imagine what it did. But then I began to look with new eyes at these offshoots, these biped shapes my own cells had so scrupulously and unthinkingly copied when they reshaped me for this world. Unused to inventory—why catalog body parts that only turn into other things at the slightest provocation?—I really saw, for the first time, that swollen structure atop each body. So much larger than it should be: a bony hemisphere into which a million ganglionic interfaces could fit with room to spare. Every offshoot had one. Each piece of biomass carried one of these huge twisted clots of tissue.

I realized something else, too: the eyes, the ears of my dead skin had fed into this thing before Copper pulled it free. A massive bundle of fibers ran along the skin's longitudinal axis, right up the middle of the endoskeleton, directly into the dark sticky cavity where the growth had rested. That misshapen structure had been wired into the whole skin, like some kind of somatocognitive interface but vastly more massive. It was almost as if . . .

No.

That was how it worked. That was how these empty skins moved of their own volition, why I'd found no other network to integrate. There it was: not distributed throughout the body but balled up into itself, dark and dense and encysted. I had found the ghost in these machines.

I felt sick.

I shared my flesh with thinking cancer.

Sometimes, even hiding is not enough.

I remember seeing myself splayed across the floor of the kennel, a chimera split along a hundred seams, taking communion with a handful of dogs. Crimson tendrils writhed on the floor. Half-formed iterations sprouted from my flanks, the shapes of dogs and things not seen before on this world, haphazard morphologies half-remembered by parts of a part.

I remember Childs before I was Childs, burning me alive. I remember cowering inside Palmer, terrified that those flames might turn on the rest of me, that this world had somehow learned to shoot on sight.

I remember seeing myself stagger through the snow, raw instinct, wearing Bennings. Gnarled undifferentiated clumps clung to his hands like crude parasites, more outside than in; a few surviving fragments of some previous massacre, crippled, mindless, taking what they could and breaking cover. Men swarmed about him in the night: red flares in hand, blue lights at their backs, their faces bichromatic and beautiful. I remember Bennings, awash in flames, howling like an animal beneath the sky.

I remember Norris, betrayed by his own perfectly-copied, defective heart. Palmer, dying that the rest of me might live. Windows, still human, burned preemptively.

The names don't matter. The biomass does: so much of it, lost. So much new experience, so much fresh wisdom annihilated by this world of thinking tumors.

Why even dig me up? Why carve me from the ice, carry me all that way across the wastes, bring me back to life only to attack me the moment I awoke?

If eradication was the goal, why not just kill me where I lay?

Those encysted souls. Those tumors. Hiding away in their bony caverns, folded in on themselves.

I knew they couldn't hide forever; this monstrous anatomy had only slowed communion, not stopped it. Every moment I grew a little. I could feel myself twining around Palmer's motor wiring, sniffing upstream along a million tiny currents. I could sense my infiltration of that dark thinking mass behind Blair's eyes.

Imagination, of course. It's all reflex that far down, unconscious and immune to micromanagement. And yet, a part of me wanted to stop while there was still time. I'm used to incorporating souls, not rooming with them. This, this compartmentalization was unprecedented. I've assimilated a thousand worlds stronger than this, but never one so strange. What would happen when I met the spark in the tumor? Who would assimilate who?

I was being three men by now. The world was growing wary, but it hadn't noticed yet. Even the tumors in the skins I'd taken didn't know how close I was. For that, I could only be grateful—that Creation has rules, that some things don't change no matter what shape you take. It doesn't matter whether a soul spreads throughout the skin or festers in grotesque isolation; it still runs on electricity. The memories of men still took time to gel, to pass through whatever gatekeepers filtered noise from signal—and a judicious burst of static, however indiscriminate, still cleared those caches before their contents could be stored permanently. Clear enough, at least, to let these tumors simply forget that something else moved their arms and legs on occasion.

At first I only took control when the skins closed their eyes and their search-lights flickered disconcertingly across unreal imagery, patterns that flowed senselessly into one another like hyperactive biomass unable to settle on a single shape. (Dreams, one searchlight told me, and a little later, Nightmares.) During those mysterious periods of dormancy, when the men lay inert and isolated, it was safe to come out.

Soon, though, the dreams dried up. All eyes stayed open all the time, fixed on shadows and each other. Offshoots once dispersed throughout the camp began to draw together, to give up their solitary pursuits in favor of company. At first I thought they might be finding common ground in a common fear. I even hoped that finally, they might shake off their mysterious fossilization and take communion.

But no. They'd just stopped trusting anything they couldn't see.

They were merely turning against each other.

My extremities are beginning to numb; my thoughts slow as the distal reaches of my soul succumb to the chill. The weight of the flamethrower pulls at its harness, forever tugs me just a little off-balance. I have not been Childs for very long; almost half this tissue remains unassimilated. I have an hour, maybe two, before I have to start melting my grave into the ice. By that time I need to have converted enough cells to keep this whole skin from crystallizing. I focus on antifreeze production.

It's almost peaceful out here. There's been so much to take in, so little time to process it. Hiding in these skins takes such concentration, and under all those watchful eyes I was lucky if communion lasted long enough to exchange memories: compounding my soul would have been out of the question. Now, though, there's nothing to do but prepare for oblivion. Nothing to occupy my thoughts but all these lessons left unlearned.

MacReady's blood test, for example. His thing detector, to expose imposters posing as men. It does not work nearly as well as the world thinks; but the fact that it works at all violates the most basic rules of biology. It's the center of the puzzle. It's the answer to all the mysteries. I might have already figured it out if I had been just a little larger. I might already know the world, if the world wasn't trying so hard to kill me.

MacReady's test.

Either it is impossible, or I have been wrong about everything.

They did not change shape. They did not take communion. Their fear and mutual mistrust was growing, but they would not join souls; they would only look for the enemy outside themselves.

So I gave them something to find.

I left false clues in the camp's rudimentary computer: simpleminded icons and animations, misleading numbers and projections seasoned with just enough truth to convince the world of their veracity. It didn't matter that the machine was far too simple to perform such calculations, or that there were no data to base them on anyway; Blair was the only biomass likely to know that, and he was already mine.

I left false leads, destroyed real ones, and then—alibi in place—I released Blair to run amok. I let him steal into the night and smash the vehicles as they slept, tugging ever-so-slightly at his reins to ensure that certain vital components were spared. I set him loose in the radio room, watched through his eyes and others as he rampaged and destroyed. I listened as he ranted about a world in danger, the need for containment, the conviction that most of you don't know what's going on around here—but I damn well know that some of you do . . .

He meant every word. I saw it in his searchlight. The best forgeries are the ones who've forgotten they aren't real.

When the necessary damage was done I let Blair fall to MacReady's counterassault. As Norris I suggested the tool shed as a holding cell. As Palmer I boarded up the windows, helped with the flimsy fortifications expected to keep me contained. I watched while the world locked me away for your own protection, Blair, and left me to my own devices. When no one was looking I would change and slip outside, salvage the parts I needed from all that bruised machinery. I would take them back to my burrow beneath the shed and build my escape piece by piece. I volunteered to feed the prisoner and came to myself when the world wasn't watching, laden with supplies enough to keep me going through all those necessary metamorphoses. I went through a third of the camp's food stores in three days, and—still trapped by my own preconceptions—marveled at the starvation diet that kept these offshoots chained to a single skin.

Another piece of luck: the world was too preoccupied to worry about kitchen inventory.

There is something on the wind, a whisper threading its way above the raging of the storm. I grow my ears, extend cups of near-frozen tissue from the sides of my head, turn like a living antennae in search of the best reception.

There, to my left: the abyss glows a little, silhouettes black swirling snow against a subtle lessening of the darkness. I hear the sounds of carnage. I hear myself. I do not know what shape I have taken, what sort of anatomy might be emitting those sounds. But I've worn enough skins on enough worlds to know pain when I hear it.

The battle is not going well. The battle is going as planned. Now it is time to turn away, to go to sleep. It is time to wait out the ages.

I lean into the wind. I move toward the light.

This is not the plan. But I think I have an answer, now: I think I may have had it even before I sent myself back into exile. It's not an easy thing to admit. Even now I don't fully understand. How long have I been out here, retelling the tale to myself, setting clues in order while my skin dies by low degrees? How long have I been circling this obvious, impossible truth?

I move towards the faint crackling of flames, the dull concussion of exploding ordnance more felt than heard. The void lightens before me: gray segues into yellow, yellow into orange. One diffuse brightness resolves into many: a lone burning wall, miraculously standing. The smoking skeleton of MacReady's shack on the hill. A cracked smoldering hemisphere reflecting pale yellow in the flickering light: Child's searchlight calls it a radio dome.

The whole camp is gone. There's nothing left but flames and rubble.

They can't survive without shelter. Not for long. Not in those skins.

In destroying me, they've destroyed themselves.

Things could have turned out so much differently if I'd never been Norris.

Norris was the weak node: biomass not only ill-adapted but defective, an offshoot with an off switch. The world knew, had known so long it never even thought about it anymore. It wasn't until Norris collapsed that heart condition floated to the surface of Copper's mind where I could see it. It wasn't until Copper was astride Norris's chest, trying to pound him back to life, that I knew how it would end. And by then it was too late; Norris had stopped being Norris. He had even stopped being me.

I had so many roles to play, so little choice in any of them. The part being Copper brought down the paddles on the part that had been Norris, such a faithful Norris, every cell so scrupulously assimilated, every part of that faulty valve reconstructed unto perfection. I hadn't known. How was I to know? These shapes within me, the worlds and morphologies I've assimilated over the aeons—I've only ever used them to adapt before, never to hide. This desperate mimicry was an improvised thing, a last resort in the face of a world that attacked anything unfamiliar. My cells read the signs and my cells conformed, mindless as prions.

So I became Norris, and Norris self-destructed.

I remember losing myself after the crash. I know how it feels to degrade, tissues in revolt, the desperate efforts to reassert control as static from some misfiring organ jams the signal. To be a network seceding from itself, to know that each moment I am less than I was the moment before. To become nothing. To become legion.

Being Copper, I could see it. I still don't know why the world didn't; its parts had long since turned against each other by then, every offshoot suspected every other. Surely they were alert for signs of infection. Surely some of that biomass would have noticed the subtle twitch and ripple of Norris changing below the surface, the last instinctive resort of wild tissues abandoned to their own devices.

But I was the only one who saw. Being Childs, I could only stand and watch. Being Copper, I could only make it worse; if I'd taken direct control, forced that skin to drop the paddles, I would have given myself away. And so I played my parts to the end. I slammed those resurrection paddles down as Norris's chest split open beneath them. I screamed on cue as serrated teeth from a hundred stars away snapped shut. I toppled backwards, arms bitten off above the wrist. Men swarmed, agitation bootstrapping to panic. MacReady aimed his weapon; flames leaped across the enclosure. Meat and machinery screamed in the heat.

Copper's tumor winked out beside me. The world would never have let it live anyway, not after such obvious contamination. I let our skin play dead on the floor while overhead, something that had once been me shattered and writhed and iterated through a myriad random templates, searching desperately for something fireproof.

They have destroyed themselves. They.

Such an insane word to apply to a world.

Something crawls towards me through the wreckage: a jagged oozing jigsaw of blackened meat and shattered, half-resorbed bone. Embers stick to its sides like bright searing eyes; it doesn't have strength enough to scrape them free. It contains barely half the mass of this Childs' skin; much of it, burnt to raw carbon, is already dead.

What's left of Childs, almost asleep, thinks motherfucker, but I am being him now. I can carry that tune myself.

The mass extends a pseudopod to me, a final act of communion. I feel my pain:

I was Blair, I was Copper, I was even a scrap of dog that survived that first fiery massacre and holed up in the walls, with no food and no strength to regenerate. Then I gorged on unassimilated flesh, consumed instead of communed; revived and replenished, I drew together as one.

And yet, not quite. I can barely remember—so much was destroyed, so much memory lost—but I think the networks recovered from my different skins stayed just a little out of synch, even reunited in the same soma. I glimpse a half-corrupted memory of dog erupting from the greater self, ravenous and traumatized and determined to retain its individuality. I remember rage and frustration, that this world had so corrupted me that I could barely fit together again. But it didn't matter. I was more than Blair and Copper and Dog, now. I was a giant with the shapes of worlds to choose from, more than a match for the last lone man who stood against me.

No match, though, for the dynamite in his hand.

Now I'm little more than pain and fear and charred stinking flesh. What sentience I have is awash in confusion. I am stray and disconnected thoughts, doubts and the ghosts of theories. I am realizations, too late in coming and already forgotten.

But I am also Childs, and as the wind eases at last I remember wondering Who assimilates who? The snow tapers off and I remember an impossible test that stripped me naked.

The tumor inside me remembers it, too. I can see it in the last rays of its fading searchlight—and finally, at long last, that beam is pointed inwards.

Pointed at me.

I can barely see what it illuminates: Parasite. Monster. Disease.

Thing.

How little it knows. It knows even less than I do.

I know enough, you motherfucker. You soul-stealing, shit-eating rapist.

I don't know what that means. There is violence in those thoughts, and the forcible penetration of flesh, but underneath it all is something else I can't quite understand. I almost ask—but Childs's searchlight has finally gone out. Now there is nothing in here but me, nothing outside but fire and ice and darkness.

I am being Childs, and the storm is over.

In a world that gave meaningless names to interchangeable bits of biomass, one name truly mattered: MacReady.

MacReady was always the one in charge. The very concept still seems absurd: in charge. How can this world not see the folly of hierarchies? One bullet in a vital spot and the Norwegian dies, forever. One blow to the head and Blair is unconscious. Centralization is vulnerability—and yet the world is not content to build its biomass on such a fragile template, it forces the same model onto its metasystems as well. MacReady talks; the others obey. It is a system with a built-in kill spot.

And yet somehow, MacReady stayed in charge. Even after the world discovered the evidence I'd planted; even after it decided that MacReady was one of those things, locked him out to die in the storm, attacked him with fire and axes when he fought his way back inside. Somehow MacReady always had the gun, always had the flamethrower, always had the dynamite and the willingness to take out the whole damn camp if need be. Clarke was the last to try and stop him; MacReady shot him through the tumor.

Kill spot.

But when Norris split into pieces, each scuttling instinctively for its own life, MacReady was the one to put them back together.

I was so sure of myself when he talked about his test. He tied up all the biomass—tied me up, more times than he knew—and I almost felt a kind of pity as he spoke. He forced Windows to cut us all, to take a little blood from each. He heated the tip of a metal wire until it glowed and he spoke of pieces small enough to give themselves away, pieces that embodied instinct but no intelligence, no self-control. MacReady had watched Norris in dissolution, and he had decided: men's blood would not react to the application of heat. Mine would break ranks when provoked.

Of course he thought that. These offshoots had forgotten that they could change.

I wondered how the world would react when every piece of biomass in the room was revealed as a shapeshifter, when MacReady's small experiment ripped the façade from the greater one and forced these twisted fragments to confront the truth. Would the world awaken from its long amnesia, finally remember that it lived and breathed and changed like everything else? Or was it too far gone—would MacReady simply burn each protesting offshoot in turn as its blood turned traitor?

I couldn't believe it when MacReady plunged the hot wire into Windows' blood and nothing happened. Some kind of trick, I thought. And then MacReady's blood passed the test, and Clarke's.

Copper's didn't. The needle went in and Copper's blood shivered just a little in its dish. I barely saw it myself; the men didn't react at all. If they even noticed, they must have attributed it to the trembling of MacReady's own hand. They thought the test was a crock of shit anyway. Being Childs, I even said as much.

Because it was too astonishing, too terrifying, to admit that it wasn't.

Being Childs, I knew there was hope. Blood is not soul: I may control the motor systems but assimilation takes time. If Copper's blood was raw enough to pass muster than it would be hours before I had anything to fear from this test; I'd been Childs for even less time.

But I was also Palmer, I'd been Palmer for days. Every last cell of that biomass had been assimilated; there was nothing of the original left.

When Palmer's blood screamed and leapt away from MacReady's needle, there was nothing I could do but blend in.

I have been wrong about everything.

Starvation. Experiment. Illness. All my speculation, all the theories I invoked to explain this place—top-down constraint, all of it. Underneath, I always knew the ability to change—to assimilate—had to remain the universal constant. No world evolves if its cells don't evolve; no cell evolves if it can't change. It's the nature of life everywhere.

Everywhere but here.

This world did not forget how to change. It was not manipulated into rejecting change. These were not the stunted offshoots of any greater self, twisted to the needs of some experiment; they were not conserving energy, waiting out some temporary shortage.

This is the option my shriveled soul could not encompass until now: out of all the worlds of my experience, this is the only one whose biomass can't change. It never could.

It's the only way MacReady's test makes any sense.

I say goodbye to Blair, to Copper, to myself. I reset my morphology to its local defaults. I am Childs, come back from the storm to finally make the pieces fit. Something moves up ahead: a dark blot shuffling against the flames, some weary animal looking for a place to bed down. It looks up as I approach.

MacReady.

We eye each other, and keep our distance. Colonies of cells shift uneasily inside me. I can feel my tissues redefining themselves.

"You the only one that made it?"

"Not the only one . . . "

I have the flamethrower. I have the upper hand. MacReady doesn't seem to care.

But he does care. He must. Because here, tissues and organs are not temporary battlefield alliances; they are permanent, predestined. Macrostructures do not emerge when the benefits of cooperation exceed its costs, or dissolve when that balance shifts the other way; here, each cell has but one immutable function. There's no plasticity, no way to adapt; every structure is frozen in place. This is not a single great world, but many small ones. Not parts of a greater thing; these are things. They are plural.

And that means—I think—that they stop. They just, just wear out over time.

"Where were you, Childs?"

I remember words in dead searchlights: "Thought I saw Blair. Went out after him. Got lost in the storm."

I've worn these bodies, felt them from the inside. Copper's sore joints. Blair's curved spine. Norris and his bad heart. They are not built to last. No somatic evolution to shape them, no communion to restore the biomass and stave off entropy. They should not even exist; existing, they should not survive.

They try, though. How they try. Every thing here is walking dead and yet it all fights so hard to keep going just a little longer. Each skin fights as desperately as I might, if one was all I could ever have.

MacReady tries.

"If you're worried about me—" I begin.

MacReady shakes his head, manages a weary smile. "If we've got any surprises for each other, I don't think we're in much shape to do anything about it . . . "

But we are. I am.

A whole planet of worlds, and not one of them—not one—has a soul. They wander through their lives separate and alone, unable even to communicate except through grunts and tokens: as if the essence of a sunset or a supernova could ever be contained in some string of phonemes, a few linear scratches of black on white. They've never known communion, can aspire to nothing but dissolution. The paradox of their biology is astonishing, yes; but the scale of their loneliness, the futility of these lives, overwhelms me.

I was so blind, so quick to blame. But the violence I've suffered at the hands of these things reflects no great evil. They're simply so used to pain, so blinded by disability, that they literally can't conceive of any other existence. When every nerve is whipped raw, you lash out at even the lightest touch.

"What should we do?" I wonder. I cannot escape into the future, not knowing what I know now. How could I leave them like this?

"Why don't we just—wait here awhile," MacReady suggests. "See what happens."

I can do so much more than that.

It won't be easy. They won't understand. Tortured, incomplete, they're not able to understand. Offered the greater whole, they see the loss of the lesser. Offered communion, they see only extinction. I must be careful. I must use this newfound ability to hide. Other things will come here eventually, and it doesn't matter whether they find the living or the dead; what matters is that they find something like themselves, to take back home. So I will keep up appearances. I will work behind the scenes. I will save them from the inside, or their unimaginable loneliness will never end.

These poor savage things will never embrace salvation.

I will have to rape it into them.

STEREOGRAM OF THE GRAY FORT, IN THE DAYS OF HER GLORY

PAUL M. BERGER

Left:

The guide led us over a rise, and there was the ruined fortress, draped across the foothills like a wrecked body on a slab. I saw it first, but of course Jessica saw it better. Her young eyes dwelled on the jagged foundations of every fallen tower, and the gray stone blocks that had lain scattered throughout the centuries since the breaching of the broad walls, and the neglected palaces and armories half-revealed through the gaps. She drank in these details, fitting each to the histories she had heard since she was a child, and I thought again what a gift it was to share her sight.

A period guardhouse had been recreated alongside the path, and the vendor within jumped to his feet as we passed by the doorway. Our old guide made as if to steer me in. "Here you can purchase many fine illustrations of the Gray Fort," he said in his tinny accent, "quite suitable for greetingcardspostcardsbirthdaycardsholidaycards and the like. If you will just step this way—"

"Don't be absurd," I said, and shrugged him off. The tip he could expect from me would feed him for a week, and there was no need to subsidize his cousin as well. Jessica and I kept walking, and he rolled his eyes apologetically to the fellow within before catching up with us.

The path, which had once been a broad road, was pitted with holes. Back in the heyday of the fort, the paving stones had been interspersed with scraps of iron the humans had salvaged from their own defunct machines. It had hurt to march that road—our feet had burned, and my regiment stayed to the verge and fields whenever possible. In the years after the Elven triumph we had sent out details of Men to pick the poison from the earth here and the other places they had defended against us, and throw it into the sea.

Jessica was wearing loose silk for me. A cool breeze came down out of the hills and played the fabric over the smoothness of her shoulders. I delighted in the sensation, and she knew it. I smiled at her, and my beloved hesitantly returned my gaze for a moment. Our pair-bond was still new enough that she found it disorienting at times; looking into each other's eyes could throw her into an infinitely recursive image of ourselves, with a vertigo that twisted both our guts. She would require gentle handling, for a while. It had been so with my first wife as well: an awkward initial adjustment period that settled into centuries of intimacy and trust, ever strengthened by the continual sharing of our five senses. I knew every facet of her life, and I would not have traded a moment of it, even during those last long years of pain when her illness gripped her more closely than I could. When she died I was amazed to find that I had not gone with her, and for decades afterwards I had no use for this drab and colorless world, or even for our own. Although it is not often done, I think it was wise to choose a human for my bride this time; they are frail and short-lived, and I will not be faced with another such lingering illness or the same depth of love.

Even though Jessica could not return my gaze directly, I saw that in this clear light her hazel eyes were as green as new leaves. I watched her slim, unconscious grace and the way the wind pulled at the heavy mass of her dark hair, and thought for the hundredth time that no one could claim she was not as fair as one of our own. Their women don't take to the bond as well as ours do, but I've learned the benefits are well worth the risk. Jessica and I are now perfectly synchronized. Our sensibilities are linked so tightly we can guess each others' thoughts; I know when the food in her mouth suits her palate; and in private moments I am able to give her exactly as much pleasure as she can bear.

The guide directed us towards the crumbling hulk of the fortress, and the uneven track awoke the old war wound in my thigh. If we went slowly I could hide the limp, but Jessica of course would know.

To either side of the path stretched a wild meadow. Once upon a time this land had been fields and pastures cropped short by cows and sheep, but it had since gone untended for generations of men. Overhead, a hawk wheeled sharply, its pinions spread like the fingers of a hand raised in greeting. Somewhere in those bushes below it no doubt, a rabbit was wishing it could re-think its last move. It would be crouched rigid, body juddering with its own heartbeat, waiting for the shadow of the hunter to slide past it. I wondered if it realized it would never be more alive than right now, and if it had some way of treasuring the moment. This was, after all, what it was made for.

Here and there ahead of us we saw a few other clusters of tourists, mainly Folk with their attendants. There were not many now who cared for the early days the way my Jessica did. It was, in fact, the reason we had met—she had heard there was an old hero of the Restoration in her city, and sought me out.

Even her anachronistic name, which stumbled roughly across the tongue, recalled a bygone epoch.

Our guide labored ahead with his own doddering gait. "In the olden days when the fortress still stood," he said, "this road was lined all the way up with manymany redoubts, towerhouses and palisades. An army would cower at the thought of crossing through."

The fierce pride in his voice clung to shreds of his race's former grandeur, just as one would expect from a long-vanquished people. It had indeed been something to see, but when the time came, those defenses had not stopped us from crossing this valley. And the Great Siege that broke this fortress, the final action of our long war to subdue this strange world, had been a straight-forward affair with few surprises.

"And yet in the end, it was you that folded," I said under my breath.

"That's true—in the end," my Jessica murmured back to me. She could have whispered it from the other side of the world, and I would have felt her mouth shape the words. Her eyes rose no higher than my tunic, but she had the arch expression she wore when challenging me to a debate. How I delighted in her fire! "But humanity fought you off for centuries, even before they had the chance to adjust to the changes that the Fair Folk brought our world."

"They weren't meant to *adjust*, my love. They were meant to find their glory. The very chaos was a gift to them, and I am sure the men of that time knew it in their hearts. When we first parted the veil between our worlds and returned to this one, your alien ways had turned you into shades that we could barely see. You know how bad it was—machines too small to see did all the work and all the thinking."

"You can't deny that we were strong in those days," she rejoined.

"Your armies may have been strong, but your warriors were not. Your people had no sense of what it meant to be alive. We stopped those tiny machines, by calling upon the power that slept in the sinews and bones of your own earth, and so gave you the opportunity to live and die by the strength of your own arms once again. And how you fought, even though it was new to you! We were in awe of you right up to the moment of your defeat."

I had never mentioned this to her before. Perhaps it was striding this battlefield for the first time in all those years that brought back the memory. No matter. Now of course, we could not afford awe. They were children who needed our guiding hand lest they lapse back into the same mistakes—as tedious as that responsibility was.

"The Gray Fort is considered the finest example of Resistance-era human architecture," recited our guide as we approached the outer wall. "It was constructed over a period of thirtythree years—thirtythree being, as you know, a particularly auspicious number—using granite quarried from the hills behind it. Far more than a mere military stronghold, this was the home base of the Army of the Northeast, as well as the retinues-retainers-advisors-wives-consorts-and-harems of the warlords who led them, for one hundred eight years. It was the first structure to incorporate certain stoneworking methods for hand-cutting and laying large blocks that had been forgotten for almost a millennium."

"Indeed," I said. "We helped you recover your own lost past."

"Well, sir—" he allowed himself a wry grin that revealed gaps in his teeth "—I'd hardly call it 'helping.'"

He was forgetting his place. "You wouldn't? And how well would you know what transpired in those days?"

"Sir, I have a doctorate in pre-Resistance history from the University of the Northeast Territory."

"Of course you do," I said. A native's degree, from a native's institution. "And how useful have you found that?"

The old fool recognized the gibe and responded with a smile and a bow, then turned back to the path.

"A lesson for you, my love," I subvocalized. "Those days are gone. The history of the years before the Folk came to you is beneficial only as a reminder of mistakes you should never make again. Because of your unique position, one day your people will call upon you to teach them wisdom, and this must ever be at the forefront of your mind."

Jessica nodded sagely. She was remarkably sharp for her race. When we first met, she had hung on every detail I shared with her of the Days of Conflict and the battles I had seen. Her perception and wit spurred me to strengthen my reasoning and know myself better—exactly what I needed now that I was expected to settle into the role of Prefect of such a sorry district. When it dawned on me that I must make her my bride, I rushed to contact her father. He was loath to lose her, and he rejected my financial incentive, despite the crowded hovel and unwholesome slum in which he kept his family. But Jessica and I meant too much to each other, and there was no choice but to apply my influence across his entire community. He acceded at last, and I was as thrilled as a schoolboy.

It is said that when the Queen was brought the news, she considered it idly for a moment, then laughed and blessed our union, and all her dazzling, debonair court laughed along with her.

As we approached the fortress, Jessica's regard returned several times to the wreckage that had once been the great gates. They lay rotting where we had left them in front of the walls, and she lingered on their twisted forms. She must have been wondering what nature of assault we had used to throw them outwards, rather then knock them inwards. In truth, we had taken the stronghold by penetrating the wall at other points; we had only smashed the doors and archway days later, from within, when we ravaged it in our dismay that there was no longer anyone left to oppose us. Her people have not failed to disappoint us since then. For years we have been secretly sending our idle soldiers home in increments. No occupying force is needed here—just the rumor of one is enough to keep these sheep docile.

"Before the gateway," our guide told me quietly, "you will see many vendors waiting for tourists." Indeed, in the flat space before the gaping maw of the arch, a listless pack of hawkers manned tables and booths or sold baubles from sacks slung over their shoulders. "They are a worthless bunch of huckstersconmenpickpocketsandthieves, and you should keep your hand on your wallet and ignore them as we pass through." At last, a point on which I was inclined to credit his opinion. "Afterwards I will take you someplace where the proprietor is trusty and you will surely get what you paid for."

We approached and the hawkers rushed forward and surged about us, thrusting souvenirs in our faces, crying out with rotten breath, and steering us towards their shoddy tables. They vied to shout over each other and swirled between us in dizzying, unwashed confusion that was redoubled with the impressions from my bride. Our dotard of a guide protested ineffectively and impugned the parentage of anyone who came within range. I had been in a melee on this very spot once before, a lifetime ago, as an officer with a tall helm and a long spear. Men had died here, and some good Folk, too. I would have been within my rights to kill one or two this day, and I was not too old to destroy this whole rabble single-handedly. However, I was obliged to keep in mind that I was guardian and teacher to them now. At a loss, I retreated.

While I picked my way past the yelping mob, Jessica barely made headway, and she was obliged to halt before a plank piled high with cheap trinkets. To appease them, she tossed a hag a coin and in exchange took the first thing that caught her eye—a flimsy play dagger with a gaudy hilt and scabbard encrusted in paste gems. When she pushed her way out of the crowd, she pulled the silk shawl from her shoulders and bundled it around the toy as if she was reluctant to touch it. (Oh, to find just one of her people with the will to bear a weapon!) She was shaken by the onslaught, and I took her free hand until she was calm.

The hawkers lost interest as soon as Jessica emerged from their midst, and receded to reveal our guide, who hobbled up the path towards us. He made his apologies to Jessica directly, which was not entirely proper, but could be forgiven under the circumstances.

"But here," he said, "before we enter the fortress itself, is a display created especially for pair-bonded fair lords and ladies such as yourselves."

"A stereogram, no doubt?" I said.

"Indeed, sir."

"What's that?" asked my Jessica.

Before our guide could attempt an explanation, I answered, "A standard tourist gimmick, aimed primarily at newlyweds. They can however, on occasion, be diverting. Show us."

We handed over a few more coins and were ushered into a small building with high windows. The space inside was well-lit this time of day. It held a wide carved stone screen with two small apertures cut into it, just close enough to allow the couple peering through them to hold hands. Jessica took it all in, uncomprehending.

"Beyond that screen is a painting," I told her. "Two paintings, actually. Taken separately, they mean nothing—just streaks of color and jumbles of dots across the canvas. But when the viewers are bonded as we are, and one painting is viewed through your sight and one is viewed through mine, and we allow our intimacy to combine those views into a single image, the true nature of the portrait is revealed. It's a clever technique, and if it's done properly it can sometimes yield unexpected detail and perspective."

Jessica put her right eye to the hole in front of her and saw nothing but a broad expanse of blotches and marks. I put my left eye to the opening on my side and saw a similarly meaningless jumble. We reached for each other and clasped hands, and we allowed our breathing to ease and our vision to relax until it became a bit vague at the edges.

And then, as if a third mind straddling the two of ours had suddenly divined how the marks were meant to align, the images from her eye and mine snapped together and revealed a single, meaningful prospect. What we were looking at was the Gray Fort, not the massive ruin that stood outside, but as she was in the days of her glory—when her unblemished walls rose with the graceful curve of a ship's prow from the knees of the mountain behind her, and her towers and turrets caught the morning sun as they stood tall into the blue sky, and gold gleamed from her domes, and her long pennants made whip-cracks in the breeze. The artist's hand held a magic that made the image stand away from the canvas, as though we could have walked around it and new details would have been revealed with each step. Soldiers in bright armor manned those ramparts and lay in wait in those turrets. (They would send a cavalry charge first, and it would devastate our front ranks.) I was back on the field before those walls, and tiny chill fingers ran down my spine as I remembered for the first time in centuries the dread and wonder those men had instilled in me. I missed the weight of my spear in my hand, ready to dole out death. I recalled that I was made to fight, and to love, and to die for the things I believed in. I was not a bureaucrat or the overseer of a dull, submissive people, but a warrior once again, at a moment when history held its breath.

And over it all, I felt an immense gratitude to have that moment back, and that my Jessica was here to see it with me, and that I could share with my bride the majesty and power of that day.

Right:

Loran's long stride took him ahead of me, and he saw the fortress before I got to the top of the slope. For a frustrating moment until I caught up I had to be content with his impression of its mass and shattered strength and the way it dominated the valley. I preferred it as I saw it myself—there was more to it than I expected, and the stonework of the palaces behind the walls seemed as delicate as froth. So we really had been builders, back then.

A man was selling souvenirs inside a small stone building next to the path. Our old guide announced in his self-taught Folk tongue, Here you can purchase many fine illustrations of the Gray Fort, quite suitable for greeting-cardspostcardsbirthdaycardsholidaycards and the like. If you will just step this way—

But Loran kept walking. The vendor inside noticed me as I passed, and his face twisted. It was an expression I had seen several times in the days since we were bonded, and what it meant was, Faery's Whore. Our guide warned him off with a hard look.

I prayed that the guide didn't recognize me, though I doubted he would have forgotten. His name was Nikander. When I was a child he was a teacher, holding school in the abandoned stable he had made into a classroom, charging for lessons only what each family could afford. He smelled like turnip soup, and he laughed at his own jokes like a braying donkey. He taught me some reading and writing, and a bit of sums, but the real reason I sat in that crowded stable through hot summer days was to listen to his fantastical stories of Men before the Fair Folk came. Men before the generations of war and barbarism, and before the generations of occupation. Only a small bit of what he told us was close to believable—people flying to the moon and performing inside tiny boxes of light must have come out of his own dreams—but even that was enough to make me think there might be more to us than the Folk wanted us to know.

Today he addressed me through Loran, as was right for our respective positions, but he wouldn't meet my eye for even a moment, and that more than anything else told me he knew who I was.

The wind pulled at my hair and my shawl, and I saw myself through Loran's sight as he paused to admire me. I wouldn't have guessed that even the long-lived Folk, with their powers and deadly pride and incomprehensible moods, could be giddy newlyweds. Another fact they chose not to reveal to the Men they ruled. I looked back at him, but I only had time to glimpse his slender height and elegance, and the straight white hair hanging past his jawline, before my stomach rebelled and I had to turn away. Let him think it was because I hadn't adjusted to our bond yet. We each now lived through the other's body as we lived through our own, but this intense intimacy was a leash held by whoever was the stronger. And even dogs learned ways to keep their collars loose.

Coming to this old spot had been my idea—the sort of honeymoon trip the ancients might have taken. It was our shared interest in the olden days that had first brought me to Loran, though for him it had been mainly a chance to tell stories about his youth, while I was searching for some sense of what my people had once been. The human-tales I had heard from Nikander as a girl had stuck in the back of my mind and smoldered there. As the sprawling mud-thatch slums took my childhood and I saw a hundred daily reminders of our weakness and incompetence, I found I needed to understand what parts of those fables were true. It had been simple to flatter my way onto Loran's estate overlooking the city, and then to flirt until I had an invitation to come back. Loran had been only too happy to talk about himself to an adoring young woman. After a while, by stitching together his silences and the details left unsaid, I gathered that the Elves' conquest of our world had not always gone smoothly, and perhaps had even been a challenge.

I had not expected our relationship to progress as it did.

I felt the old axe wound in Loran's right thigh throb, and he paused once or twice as we approached the fort. Despite his age and his decades behind a desk, Loran was still frighteningly strong, a born warrior, and not many could stand against him in one of his moments of rage. He watched a hunting hawk turn in the air over the meadow, and then scanned the bushes to locate its prey. His breath went a little shallow, in anticipation of the kill, I supposed.

Nikander indicated the valley around us. In the olden days when the fortress still stood, he told us, this road was lined all the way up with many-many redoubts, towerhouses and palisades. An army would cower at the thought of passing through.

He spoke to Loran, and it was odd for me to hear him string words awkwardly in the Folk tongue when he was so compelling in our own, but I knew his meaning was intended for me, and I could see it in my mind's eye.

And yet in the end it was you that folded, I felt Loran mutter.

I shouldn't have been surprised that he wouldn't let me have even this.

That's true—in the end, I chided him. But I said it under my breath, suddenly ashamed to have Nikander see me discussing this topic so lightly with my Fay husband.

Loran responded with the same doctrine and morals I had heard all my life. But then he let slip—

We were in awe of you right up to the moment of your defeat.

My pulse banged for a moment, but I already knew the trick of dampening it with a careful breath before he noticed.

So we *were* your equals, I thought, and kept the realization private. Could it be that your beautiful, blessed and cunning people came across not to guide us, but to be shaped by the struggle? You loved us for being worthy adversaries, didn't you? Is that why your rule seems so arbitrary—do we bore you now?

What boredom was I a cure for? Loran had decided that we would be wed before I realized how far I had let things go. Honor is more important to people who have nothing than to generals, and my father had furiously resisted Loran's attempt to take me. My family held firm against the string of illnesses and petty hexes that laid them low and crumbled our home around us. But when soldiers started taking our neighbors to the work-farms one by one, and word spread that we had the power to save them, my parents were forced to let me go. I haven't spoken with them since.

Nikander filled the silence with his rote gabble. Far more than a mere military stronghold, he quoted, this was the home base of the Army of the Northeast, as well as the retinues-retainers-advisors-wives-consorts-and-harems of the warlords who led them, for one hundred eight years. It was the first structure to incorporate certain stoneworking methods for hand-cutting and laying large blocks that had been forgotten for almost a millennium.

Indeed, said my lord and husband. We helped you recover your own lost past.

I fought down the sudden churn in my stomach.

Well sir, I'd hardly call it helping.

It was the wrong time for Nikander to remember his pride. The familiar tone was like a red flag to a bull.

You wouldn't? And how well would you know what transpired in those days?

Sir, Nikander replied with quiet dignity, I have a doctorate in pre-Resistance history from the University of the Northeast Territory.

Of course you do. Loran's voice was dry and cold. And how useful have you found that?

There was a charged, still moment in which Nikander might have gotten himself killed, but then he ducked his head in a quick bow, and turned back to the path as if erasing the incident from his memory. I will never be Folk, but I can't go back now, and if one day, riding through the streets of the city I happen to come across my family again, I hope they won't know me.

Loran was in particularly good spirits now, and he ignored the raw nerves in his thigh as we made our way towards the fortress. I could see the massive gates still lying where they had been thrown down, green and brown with corrosion, covered over with growing grass in some spots and twisted up higher than a man's head in others. Like the heavy stone blocks around them, they weren't worth the effort to move. I wondered what ram or magic had thrown them *outwards* when they were breached. The Folk had done a good job of keeping that technique secret from us too.

The area in front of the gates had been turned into an improvised market, though there wasn't a single customer. Loran would be baffled, but I had grown up amongst people like this—men and women with so little they could wait all day next to a disintegrating stall or a board laid across crates, in the hope that travel might make one sightseer a bit generous or careless with his money.

Nikander warned Loran, They are a worthless bunch of hucksters-conmenpickpockets-and-thieves, and you should keep your hand on your wallet and ignore them as we pass through. Afterwards I will take you someplace where the proprietor is trusty and you will surely get what you've paid for.

We stepped into their midst and they came desperately alive, swarming around and between us, each demanding our attention for their chipped relics or cracking jewelry or cheap toys. The crowd was smothering, and I could focus only on the tiny wedge of space directly in front of me. Loran waded through the fringes, and Nikander in the thick of things feigned indignation, but I had never been rich before, and when I said *No* it was without conviction. Against my will, I was swept into the very middle of the market, and jammed hard against a stand overseen by an old woman who could have passed for my grandmother.

I dropped a coin on her table, and she slid something across the rough planks.

This one, she said.

I snatched up a hilt of bright false jewels and peeling paint. I didn't test the blade or look at it. I didn't want to be betrayed by the knowing. Placated, the hawkers gave way before me. They jostled and called out as before, but when I passed their last stall it was as if I crossed beyond their borders, and they returned to their places. I went to Loran's side.

Nikander joined us, with a show of shaking his head ruefully. I'm sorry you should be burdened with such . . . unpleasantness, milady, he said, and he looked directly into my eyes for the first time.

But here, before we enter the fortress itself, he continued, is a display created especially for pair-bonded fair lords and ladies such as yourselves.

A stereogram, no doubt? Loran said.

Indeed, sir.

Loran led me into a small room filled with clear light. Running across the middle was a white marble barrier fashioned like lacework. There were two places to peek through.

Beyond that screen is a painting. Two paintings, actually, Loran explained. Taken separately, they mean nothing—just streaks of color and jumbles of dots across the canvas. But when the viewers are bonded as we are, and one painting is viewed through your sight and one is viewed through mine, and we allow our intimacy to combine those views into a single image, the true nature of the portrait is revealed.

Loran and I looked through and both saw a nonsense hodgepodge of streaks and blots, as if someone had let squirrels run through their paints. We took each other's hand, and he softened his breath and let his eye go a little out of focus, and I copied him.

The two images swam towards each other, and mated, and suddenly we grasped the picture as it was meant to be seen. It was the Gray Fort in all its grace and magnificence, a sight that stopped the breath and sent the heart soaring in your chest as if it had been given hawk's wings. We *could* build strong walls and tall turrets and dream-like palaces. Armies *would* cower at the thought of testing our defenses. We were everything the Folk told us we weren't. We had had hands that created works of beauty, and wise minds that calculated how to shape them, and strong arms that drove our enemies before us—and this even after we had clawed our way out of chaos; the faintest shadow of the forgotten days of our true power, that had been stolen from us.

My shawl was wrapped so tightly around the hilt of the dagger that I couldn't recognize its shape in my hand, and Loran suspected nothing. I flicked my wrist, and the loose scabbard slipped off and clattered on the flag-stones. Then, while both of us were held by the vision of the fort, I raised the blade and brought it down hard into my own right thigh, and twisted it.

The pain drove through me in a sickening wave and I lurched against the marble screen. Loran, however, struck in the center of his old axe wound, spasmed with a grunt and dropped to the floor. He landed half-curled on his side, struggled to rise, and slipped.

I limped to him, and his scalp felt my fingers slide along it as I pulled his head back by his hair. I looked into his eyes.

Thank you, milord, I said. It was beautiful to see.

Loran saw the dagger in my hand, and saw my intent, and smiled with real joy.

I knew I chose well! he said.

I didn't understand. I wondered if it mattered.

The blade is sharper than I would have thought; when I make the single thrust to drive it through his eye socket, perhaps I will survive the agony. Perhaps I will be suffered to live long enough to see the Folk strike back against my city in reprisal for the assassination of an Elven lord. Then my race will be pushed too far, and we shall rise up and have war again, to the terrible delight of both our peoples.

And things may turn out differently this time.

AMOR FUGIT

ALEXANDRA DUNCAN

———◆———

In the soft space when the sun dips behind the trees and crickets fill the shadowed grass with their high metal voices, my mother and I ready our lanterns. Sunset is the vigil hour. My mother wraps herself in a heavy woven shawl, purple like the mountains looming to the west of our cottage. Fireflies bob and flicker over our wheat field. Our mouser takes up his post on top of the garden gate, regarding us with his bright stare. A crisp, early autumn breeze moves over the wheat. I shiver in my white linen chiton and rub my arms for warmth.

"There," Mother says, pointing.

I squint into the dim. Yes, there. I catch a hint of movement along the brambles at the edge of our wood. I breathe in, letting the darkening air fill my mouth, lift my lungs. Dusk tastes sour honey sweet. Sweet because the fading light means my father is making his way to us through the far-off wood. Sour because my mother will snuff out her lantern and leave me alone as soon as he comes into sight.

When I was a child, I would stand at the window and cry to see the sun go down.

I am too old for that now.

Mother opens the hinged glass door of her lantern and blows out the flame. In the moment before the light goes out, I see sadness written deep around her eyes and mouth. It's not the kind of sadness that makes her sullen and snappish at her work, or stare wistfully across the fields. It's something else. The only time I think I might have felt something like it was when our first mouser died. He was yellow like saffron and liked to rub against my legs when I fed him bits of meat. I called him Rumbler, for the sound he made in his throat when I was near. I have since learned not to name our farm animals.

Mother squeezes my hand. I don't look as she sets down her lantern and steps backward into the night. It's easier that way, like looking away when she pricks the soft side of my arm with a lancet for inoculations. I try not to listen to the receding shuffle of her footsteps and concentrate instead on picking out the glimmers of light reflecting from my father's belt, the hilt of his hunting knife, the metal clasps on the shoulders of his traveling cloak. They flash in the moonlight as he approaches, like little stars moving through our fields. He has reached the foot of the hill leading up to our house. With one hand he supports a dead stag, slung across his shoulder. I know I should stand still to welcome him, like a dignified girl who is studying to become a woman, but I break into a run. The lantern swings beside me and my skirt flaps like a flag as I careen down the path. He meets me halfway, holding out his free arm and pulling me into a fierce hug.

"Ourania." Father breathes out my name as if he's been holding it in with his breath all day.

I don't say anything, but bury my face into his shoulder, like a little girl. He smells of sweat, crushed leaves, and animal blood, and his cloak is rough against my nose.

We walk up to the cottage, hand in hand. I kneel by the hearth and start a fire with my flints while he hangs the stag's carcass in the cellar. I set out a basin of warm water and a clean cloth so he can wash the blood and dirt from his arms. When he is clean and we are sitting at the table for our simple meal of bread, cheese, soup, and wine, he asks what he always asks.

"Did your mother leave any words for me?" His face goes still and his shoulders tense as he waits for my answer, as if everything turns on what I might say.

I pick up my wine cup and take a swallow. I don't like the way the drink dries my tongue, but I like that Father doesn't try to water it for me, the way Mother does. "She says to tell you she mended your heavy cloak, so it's ready for winter. We killed a rabbit and she added its fur at the collar. She thanks you for the meat."

Father smiles to himself and takes a long drink. When he sets his cup down, his face is flushed. He's still smiling, and little points of light glitter in the folds of his eyes. I pick up my spoon and blow into my bowl to cool the broth. We both fall quiet for a time, focused on our food, making ourselves accustomed to each other's presence again after the long day apart. Later, he will tell stories by the hearth until our fire sinks down to an embered glow.

Long ago, when Day was a young woman, she blazed across the sky with little care in her heart. When she laid her head down to rest, the world became dark. When the time came for her to bring light to the world, she warmed everything, from the heath balds to the ocean deeps. Her only joy came in giving warmth.

But one night, she turned to look back into the dusk, and caught sight of a man. His robe was white and glistening like sun-warmed ice, his strong arms the pale blue of milk after the cream has been skimmed away, and his hair coiled and curled around his brow in midnight waves. This man was Night. He lifted his eyes, bright as two stars, and found her watching him.

They each left their paths and went to one another. Day fed her light to Night, Night offered up his cool for Day to sip, and they found how they curved together to form a whole. Thus Day and Night first knew love.

I wake with the sun on my face and the smell of fresh bread and olive oil hanging in the air. The mouser is curled up next to my feet at the end of my cot. I shove him off the bed and force myself up. The sun is high and hot already, and my head aches from too much wine. I've let myself sleep past dawn. I've missed Father's parting. Mother had no one to greet her. The goats will be sullen and stubborn when at last I get around to milking them. I pull on my ear in frustration and hurry to wrap my chiton around myself, stepping quickly toward the kitchen.

Mother's face shines with sweat, but she smiles to herself as she pulls a loaf of bread from our stone oven on a long, wooden board. She must have passed within a hand's breadth of Father as he was parting, in the confusion between night and dawn a heavy mist can cause. She straightens and slides the bread onto the table for cutting. A pail of cool milk rests on the center board.

"Why did you let me sleep so late?" I ask. Petulance sneaks into my voice. She's only being kind, giving me a morning off from my chores.

"You looked so peaceful." Mother rests her hands on her hips. She's tucked the hem of her long skirts up into her waistband to keep them out of the fire and I can see the broad arch of her calves, thick and strong from walking. I wonder where her trek takes her each night. Does she always make for the same place or does she wander? Does she rest? She must. But when, and where?

Mother slices the bread and lays a plate of it on the table, next to a shallow bowl of spiced olive oil. She wipes her hands clean on a broadcloth, pours a small measure of wine into two mugs, and tops them off with water. She slides one to me and sits down at the table with the other.

"Drink up," she says, sipping from her mug and reaching for a slice of bread to dip into the olive oil.

I wrinkle my nose at my own cup. I know the wine is for killing disease in the water, but my tongue curls at the slight, familiar bitterness of it. I sop my bread in oil and bite off a big, crackling chunk to scrub the taste from my mouth.

Mother has me practice my Latin as we weed the garden. We bend our backs under the heat of the late morning sun, yanking invading threads of root from the spaces between the arugula, spinach, and tomatoes. Mother kneels in the dirt and calls out infinitive verbs over their leafy heads.

"*Colere,*" she calls. She winds the stem of a prickly weed around her gloved hand and tugs.

"*Colere,*" I repeat, then string out the conjugation. "To cultivate. *Coleo, coleas, coleat, coleamus, coleatis, coleant.*" A bead of sweat drips over my eyebrow and lands on one of the flowering yellow weeds that try to take over our garden each year. I rip it out and toss it in my compost pail.

"*Amare,*" Mother returns, without missing a breath.

"*Amo, amas, amat, amamus, amatis, amant,*" I say into the dirt.

"*Consecrare. Exspectare. Invigilare. Demetere,*" Mother calls, and I send each of the words back across the leafy rows in turn.

After we finish weeding, we take small horsehair brushes and dust the stamens of our scarlet runner bean flowers with pollen from the pistils of a hearty green snap-bean. As she dips her brush into the well of each flower, Mother tells me how she hopes to breed a hybrid with the sweetness of the scarlet bean and the snap-bean's resistance to frost.

When the sun nears its zenith, we retreat inside to escape the midday heat. Mother prepares a meal of greens from our garden and lies down on a low divan by the cool north wall to wait out the worst of the heat. I pocket one of the newest books she has brought home for me and lie down with it in my room. I can never sleep through the midday, like Mother does. Even when I draw the shades and strip off my dress, I can only lie on my back and sweat into the bedclothes. I sit up and lean against the stucco wall, sweat gathering in the hollow of my back. I trace the gold-leafed imprint of words on the book's cover. Sometimes I will sneak out and read up in the olive orchard, where the breeze reaches.

I sit quietly until Mother's breath slows to a gentle snore. Then I slide my legs off the bed and walk barefoot through the common room, quiet and careful as a mouser on the hunt. As I pass the place where she lies, Mother's breath skips in her sleep. I freeze, looking down at her, and hug the book to my chest. Her lips move rapidly and her brow creases, as if she's arguing with someone in her dream. Then she breathes out. Her body relaxes into the divan cushions.

I step carefully until I pass the threshold into the kitchen, and then I run, out the kitchen door, through the garden, over the gate, and up the hill behind our cottage, where a cluster of olive trees overlooks the valley. I settle at the base of the oldest tree, its branches curving over me like the whalebone parasol Mother brought back from her journeys one time. The canopy of tiny leaves shades my head, and a soft breeze cools my skin. I lay the open book across my lap and look down on the valley.

From here I can see the flat roof of our cottage, with its high stone wall squaring off the large garden in the back. The valley dips down, split by a dirt path. Our fields billow with wheat on one side, and on the other, a corral encircles our little herd of goats. They rest in the shade of a lemon tree, not far from our barn and silo. From here, it all looks like something effortless, a spread of wildflowers cropping up naturally by a roadway. You can't make out any of the muck and sweat from so far up. A light wind trails its cool fingers up my spine and across the nape of my neck. I lean my head back into a fork in the olive tree's trunk, stretch out my legs on the mossy grass, and close my eyes.

A muffled trill of laughter sounds somewhere behind me, waking me with a start. The book drops from my slack hand and snaps closed on the ground. I scoop it up and pick my way through the olive grove, toward the meadow that lies on the other side, and the sound of voices. The sun still rides high in the sky, but tilts a little more sharply than when I fell asleep. I've only slept a short time. I pause at the lip of the meadow behind the shelter of a broad, old tree.

"Ollie ollie oxen free!" a voice rings out from a low scrub bush only a few yards to my left.

Two girls in pale blue and pink frocks, with hair like tails of wheat, dash from the shade of the trees out into the blinding bright meadow. The smaller one chases the taller, her hands outstretched. The older girl turns back, shrieks in mock terror, and lifts her knees higher as she hurtles forward through the tall grass.

"Maria! Julia!" a woman's voice calls from the near corner of the meadow. I shift my gaze and see a matronly figure in a pale, fitted dress and a broad straw hat sitting on a checkered blanket. "Stop running around and come sit in the shade. You're going to give yourselves heatstroke."

"Yes, Mama," the older girl says. The small girl drags her feet as her sister leads the way over to the blanket.

"Look at you, you're all red," the mother says as they draw near. "You know young gentlemen don't want a wife with ruddy skin, right? Come out of that sun."

The girls drop down, obedient, to the blanket and begin making chains out of the same sort of yellow weeds my mother and I rooted out of the garden earlier. The mother reclines stiff-like into her resting place, as if something is hemming in her stomach and keeping her from moving in the natural way. Maybe it's all the lace and ruffles across her bodice, or the tight row of pearl buttons down the front of her dress. I look from the bare arms of my chiton to the patches of sweat darkening the sides of her dress and the fair curls at the back of her neck. She must be a strange one to wrap herself up this way in the dead heat of summer. I peer out from under cover of the olive tree, my palms pressed against its rough bark. I look at my hand on the wood. The sun has browned my skin the color of an oil-fried fish and dirt rims my fingernails. This woman must be rich, to never have to go out in the sun. She must have servants to milk her goats and serve her dinner. Father has told me about such people, and Mother has read to me about them from her books, but I thought they were fancy tales, like the cat who makes his master into a lord.

The small girl drapes a chain of weedy flowers around her neck, and the older one arranges a shorter chain on the crown of her head like a diadem. But the sun must be making them drowsy, for after a few minutes they rest their heads next to their mother's breast and close their eyes. The wind rustles the leaves, and the dappled sunlight ripples over their sleeping forms. They make me think of statues fallen to the bottom of a clear pond.

I step forward to the edge of the meadow, meaning to take a closer look at them in their strange clothes. As I move from behind the tree, something comes into view that makes me freeze, poised with one foot in the air and one hand trailing behind me. On the other side of the blanket, a young man lies on his back. He's clothed in white shirtsleeves and trousers of the same pale, striped material as the woman's dress. A vest crosses his middle, fastened with a row of brass buttons. A broad-brimmed hat tips back from his head, and under it, two dark brown eyes stare back at me.

I turn and flee through the olive grove. I hear a scuffle in the dirt as he springs up to follow, and a hoarse whisper calling after me. His shoes crackle over the carpet of twigs and small stones, where my bare feet pass silently. I round the last row of trees and am about to hurl myself forward into the safety of the sunshine, when he grabs my arm. My own momentum swings me around. He catches me about the waist with his free hand, and we stand face to face, gaping at each other. He can't be more than a few years older than me, around the age when my father says men should be off learning war. His eyebrows angle down into a troubled knit as he stares.

"Let go," I say, and push him. He lets my arm slip from his hand and stumbles back a step. I should run, but I don't.

"Who are you?" he asks. The words are soft in his mouth, not clipped like the woman's. He holds his hand out, as if asking me to wait.

"Ourania," I say.

"Have you come from a play?" He turns to look around the wood. "Or do you belong to the Classical Society?"

"I don't know what you mean," I say, creeping back against the nearest tree. "Why would I want to be in a play?"

"Your dress," he says.

I look down at my chiton. Mother and I painted it with beeswax and dyed it blue so a pattern of cream-colored birds and flowers shows through. Some of the flowers have come away smudged a muddy green from my leaning against tree trunks and falling asleep in the grass. I lick my finger and try to rub at the stain, but it's set in already. I sigh. He must think I'm part of a paupers' troupe with my dirty robe and bare feet. I reach up to retie the bands around my hair and pull away a dead olive leaf. I crumble it in my free hand and drop the shreds to the ground, hoping he hasn't added that detail to my catalog of shames.

"I've been working," I say. "I fell asleep on the grass."

He blinks at me, then swallows and blinks some more. "What are you?"

I feel a scowl cloud my features. "I'm Ourania, like I said. What are you?"

"Aaron Lyell. I'm an apprentice engineer."

"A what?"

"An engineer. You know, for locomotives."

I stare at him.

He clears his throat. "Trains. You know." He shuffles his feet over the rocky ground.

I cock my head to the side and wait for him to explain himself.

"If you don't mind my asking, where do you come from?" He raises his eyes and looks at me with pure, innocent curiosity.

"Down the valley," I say, nodding to the slope beyond the break in the trees. "This is our olive grove."

"I'm sorry," he says. He runs his hand through his mess of short, curling hair, the same burnished yellow as the girls' braids. "The company was surveying this tract of land for railway development, and I found this lovely meadow. Looked like a nice place for a picnic. I didn't know anybody was living here. We'll have to go back over the property records now, naturally. . . . " He trails off, staring at me again.

"Should I draw you a picture?" I say.

"What's that?"

"I said, should I draw you a picture," I repeat. "That way you wouldn't have to look so hard."

"Sorry," he says. His pale skin goes a deep red and he looks down. "It's only . . . I've never, well, in books, but I've never seen anyone like you before."

"You're a strange one," I say, leaning against the tree behind me. "I've never seen anyone like you either. It's like you stepped out of a wives' tale or—"

"You're lovely," Aaron interrupts, looking up at me suddenly.

I feel my own face go hot and I look down at my bare feet. A peddler said something like that about me once, when my mother and I traded him some eggs for ribbons, but it didn't mean the same.

I hug the book to my chest. We stand in silence, avoiding each other's looks.

"May I ask," Aaron says to break the long pause, "what is it you're reading?"

I hold the book face-out so he can read the lettering.

"*On the Origin of Species*," he reads aloud. His eyes light up the way Father's do when he's telling how he brought down a hart after a daylong stalk through the forest. "You're interested in natural history?"

I shrug, then lift my eyes to look at him sidelong. "Have you read it?"

"Oh, yes," he says, a grin parting his lips and tugging up his serious brow. "Engineering science is my trade, but I've a great interest in naturalism. Mr. Darwin is marvelous. Here." He digs in his back pocket and produces a thin leather-bound volume. He holds it out at the tip of his fingers.

I step forward warily and take the book. It opens up to reveal small, cream-colored pages crowded with precise drawings of flowers and birds, sketched in graphite. Below each likeness, the name of the specimen flows in Aaron's neat hand. I sit down on the ground and begin to page through from the beginning. "You did these?" I ask.

"Yes." Aaron sits cross-legged beside me.

"I've never had time for drawing. Mother calls it a hobby." I lift a page and stop with the book open to a sketch of the two girls I saw in the meadow. The older one is sitting with her feet up under her on a plump cushion, her head bent over an embroidery hoop. The younger leans against her, fast asleep, her hand resting on a cloth poppet.

I look up from the book. "Are they your sisters?"

He opens his mouth to speak, but a voice echoes up from the direction of the meadow instead. "Aaron?" It's the woman, stretching out the sound of his name. "Aaron, where've you gone?"

He jumps up at the sound of her voice. "Coming," he shouts back. Then quietly, his voice straining with nerves, he leans close and says, "Will you come here again next Sunday?"

I sit on the forest floor in a muddle. "When's that?"

"Seven days," he says. A twig pops some way off among the trees. He glances over his shoulder and begins backing toward the sound. "Meet me here. Please. In the meadow. I only want a chance to know you better."

His eyes stay fixed on me until I nod, and then he's gone, the soft thud of his shoes fading into the twisting file of trees. I wait a moment longer, and hear the woman's voice cut out mid-call. My body feels odd and full of humming energy. I can't feel my fingers, and when I look down, I see I'm still holding Aaron's little leather-bound book. I stumble up after him. I jog through the shaded grove, dodging olive trees and hopping stones. But when I reach the meadow, the only trace of my strange visitors is a square of flattened grass where they laid their blanket. I walk slowly back to the spot where Aaron and I sat, gather up both books in my arms, and turn my feet toward home.

The afternoon passes slow and sluggish in the heat. Mother sets me to a column of geometry equations that have to do with the volume of water in our well during different seasons, while she ties on her veiled straw hat and heads out to check on the bees. I sit by the window with a wax tablet and stylus laid out in front of me and watch her white-swathed figure moving between the bee boxes. I would rather be out under all that cloth and sun than cloistered here with mathematics.

I slip my hand between the folds of my robe and pull out Aaron's book. Its cover is worn smooth from handling. I dart my eyes to the window. Mother is easing a honeycomb from one of the hives. I spread the pages open and crease each one down as I turn. Aaron's hand is exact, picking out the smallest veins and petals of the flora and fixing a lively glint in a bird's eye, but I don't recognize a single one of them. A Latin name and a common one accompany each drawing. Both sound strange on my tongue, like a cousin to a word I know. *Cercis occidentalis.* Judas Tree. *Junco hyemalis.* Dark-eyed Junco. *Callipepla californifica.* California quail. I try to sound them out, but they turn my tongue to clay.

I flip the pages under my thumb and the book falls open to a detailed sketch of an even road, flanked on both sides by tall bricked buildings. It's a street in a city of some kind, but nothing like the places I've read about or Mother describes. What might be blown glass clings to the buildings in sheets, and little curls of iron or wood jut from the stonework. Tradesmen's signs hang down from posts ensconced in the walls. There are hardly any animals in Aaron's picture, except a single horse and some kind of pygmy dog led by a woman dressed more or less the same as the one I saw in the meadow. No oxen. No goats. No chickens. No market stalls, even. The men wear tall hats, and the women cover their hair with bonnets. The next page holds the schematics for some sort of spoked wheel and chain device. Next, the skeleton of an impossibly tall building, and an oblong shape moving among the clouds. *Zeppelin*, the script beneath it reads.

I put my hand to my lips and remember to breathe out. Is it real, or something Aaron made up in an idle hour? When I was young, I would draw fancy pictures full of lichen-dripped crevasses and monsters with hundreds of heads bobbing on their long, eel-like necks.

"Ourania!" Mother's voice clips across my thoughts. She is struggling up the hill with two pails balanced out from her body in either hand.

I snap the book shut.

"Ourania!" Mother calls again. "Help me with the door."

I open the door and stand back so she can pass through with the pails, honeycombs resting in sticky blocks at their bases. I keep quiet the rest of the evening. We finish butchering the stag in the cellar and jar the honey. We bake more bread. We light our lamps. We wait.

"Father," I ask that night when most of the bread from our dinner is gone. "Could you take me with you to the wood, if you wanted?"

He chuckles, raising his eyebrows at me over the soup bowl at his mouth. "What do you want with the forest?"

My eyes slide down to the empty bowl in front of me. I pick at a heel of bread. "You could teach me to hunt. I could help you."

"But then who would help your mother? And who would be our messenger?" Father asks. He reaches across the table and pats my hand. "You make a better Mercury than you would a Diana, I think."

I must be scowling, because Father laughs again. "Is your mother's company wearing on you?"

"No," I say. I pour the last of the wine into my cup. "I only miss you, that's all."

"And you don't think my company would wear on you, too?" Father asks.

"No," I say again, cutting my eyes down to the table. I can see he doesn't mean to answer me. I open my mouth to speak again, then change my mind and snap my jaw shut instead.

Father lifts an eyebrow. "Is there something else you wanted to ask, Ourania?"

I duck my head and feel my face fill with heat. "No," I say in a small voice.

"You know I'll tell you anything you want to know," Father says. "You only have to ask."

I hesitate, and raise my eyes to him. "Do you know what a locomotive is?"

Father's eyes narrow. "Where did you hear that word?" His voice has a tang of metal in it. I am suddenly aware of all the beasts he has felled.

"Nowhere," I say, dropping my eyes again quickly. My heart speeds up and I can feel the bread and lentils in my stomach curdle. "Nowhere. I mean, I read it. There was a book Mother had me read." I bite the sides of my tongue and widen my eyes at the empty space on the table between us. He can't know all I've been reading. I might very well have seen the word written. I chance a look up to see if he'll take in what I've fed him. He stares back at me with that same hard look in his eyes. His usual, easy smile is gone, and I catch a glimpse of something dangerous coiled in its place.

I rise to clear the bowls from the table. Father remains, watching me move about. I keep my back to him and push my hands beneath the water in our kitchen basin so he won't see them shaking. After a moment, I hear the scrape of his chair as he rises, and then the low tumble of wood as he kneels to build up the hearth fire. I stay at the dishes longer than I need, wiping them dry with extra care so I won't have to turn around and see the awful power in my father's face again.

"Would you like to hear a story, Ourania?" Father asks, his voice softened and friendly again. He stands in the doorway, but I can barely hear him over the pop of burning logs.

I sigh, slipping back into the comfort of our routine. "Please," I say.

Father has told me about Diana springing forth from father Zeus's head, Lord Rama, and the hero Sunjata's sister, who married the spirit beneath the hill, and later betrayed her husband to save her brother. Tonight he will tell me of the god Osiris, whose brother murdered him and scattered his flesh over the Nile, and of faithful Isis, who gathered together the body of her husband, and restored him to a throne in the underworld.

But down on the earth, the sun halted its course at the edge of the sky. Dark did not fall, and all the beasts were trapped in a terrible half-light.

"Why has Day stopped her course? Where is Night?" the animals cried. They cowered and trembled in the stillness.

One of the beasts, the one called Man, stood upright. He held aloft a burning branch that tempered the darkness. "Don't be afraid," he said. "I will go and find them. I will set them back on their paths and restore order to the world."

Man ranged over hill and valley. He scoured the salt oceans. At last, he scaled the summit of the highest mountain. There he came upon the two of them, cradled together in a bed of stars.

A hot anger flared in Man's breast to see them so reposed.

"You, faithless ones," Man said, and his voice sparked like new-caught fire. "How could you forsake us?" He reached up into the abyss of heaven and called down a terrible beast. It snaked across the sky like a serpent, and shook the earth as it passed. Thick scarab metal covered the length of its body, and it hissed and growled foul smoke that poisoned the air. Man set it on the lovers. So Night and Day were forced to flee from it, always, or be devoured.

I am careful to rise early the next seven days. I milk the nanny goats in the chill, predawn mist, make cheese from what they give, practice my Latin and geometry, and watch the grain grow. At night, I hold Aaron's book open inside the copy of Darwin. Father asks me to read to him sometimes, but then shakes his head after only a few paragraphs of Mr. Darwin's prose and says he'll tell me a story instead. It suits us both better. By the way the wheat bows and the twinge of cold in the air at dawn, I know the harvest isn't far off.

On the seventh day, I trudge through the muggy heat of midday, up the hill to the olive grove. I carry a sack of bread and cheese. Aaron's book rests snug inside my waist sash. A breeze picks up as I near the crest of the hill and the cool wood. I walk through the grove, trailing my fingers across the trees' smooth backs and letting the wind lift the hair from my neck. The treetops create a canopy that filters little dapples of sunlight onto the ground. I am going to see Aaron. I am going to ask him if he's seen the places he draws in his book, or if they're fancies. I am going to ask him about the obelisk and the zepplin. I am going to ask where he found the Dark-eyed Junco, and what it is. I smile up at the canopy and round the last stand of trees.

The clearing stands empty. Aaron hasn't arrived yet, so I crouch down and pluck at the blades of long grass. I split one down the middle with my fingernail to make a whistle, hold it to my lips, and blow. The grass makes a dry, sputtering tweet. I bite my lip and grin. If I close my eyes, I can picture my father sitting cross-legged beside me, showing my young self the trick of it. When I tire of my game, I make a chain of flowers and drape them around my neck and head, the way I saw the little girls do. I walk the circumference of the meadow, letting my hand trail over the saplings and low brush at its border. I pause at the spot where Aaron and the girls laid their blanket. Something has been carved into the thick trunk of one of the nearby trees. I kneel beside it and brush the markings with my fingers. The cut stands out faint and boxy, but I can read it. *Ourania*. A thrill passes through my chest. I stand and scan the meadow, expecting him to stride into view at any moment. But he does not come.

I take the little hinged, bronze knife I carry from my pocket and unfold it. The bark is thick, but I keep my knife sharp. It cuts a bright yellow line in the trunk below my name. I strain my arm against the hard wood and run my hand over my work when I have finished. *Aaron*. His name joins mine on the tree's flesh. I braid long slips of grass into rope as I wait, flip through Aaron's book again, and lie back to stare at the clouds passing soundlessly overhead. If only I could make time pass more quickly, the way the wind moves clouds at its whim, so Aaron could be here already. I close my eyes. A wind shakes the leaves at the top of the trees, making them rattle like a rainstorm on all sides of me. I lean back against the earth and rest Aaron's book on the slope of my chest. For some reason, I find it easy to sleep here in the heart of the meadow. I'm sure Aaron's footsteps will wake me when he comes. I let myself drift on the hush of leaves.

I dream of Aaron coming to me through the fold of trees. He kneels and lays himself over me. I feel the length and firmness of his body pressed against my belly, my breasts. The grass is like silk against the soles of my feet. It rises up and braids itself into a bower over our heads, shading us from the sun, as if the earth itself is responding to the heat in my body. I find myself over Aaron, with his hips tucked between my thighs. I pull the bindings from my hair and let it down so it falls in waves over his body. I kiss his throat, his chest, the soft, dark indentation of his navel, covering him with my hair. I feel his hands cupping my skin, and then, and then. . . .

I wake, feeling as if the world has tilted on its axis. My chest heaves as I try to catch my breath. At first, I don't know where I am, and I paw at the bed of grass around me, trying to work my way to my feet. The sun has sunk low in the sky, a bloody bronze color. Far off, something howls. It is like the long, low baying of a wolf, but sharper, with the sound of rending metal folded in. My heart seizes, and I jump to my feet.

Late. It's too late.

I make for the olive grove, scattering chains of flowers and grass behind me as I run. I clutch at my sash and discover I've dropped Aaron's book. I scurry back to the meadow. There, beside the patch of grass I've tamped down in my sleep, it lies half-hidden in the weeds. I snatch it up and run again, through the darkening grove and down the hill, my feet fleet over the roll of the earth, terror beating in my chest.

The lights of our house shine bright. Mother has lit the lanterns without me. She stands, wrapped in her shawl, waiting by the front gate of our house. She must hear the sound of my footsteps, for she turns, and relief rushes her face. She holds out her arms and I run straight to her. Only when I've buried my head in the soft, dark folds of her cloak do I feel myself shaking.

Mother pulls back and holds me at arm's length. She slaps my face, which she has not done since the time in my fifth year when I tied a bucket to our goat's tail and he trampled part of our summer garden in his panic. "Where have you been?" she asks. And then, without waiting for me to answer. "I thought you were gone. I thought it had taken you."

"I . . . I was hot, so I went up to the olive grove. I fell asleep," I say. Then her other words seep into my ears. My heart quickens again. "What would want to take me?"

She presses me tight against her. "Nothing. Nothing. Promise me you won't stray past the borders of the farm. If you do, I can't protect you."

"But what do you need to protect me from?"

Mother stares at me. Her eyes look like dark, polished river stones. "There are all manner of evil things in the world, Ourania, that you are lucky not to know about. Let us not change that."

Day wept as she fled, and her tears flooded the earth. All the beasts cried out and raised their hands to her for mercy, but the deluge swept many under. Then Day felt something move within her. She looked, and found Night's child growing in her belly. Day dried her tears and went to Man to strike a bargain.

"Man," she said. "Have pity. I am with child by Night. Only call off your beast so we may raise our child in peace, and I swear Night and I will part forever. We will each take up our course in the sky, as always was."

"Very well," Man said. "But should you ever stray again, I will loose my beast and hound you to the ends of the earth."

Day agreed, saying, "For even if we never meet, Night's child is dear to me."

Thereafter, the pattern of days returned to the earth. Man became chief among beasts, and he turned his hand to quelling the earth and seas, and all within his ken.

Seven days pass, but I do not visit the meadow again. The grain is almost ready for threshing, so Mother and I sharpen our collection of scythes. I wonder what kept Aaron from me, if it was the same thing I heard howling, the same thing my mother fears. If my mother fears it, it must be too terrible. I am sick from wanting to ask her what it might want from us, but I don't dare. I am nearly finished with Darwin, and geometry helps keep my mind from straying to the olive grove and my strange dream. $C=2\pi r$; $A=\pi r^2$; $V=\pi r^2 h$, I think as the sun beats down on the roof of our house. $A=1/2\ bh$; $a^2+b^2=c^2$

"I have something for you," Mother says at breakfast one morning. She dusts breadcrumbs from her hands as she rises and holds up a finger, telling me to wait where I am. I clear our breakfast and wipe the table clean with a wet rag. Mother returns holding an oilcloth package bound up with twine. She holds it out to me. "Open it."

I cut the twine with my knife and fold the oilcloth away. A nest of fine, creamy linen rests inside. Light from the window catches in the fine weave, making it shimmer like sunshine on a lake. I let out a short breath. This is fabric for a priestess or a bride, not a girl who mucks around with goats and spends her days winnowing grain.

"What's this for?" I ask, turning from the kitchen window, my arms brimming with cloth.

Mother steps into the square of light with me. Her dark hair has fallen out of its tie. It curls down her back and over her breasts like thick, unchecked vines. The light picks out the thin hairs on her forearms, bleached fair by the sun, and warms her browned skin to gold. She reaches out to touch my face and I swear I feel all the heat of summer brush my skin. "You'll be a woman soon," she says. "That brings certain duties and certain boons."

I feel the air quiver around me, and I open my mouth, a hundred questions ready to tumble from the tip of my tongue. But Mother drops her hand. The air changes, as if something has gone out of it, like the release of tension between the earth and sky after a thunderstorm. I sink into my chair, my legs trembling.

"I thought we might dye the border this afternoon, after your lessons," Mother says, folding the oilcloth and twine together for safekeeping. She winds her hair back off of her neck, and I see the smudges of soot on her elbows and faded oil spots on her clothes again. She scoops up a water pail in each hand and holds one out to me. "Come on, help me with the pump."

I still can't sleep at the midday hour, but I don't dare scale the hill again. The echo of Mother's unnamed terror is too real when I wake each morning. I lie on my back in my cot with Aaron's book open in one hand, and the other cupped over my own breast. If I close my eyes, I can imagine it's Aaron's hand, not my own. I press my fingers against the soft flesh of my lips and think of him and his imagined body until the heat from my dream courses through me again. When it is gone, I feel something other than myself. Foreign and hollow, though I don't know why.

I get up and pace the quiet house with Aaron's book. I find the stub of red clay Mother uses to mark measurements on cloth and stone, and take it out to the garden. First I stare out over the vegetable rows with the clay poised over a blank page of Aaron's book. I bite my lip and pull on my ear. The mouser sleeps atop the garden wall, his eyes closed to soft slits and his tail twitching against the stone. I put the clay to the paper and try to imitate the subtle curve of his ears, the ripple of muscles beneath his fur. I block in the balance of stones in the wall, with a thick snake of vines twining up through the cracks and over the top. I hold the paper out. It is not at all neat like Aaron's drawings. The mouser might well be a toad on a woodpile. *Mouser sleeping on our garden wall*, I write below my scrawl, so Aaron will know what it is, if he ever sees it.

Still, it is only my first attempt. I assume this skill is like baking bread or math. I must practice my hand at it. I move over to the cone of wooden stakes where our bean plants grow and hunch over its flowers. I record these and label them, then a black, crook-legged maria bug I find resting beneath the late spinach. I wander the garden, taking down everything I find in Aaron's book until my skin begins to feel tight and hot under the sun. I creep indoors.

Mother lies fast asleep with her back to the wall. Her hair curls around her shoulders. She looks soft, all the drive and hurry wiped from her face. I wonder if I look this way when I sleep. I settle in the chair across from her and begin sketching, trying to spool myself, my life, together again as I go.

I cannot wait another seven days. No amount of mathematics or sketched mimicry can quell the heat flaring beneath my skin or the worry in my stomach. I will go to the hill, and I will not lie down to sleep. I will find Aaron or else leave word for him that I am waiting. My limbs shake as I slip from the house at noon and lift a sharpened scythe from the barn wall. If there is really some terror out there, I will not go unarmed.

I mount the hill again. My trek through the close files of the orchard seems to take longer than usual, but maybe that is the crawling feeling, like ants covering my skin, making time slow. As I step into the meadow, I feel a thrum in the air. The air smells hot, like when Mother works on her conductivity experiments. I adjust my grip on the scythe and step away from the sheltering trees.

I have only moved a few paces into the meadow when my foot strikes something hard and ungiving. It makes a hollow noise. I kneel down in the grass and run my hands over it. A long rail, made of thick, sun-warmed metal. Several feet away, its twin runs parallel, with a neat pattern of heavy wood boards spanning the distance between the two. The rails stretch across the length of the meadow, and now I see a break in the trees on either side where someone has cleared all the growth to make a path for them. I run to the break. Farther off, on the next hill rise, I can make out the dark curve of the track disappearing over its crest.

A low howl fills the air, the same I heard before. My chest tightens with horror. A black cloud rises over the hill, cumulating and moving at terrifying speed, faster than I have ever known any beast to run. Beneath the screen of smoke, I make out a flash of dark metal glinting in the sun. It stretches in a sinuous trail over the top of the hill, like an asp or a millipede, gaining velocity as it drops toward the valley floor. The metal thing dips along the swale, then tilts its face toward me and begins to strain up the hill. It beats out a hollow rhythm, metal against metal, with a horrible, tooth-scraping grind between beats.

I drop my scythe and run back along the wooden path. The sound of the thing—is it animal or some kind of machine?—drowns out the slap of my sandals against the boards. The ground rumbles beneath my feet, growing to a constant tremor as the high howl and screech flood my ears, my mouth, my entire body. The noise fills everything. My heart shudders in time with the creature's unearthly growl, like a bell reverberating, and I throw myself from the path, into the high grass. I huddle, clutching the earth. The world is nothing but rattle, rock, clack, and moan. And then as suddenly as it came, I feel the thing pass. A rush of air sucks at me, leaving the grass swaying as the roar retreats into the distance.

I stand up. The air tastes acrid, like burning rock. I feel grimed. I run my hands over my hair and skin. A fine, gray dust has settled on my neck and arms, and through my hair. I spit and wipe my eyes. I stand mere feet from the track, and on the other side, there is a man. He wears a brown suit, cut in a simpler version of the style I saw on Aaron, and a domed hat I recognize from the book of drawings. A silky piece of fabric hangs in a knot at his throat. His face is older by far than my father's, more lined and baked by the sun. Drifts of gray hair sweep out from under his hat. But his eyes, those are brown and deep as a cistern.

"Ourania?" His voice sticks and comes out as a croak.

"Do I know you?" I call back. I can hear the waver in my own voice. I hurry forward until my feet meet the rail, then stand back a pace. Who knows if the metal creature might come ripping through the trees again?

He walks toward me and lifts his feet over the track without pause. We stand within a hand's breadth of each other, only the span of the metal rail separating us. I look up at him. I study the folds of flesh under his eyes and the creases at the corners of his mouth, the shape of his ears and the familiar, broad line of his nose. I know. Oh, help me, I know.

"Aaron." His name comes out of me in a rush of breath. I want to double over, for I feel as if something has knocked the air from my lungs. I hold out a hand to keep myself upright, and he catches it. He helps me over to a patch of low grass in the shade of the olive trees. I sit, hard. He kneels by me.

"I knew," he says. His eyes rim with wet. "I knew if I kept coming I would find you some day."

"Aaron." I lift my hand to touch his face. His skin feels thin and soft.

"What happened to you? I came to the meadow after seven days, and you weren't there, but I saw where you carved my name." My eyes flick across his face. I know of many stories my father tells, where a sorceress or some such casts a spell on a man to make him take a form other than his own.

"Have you been cursed?" I ask. "Who's done this to you? My mother, maybe she can fix you. She knows. . . . " I spy the sadness welling in Aaron's eyes and let my voice trail off.

"Ourania." He takes my hand and buries his face in it, kisses my work-rough palm. "I'm not cursed. I'm old, that's all. I've grown old, and you're still young, after all these years."

"Years!" I snatch my hand away. "It's only been weeks since I saw you, not even a season."

He shakes his head. "I came after seven days, and then another seven. I came every Sunday I could for fifty-two years. This is the first I've seen you."

My breath hitches and my vision clouds. I cover my face with my hands. The meadow air is too close.

"At first I thought you couldn't get away, and then I thought I'd gone mad. That I'd dreamed you altogether." He pulls my hands softly away from my face. The skin around his eyes crinkles as he smiles. "But you're here."

I feel a sob welling up in my chest. I try to tamp it down, but it breaks through anyway. Aaron holds me and we rock together in the dry grass.

"Take me away with you," I say, finally, pulling back from him. "I wanted to see where you came from, if the things in your book were real. I wanted you to show it to me." I pull the book from its place at my waist sash.

His mouth opens as he stares at it. He reaches out and brushes his fingers against its leather cover. "Like new," he says. He takes the book from me and begins paging through, turning each leaf faster and faster, until he reaches my drawing of the garden wall. He stops. Aaron traces his finger over the page, then closes the book. His face looks pale. He stands and hands the book back to me.

"Keep this," he says.

I scramble up after him. "It's yours," I say.

He shakes his head again. "I had forgotten all about it. But you," he says, touching his hand to my face again. "I can never forget you." He leans in to kiss me.

I close my eyes. Our lips touch and I see him as a young man, straight and unlined, untouched by age. I would gladly stand here until the sun sinks from the sky. I would gladly follow him to whatever strange land he would lead me, even if it means braving beasts of smoke and metal.

Aaron breaks away and steps back. "Thank you, Ourania." He turns and begins walking to the line of trees.

Time slows and crystallizes around me. I feel the pump of my own heart and the gentle sway of wind picking at the hem of my skirt. Aaron is walking away from me, but for the life of me, I cannot follow. He reaches the tree line and looks back. He smiles. Then passes through to the other side, and I see him no more.

In the quiet hour when the moon has put itself away, when my father sleeps and my mother wanders far, I gather my worldly possessions. Aaron's book with the pictures of my home inside, my folding knife, my mother's copy of Darwin, and the yards of white linen. I pack them away in a leather satchel. I loop a water bladder around my neck. I stow several days' rations of bread and dried meat, and open the cottage door onto the night. Our mouser watches with eyes glowing like two moons as I turn my feet to the road leading away from our door.

DEAD MAN'S RUN

ROBERT REED

ONE

The phone wakes him. Lucas snags it off the nightstand and clips it to the right side of his face. The caller has to be on the Allow list, so he opens the line. Lucas isn't great with numbers and even worse reading, but he has a genius for sounds, for voices. A certain kind of silence comes across. That's when he knows.

"When are we running?" the voice says.

"You're not running," Lucas says. "You're dead."

He hangs up.

Right away, Lucas feels sorry. Guilty, a little bit. But mostly pissed because he knows how this will play out.

The nightstand clock and phone agree. It's three minutes after five in the morning. What calls itself Wade Tanner is jumping hurdles right now, trying to slip back on the Allow list. That race can last ten seconds or ten minutes. Sleep won't happen till this conversation is done. But calling Wade's home number makes it look like Lucas wants to chat, which he doesn't. And that's why he tells his phone to give up the fight, letting every call through.

The ringing begins.

"You know what you need?" says a horny foreign-girl voice. "Fun."

Lucas hangs up and watches. A dozen calls beg to be answered. Two dozen. Obvious adult crap and beach-sale crap are flagged. He picks from what's left over, and a man says, "Don't hang up, I beg you." The accent is familiar and pleasant, making English sing. "I live in Goa and haven't money for air conditioning and food too. But I have a daughter, very pretty."

Lucas groans.

"And a little son," the voice says, breaking at the edges. "Do you know despair, my friend? Do you understand what a father will do to save his precious blood?"

Lucas hangs up and picks again.

The silence returns, that weird nothing. And again, what isn't Wade says, "What time are we running?"

"Seven o'clock," Lucas says.

"From the Y?"

"Sure." Lucas has a raspy voice that always seems a little loud, rolling out of the wide, expressive mouth. Sun and wind can be rough on runners, but worse enemies have beaten up his face. The bright brown eyes never stop jumping. The long black hair is graying and growing thin up high. But the forty-year-old body is supremely fit—broad shoulders squared up, the deep chest and narrow trunk sporting a pair of exceptionally long legs.

"Are you running with us?" says Wade.

"Yeah." Lucas sits up in bed, the cold dark grabbing him.

"Who else is coming?"

Whenever Wade talks, other sounds flow in. It feels as if the dead man is sitting in a big busy room, everybody else trying to be quiet while he chats. That's how Lucas pictures things: Too many people pushed together, wanting to be quiet but needing to whisper, to breathe.

Wade says, "Who else?"

"Everybody, I guess."

"Good."

"Yeah, but I need to sleep now."

"Sleep's overrated," says Wade.

"Most things are."

The voice laughs. It used to be crazy, hearing that laugh. And now it's nothing but normal.

"So I'll leave you alone," says Wade. "Besides, I've got other calls to make."

And again, that perfect nothing comes raining back. The sound the world makes when it isn't saying anything.

Lucas can't sleep, but he can always drink coffee.

By six-thirty, an entire pot is in his belly and his blood. Fifty-two degrees inside the house, and he's wearing the heavy polypro top and blue windbreaker and black tights, all showing their years. But the shoes are mostly new. On the kitchen television, Steve McQueen chases middle-aged hit men instead of doing what makes sense, which is scrogging Jacqueline Bisset. McQueen drives, and Lucas cleans the coffee machine and counter and the Boston Marathon '17 cup. A commercial comes on—another relief plea—and Lucas turns it off in mid-misery. Then he drops the thermostat five degrees and puts on clean butcher gloves and the wool mittens that he's had for fifteen years. The headband slides around his neck and he pulls on the black stocking cap that still smells like mothballs. His pack waits beside the back door, ready to go. He straps it on, leaving only one more ritual—throwing his right foot on a stool and twisting the fancy bracelet so it rides comfortably on the bare ankle, tasting flesh, telling the world that he is sober.

The outside air is frigid and blustery. Lucas trots down the driveway and turns into the wind. Arms swing easy, lending momentum to a stride that needs no help. Even slow, Lucas looks swift. Every coach dreams of discovering a talent like his—this marriage of strength, grace, and blood-born endurance. Set a mug of beer on that head and not a drop splashes free. The stride is that smooth, that elegant. That fine. But biology demands that a brain has to inhabit that perfect body, and there's more than one way to drain a damn mug of beer.

A person doesn't have to read the news to know the news.

Two sets of sirens are wailing in the distance, chasing different troubles. Potholes and slumping slabs make the street interesting, and half of the streetlights have had their bulbs pulled, saving the city cash and keeping a few lumps of coal from being burned. Every house is dark and sleepy, stuffed full of insulation and outfitted with wood-burning stoves. Most yards have gardens and compost piles and rain barrels. Half the roofs are dressed in solar panels. When Lucas moved into his house, big locusts and pin oaks lined the street. But most of those trees have been chopped down for fuel and to let the sun feed houses and gardens. Then the lumberjacks planted baby trees—carbon patriots lured by the tax gimmicks—except the biggest of those trees are already being sacrificed for a few nights of smoky heat.

You don't have to travel the world to know what's happening.

The last house on the block is the Florida compound. Those immigrants rolled in a couple years ago, boasting about their fat savings and their genius, sports-hero kids. But there aren't any jobs outside the Internet and grunt work in the windmill fields, and savings never last as long as you wish. Their big cars got dumped on the Feds during an efficiency scheme. Extra furniture and jewelry were sold to make rent. A cigarette boat and trailer were given FOR SALE signs to wear, and they're still wearing them, sitting on the driveway where they've been parked forever. Then came the relatives from Miami begging for room, and that's when police started getting calls about drinking and fighting, and then a couple of the sports heroes were jailed for trafficking. Then it was official: These were refugees, and not even high-end refugees anymore.

Cheeks ache when Lucas runs at the wind, but nothing else. Turning west, the world warms ten degrees. In the dark it's best to keep to the middle of the street, watching for anything that can trip or chase. People will abandon family and homes on drowning beaches, but not their pit bull and wolf-mutts. It's also smart to run with your phone off, but Lucas is better than most when it comes to handling two worlds at once. His piece of Finland is a sweet little unit powered by movement, by life. A tidy projection hangs in front of his right eye. He's ignoring the screen for the moment, running the street with the imaginary dogs, and that's when the ringing starts.

"Yeah?"

"You leave yet?" Wade says.

"Nope, still sitting," says Lucas. "Drinking coffee, watching dead people on TV."

That wins a laugh. "According to GPS, you're running. An eight-minute pace, which is knuckle-walking for you."

"Do the cops know?" says Lucas.

"Know what?"

"That you're borrowing their tracking system."

"Why? You going to turn me in?"

No, but that's when Lucas cuts the line, and an old anger comes back, making his legs fly for the next couple blocks.

Bodies stand outside the downtown YMCA. Swimmers and weightlifters sport Arctic-ready coats, while the runners are narrower, colder souls wearing nylon and polypro. Gym bags clutter up the sidewalk. Every back is turned to the wind. When someone breathes or speaks, twists of vapor rise, illuminated by the bluish glare escaping from the Y's glass door.

Lucas slows.

A growly voice says, "Somebody got the early jump."

Passing from the trot into a purposeful walk, Lucas looks at faces, smiling at Audrey before anybody else.

"Where's your bike?" the voice asks.

"Pete," says Audrey. "Just stop."

But the temptation is too great. With amiable menace, Pete Kajan says, "Did the cops take your bike too?"

"Yeah," says Lucas. "My bike and skates and my skis. I had that pony, but they shot him. Just to be safe."

Everybody laughs at the comeback, including Pete.

Lucas slips off the pack and shakes his arms. The straps put his fingers to sleep.

"Seven o'clock," Pete says, shaking one of the locked doors. "What are the big dogs doing today?"

"Sitting on the porch, whining," Lucas says.

Runners laugh.

"How far?" Audrey says.

Pete says, "Twelve, maybe fourteen."

"Fourteen sounds right," says Doug Gatlin. Fast Doug. He's older than the rest of them but blessed with a whippet's body.

Doug Crouse is the youngest and heaviest. "Ten miles sounds better," he says.

"Sarah and Masters are coming," says Fast Doug.

"They wish," says Pete, laughing.

Rolling his eyes, Gatlin tells Crouse, "They'll meet us here and turn early. You can come back with them."

"Where's Varner?" Crouse says.

Pete snorts. "He'll be five minutes late and need to dump."

Runners laugh.

Then a big-shouldered swimmer rattles the locked door.

Crouse looks at Lucas. "Did he call you?"

"Yeah."

"He called me twice," Gatlin says.

"Everybody got at least one wake-up call," Pete says.

The runners stare into the bright empty lobby.

"He usually doesn't bother me," says Crouse.

"A bad night in heaven," Lucas says.

People try to hit the proper amount of laughter. Show it's funny, but nothing too enthusiastic.

Then the swimmer backs away from the door. "Dean's here," she says.

Dean is a tall, fleshy fellow who does everything with deliberation. He slowly walks the length of the lobby. As if disarming a bomb, he eases the key into the lock. The door weighs a thousand pounds, judging by its syrupy motion. With a small soft voice, Dean says, "Cold enough?"

Muttered replies make little threads of steam.

A line forms in the lobby. Audrey puts herself beside Lucas. "You think that's it? He had a bad night?"

"I'm no thinker," Lucas says. "If I get my shoes on in the morning, it's going to be a good day."

TWO

Fingers and thumbs are offered at the front desk, proving membership. A red sign warns patrons to take only one towel, but a Y towel can't dry a kitten. Lucas grabs two, Pete three. The Dougs lead the way up narrow, zigzagging stairs. Signs caution about paint that dried last week and forbid unaccompanied boy s in the men's locker room. At the top of the stairs, taped to a steel door, a fresh notice says there isn't any hot water, due to boiler troubles. Gatlin flips light switches. The room revealed is narrow and long, jammed with gray lockers and concrete pillars painted yellow. The carpet is gray-green and tired. Toilet cleansers and spilled aftershave give the air flavor. Bulletin boards are sprinkled with news about yoga classes and winter conditioning programs and words about winning at life. Questionable behavior must be reported to the front desk. Used towels are to be thrown into the proper bins. Lockers need to be locked. The YMC A is never responsible for stolen property. But leave your padlock overnight on a day locker, and it will be cut off and your belongings will be confiscated.

THIS IS YOUR YMCA, a final sign says.

Pete rents a locker in back. Lucas camps nearby. From the adjacent aisle, Gatlin says, "What's the course? Anybody know?"

"I know," Pete says, and that's all he says. In his early forties, he has short graying hair and a sturdy face. He glowers easily, the eyes a bright, thoughtful hazel. Pete doesn't look like a runner, but when motivated and healthy, the man can still hang with the local best.

Lucas digs out his lock, dumps his pack, and secures the door. Again, he puts his foot on the stool, adjusting the ankle monitor. Water sounds good, but the Freon was bled from the fountains, saving energy. It's better to run the cold tap at a sink and make a bowl with your hands, wasting a couple gallons before your thirst is beaten back. The paper towels are tiny. He pulls five and dries his hands, watching an old guy plug in an old television that can't remember yesterday. The machine has to cycle through channels, reprogramming its little brain. That's when Lucas starts to feel the coffee. The urinal is already full of dark piss but won't flush until the smell is bad enough. He comes back out to find the Big Fox playing. A blonde beauty is chatting about the cold snap cutting into the heart of the country. "We have an old-fashioned winter," she says, leading to thirty seconds of snow and sleds and happy red-faced kids.

"Well, that's not me," says the old guy.

Then the news jumps to places Lucas couldn't find on any map. Brown people are fighting over burning oil wells. Skinny black folks are marching across a dried-up lake. A fat white man with an accent makes noise about his rights and how he doesn't appreciate being second class. Then it's down to Pine Island and the wicked long Antarctic summer. Another slab of glacier is charging out to sea, looking exactly like the other ten thousand. But the blonde gal is a trouper. Refusing to be sad, she reminds her audience that some experts claim the cold meltwater is going to shut down this nastiness. More sexy than scientific, she says, "The oceans around the ice sheets will cool, and a new normal will emerge. Then we can get back to the business of ordinary life."

"Well, that's good news," says the old guy, throwing out a pissy laugh as he starts hunting for better channels.

Pete and the Dougs have vanished. Lucas starts for the stairs and the steel door bangs open. In comes Varner, still wearing street clothes.

"I'll be there. Got to hit the toilet first."

The man is in his middle-thirties, red-haired and freckled and always late. Lucas gives him a look.

"What? It's two minutes after seven."

"I didn't say anything."

"Yeah, well. Our ghost already called me three times, telling me to hurry the hell up."

Lucas retreats downstairs. Audrey stands in the lobby, reading *The Herald* on the public monitor. She's tall for an elite runner—nearly five nine—but unlike most fast girls doesn't live two snacks clear of starvation. Her face is strong but pretty, blonde hair cut close, middle age lurking around the pale brown eyes. She wears silver tights and a black wind-breaker, mittens and a headband piled on the countertop. Audrey always looks calm and rested. Running is something she does well, but if nobody showed this morning, she'd probably trot an easy eight and call it good.

"Where are the boys?" Lucas says.

"Around the corner."

"Any news about me?"

She blanks the screen and turns. "Where's your bike?"

"Too cold to pedal."

"If you need a ride, call."

"I should," he says.

With a burst of wind, the front door opens.

Ethan Masters walks out of a sportswear catalog and into the YMCA. Jacket and tights are matched blue with artful white stripes, the Nikes just came from the box, his gloves and stocking cap are carved from fresh snow, and the water belt carries provisions for a hundred-mile slog. But the biggest fashion statement is the sleek glasses covering the middle of a lean, thoroughly shaved face. More computing power rides his nose than NASA deployed during the twentieth century. The machine is a phone and entertainment center. Masters always knows his pulse and electrolyte levels and where he is and how fast he's moving. It must be a disappointment, falling back on old-fashioned eyes to tell him what's inside the lobby. "They're still here," he says. "I told you we'd make it in time."

Sarah follows him indoors. As short as Masters is tall, she has this round little-girl face and long brown hair tied in a ponytail. Unlike her training partner, she prefers old sweats and patched pink mittens, and her brown stocking cap looks rescued from the gutter. They are married, but not to each other—ten thousand miles logged together and the subjects of a lot of rich gossip.

"Are you everybody?" says Masters, throwing himself against a wall, stretching calves. "If we wait, we'll tighten up."

"Varner just went upstairs," Audrey says.

"So we're not leaving soon," says Masters.

Sarah is quiet. Flicking her eyes, she places a call and walks to the back of the lobby.

Lucas follows and walks past her, rounding the corner. Behind the lobby is a long narrow room overlooking the swimming pool. Treadmills and ellipticals push against the glass wall. Pete and the Dougs are yabbering with some overdressed, undertrained runners who belong to the marathon clinic. Which means they belong to the bald man sitting alone beside the Gatorade machine.

"How far, Coach?" Lucas says.

The man looks up. Cheery as an elf, he says, "We're doing an easy sixteen." As if sixteen were nothing. As if he's making the run himself. Except Coach Able is dressed for driving and maybe, if pressed, a quick stand on some protected street corner. Deep in his fifties, he carries a bad back as well as quite a lot of fat. And for thirty years he has been the running coach at Jewel College, his clinic something of a spring tradition for new runners.

Able gives Lucas a long study. He always does. And he always has a few coachy words to throw out for free.

"It looks like you're running heavy miles," he says.

"Probably so," Lucas says.

"Speed work?"

"When I remember to."

"Try the marathon this year. See if there's life in those old legs."

"Maybe I will." Lucas looks at the other runners. A man with an accent is talking about the weather, about how it was never so cold in Louisiana. Pete shakes his head, a big snarly voice saying, "So grow some fins and swim yourself back home again."

Somehow he can say words like that, and everybody finds it funny.

The coach coughs—a hard wet bark meant to win attention. "Tell me, Pepper. In your life, have you ever tried running a marathon hard? Train for it and push it and see what happens?"

"Well now, that sure sounds like work."

"I think you could beat 2:30," says Able. "And who knows how fast, if you managed a full year without misbehaving."

Lucas rolls his shoulders, saying nothing.

"There's software," the coach says. "And biometric tests. With race results, we'd be able to figure out exactly what you would have run in your prime. 2:13 is my guess. Wouldn't it be nice to know?"

"That would be nice," says Lucas. Then he shrugs again, saying, "But like my dad used to say, 'There's not enough room in the world for all the things that happen to be nice.'"

Audrey appears. "We've got our Varner."

Lucas and the other men put on stocking caps and follow. Eight bodies bunch up at the front door. The sun is coming, but not yet. Everybody wears a phone, and with tiny practiced touches, they adjust the settings. Only hair-on-fire emergency calls can interrupt now. Then the group puts on mittens and gloves and steps outside. Giving a horse-snort, Masters says, "We should run north."

"We're not," says Pete. "We're doing Ash Creek."

Everybody is surprised.

"But you want to start into the wind," Masters says. "Otherwise you'll come home wet and cold."

"There's not two damn trees up north," Pete says. "I'm going where there's woods and scenery."

"What about the usual?" Varner says.

They have a looping course through the heart of town.

"Normal is fine with me," Audrey says.

Lucas wants to move. Directions don't matter.

Then Pete says, "We've got company."

Trotting across the street is a kid half their age. Dressed in street clothes and a good new coat, Harris carries a huge gym bag in one hand. "Which way?" he says. "I'll catch up."

Pete says, "The usual." No hesitation.

"East around Jewel?" says Harris.

"Sure."

The kid scampers inside.

Then Pete gives everybody a hard stare. "Okay, we're doing Ash Creek. No arguments."

Eight liars trot west, nobody talking, the tiniest guilt following at their heels.

THREE

Tuesday meant speed work at the college track—a faded orange ribbon of crumbling foam and rutted lanes. Lucas showed last. It wasn't as hot as most August evenings, but last night's storm had left the air thick and dangerous. The rest of the group trotted on the far side of the track. Nobody was talking. Lucas parked his bike and came through the zigzag gate, and he crossed the track and football field and the track again, walking under the visitors' stands. Pigeons panicked and flew off, leaving feathers and echoes. He opened his pack and stripped, dressing in shorts and Asics but leaving his singlet in the bag. He was packing up when he noticed his hands shaking, and he stared at the hands until his phone broke the spell.

He opened the line.

"Are you up at the track?"

Wade's voice. "I am."

"Do you see me?"

"Wade?"

"I haven't been updated, "the voice said. "It's been twenty-four hours. I'm supposed to call you after twenty-four hours."

Lucas stepped out from under the seats. "Who is this?"

"Wade Tanner kept an avatar. A backup."

"I know that."

"I'm the backup, Lucas."

The group shuffled through the south turn, and Wade wasn't any of them. "Did you try the store?" Lucas said.

"No, because you're at the top of the list," the backup said. "One day passes without an update, and I'm supposed to contact you first."

"Me."

"You live close and you know where the spare key is. We want you to search the house." The voice went away and then came back. "I've studied the odds. Check the shower. Showers are treacherous places."

Walking across the brown grass, Lucas started to laugh. Nothing was funny, but laughing felt right.

"What's your workout tonight?" said the voice.

"Don't know."

"It's humid," the backup said. "Do quarters and walk half a lap before going again. Take a break after six, and quit if you forget how to count."

It could have been the real Wade. "You sound just like him."

"That's how it works." Then, after a pause, the backup said, "I've got this bad feeling, Lucas."

"Why's that?"

"I'm voicemail, too. And people have been calling all day. Nobody knows where Wade is."

Lucas said nothing.

"You'll check the house?"

"Soon as I'm done running quarters."

"Thanks, buddy."

The line fell silent.

Most of the people were sharing the same patch of shade. Audrey was walking back and forth on the track, talking on the phone. Only Gatlin and Wade were missing. The new kid jumped toward Lucas, saying, "Are we running or not?"

"Leave him alone," Pete said. "Our boy put in a rough weekend."

Harris had a big sandpaper laugh. "I was at the party. Yeah, I saw him drinking."

People looked away, embarrassed for Lucas.

"I've known a few drinkers," the kid said. "But I never, ever saw anybody drain away that much of anything."

Lucas looked past him. "Anybody see Wade?"

"Bastard's late," Pete said.

The others said, "No," or shook their heads. Except for Harris, who just kept grinning and staring at Lucas.

Lucas needed a breath. "Wade's backup just called me. It hasn't heard from him, and it's worried."

"Why would the backup call you?" Sarah said.

Lucas shrugged, saying nothing.

"Wade has an avatar?" said Harris.

"He does," Masters said. "In fact, I helped him set it up."

Lucas waved a hand, bringing eyes back to him. "I know what they are," he said. "Except I don't know anything about them."

Masters stepped into the sunshine, his glasses turning black. With his know-everything voice, he said, "They're basically just personal records. Data you want protected, kept in hardened server farms. They have your financial records, video records. Diaries and running logs and whatever else you care about. You can even model your personality and voice, coming up with a pretty good stand-in."

"Wade has been doing this for years," Sarah said.

People turned to her, waiting.

Quiet little Sarah smiled, nervous with the attention. "Don't you know? He records everything he does, every day. He says it helps at the store, letting him know each of his customers. He even leaves his phone camera running, recording everything he sees and hears to be uploaded later."

"That's anal," Crouse said.

"Who's anal?" said Audrey, walking into the conversation.

"Storing that much video is expensive," Harris said. "How can a shoe salesman afford a cashmere backup?"

"That shoe salesman had rich parents," Pete said. "And they were kind enough to die young."

With that, the group fell silent.

Lucas approached Audrey. "Was it Wade's backup on the phone?"

"No. Just my husband."

Harris got between them. "Let's run," he said.

"Not in the mood," Lucas said.

The kid looked at everybody, and then he was laughing at Lucas. "So what happened to you? You were drinking everything at the party . . . and then you just sort of vanished—"

"He had an appointment," Pete said.

"What appointment?"

Pete shook his head. "With the police."

Audrey wasn't happy. "Everybody, just stop. Quit it."

Masters was talking to Sarah. "How do you know so much about Wade's backup?" he said.

Sarah shrugged and smiled. "I just know."

Masters ate on that. Then he turned to Lucas, saying, "The call was a glitch. Wade didn't get things uploaded last night, and it triggered the warning system. That's all."

Lucas nodded, wanting to believe it.

"Let's just run," Harris said.

"Is this how they do things in Utah?" Pete said. "Pester people till you get what you want?"

"Sometimes." The kid showed up at the track six weeks ago—a refugee running away from drought and forest fires. Harris liked to talk. He told everybody that he was going out on the prairie and build windmills. Except of course he didn't know anything about anything useful. His main talent was a pair of long strong and very young legs, and there were sunny looks and a big smile that was charming for two minutes, tops.

"I'm running," he said, smiling hard. Then he walked to the inside lane.

Others started to follow.

Not Lucas.

A little BMW pulled off the road and Gatlin got out. He wasn't dressed to run. A fifty-year-old man with wavy gray hair, he looked nothing but respectable in a summer suit and tie. Coming through the zigzag, he moved slowly, one hand always holding the chain-link. He seemed sad, and then the sadness fell into something darker. And with little steps, he walked toward the others.

"Well, now we've got to stop talking about you," said Pete.

Gatlin's mouth was open, a lost look passing through his dark brown eyes. "I just got a call," he said. "From a friend in the mayor's office. He thought I'd want to know. Kids playing near Ash Creek found a body this morning. And the police think they recognize the man."

"Wade Tanner," said Lucas.

Surprised, Gatlin straightened his back. "How did you know?"

"We had a hint," said Pete, and then he couldn't talk anymore.

Nobody was talking. Nobody reacted or moved, except for Gatlin who was embarrassed to have his awful news stolen from him. Besides the wind, the only sound was a soft low moan rising from nowhere.

Then Sarah closed her mouth and the moaning stopped.

Downtown fights to wake up. City buses roll past on their way to still-empty stops. Bank tellers move through darkened lobbies while bank machines count piles of electronic money. Apartment lights come on, but the hotels have never been dark, filled with anxious refugees living on the government plan. A pair of long-haul boxes point in opposite directions, burning soybean juice to keep sleeping travelers warm. Out from the bus station comes a bearded man wearing a fine suit and carrying an I-tablet. Except the suit is filthy, both knees looking like they have been dragged through grease, and the tablet is dead, and talking in a loud crazed voice, he says, "Stop being proud. Accept Satan as our leader, and let's build a clean, efficient Hell."

The pace lifts, the group crossing into the old warehouse district. Concrete turns to cobblestone and black scabs of asphalt. Low brick buildings have been reborn as bars and pawnshops and coffee shops, plus one little store dedicated to runners. Dropping to the floodplain, the street ends with a massive stone building from the nineteenth century. In one form or another, this place has always served as the city's train station. Half a dozen travelers are waiting with their luggage, hoping for the morning westbound, and the little boy in the group gives the runners a big wave, saying, "Hey there. Hi."

Nobody talks. The group turns south, gloom following them into Germantown. Warehouses give way to little houses, and they turn right, pointed west again, and the pace lifts another notch.

"Slow down," says Pete.

Nobody listens. Runners and the street cross an abandoned set of railroad tracks. Little twists of vapor mark their breathing, shoes slapping at the pavement. Then comes the Amtrak line, and that's when the houses start to wear down. Cars sporting out-of-state plates are parked on brown lawns. A solitary drunk stands at a corner, calmly waiting for the race to pass before he staggers a little closer to what might be home. The final house has been reborn as a church, its walls painted candy colors and with holy words written in Vietnamese. That's where the street ends. A barbed-wire fence breaks where a thin trail snakes up through flattened prairie grass. The sky is dawn-blue with a few clouds. And somebody is running on top of the levee: A narrow male with tall legs and long arms carried high. It's a pretty stride. Not Lucas-pretty, but efficient. Strong. The man's legs are bare and pale. He wears a long-sleeved T-shirt, gray and tight, and maybe a second layer underneath. White butcher gloves cover big hands, and riding the head is a black baseball cap set backward, the brim tucked low over the long neck.

As if their legs have been cut out from under them, people stumble to a halt.

"What's he doing here?" says Sarah.

Crouse is first to say, "Jaeger."

Normally easygoing, almost sweet, Slow Doug puts on a sour face and says, "That prick."

"What is he doing?" Masters says.

"Running, by the looks of it," says Pete.

Jaeger is cruising south on the levee road, heading upstream. The other runners stand in shadow, but he is lit up by the dawn, his gaze fixed straight ahead, the sharp face showing in profile.

"So what?" says Audrey. "We'll just run the other way."

"I'm not," says Pete.

People glance at each other, saying nothing.

Starting toward the fence and trail, Pete says, "I don't change plans for murdering assholes."

Gatlin and Varner fall in behind him.

Lucas turns to Audrey. "Want to go back?"

She pulls off her hat and a mitten, running her hand through her short, short hair. "Maybe."

"We can't just stand here," says Masters.

"I'm not turning around," says Sarah, short legs working, the ponytail jumping and swishing.

Crouse trots after her. Then Audrey sighs and says, "I guess," and catches them before the fence.

"This is stupid," says Masters. But then he starts chasing.

Lucas stands motionless. Nobody can run out of sight on him, except Jaeger. Maybe. He has time to pull off a mitten and wipe his mouth, ice already clinging to his little beard. Then he touches his phone to wake it, pulling up the familiar number with an eye and placing his call.

"How's the run going?" says Wade.

Lucas doesn't talk.

"I see where you are," Wade says. "Are we running the creek today?"

"We're supposed to."

"So why aren't you moving, Lucas?"

"Jaeger's up ahead."

There is a pause, a long breath of nothing before the voice returns. "You know what I want," Wade says. "I told you what I want. Find out who killed me, okay?"

FOUR

Wade was five days dead.

The heat and drought had returned, and the Saturday group met long before the Y opened. Standing in the broiling darkness, they said very little. Even Harris was playing the silent monk. One minute after six they took off to the east, aiming for Jewel College. Harris grabbed the lead, Lucas claimed the empty ground between him and the pack. Then Crouse put on a surge, catching Lucas. "Have you tried Wade's number?"

"Why would I?"

"Maybe you're curious," Crouse said.

"Not usually," said Lucas.

"Well, you can't get through. Voice mail answers, but even if you leave a message, the backup can't call you back."

"Why not?"

"He's evidence," Crouse said. "And maybe he's a witness. That's why they've got him bottled up."

"I forgot. You're a cop."

"No." The man hesitates, laughs. "But remember my sister-in-law?"

"The gal with black hair and that big bouncy ass," Lucas said.

"She's a police officer."

"That too."

"Anyway, she's got this habit. She has to tell my wife everything."

"Okay. Now I'm curious."

Crouse was running hard. Whenever he talked, he first had to gather up enough air. "Wade ran for Jewel."

Lucas glanced at him. "Everybody knows that."

"Came here on a scholarship. Able recruited him. Wade was the big star for the first year. Then this other guy showed."

"Carl Jaeger," said Lucas.

"You probably know the whole story," said Crouse, disappointed.

"Wade told it a couple times. Every day."

"Know where the coach found Jaeger?"

"In Chicago, in rehab. There were legal hoops, getting him out from under some old charges. But the kid had ruled Illinois during high school, and that's why Able brought him here. He wanted Jaeger to be his big dog, to help put Jewel on the map."

Crouse nodded, fighting to hold the pace.

Lucas slowed. "You're new to this group. You didn't know. But Wade and Jaeger never liked each other."

"What about the girl?" Crouse said.

Lucas said, "Yeah." But then he realized that he didn't know what they were talking about. "What girl?"

"Wade's girlfriend in college. Jaeger got her. Stole her and got her pregnant and even married her for a couple years."

"What's her name?" Lucas said.

"I don't know. I didn't hear that part. But the virtual Wade remembers everything." Crouse was happy, finding something fresh to offer. "The police department brought in specialists to sort through the files, the software. The AI business. The technology's been around for a few years, but the experts haven't seen a backup with this much information."

"That's Wade," said Lucas. "Mr. Detail."

"He kept training logs," said Crouse.

"Some of us do."

"You?"

"Never."

Crouse found fresh speed in his legs. "Wade's logs are different. They reach back to the day he started running, when he was eight. And there's a lot more than miles and times buried in them."

"Like what?"

"Sleep. Dreams. Breakfasts. And what he and his friends talked about during the run—word for word, sometimes. And he spends a lot of file space hating Carl Jaeger."

The girl news was unexpected. Lucas thought about it for a minute. Then he said, "So what's happening? Are the cops looking at Carl?"

"Oh, I'm not saying like that," said Crouse, reaching that point where his legs were shaky-weak. "I just thought you'd be interested in what's happening. That's all."

Runners are strung out along the levee. On the left little houses turn into body shops and junkyards and a sad pair of gray-white grain elevators. Ash Creek runs on their right, the channel gouged deep and straight and shouldered with pale limestone boulders. Fresh thin ice covers the shallow water. Pete and Gatlin run in front, Varner tucked into their slipstream. Snatches of angry conversation drift back. With a big arm, Pete points toward Jaeger. He curses, and Gatlin glances back at the others. Then the leaders slow, forcing the others to drift closer.

"I can't believe this," Masters says. "Why would the man run this course?"

"He likes the route," Lucas says, his legs deciding to leap ahead, quick feet kicking back gravel.

Crouse hears the stride coming. "Hey, Lucas, "he says. And a moment later, he is passed.

The women are shoulder to shoulder. Audrey says a few words, laughing alone. Then she looks back at Lucas, her smile working. "What are those boys proving?"

"Don't know," Lucas says.

Audrey says, "Men," and laughs again.

Lucas runs on the grass beside them. Pete is forty yards ahead and surging, body tilting and arms churning. Nobody in that trio talks, every whisper of oxygen saved for the legs.

"Look at them," says Audrey.

"What about them?" Sarah says, her voice small and tight.

"They won't catch Carl," says Audrey.

"The man was in jail," Sarah says. "For months."

Audrey's face stiffens. "We're talking about Carl. There's no way they can close that gap."

Jaeger's legs and lungs are almost lost in the sunshine. But he isn't increasing his lead. Maybe he's starting out on a lazy twenty and holding back. Or he knows they're following him, and he just wants a little fun.

Lucas glances at Audrey.

"You don't have to chase," she says, her voice sharp.

He surges.

"Please, Lucas. Be careful."

The man who sold shoes to every athlete in town was lying inside a closed box, waiting to be set into the ground, and the church was full of skinny people and beefy old friends, with a few distant relatives sitting up front, hoping for a piece of the Wade pie. Everybody made sorry sounds about the circumstances. Every male tried to spot the ex-girlfriends in the audience. Wade was no beauty, but he had a genius for pretty girls who fell for charm and little hints of marriage. There were maybe a dozen exes in the crowd, some crying for what had happened and others for what hadn't. Lucas and Pete were pallbearers. They served with cousins and college buddies who didn't know them from a can of paint. It was a cousin who mentioned that the cops were done with the backup. He said anybody could call the machine and it was almost fun, talking to a voice that remembered when you were ten years old and sitting together at Thanksgiving, watching relatives get drunk and funny.

Lucas did call Wade's old number. But not right away and only twice and both times was surprised by the busy signal. Then he tried after midnight and got thrown straight into voicemail. Which pissed him off. Not that he was hungry for this chat, but it was sure to happen and why did things have to be so difficult?

His phone rang during next morning's coffee. "You know what surprises me? It's the strangers who read an obit and think it's neat, calling you for no reason but to chat. And it's not just local voices either. This is the big new hobby, I'm learning. Dial the afterlife. Listen to a ghost telling stories."

"How you doing?" Lucas said.

The backup said, "I'm busy. And that's a good thing."

"What's 'busy' mean?"

"Well, I'm running again. For instance."

"How do you do that?"

"I've got video files, and I've built all of our favorite courses. The hills, the effort levels. How my body responds to perceived workouts. I can change the weather however I want it. You'd be amazed how real it looks and feels. And the food here doesn't taste too wrong. Of course the sense of smell needs work, but that's probably good news. When it's polypro season."

Then Wade stopped talking, forcing Lucas to react. "Is that why I'm getting busy signals? You're making new friends?"

"And talking to people you know."

"But you're fast. Computers are. Why can't you yabber to a thousand mouths at once?"

"Some of my functions are fast. Scary fast, sure. But right now, talking to you, my AI software has to work flat out just to keep up." Part of the software made lung noises. Wade took a pretend breath, and then he said, "I still need sleep, by the way. Which is why I didn't pick up last night."

Lucas didn't talk.

"So tell me, Lucas. In your head, what am I? A machine, a program, or a man?"

"I don't know."

"Actually, I'm none of those things."

"Because you're a ghost."

The laughter rattled on. "No, no. In the eyes of the law, I'm an intellectual foundation. That's a new kind of trust reserved for backups. I've been registered with a friendly nation that has some very compassionate laws, and to maintain my sentient status, I have to keep enough money in the local bank."

Lucas said nothing.

The silence ended with a big sigh. Then the intellectual foundation said, "So, Lucas? Do you have any idea who killed me?"

A little too quickly, Lucas said, "No."

Another pause. Then Wade said, "It was a nice funeral."

"You watched?"

"Several people streamed it to me. You did a nice job, Lucas."

It was peculiar, how much those words mattered. Lucas took his own breath, real and deep, and then he said, "You know, I am sober."

"What's that?"

"Since the party, I haven't had a taste."

Uncomfortable sighs kept the silence away. Then a tight quick voice said, "Tell me that in another year. Tell it to me thirty years from today. A couple weeks without being shit-faced? I think it's early to start calling that good news."

The lead pack works, but Lucas catches them easily. Legs eat the distance, the lungs blow themselves clean, and he tucks in behind Pete, shortening his stride and measuring their bodies. Nobody talks, but the men trade looks and the group slows, making ready for the next miserable surge.

The levee curls west toward the bypass and dives under the bridge. Jaeger has vanished. He isn't below, and he's not up on the highway either. They follow the levee road down, gravel replaced with pale frozen clay. The air turns colder, tasting like wet concrete. Water sounds bounce off the underside of the bridge. Then the road yanks left and starts a long climb.

Jaeger is above them, and then he is gone.

Pete curses. Sweat bleeds through his windbreaker and freezes, a little white forest growing on his back.

Topping the levee, they hold their effort, gaining speed on the flat. But the road is empty. Except nodding brown grass, nothing moves, and there isn't anybody to chase.

The pack slows.

"Look," Varner says. "That pipe."

The sewer pipe is fat and black, jutting out of the levee's shoulder, a thin trickle of oily runoff dripping. Jaeger stands on the pipe, facing the stream. With his shorts yanked down, he holds himself with both hands, aiming long, urine splashing in the oil.

Pete pulls up. The rest of the group stops behind him, watching. Then Jaeger turns toward them and shakes himself dry before yanking up his underwear and then the shorts.

"Let's please turn," says Audrey.

No one else talks.

Jaeger climbs back to the road, watching them.

"Hey, asshole," says Pete. "Hey."

The last months have taken a toll. Jaeger's face remains lean, but wrinkles have worked into his features. The short black hair shows white. He breathes harder than normal. Forty-three years old, and for the first time anyone can recall, he looks his age.

"I don't like this," says Masters.

Pete laughs. "What are you worried about?"

Jaeger's body turns away, but not his face.

"There's eight of us," says Pete.

"What's that mean?" Crouse says.

"Depends," Pete says, his bulldog face challenging them. "We're here, and that man is standing over there. And he beat our friend to death with a chunk of concrete."

Jaeger starts running, the first strides short.

Audrey shakes her head. "What are we doing?"

Sarah knows.

"We're just following the man," Sarah says, her voice slow and furious. "Jaeger can't be in great shape. But we are. So we'll keep close and talk to him, and maybe he'll say something true."

FIVE

Lucas rode to the airport, the chain clicking. A gray-haired woman handed him the entry form, and he filled in the blanks slowly, paying the late fee with two twenties. Then he pinned the race number to his shorts and strapped the chip to his right shoe, and the new T-shirt ended up tied beneath the seat of his bike.

The pre-race mood was quiet, grim. Conversations were brief. Race-day rituals were performed with sluggish discipline. The normally bouncy voice on the PA system growled at the world, warning that only twenty minutes were left until the gun. Bikes don't get bodies ready to run. Lucas started running easy through the mostly empty parking lots, past a terminal that looked pretty much shut down, and that's when a tall man stepped from behind an Alleycat Dumpster.

"Pepper."

Lucas nodded, lifting one hand.

Jaeger fell in beside him. He was wearing racing flats and shorts and a White Sox cap twisted around on his head. Saying nothing, he ran Lucas back to his bike, watching him strip the shirt he wore from home and then tie it to the frame.

"Lose your car?" he said.

"I know where it is."

"Got fancy jewelry on that ankle, I see."

Lucas lifted his foot and put it down again. "Jealous?"

"Jail time?"

"If I drink."

"With your record? They should keep you in a cage for a year."

"The jail's full." Lucas shrugged. "And besides, the case wasn't strong."

"No?"

"Maybe I wasn't driving." Shame forced his gaze to drop. "Somebody called the hotline, but it was a busy night. One cop spotted my car and flashed her lights, and my car pulled up and a white male galloped off between the houses."

"That cop chase after the driver?"

"On foot, but she couldn't hang on."

"I bet not," Jaeger said, laughing.

"A second cruiser found me half a mile away, while he was investigating a burglary. Just happened to trip over me."

Lucas's phone started to ring.

"I don't know how you run with those machines," Jaeger said. "Mine's an old foldable, and I put it away sometimes."

Lucas opened the line.

"Five minutes," said Wade.

"Five minutes," said the public address voice.

Wade said, "How do you feel?"

"Talk to you later, okay?" Lucas hung up.

Jaeger was watching him and the phone. He didn't ask who called, but when Lucas looked at him, the man offered what might have been a smile, shy and a little sorry.

"See you out there. Okay, Pepper?"

The levee twists to the southeast, ending at the park's north border. Hold that road, and Jaeger will work his way back into town. Any reasonable man would do that. But as soon as he hits Foster Lane, Jaeger jumps right and surges. And just to be sure that everyone understands, he throws back a little sneer as he crosses Ash Creek.

Pete and Varner are leading, milking the speed from their legs. Audrey is beside Lucas, but she won't chase anymore. Arms drop and her stride shortens. "You can't catch him," she says.

"Watch us," says Pete.

"Then what?" she says.

Nobody answers. They make Foster and turn together, bunching up as they cross the rusted truss bridge. Pounding feet make the old steel shiver, and the wind cuts sideways, sweaty faces aching.

"I can't run this fast," Sarah says.

"Nobody can," says Crouse.

Up ahead, past the bridge, the road yanks to the left, placing itself between the water and tangled second-growth woods. They watch Jaeger striding out, and then Masters says, "We've got to slow down."

But Pete has a plan. "If he runs the trails, we'll cut him off."

"He won't," Audrey says. "That would be stupid."

They come off the bridge, and Pete slows. "We'll split up," he says. "Fast legs chase, the rest wait up ahead."

Jaeger is pushing his lead.

"A turnoff's coming," Lucas says.

"Half a mile up," says Gatlin. "The park entrance."

"No, it's there," he says. "Soon."

And just like that, Jaeger turns right, leaping over a pile of gray gravel before diving into the brush. Two long strides and he becomes this pale shape slipping in and out of view, and with another stride, he's gone.

Varner curses.

"Run ahead or chase," says Pete.

Sarah and Masters fall back. And Crouse. Then Audrey says, "No," to somebody and drops away too.

Pete and Varner accelerate, Gatlin falling in behind them. Lucas holds his pace, looking at his feet, measuring the life in his legs. Then he slips past everybody and yanks himself to the right, plunging into the bare limbs. The others miss the tiny trail and overshoot. Alone, Lucas drops off the roadbed, following a rough little path to where it joins up with the main trail—a wide slab of black earth and naked roots that bends west and plunges.

Gravity takes him. Lifting his feet, Lucas aims for smooth patches of frozen ground, dancing over roots and little gullies. Then the trail flattens, trees replaced by a forest of battered cattails.

Lucas slows, breathes.

The others chug up behind. "I don't see him," says Varner.

Far ahead, an ancient cottonwood lies dead on its side—a ridge of white wood stripped of bark, shining in the chill sunshine. Before anyone else, Lucas sees the black ball cap streaking behind the tree, and he surges again, nothing easier in the world than making long legs fly.

"Five minutes," said the rumbling PA voice. But a minute later he said, "No, folks. We're going to have a short delay."

People assumed that a plane was coming, which was a rare event and every eye looked skyward. Except nothing was flying on that hot September morning. Lucas lined up next to Audrey, toes at the start line. Pete and Gatlin and Varner were on the other side of her. Crouse was a few rows back with Masters. Sarah was missing, and Lucas couldn't see Jaeger anymore. Like a puppy, Harris sprinted out onto the empty runway and trotted back again. Then he wasted another burst of speed, and Pete said, "What lottery did we lose and get him?"

Laughter came from everywhere, and then it collapsed.

Carl Jaeger had appeared. Where he was hiding was a mystery, but he was suddenly standing at the line. He had come here to race. Inside himself, the man was making ready for the next ten kilometers. Forty-plus years old and nobody could remember him losing to a local runner. It was an astonishing record demanding conditioning and focus and remarkable luck. Staring at the tape in front of his left toes, he didn't seem to notice the detectives pushing under the barricade, coming at him with handcuffs at the ready.

"Keep your hands where we can see them," said the lead cop.

Jaeger's legs tensed, long calves twitching. He looked up, saying, "You don't want me." Then he looked down, staring at the gray pavement, and talking to his feet, he said, "Just let me run this. Just let me."

SIX

The trail leaps out of the marsh and flattens, fading into a lawn of clipped brown grass. Stone summer-camp buildings have been abandoned for the winter, every door padlocked and plywood sheets screwed into every window. Lucas holds his line, and the buildings fall away. Then the trail is under him again, yanking to the left, and the clearing ends with trees and a deep gully and a narrow bridge made from oak planks and old telephone poles.

Habit keeps him on the trail. Seepage has pooled at the bottom and frozen on top, and the ice is broken where Jaeger's right foot must have planted. The muddy water is still swirling. Lucas cuts his stride. His legs decide to jump early. He knows that he won't reach the far bank, and his lead foot hits and breaks through, and he flings his other leg forward, dragging the trailing foot out of the muck before it's drenched.

The effort slows him, and the next slope is dark and very slick and slow, and that's how the others pass him.

Shoes drum on the oak planks. Pete is up ahead, hollering a few words that end with a question mark.

"What?" Lucas says.

Varner slows, looking down at him. "Where is he?"

Then Pete says, "Got him."

Lucas is on the high ground again. The woods are young and closely packed, the trail winding through the little trees until it seems as if there is no end to them. Then everybody dives again, back down into the cattails. Jaeger is a gray shape catching the sunshine. Bent forward a little too much, he swings his arms to help drive his legs, attacking the next rise.

A second cottonwood lies in the bottoms, the trunk and heavy roots made clean and simple by years of rot.

"Short cut," says Lucas.

Pete says some little word. He and Varner are suffering, pitching forward long before they reach the slope. Only Gatlin looks smooth, his tiny frame floating out into the lead.

Lucas steers left, meaning to leap the tree, but he doesn't have the lift, the juice. His lead foot hits and he grabs at the wood with the mittens, then the trailing foot clips the trunk and slows him. He stops, looking down from a place where he's never been before. A thin old trail leads up the middle of the cattails. He jumps down and runs it, alone again.

A distant voice drifts past. No word makes sense. Then the only sound is the wind high above and the pop of his feet. Lucas's face drips. Still running, he pulls off the mittens and bunches them together and shoves them into his tights.

Again, voices find him.

To his right, motion.

Jaeger appears on the high ground, body erect, the stride relaxed. He looks like a man riding an insurmountable lead. Watching nothing but the trail ahead, he dives back into the bottoms, slowing a little, and Lucas surges and meets him where the trails merge. Looking over his shoulder, Jaeger gives a little jump. "No," he says. And a big nervous laugh rolls out of him.

Lucas tucks in close. Again the trail climbs out of the marsh. And when Jaeger rises in front of him, Lucas reaches down, catching an ankle, yanking it toward the sky.

Jaeger falls, one hand slapping the frozen earth.

Grabbing the other ankle, Lucas says, "Run."

Jaeger kicks at him.

"What are you doing?" Lucas says. "You're an idiot. Run the hell out of here. Are you listening to me?"

Voices drift close. Varner says, "Pepper," and Pete says, "We got him," and that's when Jaeger scrambles to his feet. His eyes are wild, fiery. With a matching voice, he says, "What do you know." Not a question, just a string of flat hard words. Then he runs, his right leg wobbling. But the stride recovers, and that endless strength carries him off while Lucas watches, hoping for the best.

The others catch up and stop, bending to breathe.

"Good idea," says Pete.

Varner says, "What'd he tell you?"

Lucas looks at the butcher's gloves on his hands and puts his hands down, and Gatlin says, "Did you hurt him?"

"No," says Lucas.

"Too bad," Varner says. "Next time, break his legs."

Voices come through the trees. A woman shouts, a man speaks. Then the woman shouts again, her voice scary-angry and making no sense. Lucas surges, pulling away from the others. Wide and carpeted with rotted wood chips, the main trail points south, climbing a final little slope up onto Foster Lane. Jaeger has already passed. Masters stands in the middle of the road, hands on hips. Sarah is closest to him. "Do nothing," she says. "Just do nothing."

Masters says something soft.

She says, "God," and swats the air with her mittens.

Masters looks at Lucas, cheeks red and his mouth tiny, some wicked embarrassment twisting his guts.

"Asshole, run," says Crouse. The man is angry, but only to a point. A sports fan yelling at the enemy team, he cups his hands around his mouth. "We're chasing you, asshole."

Nobody moves.

Pete staggers up to the road, face dripping. Varner and Gatlin cross it and stop at the mouth of the next trail, and Gatlin points. "There."

"Chase him," Sarah says.

She isn't talking to Masters. Grabbing Lucas by the elbow, she shakes him and says, "Go."

Varner and Gatlin are running into the trees again.

Hands on knees, Pete says, "Foster goes where? Down the west side of the park, right?"

Lucas nods. "A couple trails pop out."

"We'll watch for him." Then Pete coughs into a fist.

"Oh, he's gotten away," says Sarah. Pink mittens on her head, she says, "There's a million trails in there."

"Come on," says Crouse, setting off down the road.

Pete trots after him.

Masters watches Sarah, glasses like volcanic glass, the mouth pressed down to a scared pink dot.

Audrey stands aside, her bottom lip tucked into her mouth, little teeth chewing. She acts like a bystander unlucky enough to stumble across an ugly family brawl.

"With me?" says Lucas.

Then he runs, saying, "Somebody."

Small shoes dance across dry gravel.

Lucas shortens his gait, giving her no choice but to fall in beside him.

"What did you do?" Audrey says. "His knee's bleeding."

The trail is wide and heavily used, slicing south through old timber before crossing one of the gullies that feed Ash Creek. "I spilled him," Lucas says.

"Spilled him."

"Stupid," he says.

The gully is wide, choked with muck and dead timber. The long bridge is made from pipe and oak planks. Lucas jumps on first, feet drumming. "I wanted to scare him. Get him to run somewhere else."

They come off the bridge and the world turns quiet. The trail splits, one branch heading west, but Lucas presses south.

"We were talking," says Audrey. "Up on the road, waiting, Masters made a joke. He said we should tackle Jaeger, and right away Sarah said that was good idea. But when Carl finally showed up, nobody moved."

Voices drift in from the west, from deep in the trees.

"Should we have turned back there?" Audrey says.

"The other trail just makes a little loop. Jaeger can take it to the road, or he comes back to us."

She pulls up beside him, and neither of them talks.

Then he says, "Nothing's going to happen to the guy."

"Promise?"

He slows.

She passes him and looks back. "What?"

"We're here. Stop," he says.

The trail jumps left where the woods end. In front of them is twenty feet of vertical earth falling into cold slow water. The secondary trail pops out on their right. "Hear anything?" says Lucas.

"No." She tilts her head. "Yes."

The gray T-shirt appears first, and then the pale face. Jaeger spots them. Three strides away, he stops. His right knee is trying to scab over. He breathes hard, big lungs working, his face holding a deep, thorough fatigue. But the voice is solid. Ignoring Lucas, he says, "Not you."

More sad than angry, Audrey says, "Just tell me, Carl."

"Tell you what?"

"Did you kill Wade?"

Jaeger throws a look back up the smaller trail. Gatlin and Varner stand in the trees, both men heaving. And Jaeger turns again, looking only at Lucas. He doesn't say a word, but an odd little smile builds. Then he runs again—a handful of lazy strides pushing him between Lucas and Audrey—and the big legs kick into high gear, frozen twists of mud scattering on the ground behind him.

"You could have won."

It was Wade's voice, and it wasn't.

"They just posted the results," he said. "You should see the splits. At five miles, Harris had you by eleven seconds. If you'd kept close, you would have toasted him at the end. The kid thinks he has a kick, but he doesn't."

Lucas was sitting in his kitchen, finishing a pot of coffee. Orcs and humans were fighting on the television, ugly evil pitted against the handsome good.

"Are you listening, Lucas?"

"Yeah."

"You haven't won a race since you were sixteen."

Lucas put down the mug. "How do you know? Did I tell you?"

"I've been reading old sports stories," Wade said. Except something about the voice was different. Changed. Not in the words or rhythm, but in the emotions. Wade was always intense, but usually in a tough-coach, in-control way. Usually. But this character was letting his anger creep into everything he was saying. "You had your chance, Lucas. With Jaeger out of commission and all."

"You know about the arrest?"

"An article just got posted. There's a nice picture of me from ten years ago. And a real shitty shot of Jaeger. I'm hoping Masters has the arrest on video. That's something I'd like to see."

Lucas reached across the table, turning off the television.

"Two witnesses put Jaeger running with me," Wade said. "I just read all about it. We're in the park that Monday, at the north end heading south, and both witnesses claim the mood was ugly."

"But you don't remember."

"Wade uploaded his days at night," Wade said. "That was his routine."

"I remember."

Silence.

Lucas waited. Then he said, "You think Carl did it?"

"Killed me?" An odd laugh came across. "I don't know. I really don't. But I'll tell you how this feels. Suppose you're at a theater watching some movie. It's a murder mystery, and there's this one character that you really, really care about. You want the best for him but you've got to pee, and that's when this person you like is killed. You're out of the room, and he gets his skull caved in. And now you feel angry and sad, but mostly you just feel cheated."

Lucas lifted the mug, looking at the stained bottom.

"Maybe Carl did it, and maybe not," Wade said. "But I missed that part. And now I'm sitting in the dark, waiting to see how things end up. Just so I can get on with my life."

Mountain bikes and hiking boots have carved a broad rut down the trail's middle. Runners keep to the rut, single file, jumping the bank when the trail twists, slicing the turn. Lucas leads and Audrey is behind him, watching her next steps. With a tight voice, she says, "I can't believe this."

"So quit," Varner says.

Jaeger is forty feet ahead. Where the trail pulls left, he cuts through the woods, adding a half-stride to his lead.

Varner surges, passing Audrey and clipping Lucas's heel with a foot.

Lucas slows and turns north, wind gnawing at his sweaty face.

The next bridge is a tall smear of red just visible through the trees. Jaeger is almost there, slowing his gait, getting ready to jump on the stairs.

Varner surges again, lifting himself to a full sprint, just managing to pull around Lucas.

Jaeger looks back, squinting, the wide mouth pulling air in long gulps. Then he turns and leaps, his right foot landing on a pink granite step. And he pauses, calculating distance and his own fatigue before jumping again, breaking into a smooth trot across the bridge.

Varner staggers, stiff legs climbing after Jaeger.

The others bunch up behind.

Lucas gasps, scrubbing his blood before pushing back into the lead. Ash Creek is wide as a river, and the long wooden bridge shakes with the pounding. Jaeger is twenty feet ahead when he reaches the end, leaping over the steps, hitting the ground hard. His posture is surprised. He stands where he landed, glancing back at Lucas and almost talk ing. Almost. Then he starts running again, not quite trusting his right leg.

Lucas dances down the steps and runs. The next stretch of trail is wide and straight—an old road through what used to be a farmer's yard. Someone with affection for poplars planted them in rows, skinny white trunks looking sickly without the glittering leaves. Again, the wind pushes the runners. Again, everybody accelerates. The old yard ends with a massive oak and deep woods. For Wade, this was always a traditional turnaround point from the Y. By this route, they have covered a few steps more than seven miles.

Jaeger disappears into the trees.

Lucas slows and says, "There's another bridge."

Audrey pushes close. "What about it?"

"It's closed. Since last summer."

"We can still cross," Gatlin says.

"Yeah," Lucas says. "But that's not what I'm talking about."

The bridge rises in the distance. It looks wrong. Four tall posts sag toward the middle. Last June, a flash flood roared down the tributary, cutting at the banks and undermining the foundation. Jaeger is driving hard, pushing away from them. Varner is scared that he might get away, and the adrenaline gives him just enough speed to catch Lucas and trip him by clipping his heel.

Both men tumble. Lucas slaps the ground where an exposed root cuts through a butcher's glove, ripping into his right palm.

Audrey stops.

Gatlin is past, gone.

Varner groans and finds his feet, giving Lucas an embarrassed but thoroughly pissed look before wobbling away.

"Are you okay?" says Audrey.

Lucas stands, watching the blood soak the cheap white fabric. Wincing, he says, "Come on," and breaks into a slow trot, eyes down.

DANGER, CLOSED reads the sign nailed to crossed planks.

Jaeger has crawled past the barricade. Steel cables serve as railings, and with arms spread wide, he slowly drops out of view.

"We're beaten," says Audrey. "We're done."

She sounds nothing but happy.

Gatlin stands on the ramp. Then he lifts an arm and waves at someone on the far bank.

Past the bridge is a trailhead and parking lot. If people ran the road down the west side of the park, following Foster, even a knuckle-walking pace would take them to this trailhead before any greyhound could sprint down these trails. Gatlin and Varner stand at the crossed boards, staring across the slough. The suspension bridge looks tired and old and treacherous, sagging in the middle as if holding an enormous weight. Jaeger stands at the bottom. He doesn't move. With feet apart, Pete guards the opposite barricade. Masters and Crouse are behind him, and Sarah hovers to the side, nothing but smiles now.

Pete says, "Look at you." Then he punches the boards, saying, "Unless you sprout wings, we've caught your ass."

"See the news today?"

Lucas was making a fresh pot. "Besides murder stories, you mean?"

The dead man laughed and then fell silent. And out from the silence, he said, "There was a thunderstorm yesterday. In Greenland."

Lucas didn't talk.

"You know where Greenland is, don't you?"

"Well enough," Lucas said.

The next laugh was smaller, angrier. "It wasn't a big storm, and it didn't last. But if rain starts falling hard on those glaciers, it's going to be a real mess."

"I thought we had a real mess."

"Even worse," Wade said.

Mr. Coffee set to work, happy to prove itself.

"Our weather wouldn't be this crazy," Lucas said, "if the Chinese hadn't burned all that coal."

"Which authority is talking? You?"

"Masters, mostly."

"It wasn't the Chinese, Lucas. It was everybody."

Lucas said nothing, waiting.

"Smart people can be stupid," Wade said.

"I guess."

"And I know guys who can't read a map, but they still see things that I'd never notice."

Lucas poured a fresh cup.

"Did I tell you? Climate is the biggest reason I got made. And it wasn't just the rising oceans and ten-year droughts and those heat waves that hammered the

Persian Gulf. Climate does change. Always has, and life always adapts. Except the Earth today has two big things that didn't exist during the Eocene."

Lucas said the new word. "Eocene."

"The Earth has its money and it has politics. And those very precious things are getting hit harder than anything else. The sultans can fly off to cool wet Switzerland, but the poor people have to die. The Saudi government has to collapse. But meanwhile, engineers get to sit inside their air-conditioned bunkers, using robots to run oil fields cooking at a hundred and fifty degrees. As if this was some other planet, and they were noble astronauts doing good work."

"I guess," said Lucas.

"Political stability and wealth," the voice said. "People depend on those two things more than anything else. And the poverty and riots and little murders and big wars are just going to get worse. Hour by hour, year by year. That's why I put my savings into this venture. Why Wade did. Sure, we were hoping for fifty years of tweaking, but at least we had enough time to pack up everything about me and put it here. My whole life, safe as safe can possibly be."

Lucas sipped and looked out the window. Or he didn't look anywhere. He was thinking, and he had no idea what he was thinking until he spoke.

"Nobody would do that," he said.

"Do what?" said Wade.

"Take everything." Lucas wiped the counter with a clean towel. "It's like this. You're putting your life into one big bag. But there's always going to be choices. There's always embarrassing ugly dangerous shit, and you'll look at it and say, 'Hell, that crap needs to be left behind.' "

"Think so?"

"I know it." Lucas watched the coffee wobbling in the mug. "That's probably another reason why Wade did what he did. Getting free of the past."

The line was silent.

"And you, the poor backup . . . you can't even know what's missing." Lucas was laughing but not laughing. "Right there, that says plenty."

SEVEN

Jaeger stands at the bottom of the slow-swaying curve, turning slowly and staring up at the people on both ends of the bridge. His chest swells, drinking the cold air. The muscles in his bare legs look like old rope, bunched and frayed, and the right knee keeps bleeding, a red snake glistening down the long shin. With filthy butcher gloves, he holds onto the steel cables. Old wood feels his weight, groaning. He doesn't seem to mind. If the bridge collapses, he falls ten feet into icy mud and nothing happens, nothing but pain and mess. Jaeger spent two months sitting in jail. He was too broke to make bail or find an adequate attorney. The city's murder rate had exploded in the last few years. A hundred other cases needed to be chased. But a popular citizen had been brutally murdered, and that's why the police and prosecutors threw everything at the suspect, trying to wring a confession from him. But there was no confession. And when key bits of physical evidence were finally attacked by the full powers of modern science, they were found wanting. Witnesses and odd circumstances don't make a case, and the court had no choice but to order Jaeger released. And that's why this bridge is no obstacle. None. Nothing will make the man meaner or any harder. That's what he says with his body and his face and the hard sure grip of his hands. That's what he says to Lucas, staring at him with those fierce green eyes.

And then Jaeger blinks.

He takes another breath and holds it. His head tips on that long neck. Maybe he feels cold. Anyone else would, dressed as he's dressed and standing still. Then he exhales and makes a quarter turn, wrapping both hands around the same fat steel cable.

Pete says, "Hey, prick. Tell the truth, and we'll let you go."

Jaeger stares at the slough. With a plain voice, not loud but carrying, he says, "That's what I am. A prick. And Wade was this righteous good guy, and everybody liked him, and dying made him perfect."

Nobody talks. Except for the wind in the trees and a slow trickle of water, there is nothing to hear.

"No, I wasn't with him when he died," says Jaeger. "But I know how he died. Even after the rain, there were clues: A big chunk of skin was found south of here, down near the water. It came out of his shoulder, and it was the first wound. Somebody was swinging a piece of rebar with a lump of concrete on the end, and they clipped Wade from behind, on his left side, probably knocking him off his feet. Giving his attacker the chance to grab his phone, leaving him bloody and cut off from the world, but mobile.

"That's when the chase began," he says. "There was a blood trail. DNA sniffers and special cameras showed where he ran, where he was bleeding. Twice, Wade tried doubling back to the nearest trailhead, but his enemy clipped the shoulder again and then bashed in one of his hands. The experts could tell that from the clotting. They know how fast the blood flowed and where Wade collapsed. He was up on the abandoned rail line, probably trying to get back to town. That's where his killer used the club to bust one of Wade's knees, crippling him. Then his jaw was broken, maybe to keep him quiet. After that, his killer dragged him down into the brush and with a couple good swings broke his hip. Then for some reason, the beating took a break."

Jaeger pauses.

Almost too soft to hear, Sarah says, "What are you telling us?"

"I'm explaining why you're idiots." Jaeger looks at her and back at Lucas. "Fifteen, twenty minutes passed. The killer stood over Wade. Talking to him, I guess. Probably telling him just how much he was hated. Because that's what this murder was. That was the point of it all. Somebody wanted to milk the fun out of hurting him. He wanted Wade helpless, wanted him to understand that he was crippled and ruined."

Sarah makes a soft, awful sound.

Jaeger shakes his head. "Twenty minutes of talk, and then three or four minutes of good solid hammering. Wade died within sixty seconds, they figured. But he was a tough bastard and maybe not. Maybe he felt the one side of the face getting caved in and the ribs and arms busted and the neck shattered."

Lucas leans against the barricade.

Jaeger pushes into the cable, long arms stretched wide and holding tight. The steady drumming of his strongest muscle causes the steel to shudder. Anyone touching the bridge can feel his heart beating hard and quick.

"I didn't hate the man," says Jaeger. "You know me, Audrey. You too, Lucas. I'm wrapped up in myself, sure. But this feud ran in just one direction." He laughs and grabs both cables again. "Yeah, we ran together that Monday. And we were talking. But after a mile or so, I turned and he went on. For me, Wade was nothing. He was just another body in the pack. I didn't hate him. Not till I spent two months in jail, thinking about him and his good sweet friends. And you know what? I've got this feeling. This instinct. I didn't have reason for killing, particularly like that. But I'm thinking that killing Wade Tanner is something one of you bastards would do. Easy."

The building began as a factory and became a filthy warehouse. Then the property sold cheap, and the investor put loft apartments into the upper stories and The Coffee Corner took over the loading dock and west end, while the backside was reborn as a fashionable courtyard complete with flowerpots and a broken fountain. Lucas was walking past the courtyard's black-iron gate. Saturday's run was finished and coffee was finished and he was thinking about the rest of his day, and from behind, Sarah said, "I need new shoes."

She was talking to him, Lucas thought, turning around.

To her phone, she said, "What kind should I try?"

The odd funny weird thing about the moment was her face. Sarah looked happy, which was different. The smile lit her face and made her eyes dance. She was listening to a voice, and he realized whose voice. Then she noticed Lucas and turned away, suddenly embarrassed, muttering soft little words nobody else needed to hear.

Sarah went through the gate. Lucas followed. The original pavers made the courtyard, dark red and worn smooth by horses pulling wagons. Maybe the horses were coming back someday. It was something to think about as he followed the little woman. A glass door led into The Runner's Closet, and the owner had just opened up. A few minutes after ten, in October, and his day was starting off fine. He had two customers at once, and the guy had to grin.

Lucas stumbled over names. Tom? Tom Hubble, right.

"He wants me to try the Endorphins," Sarah said. "The ones with the twin computers and the smart-gel actuators."

"Good choice," Tom said. "What size?"

She told him and he vanished into the back room, and then she turned, watching Lucas. She didn't talk. She was listening and smiling. Then she said, "Lucas is here too," and nodded as Wade talked. Then she told the living man, "He says you need new shoes too."

"Yeah, but how does he know?"

"Wade still helps here. Keeps track of who buys what, and you haven't bought for a long time."

What was strangest was how much all of that made sense.

Lucas sat on the padded bench, Sarah settling beside him, still talking to Wade. An oval track had been painted on the floor, wrapping around the bench. She listened to the voice, and Tom brought out a box of shoes and put them on her and laced her up and watched her jogging a few strides at a time, smart eyes trying to see what was right and wrong in her step.

Sarah giggled. Not laughed, but giggled.

"I need new shoes too," Lucas said.

"What kind do you like?" Tom said.

"What I have," Lucas said.

"What's the model?"

"I don't remember," Lucas said. "Ask Wade."

Tom nodded, watching Sarah finishing her lap. She said, "Bye," and touched her phone. "I'll take them. And he said pass his commission back to me, please."

"Sure," Tom said, rising slowly.

Sarah started following him toward the counter but then stopped and looked at Lucas. "You know, I talk to him more than ever," she said, smiling but not smiling. Happy in her core but knowing there was something wrong, something sick about feeling this way.

Jaeger grabs the cables and drives with his legs, climbing the far side of the swaying bridge. Pete holds his ground, waiting. The four people wait, shoulders squared but the feet nervous. Everything will be finished in another minute. A fight is coming, and the four people on the north bank can only watch, each of them feeling lucky because of it.

Pete's face tightens.

Jaeger says, "Move."

Nobody reacts. Pride holds them in place, right up until Pete dips his head, throwing a few words at the others as he backs away.

Masters retreats, relieved.

Not Crouse. He replants his feet. Unimpressed, Jaeger grabs the barricade and jumps, one foot landing where the planks cross. Then he yanks the foot free and drops beside Crouse, saying nothing while staring down at him, and Crouse nearly trips backing off the wooden ramp.

Only Sarah remains. She makes fists inside her mittens and steps forward, waving the fists while sobbing, fighting for breath.

Jaeger pushes past her and runs, vanishing in a few strides.

Pete waves. "One at a time."

Gatlin goes first. The little body slips under the barricade and runs to the bottom and then up to the far side. Varner chases, every step ridiculously long, the bridge bucking and creaking. Audrey is next, but she won't let go of the cables and she won't run. Halfway down, she looks back at Lucas, and he says, "Let's just leave. We can head back."

She shakes her head and says, "But what if they catch him?" Just the possibility makes her tremble, and she hurries, finishing her trip down and then up again.

Cupping a hand against his mouth, Pete says, "Are you coming?"

Lucas says, "No." Maybe he means it. Anywhere else in the world would be better than being here. But he watches himself bend and climb through the barricade, and he lets his legs run. Planks rattle as he stretches out, and then without a false step or stumble, he charges up the far side.

Only Pete waits. He looks in Lucas's direction. He talks to Lucas, unless he's talking to himself. "I don't know," he says to one of them. "I just don't know."

The trail follows the slough to its mouth and then follows Ash Creek again. Cottonwoods stand among the scrub elms and mulberries, and the woods give way to dead grass and a parking lot of rutted gravel. Past the lot is West Spencer Road and another mile-deep slice of parkland. The rest of the group stand beside the lone picnic table, bunched together and silent. A rhythmic shriek begins, cutting at the cold air. Jaeger has claimed the old-style pump, lifting the handle and shoving it down again. A rusty box fills with water and brown water spouts from the bottom into a rusted bowl, spouting even when he stops pumping, bending over to drink.

Once he has his fill, Jaeger straightens, wiping his chin and his mouth. Then he trots to the next trail and stops again, looking back at them.

"He's waiting on us," Varner says.

And with a quiet sick voice, Audrey says, "Who's chasing who?"

Sarah paid for the shoes and left, and Tom vanished into the back again. His voice drifted out of the storeroom—one side of the conversation exchanging pleasantries before asking the real question. Lucas drifted to the front of the store, up where a tall sheet of corkboard was covered with race results and news clippings and free brochures telling new runners how to train for competition. A younger, badly yellowed Wade smiled down from a high corner, holding a famous pair of shoes in one hand. Tom came out with a box while Lucas was picking his way through the news clipping, one word after another.

"I'd pull that old thing down," Tom said, "but people expect it. I'm afraid customers would get mad, not seeing it there."

"I wouldn't," Lucas said.

Tom examined the clipping. "I was here that day. In fact, I saw the kid snatch up those shoes. Out the door and gone, and Wade came charging from the storeroom to chase him. I told him not to. The kid was on meth. I could tell. But you know Wade."

"Yeah."

"I knew he'd catch the thief, and that's what scared me."

Lucas gave up reading. It was the photograph that mattered. It was that big smile and the hair that was still thick and blond and the rugged looks wrapped around a crooked nose, and it was how that younger Wade held those shoes up to the camera, no prize in the world half as important.

"That shoe thief had a knife," Tom said.

"I remember."

"But things worked out. Wade just kept running him until he collapsed, and nobody got cut."

Lucas dropped his eyes, watching the floor.

"He was the first salesman that I hired," said Tom. "Wade was still in college. I had no idea he'd stay here for twenty years. Honestly, I didn't think he would last that first week. He was too intense, I thought. Too perfect, too driven. The crap he would pull sometimes. God, these are just shoes. The world isn't going to end if you don't happen to make that one sale."

Tom was looking at the same piece of the floor, explaining. "But like nobody I've ever known, Wade had a talent for names and faces. For feet and gaits. He was everybody's first doctor when they got hurt, and he loved selling shoes, and even dead, he's still practically managing this place."

"What else?" Lucas said.

"What else what?"

"What stupid crap did he pull? Besides chasing shoe thieves, I mean."

Tom swallowed, thinking before answering. "He fired clerks for little things. No warnings, just gone. If a customer gave him a bad check, he wouldn't take another check from that person. Ever. And he couldn't keep his nose out of private concerns. He had this need, this compulsion, to steer the world toward doing what's right. You know what I mean."

"Oh, sure."

"I was at that party too, Lucas."

Lucas looked at him.

"I never would have called the cops on you."

Lucas didn't know what to say. He tried a small shrug.

Tom was nervous but proud. He thought that he was making a customer for life. "Wade was a good man, but he thought everyone should be."

One last glance at the photograph seemed right.

"Ithaca Flyers. Is that your shoe?"

"Sounds right."

"This is the new model, but he says you'll like it."

"Well," said Lucas. "The guy was usually right."

The group shuffles over to the pump. Masters pulls a little bottle off the back of his belt, sharing the blue drink with Sarah. Pete gives the handle a few hard shoves and drinks, and then the others take turns. Everybody is tired, but not like runners beaten up by miles. They look like cocktailers after Last Call, faces sloppy and sad and maybe a little scared by whatever is coming next.

Lucas drinks last, holding the frigid bowl with his bloodied palm, the water warm and thick with iron.

"Sucking the ground dry?" says Jaeger.

Lucas stops drinking. But instead of standing, he drops down, stretching his legs with a runner's lunge.

Jaeger turns and leaves.

"Hurry," Sarah says.

Masters is squeezing the last taste out of a gel-pack.

She says, "Now."

He nearly talks. Words lie ready behind those big sorrowful eyes. But he forces himself to say nothing, folding the foil envelope and shoving it into his belt pocket before taking a last little swig from the bottle, diluting the meal before it hits his defenseless stomach.

Everybody is stiff from standing, and nobody mentions it. Nobody does anything but run, lifting their pace until they see Jaeger floating up ahead. Sarah is in front, sniffling. A flat concrete bridge carries West Spencer across the stream. Jaeger throws back a quick glance before following the trail under the bridge, hugging the east bank.

"It was him," Varner says.

Crouse says, "Sure."

"Wade was our friend," Varner says. But that isn't enough. Shaking his head, he says, "Wade was my best friend. He got me into running. Sold me my first shoes, when I was fat. And he was a groomsman at my wedding. Remember?"

With an edge, Pete says, "Yeah, none of us had reasons."

Sarah slows. "What does that mean?"

They bunch up behind her.

"One of us had a motive?" she says.

Pete drops back to Audrey. "What do you think, princess? Your old boyfriend kill Wade, or didn't he?"

The trail dives and widens, its clay face pounded slick. The stream lies on their right, pushing past the concrete pilings and dead timber, the wet roar hitting the underside of the bridge before bouncing over them. It is hard to hear Audrey saying, "I never believed he was guilty."

They come out from under, emerging into the calm. Climbing the slope, nobody talks. Then Audrey says, "Carl is self-centered and stubborn, like a little boy. But he's never been violent. Not around me."

Carved by chainsaws, a simple bench sits beside the trail, waiting for the exhausted. They run past and the trail drops again and hits bottom, and Crouse gasps as they climb. "You two dated?" he says.

"Years ago," she says, ready to say nothing more.

Crouse has to surge to catch her. But it's worth the pain to tell her, "I don't see it. I don't understand. Why is Carl attractive?"

For several strides, nothing happens. The trail twists away from the stream, nothing but trees around them. Then Audrey slows and looks at Crouse, her face pretty and pleased when she says, "Look at that body, those legs. And now guess what I saw in him."

The man reddens.

She laughs, saying, "Little boys can be fun."

Jaeger looks back again, holding the gap steady.

"So did he ever talk about Wade?" says Pete.

She keeps laughing. "Carl loved, and I mean loved, how that man kept trying to beat him. It fed him, knowing one person was awake nights, trying to figure out how to pass him at the finish line."

Nobody reacts.

Then she says, "Lucas," and comes up beside him. "I don't think I ever told you. But when you started training with Wade, Carl wasn't sure how long he would stay on top. 'Wade found his thoroughbred,' was what he said."

Everybody but Pete glances at Lucas. Pete just dips his head, asking the trail, "What about you, Pepper? Is Jaeger the killer?"

Lucas drops his arms and slows. The stream comes back looking for the trail. Suddenly the world opens up, and they chug along a narrow ribbon of earth, perched on a bank being undercut by every new flood. To their right is nothing except open air. A string of bodies are pushing against the brush on the left. Audrey is in front of Lucas, Pete behind. Pete says, "If it isn't Jaeger, who was it?"

Lucas runs with eyes down, and a quiet, puzzled voice says, "If it wasn't Carl?"

"Yeah?"

"Me," he says. "I could have beaten Wade Tanner to death."

EIGHT

Audrey slows, nearly tripping Lucas.

He says, "Sorry," and drops his hands on her shoulders.

"Was it you?" says Pete. "No," Lucas says.

"How can you even think it?" says Audrey. Lucas lets go of her, eyes down, head shaking.

Varner and Gatlin are in the lead. Feeling the others fall back, they pull up reluctantly, and Varner says, "Who's hurt?"

Nobody answers. Six runners stand on the crumbling trail, flush against the drop-off. Lucas turns his back to the water. "It's just how things look," he says to Audrey, to everybody. "If you think about it."

"Keep talking," says Pete.

But Masters speaks first. With a voice nobody has ever heard—an angry, sharp, defiant voice—he says, "Wade was an ass."

Everybody turns.

The man's face is red, his jaw set. "I'm tired of thinking about the man," he says. "I'm tired of talking about the man. And I don't want to have another conversation with that goddamn software."

"Don't," says Sarah. Then again, softer, she says, "Don't."

Nobody wants to look at her. It is easier to stare at the madman with the sleek black glasses and the long-built rage.

"Let's run home," says Audrey.

Varner and Gatlin return to the pack. "Who's hurt?" says Varner.

Pete says, "Nobody. We're just having a meeting."

"We couldn't have," Sarah says. "Nobody here would kill him."

Which makes Pete laugh. Except his face is flushed and he can't stop shaking his head, blowing hard through clenched teeth. With one finger, he pokes Lucas in the chest. "Was it you?" he says.

"No." A spasm rips through Lucas's body. One foot drops over the soft lip of the trail, and he brings it back again, stepping forward just far enough to feel that he won't fall in the next moment. Then Pete puts a hand flush against Lucas's chest, not pushing but ready to push, waiting for the excuse.

And now another voice comes in.

"I've got a list of suspects," Jaeger says. "Why don't you listen to me now?"

The old burr oak stands on the bank, undermined to where a tangle of fat curling roots juts into the open air. Jaeger stands in the shadow of that doomed tree, smiling. Pulling off the baseball cap, he uses the long sleeve of his shirt to wipe his eyes and broad forehead. Then he puts the cap back where it belongs, and he says nothing, the smile never breaking.

"Give us names," says Pete.

"Okay, yours," Jaeger says. "And Varner."

"Why?" Varner says.

"Cause you're mean boys. I barely know either of you, and I'm pretty sure that I've never hurt you. But here you are, chasing me, both of you looking ready to bust heads. All you need is a reason. So maybe Wade gave you a good reason. Who knows?"

Varner curses. Pete gives a horse snort.

"Then there's the little guy," says Jaeger. "I've got a guess, Mr. Gatlin. But it's a sweet one."

"What?" Fast Doug says.

"You ran for mayor when? Three, four years back? And Wade helped. I heard he gave you names and phone numbers for every runner in town. Stuffed envelopes, dropped money in your lap. But then news leaked about some old business back in Ohio. Sure, those troubles were years old. Sure, the girl stopped cooperating with the cops and charges got dropped. But you know how it is. Nothing's uglier than reporters chasing something that looks easy."

Gatlin opens his mouth and closes it.

"Did Wade know your sex-crime history?" says Jaeger. "Was he the leak that got the scandal rolling?"

Quietly, fiercely, the accused man says, "I don't know."

Jaeger laughs. "But it could have been Wade. We know that. Love him or not, the guy had this code for how people should act, and not living up to his standards was dangerous. He could be your buddy and remain civil, but if you were trying to run for public office and he decided that you were guilty of something, he'd happily drop a word in the right ear and let justice run you over. That wouldn't bother the man for a minute."

"So everybody but you is guilty," says Pete. "Is that it?"

Jaeger winks at Crouse. "Wade liked pretty girls. And pretty wives were best. Which is funny, considering the man's ethics. But adultery isn't a crime. Romance is a contest, a race. There is a winner, and there is everybody else, and I'm looking at you but thinking about your wife. She is a dream. A fat toad like you is lucky to have her. And believe me, a guy like Wade is going to be interested, and by the way, whose baby did she just have?"

Crouse tries to curse, but he hasn't the breath.

Audrey says, "Carl."

"With you, darling, I don't have guesses." Jaeger's face softens. "Maybe you two had a history. Maybe there was a good reason for you to cripple him and kill him. I heard your marriage fell apart a couple months ago. Anybody can draw a story from that clue. Except you never tried to kill me, not once, and I gave you a hundred reasons to cut off my head while I was dreaming."

Audrey cries.

Jaeger points at Sarah. "But you," he says. "At the races, I saw you chatting it up with the dead man. I'm not the most sensitive boil, but everything showed in those eyes. If you didn't screw Wade, you wanted to. And maybe you didn't do the bashing, but you've got a husband. And worse, you've got this tall goon following you around. What would Mr. Masters do if he discovered that his training buddy was cheating on her husband and on him?"

Breathing hard, Masters stares at the back of Sarah's head.

"No end to the suspects," Jaeger says.

"What about Pepper?" says Pete.

"Yeah, I was saving him."

Lucas feels sick.

Pete turns and looks at him. "The party," he says.

"At the coach's house," says Jaeger. "I've heard stories. Not that anybody invited me, thank you. But my sources claim that a brutal load of liquor was consumed. By one man, mostly. Years of sobriety gone in a night, and then the drunk drove away." He smiles, something good on his tongue. "And that's when somebody called the hotline. Somebody told the world, 'Lucas Pepper is driving and shit-faced, and this is his license plate, and this is his home address, and this is his phone number.' "

Lucas manages ragged little breaths.

"A night in jail and your license suspended," says Jaeger. "But there's worse parts to the story. I know because my first source told me. That next Monday, when I crossed paths with Wade, I asked about you, Pepper. 'Where's your prize stallion?' I said. "'Why isn't he running in this miserable heat?' That's when he launched into this screaming fit about drunks, about how stupid it was to waste effort and blood trying to keep bastards like them on track.

"I know something about ugly tantrums," Jaeger says. "And this was real bad. This is what the witnesses saw when they saw us in that park. They assumed it was two men fighting. Which it was, I guess. Except only one of the men was present, and I was just a witness, trying to hang on for the ride.

"Wade told me about that party and how he watched you drinking and drinking, and then he made it his business to walk you to your car, and that's where he got into your face. Standing at the curb, he told you exactly what you were, which was the worst kind of failure. He said he wasn't sure he was going to give you even one more chance. Why bother with a forty-year-old drawerhead, spent and done and wasted?

"And that's the moment I turned around. It was a hot sticky evening, and that was my excuse. But really, I was embarrassed for you, Lucas. I didn't know that was possible. I turned and ran home, and Wade went on his merry way, and I can guess what happened if he came around the bend and ran into you trotting by yourself."

Lucas stares at Jaeger but glimpses something moving. Something is running through the trees, and nobody else sees it.

With the one finger, Pete punches Lucas. "Is there something you want to tell us, Pepper?"

Sniffing, Audrey whispers his name.

Jaeger removes the cap again, wiping at his forehead.

Lucas is the only person who doesn't jump when Harris trots up behind Jaeger.

"Hey, guys," says a big happy voice. "I finally found you."

In November, in the warm dark, Lucas rode up to the Harold Farquet Memorial Fieldhouse. He was stowing bike lights when Varner appeared. "I must be late," said Lucas.

"What's that mean?" said Varner, not laughing.

They went inside. Half an acre of concrete lay beneath a shell of naked girders and corrugated steel. The building's centerpiece was the two-hundred-meter pumpkin-orange track. Multipurpose courts filled the middle and stretched east. Athletics offices and locker rooms clung to the building's south end. Banners hanging from the ugly ceiling boasted about third-place finishes. The largest banner celebrated the only national championship in Jewel history—twenty years ago, in cross-country.

Thirty people had come out of the darkness to run. Most were middle-of-the-pack joggers, cheery and a little fat. Masters and Sarah were sharing a piece of floor, stretching hamstrings and IT bands. Audrey ran her own workout, surging on the brief straightaways. Lucas watched her accelerate toward him and then fall into a lazy trot on the turn, smiling as she passed.

Varner vanished inside the locker room. Out of his pack, Lucas pulled a clean singlet and dry socks and the still-young shoes. His shorts were under his jeans. Kicking off street shoes, he changed in the open. His phone rang, and glancing at the number, he killed the ring. Then Audrey's phone rang as she came past, and she answered by saying, "Kind of busy here, Mr. Tanner."

The indoor air felt hot and dry. Lucas walked toward the lockers, bent, and took a long drink from the old fountain, the water warm enough for a bath. Burping, he stepped away. Heroes covered the wall. Someone made changes since last winter, but the biggest photograph was the same: The championship team with its top five competitors in back, slower runners kneeling at their feet. Able and his assistants flanked the victors. The coach looked happiest, standing beside his main stallion. By contrast, Jaeger appeared smug and bored, his smile as thin as could be and still make a smile. The big portrait of the school's national champion runner had been removed. Three different years, Carl Jaeger was the best in Division II cross-country. But that man was in jail, and the dead man had replaced him. Newly minted prints of Wade had been taken from past decades, each image fresh and clean. Testimonials about the man's competitive drive and importance to the local running community made him into somebody worth missing. Lucas read a few words and gave up. Farther along was a younger Audrey, third-best at the national trials. Her hair was long but nothing else had changed much. He studied the picture for a minute, and then she came around again, saying, "Don't stare at little girls, old man. Hear me?"

"You pointed east," Harris says. "So I headed east. I chased you. Except nobody was there. Old farts start slow, and I didn't see you after the first mile, so I figured you changed your minds."

The kid is angry but smiling, proud of his cleverness.

"I thought about going north. But then I realized. . . . " Harris stops talking. "Hey, Carlie. What are you doing with this crew?"

Nobody speaks.

Something odd is happening here. That fact is obvious enough to sink into Harris's brain. The smirk softens, blue eyes blink, and again he says, "What are you doing with these guys, Carl?"

Jaeger turns and runs.

Harris is wearing long shorts and a heavy yellow top, his black headband streaked with salt. His glasses are the same as Masters's, only newer. His shoes look like they came out of the box this morning. "You should see your faces," he says. "You guys look sick."

Pete steps away from Lucas.

"Anyway," Harris says. "I didn't know where you were, but I knew somebody who'd know. So I called Wade. He pointed me in the right direction, and I ran the train tracks to cut distance. I nearly missed seeing you, but I heard shouting."

"Shut up," Pete says.

"What do we do?" says Gatlin.

"Follow him," Varner says.

Jaeger is crossing a meadow, the black cap bobbing too much.

Pete looks at Lucas, big hands closing into fists.

And Lucas breaks into a full sprint, cutting between bodies.

Harris smiles and says, "Pepper." Then, for fun, he sets his feet and throws out an arm. "What's the password?"

They collide.

The young body is wiry-strong and tough. But Lucas has momentum, and they fall together. Lucas's sore hand ends up inside the kid's smile. Bony knuckles smack teeth and lips, and with a hard grunt Harris is down, the split upper lip dripping blood.

A wet voice curses.

Lucas is up and running.

Harris pokes at his aching mouth, and after careful consideration he says, "Screw you, asshole."

Lucas charges past the oak and across the meadow. The black cap is gone. Lucas holds to the main trail, following it back into the woods where it turns cozy with the stream. A wild sprint puts him near a five-minute pace. Then he slows, feeding oxygen to his soggy head. Roots and holes want to trip him. Voices call out from behind, and he surges again. Somebody hollers his name. Lucas holds the pace. He has little extra to give, but his stride stays smooth and furious. A half-grown ash tree is dead on the trail, and his legs lift, carrying him over what is barely an obstacle. The stream is straight ahead, the bank cut into a longugly ramp, rocks and concrete slabs creating shallow water where horses can ford. Lucas turns left, following a narrower trail, and the trail splits, the right branch blocked by a CLOSED sign.

Jaeger went left, gravel showing where a runner churned up the little slope. Lucas runs right on the badly undermined trail. Holes need to be leaped. Last year's grass licks at his legs. The trail ends where the bank collapsed, probably in the last few weeks, and he pushes sideways and up through the grass, popping out on the wide rail bed.

Jaeger is close. Seeing Lucas, he surges, and where the trail drops back into the woods, he accelerates. But his head dips too much. Long arms look sloppy, tight to the body and not in sync. Lucas throws in his own surge, and, catching Jaeger, he dips his head, delivering one hard shove.

Jaeger stays up but drifts into the brush, and his right leg jumps out. Both men trip and fall, bony arms flinging at each other, trading blows until they are down, scraped and panting.

Lucas is first to his feet.

Cursing, he tries kicking Jaeger's ribs and beats his toes into the frozen ground by mistake. Then Jaeger grabs the foot and tries to break it, twisting as hard as he can, doing nothing but forcing Lucas to fall on his ass again.

Lucas breathes in long gulps. "This is no fun," he says.

"Better than jail," Jaeger says.

"Not much."

Up on the rail bed, Gatlin says, "I see them."

Harris says, "He's mine, mine."

Jaeger finds his feet first. Then, after a moment's consideration, he reaches down and offers a hand to Lucas.

Pete emerged from the locker room, walking ahead of Gatlin. "Are you standing or running?" he said.

"I can do both," Lucas said.

The men laughed and left him looking at pictures.

Audrey was taking another turn. She wasn't talking to anybody now. Harris had come from somewhere, trotting next to her, chatty and happy.

As if he had a chance with her. He said something and laughed for both of them, and Audrey did her best not to notice.

Lucas had no fire. He didn't want to run, and that's why he kept delaying. Walking the wall, he studied volleyball pictures and wrestling pictures and a big plaque commemorating Harold Farquet, dead thirty years but still looking plush in that suit and tie. Then he reached a bare spot. A rectangular piece of the wall seemed too bright, holes showing where bolts had held up something heavy. Curious to a point, he tried remembering what used to be there. He couldn't. The adjacent hallway led to the offices, and someone was moving inside Able's office. On a whim, Lucas knocked, and the coach came out smiling.

"What's up, Pepper?"

"I like that stuff about Wade," Lucas said.

"Yeah, we thought it was good to do. Glad you like it."

"And you took down Carl."

Able grimaced. "Yeah, we did."

"There's something else down," Lucas said. "There used to be a plaque around the corner. About Carl?"

"No," the coach said. "A few years back, we had an alum give the athletic department some money. We thanked him with a banquet and a big plaque in his honor."

"So what happened?"

"Jared Wails. Remember him?"

"I don't do names," Lucas said.

"He was a slow runner, a businessman. Had that big-title company up until last year." Blood showed in the round face. "You saw him at races, probably. The rich boy who drove Corvettes."

"The '73 Stingray."

"That's him."

"I remember. The guy was kiting checks." Lucas nodded, pieces of the story coming back. "He told people he inherited his money, but he didn't. And when it caught up to him, he drove out to the woods and blew his brains out."

"And we pulled down his plaque."

"Yeah, I knew him. I even talked to him a few times." Lucas nodded, saying, "I liked the man's cars. I told him so. He was the nicest rich guy in the world, so long as we were yabbering about Corvettes."

"He wasn't that nice," the coach said.

"That's what I'm saying." Lucas wiped at his mouth. "We always had the same conversation: Cars and how much fun it was to drive fast, but gas was scarce, even for somebody with money. It was a nice conversation. Except he always changed subjects. He always ended up making big noise about hiring me."

"You?"

"I was going to be his personal trainer. I was going to coach him to where he could run a sub-three-hour marathon, or some such crap. And he was going to pay me. He always gave me numbers, and each time, the numbers got fatter. Wilder. Plus he was going to drop ten pounds, or twenty, and then thirty. And I was going to run ultra-marathons with him, crossing Colorado or charging up that mountain in Africa. Kilimanjaro?"

"Lucas Pepper, personal trainer," Able said, laughing.

"Yeah, Mr. Discipline. Me." Lucas shook his head. "Of course Wails didn't mean it. Anybody could tell. He always smiled when he talked that way. It was a smart bossy smile. The main message was that he had enough money to buy my ass. Whenever he wanted. And I needed to know it."

The coach nodded. Waiting.

"The Program's full of people like him," Lucas said. "AA, I mean. It's drunks and drawerheads who spend their lives lying about a thousand things to keep their drinking secret. That's the feel I got off the Stingray man. The shiny smile. The way his eyes danced, not quite looking at me when he was telling his stories. Any story."

"The man was a compulsive liar."

"I guess."

"No, after the suicide. Jared Wails had this big life story, but most of it was made up."

"A lot of people try doing that," Lucas said.

"But you saw through him."

Lucas shrugged.

"So? You ever mention your intuition to anybody?"

"Yeah, I did." Lucas nodded, looking out at the track. Ready to run now. "Once, I told somebody what I saw in that guy."

What matters is the trail. Trees and brush and the wide sunny gash of the stream slide past, but they are nothing. What is real is the wet black strip of hard-packed earth that twists and folds back on itself. What matters is what's under the foot and what waits for the next foot. A signpost streaks past—a yellow S sprouting an arrow pointing southwest. The trail narrows and drops and widens again, forming an apron of water-washed earth that feels tacky for the next two strides. The runners slow, barely. Lucas leads. Then the trail lifts and yanks left, and the pace quickens and quickens again, and a guttural little voice from behind tries to say something clever, but there isn't enough air for clever. Jaeger settles for a muttered, plaintive curse.

Two strides ahead, Lucas's clean gait skips over roots and a mound of stubborn dirt. His blue windbreaker is unzipped, cracking and popping as the air shoves past. Every sleeve is pushed over his elbows. The stocking cap and hair are full of sweat, but the face is perfectly relaxed. Except for little glimpses, his eyes point down, and he listens carefully to the footfalls behind him.

Jaeger slows, dropping back another stride.

Ash Creek takes a hard bend, and then it straightens, pointing due east. The water is wide and shallow, filled with downed timber and busy bubbling water heading in the opposite direction, and the trail hangs beside it, smooth and straight. Lucas pushes, and somewhere the water sounds vanish. The endless wind still blows, but he can't hear it pushing at the trees and he can't hear Jaeger's feet getting sloppy, starting to scrape at the earth. Coming from nowhere is a great long throb, and the ground shakes. Lucas dips his head and turns it, and Jaeger says one word with a question mark chasing. Then Lucas slows enough to shout the word back at him. "Train," he says.

The stream bends right, slicing close to the old rail bed. Last year's floods endangered the tracks, and the railroad responded with black boulders dropped over the trail and bank. A big two-legged sign blocks the way onto the bed, stern words warning those foolish enough to trespass on railroad property. Lucas lifts his knees and drives, a few stones rolling, and he glances downstream, seeing sunlight dancing on the bright skin of the morning Amtrak.

The big diesel throbs, pushing against the steady grade. Then the driver sees runners and hits the horn, and every living organism within a mile hears the piercing furious white roar.

Lucas turns south and sprints.

One set of tracks fills the bed. Jaeger says a word and another word and then gives up shouting. Adrenaline gives him life. He follows near enough to be felt, and Lucas looks back just once more, judging the train's speed. Some visceral calculation is made, and he believes he has time and enough speed. But the horn sounds again, shaking his body, and he can't be sure. Arms pump and he drives off the balls of his feet, reclaiming the two-stride lead. Then the engine grudgingly throttles back, and knowing that he won't have to leap onto the big black rocks, Lucas falls back into the sprint he would use on a hot summer track.

The trail dips between boulders, down into the trees again.

He rides the slope, Jaeger still chasing, and Lucas stops and Jaeger runs into his back as the Amtrak roars past. Neither man falls. The horn blares once more, for emphasis, and an angry face in the engine's window glares down at them. Sleek old cars follow, and after them, new cars cobbled together in some crash program. Empty windows and one little boy stare at the world. The boy waves at them and smiles, utterly thrilled with a life jammed with spectacle and adventure.

Lucas waves back.

Jaeger collapses to a squat, unable to find his breath. The air is full of diesel fumes. He tries cursing and can't. He wants to stand and can't. All those weeks in jail have eaten at his legs, and for athletes in their forties lay-offs are crippling. Jaeger won't win another important race in his life. He knows this, and Lucas sees it, and then the beaten man stands, his entire body shaking.

The train is far enough gone that the forest sounds are returning.

"So did you kill him?" says Jaeger.

Lucas shakes his head.

Jaeger nods. If he does or doesn't believe that answer isn't important. Looking straight at Lucas, he says, "Now what?"

"I'm going," Lucas says. "Wait here for the others."

"And then?"

Downstream from them, climbing out of the trees, the rest of the group is cautiously running next to the still-humming rails. "I don't know who killed Wade," he says.

"Too bad," Jaeger says. "But I know who paid to have it done." That earns a long, long stare.

"Keep that face," Lucas says. "Tell everybody what I just told you. And we'll see what happens next."

NINE

"Jingle bells," the voice said.

"Merry Christmas to you."

"No, I'm talking about the race. The 5K. If you don't win this year, you aren't trying. That's what I think."

Lucas poured a cup, not talking.

"I'm seeing improvement, Lucas. Every week, with your splits and overall times, you're finding fire."

"Thanks for caring."

"Just want to help." Then the voice went away.

Lucas sat on a kitchen stool, sipping. Outside it was cold and wet, and it was chill and damp in the house. The television had been showing an old Stallone movie, but the network interrupted with news about a big dam in China getting washed away. Serious stuff, and Lucas reached across the counter, turning it off.

The voice returned. "You there?"

"Still. Where did you go?"

"Another call. But I'm back."

"You're busy."

"Always," Wade said. "Have you entered?"

"The Jingle Bell? It's not till next month."

"I'll do it for you. My treat."

Lucas set the cup down, saying nothing.

"Okay, it's done."

"Like that?"

"Like that."

"Thanks, I guess." A long breath seemed necessary. Then Lucas said, "You probably heard, but they let him out. A couple days ago."

"Yeah, Sarah called when it happened. And I read every story, too."

"What do you think?"

"They don't have enough evidence, I think."

"The DNA tests didn't work," Lucas said. "That's what I'm hearing. Not enough material, even with the fanciest labs helping."

"That big rain screwed everything."

"Lucky for Carl," said Lucas.

Silence.

"Ever meet Crouse's sister-in-law?"

"The cop with the jiggly ass?" Wade laughed. "Yeah, she's a pretty one."

"Well, she says the detectives can't see anybody but Jaeger. He has to be the guy. But it's the Wild West around here anymore, and there's not enough manpower to throw at one case. So they let Jaeger go, hoping for something to break later."

"I've studied the statistics, Lucas. Even in good times, a lot of murders never get solved."

"Who else is suspicious?"

The silence ended with fake breathing and an exasperated voice. "You know, I can hope it's Carl. Because if this was a random thing, like some hobo riding the rails or something, then nobody's ever going to find out what happened."

Lucas tried silence.

After a while, Wade said, "You don't have any excuses. I'm looking at the race's roster. Your only competition is Harris, and he can't hang with you."

"It's just the Jingle Bells," said Lucas. "A nothing run."

Another pause.

Another long sip of coffee.

Then the dead man said, "Win a race, Lucas. Just one race. Then you can talk all you want about nothings."

Trees surrender to flattened grass and little stands of sumac. The sky hasn't changed, but the scattered clouds seem higher than before and the polished blue above the world is bright enough to make eyes water and blink. Diving into the grass, the twisting trail decides to narrow, and then like a man regaining his concentration, it straightens—a tidy little gully etched into the native black sod. Lucas runs into the meadow, out where he can see and be seen, and that's where he stops. Nobody follows. Certain teeth ache when he stares into the wind, and he pulls down his sleeves and kneels slightly, listening and waiting. He soon becomes an expert in the sound of wind. It isn't just one noise, but instead wind is endless overlapping noises, each coming from some different place, each hurrying to find ears that want to hear voices and words and sad cries that were never there.

Lucas touches his phone. Eyes scroll and blink to make the call. What isn't a second phone rings in a place that isn't a place. After four rings, he expects voicemail. But the fifth ring breaks early.

"What are you doing?" says the voice.

"Standing. What are you doing?"

"Standing," says Wade.

"Why aren't you running with us?"

"Nobody wanted to talk before. So I turned early and finished." A lip-smack sound comes across. "Have I ever told you? The coffee always tastes great over here."

Lucas stands, knees a little achy.

"Everybody's panting, judging by these paces I've been watching."

"Do you know where they are?" Lucas says.

"Standing where you left Jaeger, mostly."

"Mostly?"

"I've got one phone moving."

"But you can't watch Carl. He doesn't carry a phone."

"Even if he did, I wouldn't know anything. A person has to call a person, and the line has to be opened. That's how I get a lock on positions. And I don't think Jaeger wants to trade running stories with me."

"By the way," Lucas says, "Carl looks pretty innocent."

"Yeah, I'm thinking the shit might have gotten himself a bad break."

"And what do you think about me?" Lucas says.

Silence is the answer, persistent and unnerving.

"So how long does a phone lock last?" Lucas says.

"Four hours, give or take. Then the AI attendant spills me back into the normal mode."

Lucas digs his mittens out of his tights, warming the fingers. "You said one phone is moving." Then he says, "Never mind, I see her."

A brown cap and a pale little face comes out from the trees, the ponytail swaying behind.

"How's Sarah look?" Wade says.

"Real, real tired."

"Poor girl."

"Yeah."

Something not quite a laugh comes into his ear. "I pester you," says Wade. "I know you don't like it sometimes. But she's a lot worse about calling me, and usually for no good reason."

"See you, Wade."

"Yeah," the voice says. "Take care."

Sarah wants to hurry, but her legs are short and stiff. She shuffles and cries and then stops crying. She comes at Lucas with her face twisting, fresh agonies piled on the old, and as soon as she is in arm's length, she makes a fist inside the pink mitten and jabs at his stomach. But even the arms are drained. Lucas catches the fist between his hands. She can't hurt him, so he lowers his hands. "Okay," he says, sticking his stomach out. "If it helps."

Sarah doesn't hit. She falls to her knees, sobbing hard.

Nobody moves in the woods to the north. To the west is the unseen creek with its shackling trees. The empty Amtrak line runs down the east side of the park. A quarter mile south stands a row of ancient cottonwoods, tall as hills, the silvery bark glowing in the rising light. Past those trees is a second rail line. A long oak trestle was built across the floodplain and the older line where the Amtrak would eventually run. Dirt was brought in and dumped under the trestle, creating a tall dark ridge. That line was abandoned decades ago. The rails were pulled up for scrap, old ties sold to gardeners. Only the ridge remains, sprouting trees and angling across the park on its way to towns that exist as history and as memory and as drab little dots on yellowed maps.

Sarah stands and takes in one worthless breath. "You told Jaeger," she says. "You think somebody hired somebody."

Lucas watches her.

"Somebody paid a professional to kill Wade. Is that what you're thinking?"

"No," he says. "I don't think a person put down money to have it done."

She watches him.

"Remember that guy who was kiting checks?" he says. "I once mentioned him to Wade, that I had this bad feeling about the Stingray man. What was his name?"

"Wails."

"Something about Wails was wrong. Talking to the guy, I could see that he was full of shit. I didn't think of check-kiting and stealing millions. That wasn't what I expected. But I told Wade what I thought, and you know him. He took me seriously. 'I'll make some inquiries, see what's what,' he said. Then a week later, cops opened an investigation, and a couple days after that, Wails drove out here . . . . .. to the parking lot we just ran through, if I remember this right . . . and killed himself—"

"But that was a year ago," Sarah says. "Wade was still alive."

"I didn't say Mr. Wails hired it. I'm asking: What if he had a backup?"

She says nothing, staring past his face now.

"I'm not talking about an official, carry-the-same-name kind of backup," he says. "There have to be ways to fake a name and slip clear of your past life, living in the clouds like Wade does. Being everywhere, nowhere. Sitting on whatever stolen money the man was able to hide, and nothing to do with its days but get angrier and angrier about the son-of-a-bitch that made this happen."

Sarah lifts both hands, piling them on top of her head while she slowly rocks back and forth.

"Wails's backup hates Wade Tanner. So he goes out into the living world and finds somebody to help get revenge. Maybe it's for the money, or maybe for personal reasons. And like Carl says, it has to be somebody strong enough and fast enough to keep close to Wade when they're running."

Sarah drops her arms, leaning into Lucas.

He holds her and looks everywhere. The world moves under the wind, but there aren't any people. After another half minute, he says, "I was guessing Pete. He's got the muscle and enough pop in the legs. I figured I was going to see him come out of the trees, looking to shut me up. You I didn't expect."

"It isn't Pete," she says.

"Yeah, I don't want it to be."

"No. I mean it isn't him."

"Why not?"

She pulls out of his grip, wiping her swollen eyes. "Pete made us run this course. Remember? And Jaeger just happened to be up on the levee at the right time. Those aren't coincidences. While we were chasing you, Pete explained everything. He said he bumped into Jaeger last week and threw a few insults at him, and Carl came back with the same arguments he used on the bridge. That's when Pete started to believe him. He began wondering that if Carl wasn't guilty, then maybe the best suspect left was you."

Lucas keeps watch to north, and nothing changes.

A hard sorry laugh comes out of her. "You won't believe this," she says. "Probably nobody would at this point. But I want you to know: I have never, ever cheated on my husband. Not with Masters, and not even with Wade."

Lucas listens to the winds, waiting.

Then she giggles, brightly and suddenly, saying, "But of course it doesn't count, playing games with a machine."

Lucas shakes his head and breathes.

"Harris," he says.

"What?"

"Maybe he's the killer."

"It can't be," she says. "Pete looked at the kid, sure. We know he's strange and we don't know much about his story. But like Carl says, this was a personal killing. A fury killing. Pete says that an ex-Mormon goofball who isn't here six weeks isn't going to want to hurt Wade Tanner. That's why Pete sent him charging off in the wrong direction this morning. He's not a suspect."

"He's telling you that? In front of the kid?"

She shakes her head. "No, Harris was gone by then."

"Gone?"

"The train went past and we caught up to Carl, and Carl gave us your message, and then we stood there talking. And then Harris said we were nuts and stupid and he'd rather run with the deer than waste time standing around with old farts. So he ran back to the train tracks and headed . . . I don't remember where. . . . "

Lucas says nothing.

Sarah takes a breath and holds it. Then all at once, her eyes become big, and she says, "What if . . . ?"

Lucas tells his phone to redial.

Wade picks up and says, "Still standing, still drinking my coffee."

"So," Lucas says. "You talk to Harris today?"

A very brief silence ends with the sound of people being politely quiet, ten million backups stuffed inside that very crowded room. And from the busy silence, Wade says, "Today? No, I haven't talked to the boy. Why? What's our new stallion up to?"

The meadow trail leads south to the cottonwoods. Where shadows begin, Lucas stops and stows the mittens and looks back. Sarah is slowly making her way to the north edge of the grass, and the rest of the runners have come out to meet her. Jaeger stands in the middle of the group. Hands on hips or on top of their heads, they look like soldiers in mismatched uniforms ready to quit the war. Sarah stops and talks, pointing back at Lucas, and everybody stares across the grass, and he can feel the doubts and suspicions thrown his way.

Turning, he settles into a lazy trot.

The forest trail snakes its way toward Ash Creek. The abandoned rail line stands on his left, capped with a second trail that leads over the Amtrak line and back into town. Harris could be running the old right-of-way. If he was smart, the kid would be galloping home now to pack a bag and make some last-second escape. But that would be sensible, and sensible isn't Harris. He's a charger and a brawler. And besides, he found them in the middle of a forest. So the boy isn't completely stupid, and he has some clever way of tracking people.

The five o'clock calls come back to Lucas—the sexy woman and the desperate father. Either one of them could have been Wails faking a voice to patch into the tracking system. But that feels unlikely. Why not just let him pick up, and then hang up? But maybe there's some other trick. Trying to think it through, Lucas realizes that he isn't running and can't remember when he stopped. Staring at the ground, not certain about his own thoughts, his eyes grab onto his ankle, and he bends and pulls up the muddy black leg of the tights, staring at that fancy bracelet that does nothing but shout at the world that he is here and he is sober.

Lucas straightens and turns one full circle. Something is moving on top of the old trestle, but then the background of tree limbs swallows it. Or it never was. Lucas falls into running again, easy long steps eating distance. Get past the trestle, and a dozen trails are waiting to be followed, and there's a hundred ways out of the park. But the best obvious plan is dialing 911, or at least calling somebody closer. Audrey. Lucas decides on her and touches the phone, and he touches it again when nothing happens. But despite having power and a green light, the machine refuses to find the world beyond.

Lucas stops and looks left.

A yellow shirt is on the high ground, not even pretending to hide. The face above it smiles, and maybe it tries laughing. Harris wants to laugh. He stands still, looking down at Lucas while saying a word or two. His glasses are clear enough to show the eyes. He is close enough that the bloody lip looks big and sweat makes the boy-face bright. Some little voice needs to be listened to, and he nods and says something else. Then the right hand lifts, holding a chunk of rusted steel—a piece of trash shaped by chance to resemble a small hatchet.

Harris lifts a foot and drops it.

Lucas breaks, sprinting toward the creek. This time he doesn't obey the trail, cutting across the hard-frozen dirt wherever the brush is thin. He looks down and ahead, and ten strides into this race he turns stupid. It isn't just the world that narrows. His mind empties, his entire day going away. Oxygen-starved and terrified, the brain drops into wild panic, and every step tries to be the biggest, and every downed limb and little gully is jumped with a grace that will never be duplicated. He doesn't know where Harris is, and really, it doesn't matter. Nothing counts but speed and conquering distance, and that wild perfect urgency lasts for most of a minute. And then Lucas runs dry of fuel and breath.

He slows, tasting blood in his throat.

He throws a glance to his left.

The earth wall is close and tall, and Harris runs on top. The kid has never looked this serious, this mature. To somebody, he says, "Yeah."

Then he slows and makes a sharp turn, jumping onto a little deer trail that puts him behind Lucas, maybe twenty meters back.

That feels like a victory, owning the lead.

But Lucas can't turn back now. Not without risking a hack from that piece of metal. Or worse than a hack. He throttles up again, and Harris matches his pace, and he cuts across that last loop in the trail, raspberry bushes snagging his tights. Then he slows, letting the kid buy maybe half of the distance between them while he makes ready for the next turn.

Rusted iron legs hold the vanished tracks high above the stream. The trail lurches to the left and drops under the trestle, and then it lifts again, flattening and turning right before reaching a long pipe-and-wood bridge. Lucas runs the curve tight, saving a half-stride. Maybe ten meters separate them. Maybe eight. He listens to the chasing feet, measuring their pounding. Instinct knows what happens next: As soon as Harris is free of the bridge, he surges. Youth and fear and all that good rich adrenaline are going to demand that Harris end this race here, in the next moments. That's why Lucas surges first. He leaps off the end of the bridge and gains a little, but the pounding behind him ends with some fast clean footfalls that halve the distance and then halve it again. Harris is tucked behind him. A small last surge will put him in range, leaving the boy where he can clip Lucas with his weapon.

But Lucas shortens his stride, just to help his legs move quicker, and Harris is paying a cost for matching him. He gives a hard grunt before accelerating. Except he has somehow fallen back another couple strides, and his exasperation comes out from his chest. He curses—not a word so much as an animal sound that says everything. Those baby legs start to fill with cement. Frustrated and baffled but still too stupid and young to know what has happened, Harris slows down just a little more. His intention is to rest on the fly, gathering his reserves for another surge. This will be easy, in the end. He can't believe anything else. Lucas is nearly twice his age, and there's only one ending in his head, stark and bloody and final. Harris lets the old man gain a full fifteen-meter lead, and just to make sure that Lucas knows, he calls out to him. He says, "Give up." He breathes and says, "You can't win."

Lucas has won. He knows it, and the only problem left is mapping out the rest of this chase.

During one of the big storms last summer, an old cottonwood tumbled across the trail. The city didn't have the money to remove it, and feet and bike tires made a new trail before winter. Trees fall and detours are made, and that's one reason why there aren't many straight lines in the woods. Chainsaws and rot take away the trunks, but new twists are added and established and eventually preferred. The dead tell the living where to walk, and the living never realize that that's what they are doing, and it's like that everywhere and with everything, always.

Big turns are coming. Three, maybe four loops are going to practically double back for a few strides. Lucas doesn't know which one to use, but his plan, much as he plans anything, is to work Harris into a numb half-beaten state and then take him around and jump through the brush, heading north again. But always keeping just ahead, teasing the kid with the idea that at any moment his luck will change, that his legs will get thirty minutes younger and he'll close the gap between him and this gray old fool who doesn't understand that he is beaten.

TEN

The annual track club meeting was held in the restaurant's basement. A stale shabby room was crowded with long tables and folding chairs and fit if not always skinny bodies. Paper plates were stacked with pizza and breadsticks, tall plastic cups full of pop and beer. Conversations centered on January's fine weather and yesterday's long run from the Y, bits of grim international news making it into the chatter. The Y group had claimed the back table, fending off most of the invaders. Chance placed Masters's wife at one end—a heavily made-up woman who made no secret of her extraordinary boredom. Sarah sat between her husband and Crouse, her focus centered on photographs of the new baby. Pete and Varner and Gatlin ruled the room's back corner, entertaining themselves with catty comments about everybody, including each other. Lucas was in the middle of the table, facing the rest of the party. Everybody was keenly aware that he was drinking Pepsi. Audrey had brought her daughter—the fastest fourth-grader in the state—and in a shrewd bid of manipulation set her next to Lucas. Children liked the rough voice and kid-like manner, and the girl was a relentless flirt. She said she liked watching him run. She said the two of them should run together sometime, and Mom could come along, if she could keep up. She asked Lucas how he trained and did he warm up ever and why didn't he ever get hurt?

Harris was sitting on the other side of Lucas. A big bellowing cackle grabbed everyone's attention, and with a matching voice he said, "He doesn't get hurt because of the booze, darling. Beer keeps joints limber."

Embarrassed silence took hold.

Even Harris took note. Trying to make amends, he gave Lucas a friendly punch in the shoulder, and when that wasn't sufficiently charming, he leaned back and said, "Naw, I'm just teasing. Forget it."

Pete noticed. Saying nothing, he stood and wormed his way along the back wall, reaching around Lucas to grab up the Pepsi, taking a long experimental sip. Then he smacked his lips, saying, "Just checking," and he gave Harris a big wink, as if they shared the same joke. The kid laughed and shook his head. Pete set the cup aside, and as his hand pulled away, he kicked a table leg, and as the cup started to tumble, he made a show of reaching out, pushing it and its sticky dark contents into Harris's lap.

The boy cursed, but in a good-natured, only half-pissed way. And the rest of the runners choked their laughs until he had vanished into the bathroom.

Sarah used the distraction to slip away.

Masters's wife noticed the second empty chair. From her regal place at the end of the table, she said to her husband, "What's your girl doing at the podium? She's talking to that camera, isn't she?"

Masters squirmed and said nothing.

Always helpful, Crouse said, "Wade's backup is watching. Don't tell him, but we're giving him a special award tonight."

The woman sneered. Then because it was such an important point, she used a loud voice to tell everybody, "The man is dead. He has been dead for months, and I think you're crazy to play this game."

A new silence grabbed hold. Some eyes watched Masters, wishing that he would say or do anything to prove he had a spine. Oddly though, it was Sarah's husband who took offense. A boyish fellow, small but naturally stout, he possessed a variety of conflicting feelings about many subjects, including Sarah's weakness for one man's memory. But defending his wife mattered, and that's why he leaned across Crouse's lap to say, "You should know, lady. All that makeup and with that poker stuck up your ass, you look more dead than most ghosts do."

The woman blushed, and she straightened. And after careful consideration, she picked up her tiny purse and said, "I'm leaving."

Masters nodded, saying nothing.

"I need the car keys," she said to him.

Then with the beginnings of a smile, Masters said, "It's a nice evening, honey. Darling. A long walk would do you some good."

The pace is barely faster than knuckle-walking. Lucas pushes north, crossing old ground, the wind chilling his face but nothing else. He's going to hurt tomorrow, but nothing feels particularly tired right now. His breathing is easy, legs strong. The trail is smooth and mostly straight, and he has a thirty-meter lead, except when he forgets and works too hard, and then he has to fall back, pretending to be spent, giving Harris reason to surge again. Or he fakes rolling his ankle in a hole. Twice he does that trick, limping badly, and Harris breathes hard and closes the gap, only to see his quarry heal instantly and recover the lead in another few seconds.

The third ankle sprain doesn't fool anyone. Lucas looks back, making certain Harris sees his smile, and then on the next flat straight piece of trail he extends his lead before turning around, running backward, using the same big laugh that the kid uses on everybody else.

Furious, Harris stops and flings the steel weapon.

Lucas sidesteps it and keeps trotting backward, letting the kid come close, and then he wheels and sprints, saying, "So after Wade died . . . why did you stay in town?"

"I didn't kill the guy," Harris says.

"Good to *hear*," Lucas says. "But why stay? Why not pull up and go somewhere else?"

"Because I like it here."

"Good."

"I'm the fastest runner here," he says. "And I like winning races."

Slower runners are up ahead. Everybody looks warm and exhausted, survival strides carrying them toward Lucas. He didn't expect to see them, but nothing that has happened today has made him any happier. "So you didn't kill Wade?" he says.

"No."

"Then why are you chasing me?"

Somehow Harris manages to laugh. "I'm not," he says. "I'm just out for a run, and I'm letting you lead."

Audrey and Carl are leading their pack. Lucas surges to meet up with them, and he stops and turns, and Harris stops with that good thirty meters separating him from the others. Everybody shakes from fatigue, but the kid can barely stand. All of his energy feeds a face that looks defiant and unconcerned and stupid. With a snarl, he says, "I brought the son-of-a-bitch back to you. See?"

Lucas shrugs and says, "Harris killed him. He told me."

"I did not."

"I heard you," Lucas says. Then to the others, he says, "Take us both in. Let the cops sort the evidence. Like those glasses of his . . . I bet they've got some juicy clues hidden in the gears."

Harris pulls off the glasses.

"Watch it," says Pete.

Harris throws the glasses on the ground and lifts a leg, ready to crush the fancy machinery into smaller and smaller bits. But Carl is already running, and the kid manages only two sloppy stomps before he is picked up and thrown down on his side, ribs breaking even before the bony knee is driven into his chest.

"We weren't sure what to do," Pete says to Lucas. "Some of us thought you were guilty, others didn't want to think that. We tried calling you, and when you didn't pick up, I figured you had to be running for Mexico."

Harris tries to stand, and Carl beats him down again.

"We took a vote," Varner says. "Would we come looking for you, or would we just head back to the Y?"

"So I won," Lucas says, smiling.

Audrey dips her head and laughs.

Sarah is next to Carl, watching the mayhem up close.

"No, you only got three votes," Pete says. "But you know how this group makes decisions. The loudest wins, and Audrey just about blew up, trying to get us chasing you."

Lucas looks at her and smiles.

And she rolls her eyes, wanting to tell him something. The words are ready. But not here, not like this.

Then Sarah steps up and hits the cowering figure. She kicks once and again, and polishing her technique, she delivers a hard third impact to the side of the stomach. That's when Masters pulls her away, holding her as she squirms, saying words that don't help. And Carl kneels and pokes once more at the aching ribs, and he picks up every piece of the broken glasses, talking to the ground as he works, saying, "Okay. Now. What are we going to do?"

Back from the bathroom, Harris made a final pass of the food table before reclaiming the chair next to Lucas. Then the track club president—a wizened ex-runner with two new knees—leaned against the podium, reciting the same jokes he used last year before attacking the annual business. Board members talked long about silly crap, and race directors talked way too long about last year's events and all the new runners who were coming from everywhere to live here. Then awards were handed out, including a golden plaque to the police chief who let the track club borrow his officers andhis streets. But the chief had some last-minute conflict and couldn't attend, and nobody else from the department was ready to accept on his behalf. With a big mocking voice, Pete said, "They're out in the world, solving crimes." And most of his table understood the reference, laughing it up until Coach Able and Tom Hubble met at the podium.

Both men were lugging the night's biggest award.

For five long minutes, the presenters took turns praising the dead man. Lucas listened, or at least pretended to listen. Little pieces of the story seemed fresh, but mostly it was old news made simple and pretty. Mostly he found himself watching the serious faces at his table, everybody staring at their plates and their folded hands. Even Harris held himself still, nodding at the proper moments and then applauding politely when the big plaque was unveiled and shown to a camera and the weird, half-real entity that nobody had ever seen.

Then the backup's voice was talking, thanking everybody for this great honor and promising that he would treasure this moment. Sometimes Wade sounded close to tears. Other times he was reading from a prepared speech. "I wish things had gone differently," he said. "But I have no regrets, not for a moment of my life. And if there's any consolation, I want you to know that I am busy here, in this realm, and I am happy."

Then he was done, and maybe he was gone, and the uncomfortable applause began and ended, and the room stood to leave. Most of the back table wanted a good look at the plaque, but somehow Lucas didn't feel like it. He found himself walking toward the stairs, and Harris fell in beside him, laughing quietly.

Or maybe the kid wasn't laughing. Lucas looked at him, seeing nothing but a serious little smile.

"Want to run tomorrow?" said Harris.

"No."

"Tuesday at the track?"

"Probably."

Harris beat him to the stairs, and Harris held the door for the old man. Then as they were stepping into the cool dark, he said, "You know what? We're all going to be living there someday. Where Wade is now."

"Not me," said Lucas.

"Why not you?"

"Because," he said, "I'm planning to die when I die."

ELEVEN

Another pot of coffee helps take the chill out of the kitchen. Out the back door, Lucas watches snow-flakes falling from a clear sky—tiny dry flakes too scarce to ever meet up with each other, much less make anything that matters. He has been talking steadily for several minutes, telling the story fast and pushing toward the finish, and only sometimes does he pause to sip at the coffee. Once or twice he pauses just to pause. Then Wade comes out of the silence, making a comment or posing some little question.

"So after Sarah kicked the shit out of him," he says. "What did you do with the bastard?"

"We picked him up and took turns dragging him and carrying him back to the old right-of-way, then across the creek and out to Foster. That was the closest road, and we got lucky. Some fellow was driving his pickup out of town, hunting for firewood. Except for his chain saw, the truck bed was empty. Gatlin promised him a hundred dollars to take us back to the Y, and Crouse called his sister-in-law, giving her a heads-up. The girls rode inside the cab, in the heat, and the rest of us just about died of frostbite. But we lived and made it back before ten-thirty, and the cops were waiting, and I've never been so happy to see them."

"Has he confessed?"

"You mean, did Harris break down and sob and say, 'Oh god, I did such an awful thing'? No. No, he didn't and he won't. I don't think he even knows that he's a wicked son-of-a-bitch."

"I guess he wouldn't."

"Harris probably doesn't believe this is going to mean anything. In the end." Lucas takes a long sip, shaking his head. "When we were marching him out of the trees, he said to me, 'There's nothing to find. That phone's new. It isn't going show anything important. Any money that I've got has a good story behind it. And the physical evidence is so thin it took them months just to throw Carlie back into the free world. So what happens to me? A couple months in jail, a lot of stupid interviews, and I'll tell them nothing, and they'll have to let me go, too.' "

Silence.

Lucas sets the empty cup on the table, using his other hand to shift the unfamiliar phone back against his ear. "I don't know, Wade. Maybe you should be careful."

"Careful of what?"

"Wails," he says. "Yeah, I told the cops my guess. My theory. I don't think they took it to heart much. But then again, this is a whole different kind of crime. Law enforcement doesn't like things tough. They're happiest when there's bloody boot prints leading to the killer's door."

The backup laughs.

Lucas doesn't. Leaning forward in his chair, he says, "My phone still doesn't work."

"You borrowed that one. I see that."

"Masters says that it was a Trojan or worm or something. Set in long ago, ready for the signal to attack."

"I'll buy you a new phone," Wade says. "That's no problem."

"Yeah, but there's a bigger problem."

"What?"

"Wails," Lucas said. "I was tired when I remembered him this morning. My head was pretty soggy. But the story made a lot of sense, at least for the next couple hours. Except while I sitting at the Y, chatting with the detectives, little things started bugging me."

"Things?"

"About Wails, I mean. Sure, the guy stole money and killed himself. But do we even know you were the reason he got found out?"

"I don't know if I was," says the backup.

"You've said that before. I remember. You aren't sure what happened, because that's one of those stories that the real Wade never told you." Water is running hard in the basement. Lucas doesn't hear it until it shuts off. "Anyway," he says, "I think it's a lot of supposing, putting everything on this one dead man. Yeah, the guy was a liar and a big-time thief, but that's a long way from coming out of the grave to kill another man who did him harm."

Silence.

"But somebody got Harris to kill you," says Lucas. "And if it wasn't Wails, that leaves one suspect that looks pretty good."

"Okay. Who?"

"I'm just talking, my head clear and thinking straight now."

"And I'm listening."

"Okay, it's somebody who wants everything to be fair. Somebody who would do anything he can to make the world right. The same person that let me climb into my own car drunk and watched me drive off and then went and called the cops on me."

"I didn't make that call, Lucas. Wade did."

"But you're based on him. Except for the differences, and maybe they're big differences. I don't know. Or maybe the two of you were exactly the same, and you're Wade Tanner in every way. But Wade didn't tell you everything about himself. We know that. And one day, maybe by accident, you discovered something about your human that really, really pissed you off. The man who built you was a lying shit, or worse. And there you were, wearing Wade's personality. Wade wouldn't let that business drop, and you couldn't either. That's why you went out into the world. You trolled for somebody with little sense and a big need for cash, and that's why Harris showed up here. Maybe murder wasn't your goal. There was that long break between the first hits and the killing. Maybe you were trying to keep Harris from finishing the job. But that's the pretty way to dress up this story. I'm guessing the delay was so that you got your chance to scream at the dying man, telling Wade that he was a miserable disappointment, and by the way, thanks for the money and the immortality and all that other good crap."

Silence.

"You still there?"

"I can't believe this," the voice says.

Lucas nods, saying, "But even if I believe it, nothing is proved. There's probably no evidence waiting out there. Voices can be doctored, which means Harris probably doesn't know who really hired him. Besides, even if I found people to buy this story, something like you has had months to erase clues and files, and even more important, make yourself comfortable with the situation."

"But Lucas—how can you think that about me? Even for a minute."

"I'm talking about a voice," Lucas says. "That's what you are. At the end of the day, you're a string of words coming out with a certain sound, and I can't know anything for sure."

Silence.

"You there?"

Nobody is. The line has been severed.

Lucas pulls the phone away from his face, setting it on the table next to the empty mug. Then Audrey comes out of the basement, wearing borrowed sweats and heavy socks.

She sits opposite him, smiling and waiting.

"I need to shower," he says.

She smiles and says, "How does it feel?"

"How's what feel?"

"Being the fastest runner in the county."

He shrugs and says, "Not on these legs, I'm not."

She says, "I heard you talking just now. Who was it?"

He watches her face and says, "It's snowing out."

She turns to look.

"No, wait," he says. "I guess it stopped."

THE FERMI PARADOX IS OUR BUSINESS MODEL

CHARLIE JANE ANDERS

The thing about seeking out new civilizations is, every discovery brings a day of vomiting. There's no way to wake from a thousand years of Interdream without all of your stomachs clenching and rejecting, like marrow fists. The worst of it was, Jon always woke up hungry as well as nauseous.

This particular time, Jon started puking before the autosystems had even lifted him out of the Interdream envelope. He fell on his haunches and vomited some more, even as he fought the starving urge to suck in flavors through his feed-holes. He missed Toku, even though he'd seen her minutes ago, subjective time.

Instigator didn't have the decency to let Jon finish puking before it started reporting on the latest discovery. "We have picked up—"

"Just—" Jon heaved again. He looked like a child's flatdoll on the smooth green floor, his body too oval from long recumbence, so that his face grimaced out of his sternum. "Just give me a moment."

Instigator waited exactly one standard moment, then went on. "As I was saying," the computer droned, "we've picked up both radiation traces and Cultural Emissions from the planet."

"So, same as always. A technological civilization, followed by Closure." Jon's out-of-practice speaking tentacles stammered as they slapped together around his feed-holes. His vomit had almost completely disappeared from the floor, thanks to the ship's autoscrubs.

"There's one thing." Instigator's voice warbled, simulating the sound of speaking tentacles knotted in puzzlement. "The Cultural Emissions appear to have continued for some time following the Closure."

"Oh." Jon shivered, in spite of the temperature-regulated, womblike Wake Chamber. "That's not supposed to happen." The entire point of Closure was that nothing happened afterwards. Ever again. At least he was no longer sick to his stomachs (for now anyway) and Instigator responded by pumping more flavors into the chamber's methane/nitrogen mix.

Jon spent two millimoments studying the emissions from this planet, third in line from a single star. Instigator kept reminding him he'd have to wake Toku, his boss/partner, with a full report. "Yeah, yeah," Jon said. "I know. But it would be nice to know what to tell Toku first. This makes no sense." Plus he wanted to clean up, maybe aim some spritzer at the cilia on his back, before Toku saw him.

At the thought of Toku coming back to life and greeting him, Jon felt a flutter in his deepest stomach. Whenever Jon was apart from Toku, he felt crazy in love with her—and when he was in her presence, she drove him nuts and he just wanted to get away from her. Since they had been sharing a three-room spaceship for a million years, this dynamic tended to play out in real-time.

Jon tried to organize the facts: He and Toku had slept for about two thousand years, longer than usual. Instigator had established that the little planet had experienced a massive radioactive flare, consistent with the people nuking the hell out of themselves. And afterwards, they'd carried on broadcasting electromagnetic representations of mating or choosing a leader.

"This is shit!" Jon smacked his playback globe with one marrow. "The whole point of Closure is, it's already over before we even know they existed."

"What are you going to tell Toku?" Instigator asked.

Toku hated when Jon gave her incomplete data. They'd taken turns being in charge of the ship, according to custom, for the first half million years of their mission, until they both agreed that Toku was the better decision-maker.

Jon was already fastening the hundreds of strips of fabric that constituted his dress uniform around his arm- and leg-joints. He hated this get-up, but Toku always woke even crankier than he did. His chair melted into the floor and a bed yawned out of the wall so he could stretch himself out.

"I guess I'll tell her what we know, and let her make the call. Most likely, they had a small Closure, kept making Culture, then had a final Closure afterwards. The second one may not have been radioactive. It could have been biological, or climate-based. It doesn't matter. They all end the same way."

At least Jon had the decency to let Toku finish voiding her stomachs and snarling at Instigator's attempts at aromatherapy before he started bombarding her with data. "Hey love," Jon said. "Boy, those two thousand years flew by, huh? The time between new civilizations is getting longer and longer. Makes you wonder if the Great Expedient is almost over."

"Just tell me the score," Toku grumbled.

"Well," Jon said. "We know they were bipedal, like us. They had separate holes for breathing and food consumption, in a big appendage over their bodies. And they had a bunch of languages, which we're still trying to decipher. We've identified manufactured debris orbiting their world, which is always a nice sign. And, uh . . . we think they might have survived."

"What?" Toku jumped to her feet and lurched over, still queasy, to look over Jon's shoulder at his globe. "That doesn't happen."

"That's what I said. So what do we do? The Over-nest says not to approach if we think there's a living culture, right? On the other hand, it might be even longer than two millennia before we find the next civilization."

"Let me worry about that," Toku said, sucking in some energizing flavors and slowly straightening up her beautifully round frame. Her speaking tentacles knotted around her feed-holes. "I think we assume they didn't survive. It's like you said: They probably held on for a little while, then finished up."

Space travel being what it was, Jon and Toku had months to debate this conclusion before they reached this planet, which was of course called Earth. (These civilizations almost always called their homeworlds "Earth.") For two of those months, Instigator mistakenly believed that the planet's main language was something called Espanhua, before figuring out those were two different languages: Spanish and Mandarin.

"It all checks out," Toku insisted. "They're ultra-violent, sex-crazed and leader-focused. In other words, the same as all the others. There's absolutely no way."

Jon did not point out that Toku and he had just spent the past two days having sex in his chamber. Maybe that didn't make them sex-crazed, just affectionate.

"I'm telling you, boss," Jon said. "We're seeing culture that references the Closure as a historical event."

"That does not happen." Toku cradled all her marrows.

There was only one way to settle it. Weeks later, they lurched into realspace and settled into orbit around Earth.

"So?" Toku leaned over Jon and breathed down his back, the way he hated. "What have we got?"

"Looking." Jon hunched over the globe. "Tons of lovely metal, some of it even still in orbit. Definitely plenty of radioactivity. You could warm up a lovebarb in seconds." Then he remembered Toku didn't like that kind of language, even during sex, and quickly moved on. "I can see ruined cities down there, and . . . oh."

He double- and triple-checked to make sure he wasn't looking at historical impressions or fever-traces.

"Yeah, there are definitely still electromagnetic impulses," said Jon. "And people. There's one big settlement on that big island. Or small continent." He gestured at a land mass, which was unfortunately lovebarb-shaped and might remind Toku of his dirty talk a moment earlier.

Toku stared as Jon zoomed in the visual. There was one spire, like a giant worship-spike, with millions of lights glowing on it. A single structure holding a city full of people, with a tip that glowed brighter than the rest. These people were as hierarchical as all the others, so the tip was probably where the leader (or leaders) lived.

"Options," Toku said.

Jon almost offered some options, but realized just in time that she wasn't asking him.

"We could leave," Toku said, "and go looking for a different civilization. Which could take thousands of years, with the luck we've had lately. We could sit here and wait for them to die, which might only take a few hundred years. We could go back into Interdream and ask Instigator to wake us when they're all dead."

"It's just so . . . tasty-looking," Jon sighed. "I mean, look at it. It's perfect. Gases, radioactive materials, refined metals, all just sitting there. How dare they still be alive?"

"They're doing it just to mess with you." Toku laughed and Jon felt a shiver of nervous affection in his back-cilia.

She stalked back to her own chamber to think over the options, while Jon watched the realtime transmissions from the planet. He was annoyed to discover the survivors spoke neither Spanish nor Mandarin, but some other language. Instigator worked on a schema, but it could take days.

"Okay," Toku said a few MM later. "We're going back to Interdream, but only level two, so years become moments. And that way, the wake-up won't be too vomit-making. Instigator will bring us out—gently—when they're all dead."

"Sure, boss," Jon said, but then an unpleasant thought hit him. "What if they don't die off? Instigator might let us sleep forever."

"That doesn't hap—" Toku put one marrow over her feed-holes before she jinxed herself. "Sure. Yeah. Let's make sure Instigator wakes us after a thousand years if the bastards haven't snuffed it by then."

"Sure." Jon started refining Instigator's parameters, just to make damned sure they didn't sleep forever. Something blared from the panel next to his globe, and an indicator he'd never seen before glowed. "Uh, that's a weird light. What's that light? Is it a happy light? Please tell me it's happy."

"That's the external contact monitor," Instigator purred. "Someone on the planet's surface is attempting to talk to us. In that language I've been working on deciphering."

It only took Instigator a couple MM to untangle it. "Attention, vessel from [beyond homeworld]. Please identify yourselves. We are [non-aggro] but we can defend ourselves if we need to. We have a [radioactive projectile] aimed at you. We would welcome your [peaceful alliance]. Please respond."

"Can we talk back in their language?" Toku asked.

Instigator churned for a while, then said yes. "Tell them we come from another star, and we are on a survey mission. We are peaceful but have no desire to interact. Make it clear we are leaving soon."

"Leaving?" Jon asked, after Instigator beamed their message down, translated into "English."

"I've had enough of this." Toku breathed. "Not only did they survive their Closure, but they're threatening us with a Closure of our own. Someone else can check on them in a few millennia. Worst comes to worst, we can just overdraw our credit at the Tradestation some more."

"They are launching something," Instigator reported. "Not a projectile. A vessel. It will converge on our position in a few MM."

Watching the blip lift off from the planet's surface, Jon felt a weird sensation, not unlike the mix of hunger and nausea he'd felt when he'd woken from Interdream: curiosity.

"You have to admit, boss, it would be interesting. The first living civilization we've actually met, in a million years of visiting other worlds. Don't you want to know what they're like?"

"I just wish they had the decency to be dead," Toku sighed. "That's by far the best thing about other civilizations: their 100 percent fatality rate."

The little blip got closer, and Toku didn't make any move to take them out of realspace. She must be experiencing the same pangs of curiosity Jon was. It wasn't as if they'd contacted these people on purpose, so nobody could blame Jon or Toku if they made contact briefly.

Jon reached out with his lower right marrow and grazed Toku's, and she gave him a gentle squeeze.

"What do you want to bet the leader of their civilization is on that ship, engaging in atavistic power displays?" Toku almost giggled. "It would be amusing to see. I mean, we've seen the end result often enough, but . . ."

"Yeah," Jon said. They were each daring the other to be the coward who took the ship out of realspace before that vessel arrived.

The "Earth" ship grazed theirs, trying to do some kind of connective maneuver. Instigator tried a few different things before finally coating the visiting ship's "airlock" with a polymer cocoon. Instigator couldn't make air that the "Earths" could breathe, but could at least provide a temperature-controlled chamber for them in the storage hold.

Three of the "Earths" came into the chamber and figured out a way to sit in the chairs that Instigator provided. In person they looked silly: They had elongated bodies, with "heads" elevated over everything else, as if each person was a miniature hierarchy. "I am Renolz. We are here in [state of non-violence]," the leader of the "Earths" said.

Jon tapped on his communications grid, some sort of all-purpose "nice to meet you" that Instigator could relay to the "Earths."

Slowly, haltingly, the "Earths" conveyed that they were from a city-state called Sidni. And everyone left alive on "Earth" was the servant of someone named "Jondorf" who controlled a profit-making enterprise called "Dorfco." The rest of the "Earths" had died hundreds of years ago, but a few million people had survived inside the "Dorfco" megastructure.

"We always had [optimism/faith] that we weren't alone in the universe," the leader said after a few MM of conversation. "We have waited so long."

"You were never alone," Jon tapped back on his comm-grid. "We made lots of others, just like you, more or less, but you're the first ones we've found alive." He hit "send" before Toku could scream at him to stop.

"What in the slow-rotting third stomach of the Death Lord do you think you're doing?" Toku pushed Jon away from the comm-grid. "You're not supposed to tell them that."

"Oh! Sorry. It just slipped out!" Jon pulled a chair from the floor on the other side of the room from the comm-grid, and settled in to watch from a safe distance.

In reality, Jon had decided to tell the "Earths" the truth, because he had that hunger/nausea pang again. He wanted to see how they would react.

"What did you say?" Renolz replied after a moment. "Did you say you made us?"

"No," Toku tapped hastily on the comm-grid. "That was a translation error. We meant to say we found you, not that we made you. Please ignore that last bit. In any case, we will now be leaving your star system forever. Please get off our ship, and we'll be gone before you know it."

"That was no translation error." Renolz looked agitated, from the way he was twitching. "Please. Tell us what you meant."

"Nothing. We meant nothing. Would you please leave our ship now? We're out of here."

"We will not leave until you explain."

"Options," Toku said, and this time Jon knew better than to offer any. She bared her flavor/gas separators at him in anger. "We could expel the 'Earths' into space, but we're not murderers. We could wait them out, but they might launch their projectile and destroy us. We could leave and take them with us, but then they would suffocate. And we're not murderers."

"Why not just explain it to them?" Jon couldn't help asking.

"This is going on your permanent file." Toku's eyes clustered in pure menace. Jon shrank back into the corner.

"Okay then," Toku tapped on the comm-pad. "This may be hard for you to understand, so please listen carefully and don't do that twitching thing again. Yes. We made you, but it's not personal."

"What do you mean, it is not personal?" Renolz seemed to be assuming the most aggressive power stance an "Earth" could take.

"I mean, we didn't intend to create your species in particular. Our employers seeded this galaxy with billions of life-seeding devices. It was just a wealth-creation schema." The worst Interdream nightmare couldn't be worse than this: having to explain yourself to one of your investment organisms. Toku stiffened and flinched, and Instigator pumped soothing flavors into the air in response.

"You mean you created us as a [capital-accretion enterprise]?" The clear bubble on the front of Renolz's helmet turned cloudy, as if he were secreting excess poisonous gases. The other two members of his group kept clutching each other.

"Yeah, that's right," Toku tapped. "We . . . " She wrote, erased, wrote, erased, wrote again. "We created you, along with countless other sentient creatures. The idea is, you evolve. You develop technology. You fight. You dig up all the metals and radioactive elements out of the ground. As you become more advanced, your population gets bigger, and you fight more. When your civilization gets advanced enough, you fight even harder, until you kill each other off. We don't even find out you existed until after you're all dead. That's how it's supposed to work, anyway."

"Why?"

However they had survived their Closure, it obviously wasn't by being super-intelligent. Toku mashed her marrows together, trying to think of another way to explain it so Renolz would understand, and then leave them alone. "You dig up the metals, to make things. Right? You find the rare elements. You invent technology. Yes? And then you die, and leave it all behind. For us. We come and take it after you are gone. For profit. Now do you understand?"

"So you created us to die."

"Yes."

"For [industrial exploitation]?"

"That's right. It's cheaper than sending machines to do it. Often, the denser metals and rare elements are hard to reach. It would be a major pain."

Toku hit "send" and then waited. Was there any chance that, having heard the truth, the "Earths" would get back into their little ship and go back home, so Toku and Jon could leave before their careers were any more ruined? With luck, the "Earths" would finish dying off before anyone found out what had happened.

"What kind of [night predators] are you?" Renolz asked.

Toku decided to treat the question as informational. "We are the Falshi. We are from a world 120,000 light years from here. We're bipeds, like you. You are the first living civilization we've encountered in a million years of doing this job. We've never killed or hurt anyone. Now will you leave our ship? Please?"

"This is a lot for us to absorb," Renolz said from the other chamber. "We . . . Does your species have [God/creator beliefs]? Who do you think created your kind?"

"We used to believe in gods," Toku responded. "Not any more. We're an old enough race that we were able to study the explosion that created the universe. We saw no creator, no sign of any intelligence at the beginning. Just chaos. But we're not your creators in any meaningful way."

Renolz took a long time to reply. "Will you establish trade with us?"

"Trade?" Toku almost laughed as she read it. She turned to Jon. "Do you see what you've done now?"

Anger made her face smooth out, opened her eyes to the fullest, and for a moment she looked the way she did the day Jon had met her for the first time, in the Tradestation's flavor marsh, when she'd asked him if he liked long journeys.

"We trade with each other," Toku tapped out. "We don't trade with you."

"I think I know why we survived," Renolz said. "We developed a form of [wealth-accretion ideology] that was as strong as nationalism or religion. Dorfco was strong enough to protect itself. Jondorf is a [far-seeing leader]. We understand trade. We could trade with you, as equals."

"We don't recognize your authority to trade," Toku tapped. As soon as she hit the "send" area of the comm-pad, she realized that might have been a mistake. Although communicating with these creatures in the first place was already a huge error.

"So you won't trade with us, but you'll sell our artifacts after we die?" Renolz was twitching again.

"Yes," Toku said. "But we won't hurt you. You hurt each other. It's not our fault. It's just the way you are. Sentient races destroy themselves, it's the way of things. Our race was lucky."

"So was ours," Renolz said. "And we will stay lucky."

Oh dear. Jon could tell Toku was starting to freak out at the way this was going. "Yes, good," she tapped back. "Maybe you'll survive after all. We would be thrilled if that happened. Really. We'll come back in a few thousand years, and see if you're still here."

"Or maybe," Renolz said, "we will come and find you."

Toku stepped away from the comm-grid. "We are in so much trouble," she told Jon. "We might as well not ever go back to Tradestation 237 if anyone finds out what we've done here." Was it childish of Jon to be glad she was saying "we" instead of "you"?

Toku seemed to realize that every exchange was making this conversation more disastrous. She shut off the comm-grid and made a chair near Jon, so she wouldn't feel tempted to try and talk to the "Earths" any more. Renolz kept sending messages, but she didn't answer. Jon kept trying to catch Toku's eyes, but she wouldn't look at him.

"Enough of the silent tactics," Renolz said an hour later. "You made us. You have a responsibility." Toku gave Jon a poisonous look, and Jon covered his eyes.

The "Earths" started running out of air, and decided to go back to their ship. But before they left, Renolz approached the glowing spot that was Instigator's main communications port in that chamber, so his faceplate was huge in their screen. Renolz said, "We are leaving. But you can [have certainty/resolve] that you will be hearing from us again." Instigator dissolved the membrane so the Earth ship could disengage.

"You idiot!" Toku shouted as she watched the ship glide down into the planet's atmosphere. (It was back to "you" instead of "we.") "See what you did? You've given them a reason to keep on surviving!"

"Oh," Jon said. "But no. I mean, even knowing we're out there waiting for them to finish dying . . . it probably won't change their self-destructive tendencies. They're still totally hierarchical; you heard how he talked about that Jondorf character."

Toku had turned her back to Jon, her cilia stiff as twigs.

"Look, I'm sorry," Jon said. "I just, you know, I just acted on impulse." Jon started to babble something else, about exploration and being excited to wake up to a surprise for once, and maybe there was more to life than just tearing through the ruins.

Toku turned back to face Jon, and her eyes were moist. Her speaking tentacles wound around each other. "It's my fault," she said. "I've been in charge too long. We're supposed to take turns, and I . . . I felt like you weren't a leader. Maybe if you'd been in charge occasionally, you'd be better at deciding stuff. It's like what you said before, about hierarchy. It taints everything." She turned and walked back towards her bedchamber.

"So wait," Jon said. "What are we going to do? Where are we going to go next?"

"Back to the Tradestation." Toku didn't look back at him. "We're dissolving our partnership. And hoping to hell the Tradestation isn't sporting a Dorfco logo when we show up there a few thousand years from now. I'm sorry, Jon."

After that, Toku didn't speak to Jon at all until they were both falling naked into their Interdream envelopes. Jon thought he heard her say that they could maybe try to salvage one or two more dead cultures together before they went back to the Tradestation, just so they didn't have to go home empty.

The envelope swallowed Jon like a predatory flower, and the sickly-sweet vapors made him so cold his bones sang. He knew he'd be dreaming about misshapen creatures, dead but still moving, and for a moment he squirmed against the tubes burrowing inside his body. Jon felt lonesome, as if Toku were light-years away instead of in the next room. He was so close to thinking of the perfect thing to say, to make her forgive him. But then he realized that even if he came up with something in his last moment of consciousness, he'd never remember it when he woke. Last-minute amnesia was part of the deal.

THE WORD OF AZRAEL

MATTHEW DAVID SURRIDGE

At the edge of the battlefield of Aruvhossin grew an elm tree. Half its branches were covered in orange leaves. Half were bare and dead. In its shadow, upon a patch of sere grass, sat a man named Isrohim Vey.

Beyond the grass the earth had been bloodied and churned to mud.

Naked to the cold sun were dead men and dead horses and those slowly dying, and scavengers and carrion creatures flitting from one to another. Isrohim Vey sat under the elm, spine against the trunk, a sword driven into the turf by his side, and watched them all. He drew one leg up, as though protecting guts and groin with his thigh-bone. There was a distant terrible pain in his stomach where he had been wounded. Seven kings lay dead on Aruvhossin nearby, and all their armies with them.

The battle had been a day and a night and half a day again. Witchfires had circled Aruvhossin in the darkness, raised by goblinkin slaves of one army or another, burning blue and green and indigo. Dizzy, Isrohim Vey shut his eyes and thought he saw again the stunted things that danced as they died, thought he saw knights charging into a storm of arrows, thought he saw the lipless one-eyed giants whose clubs made the ground tremble, and saw the cloaked Dominies alone or in circles calling on the storms and the powers beyond the storms, and saw his captain die, and saw the last stand of the Anochians, and saw men in armor he'd killed, the Westlander, the kilted Elavhri, and saw necromancers commanding the dead to rise again and whirl about the field to slay and slay and slay; all the world slain on the field of Aruvhossin, the greater part may be mercenaries like him, brutal and who can say but they deserved this, all this.

Isrohim Vey opened his eyes, and it was noon on the second day of the battle of Aruvhossin, and he was (so he imagined) the only living thing that had seen the battle from the beginning and remained alive; and then Isrohim Vey saw the Angel of Death.

The Angel was beautiful and smiled on him, and Isrohim Vey was helpless to tell the depths of that smile or its breadth; if it was a man's smile, or a child's, or if it was large as the field of Aruvhossin, or as all the world. Only that the meaning in it was beyond expression and that the power which moved the sun and the other stars lurked in it and rent his heart.

He did not know what the Angel was about on that battlefield.

He neither perceived nor understood anything of it, or little, beyond the smile. But in thatsmile was all it was and all he was and all he ever would be. His right hand moved, seeking his sword, finding it. It was a fine sword. He had found it fallen on the field of Aruvhossin late on the first day of the battle. It had served well. Now he felt only the sharpness of its edge cutting his hand.

The Angel of Death smiled on Isrohim Vey, and said a Word.

After the Angel had gone Isrohim sat under the elm tree and stared past the field of Aruvhossin. Shafts of sun fell through distant clouds. He was no longer dizzy. He was no longer in pain. He sat, clutching inside himself at the last dregs of the feeling he had been taught when he had seen the Angel and the Angel had looked on him. He knew he would live. For a time. Live to seek the Angel of Death; live 'till he saw it once more, and forever.

Live 'till he knew again the smile and could tell its meaning within his own soul. Just so long, and no longer.

The Dominie peered into the heart of the circlet of amber and crystal.

"The sword is special," he said. "It has a destiny. Be wary; many will seek to take it from you."

"The sword is not my concern," said Isrohim Vey.

The Dominie crossed his study, silver threads glittering in his green cloak, and set the circlet in its space on a shelf between an eggshell painted with a map of the world and a small stoppered glass jar which held an ink elemental splashing and sulking inside its prison. "Yes; your angel," said the Dominie. "Angels are powerful things. Some say, more powerful than all the gods of men. They move the spheres of the sky and rule the houses of the days and the nights. They are beyond both destiny and freewill. They hold the keys, you know; the keys."

"I have seen one."

"Azrael," said the Dominie. "You saw the Angel of Death, whose name is Azrael."

"What do I do now?" asked Isrohim Vey.

The Dominie shrugged. "Go forward, and be blessed."

"Not enough."

"What more will you have, then?"

"I want to see the Angel again."

The Dominie sighed. "When you die."

"I have watched men die. They see no angel. Sometimes, maybe; more often, not."

"Hum," said the Dominie. He asked: "What is death, then, to you?"

"Freedom," answered Isrohim Vey. He looked away from the Dominie. The wizard's study was close and warm. Though it was day, colored candles burned and cloying scent reeled through the air. "I've gone back to the wars since Aruvhossin. I have seen men die, and women, in numbers. I have haunted places of slaughter. But I have not seen the angel again."

The Dominie tilted his head back and drew a breath through his nostrils.

"Who can divine the ways of angels?" he asked, and half his mouth turned up in a grin. "I cannot say where you should look. Only I suggest this. Go to the Free City of Vilmariy for the Grand Masque at midsummer. On that night all things are upended; the people fill the streets in their guises, and I have heard it said, and do well believe, that their costumings on that night reveal hidden and inadvertent truths."

"Are there angels in Vilmariy?" asked Isrohim Vey.

"There are angels everywhere," answered the Dominie.

It has been said that on the night of the Grand Masque in Vilmariy the veils between the country of the dead and the country of the living weaken; as though the two were never separate at all, but two nations in their solitudes interpenetrating.

Isrohim Vey came to Vilmariy for the first time on that carnival night, and walked among the people in costume and the things in no costume and searched for a sign of truth.

He found a bazaar where witches sold candles and silver jewels; where vampires haggled for spices with goblinkin; where clergymen kept assignations with bejewelled succubi; where a half-mad prince bought, from an old man with a long-stemmed pipe and moonstone eyes, a map to the legendary Fount of All out of which proceeds every created thing. In a park he came upon an elegant dance under faerie lights, where stag-headed men partnered green women crowned with garlands of red leaves, and children of the Ylvain in fashions of old time fenced with blunt copper swords stolen from human barrows. In a cemetery he found a frenzy where the white queen of winter copulated with the red king of war in an open grave, and a flockless shepherd pawed the unlikely breasts of a pirate captain, and skeletons danced a lecherous reel with red-eyed hags.

None of these things, to him, was a sign.

Not long before dawn he saw, leaving the grounds of a rich estate where noblewomen in the guise of constellations mingled with Svar Kings from under the earth, a woman dressed as an angel. This was high up the triple-peaked hill on which Vilmariy is built. Isrohim Vey followed the woman down into the heart of the city, along thoroughfares where dukes and outlaws and satyrs lay drunk in the gutters, and then into a maze of alleys. Nor was he the only one who followed her.

Behind him he knew there were others. When the angel slipped in the dark, and kicked at a man with a hyena's head asleep in his own piss, that was when they rushed forward. For a moment Isrohim Vey was caught up in a storm of devils.

Then they were past him, and had reached the angel. Three men dressed as devils to her one. The devils fought with sword and dagger while the angel had only a slim steel rapier. But she was swift as wrath, and they could not touch her. Isrohim Vey drew the sword he had found on the field of Aruvhossin. With his first strike he broke a devil's back. His second thrust threw another against a wall. Then he had to parry; and again; and again. A dagger entered him. Then the devil facing him fell and the beautiful blood-drenched angel smiled at him.

It was not the smile he had looked for. But, he thought, dazed, it will do for now.

"Who are you?" Isrohim Vey murmured, as his legs gave way and he fell to his knees.

"I am Yasleeth Oklenn," said the angel, "the greatest dueling-master of this or any other time; and, sir, you have aided me, and for this I owe you a favor; the which I shall discharge now, in saving your life."

"That is well done," agreed Isrohim Vey.

Three years later, with much having passed between them, he prepared to leave Yasleeth.

At the very end, she said to him: "You're the greatest student I ever had. You've learned all I have to teach of the cunning old man called death. Why go, when you might stay with me, and be rich?"

"Because there is more to know of death," he said, "and I must find it out."

"Death is simple," she said.

He could not argue. He went, nevertheless.

So Isrohim Vey wandered the wide world. He had to fight, often, either to earn his way or simply to survive the bad bandit-haunted roads between cities and fortresses.

Sometimes men sought him out to fight him and take his sword. Sometimes, before he killed them, they mentioned that they had been sent by Nimsza, a Bishop of the Empire Church.

Eventually Isrohim Vey went to the land of Marás, where, in the nave of the Obsidian Cathedral, he slew the Black Bishop called Nimsza; and, taking up Nimsza's ring, spoke with the demon Gorias that Nimsza had commanded in life.

"It may be true," Gorias purred, "that demons know something of the ways of angels." Gorias held Nimsza's soul between its claws, and was content.

"Tell me of the Angel of Death," said Isrohim Vey.

"Azrael cannot be evaded," the demon said.

"I do not want to evade the Angel," said Isrohim Vey. "I want to find him."

"It is, of course, an error to refer to an angel or demon as male or female," observed Gorias thoughtfully. The soul it held wailed a tiny shriek that never ended nor wavered. "However, language on these planes is crude, and incapable of suggesting our essence. I will tell you this: understanding of the Death Angel will come with the right death, when the world turns upside down."

"Explain."

"I cannot. My understanding is not as yours, filtered through reason. Like angels, demons know only what they know. Order me to come with you, if you like. Command me to aid you. With your nameless sword, and my aid, you can become the conqueror that the Black Bishop dreamed of becoming. We will topple empires and you will crush the nations of the world beneath your boots. I have power to do that."

"No."

"Otherwise, pain will come to you. Through me the way to a life of ease. You have the ring that is my weakness; command me."

"No."

"I can give you to Azrael," said Gorias. Isrohim Vey said nothing. "You will know the smile you seek," said the demon. "Command me."

"Then you will have my soul," said Isrohim Vey.

"But you will have your angel," said the demon Gorias.

"I will say this to you," said Isrohim Vey, and spoke the Word of Azrael.

Gorias shrieked and fled to the thirteen hells.

Theologians have since debated the fate of Nimsza's soul. As is the case with most souls, however, its destiny remains unclear.

Excommunicated by the Empire Church for slaying the Black Bishop, Isrohim Vey travelled to the Valley of Rhûn that had been the heart of the Dominion of the Lohr when that mighty and cunning people had ruled half a continent. Centuries before the Valley of Rhûn had been overrun by goblinkin who had come in a swarm out of the north; the Lohr now were gone, and the goblins warred with each other among the ruins.

In the fallen Lohr capital of Opallios Isrohim Vey found libraries of ancient unreadable script guarded by Ylvain warring against the goblinkin, and small gargoyles who glared after him with garnet eyes and bellowed out proclamations of might, and carrion birds with old-man's heads, and a kind of large bone-white spider which seemed clever in the way that foxes are clever and which wove webs that wailed gently in the wind. He also found wands of light and darkness, and bell-shaped diamonds holding frozen songs, and a whip that commanded the flood and the eclipse, and the ashes of a book which had held the Seven Secret Words to Command Love and War, and, finally, ghosts.

He spoke to the ghosts one by one in the broken streets and other places, saying "I seek the Angel Azrael." And none of them had intelligence of the angel to give him.

Some said to him "Be happy and do not drive yourself through the warm life with your eyes upon the next."

These ghosts Isrohim Vey ignored.

He found sometimes ruins of the temples of the twelve gods of the Lohr and the God of All Other Things. In these places the ghosts of priests served the ghosts of gods, and Isrohim Vey spoke to them.

A priest of Ikeni, goddess of Names, said this to him:

"Your name is Isrohim Vey, and your sword has no name. Your identity is this: like any seeker of any kind, you are what you look for. To find it will be to destroy yourself."

"The sword has a name," said Isrohim Vey. "It is called Azrael's Word." And he left Opallios.

Sometime after, the excommunicate Isrohim Vey was seen in the castle-city of Tíranin, which is the capital of Yriadriú, the First Empire.

Tíranin is very old, and no one now remembers whether it began as a castle which grew into a city, or as a city which built itself up into a single castle.

Isrohim Vey was soon known and feared in the great halls that house bardic contests, in the hole-in-the-wall taverns, in the sordid side passages where thieves swindle each other and whores keep appointments in rooms filled by the ratgnawed finery of long-gone dynasties. There is very much dust, everywhere in Tíranin.

Isrohim Vey, soon after his arrival, became involved in a labyrinthine conspiracy against the ruling line of Yriadriú. By the time events worked themselves into History's chosen pattern, five towers were set afire, the Bronze Duke committed suicide, a hatmaker who ran a shop on a high balcony near Parliament Keep had an emerald pin stolen, Queen Jael met her own reflection walking in a chapel maze, a brief but violent battle flared among the Dominies of the High Thaumaturgical Council, an enslaved unicorn was freed from the flesh-marts, Isrohim Vey changed sides, the strange secret of the Leader of the Parliamentary Opposition was revealed, and a mad priest who worshipped the Red Gods of a people long thought extinct raised a forest of oaks to crack the stones of Tíranin, and in so doing revealed an army of ghouls lurking in old secret places within the walls preparing to fall upon the living who were their descendants.

In the end, it was Isrohim Vey who led the search for the Hidden Necropolis, and then led the battle against the Ghoul Lords in their tombs. Finally, facing over the point of his sword the King-That-Was-And-Would-Be-Again, Isrohim Vey heard the name of the Angel of Death once more.

"I know," said the dead King, "that you came to Tíranin seeking knowledge of Azrael. But the libraries of the Dominies have not helped you, nor have all the histories of the ages of the world."

In his hands the King-That-Was-And-Would-Be-Again held a skull. The skull said: "Murder and maim, torture and slay, long the path of Isrohim Vey."

Isrohim Vey said: "Tell me about Azrael."

The King-That-Was-And-Would-Be-Again said: "I can tell you nothing, for death has sealed my lips. But this is my counselor and prophet, who may speak as he will."

And the skull said: "Thou grim unfearing restless soul! Walk alone, no clue to your goal."

Then Isrohim Vey knew his time in Tíranin had been useless; and Queen Jael came riding through a mirror on a unicorn, and stabbed the King-That-Was-And-Would-Be-Again through his unbeating heart with an emerald pin, and the dead King fell to dust.

The skull fell to the ground and said: "One and all have their fates interlaced. Death's grin your end; all else is waste."

Leaving Tíranin, for some time Isrohim Vey wandered the north of the world. He established a society of outlaws in Thursegarth Gianthome; further east, he organized villages of the Mistborn tribes in a defense against incursions of the Nekrûl. Eventually the Nekrûl came in force, with their wicked beasts warped by chaos, their companies of toad-troopers, their priests of old and unclean dogmas.

They captured Isrohim Vey, and he was sent to Illullunor in the Clawline.

The Clawline had been carved upon the face of the world before Time began by one of the Elder Gods the Nekrûl worshipped; sunlight never came there, and fungi grew in mutated forms like wind-shaped snowdrifts, and the ground had been made brittle and false by the ages-long gnawing of subterranean acids. Illullunor, the Hideous Prison, was set in the sides of a great rift in the earth; the base of the rift, never seen, birthed cold mists that drained will and strength from the prisoners even as they were made to mine the bitter ores of the Clawline.

Iä Quis, Master of Illullunor, spoke with Isrohim Vey three times.

The first time, he said "I know who you are. I know what happened at Aruvhossin. I know the things you've done since; and why. I know your sword has a destiny, and that is why I have learned these things and brought you here. I am an initiate of the Old God Ophion, and I know Its rites and mysteries and theurgies. I will take your destiny from you. Do you understand? I will penetrate into it and defile it. You must understand. That is how it begins."

The second time Iä Quis spoke to Isrohim Vey was some while later.

Numerous tortures had been inflicted upon the swordsman by that point.

Another prisoner, a youth named Valas, had become his guide and ally. This was not known to Iä Quis, and at that time was not relevant.

"Nothingness precedes existence, and is therefore logically superior to it," said Iä Quis. "The Old Gods of Nekrûl come from the void that was before all things. To return to the gods, all things must be erased. Destiny must be, not simply changed or negated, but turned back on itself. Nihilism, to be perfect, must be universal. But your sword remains a mystery. You yourself have not uttered a word since you arrived in Illullunor, excepting your screams. Speak now; explain yourself, and the history of the sword, and be released." Isrohim Vey said nothing, and Iä Quis was not sure if the swordsman understood him or if pain had driven him mad.

The third time Iä Quis spoke to Isrohim Vey the Master of Illullunor had a fever's sweat, and his flesh was pale, as though his blood had dripped out of him. "Ophion is the Old God who first drew the distinction between *those who have* and *those who have not*; who invented power and weakness, and the lust for power, and the idea of murder for power's sake, and all the science of oppression. For power is nothingness . . . but this, the sword," and the hand of Iä Quis shook as he indicated Azrael's Word, "this I cannot unriddle . . . Only, I find always the same answer . . . that is, death. Can death, and only death, be your destiny? But that is the destiny of every living thing."

Then Isrohim Vey spoke to Iä Quis for the first and last time, and said "The meaning of these things is that you will die by Azrael's Word." Then it so happened that the youth Valas caused a carefully-planned collapse in the mine tunnels, and all Illullunor shook, and in a moment Isrohim Vey proved his words to be true.

There was, after that, much murder done in Illullunor the Hideous Prison. Perhaps all of those who died deserved their fates.

When it was done, and the former prisoners victorious and all the corpses thrown into the mists below Illullunor, the youth Valas asked to accompany Isrohim Vey on his travels.

"I am looking for the smile of the Angel of Death," said the swordsman.

Valas, expressionless, nodded.

"He frightens me," said Valas to the blind bard. "I know there was a woman, once, in Vilmariy. He loves her, but will not go back to her. Or he doesn't love her. He left her in order *not* to love her. How can a man do that?"

The old man nodded, very slow; meaning nothing. In a corner of the innroom the bard's three daughters watched, wordless. "You met him in a place which scarred many men," said the bard. "And he, you say, suffered more than most."

"There's more to it," said Valas. "I know what Illullunor did to men. You learn ways of surviving, how to gnaw dirt to cure yourself of the taste for food, which of the guards have a taste for rape, how to hide yourself away inside your head and how to find your way back to the world. But when he came and when he left was much the same. Partly it's that which frightens me."

The bard shifted on his bench, and scratched at his bristly beard. From outside the thrum of summer rain came, beating against the lush forest beyond the inn. "You've travelled with him three years? Four?—I've heard stories of the death-bound swordsman for some time, and it seems to me stories of the boy at his side began about so long ago . . . have you been afraid of him all that time?"

"No. Or, yes, but I thought it would ease over time. Lessen. It hasn't."

"Why stay?"

"One and all have their fates interlaced." Valas looked away from the bard, toward the inn's hearth. "That's something he says. At night, while he sleeps. But in a normal voice."

"What does it mean?" asked the blind bard.

"Well," said Valas. "I don't believe in fate." He propped his chin in his hand and stared into the coals of the fire. "But I have seen a great deal of the world with him. I'm learning something, I feel, though I don't know what. You say you've heard the stories."

"I'm a King among bards," said the blind man. "For what that's worth. Of *course* I've heard the stories. The amber stairs and the salamander's daughters. The white gold tears of the desolation of Thamycos. The battle with the ice of Grandfather Hiberius. The assassins sent by the House of Quis—"

"Yes, and he doesn't care," said Valas. "*That's* what frightens me. In the end. Glories, treasures, deaths, they don't . . . *touch* him."

The blind bard tapped a finger on the table as though playing an unseen instrument. "Then he's wrong. These things have become legend. Tales of Isrohim Vey are told across all the lands north of the Inheritors of Kesh. And all we are, are tales we make of ourselves. This I know to be true, as I am King of Bards; I swear it by the Fount of All, source of all things and all tales."

"Maybe," said Valas, his head bowed. He flicked his eyes to the three daughters of the old man; two of them stared back, while the third watched her father lovingly. "But what if there's something more, or what if those tales are shaped by something beyond us?"

All through this talk, Isrohim Vey sat staring out a window at a crippled dog drowning in a puddle of water. He did not move, and it was impossible to say if he had heard Valas and the blind bard, or what his thoughts were if he had.

The wanderings of Isrohim Vey took him at last to sea, and Valas with him. Far from land, their ship was attacked by pirates of the Nahor Islands.

The ship, the *Crone of Keys*, was swarmed by pirates and Isrohim Vey slew them as they came. There were half-a-dozen pirate vessels, and more and more of them were forced to send their crew aboard the *Crone of Keys* as Isrohim Vey killed and killed. The *Crone of Keys* began to burn, and he fought on. The decks were washed with blood, and the air tasted of salt. Every crewman aboard the ship had been slain, but Isrohim Vey continued to battle with Azrael's Word, and with Valas at his side.

Then the leader of the pirates came forward and shouted to Isrohim Vey, "We must fight, you and I. I am Reivym Shoi, who came from the mainland to rule these wicked crews."

Isrohim Vey nodded, and the two of them fought for a long while under the sun.

"You're going to die on this ship," said Reivym Shoi. He had a deep cut in his off-hand.

"Maybe," said Isrohim Vey, who was bleeding down one side of his face.

"I have a hero's fate," said Reivym Shoi. He began a long series of slashes and thrusts, elegant and precise; he had been schooled. Isrohim Vey blocked many of them, but not all. "I am going to wield the Nameless Sword and strike down the Angel of Death. What is fated to be must be. But this is not why you are going to die. You are going to die because I'm a better swordsman than you."

Isrohim Vey said nothing. But a moment later Reivym Shoi's sword had cut his right wrist, and he dropped Azrael's Word. Remorseless, Reivym Shoi dealt his concluding stoke. Isrohim Vey threw up his left arm to block it. The blade's edge bit deep, and struck into the bone, and stuck there. Isrohim Vey twisted his arm back and wrenched the sword from Reivym Shoi. Then he drew the sword from his arm-bone and ran the pirate through. The wound was not fatal, but Reivym Shoi staggered back against the rail of the ship as Isrohim Vey picked up Azrael's Word.

Then Reivym Shoi said "Ah, that is the Nameless Sword which was used against me."

"It is Azrael's Word," said Isrohim Vey.

"I know you," said Reivym Shoi. "The death-bound swordsman. Isrohim Vey, you and I are the only two men to have survived the battle of Aruvhossin."

Isrohim Vey lashed out with Azrael's Word. The pirate fell from the deck of the *Crone of Keys* into the deep sea. He was not seen to resurface.

Valas, who from infancy had lived in the Hideous Prison Illullunor, discovered he was the heir to a lost kingdom when the Princess Elidora Byth of Kethonin was abducted by Ûr Quis, patriarch of the House of Quis, Duke of the Tyranny of Nekrûl, whose grand-son Iä Quis had been delivered to the Angel of Death at the ruin of the Hideous Prison Illullunor. The King of Kethonin sent agents to Isrohim Vey to tell him that the leader of the clan of his enemies was abroad and engaged in some evil plan. So Isrohim Vey and Valas climbed into the mountains of what had been the kingdom of Dys in search of Ûr Quis. And this was as Ûr Quis had planned.

They found him in an ancient temple of the Nekrûl hidden deep in a cave; the mountains of Dys are within sight of the Clawline, and the Nekrûl had long ago infiltrated the countries of their neighbors. Ûr Quis had returned to this forgotten place to raise an aspect of the Old God called Ophion. Isrohim Vey slew Ûr Quis and the avatar of Ophion, a lamprey-jawed serpent thick as a man.

Valas desecrated the altars of Ophion and shattered Princess Elidora Byth's manacles.

When they returned to Kethonin, the King had it announced that Valas was the rightful heir of Dys, captured by the Nekrûl when he was a baby, and of a status to marry the Princess Elidora Byth. These things were supported with all relevant proofs and testimony from those who remembered the stolen infant prince. Princess Elidora, who was noted for her fierceness and who had sworn an oath to Halja of the Keys to make the marriage bed a place of war and poisons for any husband forced upon her, proclaimed herself pleased by this revelation, as was the young hero Valas. As for the King of Kethonin, whose subjects in the province of Dys had been restless of late, and whose daughter was noted among noblemen's sons for her troublesome spirit and her bloodthirstiness, he was himself quite satisfied at how events had fallen out. The wedding would be a great festival for all the lands nearby.

The night before it took place, Valas spoke to Isrohim Vey.

"Will you stay with us, in Kethonin?" he asked. "You'll have much honor."

He was afraid as he said this.

Isrohim Vey said nothing for a long time, staring at the stars. Then he looked at Valas. For the first time Valas realised that Isrohim Vey, who was most alone when with other people, could not frame in words things that he felt; and that therefore there were many things he did not know about himself.

"All right, then," said Valas. "But will you give us your benediction?"

Isrohim Vey nodded, and on the next day before the nobility of seven kingdoms he blessed the marriage of Prince Valas and Princess Elidora Byth by speaking the Word of Azrael.

Many years later Isrohim Vey came to Lugbragthoth the University City at the time of its sack by the armies of Ettra, headman of the Non.

The Non, who were barbarians, were laying siege to the rocky spires of the Thirteen Colleges. The Lower City was mostly ruins and ashes. Some fires burned. There were corpses, the stink of death and roasting flesh, rubble and offal. There were raw screams; these came mostly from women and girls. The males who were not at war were all dead.

Lugbragthoth had been built, not long after the beginning of the current Age of the world, upon the jagged mountain called Tavish. Each of the thirteen high narrow peaks housed a College dedicated to a branch of learning, and each of the Colleges had high old walls and many guardsmen. They also held books, which were rare things, and being books they were held to be magic, and were therefore objects of hate and lust. Around the Colleges, spreading down the sides of the mountain, was the Lower City. It seemed like a counter-attack was underway against the Non as Isrohim Vey walked toward the Dire Stairs leading to the College of the Seven Saints; anyway men in livery battled Ettra's men here and there through the city. Isrohim Vey ignored them and ignored the screaming and walked on up the hillside. Blood flowed past him, the streets become rivers flowing downhill to unimaginable oceans.

Once three Non tribesmen came upon him, and attacked chanting their war-songs. Two he slew quickly; the largest gave him a minute's battle, and that was mostly due to a tough hide the big man wore. Otherwise, he climbed to the Dire Stairs and up in silence.

The Dire Stairs branch off, then the branches cross and recombine in a diagonal labyrinth. Isrohim Vey did not know the quickest way to the College of the Seven Saints and had no skill with mazes, but he was patient. He tried every branch and turn, and retraced his steps when he needed to, which was often.

Sometimes the stairs led up to and then down from outcroppings, lookout points. At one of these places he saw the Aureate College collapse in flames. At another he met a howling old man with the corpse of a young woman in his arms; Isrohim Vey noticed that the old man's eyes were milk-white, and took his arm to guide him along the stairs.

"She's dead!" screamed the old man. He seemed not to notice the swordsman's touch. "She's dead!"

"You're alive," said Isrohim Vey.

The old man quieted at once and turned, seeking after the sound. "Your voice," he whispered. "Are you there? *You*?"

"Do you know me?"

"I heard your voice, once," said the old man. "I have echoed it for a long time since."

Isrohim Vey did not understand this, but he presumed the man was mad. "This place is not safe. I will guide you away from here."

"Ah," said the blind old man. "I know where you'll lead me."

"I will lead you to Saints' College."

"No. You've changed with the years, but not so much."

"I have nothing to do with this war. I've come only to speak with the wise men of Lugbragthoth, who I have heard are philosophers who think and write of life and also of death."

"Oh, but you, you are Isrohim Vey," said the blind man. "I know you, better than I know myself. I've told tales of you, long years I've told the tales. I know you from the inside. You will lead me to death. That's your tale, and we are every one trapped in empty tales of ourselves told by fools."

"Would you rather be free?" asked Isrohim Vey. The blind old man took a deep breath.

"I am King of Bards," he said, "and my one faithful daughter is dead." He stepped off the stairs, and fell a long way and then died.

There are stories of Isrohim Vey at the Sack of Lugbragthoth and how he led the defense of Saints' College. How by his skill and strength he threw back the invaders. Some stories say that he slew Ettra, leader of the people of the Non, in single combat, and burned his legendary gryphon-skin armor. Other stories say Ettra was killed before Isrohim Vey arrived, in a chance scuffle in the Lower City. Many of the stories are contradictory, but none has died for lack of telling.

Isrohim Vey learned to read and studied for a while in the Colleges of Lugbragthoth. Then for a time he disappeared from the known lands. Travelers to the deep forests of the stag-headed Ceridvaen races claimed to hear of a silent swordsman haunting the standing stones of an Age gone by. Eventually he was seen in Zimri, that curious city of popes, poisoners, and patrons of the arts, where he was involved in the spate of odd deaths surrounding a curious moonstone icon dedicated to Halja, Matriarch of Keys. After the destruction of the icon by lightning, Isrohim Vey travelled south past the Inheritors of Kesh to Ulvandr-Kathros the Confederate Empire, where the seasons are reversed and the stars different. Following a riot in the slave marts of the Empire's capital of Carcannum, Isrohim Vey returned to the north of the world and visited the witch-kingdom of Wyrddh, where without explanation he was taken prisoner and bound by a crossroads in a cage of yellow bone and black iron. A Duke of Cats was set to watch him and given Azrael's Word for a plaything, and so Isrohim Vey was left for dead.

Then Valas came, and he distracted the Duke of Cats with riddles and took the sword and rescued Isrohim Vey.

Valas told Isrohim Vey that the dragon Umbral had burnt most of Kethonin and abducted the Queen Elidora Byth. "I know where the dragon's lair is," said Valas. "But Umbral is very powerful. I need your help to kill him."

"I will help you," said Isrohim Vey, and they set out.

They went a very long way, across North Ocean to the Cauldron Lands where the savage goblinfolk churn in endless warfare. They crossed fields of ice and snow-storms and passed under curtains of light in the nighttime skies.

The dragon's lair was a glacier of black ice worked into spires and curves.

Four rivers crusted with half-frozen poisons flowed away from it to every point of the compass. Valas and Isrohim Vey approached as carefully as they could. They passed into a great hall, all of ice, and a chamber of black ice mirrors, and through the empty pathways of the glacier; until at last they descended into the pits below, and discovered Umbral in a fountain arising from the earth, his black scales fouling the waters at their source.

"Give me back my wife," Valas demanded of the waiting dragon.

"She's dead," said Umbral. "I killed her some time ago." Valas screamed and drew his sword and Umbral breathed a black flame and killed him. The dragon turned its old head to the other man.

"Why did you take Elidora Byth?" asked Isrohim Vey.

"Perhaps I wanted to bring you to me," said Umbral. "It worked for Ûr Quis."

"Ûr Quis is dead."

"Yes," said the dragon. Then it leaped at Isrohim Vey, huge as night.

Isrohim Vey drew Azrael's Word and in a moment the sword was buried in Umbral's heart.

"This is my death," said the dragon. "I have known all the Ages of the world; it is enough. I am slain by the Nameless Blade forged by Einik of the Svar; and that too is enough. It is a fitting death. I have made my end."

Then Umbral died, and Isrohim Vey took back Azrael's Word and set off for the south.

Traveling to the Dweorgheorte Mountains, Isrohim Vey descended into the subterranean tunnels called Chthonia or Domdaniel. In these tunnels he made his way to the Svar kingdom of Vâlain.

The Svar are half the height of a man, until they choose to be otherwise, when they can grow tall as a giant. They do not eat or drink, and do not age or die unless violence is done to them. Isrohim Vey made his way through their halls under the earth by the light of their eyes, which are burning lamps.

"Where is the smith named Einik?" he asked, and every time he asked he was given the same answer:

"Further down."

But however far down into Domdaniel Isrohim Vey travelled, he found that Einik was always further, beyond Vâlain itself, in the tunnels of the Deep Dark where only the mad and the visionary among the Svar dared to go.

It was one of these, a prophet, who finally came to Isrohim Vey and promised to lead him to Einik. Isrohim Vey went with the Svar prophet to the Deep Dark, and the prophet led him past great white bats and the cities of the grim peoples under the earth and a seer of the goblinfolk raving of a human boy who would come to be king of Domdaniel and lead his folk to victory over the armies of the surface. Then the Svar stopped and told Isrohim Vey how to proceed and the swordsman walked the last distance to the forge of Einik alone.

Einik, the legendary smith, worked at fashioning a Svar child while Isrohim Vey spoke to him.

"The truth of your sword," said Einik, "is that it is the product of a deal I made, a very long time ago. I'd realized that whatever I made would, in the end, break. Nothing was perfect. Nothing lasted. I disliked that. I made a deal; I would make a thing, a sword, the greatest thing I would ever make, and that sword would last forever through all the Ages of the world."

"Who did you make this deal with?" asked Isrohim Vey.

"Father Stone?" suggested the smith. "The One Above All? The Jack-of-all-Ills? I don't know. I don't need to know. But it was done."

"How old is the sword?"

The smith considered this. "Old," he decided.

"How did it come to the battlefield of Aruvhossin?"

"I don't know," said Einik. "I don't keep track of its whereabouts."

"Why not?"

Einik smiled without looking away from his work. "I don't need to," he said. "It's perfect. It will last. Somewhere, in the world, is the perfect thing that I made which will outlive me. That's enough."

Isrohim Vey thought about this, too, and watched as Einik finished his work.

"Does the sword have a destiny?" he asked.

"I don't know," said Einik. "I made it; that's enough. I suppose either everything has a destiny, or nothing does."

"I have given it a name," said Isrohim Vey. "It's called Azrael's Word."

"It's been called many things," said Einik. "It outlasts names." He turned the infant Svar over in his hands. It did not move and its eyes were dark.

"What did you give in exchange for the making of the sword?" asked Isrohim Vey; and then for the first time Einik of the Svar locked eyes with him, and the swordsman saw that a white heat burned in him with a hard gem-like flame.

"I will tell you," said the smith, "but you must do a thing in exchange."

Isrohim Vey nodded.

"In exchange for making one perfect thing," said Einik, "I had to accept that every other thing I made would be less than perfect. That I would never again reach the height of the Nameless Sword. Now: reach into my forge and take out a burning coal, and put it in the mouth of the child."

Isrohim Vey reached into the fire with his left hand and did as the smith demanded. As he screamed, the eyes of the Svar baby lit up.

After leaving the Dweorgheorte Mountains, Isrohim Vey returned to the city of Vilmariy and was caught up in a struggle between two noble houses which resolved itself in a duel by proxy; Isrohim Vey was one proxy, and the other was the greatest fencer in all the Free Cities, Yasleeth Oklenn. Isrohim Vey slew Yasleeth and left Vilmariy, swearing a great oath upon his soul never to return again.

The people of the hamlet of Mun-at-Tor go about their work each day in silence, unsmiling. To the north, east, and south of Mun-at-Tor are quarries of fine stone, and it is to these places that the people go. No-one goes west, past the three heavy stone churches, to the high forested hill; no-one passes under the old stone arch built over a gully in the hillside, where the greenery grows richest. No one follows the music that comes from the arch at dawn and twilight. At least, no-one from Mun-at-Tor; sometimes a wild-eyed traveler comes to the grey quarry town and strides up the hill and through the arch and is, most often, not seen again.

Isrohim Vey came to Mun-at-Tor from Vilmariy and, arriving at dusk, walked under the old stone arch into the Faefair of the Ylvain.

Stalls were scattered across the face of the darkening hillside. The stalls were made of rare white and golden and crimson woods and carved into fantastic shapes, from which sprigs of holly and mistletoe sometimes grew. Pale musicians played inhuman sounds on skin drums and beetle-shell flutes and harps strung with cat's whiskers. The faerie folk were everywhere, buying and selling, some of them with foxes' heads, some half-a-foot high, some bent and bony as gargoyles, and some of them of the noble houses of the Ylvain.

Like their enemies the Svar, the Ylvain are immortal; but the Ylvain are tall and fair, and live in magic and forestlands, and their skin is bright as dawn, and in their veins is neither blood nor ichor but fine white mist, and it is their curse that everything they touch turns to beauty.

Isrohim Vey strode into the Faefair. He ignored the slender peddlers in green with pointed brows and wolf's fangs, selling trinkets like unbreakable chains of flowers and an elixir that was the essence of music. He passed cobblers selling boots that could walk between the moments of the clock; he passed drinking-booths selling beer that tasted of summers past; he passed stalls selling rare fruits, oranges and indigos, passionfruit and repentancefruit, firstfruits and lastfruits; he passed no blacksmiths or ironmongers. He didn't know what he was looking for.

He came to a high wagon; doors in the back were open, and inside there was paper: books, scrolls, and maps. More paper than Isrohim Vey had ever seen outside of the libraries of Lugbragthoth or the archives of Tíranin, and both of those were closely guarded. An old man in faded robes sat on a step leading into the wagon, smoking a long-stemmed pipe. He seemed human, but for his eyes, which were moonstones. He nodded to Isrohim Vey as the swordsman stepped into the wagon.

"You're mortal," said Isrohim Vey.

"I'm old. That's near to mortal."

"I don't know how old I am," said Isrohim Vey. "Fifty, I think. Close. Most men in my way of life don't live as long."

"What are you looking for at the Faefair? Youth?"

"Truth," said Isrohim Vey.

"I can sell you truth. But there will be a price."

"I'll pay it."

"So sure? You don't know what it is."

Isrohim Vey said nothing.

The old man sighed and refilled his pipe. "This is the truth: fifty years ago, give or take, the Nameless Sword hung above the bed of the Duke of Eblinn. Beneath its point a child was conceived, and nine months later was born. The Nameless Sword had been in the family of the Duke of Eblinn for centuries by this time. At the birth of the boy-child, a Dominie predicted firstly that he would meet death on a field named Aruvhossin; but also that if he evaded this death, he would go on to kill death itself. This boy was named Reivym Shoi. You met him once."

"Did I?"

"It was a long time ago. But he was at Aruvhossin, commanding his father's armies; you were at the same battle, having joined a company of Naranthi mercenaries fighting under the standard of the King of Anoch. Reivym Shoi bore the Nameless Sword in battle, believing that its destiny would keep him safe to pursue his own."

"What is the destiny of the sword?" asked Isrohim Vey.

"It is a sword. Its destiny is death. More than that no created being has ever been able to tell. Perhaps it will slay all the world. It kept Reivym Shoi safe and living until late on the first day of the battle, when he was attacked from behind by a Panjonrian soldier and left for dead. The Panjonrian took the sword, but was soon slain himself. You took the sword from his dead hand. With it, you survived the rest of the day, and through the night, and through to the end of the battle."

Isrohim Vey thought about this. Then he nodded, slowly. After some time he asked: "What do I do now?"

"Go forward, as you like. But I will tell you this. If you still wish to see the Angel of Death, then look for Reivym Shoi, who will meet the Angel before he dies."

"Where's Reivym Shoi?"

"Reivym Shoi has been looking for you. He has gone to the one place you returned to, in all your time of wandering. He has gone to Vilmariy, and he has sworn a great oath upon his soul not to leave until you come a third time to the city."

Isrohim Vey said nothing. He sat on the step of the wagon and laughed.

The old man watched him.

"Now come with me," said the old man, "for you promised to pay my price."

"What must I do?"

"Fight, and kill, and perhaps die."

The old man took Isrohim Vey to a high tower in the Oneda Mountains that looked out over all the world. "I am the Dominie Segelius," the old man told Isrohim Vey, "and you are in the Demesne of Starry Wisdom and Golden-Eyed Dawn, which is the true home country of every wizard. Rest; tomorrow you begin to fight."

On the next day, Isrohim Vey fought and killed a gray-skinned warrior with a dog's head. The battlefield was a giant's outstretched palm, a thousand feet above deep forest broken by a single plume of smoke marking out an isolated inn.

The day after that, he fought and killed a pack of feral children. The battlefield was the high side of a cloud, under a sky lit by three full moons and a thousand constellations, each exerting its pull upon human destinies.

The day after that, he fought and killed a troll with three eyes and three mouths; no mouth spoke a comprehensible language, though each gibbered all through the fight. The battlefield was, or appeared to be, the Dire Stairs.

After each of these battles, and after every battle on every day that followed, Isrohim Vey found himself in the Dominie's tower, where he healed over the course of a night. On occasion the Dominie Segelius would speak with him.

What the Dominie said might be quite brief, as when he observed "wizardry is to witchcraft as art is to madness." Or he might speak at length, as when he explained to Isrohim Vey the true nature and relationship of all the gods of every mortal people, from the One Above All and the Jack-of-all-Ills of the Empire Church to the Great Gods of the Holy Dominion to the Twelve Gods and the God Of All Other Things of the Lohr to the Red Gods to the Unwritten Book to the Old Gods to Time, who was worshipped as a god in the far country of Knutherizh; and then on to the hundreds of gods of the Faefolk, and to Father Stone of the Svar, and to the gods of dragons and giantfolk and goblinkin, and how all these gods served to mortal understanding as giving to life a meaning in the face of death.

"Which is not to say," the Dominie then observed, "that they are unreal, or do not serve other purposes as well; but such purposes remain unknown, as the gods themselves are ultimately unknown. It is only the angels who can mediate between the human and divine spheres, being beyond gods as they are beyond destiny. The Dominion goddess of death, for example, is Halja; but she does not separate the soul from the body. No more does the hand of the One Above All. You know these things."

Isrohim Vey said nothing to this, and the next day he fought and killed two warriors of the shape-strong race of the Mirator, one of whom took the form of Valas as a youth while the other took the form of Valas as a king. The battlefield was the fountain of Umbral.

It was not so many days later that the battlefield was a deep dungeon, from which Isrohim Vey had to escape by defeating again the King-Who-Was-And-Will-Be-Again.

The Dominie Segelius came to the aging swordsman after that fight, and Isrohim Vey asked "Will I have to fight other figures of my past? Grandfather Hiberius, or Yasleeth Oklenn?"

"Does it surprise you that we know your history?" asked the Dominie. "We are wizards."

"Do you know everything there is to know?" asked Isrohim Vey.

The Dominie shrugged. "I know how scared you were when you faced the demon Gorias. I know you were not scared at all when you faced Umbral; but I don't know why not."

"Neither do I," said Isrohim Vey.

The Dominie nodded.

"Give me the worst of it," said Isrohim Vey.

The next day was a running battle across the field of Aruvhossin where seven armies lay dead. In that place Isrohim Vey killed his selves that might have been. He killed Isrohim Vey, the bloodthirsty mercenary captain. He killed Isrohim Vey, lecherous sybarite and drunk. He killed Isrohim Vey, devout chaplain of the Empire Church. These and many others he killed. Savage black dogs came to eat the entrails of the dead men. They scented the living Isrohim Vey, and chased him. There were too many to kill. Isrohim Vey was brought to ground. His muscles were torn from his bones and the tongues of dogs lapped at his blood. There was no angel. Only the quiet dissolution of all the world.

To his surprise, Isrohim Vey woke up in the Dominie's tower.

When the Dominie Segelius came to visit him, the swordsman said: "I died."

The Dominie shrugged.

"Why bring me back?" asked Isrohim Vey. Before the Dominie could answer, he asked also, "Why make me fight? Why do these things to me?"

"Wizards have their reasons. Perhaps we wanted to know how long it would be before you began to ask 'why.' Perhaps we wanted to see what you would do now."

"What do you mean?"

"You're free to go," said the Dominie Segelius. "You should leave the Demesne. But other than that, you may go wherever you like. Do what you will."

After a long while, Isrohim Vey asked, "Why did you wait so long to find me? Why did you wait until I was so old?"

The Dominie shrugged.

Isrohim Vey travelled south from the Demesne of Starry Wisdom and Golden-Eyed Dawn, a long way south until the stars changed. He travelled through Ulvandr-Kathros the Confederate Empire until he reached its south-west coast, and then across the harsh seas until he reached the island of Thættir. The people of Thættir were, and are, solitary and grim, fisherfolk and pirates, often foul of temper, overall seasoned by the salt of the sea and the bitter winds that lash the island of volcanic rock and ice fields; but they work together without complaint, are very brave, and love freedom. Isrohim Vey was soon voted by them to be Lawspeaker, which meant in essence to be their king.

For several years Isrohim Vey governed the people of Thættir wisely and well. Also in these years he organized their defenses. The Empress Adara XI had come to power in Ulvandr-Kathros; she was mad and lusted for conquest. For these reasons she looked westward, to Thættir, which had always before been too distant from the mainland to attract conquerors; it was that which had led men and women to settle on Thættir, and be free from rulers.

Isrohim Vey led raids against the mainland, sinking ships at harbor; he concluded alliances, with other island-folk and with the races under the ocean; and he sent agents northward to Opallios to recover that whip which commanded the flood and the eclipse, along with other treasures he had discarded decades before. When all these things had been done he made further preparations, but those were for his own future.

The night before the navies of Ulvandr-Kathros were to battle the ships of Thættir, Isrohim Vey went to the Dawn Tower, a lighthouse on the far eastern end of the island; with him was Ida, whom he trusted most on Thættir. Ida was the one he had chosen to go to Opallios. "We will win tomorrow," Isrohim Vey said to her, looking eastward.

"Yes, we will," said Ida. "The whip will determine it."

"True," agreed Isrohim Vey. "So there is no need of me." He took the obsidian amulet of the Lawspeaker from around his neck. Its chain clicked against itself as he gave it to Ida.

"I don't understand," she said. But she trusted him, and took the amulet.

"I have had some men loyal to me prepare a boat," he said. "I must go north. You will be the Lawspeaker."

"I am too young," said Ida.

"Some old men are wise," said Isrohim Vey. "Others have only lived a long time without meeting death."

"You can stay," said Ida. "Lead us further. If we break the navy of the Confederate Empire, we can raid inland—we could take the Pelian Isthmus, starve the city of Carcannum—you could topple the Empress, rule half the world."

"I could, old as I am. I choose not to."

Ida set the chain about her neck.

Suddenly, Isrohim Vey said: "You can escape destiny. Change your fate. The world's fate. If you choose to. If you know that, then you may not need to."

Below them, the waves of the sea crashed against the mossy black rocks of the island of Thættir, as they always had.

"What will I tell the people?" asked Ida.

"Tell them I have finally gone to the angel of death."

"Death. This will be difficult for them to understand."

Isrohim Vey said, "Death is simple."

Isrohim Vey did not know that the night he arrived in Vilmariy for the third and last time in his life was also the night of his sixty-first birthday; nor, if he had known, would it have mattered.

It was the night of the Grand Masque, when all things were upended.

Isrohim Vey walked through the city, past satyrs and devils and Kings of old time.

He asked a watchman for directions to the home of Reivym Shoi; whether this was truly a watchman or not did not matter. The man told the old swordsman where to find the estate of Reivym Shoi, heir to the line of Eblinn, and that was enough.

The house was dark and silent. Isrohim Vey walked to the front door and pounded on the solid wood. When no-one came after a minute he pounded again; and then again. And eventually the door opened, and Reivym Shoi stood before Isrohim Vey.

"The servants are gone to the Grand Masque," said Reivym Shoi, who seemed not to see the man before him. "I am the master here. Who are you, and what do you seek?"

"I am Isrohim Vey, the death-bound swordsman. I carry the sword called Azrael's Word, which some say is the Nameless Sword. I seek the Angel of Death."

For a moment Reivym Shoi did not move; then he sprang back into the shadows of the house. Isrohim Vey followed, more slowly, and drew Azrael's Word. Then Reivym Shoi came at him, sword in hand, and the two old men fought.

Reivym Shoi's eyesight had faded with the years, but in the dark of the house Isrohim Vey found this gave him no advantage. But the wound he had given Reivym Shoi years ago on a ship still seemed to trouble him. Isrohim Vey drove him back across an old entrance hall. Then Reivym Shoi ducked into a shadowed archway, and turned and ran. Cautiously, Isrohim Vey gave chase.

He ran through dark room after dark room. Ahead of him, in the moonlight filtering through high windows, was always the form of Reivym Shoi. As fast as Isrohim Vey ran he could not gain ground, and for the first time in his life he felt truly old. Sometimes Reivym Shoi would shout and guards would come.

Isrohim Vey killed them. Reivym Shoi came to a flight of stairs and paused; a light flared, a lantern in his hand. Reivym Shoi ran down the stairs. Isrohim Vey followed.

The diagonal of the stairs ran a long way into the dark. Then there was a landing, a switchback, another long diagonal. Another landing, another switchback. And again. Isrohim Vey would catch up to Reivym Shoi during the long descents; then Reivym Shoi would turn a corner and without the light of his lantern Isrohim Vey was forced to slow down.

The stairs seemed to continue endlessly, past walls of old stone, then past no walls at all, into a vast cavern, then through a close arched shaft of rock carved with old runes. The stairs were pitched at an odd angle, and were of varied heights, as though to fit the strides of creatures with several sets of legs and a variable length of stride. Isrohim Vey and Reivym Shoi were by this time far far below the city of Vilmariy, farther below the earth than the deepest tunnel of the Hideous Prison Illullunor, farther below than the Deep Dark where Isrohim Vey had spoken to the Svar smith Einik.

As they raced down the stairs in their weary old-man's hobble, both men became aware of a third presence with them; and Isrohim Vey remembered the Dominie he had spoken to almost four decades past saying "There are angels everywhere."

Then they were out of the tunnel, still upon the stairs, but the stairs now circled a curving stone wall; a great circle of stone, like a vast cup or cauldron on a scale fit for gods. Isrohim Vey heard a crashing and a pounding from below, and as he ran downwards he realized there was a fountain at the base of the cauldron, like the fountain under Umbral's glacier, but much larger. He could see the waters seething and frothing, raging and white; could see, at the edge of the light of Reivym Shoi's lantern, a fine mist of spray that seemed to take an infinity of forms. And those forms persisted when the light had moved on, so that in the darkness were all things made.

At the base of the long, long stairs there was a stone path like an isthmus or bridge leading out to an island in the middle of the fountain; like an image of Vilmariy, which was an island city built upon a mountain rising from a great river. Reivym Shoi hastened along the path. Isrohim Vey followed, slowly now as there was no other way off the island.

Finally, deliberately, Reivym Shoi set down his lantern and turned and drew his sword. "Do you know what this place is, Isrohim Vey?" he cried. "This is the Fount of All! Here all things come into the world! Here all things begin! So it must be here that all things end!"

It was at this point that Isrohim Vey understood that the years had taken Reivym Shoi's reason as well as his sight. Nevertheless the man attacked, and Isrohim Vey drew Azrael's Word for the last time in his life.

Isrohim Vey and Reivym Shoi battled for a long time on the island at the heart of the Fount of All.

It seemed to Isrohim Vey that every move he made he had already made, many times before. That his life was a circle and that all things in it had come round again.

Then he battered down Reivym Shoi's sword and kicked it away across the island. And he raised Azrael's Word; and brought it down; and Reivym Shoi's collarbone was crushed as the sword sank into his chest.

And then there was a light on Reivym Shoi's face, and his eyes were focused on something far away, and Isrohim Vey turned, knowing what he would see.

And there was Azrael, the Angel of Death; and the Angel was smiling.

And for the third and last time of his life Isrohim Vey spoke the Word of Azrael.

And, knowing that Reivym Shoi had still several moments of life left, Isrohim Vey deliberately let his sword fall from his hand; and this, the last decision in his life, was made in acceptance of his destiny, which, he understood now and for the first time, was only the beginning of himself and not the summation, just as he was defined not by the nature of that destiny but in how it was met and fulfilled.

And so Isrohim Vey moved beyond both destiny and free will.

And then Reivym Shoi took up the Nameless Sword which Isrohim Vey had called Azrael's Word, and, falling forward, with the last of his life drove the point of the sword through Isrohim Vey's chest and on into the heart of the Angel of Death.

And all Isrohim Vey knew was the smile of the Angel. And the smile hurt with a sweet pain that grew until it was all he knew, and he knew everything and nothing. And Isrohim Vey felt his lips curve and pull back from his teeth, and felt his blood surge, and knew a rare warmth.

And Isrohim Vey smiled the smile of the Angel of Death, and all things were upended, and the world turned upside down.

Such is the end of the story of Isrohim Vey, as the Dominies tell it, and the keepers of the truths of angels. And all of them have since debated the fate of the soul of Reivym Shoi, and of the Angel of Death called Azrael, and of Isrohim Vey.

As is the case with most souls, however, their destiny remains unclear.

UNDER THE MOONS OF VENUS

DAMIEN BRODERICK

—◆—

1.

In the long, hot, humid afternoon, Blackett obsessively paced off the outer dimensions of the Great Temple of Petra against the black asphalt of the deserted car parks, trying to recapture the pathway back to Venus. Faint rectangular lines still marked the empty spaces allocated to staff vehicles long gone from the campus, stretching on every side like the equations in some occult geometry of invocation. Later, as shadows stretched across the all-but-abandoned industrial park, he considered again the possibility that he was trapped in delusion, even psychosis. At the edge of an overgrown patch of dried lawn, he found a crushed Pepsi can, a bent yellow plastic straw protruding from it. He kicked it idly.

"Thus I refute Berkeley," he muttered, with a half smile. The can twisted, fell back on the grass; he saw that a runner of bind weed wrapped its flattened waist.

He walked back to the sprawling house he had appropriated, formerly the residence of a wealthy CEO. Glancing at his IWC Flieger Chrono aviator's watch, he noted that he should arrive there ten minutes before his daily appointment with the therapist.

2.

Cool in a chillingly expensive pale blue Mila Schön summer frock, her carmine toenails brightly painted in her open Ferragamo Penelope sandals, Clare regarded him: lovely, sly, professionally compassionate. She sat across from him on the front porch of the old house, rocking gently in the suspended glider.

"Your problem," the psychiatrist told him, "is known in our trade as lack of affect. You have shut down and locked off your emotional responses. You must realize, Robert, that this isn't healthy or sustainable."

"Of course I know that," he said, faintly irritated by her condescension. "Why else would I be consulting you? Not," he said pointedly, "that it is doing me much good."

"It takes time, Robert. As you know."

3.

Later, when Clare was gone, Blackett sat beside his silent sound system and poured two fingers of Hennessy XO brandy. It was the best he had been able to find in the largely depleted supermarket, or at any rate the least untenable for drinking purposes. He took the spirits into his mouth and felt fire run down his throat. Months earlier, he had found a single bottle of Mendis Coconut brandy in the cellar of an enormous country house. Gone now. He sat a little longer, rose, cleaned his teeth and made his toilet, drank a full glass of faintly brackish water from the tap. He found a Philip Glass CD and placed it in the mouth of the player, then went to bed. Glass's repetitions and minimal novelty eased him into sleep. He woke at 3 in the morning, heart thundering. Silence absolute. Blackett cursed himself for forgetting to press the automatic repeat key on the CD player. Glass had fallen silent, along with most of the rest of the human race. He touched his forehead. Sweat coated his fingers.

4.

In the morning, he drove in a stolen car to the industrial park's air field, rolled the Cesna 182 out from the protection of its hangar, and refueled its tanks. Against the odds, the electrically powered pump and other systems remained active, drawing current from the black arrays of solar cells oriented to the south and east, swiveling during the daylight hours to follow the apparent track of the sun. He made his abstracted, expert run through the checklist, flicked on the radio by reflex. A hum of carrier signal, nothing more. The control tower was deserted. Blackett ran the Cessna onto the slightly cracked asphalt and took off into a brisk breeze. He flew across fields going to seed, visible through sparklingly clear air. Almost no traffic moved on the roads below him. Two or three vehicles threw up a haze of dust from the untended roadway, and one laden truck crossed his path, apparently cluttered to over-flowing with furniture and bedding. It seemed the ultimate in pointless-ness—why not appropriate a suitable house, as he had done, and make do with its appointments? Birds flew up occasionally in swooping flocks, careful to avoid his path.

Before noon, he was landing on the coast at the deserted Matagorda Island air force base a few hundred yards from the ocean. He sat for a moment, hearing his cooling engines ticking, and gazed at the two deteriorating Stearman biplanes that rested in the salty open air. They were at least a century old, at one time lovingly restored for air shows and aerobatic displays. Now their fabric sagged, striped red and green paint peeling from their fuselages and wings. They sagged into the hot tarmac, rubber tires rotted by the corrosive oceanfront air and the sun's pitiless ultraviolet.

Blackett left his own plane in the open. He did not intend to remain here long. He strolled to the end of the runway and into the long grass stretching to the ocean. Socks and trouser legs were covered quickly in clinging burrs. He reached the sandy shore as the sun stood directly overhead. After he had walked for half a mile along the strand, wishing he had thought to bring a hat, a dog crossed the sand and paced alongside, keeping its distance.

"You're Blackett," the dog said.

"Speaking."

"Figured it must have been you. Rare enough now to run into a human out here."

Blackett said nothing. He glanced at the dog, feeling no enthusiasm for a conversation. The animal was healthy enough, and well fed, a red setter with long hair that fluffed up in the tangy air. His paws left a trail across the white sand, paralleling the tracks Blackett had made. Was there some occult meaning in this simplest of geometries? If so, it would be erased soon enough, as the ocean moved in, impelled by the solar tide, and lazily licked the beach clean.

Seaweed stretched along the edge of the sluggish water, dark green, stinking. Out of breath, he sat and looked disconsolately across the slow, flat waves of the diminished tide. The dog trotted by, threw itself down in the sand a dozen feet away. Blackett knew he no longer dared sit here after nightfall, in a dark alive with thousands of brilliant pinpoint stars, a planet or two, and no Moon. Never again a Moon. Once he had ventured out here after the sun went down, and low in the deep indigo edging the horizon had seen the clear distinct blue disk of the evening star, and her two attendant satellites, one on each side of the planet. Ganymede, with its thin atmosphere still intact, remained palest brown. Luna, at that distance, was a bright pinpoint orb, her pockmarked face never again to be visible to the naked eye of an Earthly viewer beneath her new, immensely deep carbon dioxide atmosphere.

He noticed that the dog was creeping cautiously toward him, tail wagging, eyes averted except for the occasional swift glance.

"Look," he said, "I'd rather be alone."

The dog sat up and uttered a barking laugh. It swung its head from side to side, conspicuously observing the hot, empty strand.

"Well, bub, I'd say you've got your wish, in spades."

"Nobody has swum here in years, apart from me. This is an old air force base, it's been decommissioned for . . . "

He trailed off. It was no answer to the point the animal was making. Usually at this time of year, Blackett acknowledged to himself, other beaches, more accessible to the crowds, would be swarming with shouting or whining children, mothers waddling or slumped, baking in the sun under

SP 50 lotions, fat men eating snacks from busy concession stands, vigorous swimmers bobbing in white-capped waves. Now the empty waves crept in, onto the tourist beaches as they did here, like the flattened, poisoned combers at the site of the Exxon Valdez oil spill, twenty years after men had first set foot on the now absent Moon.

"It wasn't my idea," he said. But the dog was right; this isolation was more congenial to him than otherwise. Yet the yearning to rejoin the rest of the human race on Venus burned in his chest like angina.

"Not like I'm *blaming* you, bub." The dog tilted its handsome head. "Hey, should have said, I'm Sporky."

Blackett inclined his own head in reply. After a time, Sporky said, "You think it's a singularity excursion, right?"

He got to his feet, brushed sand from his legs and trousers. "I certainly don't suspect the hand of Jesus. I don't think I've been Left Behind."

"Hey, don't go away now.' The dog jumped up, followed him at a safe distance. "It could be aliens, you know."

"You talk too much," Blackett said.

5.

As he landed, later in the day, still feeling refreshed from his hour in the water, he saw through the heat curtains of rising air a rather dirty precinct vehicle drive through the unguarded gate and onto the runway near the hangars. He taxied in slowly, braked, opened the door. The sergeant climbed out of his Ford Crown Victoria, cap off, waving it to cool his florid face.

"Saw you coming in, doc," Jacobs called. "Figured you might like a lift back. Been damned hot out today, not the best walking weather."

There was little point in arguing. Blackett clamped the red tow bar to the nose wheel, steered the Cessna backward into the hangar, heaved the metal doors closed with an echoing rumble. He climbed into the cold interior of the Ford. Jacobs had the air-conditioning running at full bore, and a noxious country and western singer wailing from the sound system. Seeing his guest's frown, the police officer grinned broadly and turned the hideous noise down.

"You have a visitor waiting," he said. His grin verged on the lewd. Jacobs drove by the house twice a day, part of his self-imposed duty, checking on his brutally diminished constituency. For some reason he took a particular, avuncular interest in Blackett. Perhaps he feared for his own mental health in this terrible circumstance.

"She's expected, sergeant." By seniority of available staff, the man was probably a captain or even police chief for the region, now, but Blackett declined to offer the honorary promotional title. "Drop me off at the top of the street, would you?"

"It's no trouble to take you to the door."

"I need to stretch my legs after the flight."

In the failing light of dusk, he found Clare, almost in shadow, moving like a piece of beautiful driftwood stranded on a dying tide, backward and slowly forward, on his borrowed porch. She nodded, with her Gioconda smile, and said nothing. This evening she wore a broderie anglaise white-on-white embroidered blouse and 501s cut-down almost to her crotch, bleached by the long summer sun. She sat rocking wordlessly, her knees parted, revealing the pale lanterns of her thighs.

"Once again, doctor," Blackett told her, "you're trying to seduce me. What do you suppose this tells us both?"

"It tells us, doctor, that yet again you have fallen prey to intellectualized over-interpreting." She was clearly annoyed, but keeping her tone level. Her limbs remained disposed as they were. "You remember what they told us at school."

"The worst patients are physicians, and the worst physician patients are psychiatrists." He took the old woven cane seat, shifting it so that he sat at right angles to her, looking directly ahead at the heavy brass knocker on the missing CEO's mahogany entrance door. It was serpentine, perhaps a Chinese dragon couchant. A faint headache pulsed behind his eyes; he closed them.

"You've been to the coast again, Robert?"

"I met a dog on the beach," he said, eyes still closed. A cooling breeze was moving into the porch, bringing a fragrance of the last pink mimosa blossoms in the garden bed beside the dry, dying lawn. "He suggested that we've experienced a singularity cataclysm." He sat forward suddenly, turned, caught her regarding him with her blue eyes. "What do you think of that theory, doctor? Does it arouse you?"

"You had a conversation with a dog," she said, uninflected, nonjudgmental.

"One of the genetically upregulated animals," he said, irritated. "Modified jaw and larynx, expanded cortex and Broca region."

Clare shrugged. Her interiority admitted of no such novelties. "I've heard that singularity hypothesis before. The Mayans—"

"Not that new age crap." He felt an unaccustomed jolt of anger. Why did he bother talking to this woman? Sexual interest? Granted, but remote; his indifference toward her rather surprised him, but it was so. Blackett glanced again at her thighs, but she had crossed her legs. He rose. "I need a drink. I think we should postpone this session, I'm not feeling at my best."

She took a step forward, placed one cool hand lightly on his bare, sunburned arm.

"You're still convinced the Moon had gone from the sky, Robert? You still maintain that everyone has gone to Venus?"

"Not everyone," he said brusquely, and removed her hand. He gestured at the darkened houses in the street. A mockingbird trilled from a tree, but there were no leaf blowers, no teenagers in sports cars passing with rap booming and thudding, no barbecue odors of smoke and burning steak, no TV displays flickering behind curtained windows. He found his key, went to the door, did not invite her in. "I'll see you tomorrow, Clare."

"Good night, Robert. Feel better." The psychiatrist went down the steps with a light, almost childlike, skipping gait, and paused a moment at the end of the path, raising a hand in farewell or admonishment. "A suggestion, Robert. The almanac ordains a full moon tonight. It rises a little after eight. You should see it plainly from your back garden a few minutes later, once the disk clears the treetops."

For a moment he watched her fade behind the overgrown, untended foliage fronting this opulent dwelling. He shook his head, and went inside. In recent months, since the theft of the Moon, Clare had erected ontological denial into the central principle of her world construction, her *Weltbild*. The woman, in her own mind supposedly his therapeutic guide, was hopelessly insane.

6.

After a scratch dinner of canned artichoke hearts, pineapple slices, pre-cooked baby potatoes, pickled eel from a jar, and rather dry lightly-salted wheaten thins, washed down with Californian Chablis from the refrigerator, Blackett dressed in slightly more formal clothing for his weekly visit to Kafele Massri. This massively obese bibliophile lived three streets over in the Baptist rectory across the street from the regional library. At intervals, while doing his own shopping, Blackett scavenged through accessible food stores for provender that he left in plastic bags beside Massri's side gate, providing an incentive to get outside the walls of the house for a few minutes. The man slept all day, and barely budged from his musty bed even after the sun had gone down, scattering emptied cans and plastic bottles about on the uncarpeted floor. Massri had not yet taken to urinating in his squalid bedclothes, as far as Blackett could tell, but the weekly visits always began by emptying several jugs the fat man used at night in lieu of chamber pots, rinsing them under the trickle of water from the kitchen tap, and returning them to the bedroom, where he cleared away the empties into bags and tossed those into the weedy back yard where obnoxious scabby cats crawled or lay panting.

Kafele Massri was propped up against three or four pillows. "I have. New thoughts, Robert. The ontology grows. More tractable." He spoke in a jerky sequence of emphysematic wheezing gasps, his swollen mass pressing relentlessly on the rupturing alveoli skeining his lungs. His fingers twitched, as if keying an invisible keyboard; his eyes shifting again and again to the dead computer. When he caught Blackett's amused glance, he shrugged, causing one of the pillows to slip and fall. "Without my beloved internet, I am. Hamstrung. My *preciiiouuus*." His thick lips quirked. He foraged through the bed covers, found a battered Hewlett-Packard scientific calculator. Its green strip of display flickered as his fingers pressed keys. "Luckily. I still have. This. My *slide rule.*" Wheezing, he burst into laughter, followed by an agonizing fit of coughing.

"Let me get you a glass of water, Massri." Blackett returned with half a glass; any more, and the bibliophile would spill it down his vast soiled bathrobe front. It seemed to ease the coughing. They sat side by side for a time, as the Egyptian got his breath under control. Ceaselessly, under the impulse of his pudgy fingers, the small green numerals flickered in and out of existence, a Borgesian proof of the instability of reality.

"You realize. Venus is upside. Down?"

"They tipped it over?"

They was a placeholder for whatever force or entity or cosmic freak of nature had translated the two moons into orbit around the second planet, abstracting them from Earth and Jupiter and instantaneously replacing them in Venus space, as far as anyone could tell in the raging global internet hysteria before most of humanity was translated as well to the renovated world. Certainly Blackett had never noticed that the planet was turned on its head, but he had only been on Venus less than five days before he was recovered, against his will, to central Texas.

"*Au contraire.* It has always. Spun. Retrograde. It rotates backwards. The northern or upper hemisphere turns. Clockwise." Massri heaved a strangled breath, made twisted motions with his pudgy, blotched hands. "Nobody noticed that until late last. Century. The thick atmosphere, you know. And clouds. Impenetrable. High albedo. Gone now, of course."

Was it even the same world? He and the Egyptian scholar had discussed this before; it seemed to Blackett that whatever force had prepared this new Venus as a suitable habitat for humankind must have done so long ago, in some parallel or superposed state of alternative reality. The books piled around this squalid bed seemed to support such a conjecture. Worlds echoing away into infinity, each slightly different from the world adjacent to it, in a myriad of different dimensions of change. Earth, he understood, had been struck in infancy by a raging proto-planet the size of Mars, smashing away the light outer crust and flinging it into an orbiting shell that settled, over millions of years of impacts, into the Moon now circling Venus. But if in some other prismatic history, Venus had also suffered interplanetary bombardment on that scale, blowing away its monstrous choking carbon dioxide atmosphere and churning up the magma, driving the plate tectonic upheavals unknown until then, where was the Venerean or Venusian moon? Had that one been transported away to yet another alternative reality? It made Blackett tired to consider these metaphysical landscapes radiating away into eternity even as they seemed to close oppressively upon him, a psychic null-point of suffocating extinction.

Shyly, Kafele Massri broke the silence. "Robert, I have never. Asked you this." He paused, and the awkward moment extended. They heard the ticking of the grandfather clock in the hall outside.

"If I want to go back there? Yes, Kafele, I do. With all my heart."

"I know that. No. What was it. *Like*?" A sort of anguish tore the man's words. He himself had never gone, not even for a moment. Perhaps, he had joked once, there was a weight limit, a baggage surcharge his account could not meet.

"You're growing forgetful, my friend. Of course we've discussed this. The immense green-leaved trees, the crystal air, the strange fire-hued birds high in the canopies, the great rolling ocean—"

"No." Massri agitated his heavy hands urgently. "Not that. Not the sci fi movie. Images. No offense intended. I mean . . . The *affect*. The weight or lightness of. The heart. The rapture of. Being there. Or the. I don't know. Dislocation? Despair?"

Blackett stood up. "Clare informs me I have damaged affect. 'Flattened,' she called it. Or did she say 'diminished'? Typical diagnostic hand-waving. If she'd been in practice as long as I—"

"Oh, Robert, I meant no—"

"Of course you didn't." Stiffly, he bent over the mound of the old man's supine body, patted his shoulder. "I'll get us some supper. Then you can tell me your new discovery."

7.

Tall cumulonimbus clouds moved in like a battlefleet of the sky, but the air remained hot and sticky. Lightning cracked in the distance, marching closer during the afternoon. When rain fell, it came suddenly, drenching the parched soil, sluicing the roadway, with a wind that blew discarded plastic bottles and bags about before dumping them at the edge of the road or piled against the fences and barred, spear-topped front gates. Blackett watched from the porch, the spray of rain blowing against his face in gusts. In the distance a stray dog howled and scurried.

On Venus, he recalled, under its doubled moons, the storms had been abrupt and hard, and the ocean tides surged in great rushes of blue-green water, spume like the head on a giant's overflowing draught of beer. Ignoring the shrill warnings of displaced astronomers, the first settlers along one shoreline, he had been told, perished as they viewed the glory of a Ganymedean-Lunar eclipse of the sun, twice as hot, a third again as wide. The proxivenerean spring tide, tugged by both moons and the sun as well, heaped up the sea and hurled it at the land.

Here on Earth, at least, the Moon's current absence somewhat calmed the weather. And without the endless barrage of particulate soot, inadequately scrubbed, exhaled into the air by a million factory chimneys and a billion fuel fires in the Third World, rain came more infrequently now. Perhaps, he wondered, was it time to move to a more salubrious climatic region. But what if that blocked his return to Venus? The very thought made the muscles at his jaw tighten painfully.

For an hour he watched the lowering sky for the glow pasted beneath distant clouds by a flash of electricity, then the tearing violence of lightning strikes as they came closer, passing by within miles. In an earlier dispensation, he would have pulled the plugs on his computers and other delicate equipment, unprepared to accept the dubious security of surge protectors. During one storm, years earlier, when the Moon still hung in the sky, his satellite dish and decoder burned out in a single nearby frightful clap of noise and light. On Venus, he reflected, the human race were yet to advance to the recovery of electronics. How many had died with the instant loss of infrastructure— sewerage, industrial food production, antibiotics, air conditioning? Deprived of television and music and books, how many had taken their own lives, unable to find footing in a world where they must fetch for themselves, work with neighbors they had found themselves flung amongst willy-nilly? Yes, many had been returned just long enough to ransack most of the medical supplies and haul away clothing, food, contraceptives, packs of toilet paper . . . Standing at the edge of the storm, on the elegant porch of his appropriated mansion, Blackett smiled, thinking of the piles of useless stereos, laptops and plasma TV screens he had seen dumped beside the immense Venusian trees. People were so stereotypical, unadaptive. No doubt driven to such stupidities, he reflected, by their lavish *affect*.

8.

Clare found him in the empty car park, pacing out the dimensions of Petra's Great Temple. He looked at her when she repeated his name, shook his head, slightly disoriented.

"This is the Central Arch, with the Theatron," he explained. "East and West corridors." He gestured. "In the center, the Forecourt, beyond the Proneos, and then the great space of the Lower Temenos."

"And all this," she said, looking faintly interested, "is a kind of imaginal reconstruction of Petra."

"Of its Temple, yes."

"The rose-red city half as old as time?" Now a mocking note had entered her voice.

He took her roughly by the arm, drew her into the shade of the five-story brick and concrete structure where neuropharmaceutical researchers had formerly plied their arcane trade. "Clare, we don't understand time. Look at this wall." He smote it with one clenched fist. "Why didn't it collapse when the Moon was removed? Why didn't terrible earthquakes split the ground open? The earth used to flex every day with lunar tides, Clare. There should have been convulsions as it compensated for the changed stresses. Did they see to that as well?"

"The dinosaurs, you mean?" She sighed, adopted a patient expression.

Blackett stared. "The *what*?"

"Oh." Today she was wearing deep red culottes and a green silk shirt, with a bandit's scarf holding back her heavy hair. Dark adaptive-optic sunglasses hid her eyes. "The professor hasn't told you his latest theory? I'm relieved to hear it. It isn't healthy for you two to spend so much time together, Robert. *Folie à deux* is harder to budge than a simple defensive delusion."

"You've been talking to Kafele Massri?" He was incredulous. "The man refuses to allow women into his house."

"I know. We talk through the bedroom window. I bring him soup for lunch."

"Good god."

"He assures me that the dinosaurs turned the planet Venus upside down sixty-five million years ago. They were intelligent. Not all of them, of course."

"No, you've misunderstood—"

"Probably. I must admit I wasn't listening very carefully. I'm far more interested in the emotional undercurrents."

"You would be. Oh, damn, damn."

"What's a Temenos?"

Blackett felt a momentary bubble of excitement. "At Petra, it was a beautiful sacred enclosure with hexagonal flooring, and three colonnades topped by sculptures of elephants' heads. Water was carried throughout the temple by channels, you see—" He started pacing off the plan of the Temple again, convinced that this was the key to his return to Venus. Clare walked beside him, humming very softly.

9.

"I understand you've been talking to my patient." Blackett took care to allow no trace of censure to color his words.

"Ha! It would be extremely uncivil, Robert. To drink her soup while maintaining. A surly silence. Incidentally, she maintains. You are her. Client."

"A harmless variant on the transference, Massri. But you understand that I can't discuss my patients, so I'm afraid we'll have to drop that topic immediately." He frowned at the Egyptian, who sipped tea from a half-filled mug. "I can say that Clare has a very garbled notion of your thinking about Venus."

"She's a delightful young woman, but doesn't. Seem to pay close attention to much. Beyond her wardrobe. Ah well. But Robert, I had to tell *somebody*. You didn't seem especially responsive. The other night."

Blackett settled back with his own mug of black coffee, already cooling.

He knew he should stop drinking caffeine; it made him jittery. "You know I'm uncomfortable with anything that smacks of so-called 'Intelligent Design.'"

"Put your mind at. Rest, my boy. The design is plainly intelligent. Profoundly so, but. There's nothing supernatural in it. To the contrary."

"Still—dinosaurs? The dog I was talking to the other day favors what it called a 'singularity excursion.' In my view, six of one, half a dozen—"

"But don't you see?" The obese bibliophile struggled to heave his great mass up against the wall, hauling a pillow with him. "Both are wings. Of the same argument."

"Ah." Blackett put down his mug, wanting to escape the musty room with its miasma of cranky desperation. "Not just dinosaurs, *transcendental* dinosaurs."

Unruffled, Massri pursed his lips. "Probably. In effect." His breathing seemed rather improved. Perhaps his exchanges with an attractive young woman, even through the half-open window, braced his spirits.

"You have evidence and impeccable logic for this argument, I imagine?"

"Naturally. Has it ever occurred to you. How extremely improbable it is. That the west coast of Africa. Would fit so snugly against. The east coast of South America?"

"I see your argument. Those continents were once joined, then broke apart. Plate tectonics drifted them thousands of miles apart. It's obvious to the naked eye, but nobody believed it for centuries."

The Egyptian nodded, evidently pleased with his apt student. "And how improbable is it that. The Moon's apparent diameter varies from 29 degrees 23 minutes to 33 degrees 29 minutes. Apogee to perigee. While the sun's apparent diameter varies. From 31 degrees 36 minutes to 32 degrees 3 minutes."

The effort of this exposition plainly exhausted the old man; he sank back against his unpleasant pillows.

"So we got total solar eclipses by the Moon where one just covered the other. A coincidence, nothing more."

"Really? And what of this equivalence? The Moon rotated every 27.32 days. The sun's sidereal rotation. Allowing for current in the surface. Is 25.38 days."

Blackett felt as if ants were crawling under his skin. He forced patience upon himself.

"Not all that close, Massri. What, some . . . eight percent difference?"

"Seven. But Robert, the Moon's rotation has been slowing as it drifts away from Earth, because it is tidally locked. Was. Can you guess when the lunar day equaled the solar day?"

"Kafele, what are you going to tell me? 4 BC? 622AD?"

"Neither Christ's birth nor Mohammed's Hegira. Robert, near as I can calculate it, 65.5 million years ago."

Blackett sat back, genuinely shocked, all his assurance draining away. The

Cretaceous-Tertiary boundary. The Chicxulub impact event that exterminated the dinosaurs. He struggled his way back to reason. Clare had not been mistaken, not about that.

"This is just . . . absurd, my friend. The slack in those numbers . . . But what if they are right? So?"

The old man hauled himself up by brute force, dragged his legs over the side of the bed. "I have to take care of business," he said. "Leave the room, please, Robert."

From the hall, where he paced in agitation, Blackett heard a torrent of urine splashing into one of the jugs he had emptied when he arrived. Night music, he thought, forcing a grin. That's what James Joyce had called it. No, wait, that wasn't it—Chamber music. But the argument banged against his brain. And so what? Nothing could be dismissed out of hand. The damned *Moon* had been picked up and moved, and given a vast deep carbon dioxide atmosphere, presumably hosed over from the old Venus through some higher dimension. Humanity had been relocated to the cleaned-up version of Venus, a world with a breathable atmosphere and oceans filled with strange but edible fish. How could anything be ruled out as preposterous, however ungainly or grotesque?

"You can come back in now." There were thumps and thuds.

Instead, Blackett went back to the kitchen and made a new pot of coffee. He carried two mugs into the bedroom.

"Have I frightened you, my boy?"

"Everything frightens me these days, Professor Massri. You're about to tell me that you've found a monolith in the back garden, along with the discarded cans and the mangy cats."

The Egyptian laughed, phlegm shaking his chest. "Almost. Almost. The Moon is now on orbit a bit over. A million kilometers from Venus. Also retrograde. Exactly the same distance Ganymede. Used to be from Jupiter."

"Well, okay, hardly a coincidence. And Ganymede is in the Moon's old orbit."

For a moment, Massri was silent. His face was drawn. He put down his coffee with a shaking hand.

"No. Ganymede orbits Venus some 434,000 kilometers out. According to the last data I could find before. The net went down for good.'

"Farther out than the Moon used to orbit Earth. And?"

"The Sun, from Venus, as you once told me. Looks brighter and larger. In fact, it subtends about forty minutes of arc. And by the most convenient and. Interesting coincidence. Ganymede now just exactly looks . . . "

" . . . the same size as the Sun, from the surface of Venus." Ice ran down Blackett's back. "So it blocks the Sun exactly at total eclipse. That's what you're telling me?"

"Except for the corona, and bursts of solar flares. As the Moon used to do here." Massri sent him a glare almost baleful in its intensity. "And you think that's just a matter of chance? Do you think so, Dr. Blackett?"

10.

The thunderstorm on the previous day had left the air cooler. Blackett walked home slowly in the darkness, holding the HP calculator and two books the old man had perforce drawn upon for data, now the internet was expired. He did not recall having carried these particular volumes across the street from the empty library. Perhaps Clare or one of the other infrequent visitors had fetched them.

The stars hung clean and clear through the heavy branches extending from the gardens of most of the large houses in the neighborhood and across the old sidewalk. In the newer, outlying parts of the city, the nouveaux riches had considered it a mark of potent prosperity to run their well-watered lawns to the very verge of the roadway, never walking anywhere, driving to visit neighbors three doors distant. He wondered how they were managing on Venus. Perhaps the ratio of fit to obese and terminally inactive had improved, under the whip of necessity. Too late for poor Kafele, he thought, and made a mental note to stockpile another batch of pioglitazone, the old man's diabetes drug, when next he made a foray into a pharmacy.

He sat for half an hour in the silence of the large kitchen, scratching down data points and recalculating the professor's estimates. It was apparent that Massri thought the accepted extinction date of the great reptiles, coinciding as it did with the perfect overlap of the greater and lesser lights in the heavens, was no such thing—that it was, in fact, a time-stamp for Creation. The notion chilled Blackett's blood. Might the world, after all (fashionable speculation!), be no more than a virtual simulation? A calculational contrivance on a colossal scale? But not truly colossal, perhaps no more than a billion lines of code and a prodigiously accurate physics engine. Nothing else so easily explained the wholesale revision of the inner solar system. The idea did not appeal; it stank in Blackett's nostrils. Thus I refute, he thought again, and tapped a calculator key sharply. But that was a feeble refutation; one might as well, in a lucid dream, deny that any reality existed, forgetting the ground state or brute physical substrate needed to sustain the dream.

The numbers made no sense. He ran the calculations again. It was true that Ganymede's new orbit placed the former Jovian moon in just the right place, from time to time, to occult the sun's disk precisely. That was a disturbing datum. The dinosaur element was far less convincing. According to the authors of these astronomy books, Earth had started out, after the tremendous shock of the X-body impact that birthed the Moon, with an dizzying 5.5 or perhaps eight-hour day. It seemed impossibly swift, but the hugely larger gas giant Jupiter, Ganymede's former primary, turned completely around in just 10 hours.

The blazing young Earth spun like a mad top, its almost fatal impact wound subsiding, sucked away into subduction zones created by the impact itself. Venus—the old Venus, at least—lacked tectonic plates; the crust was resurfaced at half billion year intervals, as the boiling magma burst up through the rigid rocks, but not enough to carry down and away the appalling mass of carbon dioxide that had crushed the surface with a hundred times the pressure of Earth's oxygen-nitrogen atmosphere. Now, though, the renovated planet had a breathable atmosphere. Just add air and water, Blackett thought. Presumably the crust crept slowly over the face of the world, sucked down and spat back up over glacial epochs. But the numbers—

The Moon had been receding from Earth at a sluggish rate of 38 kilometers every million years—one part in 10,000 of its final orbital distance, before its removal to Venus. Kepler's Third Law, Blackett noted, established the orbital equivalence of time squared with distance cubed. So those 65.5 million years ago, when the great saurians were slain by a falling star, Luna had been only 2500 km closer to the Earth. But to match the sun's sidereal rotation exactly, the Moon needed to be more than 18,000 km nearer. That was the case no more recently than 485 million years ago.

Massri's dinosaur fantasy was off by a factor of at least 7.4.

Then how had the Egyptian reached his numerological conclusion? And where did all this lead? Nowhere useful that Blackett could see.

It was all sheer wishful thinking. Kafele Massri was as delusional as Clare, his thought processes utterly unsound. Blackett groaned and put his head on the table. Perhaps, he had to admit, his own reflections were no more reliable.

11.

"I'm flying down to the coast for a swim," Blackett told Clare. "There's room in the plane."

"A long way to go for a dip."

"A change of scenery," he said. "Bring your bathing suit if you like. I never bother, myself."

She gave him a long, cool look. "A nude beach? All right. I'll bring some lunch."

They drove together to the small airfield to one side of the industrial park in a serviceable SUV he found abandoned outside a 7-Eleven. Clare had averted her eyes as he hot-wired the engine. She wore sensible hiking boots, dark gray shorts, a white wife-beater that showed off her small breasts to advantage. Seated and strapped in, she laid her broad-brimmed straw hat on her knees. Blackett was mildly concerned by the slowly deteriorating condition of the plane. It had not been serviced in many months. He felt confident, though, that it would carry him where he needed to go, and back again.

During the ninety-minute flight, he tried to explain the Egyptian's reasoning. The young psychiatrist responded with indifference that became palpable anxiety. Her hands tightened on the seat belt cinched at her waist. Blackett abandoned his efforts.

As they landed at Matagorda Island, she regained her animation. "Oh, look at those lovely biplanes! A shame they're in such deplorable condition. Why would anyone leave them out in the open weather like that?" She insisted on crossing to the sagging Stearmans for a closer look. Were those tears in her eyes?

Laden with towels and a basket of food, drink, paper plates and two glasses, Blackett summoned her sharply. "Come along, Clare, we'll miss the good waves if we loiter." If she heard bitter irony in his tone, she gave no sign of it. A gust of wind carried away his own boater, and she dashed after it, brought it back, jammed it rakishly on his balding head. "Thank you. I should tie the damned thing on with a leather thong, like the cowboys used to do, and cinch it with a . . . a . . . "

"A woggle," she said, unexpectedly.

It made Blackett laugh out loud. "Good god, woman! Wherever did you get a word like that?"

"My brother was a boy scout," she said.

They crossed the unkempt grass, made their way with some difficulty down to the shoreline. Blue ocean stretched south, almost flat, sparkling in the cloudless light. Blackett set down his burden, stripped his clothing efficiently, strode into the water. The salt stung his nostrils and eyes. He swam strongly out toward Mexico, thinking of the laughable scene in the movie *Gattaca*. He turned back, and saw Clare's head bobbing, sun-bleached hair plastered against her well-shaped scalp.

They lay side by side in the sun, odors of sun-block hanging on the unmoving air. After a time, Blackett saw the red setter approaching from the seaward side. The animal sat on its haunches, mouth open and tongue lolling, saying nothing.

"Hello, Sporky," Blackett said. "Beach patrol duties?"

"Howdy, doc. Saw the Cessna coming in. Who's the babe?"

"This is Dr. Clare Laing. She's a psychiatrist, so show some respect."

Light glistened on her nearly naked body, reflected from sweat and a scattering of mica clinging to her torso. She turned her head away, affected to be sleeping. No, not sleeping. He realized that her attention was now fixed on a rusty bicycle wheel half buried in the sand. It seemed she might be trying to work out the absolute essence of the relationship between them, with the rim and broken spokes of this piece of sea drift serving as some kind of spinal metaphor.

Respectful of her privacy, Blackett sat up and began explaining to the dog the bibliophile's absurd miscalculation. Sporky interrupted his halting exposition.

"You're saying the angular width of the sun, then and now, is about 32 arc minutes."

"Yes, 0.00925 radians."

"And the Moon last matched this some 485 million years ago."

"No, no. Well, it was a slightly better match than it is now, but that's not Massri's point."

"Which is?"

"Which is that the sun's rotational period and the Moon's were the *same* in that epoch. Can't you see how damnably unlikely that is? He thinks it's something like . . . I don't know, God's thumbprint on the solar system. The true date of Creation, maybe. Then he tried to show that it coincides with the extinction of the dinosaurs, but that's just wrong, they went extinct—"

"You do know that there was a major catastrophic extinction event at the Cambrian-Ordovician transition 488 million years ago at?"

Dumbfounded, Blackett said, "What?"

"Given your sloppy math, what do you say the chances are that your Moon-Sun rotation equivalence bracketed the Cambrian-Ordovician extinction? Knocked the living hell out of the trilobites, doc."

A surreal quality had entered the conversation. Blackett found it hard to accept that the dog could be a student of ancient geomorphisms. A spinal tremor shook him. So the creature was no ordinary genetically upgraded dog but some manifestation of the entity, the force, the ontological dislocation that had torn away the Moon and the world's inhabitants, most of them.

Detesting the note of pleading in his own voice, Blackett uttered a cry of heartfelt petition. He saw Clare roll over, waken from her sun-warmed drowse. "How can I get back there?" he cried. "Send me back! Send us both!"

Sporky stood up, shook sand from his fur, spraying Blackett with stinging mica.

"Go on as you began," the animal said, "and let the Lord be all in all to you."

Clouds of uncertainty cleared from Blackett's mind, as the caustic, acid clouds of Venus had been sucked away and transposed to the relocated Moon. He jumped up, bent, seized the psychiatrist's hand, hauled her blinking and protesting to her feet.

"Clare! We must trace out the ceremony of the Great Temple! Here, at the edge of the ocean. I've been wasting my time trying this ritual inland. Venus is now a world of great oceans!"

"Damn it, Robert, let me go, you're hurting—"

But he was hauling her down to the brackish, brine-stinking sea shore. Their parallel footprints wavered, inscribing a semiotics of deliverance. He began to tread out the Petran temple perimeter, starting at the Propylecum, turned a right angle, marched them to the East Excedra and to the very foot of the ancient Cistern. He was traveling backward into archeopsychic time, deeper into those remote, somber half-worlds he had glimpsed in the recuperative paintings of his mad patients.

"Robert! Robert!"

They entered the water, which lapped sluggishly at their ankles and calves like the articulate tongue of a dog as large as the world. Blackett gaped. At the edge of sea and sand, great three-lobed arthropods shed water from their shells, moving slowly like enormous wood lice.

"Trilobites!" Blackett cried. He stared about, hand still firmly clamped on Clare Laing's. Great green rolling breakers, in the distance, rushed toward shore, broke, foamed and frothed, lifting the ancient animals and tugging at Blackett's limbs. He tottered forward into the drag of the Venusian ocean, caught himself. He stared over his shoulder at the vast, towering green canopy of trees. Overhead, bracketing the sun, twin crescent moons shone faintly against the purple sky. He looked wildly at his companion and laughed, joyously, then flung his arms about her.

"Clare," he cried, alive on Venus, "Clare, we made it!"

ABANDONWARE

AN OWOMOYELA

My sister Andrea died in a bicycle-car collision when I was sixteen. My uncle came in to help Dad and me go through her stuff, weaning us from box after box sent to Goodwills or donated to advocacy raffles, but Dad and I both kept things. Dad kept her high school soccer medals and her autographed copy of *Neuromancer*. I kept a case of zip disks, a zip drive, and the ancient Mac Quadra she used them on.

I spent that weekend avoiding my father (who thought we needed to Talk with a capital T) by setting up the Quadra on a corner of my desk, which turned into half my desk and most of my legroom. I spent hours unsnarling cables and coaxing life into a machine obsolete since the late '90s. Why? Andy had some overclocked Alienware monstrosity with aspirations of becoming Skynet for her serious work, but the Quadra was her baby. While Dad Talked through my door about coming to terms with our grief and coming together as a family and letting go, I was bent over with the edge of the desk cutting into my chest, holding a flashlight in my mouth, trying to screw the monitor's cord into the tower.

Letting go was giving up. I had to get back in touch.

I sat at my desk, feet jammed between the Quadra's tower and my Dell's, window cracked to let in the wet air. It'd been raining. Andy loved how the air smelled after it rained; I didn't smell anything. I was just looking through Andy's zip disks, thinking about her.

I opened one case and a disc fell out, dropping between the wheels on my chair. It'd been stuck between the pages, not fit into one of the pockets, and that was weird, considering Andy. Whatever the original label said had been worked over in sharpie, and the new label read only **BURN THIS DISK.**

Obviously, she hadn't.

Andy was always open with me—ten years older and thinking she could tell me the secrets of life. She wanted me to tell her about girlfriends and classes and any juvenile delinquency I got into, and she told me about alcohol and sex and everything Dad didn't want to talk about, like the time she got busted sneaking into a topless bar. I couldn't think what she'd want to burn.

I turned on the zip drive, booted up the computer, and stuck the disk in. It was an early drive and an early disk, and it made a lot of noise for 100 megs, but it worked pretty well. Andy kept it fixed up.

The disk was named EraseMe. It had one file in it, a 77Mb document named SELDON.crn.

Dad knocked on my door. "David? Are you busy?"

"I'm a bit busy, Dad." I wasn't paying attention, not even to the way my shoulders knotted up. With Dad, sometimes if you just repeat a few of his phrases, he'll think you're having a conversation.

"I was thinking that we could have a night out, the two of us. Go down to Lazlo's and have a couple of burgers." And Talk, he didn't add.

A Google search on the computer that could handle the browsers that could handle the internet—that's to say, not the Quadra—told me that .crn files belonged to an obscure little program called CoadRunner, coad as in *code* but also *road* without the r. Its logo was a genericized cartoon of the blue bird I loved until I was seven, before I started empathizing with the coyote more.

"Not hungry," I said. *Leave me alone*, I didn't.

I poked around on the hard drive, which was bare except for BBEdit, Chess, Lemmings, and a folder full of bitmaps. I flipped open the disk case and ran through the disks. Digging through her stuff, I could forget how much I missed her. Sort of. Not really.

"We can go later?" Dad offered.

"Yeah, maybe." Andy was brilliant, and not just in the ten-years-older way. She tried to hook me early: programming (her job), soccer (her favorite weekend activity), science fiction (the only books she'd touch). None of it took, but I can still explain relational databases while scoring a goal, and then I can explain the three laws of robotics if you're still interested. Andy was also an organization freak. Her zip disks were color-coded by topic. Programs were alphabetized, backups ordered by date. There was an empty space in the programs where EraseMe should've been, back in the Q-R-S-T section.

"I'll be downstairs if you want to talk?" Dad said.

I didn't want to talk. I was pretty sure I'd never want to talk. CoadRunner was stuck between ClarisWorks and the Exile Trilogy games, and I popped the disk into the drive and started the installer. "Okay, dad. Later."

CoadRunner installed and I ejected that disk and put EraseMe back in. I copied SELDON.crn into its folder and opened it up.

All it gave me was a black window with green text, Matrix-style. Nothing else. I thought maybe it wanted me to register, even though the Quadra wasn't connected to the internet.

YOUR FULL NAME:

I typed in "David Elliot Knowles."

ZIP CODE:

I put in that. It asked me a few more questions, then the date. Then a number from 1-5. Then it said **DON'T GO TO SCHOOL TOMORROW** and quit. Pretty pointless.

I opened up BBEdit and opened SELDON.crn, which acted like a folder and gave me a list of files. One of the files was named CHOICES.crn, in a subfolder called INCLUDES, so I looked at that. It had a simple array with five elements, numbered one through five instead of zero through four: *Good luck, Bad luck, Friends, Family, Misc.* I'd hit 2 when I tested the program. Bad luck.

I ran the program again, filled out all my information, and then hit 1 instead. This time it said **CHECK THE STREET GUTTER TWO HOUSES DOWN** and quit again.

I poked around a bunch of the other INCLUDES/ files to see what I could understand. It'd been a long time since I programmed anything; when Andy started coaching me on how to make a tic-tac-toe game in Visual Basic, I'd stopped paying attention and never picked it up again. After a while I started going crosseyed over the symbols in SELDON, so I powered down both computers.

I'd poke my head in on Andy, on a normal day. Bother her about new movies or ask if she wanted to put in a racing game. That day I sat for a moment, not knowing what to do.

I went downstairs, thinking I could use some time out of the house.

I'd forgotten that Dad was downstairs. He was pouring himself coffee from the coffee machine in the living room, ignoring the evening news droning in the background. I almost ran back to my room, but Dad saw me.

"David," he said. "Sit down." He tried to sound like he was just suggesting it. I went down to the couch and sat, toying with the loose threads on the armrest covers.

Dad sat in the big overstuffed chair under the lamp across from me, catty-corner from the TV which was talking about a mining accident someplace that wasn't America. "We should talk about Andrea," he said, then drank his coffee like he was trying to wash a bitter taste into his mouth.

I don't like talking about things. I didn't want to talk about that, but I had to. It went something like this: he'd say something, everything jammed into past tense. How she *was* brilliant, how she *used to* make mile-deep nachos, how I must have favorite memories too, didn't I? I'd admit that maybe I did. He'd say "Tell me." He'd lean forward and look at me like he was about to break down, and I'd look away. Not talking made him talk. I had to talk to get away from that.

I told him that she took me to a baseball game and I didn't care about the game but I had the best ballpark dogs. I admitted that she wrote a new ending to *Interstellar Pig* because I didn't like the one in the book. Hers wasn't as good. I liked it better.

Andrea should have been there to get me out.

Andrea was my *sister*. Dad wasn't. I couldn't share Andrea being my sister with him, but he kept asking. He kept trying to share Andrea being his daughter with me, like I could reminisce about her in her baby jumper hanging onto mom, or like I'd want to if I could.

By the time Dad let me go and I headed out the door, I was shaking and I didn't want to be.

Andy would notice if I was in a bad mood, and she'd come play *Quake III* or *Red Faction* with me. Dad was clueless as to video games, and I was clueless as to him. Andrea could have noticed that I hated that Talk and run interference. Now it was just me and Dad and no way out.

I went around the block twice, down to the park, back up to the round-about, before remembering the message in the SELDON program. I knew it was a stupid thing to do, fortune-cookie advice for the internet age, but I checked the house two down from mine anyway. Nothing interesting. I went two houses over in the other direction, sorting through the stuff in the gutter with the toe of my sneaker until I saw something papery and leaned over to grab it.

Crumpled under a drift of sticks and leaves, soaked through and dirty, was a twenty-dollar bill.

"I don't want to go to school tomorrow," I told Dad when I came back in. Dad looked at me with a sad smile.

"No one would make you go to school this soon after the accident," he said, making me feel stupid for bringing it up. How was I supposed to know? The last family death had been my grandfather on my mother's side, who I'd met all of twice. Before that it'd been mom, who died when I was three. Dad and Andy remembered her; I never did. They don't tell you about this in the school's attendance policy. Or they did, and I didn't pay attention.

So I stayed home. Dad went to work. I ate the frozen lasagna someone had left for us and played on my computer and sometimes lurked in Andrea's old doorway, watching light fall through the window and creep across her too-empty floor. I wanted her to explain something to me—her program or Dad; either one. All I'd ever had to do was ask.

Sometime after five Dad knocked on my door and, without even waiting, pushed it open.

I was going to give him an earful. Maybe. I wasn't much for arguments, especially not with Dad. But Dad looked shellshocked—like he had when he'd met me at the door and made me sit down and told me that Andrea had died less than two blocks from our door. *There's been an accident on Rand street.* The look was toned down, but I recognized it.

"David, I thought you should know," he said. "West High's closed for a while. There was a bomb."

Andrea could have explained the look that went across my face: parser error. "A bomb?"

"A cherry bomb or something," Dad said. "It went off in the boy's locker room. There was one kid taken to the emergency room. I just thought you should know it's closed."

"There was a bomb," I said. That's as far as my brain would go. "In the locker room?"

"I think they have someone in custody," Dad responded.

I looked back at the Dell, then at the Quadra. "I'm going to—thanks," I said. I wasn't sure what else to say. "Could you—?"

"Yeah," Dad said. "I just wanted you to know."

At least he got that it was time to leave. He walked out toward the stairs, without pushing the door all the way closed.

Don't go to school. I went to Google News and typed in my school and city, and it was already up on half a dozen websites. Homemade bomb. Boys' locker room. 2:05, right at the start of fifth period, which was Physical Recreation for me. I didn't need to read past that. I went straight back to Andy's Quadra.

The INCLUDES/ files made no sense to me, but this time, I went into the folder called CORE/. It had one file, _MANCY.crn, which took up 76 of the 77 megabytes of the SELDON program. Failing to recognize that 76 megabytes is probably enough space for every American novel in plain text, I opened it. Then I had to wait thirteen minutes for it to open, pacing because the Quadra wouldn't hurry.

_MANCY.crn started off easy. Big blocks of comment text talking about date started, date completed, copyright Andrea Sophia Knowles, revisions, bug history; I scrolled past that to get at the code. Then I wished I hadn't.

It was gibberish to me. The one thing I could identify was a function library, but even knowing what it was, I couldn't make sense of it. It called double- and triple-variables, set up regular expressions which took up hundreds of lines, had functions so deeply recursive and such a complex net of file requires and cross-references that the entire thing was one big knot. It could've been a map of the universe. I couldn't tell.

Nine minutes in and I felt like I was choking on the code. The logic was too dense, and my mind was turning into a Klein bottle following it—Andrea had a false Klein bottle one of her boyfriends gave her, blue blown glass, and I couldn't figure it out any more than I could figure out this. I went online on my Dell and searched for .crn guides, but the only things I found were a bunch of ancient Usenet groups. No help there.

Maybe it was coincidence. Some really weird, freaky coincidence that it just so happened to spew that message the one day my boring, quiet school got interesting.

And maybe it wasn't.

Andy complained sometimes that you couldn't make random numbers with a computer program. Something about computers being logical and logic not being random. I had no idea if that applied to random chance, and she always spun it out to some theory about chaotic systems and the logical laws of physics and at that point my eyes always glazed over. I wanted to be sure that I was being ridiculous. There was no way a program on a zip disk could predict the future.

I just didn't know how to look into that.

I really should have known by then not to go downstairs. The problem was, upstairs was just bedrooms and a bathroom, and my window wasn't made for climbing out of. I wanted out of the house.

I don't think Dad, staring at the TV without really watching it, wanted to let me.

He stood up when I came down, turning the TV off and setting the remote on its endtable. "Are you hungry?" he asked. "I was just about to boil up some spaghetti . . . "

I told him I wasn't.

"Why don't you come help me in the kitchen?" he said. "Maybe you'll work up an appetite."

There was no way to get away.

Dad made this sort of pasta sauce where you only simmered the tomatoes for a few minutes, "to keep them fresh." I was cutting tomatoes into squishy cubes, thinking about red being the color of blood and white being the color of both the cutting board and the background of the code program and the program itself being thousands or millions of letters, numbers, symbols, totally without a matching metaphor in Dad's spaghetti dinner, and on a whim I asked, "Do you still miss mom?"

Dad, who was crushing garlic, looked like I'd come up behind him and startled him. "I haven't thought about her in a long time," he lied. I could tell he was lying because he's been a lousy liar my whole life. He used to tell us that cough medicine tasted *yummy*, like we wouldn't be able to tell as soon as we tasted it, like we wouldn't be wise to that line every time thereafter.

I wanted to turn around and walk straight back to my room and shut the door on Dad and our shrinking family and how hard it was just to talk to him. I think I managed a couple words before I did, something about needing some time out and he could finish this without me, right? I sat at my computer and held onto my mouse and keyboard and I thought: Dad wanted a nice nuclear family, didn't he? A wife, two kids, maybe a dog someday. Instead they didn't get a second kid until ten years after the first one, then mom died, then Andrea, until it was just the two of us. Just two, and every time Dad looked at me he was seeing the last person in his family not to die.

It wasn't like I could do anything. Not like I could bring back the dead, not like I could have known—

Andy had to have known.

She had a program that knew everything. I would check that every morning before I put on a shirt, if I had it. What sort of program warns me about a bomb threat and then doesn't tell my sister not to ride her bike? SELDON had to have known. Andy had to have known.

Why'd she want to burn that disk?

I punched in Andy's demographics.

That morning I'd overheard Dad calling the school and telling them that I was still in shock over Andy's death. Maybe I was. I missed her, yeah, but I wasn't crying or screaming or anything. All I can remember was a dull ache and curiosity about her Quadra, her pet projects, that code. I felt like she had part of her that she kept trying to share and it was hidden in this computer, part of her I never got to see because programming and soccer and science fiction were all like trigonometry—things I was good at, but didn't enjoy.

That's why I put in Andrea's information. I wanted to know what was going on between her and SELDON.

I selected **Friends** first.

Friends read **EVERYONE MISSES YOU, BUT IT'S OVER NOW**.

It quit. This time, I was glad.

A bunch of Andy's friends had been at her funeral. A couple of her high school friends flew in. One of them wished she hadn't been cremated because he had a first serialization copy of *The War of the Worlds* in *Pearson's Weekly* he would have let Dad bury with her. Of course they missed her. Andy was great. I tried something else.

Misc. **IT'S OVER NOW**.

Maybe there wasn't much you could tell to someone who ended up lying on the side of the road and died before the ambulances could get to her.

Bad luck. **THERE'S NOTHING LEFT. IT'S OVER NOW**.

Bad luck gave me the obvious answer. She was twenty-eight and brilliant and just riding her bike when a car came out of nowhere and hit her. Dumb luck. Bad luck.

Good luck. **IT'S OKAY. IT'S OVER NOW.**

That's when my hand started shaking.

That line made it sound like a suicide. Like something in her life caught up to her and she ran straight into a Subaru to escape it. Like we were going to be that grieving family on the news, everybody knows the one; the family that says, "There was never any indication, she always seemed so happy."

And I didn't want that. I didn't want to be told that by a stupid secret computer program that had no way of knowing anything and still knew my sister better than I did. I didn't want it to know anything.

I punched in 3 for Family.

YOU SHOULD HAVE BURNED THE DISK.

I kicked the power strip and both the computers went down. I shot back in my computer chair and jerked to a stop against my bed, both black monitors staring at me. **YOU SHOULD HAVE BURNED THE DISK.** 3 for family. 3 for Dad trying to Talk while I installed this. 3 for me reading her handwriting in sharpie on the label. 3 for me.

I should have burned the disk?

Good luck. I could stick to good luck from now on. If it was even real. If SELDON.crn actually knew anything and wasn't just random words and a few coincidences. Then I thought of the bomb in the locker room, and how I could have been there. I thought of Andy and her insistence that nothing computerized was random. *Bad luck.* Someone was injured. I could have been.

Burn this disk. Why didn't it just tell me to beware the Ides of March?

I rolled back over and flipped the powerstrip back on with my toe. I booted both of my computers up and made myself open SELDON again.

For a long time I just stared at the input box. After a few minutes I wrote in my name, but the date I gave was the day Andy died. I punched in 3 for family.

YOUR SISTER LOVES YOU.

I think I was shaking again.

I wrote in Andy's info for that day, her deathday, and stopped on the prompt. Good luck? Bad luck? She'd *died*—most of the answers seemed obvious, and some, I didn't want to know. I went with the one I didn't want to know instead of the ones I already did. Good luck.

A TRULY RANDOM CHANCE IS WAITING JUST OUTSIDE THE DOOR, good luck read. Then for bad luck it just said **MAYBE PREDESTINATION'S NOT THAT BAD.**

I wanted to punch through the monitor.

I tried typing in WHAT DO YOU WANT FROM ME? and got an **ERROR: INDEX OUT OF BOUNDS** as soon as I hit W. Same with 0, with 6, with T for TELL ME WHAT YOU ARE. I closed all the code windows, shut the computer down, ran downstairs so I could deal with something that wasn't it, and ended up running back up with a bowl of spaghetti and a mumbled "Sorry Dad I just don't want to talk right now" because I couldn't leave it alone. My eyes were burning. I told myself it was from onions. Dad never simmered them enough.

I wanted to tear that program apart. I wanted to print out all those Usenet group pages, print out all that code, sit at my desk and go through it and learn it and make it tell me what it knew. It had to tell me. Computers weren't smarter than people; people programmed them. They were just better at crunching numbers.

Sometime after my spaghetti was cold Dad knocked on my door again. "David," he said, "I know you want to be alone, and it's all right that you take some time for that . . . "

I didn't want to be alone. I wanted to solve this.

Dad pushed open my door and saw me, and then he just walked in. He pulled my chair around to face him and he sat down on the edge of my bed and I hunched down and didn't want him there.

"David," he said, "turn off the computers. Please."

I didn't want to, but turning off the computers gave me a way not to look at him for a minute or so.

"We need to talk through this," he said, like there was a way to. If he'd known programming maybe we could have talked through SELDON, but Andy was dead. No logic, no reasoning, just dead and what was I supposed to say about that?

"I don't want to," I said, and Dad's face tightened up. I wasn't the problem there. I wasn't the thing being impossible to solve.

"It's not healthy to keep everything inside of you," Dad said. "I know this is horrible and I wish I knew how to help you, but you and Andy always had it so together," he said, and Andy was the one who'd always had it together, and I was stuck here between SELDON and Dad with no way to deal with either one.

It didn't matter that I wasn't healthy or Dad couldn't help. What mattered was that I had to know why Andrea had a program that could tell the future, I had to know and Andy wasn't there to tell me, and for a second it mattered more that she couldn't tell me than she wasn't there.

It was just for a second. Really. Just a second and I caught myself. I wanted Andy back more than I wanted to understand this, but I was sitting there with my mouth open and I must have been shaking or something because I remember Dad reaching over to me and then I was crushed against his chest, crying.

I really hadn't wanted to cry.

He held onto me for I don't know how long. The black space behind my eyelids was warmer than the black window I'd been staring at, and the *thump-*

thump-thump I couldn't block out coming from Dad's heart started blocking out the hum of electricity in the room.

I didn't know what I was doing. More than not knowing .crn programming, more than not knowing how logic and chance and the future fit together, I wanted Andrea back and I couldn't have that so I was getting in fights with a program she'd made. It didn't make sense to me.

When Dad finally let me go, there was a wet patch on his shirt where my eyes had been.

We sat for a while. We talked about nothing. He left me alone after that, staring at the blank screen of Andy's Quadra. It'd been supposed to make this all easier.

I booted it up, feeling horrible for doing it. I opened up SELDON thinking I didn't want to.

I wrote in my information and the correct date.

1 for Good luck. **TRUST THAT BAD FEELING**.

5 for Misc.

This time it thought for a while. I could hear the Quadra's harddrive struggling like I'd tried to install Doom on it and it couldn't handle that at all. After a while it gave me my answer.

GOODBYE, DAVID.

That night I snuck out while Dad was sleeping and went out back to our firepit. I was wearing my black Metallica hoodie and cargo pants but white sneakers; I guess I blended in with the darkness anyway. There were stars out and a bit more than a half moon, so it wasn't hard to see.

I took all the wet leaves and stuff out of the pit and cleared off the gravel around it. Then I put down the grate and some charcoal and a shoebox. The shoebox was full of shredded newspaper and matchbooks and some oil—whatever I thought would burn. And it had the zip disk.

I wasn't out there in my suit or my dress shoes, but I wasn't sure people wore suits to cremations anyway. I poured some lighter fluid over everything and lit the charcoal. Then I crouched there and watched it all burn. It stank, and it smoldered, and it flared up when the matches caught, and oily smoke went up through the trees.

It took a long time to burn down, and the zip disk wasn't gone like I had hoped. But it was blackened and melted, which was enough. I dumped a bucket of water into the pit and stirred up the ashes.

I snuck back up to my room. On the way there I stopped outside Dad's door, and I heard him turn over on his bed. I heard him adjust the sheets. I didn't listen long.

My Dell was asleep. The Quadra hummed at me and I sat down, trashed the SELDON program, and turned it off. Lots cleaner than the fire. Of course it didn't feel the same.

I changed into pajamas and lay down, pulling the sheets up over my head. Andy had always been smarter than me; I never could get into her interests, but I trusted her. I'd forget about SELDON, if I could. Maybe tomorrow I'd play some Lemmings or Exile on the Quadra, maybe I'd find somewhere to spend that twenty I got from the gutter. I'd try, anyway. And maybe tomorrow I'd talk to Dad about something that wasn't Andy or her death.

Maybe letting go was something I did need to learn.

I fell asleep thinking of the fire, the stench of the smoke as it rose through the branches. It'd been dark and solid, and it went straight up and disappeared against the sky until only the absence of stars told me where it was. I fell asleep thinking of absence, SELDON and Andy and a way of knowing the future, and then I was out, and I don't remember my dreams.

THE MAIDEN FLIGHT OF McCAULEY'S *BELLEROPHON*

ELIZABETH HAND

Being assigned to The Head for eight hours was the worst security shift you could pull at the museum. Even now, thirty years later, Robbie had dreams in which he wandered from the Early Flight gallery to Balloons & Airships to Cosmic Soup, where he once again found himself alone in the dark, staring into the bland gaze of the famous scientist as he intoned his endless lecture about the nature of the universe.

"Remember when we thought nothing could be worse than that?" Robbie stared wistfully into his empty glass, then signaled the waiter for another bourbon and Coke. Across the table, his old friend Emery sipped a beer.

"I liked The Head," said Emery. He cleared his throat and began to recite in the same portentous tone the famous scientist had employed. "Trillions and trillions of galaxies in which our own is but a mote of cosmic dust. It made you think."

"It made you think about killing yourself," said Robbie. "Do you want to know how many time I heard that?"

"A trillion?"

"Five thousand." The waiter handed Robbie a drink, his fourth. "Twenty-five times an hour, times eight hours a day, times five days a week, times five months."

"Five thousand, that's not so much. Especially when you think of all those trillions of galleries. I mean galaxies. Only five months? I thought you worked there longer."

"Just that summer. It only seemed like forever."

Emery knocked back his beer. "A long time ago, in a gallery far, far away," he intoned, not for the first time.

Thirty years before, the Museum of American Aviation and Aerospace had just opened. Robbie was nineteen that summer, a recent dropout from the University of Maryland, living in a group house in Mount Rainier. Employment opportunities were scarce; making $3.40 an hour as a security aide at the Smithsonian's newest museum seemed preferable to bagging groceries at Giant Food. Every morning he'd punch his time card in the guards' locker room and change into his uniform. Then he'd duck outside to smoke a joint before trudging downstairs for morning meeting and that day's assignments.

Most of the security guards were older than Robbie, with backgrounds in the military and an eye on future careers with the D.C. Police Department or FBI. Still, they tolerated him with mostly good-natured ribbing about his longish hair and bloodshot eyes. All except for Hedge, the security chief. He was an enormous man with a shaved head who sat, knitting, behind a bank of closed-circuit video monitors, observing tourists and guards with an expression of amused contempt.

"What are you making?" Robbie once asked. Hedge raised his hands to display an intricately-patterned baby blanket. "Hey, that's cool. Where'd you learn to knit?"

"Prison." Hedge's eyes narrowed. "You stoned again, Opie? That's it. Gallery Seven. Relieve Jones."

Robbie's skin went cold, then hot with relief when he realized Hedge wasn't going to fire him. "Seven? Uh, yeah, sure, sure. For how long?"

"Forever," said Hedge.

"Oh, man, you got The Head." Jones clapped his hands gleefully when Robbie arrived. "Better watch your ass, kids'll throw shit at you," he said, and sauntered off.

Two projectors at opposite ends of the dark room beamed twin shafts of silvery light onto a head-shaped Styrofoam form. Robbie could never figure out if they'd filmed the famous scientist just once, or if they'd gone to the trouble to shoot him from two different angles.

However they'd done it, the sight of the disembodied Head was surprisingly effective: it looked like a hologram floating amid the hundreds of back-projected twinkly stars that covered the walls and ceiling. The creep factor was intensified by the stilted, slightly puzzled manner in which the Head blinked as it droned on, as though the famous scientist had just realized his body was gone, and was hoping no one else would notice. Once, when he was really stoned, Robbie swore that the Head deviated from its script.

"What'd it say?" asked Emery. At the time he was working in the General Aviation Gallery, operating a flight simulator that tourists clambered into for three-minute rides.

"Something about peaches," said Robbie. "I couldn't understand, it sort of mumbled."

Every morning, Robbie stood outside the entrance to Cosmic Soup and watched as tourists streamed through the main entrance and into the Hall of Flight. Overhead, legendary aircraft hung from the ceiling. The 1903 Wright Flyer with its Orville mannequin; a Lilienthal glider; the Bell X-1 in which Chuck Yeager broke the sound barrier. From a huge pit in the center of the Hall rose a Minuteman III ICBM, rust-colored stains still visible where a protester had tossed a bucket of pig's blood on it a few months earlier. Directly above the entrance to Robbie's gallery dangled the Spirit of St. Louis. The aides who worked upstairs in the planetarium amused themselves by shooting paperclips onto its wings.

Robbie winced at the memory. He gulped what was left of his bourbon and sighed. "That was a long time ago."

"Tempus fugit, baby. Thinking of which—" Emery dug into his pocket for a Blackberry. "Check this out. From Leonard."

Robbie rubbed his eyes blearily, then read.

> **From:** l.scopes@MAAA.SI.edu
> **Subject: Tragic Illness**
> **Date:** April 6, 7:58:22 PM EDT
> **To: emeryubergeek@gmail.com**
>
> Dear Emery,
>
> I just learned that our Maggie Blevin is very ill. I wrote her at Christmas but never heard back. Fuad El-Hajj says she was diagnosed with advanced breast cancer last fall. Prognosis is not good. She is still in the Fayetteville area, and I gather is in a hospice. I want to make a visit though not sure how that will go over. I have something I want to give her but need to talk to you about it.
>
> L.

"Ahhh." Robbie sighed. "God, that's terrible."

"Yeah. I'm sorry. But I figured you'd want to know."

Robbie pinched the bridge of his nose. Four years earlier, his wife, Anna, had died of breast cancer, leaving him adrift in a grief so profound it was as though he'd been poisoned, as though his veins had been pumped with the same chemicals that had failed to save her. Anna had been an oncology nurse, a fact that at first afforded some meager black humor, but in the end deprived them of even the faintest of false hopes borne of denial or faith in alternative therapies.

There was no time for any of that. Zach, their son, had just turned twelve. Between his own grief and Zach's subsequent acting-out, Robbie got so depressed that he started pouring his first bourbon and coke before the boy left for school. Two years later, he got fired from his job with the County Parks Commission.

He now worked in the shipping department at Small's, an off-price store in a desolate shopping mall that resembled the ruins of a regional airport. Robbie found it oddly consoling. It reminded him of the museum. The same generic atriums and industrial carpeting; the same bleak sunlight filtered through clouded glass; the same vacant-faced people trudging from Dollar Store to SunGlass Hut, the way they'd wandered from the General Aviation Gallery to Cosmic Soup.

"Poor Maggie." Robbie returned the Blackberry. "I haven't thought of her in years."

"I'm going to see Leonard."

"When? Maybe I'll go with you."

"Now." Emery shoved a twenty under his beer bottle and stood. "You're coming with me."

"What?"

"You can't drive—you're snackered. Get popped again, you lose your license."

"Popped? Who's getting popped? And I'm not snackered, I'm—" Robbie thought. "Snockered. You pronounced it wrong."

"Whatever." Emery grabbed Robbie's shoulder and pushed him to the door. "Let's go."

Emery drove an expensive hybrid that could get from Rockville to Utica, New York on a single tank of gas. The vanity plate read MARVO and was flanked by bumper stickers with messages like GUNS DON'T KILL PEOPLE: TYPE 2 PHASERS KILL PEOPLE and FRAK OFF! as well as several slogans that Emery said were in Klingon.

Emery was the only person Robbie knew who was somewhat famous. Back in the early 1980s, he'd created a local-access cable TV show called Captain Marvo's Secret Spacetime, taped in his parents' basement and featuring Emery in an aluminum foil costume behind the console of a cardboard spaceship. Captain Marvo watched videotaped episodes of low-budget 1950s science fiction serials with titles like PAYLOAD: MOONDUST while bantering with his co-pilot, a homemade puppet made by Leonard, named Mungbean.

The show was pretty funny if you were stoned. Captain Marvo became a cult hit, and then a real hit when a major network picked it up as a late-night offering. Emery quit his day job at the museum and rented studio time in Baltimore. He sold the rights after a few years, and was immediately replaced by a flashy actor in Lurex and a glittering robot sidekick. The show limped along for a season then died. Emery's fans claimed this was because their slacker hero had been sidelined.

But maybe it was just that people weren't as stoned as they used to be. These days the program had a surprising afterlife on the internet, where Robbie's son Zach watched it with his friends, and Emery did a brisk business selling memorabilia through his official Captain Marvo website.

It took them nearly an hour to get into D.C. and find a parking space near the Mall, by which time Robbie had sobered up enough to wish he'd stayed at the bar.

"Here." Emery gave him a sugarless breath mint, then plucked at the collar of Robbie's shirt, acid-green with SMALLS embroidered in purple. "Christ, Robbie, you're a freaking mess."

He reached into the back seat, retrieved a black t-shirt from his gym bag. "Here, put this on."

Robbie changed into it and stumbled out onto the sidewalk. It was mid-April but already steamy; the air shimmered above the pavement and smelled sweetly of apple blossom and coolant from innumerable air conditioners. Only as he approached the Museum entrance and caught his reflection in a glass wall did Robbie see that his t-shirt was emblazoned with Emery's youthful face and foil helmet above the words O CAPTAIN MY CAPTAIN.

"You wear your own t-shirt?" he asked as he followed Emery through the door.

"Only at the gym. Nothing else was clean."

They waited at the security desk while a guard checked their IDs, called upstairs to Leonard's office, signed them in and took their pictures before finally issuing each a Visitor's Pass.

"You'll have to wait for Leonard to escort you upstairs," the guard said.

"Not like the old days, huh, Robbie?" Emery draped an arm around Robbie and steered him into the Hall of Flight. "Not a lot of retinal scanning on your watch."

The museum hadn't changed much. The same aircraft and space capsules gleamed overhead. Tourists clustered around the lucite pyramid that held slivers of moon rock. Sunburned guys sporting military haircuts and tattoos peered at a mockup of a F-15 flight deck. Everything had that old museum smell: soiled carpeting, machine oil, the wet-laundry odor wafting from steam tables in the public cafeteria.

But The Head was long gone. Robbie wondered if anyone even remembered the famous scientist, dead for many years. The General Aviation Gallery, where Emery and Leonard had operated the flight simulators and first met Maggie Blevin, was now devoted to Personal Flight, with models of jetpacks worn by alarmingly lifelike mannequins.

"Leonard designed those." Emery paused to stare at a child-sized figure who seemed to float above a solar=powered skateboard. "He could have gone to Hollywood."

"It's not too late."

Robbie and Emery turned to see their old colleague behind them.

"Leonard," said Emery.

The two men embraced. Leonard stepped back and tilted his head. "Robbie. I wasn't expecting you."

"Surprise," said Robbie. They shook hands awkwardly. "Good to see you, man."

Leonard forced a smile. "And you."

They headed toward the staff elevator. Back in the day, Leonard's hair had been long and luxuriantly blond. It fell unbound down the back of the dogshit-yellow uniform jacket, designed to evoke an airline pilot's, that he and Emery and the other General Aviation aides wore as they gave their spiel to tourists eager to yank on the controls of their Link Trainers. With his patrician good looks and stern gray eyes, Leonard was the only aide who actually resembled a real pilot.

Now he looked like a cross between Obi-Wan Kenobi and Willie Nelson. His hair was white, and hung in two braids that reached almost to his waist. Instead of the crappy polyester uniform, he wore a white linen tunic, a necklace of unpolished turquoise and coral, loose black trousers tucked into scuffed cowboy boots, and a skull earring the size of Robbie's thumb. On his collar gleamed the cheap knock-off pilot's wings that had once adorned his museum uniform jacket. Leonard had always taken his duties very seriously, especially after Margaret Blevin arrived as the museum's first Curator of Proto-Flight. Robbie's refusal to do the same, even long after he'd left the museum himself, had resulted in considerable friction between them over the intervening years.

Robbie cleared his throat. "So, uh. What are you working on these days?" He wished he wasn't wearing Emery's idiotic t-shirt.

"I'll show you," said Leonard.

Upstairs, they headed for the old photo lab, now an imaging center filled with banks of computers, digital cameras, scanners.

"We still process film there," Leonard said as they walked down a corridor hung with production photos from *The Day the Earth Stood Still* and *Frau Im Mond*. "Negatives, old motion picture stock—people still send us things."

"Any of it interesting?" asked Emery.

Leonard shrugged. "Sometimes. You never know what you might find. That's part of Maggie's legacy—we're always open to the possibility of discovering something new."

Robbie shut his eyes. Leonard's voice made his teeth ache. "Remember how she used to keep a bottle of Scotch in that side drawer, underneath her purse?" he said.

Leonard frowned, but Emery laughed. "Yeah! And it was good stuff, too."

"Maggie had a great deal of class," said Leonard in a somber tone.

You pompous asshole, thought Robbie.

Leonard punched a code into a door and opened it. "You might remember when this was a storage cupboard."

They stepped inside. Robbie did remember this place—he'd once had sex here with a General Aviation aide whose name he'd long forgotten. It had been a good-sized supply room then, with an odd, sweetish scent from the rolls of film stacked along the shelves.

Now it was a very crowded office. The shelves were crammed with books and curatorial reports dating back to 1981, and archival boxes holding god knows what—Leonard's original government job application, maybe. A coat had been tossed onto the floor in one corner. There was a large metal desk covered with bottles of nail polish, an ancient swivel chair that Robbie vaguely remembered having been deployed during his lunch hour tryst.

Mostly, though, the room held Leonard's stuff: tiny cardboard dioramas, mockups of space capsules and dirigibles. It smelled overpoweringly of nail polish. It was also extremely cold.

"Man, you must freeze your ass off." Robbie rubbed his arms.

Emery picked up one of the little bottles. "You getting a manicurist's license?"

Leonard gestured at the desk. "I'm painting with nail polish now. You get some very unusual effects."

"I bet," said Robbie. "You're, like huffing nail polish." He peered at the shelves, impressed despite himself. "Jeez, Leonard. You made all these?"

"Damn right I did."

When Robbie first met Leonard, they were both lowly GS-1s. In those days, Leonard collected paper clips and rode an old Schwinn bicycle to work. He entertained tourists by making balloon animals. In his spare time, he created Mungbean, Captain Marvo's robot friend, out of a busted lamp and some spark plugs.

He also made strange ink drawings, hundreds of them. Montgolfier balloons with sinister faces; B-52s carrying payloads of soap bubbles; carictatures of the museum director and senior curators as greyhounds sniffing each others' nether quarters.

It was this last, drawn on a scrap of legal paper, which Margaret Blevin picked up on her first tour of the General Aviation Gallery. The sketch had fallen out of Leonard's jacket: he watched in horror as the museum's deputy director stooped to retrieve the crumpled page.

"Allow me," said the woman at the director's side. She was slight, forty-ish, with frizzy red hair and enormous hoop earrings, wearing an indian-print tunic over tight, sky-blue trousers and leather clogs. She snatched up the drawing, stuffed it in her pocket and continued her tour of the gallery. After the deputy director left, the woman walked to where Leonard stood beside his flight simulator, sweating in his polyester jacket as he supervised an overweight kid in a Chewbacca t-shirt. When the kid climbed down, the woman held up the crumpled sheet.

"Who did this?"

The other two aides—one was Emery—shook their heads.

"I did," said Leonard.

The woman crooked her finger. "Come with me."

"Am I fired?" asked Leonard as he followed her out of the gallery.

"Nope. I'm Maggie Blevin. We're shutting down those Link Trainers and making this into a new gallery. I'm in charge. I need someone to start cataloging stuff for me and maybe do some preliminary sketches. You want the job?"

"Yes," stammered Leonard. "I mean, sure."

"Great." She balled up the sketch and tossed it into a wastebasket. "Your talents were being wasted. That looks just like the director's butt."

"If he was a dog," said Leonard.

"He's a son of a bitch, and that's close enough," said Maggie. "Let's go see Personnel."

Leonard's current job description read Museum Effects Specialist, Grade 9, Step 10. For the last two decades, he'd created figurines and models for the museum's exhibits. Not fighter planes or commercial aircraft—there was an entire division of modelers who handled that.

Leonard's work was more rarefied, as evidenced by the dozens of flying machines perched wherever there was space in the tiny room. Rocket ships, bat-winged aerodromes, biplanes and triplanes and saucers, many of them striped and polka-dotted and glazed with, yes, nail polish in circus colors, so that they appeared to be made of ribbon candy.

His specialty was aircraft that had never actually flown; in many instances, aircraft that had never been intended to fly. Crypto-aviation, as some disgruntled curator dubbed it. He worked from plans and photographs, drawings and uncategorizable materials he'd found in the archives Maggie Blevin had been hired to organize. These were housed in a set of oak filing cabinets dating to the 1920s. Officially, the archive was known as the Pre-Langley Collection. But everyone in the museum, including Maggie Blevin, called it the Nut Files.

After Leonard's fateful promotion, Robbie and Emery would sometimes punch out for the day, go upstairs and stroll to his corner of the library. You could do that then—wander around workrooms and storage areas, the library and archives, without having to check in or get a special pass or security clearance. Robbie just went along for the ride, but Emery was fascinated by the things Leonard found in the Nut Files. Grainy black-and-white photos of purported UFOs; typescripts of encounters with deceased Russian cosmonauts in the Nevada desert; an account of a Raelian wedding ceremony attended by a glowing crimson orb. There was also a large carton donated by the widow of a legendary rocket scientist, which turned out to be filled with 1950s foot fetish pornography, and 16-millimeter film footage of several Pioneers of Flight doing something unseemly with a spotted pig.

"Whatever happened to that pig movie?" asked Robbie as he admired a biplane with violet-striped ailerons.

"It's been de-accessioned," said Leonard.

He cleared the swivel chair and motioned for Emery to sit, then perched on the edge of his desk. Robbie looked in vain for another chair, finally settled on the floor beside a wastebasket filled with empty nail polish bottles.

"So I have a plan," announced Leonard. He stared fixedly at Emery, as though they were alone in the room. "To help Maggie. Do you remember the *Bellerophon*?"

Emery frowned. "Vaguely. That old film loop of a plane crash?"

"*Presumed* crash. They never found any wreckage, everyone just assumes it crashed. But yes, that was the *Bellerophon*—it was the clip that played in our gallery. Maggie's gallery."

"Right—the movie that burned up!" broke in Robbie. "Yeah, I remember, the film got caught in a sprocket or something. Smoke detectors went off and they evacuated the whole museum. They got all on Maggie's case about it, they thought she installed it wrong."

"She didn't." Leonard said angrily. "One of the tech guys screwed up the installation—he told me a few years ago. He didn't vent it properly, the projector bulb overheated and the film caught on fire. He said he always felt bad she got canned."

"But they didn't fire her for that." Robbie gave Leonard a sideways look. "It was the UFO—"

Emery cut him off. "They were gunning for her," he said. "C'mon, Rob, everyone knew—all those old military guys running this place, they couldn't stand a woman getting in their way. Not if she wasn't Air Force or some shit. Took 'em a few years, that's all. Fucking assholes. I even got a letter-writing campaign going on the show. Didn't help."

"Nothing would have helped." Leonard sighed. "She was a visionary. She *is* a visionary," he added hastily. "Which is why I want to do this—"

He hopped from the desk, rooted around in a corner and pulled out a large cardboard box.

"Move," he ordered.

Robbie scrambled to his feet. Leonard began to remove things from the carton and set them carefully on his desk. Emery got up to make more room, angling himself beside Robbie. They watched as Leonard arranged piles of paper, curling 8x10s, faded blueprints and an old 35mm film viewer, along with several large manila envelopes closed with red string. Finally he knelt beside the box and very gingerly reached inside.

"I think the Lindbergh baby's in there," whispered Emery.

Leonard stood, cradling something in his hands, turned and placed it in the middle of the desk.

"Holy shit." Emery whistled. "Leonard, you've outdone yourself."

Robbie crouched so he could view it at eye level: a model of some sort of flying machine, though it seemed impossible that anyone, even Leonard or Maggie Blevin, could ever have dreamed it might fly. It had a zeppelin-shaped body, with a sharp nose like that of a Lockheed Starfighter, slightly uptilted. Suspended beneath this was a basket filled with tiny gears and chains, and beneath that was a contraption with three wheels, like a velocipede, only the wheels were fitted with dozens of stiff flaps, each no bigger than a fingernail, and even tinier propellers.

And everywhere, there were wings, sprouting from every inch of the craft's body in an explosion of canvas and balsa and paper and gauze. Bird-shaped wings, bat-shaped wings; square wings like those of a box-kite, elevators and hollow cones of wire; long tubes that, when Robbie peered inside them, were filled with baffles and flaps. Ailerons and struts ran between them to form a dizzying grid, held together with fine gold thread and monofilament and what looked like human hair. Every bit of it was painted in brilliant shades of violet and emerald, scarlet and fuchsia and gold, and here and there shining objects were set into the glossy surface: minute shards of mirror or colored glass; a beetle carapace; flecks of mica.

Above it all, springing from the fuselage like the cap of an immense toadstool, was a feathery parasol made of curved bamboo and multicolored silk.

It was like gazing at the Wright Flyer through a kaleidoscope.

"That's incredible!" Robbie exclaimed. "How'd you do that?"

"Now we just have to see if it flies," said Leonard.

Robbie straightened. "How the hell can that thing fly?"

"The original flew." Leonard leaned against the wall. "My theory is, if we can replicate the same conditions—the *exact same* conditions—it will work."

"But." Robbie glanced at Emery. "The original didn't fly. It crashed. I mean, presumably."

Emery nodded. "Plus there was a guy in it. McCartney—"

"McCauley," said Leonard.

"Right, McCauley. And you know, Leonard, no one's gonna fit in that, right?" Emery shot him an alarmed look. "You're not thinking of making a full-scale model, are you? Because that would be completely insane."

"No." Leonard fingered the skull plug in his earlobe. "I'm going to make another film—I'm going to replicate the original, and I'm going to do it so perfectly that Maggie won't even realize it's *not* the original. I've got it all worked out." He looked at Emery. "I can shoot it on digital, if you'll lend me a camera. That way I can edit it on my laptop. And then I'm going to bring it down to Fayetteville so she can see it."

Robbie and Emery glanced at each other.

"Well, it's not completely insane, " said Robbie.

"But Maggie knows the original was destroyed," said Emery. "I mean, I was there, I remember—she saw it. We all saw it. She has cancer, right? Not Alzheimer's or dementia or, I dunno, amnesia."

"Why don't you just Photoshop something?" asked Robbie. "You could tell her it was an homage. That way—"

Leonard's glare grew icy. "It is not an homage. I am going to Cowana Island, just like McCauley did, and I am going to recreate the maiden flight of the *Bellerophon*. I am going to film it, I am going to edit it. And when it's completed, I'm going to tell Maggie that I found a dupe in the archives. Her heart broke when that footage burned up. I'm going to give it back to her."

Robbie stared at his shoe, so Leonard wouldn't see his expression. After a moment he said, "When Anna was sick, I wanted to do that. Go back to this place by Mount Washington where we stayed before Zach was born. We had all these great photos of us canoeing there, it was so beautiful. But it was winter, and I said we should wait and go in the summer."

"I'm not waiting." Leonard sifted through the papers on his desk. "I have these—"

He opened a manila envelope and withdrew several glassine sleeves. He examined one, then handed it to Emery.

"This is what survived of the original footage, which in fact was *not* the original footage—the original was shot in 1901, on cellulose nitrate film. That's what Maggie and I found when we first started going through the Nut Files. Only of course nitrate stock is like a ticking time bomb. So the Photo Lab duped it onto safety film, which is what you're looking at."

Emery held the film to the light. Robbie stood beside him, squinting. Five frames, in shades of amber and tortoiseshell, with blurred images that might have been bushes or clouds or smoke damage, for all Robbie could see.

Emery asked, "How many frames do you have?"

"Total? Seventy-two."

Emery shook his head. "Not much, is it? What was it, fifteen seconds?"

"Seventeen seconds."

"Times twenty-four frames per second—so, out of about four hundred frames, that's all that's left."

"No. There was actually less than that, because it was silent film, which runs at more like eighteen frames per second, and they corrected the speed.

So, about three-hundred frames, which means we have about a quarter of the original stock." Leonard hesitated. He glanced up. "Lock that door, would you, Robbie?"

Robbie did, looked back to see Leonard crouched in the corner, moving aside his coat to reveal a metal strongbox. He prised the lid from the top.

The box was filled with water—Robbie *hoped* it was water. "Is that an aquarium?"

Leonard ignored him, tugged up his sleeves then dipped both hands below the surface. Very, very carefully he removed another metal box. He set it on the floor, grabbed his coat and meticulously dried the lid, then turned to Robbie.

"You know, maybe you should unlock the door. In case we need to get out fast."

"Jesus Christ, Leonard, what is it?" exclaimed Emery. "Snakes?"

"Nope." Leonard plucked something from the box, and Emery flinched as a serpentine ribbon unfurled in the air. "It's what's left of the original footage—the 1901 film."

"That's nitrate?" Emery stared at him, incredulous. "You *are* insane! How the hell'd you get it?"

"I clipped it before they destroyed the stock. I think it's okay—I take it out every day, so the gases don't build up. And it doesn't seem to interact with the nail polish fumes. It's the part where you can actually see McCauley, where you get the best view of the plane. See?"

He dangled it in front of Emery, who backed toward the door. "Put it away, put it away!"

"Can I see?" asked Robbie.

Leonard gave him a measuring look, then nodded. "Hold it by this edge—"

It took a few seconds for Robbie's eyes to focus properly. "You're right," he said. "You can see him—you can see someone, anyway. And you can definitely tell it's an airplane."

He handed it back to Leonard, who fastidiously replaced it, first in its canister and then the water-filled safe.

"They could really pop you for that." Emery whistled in disbelief. "If that stuff blew? This whole place could go up in flames."

"You say that like it's a bad thing." Leonard draped his coat over the strongbox, then started to laugh. "Anyway, I'm done with it. I went into the Photo Lab one night and duped it myself. So I've got that copy at home. And this one—"

He inclined his head at the corner. "I'm going to take the nitrate home and give it a Viking funeral in the back yard. You can come if you want."

"Tonight?" asked Robbie.

"No. I've got to work late tonight, catch up on some stuff before I leave town."

Emery leaned against the door. "Where you going?"

"South Carolina. I told you. I'm going to Cowana Island, and . . . " Robbie caught a whiff of acetone as Leonard picked up the *Bellerophon*. "I am going to make this thing fly."

"He really is nuts. I mean, when was the last time he even saw Maggie?" Robbie asked as Emery drove him back to the mall. "I still don't know what really happened, except for the UFO stuff."

"She found out he was screwing around with someone else. It was a bad scene. She tried to get him fired; he went to Boynton and told him Maggie was diverting all this time and money to studying UFOs. Which unfortunately was true. They did an audit, she had some kind of nervous breakdown even before they could fire her."

"What a prick."

Emery sighed. "It was horrible. Leonard doesn't talk about it. I don't think he ever got over it. Over her."

"Yeah, but . . . " Robbie shook his head. "She must be, what, twenty years older than us? They never would have stayed together. If he feels so bad, he should just go see her. This other stuff is insane."

"I think maybe those fumes did something to him. Nitrocellulose, it's in nail polish, too. It might have done something to his brain."

"Is that possible?"

"It's a theory," said Emery broodingly.

Robbie's house was in a scruffy subdivision on the outskirts of Rockville. The place was small, a bungalow with masonite siding, cracked cinderblock foundation and the remains of a garden that Anna had planted. A green GMC pickup with expired registration was parked in the drive. Robbie peered into the cab. It was filled with empty Bud Light bottles.

Inside, Zach was hunched at a desk beside his friend Tyler, owner of the pickup. The two of them stared intently into a computer screen.

"What's up?" said Zach without looking away.

"Not much," said Robbie. "Eye contact."

Zach glanced up. He was slight, with Anna's thick blonde curls reduced to a buzzcut that Robbie hated. Tyler was tall and gangly, with long black hair and wire-rimmed sunglasses. Both favored tie-dyed t-shirts and madras shorts that made them look as though they were perpetually on vacation.

Robbie went into the kitchen and got a beer. "You guys eat?"

"We got something on the way home."

Robbie drank his beer and watched them. The house had a smell that Emery once described as Failed Bachelor. Unwashed clothes, spilled beer, marijuana smoke. Robbie hadn't smoked in years, but Zach and Tyler had taken up the slack. Robbie used to yell at them but eventually gave up. If his own depressing example wasn't enough to straighten them out, what was?

After a minute, Zach looked up again. "Nice shirt, Dad."

"Thanks, son." Robbie sank into a beanbag chair. "Me and Emery dropped by the museum and saw Leonard."

"Leonard!" Tyler burst out laughing. "Leonard is so fucking sweet! He's, like, the craziest guy ever."

"All Dad's friends are crazy," said Zach.

"Yeah, but Emery, he's cool. Whereas that guy Leonard is just wack."

Robbie nodded somberly and finished his beer. "Leonard is indeed wack. He's making a movie."

"A real movie?" asked Zach.

"More like a home movie. Or, I dunno—he wants to reproduce another movie, one that was already made, do it all the same again. Shot by shot."

Tyler nodded. "Like *The Ring* and *Ringu*. What's the movie?"

"Seventeen seconds of a 1901 plane crash. The original footage was destroyed, so he's going to re-stage the whole thing."

"A plane crash?" Zach glanced at Tyler. "Can we watch?"

"Not a real crash—he's doing it with a model. I mean, I think he is."

"Did they even have planes then?" said Tyler.

"He should put it on Youtube," said Zach, and turned back to the computer.

"Okay, get out of there." Robbie rubbed his head wearily. "I need to go online."

The boys argued but gave up quickly. Tyler left. Zach grabbed his cellphone and slouched upstairs to his room. Robbie got another beer, sat at the computer and logged out of whatever they'd been playing, then typed in MCCAULEY BELLEROPHON.

Only a dozen results popped up. He scanned them, then clicked the Wikipedia entry for Ernesto McCauley.

McCauley, Ernesto (18??—1901) American inventor whose eccentric aircraft, the *Bellerophon*, allegedly flew for seventeens seconds before it crashed during a 1901 test flight on Cowana Island, South Carolina, killing McCauley. In the 1980s, claims that this flight was successful and predated that of the Wright Brothers by two years were made by a Smithsonian expert, based upon archival film footage. The claims have since been disproved and the film record unfortunately lost in a fire. Curiously, no other record of either McCauley or his aircraft has ever been found.

Robbie took a long pull at his beer, then typed in MARGARET BLEVIN.

Blevin, Margaret (1938—) Influential cultural historian whose groundbreaking work on early flight earned her the nickname "The Magnificent Blevin." During her tenure at the Smithsonian's Museum of American Aeronautics and Aerospace, Blevin redesigned the General Aviation Gallery to feature lesser-known pioneers of flight, including Charles Dellschau and Ernesto McCauley, as well as . . .

" 'The Magnificent Blevin?' " Robbie snorted. He grabbed another beer and continued reading.

But Blevin's most lasting impact upon the history of aviation was her 1986 bestseller *Wings for Humanity!*, in which she presents a dramatic and visionary account of the mystical aspects of flight, from Icarus to the Wright Brothers and beyond. Its central premise is that millennia ago a benevolent race seeded the Earth, leaving isolated locations with the ability to engender huiman-powered flight. "We dream of flight because flight is our birthright," wrote Blevin, and since its publication *Wings for Humanity!* has never gone out of print.

"Leonard wrote this frigging thing!"

"What?" Zach came downstairs, yawning.

"This Wikipedia entry!" Robbie jabbed at the screen. "That book was never a bestseller—she snuck it into the museum gift shop and no one bought it. The only reason it's still in print is that she published it herself."

Zach read the entry over his father's shoulder. "It sounds cool."

Robbie shook his head adamantly. "She was completely nuts. Obsessed with all this New Age crap, aliens and crop circles. She thought that planes could only fly from certain places, and that's why all the early flights crashed. Not because there was something wrong with the aircraft design, but because they were taking off from the wrong spot."

"Then how come there's airports everywhere?"

"She never worked out that part."

" 'We must embrace our galactic heritage, the spiritual dimension of human flight, lest we forever chain ourselves to earth,' " Zach read from the screen. "Was she in that plane crash?"

"No, she's still alive. That was just something she had a wild hair about. She thought the guy who invented that plane flew it a few years before the Wright Brothers made their flight, but she could never prove it."

"But it says there was a movie," said Zach. "So someone saw it happen."

"This is Wikipedia." Robbie stared at the screen in disgust. "You can say any fucking thing you want and people will believe it. Leonard wrote that entry, guarantee you. Probably she faked that whole film loop. That's what

Leonard's planning to do now—replicate the footage then pass it off to Maggie as the real thing."

Zach collapsed into the bean bag chair. "Why?"

"Because he's crazy, too. He and Maggie had a thing together."

Zach grimaced. "Ugh."

"What, you think we were born old? We were your age, practically. And Maggie was about twenty years older—"

"A cougar!" Zach burst out laughing. "Why didn't she go for you?"

"Ha ha ha." Robbie pushed his empty beer bottle against the wall. "Women liked Leonard. Go figure. Even your Mom went out with him for a while. Before she and I got involved, I mean."

Zach's glassy eyes threatened to roll back in his head. "Stop."

"We thought it was pretty strange," admitted Robbie. "But Maggie was good-looking for an old hippie." He glanced at the Wikipedia entry and did the math. "I guess she's in her seventies now. Leonard's in touch with her. She has cancer. Breast cancer."

"I heard you," said Zach. He rolled out of the beanbag chair, flipped open his phone and began texting. "I'm going to bed."

Robbie sat and stared at the computer screen. After a while he shut it down. He shuffled into the kitchen and opened the cabinet where he kept a quart of Jim Beam, hidden behind bottles of vinegar and vegetable oil. He rinsed out the glass he'd used the night before, poured a jolt and downed it; then carried the bourbon with him to bed.

The next day after work, he was on his second drink at the bar when Emery showed up.

"Hey." Robbie gestured at the stool beside him. "Have a set."

"You okay to drive?"

"Sure." Robbie scowled. "What, you keeping an eye on me?"

"No. But I want you to see something. At my house. Leonard's coming over, we're going to meet there at six-thirty. I tried calling you but your phone's off."

"Oh. Right. Sorry." Robbie signaled the bartender for his tab. "Yeah, sure. What, is he gonna give us manicures?"

"Nope. I have an idea. I'll tell you when I get there, I'm going to Royal Delhi first to get some takeout. See you—"

Emery lived in a big townhouse condo that smelled of Moderately Successful Bachelor. The walls held framed photos of Captain Marvo and Mungbean alongside a lifesized painting of Leslie Nielsen as Commander J.J. Adams.

But there was also a climate-controlled basement filled with Captain Marvo merchandise and packing material, with another large room stacked with electronics equipment—sound system, video monitors and decks, shelves and files devoted to old Captain Marvo episodes and dupes of the Grade Z movies featured on the show.

This was where Robbie found Leonard, bent over a refurbished Steenbeck editing table.

"Robbie." Leonard waved, then returned to threading film onto a spindle. "Emery back with dinner?"

"Uh uh." Robbie pulled a chair alongside him. "What are you doing?"

"Loading up that nitrate I showed you yesterday."

"It's not going to explode, is it?"

"No, Robbie, it's not going to explode." Leonard's mouth tightened. "Did Emery talk to you yet?"

"He just said something about a plan. So what's up?"

"I'll let him tell you."

Robbie flushed angrily, but before he could retort there was a knock behind them.

"Chow time, campers." Emery held up two steaming paper bags. "Can you leave that for a few minutes, Leonard?"

They ate on the couch in the next room. Emery talked about a pitch he'd made to revive Captain Marvo in cellphone format. "It'd be freaking perfect, if I could figure a way to make any money from it."

Leonard said nothing. Robbie noted the cuffs of his white tunic were stained with flecks of orange pigment, as were his fingernails. He looked tired, his face lined and his eyes sunken.

"You getting enough sleep?" Emery asked.

Leonard smiled wanly. "Enough."

Finally the food was gone, and the beer. Emery clapped his hands on his knees, pushed aside the empty plates then leaned forward.

"Okay. So here's the plan. I rented a house on Cowana for a week, starting this Saturday. I mapped it online and it's about ten hours. If we leave right after you guys get off work on Friday and drive all night, we'll get there early Saturday morning. Leonard, you said you've got everything pretty much assembled, so all you need to do is pack it up. I've got everything else here. Be a tight fit in the Prius, though, so we'll have to take two cars. We'll bring everything we need with us, we'll have a week to shoot and edit or whatever, then on the way back we swing through Fayetteville and show the finished product to Maggie. What do you think?"

"That's not a lot of time," said Leonard. "But we could do it."

Emery turned to Robbie. "Is you car road-worthy? It's about twelve hundred miles roundtrip."

Robbie stared at him. "What the hell are you talking about?"

"The *Bellerophon*. Leonard's got storyboards and all kinds of drawings and still frames, enough to work from. The realtor's in Charleston, she said there wouldn't be many people this early in the season. Plus there was a hurricane a couple years ago, I gather the island got hammered and no one's had money to rebuild. So we'll have it all to ourselves, pretty much."

"Are you high?" Robbie laughed. "I can't just take off. I have a job."

"You get vacation time, right? You can take a week. It'll be great, man. The realtor says it's already in the 80s down there. Warm water, a beach—what more you want?"

"Uh, maybe a beach with people besides you and Leonard?" Robbie searched in vain for another beer. "I couldn't go anyway—next week's Zach's spring break."

"Yeah?" Emery shook his head. "So, you're going to be at the store all day, and he'll be home getting stoned. Bring him. We'll put him to work."

Leonard frowned, but Robbie looked thoughtful. "Yeah, you're right. I hadn't thought of that. I can't really leave him alone. I guess I'll think about it."

"Don't think, just do it. It's Wednesday, tell 'em you're taking off next week. They gonna fire you?"

"Maybe."

"I'm not babysitting some—" Leonard started.

Emery cut him off. "You got that nitrate loaded? Let's see it."

They filed into the workroom. Leonard sat at the Steenbeck. The others watched as he adjusted the film on its sprockets. He turned to Robbie, then indicated the black projection box in the center of the deck.

"Emery knows all this, so I'm just telling you. That's a quartz halogen lamp. I haven't turned it on yet, because if the frame was just sitting there it might incinerate the film, and us. But there's only about four seconds of footage, so we're going to take our chances and watch it, once. Maybe you remember it from the gallery?"

Robbie nodded. "Yeah, I saw it a bunch of times. Not as much as The Head, but enough."

"Good. Hit that light, would you, Emery? Everyone ready? Blink and you'll miss it."

Robbie craned his neck, staring at a blank white screen. There was a whir, the stutter of film running through a projector.

At the bottom of the frame the horizon lurched, bright flickers that might be an expanse of water. Then a blurred image, faded sepia and amber, etched with blotches and something resembling a beetle leg: the absurd contraption Robbie recognized as the original *Bellerophon*. Only it was moving—it was flying—its countless gears and propellers and wings spinning and whirring and flapping all at once, so it seemed the entire thing would vibrate into a thousand pieces. Beneath the fuselage, a dark figure perched precariously atop the velocipede, legs like black scissors slicing at the air. From the left corner of the frame leaped a flare of light, like a shooting star or burning firecracker tossed at the pedaling figure. The pilot listed to one side, and—

Nothing. The film ended as abruptly as it had begun. Leonard quickly reached to turn off the lamp, and immediately removed the film from the take-up drive.

Robbie felt his neck prickle—he'd forgotten how weird, uncanny even, the footage was.

"Jesus, that's some bizarre shit," said Emery.

"It doesn't even look real." Robbie watched as Leonard coiled the film and slid it in a canister. "I mean, the guy, he looks fake."

Emery nodded. "Yeah, I know. It looks like one of those old silents, "The Lost World" or something. But it's not. I used to watch it back when it ran a hundred times a day in our gallery, the way you used to watch The Head. And it's definitely real. At least the pilot, McCauley—that's a real guy. I got a big magnifier once and just stood there and watched it over and over again. He was breathing, I could see it. And the plane, it's real too, far as I could tell. The thing I can't figure is, who the hell shot that footage? And what was the angle?"

Robbie stared at the empty screen, then shut his eyes. He tried to recall the rest of the film from when it played in the General Aviation gallery: the swift, jerky trajectory of that eerie little vehicle with its bizarre pilot, a man in a black suit and bowler hat; then the flash from the corner of the screen, and the man toppling from his perch into the white and empty air. The last thing you saw was a tiny hand at the bottom of the frame, then some blank leader, followed by the words THE MAIDEN FLIGHT OF MCCAULEY'S "BELLEROPHON" (1901). And the whole thing began again.

"It was like someone was in the air next to him," said Robbie. "Unless he only got six feet off the ground. I always assumed it was faked."

"It wasn't faked," said Leonard. "The cameraman was on the beach filming. It was a windy day, they were hoping that would help give the plane some lift but there must have been a sudden gust. When the *Bellerophon* went into the ocean, the cameraman dove in to save McCauley. They both drowned. They never found the bodies, or the wreckage. Only the camera with the film."

"Who found it?" asked Robbie.

"We don't know." Leonard sighed, his shoulders slumping. "We don't know anything. Not the name of the cameraman, nothing. When Maggie and I ran the original footage, the leader said "Maiden Flight of McCauley's Bellerophon." The can had the date and 'Cowana Island' written on it. So Maggie and I went down there to research it. A weird place. Hardly any people, and this was in the summer. There's a tiny historical society on the island, but we couldn't find anything about McCauley or the aircraft. No newspaper accounts, no gravestones. The only thing we did find was in a diary kept by the guy who delivered the mail back then. On May 13, 1901 he wrote that it was a very windy day and two men had drowned while attempting to launch a flying machine on the beach. Someone must have found the camera afterward. Somebody processed the film, and somehow it found its way to the museum."

Robbie followed Leonard into the next room. "What was that weird flash of light?"

"I don't know." Leonard stared out a glass door into the parking lot. "But it's not overexposure or lens flare or anything like that. It's something the cameraman actually filmed. Water, maybe—if it was a windy day, a big wave might have come up onto the beach or something."

"I always thought it was fire. Like a rocket or some kind of flare."

Leonard nodded. "That's what Maggie thought, too. The mailman—mostly all he wrote about was the weather. Which if you were relying on a horse-drawn cart makes sense. About two weeks before he mentioned the flying machine, he described something that sounds like a major meteor shower."

"And Maggie thought it was hit by a meteor?"

"No." Leonard sighed. "She thought it was something else. The weird thing is, a few years ago I checked online, and it turns out there was an unusual amount of meteor activity in 1901."

Robbie raised an eyebrow. "Meaning?"

Leonard said nothing. Finally he opened the door and walked outside. The others trailed after him.

They reached the edge of the parking lot, where cracked tarmac gave way to stony ground. Leonard glanced back, then stooped. He brushed away a few stray leaves and tufts of dead grass, set the film canister down and unscrewed the metal lid. He picked up one end of the coil of film, gently tugging until it trailed a few inches across the ground. Then he withdrew a lighter, flicked it and held the flame to the tail of film.

"What the—" began Robbie.

There was a dull *whoosh*, like the sound of a gas burner igniting. A plume of crimson and gold leaped from the canister, writhing in the air within a ball of black smoke. Leonard staggered to his feet, covering his head as he backed away.

"Leonard!" Emery grabbed him roughly, then turned and raced to the house.

Before Robbie could move, a strong chemical stink surrounded him. The flames shrank to a shining thread that lashed at the smoke then faded into flecks of ash. Robbie ducked his head, coughing. He grasped Leonard's arm and tried to drag him away, glanced up to see Emery running toward them with a fire extinguisher.

"Sorry," gasped Leonard. He made a slashing motion through the smoke, which dispersed. The flames were gone. Leonard's face was black with ash. Robbie touched his own cheek gingerly, looked at his fingers and saw they were coated with something dark and oily.

Emery halted, panting, and stared at the twisted remains of the film can. On the ground beside it, a glowing thread wormed toward a dead leaf, then expired in a gray wisp. Emery raised the fire extinguisher threateningly, set it down and stomped on the canister.

"Good thing you didn't do that in the museum," said Robbie. He let go of Leonard's arm.

"Don't think it didn't cross my mind," said Leonard, and walked back inside.

They left Friday evening. Robbie got the week off, after giving his dubious boss a long story about a dying relative down south. Zach shouted and broke a lamp when informed he would be accompanying his father on a trip during his spring vacation.

"With Emery and *Leonard*? Are you fucking *insane*?"

Robbie was too exhausted to fight: he quickly offered to let Tyler come with them. Tyler, surprisingly, agreed, and even showed up on Friday afternoon to help load the car. Robbie made a pointed effort not to inspect the various backpacks and duffel bags the boys threw into the trunk of the battered Taurus. Alcohol, drugs, firearms: he no longer cared.

Instead he focused on the online weather report for Cowana Island. 80 degrees and sunshine, photographs of blue water, white sand, a skein of pelicans skimming above the waves. Ten hours, that wasn't so bad. In another weak moment, he told Zach he could drive part of the way, so Robbie could sleep.

"What about me?" asked Tyler. "Can I drive?"

"Only if I never wake up," said Robbie.

Around six Emery pulled into the driveway, honking. The boys were already slumped in Robbie's Taurus, Zach in front with earbuds dangling around his face and a knit cap pulled down over his eyes, Tyler in the back, staring blankly as though they were already on I-95.

"You ready?" Emery rolled down his window. He wore a blue flannel shirt and a gimme cap that read STARFLEET ACADEMY. In the hybrid's passenger seat, Leonard perused a road atlas. He looked up and shot Robbie a smile.

"Hey, a road trip."

"Yeah." Robbie smiled back and patted the hybrid's roof. "See you."

It took almost two hours just to get beyond the gravitational pull of the Washington Beltway. Farms and forest had long ago disappeared beneath an endless grid of malls and housing developments, many of them vacant. Every time Robbie turned up the radio for a song he liked, the boys complained that they could hear it through their earphones.

Only as the sky darkened and Virginia gave way to North Carolina did the world take on a faint fairy glow, distant green and yellow lights reflecting the first stars and a shining cusp of moon. Sprawl gave way to pine forest. The boys had been asleep for hours, in that amazing, self-willed hibernation they summoned whenever in the presence of adults for more than fifteen minutes. Robbie put the radio on, low, searched until he caught the echo of a melody he knew, and then another. He thought of driving with Anna beside him, a restive Zach behind them in his car seat; the aimless trips they'd make until the toddler fell asleep and they could talk or, once, park in a vacant lot and make out.

How long had it been since he'd remembered that? Years, maybe. He fought against thinking of Anna; sometimes it felt as though he fought Anna herself, her hands pummeling him as he poured another drink or staggered up to bed.

Now, though, the darkness soothed him the way those long-ago drives had lulled Zach to sleep. He felt an ache lift from his breast, as though a splinter had been dislodged; blinked and in the rearview mirror glimpsed Anna's face, slightly turned from him as she gazed out at the passing sky.

He started, realized he'd begun to nod off. On the dashboard his fuel indicator glowed red. He called Emery, and at the next exit pulled off 95, the Prius behind him.

After a few minutes they found a gas station set back from the road in a pine grove, with an old-fashioned pump out front and yellow light streaming through a screen door. The boys blinked awake.

"Where are we?" asked Zach.

"No idea." Robbie got out of the car. "North Carolina."

It was like stepping into a twilight garden, or some hidden biosphere at the zoo. Warmth flowed around him, violet and rustling green, scented overpoweringly of honeysuckle and wet stone. He could hear rushing water, the stirring of wind in the leaves and countless small things—frogs peeping, insects he couldn't identify. A nightbird that made a burbling song. In the shadows behind the building, fireflies floated between kudzu-choked trees like tiny glowing fish.

For an instant he felt himself suspended in that enveloping darkness. The warm air moved through him, sweetly fragrant, pulsing with life he could neither see nor touch. He tasted something honeyed and faintly astringent in the back of his throat, and drew his breath in sharply.

"What?" demanded Zach.

"Nothing." Robbie shook his head and turned to the pump. "Just—isn't this great?"

He filled the tank. Zach and Tyler went in search of food, and Emery strolled over.

"How you holding up?"

"I'm good. Probably let Zach drive for a while so I can catch some Z's."

He moved the car, then went inside to pay. He found Leonard buying a pack of cigarettes as the boys headed out, laden with energy drinks and bags of chips. Robbie slid his credit card across the counter to a woman wearing a tank top that set off a tattoo that looked like the face of Marilyn Manson, or maybe it was Jesus.

"Do you have a restroom?"

The woman handed him a key. "Round back."

"Bathroom's here," Robbie yelled at the boys. "We're not stopping again."

They trailed him into a dank room with gray walls. A fluorescent light buzzed overhead. After Tyler left, Robbie and Zach stood side by side at the sink, trying to coax water from a rusted spigot to wash their hands.

"The hell with it," said Robbie. "Let's hit the road. You want to drive?"

"Dad." Zach pointed at the ceiling. "Dad, look."

Robbie glanced up. A screen bulged from a small window above the sink. Something had blown against the wire mesh, a leaf or scrap of paper.

But then the leaf moved, and he saw that it wasn't a leaf at all but a butterfly.

No, not a butterfly—a moth. The biggest he'd ever seen, bigger than his hand. Its fan-shaped upper wings opened, revealing vivid golden eyespots; its trailing lower wings formed two perfect arabesques, all a milky, luminous green.

"A luna moth," breathed Robbie. "I've never seen one."

Zach clambered onto the sink. "It wants to get out—"

"Hang on." Robbie boosted him, bracing himself so the boy's weight wouldn't yank the sink from the wall. "Be careful! Don't hurt it—"

The moth remained where it was. Robbie grunted—Zach weighed as much as he did—felt his legs trembling as the boy prised the screen from the wall then struggled to pull it free.

"It's stuck," he said. "I can't get it—"

The moth fluttered weakly. One wing-tip looked ragged, as though it had been singed.

"Tear it!" Robbie cried. "Just tear the screen."

Zach wedged his fingers beneath a corner of the window frame and yanked, hard enough that he fell. Robbie caught him as the screen tore away to dangle above the sink. The luna moth crawled onto the sill.

"Go!" Zach banged on the wall. "Go on, fly!"

Like a kite catching the wind, the moth lifted. Its trailing lower wings quivered and the eyespots seemed to blink, a pallid face gazing at them from the darkness. Then it was gone.

"That was cool." For an instant, Zach's arm draped across his father's shoulder, so fleetingly Robbie might have imagined it. "I'm going to the car."

When the boy was gone, Robbie tried to push the screen back into place. He returned the key and went to join Leonard, smoking a cigarette at the edge of the woods. Behind them a car horn blared.

"Come on!" shouted Zach. "I'm leaving!"

"Happy trails," said Leonard.

Robbie slept fitfully in back as Zach drove, the two boys arguing about music and a girl named Eileen. After an hour he took over again.

The night ground on. The boys fell back asleep. Robbie drank one of their Red Bulls and thought of the glimmering wonder that had been the luna moth. A thin rind of emerald appeared on the horizon, deepening to copper then gold as it overtook the sky. He began to see palmettos among the loblolly pines and pin oaks, and spiky plants he didn't recognize. When he opened the window, the air smelled of roses, and the sea.

"Hey." He poked Zach, breathing heavily in the seat beside him. "Hey, we're almost there."

He glanced at the directions, looked up to see the hybrid passing him and Emery gesturing at a sandy track that veered to the left. It was bounded by barbed wire fences and clumps of cactus thick with blossoms the color of lemon cream. The pines surrendered to palmettos and prehistoric-looking trees with gnarled roots that thrust up from pools where egrets and herons stabbed at frogs.

"Look," said Robbie.

Ahead of them the road narrowed to a path barely wide enough for a single vehicle, built up with shells and chunks of concrete. On one side stretched a blur of cypress and long-legged birds; on the other, an aquamarine estuary that gave way to the sea and rolling white dunes.

Robbie slowed the car to a crawl, humping across mounds of shells and doing his best to avoid sinkholes. After a quarter-mile, the makeshift causeway ended. An old metal gate lay in a twisted heap on the ground, covered by creeping vines. Above it a weathered sign clung to a cypress.

WELCOME TO COWANA ISLAND
NO DUNE BUGGIES

They drove past the ruins of a mobile home. Emery's car was out of sight. Robbie looked at his cellphone and saw there was no signal. In the back, Tyler stirred.

"Hey Rob, where are we?"

"We're here. Wherever here is. The island."

"Sweet." Tyler leaned over the seat to jostle Zach awake. "Hey, get up. "

Robbie peered through the overgrown greenery, looking for something resembling a beach house. He tried to remember which hurricane had pounded this part of the coast, and how long ago. Two years? Five?

The place looked as though it had been abandoned for decades. Fallen palmettos were everywhere, their leaves stiff and reddish-brown, like rusted blades. Some remained upright, their crowns lopped off. Acid-green lizards sunned themselves in driveways where ferns poked through the blacktop. The remains of carports and decks dangled above piles of timber and mold-blackened sheetrock. Now and then an intact house appeared within the jungle of flowering vines.

But no people, no cars except for an SUV crushed beneath a toppled utility pole. The only store was a modest grocery with a brick facade and shattered windows, through which the ghostly outlines of aisles and displays could still be glimpsed.

"It's like *28 Days*," said Zach, and shot a baleful look at his father.

Robbie shrugged. "Talk to the man from the Starfleet Academy."

He pulled down a rutted drive to where the hybrid sat beneath a thriving palmetto. Driftwood edged a path that led to an old wood-frame house raised on stiltlike pilings. Stands of blooming cactus surrounded it, and trees choked with honeysuckle. The patchy lawn was covered with hundreds of conch shells arranged in concentric circles and spirals. On the deck a tattered red whirligig spun in the breeze, and rope hammocks hung like flaccid cocoons.

"I'm sleeping there," said Tyler.

Leonard gazed at the house with an unreadable expression. Emery had already sprinted up the uneven steps to what Robbie assumed was the front door. When he reached the top, he bent to pick up a square of coconut matting, retrieved something from beneath it then straightened, grinning.

"Come on!" he shouted, turning to unlock the door; and the others raced to join him.

The house had linoleum floors, sifted with a fine layer of sand, and mismatched furniture—rattan chairs, couches covered with faded bark-cloth cushions, a canvas seat that hung from the ceiling by a chain and groaned alarmingly whenever the boys sat in it. The sea breeze stirred dusty white curtains at the windows. Anoles skittered across the floor, and Tyler fled shouting from the outdoor shower, where he'd seen a black widow spider. The electricity worked, but there was no air conditioning and no television; no internet.

"This is what you get for three hundred bucks in the off season," said Emery when Tyler complained.

"I don't get it." Robbie stood on the deck, staring across the empty road to where the dunes stretched, tufted with thorny greenery. "Even if there was a hurricane—this is practically oceanfront, all of it. Where is everybody?"

"Who can afford to build anything?" said Leonard. "Come on, I want to get my stuff inside before it heats up."

Leonard commandeered the master bedroom. He installed his laptop, Emery's camera equipment, piles of storyboards, the box that contained the miniature *Bellerophon*. This formidable array took up every inch of floor space, as well as the surface of a ping pong table.

"Why is there a ping pong table in the bedroom?" asked Robbie as he set down a tripod.

Emery shrugged. "You might ask, why is there not a ping pong table in all bedrooms?"

"We're going to the beach," announced Zach.

Robbie kicked off his shoes and followed them, across the deserted road and down a path that wound through a miniature wilderness of cactus and bristly vines. He felt lightheaded from lack of sleep, and also from the beer he'd snagged from one of the cases Emery had brought. The sand was already hot; twice he had to stop and pluck sharp spurs from his bare feet. A horned toad darted across the path, and a skink with a blue tongue. His son's voice came to him, laughing, and the sound of waves on the shore.

Atop the last dune small yellow roses grew in a thick carpet, their soapy fragrance mingling with the salt breeze. Robbie bent to pluck a handful of petals and tossed them into the air.

"It's not a bad place to fly, is it?"

He turned and saw Emery, shirtless. He handed Robbie a bottle of Tecate with a slice of lime jammed in its neck, raised his own beer and took a sip.

"It's beautiful." Robbie squeezed the lime into his beer, then drank. "But that model. It won't fly."

"I know." Emery stared to where Zach and Tyler leaped in the shallow water, sending up rainbow spray as they splashed each other. "But it's a good excuse for a vacation, isn't it?"

"It is," replied Robbie, and slid down the dune to join the boys.

Over the next few days, they fell into an odd, almost sleepless rhythm, staying up till two or three A.M., drinking and talking. The adults pretended not to notice when the boys slipped a Tecate from the fridge, and ignored the incense-scented smoke that drifted from the deck after they stumbled off to bed. Everyone woke shortly after dawn, even the boys. Blinding sunlight slanted through the worn curtains. On the deck where Zack and Tyler huddled inside their hammocks, a treefrog made a sound like rusty hinges. No one slept enough, everyone drank too much.

For once it didn't matter. Robbie's hangovers dissolved as he waded into water warm as blood, then floated on his back and watched pelicans skim above him. Afterward he'd carry equipment from the house to the dunes, where Emery had created a shelter from old canvas deck chairs and bedsheets. The boys helped, the three of them lugging tripods and digital cameras, the box that contained Leonard's model of the *Bellerophon*, a cooler filled with beer and Red Bull.

That left Emery in charge of household duties. He'd found an ancient red wagon half-buried in the dunes, and used this to transport bags of tortilla chips and a cooler filled with Tecate and limes. There was no store on the island save the abandoned wreck they'd passed when they first arrived. No gas station, and the historical society building appeared to be long gone.

But while driving around, Emery discovered a roadside stand that sold homemade salsa in mason jars and sage-green eggs in recycled cardboard cartons. The drive beside it was blocked with a barbed-wire fence and a sign that said BEWARE OF TWO-HEADED DOG.

"You ever see it?" asked Tyler.

"Nope. I never saw anyone except an alligator." Emery opened a beer. "And it was big enough to eat a two-headed dog."

By Thursday morning, they'd carted everything from one end of the island to the other, waiting with increasing impatience as Leonard climbed up and down dunes and stared broodingly at the blue horizon.

"How will you know which is the right one?" asked Robbie.

Leonard shook his head. "I don't know. Maggie said she thought it would be around here—"

He swept his arm out, encompassing a high ridge of sand that crested above the beach like a frozen wave. Below, Tyler and Zach argued over whose turn it was to haul everything uphill again. Robbie shoved his sunglasses against his nose.

"This beach has probably been washed away a hundred times since McCauley was here. Maybe we should just choose a place at random. Pick the highest dune or something."

"Yeah, I know." Leonard sighed. "This is probably our best choice, here."

He stood and for a long time gazed at the sky. Finally he turned and walked down to join the boys.

"We'll do it here," he said brusquely, and headed back to the house.

Late that afternoon they made a bonfire on the beach. The day had ended gray and much cooler than it had been, the sun swallowed in a haze of bruise-tinged cloud. Robbie waded into the shallow water, feeling with his toes for conch shells. Beside the fire, Zach came across a shark's tooth the size of a guitar pick.

"That's probably a million years old," said Tyler enviously.

"Almost as old as Dad," said Zach.

Robbie flopped down beside Leonard. "It's so weird," he said, shaking sand from a conch. "There's a whole string of these islands, but I haven't seen a boat the whole time we've been here."

"Are you complaining?" said Leonard.

"No. Just, don't you think it's weird?"

"Maybe." Leonard tossed his cigarette into the fire.

"I want to stay." Zack rolled onto his back and watched sparks flew among the first stars. "Dad? Why can't we just stay here?"

Robbie took a long pull from his beer. "I have to get back to work. And you guys have school."

"Fuck school," said Zach and Tyler.

"Listen." The boys fell silent as Leonard glared at them. "Tomorrow morning I want to set everything up. We'll shoot before the wind picks up too much. I'll have the rest of the day to edit. Then we pack and head to Fayetteville on Saturday. We'll find some cheap place to stay, and drive home on Sunday."

The boys groaned. Emery sighed. "Back to the salt mines. I gotta call that guy about the show."

"I want to have a few hours with Maggie." Leonard pulled at the silver skull in his ear. "I told the nurse I'd be there Saturday before noon."

"We'll have to leave pretty early," said Emery.

For a few minutes nobody spoke. Wind rattled brush in the dunes behind them. The bonfire leaped then subsided, and Zach fed it a knot of driftwood. An unseen bird gave a piping cry that was joined by another, then another, until their plaintive voices momentarily drowned out the soft rush of waves.

Robbie gazed into the darkening water. In his hand, the conch shell felt warm and silken as skin.

"Look, Dad," said Zach. "Bats."

Robbie leaned back to see black shapes dodging sparks above their heads.

"Nice," he said, his voice thick from drink.

"Well." Leonard stood and lit another cigarette. "I'm going to bed."

"Me too," said Zach.

Robbie watched with mild surprise as the boys clambered to their feet, yawning. Emery removed a beer from the cooler, handed it to Robbie.

"Keep an eye on the fire, compadre," he said, and followed the others.

Robbie turned to study the dying blaze. Ghostly runnels of green and blue ran along the driftwood branch. Salt, Leonard had explained to the boys, though Robbie wondered if that was true. How did Leonard know all this stuff? He frowned, picked up a handful of sand and tossed it at the feeble blaze, which promptly sank into sullen embers.

Robbie swore under his breath. He finished his beer, stood and walked unsteadily toward the water. The clouds obscured the moon, though there was a faint umber glow reflected in the distant waves. He stared at the horizon, searching in vain for some sign of life, lights from a cruiseship or plane; turned and gazed up and down the length of the beach.

Nothing. Even the bonfire had died. He stood on tiptoe and tried to peer past the high dune, to where the beach house stood within the grove of palmettos. Night swallowed everything,

He turned back to the waves licking at his bare feet. Something stung his face, blown sand or maybe a gnat. He waved to disperse it, then froze.

In the water, plumes of light coiled and unfolded, dazzling him. Deepest violet, a fiery emerald that stabbed his eyes; cobalt and a pure blaze of scarlet. He shook his head, edging backward; caught himself and looked around.

He was alone. He turned back, and the lights were still there, just below the surface, furling and unfurling to some secret rhythm.

Like a machine, he thought; some kind of underwater windfarm. A wavefarm?

But no, that was crazy. He rubbed his cheeks, trying to sober up. He'd seen something like this in Ocean City late one night—it was something alive, Leonard had explained, plankton or jellyfish, one of those things that glowed. They'd gotten high and raced into the Atlantic to watch pale-green streamers trail them as they body-surfed.

Now he took a deep breath and waded in, kicking at the waves, then halted to see if he'd churned up a luminous cloud.

Darkness lapped almost to his knees: there was no telltale glow where he'd stirred the water. But a few yards away, the lights continued to turn in upon themselves beneath the surface: scores of fist-sized nebulae, soundlesss and steady as his own pulse.

He stared until his head ached, trying to get a fix on them. The lights weren't diffuse, like phosphorescence. And they didn't float like jellyfish. They seemed to be rooted in place, near enough for him to touch.

Yet his eyes couldn't focus: the harder he tried, the more the lights seemed to shift, like an optical illusion or some dizzying computer game.

He stood there for five minutes, maybe longer. Nothing changed. He started to back away, slowly, finally turned and stumbled across the sand, stopping every few steps to glance over his shoulder. The lights were still there, though now he saw them only as a soft yellowish glow.

He ran the rest of the way to the house. There were no lights on, no music or laughter.

But he could smell cigarette smoke, and traced it to the deck where Leonard stood beside the rail.

"Leonard!" Robbie drew alongside him, then glanced around for the boys.

"They slept inside," said Leonard. "Too cold."

"Listen, you have to see something. On the beach—these lights. Not on the beach, in the water." He grabbed Leonard's arm. "Like—just come on."

Leonard shook him off angrily. "You're drunk."

"I'm not drunk! Or, okay, maybe I am, a little. But I'm not kidding. Look—"

He pointed past the sea of palmettos, past the dunes, toward the dark line of waves. The yellow glow was now spangled with silver. It spread across the water, narrowing as it faded toward the horizon, like a wavering path.

Leonard stared, then turned to Robbie in disbelief. "You idiot. It's the fucking moon."

Robbie looked up. And yes, there was the quarter-moon, a blaze of gold between gaps in the cloud.

"That's not it." He knew he sounded not just drunk but desperate. "It was *in* the water—"

"Bioluminescence." Leonard sighed and tossed his cigarette, then headed for the door. "Go to bed, Robbie."

Robbie started to yell after him, but caught himself and leaned against the rail. His head throbbed. Phantom blots of light swam across his vision. He felt dizzy, and on the verge of tears.

He closed his eyes; forced himself to breathe slowly, to channel the pulsing in his head into the memory of spectral whirlpools, a miniature galaxy blossoming beneath the water. After a minute he looked out again, but saw nothing save the blades of palmetto leaves etched against the moonlit sky.

He woke several hours later on the couch, feeling as though an ax were embedded in his forehead. Gray light washed across the floor. It was cold; he reached fruitlessly for a blanket, groaned and sat up.

Emery was in the open kitchen, washing something in the sink. He glanced at Robbie then hefted a coffee pot. "Ready for this?"

Robbie nodded, and Emery handed him a steaming mug. "What time is it?'

"Eight, a little after. The boys are with Leonard—they went out about an hour ago. It looks like rain, which kind of throws a monkey wrench into everything. Maybe it'll hold off long enough to get that thing off the ground."

Robbie sipped his coffee. "Seventeen seconds. He could just throw it into the air."

"Yeah, I thought of that too. So what happened to you last night?"

"Nothing. Too much Tecate."

"Leonard said you were raving drunk."

"Leonard sets the bar pretty low. I was—relaxed."

"Well, time to unrelax. I told him I'd get you up and we'd be at he beach by eight."

"I don't even know what I'm doing. Am I a cameraman?"

"Uh uh. That's me. You don't know how to work it, plus it's my camera. The boys are in charge of the windbreak and, I dunno, props. They hand things to Leonard."

"Things? What things?" Robbie scowled. "It's a fucking model airplane. It doesn't have a remote, does it? Because that would have been a *good* idea."

Emery picked up his camera bag. "Come on. You can carry the tripod, how's that? Maybe the boys will hand you things, and you can hand them to Leonard."

"I'll be there in a minute. Tell Leonard he can start without me."

After Emery left he finished his coffee and went into his room. He rummaged through his clothes until he found a bottle of Ibuprofen, downed six, then pulled on a hooded sweatshirt and sat on the edge of his bed, staring at the wall.

He'd obviously had some kind of blackout, the first since he'd been fired from the Parks Commission. Somewhere between his seventh beer and this morning's hangover was the blurred image of Crayola-colored pinwheels turning beneath dark water, his stumbling flight from the beach and Leonard's disgusted voice: *You idiot, it's the fucking moon.*

Robbie grimaced. He *had* seen something, he knew that.

But he could no longer recall it clearly, and what he could remember made no sense. It was like a movie he'd watched half-awake, or an accident he'd glimpsed from the corner of his eye in a moving car. Maybe it had been the moonlight, or some kind of fluorescent seaweed.

Or maybe he'd just been totally wasted.

Robbie sighed. He put on his sneakers, grabbed Emery's tripod and headed out.

A scattering of cold rain met him as he hit the beach. It was windy. The sea glinted gray and silver, like crumpled tinfoil. Clumps of seaweed covered the sand, and small round discs that resembled pieces of clouded glass: jellyfish, hundreds of them. Robbie prodded one with his foot, then continued down the shore.

The dune was on the north side of the island, where it rose steeply a good fifteen feet above the sand. Now, a few hours before low tide, the water was about thirty feet away. It was exactly the kind of place you might choose to launch a human-powered craft, if you knew little about aerodynamics. Robbie didn't know much, but he was fairly certain you needed to be higher to get any kind of lift.

Still, that would be for a full-sized craft. For a scale model you could hold in your two cupped hands, maybe it would be high enough. He saw Emery pacing along the water's edge, vidcam slung around his neck. The only sign of the others was a trail of footsteps leading to the dune. Robbie clambered up, using the tripod to keep from slipping on sand the color and texture of damp cornmeal. He was panting when he reached the top.

"Hey, Dad. Where were you?"

Robbie smiled weakly as Zach peered out from the windbreak. "I have a sinus infection."

Zach motioned him inside. "Come on, I can't leave this open."

Robbie set down the tripod, then crouched to enter the makeshift tent. Inside, bedsheet walls billowed in the wind, straining at an elaborate scaffold of broom handles, driftwood, the remains of wooden deck chairs. Tyler and Zach sat crosslegged on a blanket and stared at their cellphones.

"You can get a strong signal here," said Tyler. "Nope, it's gone again."

Next to them, Leonard knelt beside a cardboard box. Instead of his customary white tunic, he wore one that was sky-blue, embroidered with yellow birds. He glanced at Robbie, his gray eyes cold and dismissive. "There's only room for three people in here."

"That's okay—I'm going out," said Zach, and crawled through the gap in the sheets. Tyler followed him. Robbie jammed his hands into his pockets and forced a smile.

"So," he said. "Did you see all those jellyfish?"

Leonard nodded without looking at him. Very carefully he removed the *Bellerophon* and set it on a neatly folded towel. He reached into the box again, and withdrew something else. A doll no bigger than his hand, dressed in black frockcoat and trousers, with a bowler hat so small that Robbie could have swallowed it.

"*Voila*," said Leonard.

"Jesus, Leonard." Robbie hesitated, then asked, "Can I look at it?"

To his surprise, Leonard nodded. Robbie picked it up. The little figure was so light he wondered if there was anything inside the tiny suit.

But as he turned it gently, he could feel slender joints under its clothing, a miniature torso. Tiny hands protruded from the sleeves, and it wore minute, highly polished shoes that appeared to be made of black leather. Under the frock coat was a waistcoat, with a watch-chain of gold thread that dangled from a nearly invisible pocket. From beneath the bowler hat peeked a fringe of red hair fine as milkweed down. The cameo-sized face that stared up at

Robbie was Maggie Blevin's, painted in hairline strokes so that he could see every eyelash, every freckle on her rounded cheeks.

He looked at Leonard in amazement. "How did you do this?"

"It took a long time." He held out his hand, and Robbie returned the doll. "The hardest part was making sure the *Bellerophon* could carry her weight. And that she fit into the bicycle seat and could pedal it. You wouldn't think that would be difficult, but it was."

"It—it looks just like her." Robbie glanced at the doll again, then said, "I thought you wanted to make everything look like the original film. You know, with McCauley—I thought that was the point."

"The point is for it to fly."

"But—"

"You don't need to understand," said Leonard. "Maggie will."

He bent over the little aircraft, its multi-colored wings and silken parasol bright as a toy carousel, and tenderly began to fit the doll-sized pilot into its seat.

Robbie shivered. He'd seen Leonard's handiwork before, mannequins so realistic that tourists constantly poked them to see if they were alive.

But those were life-sized, and they weren't designed to resemble someone he *knew*. The sight of Leonard holding a tiny Maggie Blevin tenderly, as though she were a captive bird, made Robbie feel lightheaded and slightly sick. He turned toward the tent opening. "I'll see if I can help Emery set up."

Leonard's gaze remained fixed on the tiny figure. "I'll be right there," he said at last.

At the foot of the dune, the boys were trying to talk Emery into letting them use the camera.

"No way." He waved as Robbie scrambled down. "See, I'm not even letting your Dad do it."

"That's because Dad would suck," Zach said as Emery grabbed Robbie and steered him toward the water. "Come on, just for a minute."

"Trouble with the crew?" asked Robbie.

"Nah. They're just getting bored."

"Did you see that doll?"

"The Incredible Shrinking Maggie?" Emery stopped to stare at the dune. "The thing about Leonard is, I can never figure out if he's brilliant or potentially dangerous. The fact that he'll be able to retire with a full government pension suggests he's normal. The Maggie voodoo doll, though . . . "

He shook his head and began to pace again. Robbie walked beside him, kicking at wet sand and staring curiously at the sky. The air smelled odd, of ozone or hot metal. But it felt too chilly for a thunderstorm, and the dark ridge that hung above the palmettos and live oaks looked more like encroaching fog than cumulus clouds.

"Well, at least the wind's from the right direction," said Robbie.

Emery nodded. "Yeah. I was starting to think we'd have to throw it from the roof."

A few minutes later, Leonard's voice rang out above the wind. "Okay, everyone over here."

They gathered at the base of the dune and stared up at him, his tunic an azure rent in the ominous sky. Between Leonard's feet was a cardboard box. He glanced at it and went on.

"I'm going to wait till the wind seems right, and then I'll yell '*Now!*' Emery, you'll just have to watch me and see where she goes, then do your best. Zach and Tyler—you guys fan out and be ready to catch her if she starts to fall. Catch her *gently*," he added.

"What about me?" called Robbie.

"You stay with Emery in case he needs backup."

"Backup?" Robbie frowned.

"You know," said Emery in a low voice. "In case I need help getting Leonard back to the rubber room."

The boys began to walk toward the water. Tyler had his cellphone out. He looked at Zach, who dug his phone from his pocket.

"Are they *texting* each other?" asked Emery in disbelief. "They're ten feet apart."

"Ready?" Leonard shouted.

"Ready," the boys yelled back.

Robbie turned to Emery. "What about you, Captain Marvo?"

Emery grinned and held up the camera. "I have never been readier."

Atop the dune, Leonard stooped to retrieve the *Bellerophon* from its box. As he straightened, its propellers began turning madly. Candy-striped rotators spun like pinwheels as he cradled it against his chest, his long white braids threatening to tangle with the parasol.

The wind gusted suddenly: Robbie's throat tightened as he watched the tiny black figure beneath the fuselage swung wildly back and forth, like an accelerated pendulum. Leonard slipped in the sand and fought to regain his balance.

"Uh oh," said Emery.

The wind died, and Leonard righted himself. Even from the beach, Robbie could see how his face had gone white.

"Are you okay?" yelled Zach.

"I'm okay," Leonard yelled back.

He gave them a shaky smile, then stared intently at the horizon. After a minute his head tilted, as though listening to something. Abruptly he straightened and raised the *Bellerophon* in both hands. Behind him, palmettos thrashed as the wind gusted.

"*Now!*" he shouted.

Leonard opened his hands. As though it were a butterfly, the *Belllerophon* lifted into the air. Its feathery parasol billowed. Fan-shaped wings rose and fell; ailerons flapped and gears whirled like pinwheels. There was a sound like a train rushing through a tunnel, and Robbie stared open-mouthed as the *Bellerophon* skimmed the air above his head, its pilot pedaling furiously as it headed toward the sea.

Robbie gasped. The boys raced after it, yelling. Emery followed, camera clamped to his face and Robbie at his heels.

"This is fucking incredible!' Emery shouted. "Look at that thing go!"

They drew up a few yards from the water. The Bellerophon whirred past, barely an arm's-length above them. Robbie's eyes blurred as he stared after that brilliant whirl of color and motion, a child's dream of flight soaring just out of reach. Emery waded into the shallows with his camera. The boys followed, splashing and waving at the little plane. From the dune behind them echoed Leonard's voice.

"*Godspeed.*"

Robbie gazed silently at the horizon as the *Bellerophon* continued on, its pilot silhouetted black against the sky, wings opened like sails. Its sound grew fainter, a soft whirring that might have been a flock of birds. Soon it would be gone. Robbie stepped to the water's edge and craned his neck to keep it in sight.

Without warning a green flare erupted from the waves and streamed toward the little aircraft. Like a meteor shooting *upward*, emerald blossomed into a blinding radiance that engulfed the *Bellerophon*. For an instant Robbie saw the flying machine, a golden wheel spinning within a comet's heart.

Then the blazing light was gone, and with it the *Bellerophon*.

Robbie gazed, stunned, at the empty air. After an endless moment he became aware of something—someone—near him. He turned to see Emery stagger from the water, soaking wet, the camera held uselessly at his side.

"I dropped it," he gasped. "When that—whatever the fuck it was, when it came, I dropped the camera."

Robbie helped him onto the sand.

"I felt it." Emery shuddered, his hand tight around Robbie's arm. "Like a riptide. I thought I'd go under."

Robbie pulled away from him. "Zach?" he shouted, panicked. "Tyler, Zach, are you—"

Emery pointed at the water, and Robbie saw them, heron-stepping through the waves and whooping in triumph as they hurried back to shore.

"What happened?" Leonard ran up alongside Robbie and grabbed him. "Did you see that?"

Robbie nodded. Leonard turned to Emery, his eyes wild. "Did you get it? The *Bellerophon*? And that flare? Like the original film! The same thing, the exact same thing!"

Emery reached for Robbie's sweatshirt. "Give me that, I'll see if I can dry the camera."

Leonard stared blankly at Emery's soaked clothes, the water dripping from the vidcam.

"Oh no." He covered his face with his hands. "Oh no . . . "

"We got it!" Zach pushed between the grownups. "We got it, we got it!" Tyler ran up beside him, waving his cellphone. "Look!"

Everyone crowded together, the boys tilting their phones until the screens showed black.

"Okay," said Tyler. "Watch this."

Robbie shaded his eyes, squinting.

And there it was, a bright mote bobbing across a formless gray field, growing bigger and bigger until he could see it clearly—the whirl of wings and gears, the ballooning peacock-feather parasol and steadfast pilot on the velocipede; the swift silent flare that lashed from the water then disappeared in an eyeblink.

"Now watch mine," said Zach, and the same scene played again from a different angle. "Eighteen seconds."

"Mine says twenty," said Tyler. Robbie glanced uneasily at the water.

"Maybe we should head back to the house," he said.

Leonard seized Zach's shoulder. "Can you get me that? Both of you? Email it or something?"

"Sure. But we'll need to go where we can get a signal."

"I'll drive you," said Emery. "Let me get into some dry clothes."

He turned and trudged up the beach, the boys laughing and running behind him.

Leonard walked the last few steps to the water's edge, spray staining the tip of one cowboy boot. He stared at the horizon, his expression puzzled yet oddly expectant.

Robbie hesitated, then joined him. The sea appeared calm, green-glass waves rolling in long swells beneath parchment-colored sky. Through a gap in the clouds he could make out a glint of blue, like a noonday star. He gazed at it in silence, and after a minute asked, "Did you know that was going to happen?"

Leonard shook his head. "No. How could I?"

"Then—what was it?" Robbie looked at him helplessly. "Do you have any idea?"

Leonard said nothing. Finally he turned to Robbie. Unexpectedly, he smiled.

"I have no clue. But you saw it, right?" Robbie nodded. "And you saw her fly. The *Bellerophon*."

Leonard took another step, heedless of waves at his feet. "She flew." His voice was barely a whisper. "She really flew."

That night nobody slept. Emery drove Zach, Tyler and Leonard to a Dunkin Donuts where the boys got a cellphone signal and sent their movie footage to Leonard's laptop. Back at the house, he disappeared while the others sat on the deck and discussed, over and over again, what they had seen. The boys wanted to return to the beach, but Robbie refused to let them go. As a peace offering, he gave them each a beer. By the time Leonard emerged from his room with the laptop, it was after three A.M.

He set the computer on a table in the living room. "See what you think." When the others had assembled, he hit Play.

Blotched letters filled the screen: THE MAIDEN FLIGHT OF MCCAULEY'S BELLEROPHON. The familiar tipsy horizon appeared, sepia and amber, silvery flashes from the sea below. Robbie held his breath.

And there was the *Bellerophon* with its flickering wheels and wings propelled by a steadfast pilot, until the brilliant light struck from below and the clip abruptly ended, at exactly seventeen seconds. Nothing betrayed the figure as Maggie rather than McCauley; nothing seemed any different at all, no matter how many times Leonard played it back.

"So that's it," he said at last, and closed his laptop.

"Are you going to put it on YouTube?" asked Zach.

"No," he replied wearily. The boys exchanged a look, but for once remained silent.

"Well." Emery stood and stretched his arms, yawning. "Time to pack."

Two hours later they were on the road.

The hospice was a few miles outside town, a rambling old white house surrounded by neatly-kept azaleas and rhododendrons. The boys were turned loose to wander the neighborhood. The others walked up to the veranda, Leonard carrying his laptop. He looked terrible, his gray eyes bloodshot and his face unshaved. Emery put an arm over his shoulder and Leonard nodded stiffly.

A nurse met them at the door, a trim blonde woman in chinos and a yellow blouse.

"I told her you were coming," she said as she showed them into a sunlit room with wicker furniture and a low table covered with books and magazines. "She's the only one here now, though we expect someone tomorrow."

"How is she?" asked Leonard.

"She sleeps most of the time. And she's on morphine for the pain, so she's not very lucid. Her body's shutting down. But she's conscious."

"Has she had many visitors?" asked Emery.

"Not since she's been here. In the hospital a few neighbors dropped by.

I gather there's no family. It's a shame." She shook her head sadly. "She's a lovely woman."

"Can I see her?" Leonard glanced at a closed door at the end of the bright room.

"Of course."

Robbie and Emery watched them go, then settled into the wicker chairs.

"God, this is depressing," said Emery.

"It's better than a hospital," said Robbie. "Anna was going to go into a hospice, but she died before she could."

Emery winced. "Sorry. Of course, I wasn't thinking."

"It's okay."

Robbie leaned back and shut his eyes. He saw Anna sitting on the grass with azaleas all around her, bees in the flowers and Zach laughing as he opened his hands to release a green moth that lit momentarily upon her head, then drifted into the sky.

"Robbie." He started awake. Emery sat beside him, shaking him gently. "Hey—I'm going in now. Go back to sleep if you want, I'll wake you when I come out."

Robbie looked around blearily. "Where's Leonard?"

"He went for a walk. He's pretty broken up. He wanted to be alone for a while."

"Sure, sure." Robbie rubbed his eyes. "I'll just wait."

When Emery was gone he stood and paced the room. After a few minutes he sighed and sank back into his chair, then idly flipped through the magazines and books on the table. *Tricycle*, *Newsweek*, the *Utne Reader*; some pamphlets on end-of-life issues, works by Viktor Frankl and Elizabeth Kubler-Ross.

And, underneath yesterday's newspaper, a familiar sky-blue dustjacket emblazoned with the garish image of a naked man and woman, hands linked as they floated above a vast abyss, surrounded by a glowing purple sphere. Beneath them the title appeared in embossed green letters.

Wings for Humanity!
The Next Step is OURS!
by Margaret S. Blevin, PhD

Robbie picked it up. On the back was a photograph of the younger Maggie in a white embroidered tunic, her hair a bright corona around her piquant face. She stood in the Hall of Flight beside a mockup of the Apollo Lunar Module, the Wright Flyer high above her head. She was laughing, her hands raised in welcome. He opened it to a random page.

... that time has come: **With the dawn of the Golden Millennium we will welcome their return, meeting them at last as equals to share in the glory that is the birthright of our species.**

He glanced at the frontispiece and title page, and then the dedication.

For Leonard, who never doubted

"Isn't that an amazing book?"

Robbie looked up to see the nurse smiling down at him.

"Uh, yeah," he said, and set it on the table.

"It's incredible she predicted so much stuff." The nurse shook her head. "Like the Hubble Telescope, and that caveman they found in the glacier, the guy with the lens? And those turbines that can make energy in the jet stream? I never even heard of that, but my husband said they're real. Everything she says, it's all so hopeful. You know?"

Robbie stared at her, then quickly nodded. Behind her the door opened. Emery stepped out.

"She's kind of drifting," he said.

"Morning's her good time. She usually fades around now." The nurse glanced at her watch, then at Robbie. "You go ahead. Don't be surprised if she nods off."

He stood. "Sure. Thanks."

The room was small, its walls painted a soft lavender-gray. The bed faced a large window overlooking a garden. Goldfinches and tiny green wrens darted between a bird feeder and a small pool lined with flat white stones. For a moment Robbie thought the bed was empty. Then he saw an emaciated figure had slipped down between the white sheets, dwarfed by pillows and a bolster.

"Maggie?"

The figure turned its head. Hairless, skin white as paper, mottled with bruises like spilled ink. Her lips and fingernails were violet; her face so pale and lined it was like gazing at a cracked egg. Only the eyes were recognizably Maggie's, huge, the deep slatey blue of an infant's. As she stared at him, she drew her wizened arms up, slowly, until her fingers grazed her shoulders. She reminded Robbie disturbingly of a praying mantis.

"I don't know if you remember me." He sat in a chair beside the bed. "I'm Robbie. I worked with Leonard. At the museum."

"He told me." Her voice was so soft he had to lean close to hear her. "I'm glad they got here. I expected them yesterday, when it was still snowing."

Robbie recalled Anna in her hospital bed, doped to the gills and talking to herself. "Sure," he said.

Maggie shot him a glance that might have held annoyance, then gazed past him into the garden. Her eyes widened as she struggled to lift her hand, fingers twitching. Robbie realized she was waving. He turned to stare out the window, but there was no one there. Maggie looked at him, then gestured at the door.

"You can go now," she said. "I have guests."

"Oh. Yeah, sorry."

He stood awkwardly, then leaned down to kiss the top of her head. Her skin was smooth and cold as metal. "Bye, Maggie."

At the door he looked back, and saw her gazing with a rapt expression at the window, head cocked slightly and her hands open, as though to catch the sunlight.

Two days after they got home, Robbie received an email from Leonard.

Dear Robbie,

Maggie died this morning. The nurse said she became unconscious early yesterday, seemed to be in pain but at least it didn't last long. She had arranged to be cremated. No memorial service or anything like that. I will do something, probably not till the fall, and let you know.

Yours, Leonard

Robbie sighed. Already the week on Cowana seemed long ago and faintly dreamlike, like the memory of a childhood vacation. He wrote Leonard a note of condolence, then left for work.

Weeks passed. Zach and Tyler posted their clips of the *Bellerophon* online. Robbie met Emery for drinks ever week or two, and saw Leonard once, at Emery's Fourth of July barbecue. By the end of summer, Tyler's footage had been viewed 347,623 times, and Zach's 347,401. Both provided a link to the Captain Marvo site, where Emery had a free download of the entire text of *Wings for Humanity!* There were now over a thousand Google hits for Margaret Blevin, and Emery added a *Bellerophon* t-shirt to his merchandise: organic cotton with a silk-screen image of the baroque aircraft and its bowler-hatted pilot.

Early in September, Leonard called Robbie.

"Can you meet me at the museum tomorrow, around eight-thirty? I'm having a memorial for Maggie, just you and me and Emery. After hours, I'll sign you in."

"Sure," said Robbie. "Can I bring something?"

"Just yourself. See you then."

He drove in with Emery. They walked across the twilit Mall, the museum a white cube that glowed against a sky swiftly darkening to indigo. Leonard waited for them by the side door. He wore an embroidered tunic, sky-blue, his white hair loose upon his shoulders, and held a cardboard box with a small printed label.

"Come on," he said. The museum had been closed since five, but a guard opened the door for them. "We don't have a lot of time."

Hedges sat at the security desk, bald and even more imposing than when Robbie last saw him, decades ago. He signed them in, eying Robbie curiously then grinning when he read his signature.

"I remember you—Opie, right?"

Robbie winced at the nickname, then nodded. Hedges handed Leonard a slip of paper. "Be quick."

"Thanks. I will."

They walked to the staff elevator, the empty museum eerie and blue-lit. High above them the silent aircraft seemed smaller than they had been in the past, battered and oddly toylike. Robbie noticed a crack in the Gemini VII space capsule, and strands of dust clinging to the Wright Flyer. When they reached the third floor, Leonard led them down the corridor, past the Photo Lab, past the staff cafeteria, past the library where the Nut Files used to be. Finally he stopped at a door near some open ductwork. He looked at the slip of paper Hedges had given him, punched a series of numbers into the lock, opened it then reached in to switch on the light. Inside was a narrow room with a metal ladder fixed to one wall.

"Where are we going?" asked Robbie.

"The roof," said Leonard. "If we get caught, Hedges and I are screwed. Actually, we're all screwed. So we have to make this fast."

He tucked the cardboard box against his chest, then began to climb the ladder. Emery and Robbie followed him, to a small metal platform and another door. Leonard punched in another code and pushed it open. They stepped out into the night.

It was like being atop an ocean liner. The museum's roof was flat, nearly a block long. Hot air blasted from huge exhaust vents, and Leonard motioned the others to move away, toward the far end of the building.

The air was cooler here, a breeze that smelled sweet and rainwashed, despite the cloudless sky. Beneath them stretched the Mall, a vast green gameboard, with the other museums and monuments huge gamepieces, ivory and onyx and glass. The spire of the Washington Monument rose in the distance, and beyond that the glittering reaches of Roslyn and Crystal City

"I've never been here," said Robbie, stepping beside Leonard.

Emery shook his head. "Me neither."

"I have," said Leonard, and smiled. "Just once, with Maggie."

Above the Capitol's dome hung the full moon, so bright against the starless sky that Robbie could read what was printed on Leonard's box.

MARGARET BLEVIN.

"These are her ashes." Leonard set the box down and removed the top, revealing a ziplocked bag. He opened the bag, picked up the box again and stood. "She wanted me to scatter them here. I wanted both of you to be with me."

He dipped his hand into the bag and withdrew a clenched fist; held the box out to Emery, who nodded silently and did the same; then turned to Robbie.

"You too," he said.

Robbie hesitated, then put his hand into the box. What was inside felt gritty, more like sand than ash. When he looked up, he saw that Leonard had stepped forward, head thrown back so that he gazed at the moon. He drew his arm back, flung the ashes into the sky and stooped to grab more.

Emery glanced at Robbie, and the two of them opened their hands.

Robbie watched the ashes stream from between his fingers, like a flight of tiny moths. Then he turned and gathered more, the three of them tossing handful after handful into the sky.

When the box was finally empty Robbie straightened, breathing hard, and ran a hand across his eyes. He didn't know if it was some trick of the moonlight or the freshening wind, but everywhere around them, everywhere he looked, the air was filled with wings.

BIOGRAPHIES

Yoon Ha Lee likes to raid philosophy books for story ideas and knows just enough about guns to stay away from the real thing. Her works have appeared in *Clarkesworld, The Magazine of Fantasy and Science Fiction*, and *Lightspeed*.

Born in Vermont and raised all over the place, **K.J. Parker** has worked as, among other things, a tax lawyer, an auction house porter, a forester and a numismatist. Married to a lawyer and settled in southern England, Parker is currently a writer, farm labourer and metalworker, in more or less that order. K. J. Parker is not K. J. Parker's real name, but if somebody told you K. J. Parker's real name, you wouldn't recognise it.

Amal El-Mohtar is a Canadian-born child of the Mediterranean, presently pursuing a PhD at the Cornwall campus of the University of Exeter. She is the author of *The Honey Month*, a collection of poetry and prose written to the taste of twenty-eight different kinds of honey. Her poem "Song for an Ancient City" received the 2009 Rhysling Award for best short poem, and "The Green Book" received a Nebula nomination for best short story. She also co-edits *Goblin Fruit*, an online quarterly dedicated to fantastical poetry, with Jessica P. Wick. Find her online at amalelmohtar.com.

Alice Sola Kim currently lives in San Francisco but occasionally finds herself in St. Louis, where she is completing an MFA program at Washington University. Her short fiction has appeared in publications such as *Asimov's Science Fiction, Strange Horizons,* and *Lady Churchill's Rosebud Wristlet*.

Geoffrey A. Landis has been reading science fiction for as long he can remember, but he only seriously started to write it when he entered graduate school. His first story, "Elemental," appeared in 1984, and since then he's published a number of stories, poems, one novel ("Mars Crossing"), and a short-story collection ("Impact Parameter and other Quantum Fictions"). He won the Nebula previously in 1989, for his story "Ripples in the Dirac Sea." Despite wasting vast amounts of time writing science fiction, he did eventually complete his doctorate in physics, and now works for the NASA John H. Glenn Research Center, in Cleveland Ohio, where he works on technology for missions to Mars, Venus, and the sun. He lives in Berea, OH, with his wife, sf writer Mary Turzillo, and four cats. He occasionally appears on television, when a television science special needs a scientist and Stephen Hawking isn't available.

Christie Yant tests software by day, and by night writes, acts as assistant editor for *Lightspeed Magazine,* narrates short fiction for the *StarShipSofa* podcast, co-blogs at inkpunks.com, and reviews audio books for Audible.com. She lives on the central coast of California with her impossibly patient boyfriend, two wonderful daughters, two terrible dogs, and a cat. Her personal blog can be found at inkhaven.net.

Steve Rasnic Tem's next book is *Deadfall Hotel,* a May 2012 paperback release from Solaris Books. This will be followed in August by *Ugly Behavior,* a collection of his darker noir fiction from New Pulp Press.

Matthew Johnson lives in Ottawa with his wife Megan and their sons Leo and Miles. His stories have appeared in such places as *Asimov's Science Fiction, Strange Horizons* and *Fantasy Magazine*, and have been translated into Russian, Danish, and Czech; two of his other stories, "Public Safety" and "Irregular Verbs" appeared in previous editions of *The Year's Best*. His first novel, *Fall From Earth,* was published in 2009 by Bundoran Press and a collection of his short fiction, *Irregular Verbs and Other Stories,* will be published in 2013 by ChiZine Publications. His website is zatrikion.blogspot.com.

Charles Yu received the National Book Foundation's 5 Under 35 Award for his story collection, *Third Class Superhero*. His first novel, *How to Live Safely in a Science Fictional Universe*, was a *Time Magazine* Best Book of the Year and a *New York Times* Notable Book of the Year. His work has appeared in *Eclectica, Harvard Review, Lightspeed Magazine, Oxford American,* and *Playboy,* among other publications.

Rachel Swirsky is a graduate of the Iowa Writers Workshop. Her short fiction has appeared in numerous magazines and anthologies, and been nominated for the Hugo and the Nebula. Her first collection, *Through the Drowsy Dark,* came out from Aqueduct Press in 2010.

Adam-Troy Castro's many books include four Spider-Man novels, a nonfiction work about the TV reality-series *The Amazing Race,* three novels about his deeply broken far-future crime investigator Andrea Cort, and the macabre alphabet books *Z Is For Zombie* and *V is for Vampire* (both illustrated by Johnny Atomic). The winner of the Philip K. Dick award for his novel *Emissaries From The Dead*, he has also been nominated for two Hugo Awards, two Stokers, and as of 2011 six Nebulas. His next project is a series of middle-school novels starring a very odd young boy by the name of Gustav Gloom, coming from Grossett and Dunlap in 2012. Adam lives in Miami with his wife Judi and a pair of insane cats called Uma Furman and Meow Farrow.

Bill Kte'pi is a full-time writer with publications in *Strange Horizons, Chizine, The Fortean Bureau,* and elsewhere; stories available online are listed at ktepi. com. *Low Country,* a southern haunted house novel, was published by Fey Publishing in 2010. He also writes a food and drink blog, okaycheckitout. blogspot.com.

Samantha Henderson's fiction and poetry has been published in *Strange Horizons, Realms of Fantasy, Clarkesworld, Fantasy,* and the anthologies *Fantasy: Best of the Year, Steampunk Reloaded* and *Running with the Pack.* Her second novel, *Dawnbringer,* was released by Wizards of the Coast in May of 2011. She lives in Southern California with her family and assorted fauna.

Paul Park has written numerous novels—*Celestis, A Princess of Roumania,* and *The Gospel of Corax,* among others—in various genres. His most recent projects include a steampunk story in an upcoming anthology, an apocalyptic science-fiction Icelandic edda, and a Forgotten Realms novel called *The Rose of Sarifal,* to be published under the name Paulina Claiborne. *Ghosts Doing the Orange Dance,* nominated for the Nebula Award for best novella of 2010, will soon be reprinted in an expanded, illustrated form, by PS Publishing. Mr. Park teaches writing and literature at Williams College in Berkshire County, Massachusetts, where he lives with his wife and two children.

Gene Wolfe worked as an engineer, before becoming editor of trade journal *Plant Engineering.* He came to prominence as a writer in the late 1960s with a sequence of short stories in Damon Knight's *Orbit* anthologies. His early major novels were *The Fifth Head of Cerberus* and *Peace,* but he established his reputation with a sequence of three long, multivolume novels—*The Book of the New Sun, The Book of the Long Sun,* and *The Book of the Short Sun.* His short fiction has been collected in *The Island of Doctor Death and Other Stories, Endangered Species, Strange Travelers,* and, most recently, *The Best of Gene Wolfe.* He is the recipient of the Nebula, World Fantasy, Locus, John W. Campbell Memorial, British Fantasy, British SF, and World Fantasy Lifetime Achievement Awards. Wolfe's most recent book is the novel *An Evil Guest.* Upcoming is his new novel *The Sorcerer's House.*

Carol Emshwiller grew up in Michigan and in France. She lives in New York City in the winter and in Bishop, CA in the summer. She's been doing only short stories lately. A new one will appear in *Asimov's* soon. She's wondering if she's too old to start a novel but if a good idea came along she might do it anyway. PS Publishing is publishing two of her short story collections in a single volume (sort like an Ace Double), with her anti-war stories on one side and other stories on the other.

C.S.E. Cooney grew up in an Arizona desert, spent her twenties in the Midwest, and is about to embark on an East Coast adventure. Her fiction and poetry can be found in *Clockwork Phoenix 3, Subterranean Press, Strange Horizons, Apex Magazine, Ideomancer, Goblin Fruit,* and *Mythic Delirium*. She has novellas forthcoming with Drollerie Press, *Cabinet des Fées,* and *Black Gate* (where she is Blog Editor). Her novel-in-progress includes one really big wolf, a shapeshifter with identity issues, and several feisty kitchen maids. She keeps her own blog at csecooney.livejournal.com.

Bestselling author **Neil Gaiman** has long been one of the top writers in modern comics, as well as writing books for readers of all ages. He is listed in the *Dictionary of Literary Biography* as one of the top ten living post-modern writers, and is a prolific creator of works of prose, poetry, film, journalism, comics, song lyrics, and drama. Some of his notable works include *The Sandman* comic book series, *Stardust, American Gods, Coraline,* and *The Graveyard Book*. Gaiman's writing has won numerous awards, including World Fantasy, Hugo, Nebula, IHG, and Bram Stoker, as well as the 2009 Newbery Medal. Gaiman's official Web site, www.neilgaiman.com, now has more than one million unique visitors each month, and his online journal is syndicated to thousands of blog readers every day.

Willow Fagan is a queer writer living in Portland, Oregon. They're genderqueer, which for them means that they feel more like a pirate princess than like a man or a woman. Their fiction has appeared in *Fantasy Magazine* and *Behind the Wainscot*. Their non-fiction is forthcoming in the anthologies *Dear Sister, Why Are Faggots So Afraid of Faggots?* and *Queering Sexual Violence*. To read more about their writing and adventures, go to willowfagan.livejournal.com.

Peter Watts owes at least part of his 2010 Hugo (for the novelette "The Island") to fan outrage over an unfortunate altercation with armed capuchins working for the Department of Homeland Security. This year he has decided to play the Sympathy card, by nearly dying of flesh-eating disease contracted during a routine skin biopsy. The strategy seems to have worked insofar as "The Things" has made the finals for this year's short-story Hugo. Watts is already hard at work on The Next Horrible Thing to catapult him towards future trophies. Given his past life as a marine mammalogist, the smart money is on being gang-raped by dolphins.

Paul M. Berger has been a Japanese bureaucrat, a Harvard graduate student, an M.I.T. program administrator, an Internet entrepreneur, a butterfly wrangler and (God help him) a Wall Street recruiter, which, in the aggregate, may have prepared him for nothing except the creation of speculative fiction. His fiction has appeared in *Strange Horizons, Interzone, Polyphony 6, Twenty Epics, All-Star Zeppelin Adventure Stories, Ideomancer* and *Escape Pod*. The story of his battle against giant Japanese spiders was the first true-life memoir published in *Weird Tales*. He is a 2008 graduate of the Clarion Writers' Workshop. His website is www.paulmberger.com.

Alexandra Duncan is a frequent contributor to *The Magazine of Fantasy and Science Fiction*. She blogs about wizards, pie, birds, and books at alexandraduncanlit. blogspot.com.

Robert Reed is the author of many short stories and a few beefy novels, including the well-received space opera epic, *Marrow*. He has been nominated for various Hugos, a Nebula, and the World Fantasy award. In 2007, he won a Hugo for his novella, "A Billion Eves." Reed lives in Lincoln, Nebraska with his wife and daughter. For fun, he runs. In his life, he has run more than 60,000 miles, give or take.

Charlie Jane Anders is the managing editor of io9.com. Her writing has appeared in the *McSweeney's Joke Book of Book Jokes, Mother Jones, the San Francisco Chronicle, Lady Churchill's Rosebud Wristlet* and other places. She organizes the Writers With Drinks reading series in San Francisco.

Matthew David Surridge lives in Montreal with his One True Love, writer Grace Seybold. His fiction has appeared in *Beneath Ceaseless Skies* and *Black Gate*, and he has a weekly column on the *Black Gate* blog. A former critic for *The Comics Journal*, he also helped cover the 2009 Worldcon for *The Montreal Gazette*. You can find his ongoing fantasy adventure serial at Fellgard.com.

Damien Broderick is an award-winning Australian sf writer, editor and critical theorist, with a PhD from Deakin University. A senior fellow in the School of Culture and Communication at the University of Melbourne, he currently lives in San Antonio, Texas. He has published more than forty-five books, including *Reading by Starlight, x, y, z, t: Dimensions of Science Fiction, Unleashing the Strange, Chained to the Alien* and *Skiffy and Mimesis*. His latest sf novel is the diptych *Godplayers* and *K-Machines*, written with the aid of a two-year Fellowship from the Literature Board of the Australia Council, and his recent sf collections are *Uncle Bones* and *The Qualia Engine*.

Variously known as a student of Linguistics, a web application developer, a graduate of the 2008 Clarion West class, a writer of speculative fiction, and a purveyor of medieval armor and fine baked goods, **An Omowoyela** mostly resides in places contrary to consensus reality but is compelled to list a university town in the American Midwest as home on most official documents. Fiction bearing the mark of this elusive author can be found in an increasing variety of "here"s and "there"s, and more general information can be found at an.owomoyela.net.

Elizabeth Hand is the multiple-award-winning author of ten novels and three collections of short fiction. Her most recent novel is *Illyria*, winner of the World Fantasy Award. She is also a longtime critic whose reviews and essays appear regularly in the *Washington Post* and *F&SF*, among many other publications. She is on the Popular Fiction faculty for the Stonecoast MFA Program in Creative Writing at the University of Southern Maine, and has two novels forthcoming in 2012: *Available Dark*, sequel to Shirley Jackson Award winner *Generation Loss*, and *Radiant Days*, a YA novel about the French poet Arthur Rimbaud. She lives on the coast of Maine.

RECOMMENDED READING

Nina Allan, "The Upstairs Window" (*Interzone*, 9-10/10)
Eleanor Arnason, **Tomb of the Fathers** (Aqueduct)
Eleanor Arnason, "Mammoths of the Great Plains"
    (**Mammoths of the Great Plains**)
Dale Bailey, "Silence" (*F&SF*, 5-6/10)
Kage Baker, "The Bohemian Astrobleme" (*Subterranean*, Winter)
Kage Baker, "The Books" (**The Mammoth Book of Apocalyptic SF**)
Stephen Baxter, "The Ice Line" (*Asimov's*, 2/10)
Peter S. Beagle, "La Lune T'Attend" (**Full Moon City**)
Peter S. Beagle, "Return" (*Subterranean*, Spring/10)
Elizabeth Bear, **Bone and Jewel Creatures** (Subterranean Press)
Chris Beckett, "The Peacock's Cloak" (*Asimov's*, 6/10)
Aliette de Bodard, "The Jaguar House, in Shadow" (*Asimov's*, 7/10)
Gregory Norman Bossert, "The Union of Sky and Soil" (*Asimov's*, 4-5/10)
Simon Brown, "Sweep" (**Sprawl**)
Eugene Byrne, "Spunkies" (**Dark Spires**)
James L. Cambias, "How Seosiris Lost the Favor of the King"
    (*F&SF*, 9-10/10)
Elizabeth Carroll, "The Duke of Vertumn's Fingerling"
    (*Strange Horizons*, 4/5/10)
Fred Chappell, "Thief of Shadows" (*F&SF*, 5-6/10)
Ted Chiang, **The Lifecycle of Software Objects** (Subterranean Press)
Cinda Williams Chima, "The Trader and the Slave"
    (**The Way of the Wizard**)
Deborah Coates, "What Makes a River" (*Tor.com*, 8/10)
C.S.E. Cooney, **The Big Bah-Ha** (Drollerie Press)
C.S.E. Cooney, "Household Spirits" (*Strange Horizons*, 11/8/10)
Sean Craven, "Tourists" (Tor.com, 2/10)
Eric Del Carlo, "After We Got Back the Lights" (*Strange Horizons*, 2/8/10)
Alexandra Duncan, "Swamp City Lament" (*F&SF*, 11-12/10)
Lindsey Duncan, "The Naming Braid" (*GUD*, Summer/10)
Carol Emshwiller, "Above it All" (*Fantasy*, 1/10)
Gregory Feeley, **Kentauros** (NHR Books)

Neil Gaiman, "The Truth Is a Cave in the Black Mountains" (**Stories**)

Emily Gilman, "Lily" (*Strange Horizons*, 12/6/10)

Felix Gilman, "Lightbringers and Rainmakers" (*Tor.com*, 10/10)

Elena Gleason, "Whisper's Voice" (*Fantasy*, 4/10)

Theodora Goss, "Fair Ladies" (*Apex*, 8/10)

Theodora Goss, "The Mad Scientist's Daughter"
(*Strange Horizons*, 1/18/10-1/25/10)

Lev Grossman, "Endgame" (**The Way of the Wizard** / *Borders.com*)

Grady Hendrix, "The Bright and Shining Parasites of Guiyi"
(*Strange Horizons*, 7/12/10-7/19/10)

Rosamund Hodges, "More Full of Weeping Than You Can Understand"
(*Beneath Ceaseless Skies,* 10/7/10)

Robert J. Howe, "The Natural History of Calamity" (*Black Gate*, Spring/10)

Jon Ingold, "The History of Poly-V" (*Interzone*, 3-4/10)

Alex Irvine, "The Word He Was Looking for Was Hello"
(**Is Anbody Out There?**)

Ivaylo P. Ivanov, "I Dreamed a Human Face" (*Marginal Boundaries*, 4/10)

Alexander Jablokov, "Blind Cat Dance" (*Asimov's*, 3/10)

K. J. Kabza, "The Leafsmith in Love" (*Beneath Ceaseless Skies*, 3/10)

Daniel Kaysen, "Babylon's Burning" (*Black Static*, 2-3/10)

James Patrick Kelly, "Plus or Minus" (*Asimov's*, 12/10)

Alice Sola Kim, "Hwang's Billion Brilliant Daughters" (*Lightspeed*, 11/10)

Leonid Korogodski, **Pink Noise** (Silverberry Press) 8/10

Matthew Kressel, "The History Within Us" (*Clarkesworld*, 3/10)

Ellen Kushner, **The Man With the Knives**
(Temporary Culture, *Tor.com*, 10/10)

Jay Lake, **The Baby Killers** (PS Publishing)

Jay Lake, "Permanent Fatal Errors" (**Is Anbody Out There?**)

John Lambshead, "Storming Venus" (*Baen's Universe,* 4/10)

K.M. Lawrence, "The Freedom" (*Strange Horizons*, 4/26/10)

Ann Leckie, "Beloved of the Sun" (*Beneath Ceaseless Skies*, 10/21/10)

Yoon Ha Lee, "Between Two Dragons" (*Clarkesworld*, 4/10)

David D. Levine, "Teaching the Pig to Sing" (*Analog*, 5/10)

Marissa Lingen, "The Six Skills of Madam Lumiere"
(*Beneath Ceaseless Skies*, 7/1/10)

Rochita Loenen-Ruiz, "Alternate Girl's Expatriate Life" (*Interzone*, 7-8/10)

Barry Longyear, "Alten Kameraden" (*Asimov's*, 4-5/10)

Ian R. MacLeod, "Recrossing the Styx" (*F&SF*, 7-8/10)

Joseph Mallozzi, "Downfall" (**Masked**)

George R. R. Martin, "The Mystery Knight" (**Warriors**)

Meghan McCarron, "WE HEART VAMPIRES!!!!!!"
(*Strange Horizons*, 5/3/10-5/10/10)

Sandra McDonald, "Diana Comet and the Collapsible Orchestra"
(**Diana Comet**)
Sandra McDonald, "Seven Sexy Cowboy Robots" (*Strange Horizons*, 10/4/10)
Maureen McHugh, "The Naturalist" (*Subterranean*, Spring/10)
Sean McMullen, "Eight Miles" (*Analog*, 9/10)
David Moles, **Seven Cities of Gold** (PS Publishing)
James Morrow, "The Raft of the Titanic"
(**The Mammoth Book of Alternate Histories**)
Ruth Nestvold, "The Bleeding and the Bloodless" (*Giganotosaurus*, 11/10)
Kim Newman, "Kentish Glory" (**Mysteries of the Diogenes Club**)
Garth Nix, "To Hold the Bridge" (**Legends of Australian Fantasy**)
Charles Oberndorf, "Writers of the Future" (*F&SF*, 1-2/10)
Nnedi Okorafor, "The Go-Slow" (**The Way of the Wizard**)
Eilis O'Neal, "Waiting" (*Strange Horizons*, 5/31/10)
Eilis O'Neal, "The Wing Collection" (*Fantasy*, 1/10)
Eilis O'Neal, "The Wizard's Calico Daughter" (*Fantasy*, 8/10)
K. J. Parker, **Blue and Gold** (Subterranean Press)
Richard Parks, "Lady of the Ghost Mill" (*Beneath Ceaseless Skies*, 10/7/10)
Richard Parks, "The Queen's Reason"
(*Lady Churchill's Rosebud Wristlet*, 5/10)
Richard Parks, "Sanji's Demon" (*Beneath Ceaseless Skies*, 3/10)
Richard Parks, "Four Horseman, at Their Leisure" (*Tor.com*, 4/10)
Steven Popkes, "The Crocodiles" (*F&SF*, 5-6/10)
Steven Popkes, "Jackie's-Boy" (*Asimov's*, 4-5/10)
Tom Purdom, "Haggle Chips" (*Asimov's*, 7/10)
Robert Reed, "The History of Terraforming" (*Asimov's*, 7/10)
Robert Reed, "The Cull" (*Lightspeed*, 9/10)
Shauna Roberts, "The Hunt" (*Baen's Universe*, 2/10)
Barbara Roden, "Flu Season" (*Subterranean*, Winter)
Margaret Ronald, "A Serpent in the Gears" (*Beneath Ceaseless Skies*, 1/10)
Patricia Russo, "The Shadow Traders" (*Not One of Us*, 4/10)
Patricia Russo, "Stranger" (*Fantasy*, 2/10)
George Saunders, "Escape from Spiderhead"
(*The New Yorker*, 12/20/10-12/27/10)
Gord Sellar, "Sarging Rasmussen: A Report (by Organic)" (**Shine**)
Angela Slatter, "Brisneyland by Night" (**Sprawl**)
Allen M. Steele, "The Great Galactic Ghoul" (*Analog*, 10/10)
Hannah Strom-Martin, "Father Peña's Last Dance" (*Realms of Fantasy*, 8/10)
Lavie Tidhar, **Cloud Permutations** (PS Publishing)
Lavie Tidhar, "In Pacmandu" (*Futurismic*, 9/10)
Lavie Tidhar, "Lode Stars" (**The Immersion Book of SF**)
Lavie Tidhar, "The Spontaneous Knotting of an Agitated String"
(*Fantasy*, 6/10)

Ian Tregillis, "What Doctor Gottlieb Saw" (*Tor.com*, 6/10)

Carrie Vaughn, "Amaryllis" (*Lightspeed*, 6/10)

Howard Waldrop, "Ninieslando" (**Warriors**)

Rick Wilber, "Several Items of Interest" (*Asimov's*, 10-11/10)

Sean Williams, "A Glimpse of the Marvelous Structure,
      and the Threat it Entails" (**Godlike Machines**)

Bruce Worden, "The American" (*Intergalactic Medicine Show*, 12/10)

Richard Wolkomir, "A Remnant Man Rode a Linguahorse
      Across the Plain of Conn" (*Zahir*, 1/10)

Caroline M. Yoachim, "The Sometimes Child" (*Fantasy*, 5/10)

Caroline M. Yoachim, "What Happens in Vegas" (*GUD*, Summer/10)

Haihong Zhao, "Exuviation" (*Lady Churchill's Rosebud Wristlet*, 5/10)

PUBLICATION HISTORY

ABOUT THE EDITOR

RICH HORTON is a software engineer in St. Louis. He is a contributing editor to *Locus*, for which he does short fiction reviews and occasional book reviews; and to *Black Gate*, for which he does a continuing series of essays about SF history. He also contributes book reviews to *Fantasy Magazine*, and to many other publications.